THE MARTYR TIDES

BOOK ONE
OF THE TIDES SERIES

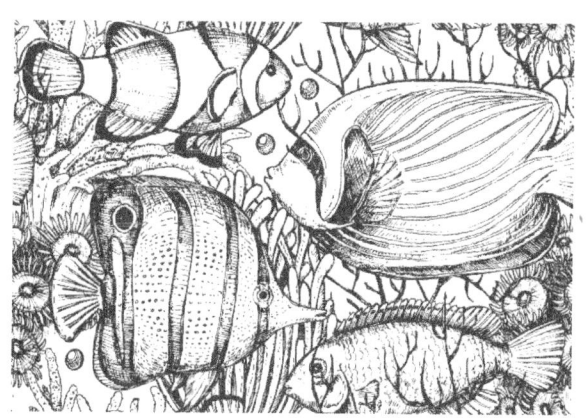

PENELOPE AUSTIN

This book is a work of fiction.
Any references to historical events, real
people, or real locations are used fictitiously.
Other names, characters, places, and
Incidents are the product of the author's
imagination, and any resemblance to actual
events locations, or persons living or
dead, is entirely coincidental.

THE MARTYR TIDES
Book One
Of the Tides Series
Copyright © 2023
by Penelope Austin
All rights reserved.

No portion of this book may be reproduced
in any form without written permission
from the publisher or author.

DEDICATION & THANKS

I would like to thank my husband for
putting up with me while I'm busy
writing (and for supporting my content)
He always has something clever to add,
just one of the reasons he's the best.

Thank you, Susan, for helping me in
so many ways to make this book special.
I hope you enjoy seeing your contributions
and know that I really appreciate your help.

And most of all, I'd like to thank Heidi Fast
for reaching into my head, plucking out
the characters, and bringing them to life.
Her work Is amazing, and I hope you enjoy
the image gallery on our Author page.

I should also take the time to thank the
people and the critters of the Florida Keys.
If you've never been there, you should go.
It's like no other place on earth, and someday,
I'll live there with my hubby and the dogs.

This book is dedicated to Bill,
who inspired so many and
asked for nothing in return.
And did go to Oregon—twice.

PROLOGUE

With an open book to hide my face, I watched Edaline, my eyes casually following the athletic, silver-haired waitress as she bustled around the diner. Her sparkling gray eyes smiled at every guest she served—like fingernails on a chalkboard to me. The good-girl vibes she projected made my hackles lift. I hated her, yet longed to get my claws on all that power. *Ahh, the irony.*

The thought of seeing her crawl made my gums ache. I pursed my lips to hide the tips of thirty-two rebellious fangs suddenly poking into my mouth, my lips bulging over the emerging spikes. I covered the lumpy mess with one hand and held back a smile, pulling myself together before fur sprouted and joined the fangs.

I must hide my presence a little longer. It wouldn't be wise to reveal myself, at least not yet. I turned the page I hadn't read as my eager eyes tracked the clueless mongrel.

As the minutes slipped away, so did my overly eager fangs. With a contented sigh, I sipped from the porcelain mug, relieved when nothing clinked to give me away. At least the coffee was hot, and the food was as good as could be expected from a greasy spoon like the Crazy Conch Diner.

Lifting a knife and the pat of jam, I carefully spread it on the two slices of toast cooling on my plate. Soon, very soon. The hunt to make her mine had been a long one. Twenty-six years of stalking my prey was a personal best. If I got cocky again, the Gryphon would sweep the silver-haired bitch out of my reach, and I'd be back to square one. I couldn't let that happen.

As if hearing my thoughts, Eddi glanced in my direction and raised the coffee pot, her dark eyebrows lifting in question. I shook my head and smiled. She just offered coffee to something that could easily tear off her head and crunch on it like a candy apple. Red flashed across the book's pages; with a quiet hiss, I closed my eyes and reeled in my thoughts.

Soon, I would add her to my collection of *Others*, each creature a piece of the masterful puzzle that would bring me to power. I could barely wait to see her face when Eddi realized she was mine until the day she died. When the time was right, all my years of patience would finally bear fruit.

I grinned and closed my book, digging into the scrambled eggs while imagining all the fun I'd have with her once my trap was sprung. She had absolutely no idea of the hell that awaited her.

CHAPTER 1

With the Atlantic at my back, the cool morning air kissed me goodbye as I headed to work on my pink vintage Raleigh. Behind me, the fiery orange ball at the horizon painted the trailers lining the crumbled edges of my street. Today would be hot, with a chance of hotter.

As I pedaled along beneath the scattered palm trees, a disturbance ahead caught my eye. As I approached, I saw it was a police cruiser—parked haphazardly on the shoulder. Something was about to go down.

When I got closer, I watched a cop struggling to press a guy onto the hood of his car. Not yet in cuffs, the man fought desperately to escape. I hesitated, then crossed the road to give them a wide berth, weaving carefully around the potholes waiting to swallow me.

My timing was impeccable. As I passed, the cop was left holding a jean jacket as his suspect slipped from the sleeves and bolted. Boots pounded; I looked up; the guy's unfocused stare registered nothing—*including me.*

The impact sent my bike clattering across the pavement as I was thrown clear. Well, almost. With a grunt, a sweaty body pinned me to the ground.

I lay there, stunned, my horrified gaze zig-zagging across the face of the guy panting all over me. Through greasy, tousled hair, he peered down at my ear. He couldn't focus.

A glazed-over white, his eyes rolled back and forth, his pink tongue licking at nothing. A slack jaw, his tight neck, the weird moans—I didn't put it all together until the thick ridge of his arousal pegged my thigh.

OH MY GOD!

I wanted to scream, but shock froze me in place as the freak of nature dry-humped my leg hard enough to hurt—and then he was gone.

Right. The officer. Keep it together, Eddi.

Flinging gravel showered me as the snarling cop wrestled his perp into a headlock, finally restraining him. The officer was a mess. One swollen eye bloomed a bluish cast, and long scratches furrowed his face. With muffled grunts and scuffling feet, he managed to cram the weirdo, still moaning and thrusting, into the back of his cruiser.

Scrambling to my feet, I hauled up my bike and hopped on, taking off like the hounds of hell were on my heels. I didn't want to be late for work—

"Ma'am. Ma'am. *Stop!*"

Pedaling harder, I looked over my shoulder, caught the cop's eye, and yelled back, "I'm sorry! I'm late for work!" I pointed. "At the diner!"

As I rolled out of sight around the corner, the officer shook his head and doubled over, his hands propped on his thighs while he caught his breath. The shiner, now a deep purple, was already closing in on the slit of his eye. Man, that had to hurt.

What the hell was that guy on? His behavior was so ... unnatural.

The chills curling up my spine told me—it was nothing good. *Nothing good at all.*

***

There it was again—the unmistakable odor of something foul. Mingled with the smell of fryer grease, I wondered if I imagined it.

Bert was making friends again.

Bellied up to the ancient grill tucked behind the counter, our cook was all business this morning. I scowled at the back of his neck, the untrimmed stubble and generous folds shining with sweat. Feeling my stare, Bert shot me some side-eye, his lips turning up in one corner before looking away.

The grill hissed and popped with bacon and eggs as customers swiveled on their padded stools; the guy closest to Bert sported a strange expression.

So I didn't imagine it.

Across the diner, Ada lifted her head. The generous wrinkles on her face disappeared, her eyes shooting wide in disbelief. I laughed. With a shake of her bright pink curls, she resumed taking orders for her table of tourists fresh from Sombrero Beach.

The group sat by the panoramic front windows, where customers enjoyed watching the constant flow of traffic roaring by a few yards away on Highway 1—the only way in or out of the Florida Keys.

I turned to see Bert slip a silver flask back under the counter. Awesome. A drinking problem, too. The man was a menace. He was lucky there were labor shortages, and our boss Patsy was desperate for a cook.

The bell over the door tinkled, and a slitted eye surrounded by a wicked shade of prune pinned me where I stood. The magnificent purple contusion belonged to a handsome middle-aged officer—the one from this morning. I cringed at the scratches marring his face.

OH SHIT.

I combed fingers through my short hair and tucked my silvery bangs behind one ear. Tension shot down my spine, and the cloying smell of diesel flooded my senses. I froze, saliva flooding my mouth. Ghostly shouts and screams raised goosebumps, but I wrestled the memories into submission and focused on the cop thumping toward me.

Breathe. Stay calm. You're fine, Eddi.

"You do realize leaving the scene is illegal, right?"

"I'm sorry, sir. I was late for work. I can't afford to lose my job."

He sighed. "Fine. I get it. Where can we sit so I can take your statement?" He looked around the diner as I grabbed him a coffee, then we sat by the window.

"I'm sorry, officer"—I read his tag—*"Henson*. I guess I was flustered. The whole thing was so weird. What was that guy on, anyway?"

"Nothing you need to concern yourself with, ma'am."

Officer Henson took my statement and, thankfully, didn't push me to press charges.

"So, is he alright? The guy? He was pretty messed up."

Gingerly feeling the bruise around his eye, the officer gave me a wry smile. "He was wild, I'll say that."

With a thoughtful expression, he watched me chew my lips. "Look. I spent my twenties partying and having a good time, too. I know what you kids get up to on the weekend. Just be careful, alright? You and your friends need to stick to drinks—not drugs. And stay out of dark alleys."

Well, that wasn't ominous at all.

Gathering up his pad, Officer Henson slipped his pen back into a pocket. His eyes flicked over my face, and his lips tightened. "You didn't hear this from me, but there's a new drug popping up here and there, and it's bad news. I'm not at liberty to say much, but ..."

He stood, staring down at me, his feet restless. Then, his eyes softened. "I have a daughter almost your age. I'd hate to see anything bad—" He ran his fingers through his short, damp hair. "You saw the way he behaved, Edaline. Users have no control. It's causing some really— *ah, shit*. Just behave yourself, ok?" He smiled, then turned to leave.

I waved and mouthed, *"Thank you,"* as he stepped through the scuffed glass door. Ada slid up beside me to grab some napkins. "Wow. He was *cute!*" She watched him through the windows as he climbed into his cruiser, then nodded at my leg. "Did you get the gravel picked out?"

"Yeah, I'm fine." I looked down at the bandaids covering the scrape. "I don't understand. My neighborhood is usually quiet. Where the hell did that guy come from this morning?"

"Who the hell knows? But your hero was *hot*. I would have given your statement *for you* if it got me closer to *that!* I love a man in uniform." With a sly grin, she added, "and handcuffs." With a click of her pen, Ada headed back to her section.

I laughed, wondering if she realized he was old enough to be my father. Uninvited tears pushed against my lids at the thought, but I dashed them away. Letting out a long, soothing breath, I motioned to Ada that I would take the customers coming through the door.

As I fixed my apron, I glanced at Bert, who sat down and wiped the back of his neck with a hand towel before running it over his shiny scalp. I frowned as I thought about how uncomfortable he must be carrying that extra weight. A pang of guilt shot through me.

I shouldn't tease him so much. Like me, he had no one to go home to and never spoke about family or friends. He kept pretty much to himself, the poor guy.

My charitable thoughts were premature. A few hours later, I walked in on him smoking in the dishwashing area, his yellowed fingers pinching a hand-rolled that was seventy percent ash.

"BERT!" I hissed. "What the hell are you doing? You can't smoke in here!" I glanced over at the stainless counter and saw red when I noticed ashes scattered over the surface.

"My God, we've already had one health code violation when they found your butts in a coffee mug back here!"

Bert's face creased as he grinned around the butt clenched in his teeth. "Whatcha going to do about it, *princess?*"

"You better hope Patsy doesn't come in and see that. In fact, put that thing out before I make you eat it," I growled. "She doesn't need any more trouble. How could you?"

Grumbling, he shuffled outside to the parking lot to finish his smoke. The word *hate* was pretty strong, *but some days*—

With a stack of plates in her hands and a receipt in her teeth, Ada bustled through the swinging kitchen door. I grabbed the load before she dropped it and plunked it down near the stainless dishwasher.

Ada groaned, bent over, removed one of her sensible shoes, and rubbed her foot. She sniffed the air, and her thin penciled eyebrows shot up. "Oh my God, again? Lordy, I HATE that guy! Where is he *now?*"

I nodded my head towards the back parking lot. Rolling her eyes, she slipped her shoe back on, washed her manicured hands, and headed to wipe her tables. Ada paused at the swinging door and looked back at me.

"Eddi, why don't you find yourself a nice guy and have some fun for a change? Go to a movie. Kiss him over some popcorn. Live a little! All you do is work."

I laughed and tossed the diner keys onto the counter. "Thanks for the suggestion, but there's no time for that nonsense. Do you mind locking up?"

"Sure, hun," Ada tossed over her shoulder. "Watch the tide today. It's going to be a strong one."

I grinned at her retreating form and chucked my dirty waitress apron in the bin, shoving past Bert as he opened the screen door.

"Where are you going in such a hurry, Eddi?" he grumbled. "You got a shift at Davy Jones Locker this afternoon? Or are you going out to fight more *crime?*"

Halfway to the bike rack, I stopped and looked back at him. Bert watched me, a hammy fist flexing on the desiccated wood of the screen door. His eyes tracked the beads of sweat rolling down my chest before soaking into my tank top.

"Not that it's any of your business, *Bert*, but in case you haven't noticed, it's hot. I'm going for a paddle and a swim."

No response.

"And Bert?"

He raised one bushy eyebrow.

"I'm not going to have to turn the rinse hose on you again, am I?"

He retreated into the restaurant with a snort, letting the door slam shut behind him. "That was a misunderstanding!" he hollered, his voice filtering through the tattered screen.

Unlocking my bike, I pushed it down the oil-stained alley. The mangled restaurant exhaust thumped to life behind me, the smell of bacon filling the humid air. My stomach rumbled, and I decided to hit the Dunkin Donuts across the way.

I glanced down our side street and soaked in the view. Framed by palms and the guard rail at the dead end, the ocean's Van Gogh blues turned my frown into a smile. The salty breeze of the Atlantic reached me, lifting my bangs and cooling my flushed face. It reminded me of my afternoon plans, and I picked up the pace.

Crossing the patched street, I pushed my bike over the newly paved lot at Dunkin. The hot smell of fresh asphalt wafted up but couldn't compete with the aroma of freshly baked donuts. My mouth watered.

They had been my favorite treat ever since Cal rescued me from behind the dumpster here almost a decade ago. I should have hated the sweet snack. It was all I ate for months as I found my way south from Tennessee. Searching—*always searching*—and running from the black hole of my empty past.

Yep. Donuts should have been my least favorite food.

A quick dash into the modern, air-conditioned oasis, and I had my sugary prize. I set the bag full of warm dough into my handlebar basket and wondered if the chocolate dip, Cal's favorite, was a bad idea today.

***

I pedaled over to Davy Jones Locker, the aging business perched on the edge of Vaca Key, not far from my tiny apartment. It was my afternoon off, and the ocean waited for me.

As I pushed my bike past the enormous mural covering the side of the building, I admired the hand-painted sharks, rays, and dolphins covering the aqua-blue scene. Cool and Keysie, I never tired of gazing at the sea life it depicted.

It was four-thirty, so I hustled to lock up my bike and hit the docks. Captain Brian was due back any time now with his load of tourists and today's catch. I rounded the corner onto the shady veranda and ducked inside the bait shop entrance. Writing "help yourself" on the paper bag of carby goodness, I sat the donuts behind the till, then popped outside.

The charter was back. A festive crowd swarmed the dock around the *High Society*. Evan, a new hire at the marina, finished rinsing the fish blood from the deck of the magnificent 49' Carolina as Captain Brian cleaned fish. The vessel's fishing tower and outriggers rocked gently back and forth. I envied the lucky folks who enjoyed the luxury of heading offshore for Mahi Mahi.

Smiles were everywhere as tourists clustered around the fish-cleaning station, admiring the catch while customers posed for pictures with their fish. A massive Wahoo hung from the pegs, and my pulse raced at the size of it. At least one fisherman would celebrate tonight.

I scanned the marina for Cal, wispy tendrils of unease spreading through me when I didn't see him. Forcing myself to breathe, I rubbed my chest to ease the tightness there. The two of us shared something special. He was my rock, my safe harbor. Without his kindness and tenacity, I'd still be living on the street eating donuts from dumpsters.

Ten years ago, police in Tennessee found me on the highway, wandering and confused, a blinding headache doubling me over. I had no idea who I was or where I came from. In my mind, that was the day I was born—in a grassy ditch outside Knoxville, wearing a bloody jean jacket with a hole in it. The cops picked me up, welcomed me into the system, and that was that.

A year or so later, I aged out of foster care and wandered down to the Keys, my past still a complete mystery. I had fragments of recollection: a fire, screams, and someone shouting, *"Run, Edaline. RUN!*

Was that my real name—or part of a dream? Such a simple question. A name wasn't much, but I took it for my own.

I had no family unless you counted my case worker. Yes, I was an embarrassing sob story, and I kept quiet about it. Whatever I did back in Tennessee must have been pretty damn horrible if no *loving parents* ever showed up to claim me from the system. Moisture beaded my eyelashes, even as I tried to convince myself I didn't care. It didn't matter. I had Cal. I was good now.

To this day, my friend never revealed a thing about his own past, and I was okay with that, too. We both understood that some things were better left unsaid—especially when it came to family.

Now, if I could get rid of the nightmares once and for all, everything would be ducky. They followed me from Tennessee, unfortunately, and I couldn't shake them. Aspirin was my best friend, next to Cal.

Now, where is he? There.

Down on the kayak beach, busy with a family, the gigantic brim of his dorky cotton sun hat flopped in the breeze like a tan-colored beacon. Designed for maximum coverage, the weirdly flamboyant but entirely practical headgear was necessary for white blondes like my friend. On anyone else, it would look ridiculous. Cal rocked it.

"You have to own it, Eddi. That's the key to good living." With a straight face, he would shoot me a line of total BS, and I would eat it up, hook, line, and sinker. I asked him once what "Cal" was short for, and he wiggled his eyebrows and said, "Calamari." *Classic Cal.*

Right now, he set up some tourists with a kayak rental. A chubby mom in a brightly flowered bathing suit struggled to get herself onto a kayak without flipping it. Cal, lean but athletic, tried valiantly to keep a firm grip on the boat, which bucked like a wild thing from all the awkward attempts.

Oh yeah. Someone was going for an unplanned swim. He looked up, saw me watching, and grinned. I let out a long, slow sigh and sent him a finger wave before heading down to the staff-only end of the kayak rack.

James, the marina's owner, nodded to me as he flip-flopped up the grassy knoll to the shop, his sandy-colored hair waving in the light breeze. Reaching out a hand, he gently tweaked my arm on his way by.

Born in the Keys, my boss had the classic laid-back vibe of a local. Kind and quick with a smile, he generously let me store my kayak next to the rentals. With my overstuffed schedule, it made hitting the water that much easier.

Carrying my Cobra kayak down the gentle slope to the sandy beach, I hid my smile as I watched Cal help his dripping customer back up for another try. Everyone grinned, their laughter ringing out across our sheltered cove.

In no time, I pushed off and sliced through the water, the salty ocean air whisking away my tension. My favorite fishing spot was on the Atlantic side of the island. I went out with the tide today, letting the strong current push me along. Peering into the crystal-clear water below, I watched for interesting sea life.

I spotted a four-foot nurse shark, and as I drifted over her, she startled and bolted to safety. Around the islands, you often ran into young sharks pupped in the protection of the mangroves. Harmless if you let them be.

The forceful bounce of the tide took me on quite a ride under the bridge before releasing me into calmer water on the Atlantic side. I paddled for the small coastal island that I favored. As I passed a sandy gap in the mangroves surrounding it, I noticed the white homemade swing rocking back and forth in the breeze.

Locals had lugged out two green plastic chairs with only six solid legs between them, tying them together in front of the blackened fire pit. The island was well-loved, and Cal and I spent many an afternoon here, swinging in the shade.

I anchored my kayak on the south side and waded into the sandy waist-deep pool to cool off. Today, the shallows surrounding the island were crystal clear. I relaxed, knowing the bright sandy bottom made nosy sea critters easy to spot.

Thirty feet away, the shallows turned a cobalt blue as they fell away into a deep water drop-off. The beach nudging the opposite bank of the channel gleamed brightly in the afternoon sun, with not a soul in sight. I was alone.

My body cooled as I melted into the water, submerging to the chin. I leaned back, dunking my head with a contented grin. Automatically, my eyes roamed the vast expanse of turquoise spreading all the way to the horizon.

If you lived on the ocean, you developed an eye for movement on the water. Cool things lived out there, a keen eye needed to spot them.

As I floated, I saw a loggerhead turtle pop up in the distance, swiveling its bulky head as it drifted. Then, with a blip and a swirl, he was gone, his massive three-foot shell leaving a wake. He was lucky that the turtle soup days were long gone.

I thought about grabbing my rod, but something caught my eye. A dorsal fin appeared in the middle of the channel, and I stiffened. Another followed it, then another, the water churning as several flat horizontal tails tipped into the air.

Dolphins.

Letting out my breath, I counted a pod of five or six. Judging by the swirling water and random fins flopping about, the randy buggers took turns breeding a female as they moved down the channel. My bright smile didn't last long, though.

A human head bobbed up beside them—a male head. Even silhouetted by the bright afternoon sun, his dark hair and chiseled features gave him away. Every muscle in my body tensed. What the hell was this idiot doing?

A long, muscular arm came up, and I got a clear visual of him throwing a fish. A freakin' fish! What the hell? Did this moron not know he'd get a minimum $5000 fine if a Conservation Officer caught him feeding dolphins?

The gray torpedoes took off after the fish, and the swimmer dove, presumably to follow and harass them further. I was so angry that I grabbed my anchor, tossed it in the foot well, jumped on the Cobra, and paddled out into the current.

I mean, come on! Tourists did some pretty dumb things, but getting up close and personal with a pod of mating dolphins and feeding them was a recipe for trouble. Dolphins weren't always the gentle creatures the movies portrayed. They were downright dangerous when provoked. If I found him, I would give this guy a piece of my mind. Feeding dolphins made career beggars out of them, which ended tragically for the smiley critters.

Nothing was there when I got to where I'd last seen them. Not a ripple. At this time of day, the waves reflected a million glittering lights, which made spotting a swimmer damn near impossible. I drifted with the now gentle tide as I scanned the water. No luck. He was gone.

Cursing and grumbling to myself, I paddled back to the island, re-anchored in the shallows, and dug out my cast net to catch some bait fish. I couldn't shake the odd sense that I should have looked further for the troublemaker.

Was he ok? Did the dolphins get pissed and hurt him? Was he injured and floating just under the water, and I let him drown?

Nah. He looked like a strong swimmer. At least I didn't have to rip him a new one for messing with the local wildlife.

Dragging my kayak behind me, I concentrated on watching for the shadows of bait fish in the clear, shallow water. It took sharp eyes because you wouldn't see the pale minnows against the sand—only their shadow. I looped my bait net over my arm and slowly moved along the shoreline.

There. In front of the mangroves, a school of Pilchards darted past. With a wind-up and a practiced throw, I cast my net, grinning as I dragged in a ball of squirming minnows.

I shook them into the bait pail, letting the rest plop back into the ocean, where they scattered for cover. We sold frozen bait at the shop, but nothing worked as well as live Pilchards. Being broke, fresh fish was a necessity, and these little wrigglers were just the thing to catch a tasty entrée.

Wading deep enough to turn my kayak around, I stowed my net and was about to go catch my dinner when a flash of movement caught my eye.

Instinctively, I froze. Turning my head, I sucked in a breath.

CHAPTER 2

Standing in the tidal current, just past where I had been lounging a short time ago, was a guy. Correction. An incredibly beautiful guy. And he watched me—*intently*. With the turquoise ocean behind him, I barely concealed a double take at my sudden, visceral reaction to what I was seeing.

His mesmerizing green eyes caught my gaze and held it, their penetrating intensity making my skin pebble. And not just my skin. My ladies flushed to full attention, too.

Standing waist-deep in the water, the tide caressed his 'V' muscle as it slipped past. His slim waist tapered into 3D abs that stopped abruptly at a pair of the most delicious pecs, his hard frame bronzed by the tropical sun. A pair of brilliant green swim trunks peeked above the waterline. And the entire, incredibly edible package of this guy's body glistened with salty water droplets. I licked my lips in some sort of weird Pavlovian response.

Holy crap! This guy is HOT.

His head was cocked slightly to the side, his short dark hair plastered down and still dripping. Slightly longer bangs stuck up here and there as if he had just shaken his head to get rid of the salt water. A chiseled, completely hairless jawline ended in a pair of the cutest ears, which were small and slightly oval but somehow worked perfectly with his almond-shaped eyes and straight nose.

This guy oozed an off-the-charts confidence and masculinity that set me back on my heels. He looked like he stepped out of a Greek art exhibit. Well, if art exhibits were crafted with a full-on scowl framed by the most perfect lips. Luscious, full lips that looked really soft and kissable.

I dropped the anchor rope and, mesmerized, pushed toward him, rubbing my thighs together at each step. The friction was heavenly. Then, I was there, reaching up and sliding my hands over his warm, wet chest, tangling my fingers in his hair and yanking his lips to mine. He grunted, his fingers reaching down to stroke me through my wet shorts. I moaned, pressing into his hand as I crushed him to me. My kayak rubbed against my leg, and I pushed it away, but it kept bumping—bumping. Annoyed, I looked down.

What the fuck?

My kayak bounced against my leg alright, thanks to the wake from a boat passing down the channel. I wasn't hanging on my strange visitor like a porn star, though. I stood exactly where I was moments ago, my kayak tied around my waist.

Confused, I looked up. He was still there. The scowl was still there, too, only now, his expression said I was a complete idiot.

I shook my head, then shook it again. What was I doing? Staring, that's what. And having freaky sex in my head with a stranger, even though he seemed angry at me about something.

Judging by the glare he threw my way, I would hear about it. Where the hell did he come from?

Slamming my gaping mouth closed, I cleared my throat and tried to compose myself, but the tramp in my pants wasn't having it. Vagellina was throwing a hissy downstairs, and I had to resist the urge to clamp my legs together. I was pretty sure if I didn't, she would stomp down my leg, swim the short distance, and impale herself on whatever was hidden below the waterline.

"What."

Yep, that was all I managed to croak out. Apparently, my brain was on strike.

Absolutely no response from this guy. A breeze caressed us both as he stood there, staring at me. The *unnaturally still* sort of staring that gave you the willies.

He cocked his head back the other way, and the image of a curious iguana popped into my head. Shaking off the thought, I gathered my traitorous tongue and tried again.

"Do we have a problem?"

Nothing but frowning. He still stared, but now he focused on my chest.

"What can I do for you?"

My eyes trailed down to the green trunks shimmering beneath the water, his Adonis belt drawing me along its fascinating downward slope.

"I would love to see what you're packing in your banana hammock under the water there—"

I cringed. Wait, *WHAT!?* Did I just say that out loud? *Fuck!*

No, I did NOT say that out loud. *Did I?*

Confused, I raised my hands, rubbed my eyes with my palms, then dropped them. Nope, he was still there. I wasn't enjoying some weird afternoon sex fantasy. This guy was REAL. And still staring at me.

His gaze flicked over my body, which was covered by a pink pair of eensy spandex boy shorts and a wet, clingy rash guard. In white. Regretting my choice to skip the bra today, I became very aware that my headlights were flashing this guy.

Was this seriously happening right now, or was I stuck in some weird alternate universe?

Those panty-melting eyes made a few circuits up and down, pausing briefly on my pink shorts. He narrowed his eyes. I thought the fish scale pattern was cute, but they seemed to displease Mr. Tall Dark and Wet.

Very wet. Oh my god—so freaking wet.

Slapping my hand over my mouth in case it spewed more embarrassing nonsense, I gurgled out a mortified noise. It was somewhere between a cough and a moan, which made him glower even harder.

As his scowl deepened, his dark, finely arched brows dipped low, his jaw pulling tight. We were now officially in the territory of *dude, you're making me nervous.*

Snapping out of it and realizing he still hadn't said a word, and was clearly sizing me up and finding me wanting, I did what any self-respecting girl would do. I got *MAD*.

The heat he had generated in the boy shorts basement snuffed out with an almost audible sizzle. The Polar Express had arrived in the Keys and pulled into Nether Station just in time.

Now, I was the one who was pissed.

"You have some sort of problem with my *SHORTS*, pal?"

His eyes flashed to mine, and I almost faltered at the glittery green of them as they drilled into me.

"Are you that freaking idiot that hassled the dolphins earlier? Because if you were, you clearly don't understand the whole conservation thing we've got going on down here. You'll get them killed, you know that, right?"

I was so angry I stomped toward him, which was hard to pull off gracefully in thigh-deep water. A sharp, angry look replaced his glare, and I stopped. My kayak, still tied around my waist, hit me in the butt.

I thought he would react, but there was still nothing. Not one word. He curled his lip at my gear like it was the dumbest thing he had ever seen.

For some ridiculous reason, I felt the urge to defend my stuff, so I shoved it behind me. Like, what the fuck, you incredibly insolent asshat.

"Listen here, Aquaman. I don't care who you think you are, but messing with dolphins is bad news." I circled my finger in the air at him while he tracked it with his eyes. "So take that Ryan Reynolds thing you've got going on and move it along. I just want to enjoy some PRIVACY."

Aannndd now he's moved on to a perplexed look.

"You understand PRIVACY, right?" Furious, I did air quotes with my fingers. And then it hit me. This guy didn't speak English. That had to be it. So I tried a new tack.

"Mi privacidad?" No response and an even more puzzled look. I circled my finger around my ear and asked *"Eres un idiota?"* No headway there, just the same dumb look again. I sighed. This was getting me nowhere.

"Ok, Mystery Man. Let me put it this way. If I see you feeding them again, I'm calling the FWC. You know, *Florida Wildlife Conservation?* The ones who can take your truck, your house, and your firstborn?"

My voice came out way louder and more shrill than I intended, and I grimaced at how bitchy I sounded. Oh well, he deserved it. He had ticked me off now, and *Karen* was coming to the rescue.

At my sharp tone, his attention snapped back to my face, and he jerked back in surprise. I saw the wheels turning as he mulled over my threat. Those sparkling eyes of his were so INTENSE. I didn't get it. What was this dude's problem, anyway?

Spurred on by my anger over the dolphins, the silent staring contest, and the obvious disdain he threw my way, I lost it. Eye candy or not, this guy crossed the line. I don't know what came over me. It was an involuntary reaction that just—*happened.*

Without thinking, I picked my bait pail up off the kayak, stomped closer, and tossed the contents at him. As the Pilchards slid down his torso in a fishy waterfall, I dropped the empty pail back on my kayak and crossed my arms to see what he thought of *that.*

He looked down at his chest, plucked a stranded minnow from it, and lowered his hand into the ocean, calmly watching it dart away. Then, he looked up at me.

I braced for what was coming, but to my utter disbelief, his scowl disappeared. In a complete about-face, he relaxed, the tension leaving his shoulders. Then, he *smiled.*

Not just any smile, but the panty-burning kind of smile that transformed him into something ethereal, making me feel a little light-headed. He was smiling—*at me*. And apparently, at my vagina, which once again had abandoned common sense and was throwing a party in my pants without inviting my brain.

Wait a minute. Why was I practically drooling, and wanting to run home to grab Buzz Nightgear for some *"me"* time? *Gahhhh!!*

Flustered, and thoroughly alarmed at my suddenly unstable behavior, I did the only thing I could think of. I made a break for it.

Yanking up my anchor and hopping onto my kayak, I launched it into the current, the now rising tide pushing toward home. Unable to help myself, I glanced over my shoulder.

He was gone.

CHAPTER 3

Back at Davy Jones, Cal and I hung out behind the bait shop, enjoying a beer in the shade of the Tiki while catching up on our day. I told him about my crazy morning, then went over the island incident with him. Instead of being helpful, he laughed. *Hard*. I gave him an exasperated slap.

"Have you seen this guy around, or is he a tourist? I mean, it was odd. He pops up out of nowhere, doesn't say a word, gawks at me like he'd like to wring my neck, and then thinks it's hilarious when I assault him. I *assaulted* him! And it *amused* him!"

I covered my eyes, propped my elbows on the Tiki counter, and let out a loud, frustrated sigh.

Cal rubbed his baby-smooth chin and shook his head with a thoughtful expression. "I have no idea who he is. I know a couple of locals who fit the description, but they aren't that HOT," he said, making me laugh with an exaggerated flutter of his white lashes. "Man, I wish I could have gone with you today. He sounds *amazing.*"

I couldn't help but laugh as Cal tried to cheer me up. "I don't know. This guy was different. And what's with the porno playing in my pants? I mean, you know me. I'm practically *virginal* these days."

He laughed and put his hand on my shoulder. "Don't worry Edster. Meeting a hot guy is everybody's wet dream. It will give you and *Buzz* some fantasy material tonight. Or should I say *materiales de fantasia?*" He burst out laughing, and I walloped him, the jerk.

"Whatever. Enough about my mysterious hottie. *Moving on*. What are you up to tonight? Wanna come over for a movie?"

"Sure, sounds awesome. But first, I have a surprise for you." He grabbed my arm, and setting my beer down, Cal hauled me toward the line of docks.

"Where are we going? I'm tired and want to head home. Can't it wait?" Cal dragged me down the stairs toward the liveaboard section, our feet thumping on the desiccated boards.

"Oh, no, no, no. This definitely can't wait," Cal said with a sly grin as he frog-marched me down the dock. I knew there was an ambush in progress by the expression on his face.

At the end of the row of slips, tucked up against the mangroves, was the ugliest liveaboard I had ever seen. It was every marina owner's nightmare.

The 1980s Ranger Tug Boat was one stiff breeze away from its final voyage—*to the bottom*. At one time, someone had made it into a decent liveaboard, and I'm sure it could haul ass in its day. But those days were long gone.

The rear deck had a canvas shade cover that may have been tan once but was now a rotting gray drab. Algae slime covered the edge of every grommet, window, and piece of trim. The stern deck was pretty sweet, but the railing was no longer silver; it was more of a classic rust. If this boat had a name, it was probably *Pissed and Broke*.

Oh, wait. No, there it was. The name on her hull, proudly displayed in peeling vinyl, was the *Predator II*. I gaped at Cal, who grinned back.

"I'd hate to see what *Predator I* looks like," he panned.

Cal was loving it, but I wasn't sure why. I mean, yeah, it was ugly. It was bringing down property values. But why the big fuss?

What are you up to, Cal?

"Doesn't the marina have rules about this sort of thing? Who the heck owns this piece of shit?" I whispered.

Cal giggled. "You'll see in a sec! You're gonna love it!" We stopped at the slip holding the eyesore, and I heard a voice.

"Bend over, Honey," someone hissed.

I glanced at Cal, who looked confused. Then we heard it again.

"That's it, BABY. Right there, BABY. Oh, YA baby!"

We swung our heads around to see who spoke. Cal shot me an embarrassed look and shrugged.

"I have NO idea," he whispered.

I looked up, and perched on the upper deck railing was a ratty blue and gold macaw parrot with most of the feathers missing from his chest. With a flap of its wings, it fluttered down to the lower railing, almost crash-landing into the ocean. Having regained its balance, the parrot inched along the rusty bow rail, turning his body back and forth, his head bobbing. It cocked its head to the right and leaned out at us as if to come for a visit.

"HARDER BABY!" the parrot screeched and bobbed its head up and down.

Cal gawked at me, his mouth opening and closing like a fish. "Oh boy. I had NO idea, I swear!" He doubled over with laughter at the expression on my face.

The tattered bird, who in no way resembled any of his majestic brethren, reached our location. For some foolish reason, I thought reaching out and rubbing the poor bird's bare chest would be a good idea. As I moved to do so, several things happened at once.

From the corner of my eye, I saw movement on board, and a baritone voice yelled, *"Nooooooo!"*

It was too late. That ratty little excuse for a parrot struck, sinking its black, razor-sharp beak into the flesh of my index finger and clamped down—*hard*.

The parrot had no intention of letting go, even though blood gushed from my finger. You've never lived until you've had a bald parrot with a razor-sharp beak hanging off your most important digit as a red waterfall splattered the dock.

Screeching loud enough to be heard in the next county and instinctively trying to pull back my hand, I got more than I bargained for when the whole damn parrot came with it. Now, the two-pound monster hung from my finger while I tried to shake it loose and hopped around on the dock.

A hulking brute of a man appeared from nowhere and leaned over me. Too occupied trying to get the flying buzz saw off my finger, I didn't notice the two meaty hands reaching out to help. One grabbed my arm to hold it still while the other wrapped around the parrot.

Then, Cal was there, prying Jack the Ripper's blood-stained maw off my mangled finger.

Hissing in pain, I clamped my eyes shut. With my good hand putting pressure on the bleeding, I bent over and pressed my hands between my knees as I gasped for air.

"Holy crap! Whose fucking monster *IS* that!?"

I opened my eyes, my finger throbbing with a life of its own. And there, standing on the deck, holding a very disgruntled parrot, *was Bert*.

***

"What the HELL, Cal?"

Bert retreated with the angry parrot, and Cal and I went to the office. My friend apologized as he helped stop the bleeding on my poor, abused finger.

"Eddi, I'm so sorry. I didn't know Bert had a parrot! I only knew that he moved in today. I thought you'd get a kick out of it." He suppressed a laugh. "Ok, I knew you'd be pissed. I'm sorry. I have no idea why James let him move his derelict piece of crap here, but he's staying for six months."

I didn't know if I was queasy from the pain, or the knowledge that Bert would be an everyday fixture in my happy place.

Great, just great.

Cal hissed with laughter. "The bird's name is *Mr. Darcy*, of all things. I mean, who names a ratty embarrassment like that Mr. Darcy?"

I couldn't laugh. I wanted to, but I was too distracted by my finger, which was auditioning as a drummer for *RUSH* at the moment. After promising to meet up at my place later, Cal and I parted ways, and I headed home. One-handed.

Rotten parrot. I'm looking up recipes for you, pal.

Alone in my apartment, I made a salad and a grilled cheese and sat down at my small window table to eat. Visible at the end of my road, I watched the sea birds hovering over the ocean. I couldn't stop my thoughts from drifting to the stranger at the island today. My reaction to him was so weird, and I had a sick feeling that I was missing something important.

Did I know him from somewhere? Maybe I'd seen him at the grocery store. His not talking to me was odd. Perhaps he wasn't Spanish *or* English. Ordinary people would at least *try* to communicate, wouldn't they?

And oh my god, *Bert*. What were the chances? Somehow, I wasn't surprised that his parrot was a prick. James letting him park his floating disaster at the marina was odd, though.

Shrugging off today's unusual events, I tidied up and waited for Cal. Of course, I had to wash my dishes with one hand so I didn't get my bandage wet. A few minutes later, there was a knock, followed by Cal popping his head in.

"Some wine and cheese for *m'lady?*"

Dropping the bag of munchies on the counter, he draped the wine bottle across his arm with a flourish. "Perhaps my princess would like this exquisite three-dollar bottle of Oyster Bay Sauvignon Blanc?"

I couldn't help but laugh. "Yes, please. And for the love of all that is holy, tell me you brought two bottles?"

Cal smiled and reached for my Finding Nemo beer glasses. It may have been a hellish day, but nothing a replay of *Pride and Prejudice* with my partner in crime wouldn't fix.

CHAPTER 4

The following week was uneventful, and there were no more sightings of Mr. Tall, Dark, and Dishy. The parrot lay low, too.

I paddled to the Island several times but had no unexpected company, which was strangely disappointing. I did catch some nice mangrove snapper and a beautiful grouper. I let the Grouper go because it wasn't in season.

Constantly thinking about this guy stressed me out. Cal said I was horny, the smart ass. But I couldn't get the devilishly handsome guy out of my head.

Charter bookings were plentiful over the next few weeks, so I stayed busy. A year or so ago, my boss, James, urged me to get my captain's license. That way, I would make more money, and he could book the more lucrative private gigs. He trained me, and two months ago, I passed my test. I'd already taken several family charters, becoming more comfortable with every trip. Of course, James gave me the oldest boat in the fleet to drive.

The *Wanderlust* may have been old, but unlike Bert's boat, it was in fantastic shape. A navy blue and white beauty, it was a 1994 Grady-White Explorer with a cuddy cabin. And at twenty-four feet, it was the perfect size for me to handle. It had a porta potty tucked into the tiny cabin below, separated from the main deck by a plastic shutter door. The hard top over the helm kept the sun off everyone's heads, and I adored the antique wooden captain's wheel installed by a previous owner.

It was perfect for day trips. The stern deck was big, so if kids were on board, they could move around. The parents loved the space, and teenage girls used the walkaround to sunbathe on the nice flat bow. The livewell in the stern was convenient. For an older boat, it was the perfect setup for small charters.

Sometimes, I brought Cal as my first mate to help bait the lines and take off fish. I had to put up with him constantly grinning, giving me military salutes, and shouting, "Yes sir, Captain Ed, sir!" Neither of us was a tournament fisherman, but we always came home with lots of Yellowtail Snapper for our clients.

Today was quiet, so I staffed the bait shop. Cal was offshore helping Captain Brian on the *High Society*. After an uneventful morning selling tackle and bait, I headed outside to eat lunch.

It was your typical April day in the Keys—cloudless blue skies and hot without being humid. The water had a light chop, making it the perfect weather.

After eating, I headed down to the tiny beach we used to launch kayaks. A giant chunk of coral was buried in the sand by the water in the shade of some palms. I loved to bring a folded towel and relax on it, watching the seabirds or the colorful Iguanas lounging in the Mangroves.

The marina hugged the edge of the channel, so the Atlantic was visible through the palms. I lived inside a postcard, and sometimes, I got a lump in my throat looking out at that unbelievable turquoise color.

As I sipped my water, a woman walked along the seawall on the far side of the channel. When she looked familiar, I realized it was Myrtle from the restaurant. She noticed me, and we exchanged friendly waves.

Seeing her reminded me of our chat at the restaurant. I hated thinking about my missing past. Quiet moments like these hollowed me out, a lonely ache filling my empty—

Don't do this to yourself, Eddi. There's no point.

My eyes lost focus as my thoughts turned to the past. I had more questions than memories. What happened in Tennessee? I kept smelling something burning. Why wasn't I hurt in the fire?

I had no burns, so I got out somehow. Who was the woman in the fire? I shuddered at the thought of some poor woman burning alive. Because she was alive, alright. Dead people didn't scream.

It was nighttime. The mystery woman yelled at me, *"RUN, Edaline! Run!"* Was it a real memory? Or was it a recurring nightmare?

Big fires made your skin bubble if you got close. I know because a boat burned at the marina a few years ago, and no one could get close enough to do anything. We let it burn until it sank.

And why do I always smell diesel? People used diesel to set fires. Did I burn something? Is that why my parents abandoned me? Deep down, I knew I would never do something so horrible. But somehow, I felt responsible. Cal said I was a rescuer at heart. I hoped he was right.

I sighed. As usual, all questions and no answers. Trying to remember never got me anywhere. Did I even *want* to know the truth? I might not like the answers. And I was content here—*right?*

I looked up the meaning of the name Edaline once. It meant *warrior, or fighter*. I snorted. Here I was, hiding in the Keys from a past I couldn't remember, and never tried to pursue.

Ya, I was brave, alright.

Cal had saved me. I'd run into him one day as I fished through the dumpster at the donut shop. Being the kind guy he is, he took me in and helped me get on my feet. I don't know what I would have done without him.

I sighed, and relaxing my shoulders, I closed my eyes and let the sun and the fresh smell of salt water ease me back into my peaceful reality.

Opening my eyes, I rubbed my neck and watched a land crab who thought he was invisible walk across the grass near the mangroves. It made me smile. Life was quiet and simple here.

Time to get back to work. I crunched my can into a ball, and as I stood, I looked up one last time—and sat back down with a thump.

Standing in the water across from me, at the mouth of the channel, with the glorious colors of the Atlantic as a backdrop, was Mr. Wet Dream.

He wasn't close, but I knew it was him. Once again, he stood there, watching me. Instead of being afraid, my heart leapt at the sight of him. I couldn't help the smile that spread across my face.

There he is. He's watching me again. Will he come over and talk to me?

The point of land behind him was a small sand spit with palm trees. Seeing him standing against that backdrop made me think of a postcard.

"Hi, Mom! Having a great time. Had sex with a total stranger today on the beach under a palm tree. I'm never coming back. Give my regards to Dad!"

I huffed out a breath, realizing I'd been holding it. As we stood there, locked in a staring contest, I swore I sensed a voice whispering down my spine. I shrugged off the ticklish sensation.

Why didn't this guy give me the creeps? Because he's hot, that's why.

"You're so desperate, *Eddi*," I whispered to myself.

What was he doing out there? I looked around. Was he staying at the campground on the other side of the channel?

Tourists always got themselves into trouble. That sand spit wouldn't be my first choice for swimming because the chunky coral retaining wall held patches of fire coral and the odd sea urchin. If you stepped on one of those, you'd never forget it.

As I watched, he sank into the water and slowly swam toward me. My pulse hammered.

He's coming over. SHIT.

Wildly, I looked around, relaxing when I saw Myrtle and Henry sitting on a bench under a palm tree on the other side of the channel.

Mr. Postcard disappeared briefly, and I caught a tantalizing visual of his firm buttocks covered by the same vibrant green suit from our last encounter. Those bulging, sexy thighs slipped under the water as he dove, and I realized he wore an ankle-length pair of dive skins. Judging by how they shimmered under the water, they were pricey.

He surfaced, this time in the middle of the channel. As he closed the distance, I tensed. What would I say to him? Would he speak to me this time or ignore my questions? My heart pounded.

Yep, you never know what will pop out of the ocean, alright.

I stood up, walked to the edge of our kayak beach, and waited for him to appear. I scanned the channel for ripples or a flash of green, but he was gone.

I waited a minute or two, but that was all I saw of him. It left me wondering if I had imagined it.

When I turned my head, I knew I hadn't been dreaming. Bert stood on his deck, and he watched, too. The cook looked at me, and even from this distance, I saw his frown.

***

~ RONAN ~

There she was, down by the water, sitting on a chunk of coral. As I stood across the channel and watched her daydreaming under the palm tree, my longing for her excited and terrified me. Not since my mother was alive had a woman meant anything to me.

These days, I kept to my grumpy self. But that meant no one for company. No lovers. No friends. Loneliness was an anchor around my neck, dragging me to the bottom.

When I saw the beautiful silver-haired girl so many years ago, sleeping by the mangroves on the edge of the sea, I sensed a chaotic energy dancing around her. I knew right away she was special.

I paid no attention to the fairer sex as they threw themselves at me out at the reef. I wasn't interested. With *this* girl, things were different.

You've got it wrong, you fool. You're going to regret it.

I tried to be smart and stay out of this one's sphere—out of her life. But lately, I drew closer and closer, wanting to speak to her, but failing miserably. And here I was again, staring at her and wishing more than anything in the world that I could talk to her.

Her silver bangs fluttered in the breeze, and her light gray eyes made my heart skip when she looked up and saw me watching her. The sad thoughts flitting over her face flew away when she smiled at me. My chest thumped hard enough to force a grimace.

Gods, Ronan, you are pathetic.

Even when she was sad, like today, she appeared so vibrant that I tasted her energy on my tongue. I wanted more of her. I couldn't stop myself.

I thought about all the places I could show her out on the mayan-blue waters of the Atlantic. The beautiful creatures that the warm Gulf Stream brought to our shores. These islands were my home, and I would love to share them with her. A silly, useless daydream that would end only one way.

Drawn irresistibly closer, I dove into the warm water of the channel and swam toward her. What would I say? What clever, eloquent words would I speak to convey my thoughts to her? I could barely speak, especially to girls. I had no idea what to say or how to say it. I would only have one chance to sweep her off her feet. I would be sure to plan it well.

Her curious eyes latched onto me when I bobbed up in the center of the channel, not far from where she sat. Her beautiful eyes called to me.

I was torn. Go to her and look like a fool? NO. Not with this girl. Not yet, anyway.

Sighing, I swam back the way I had come.

***

By five o'clock, *High Society* was back, the happy clients had taken their photos with their catch, and Captain Brian was cleaning fish while Cal hosed down the boat. I headed down to the dock to help rinse and hang up the gear, and we chatted while we worked.

"He was here? At the Marina?" Cal took his sweat-stained sun hat off in the shade of the boat top and rubbed his itching scalp. "And he didn't come and talk to you, huh? That is a little weird."

I nodded. "It was the strangest thing. One minute he was here, and then, poof, he was gone. Bert saw him, too."

"Maybe he likes you, Ed. Maybe he wants to play Hide the *Cigar Fish* with you?" Cal put his hat down by his groin and made a suggestive move with his hips. When he looked up, he got a squirt in the face for razzing me.

"Maybe he knows your favorite cook and was coming over for an early dinner?" We both laughed at that one.

"I know this sounds silly, but I got a bit nervous when I saw him. I wondered if he was coming to see *ME*. Isn't that dumb? I don't know who he is or anything about him, and he keeps popping up in my bubble. Should I mention it to James?"

"Well, how does he make you feel? I always figure that's a great indicator. If you feel comfortable, don't worry about it. See how it plays out, but just make sure there are people around if he comes back again. And if you feel scared, or like he's a threat or something, then *run like hell* and tell someone. He could just be a guy from the mainland who thinks that silver doo you're rocking is sexy—and *intriguing*."

I rolled my eyes and squirted him again. "As intriguing as the *Silver Surfer* in a dorky sun hat?"

Cal grabbed the brim of his hat, pulled both sides under his chin, puckered his lips, and batted his white eyelashes at me. I tried not to react, but I couldn't help smiling. I honestly didn't know where he got the energy when it was this bloody hot.

"I don't know, Cal. This whole thing has me on edge. There's something weird about this guy. Hell, I don't even know his name!"

Cal grinned. "Who needs names, sweetheart?"

I laughed and threw a rag at his head, which he caught out of the air with a flourish. We finished cleaning up the boat, then Cal collected his share of the tips and said goodbye to Brian.

Walking together, we headed down the dock to the stairs that led to the bike racks. As we reached the bottom of the steps, I noticed Bert standing at the stern of his tug boat. The delicious smell of barbecue wafted from the railtop grill hanging over the water. On his shoulder, my arch nemesis snuggled up to his neck, talking a blue streak.

Bert tracked us as we walked up the stairs, and as we passed, I pointed my injured finger at Mr. Darcy, then turned my hand so that it looked like a gun and pretended to fire. To my surprise, Bert chuckled and gave us a wave of his greasy flipper.

"He's not so bad, you know." Cal threw his leg over his bike and tossed his lunch box in the basket. "I talk to him once in a while. He's got some pretty cool stories. Did you know he's from Greece?"

I gave him a funny look. "You chatted—with Bert?" I glanced over my shoulder to see Mr. Darcy nibbling on Bert's earlobe. "I guess I am a little hard on him. I can't get past his personal hygiene. And he smokes!"

Cal gave me his *"Eddi, be nice"* look, and we parted ways for the night.

The sun was lower now, the evening offering a cooling breeze. As I biked past the kayak beach, I found my eyes scanning the mouth of the channel, hoping to catch a flash of green in the darkened water. All I saw were a bunch of Pelicans. And Bert, standing on his upper deck with a carnivorous parrot on his shoulder, watching me leave.

CHAPTER 5

A few days later, Cal and I were scheduled to work at the Bait & Dive Shop, which sold fishing tackle, swimwear, and other helpful things. Heat whorls shimmered from the pavement as we crossed the parking lot and stepped through the door into the blessed relief of the air conditioning. The day bustled with customers, but during the lulls, Cal and I discussed a Key West trip we had been planned for ages—the Dry Tortugas.

"The color of the water way out in the middle of nowhere will be sublime," Cal said as he folded a t-shirt. "I heard the Fort is so quiet after the tourists leave that it's a bit creepy at night. At least there's a handful of other campers out there."

"I'm just glad camping is only fifteen bucks a night. I can handle lugging gallons of drinking water along for the trip since it's so affordable. The two hundred bucks for the Yankee Freedom will pretty much break me, though."

Cal grabbed my shoulder and crouched, spreading his other arm out like a film producer. "Just imagine, Ed. Beautiful sandy beaches, untouched by the feet of millions of tourists—and it's all yours, for days." He laughed and grabbed another shirt to fold. "I'm glad we can lug your kayak along. The fishing must be amazing way out there."

I finished my stack of shirts and put them on the shelf. "At least we can shower on the ferry every day. That will be handy. Heading seventy miles offshore to camp at a historic fort in the Gulf of Mexico is a dream vacation. But in the middle of nowhere? I can't imagine how cool it will be."

The bell on the door jingled, and Cal headed to the till to service the customer. When I emerged from the t-shirt racks, I got the shock of my life. Standing in the middle of the store, talking to Cal, was my close encounter of the edible kind.

An embarrassing heat sizzled up the back of my neck. God, was my face going red? Why yes—*yes it was*. I let out a breath and tried to look natural.

Ha! Right!

I stood there with my mouth open. Luckily, they hadn't noticed me yet. I struggled to breathe as I gathered my courage and headed over to the cash.

Did this guy ever wear a shirt? Was he here to see ME?

I was tempted to bolt. Looking down, I checked my tank top and smoothed it out before realizing I was acting like an idiot. My cheeks turned crimson. Heat rose from my face in waves. I looked at Cal, who sent me a questioning look.

Coming to my senses, I moved behind the counter with him. My heart pounded so hard I choked on it. I could be professional. The guy was a customer. That's all—*a customer*. A very hot, desirable customer.

Cal covered his mouth with his hand to hide his smile. Judging by the twinkle in his eye, he had noticed my flushed face and struggled to keep his smart-ass comments to himself. I resisted the urge to kick him behind the counter.

I gave our visitor a quick once-over, surprised to see he looked—*normal*. His tanned chest was bare, and he wore those skin-tight ankle-length dive skins again. But now that I got a good look at them, I knew this guy had money. Those tights must have cost a fortune because they were thicker and more rugged than the cheaper brands, fitting him like a second skin.

At the ankle, they were a dark, almost black-green. A tiny, iridescent scale pattern, beautifully irregular, climbed to the guy's trim hips and faded to chartreuse before ending in a thin tan-colored seam. I saw no label, so they were custom-made or came from some exclusive European dive shop. Yep, we had a wealthy visitor from the mainland here, alright.

Man, that bulge in his tights is impressive.

Someone choked, and when I looked up, Cal's lips curled together as he tried not to burst out laughing.

Sweat trickled down the back of my neck. I gathered my courage to speak, but what came out made me wish I hadn't.

"So, where exactly do you keep your *wallet?*"

Oh my GOD, *Eddi!* No greeting, no filter. Just put it right out there. In the awkward silence that followed, I wanted to cover my face and find a hole somewhere.

Cal interjected on my behalf, thank goodness.

"Hey, Eddi. This is Ronan. He's here for *some bait.*"

My head whipped around to gawk at Cal, my face in flames. Oh my God. He was here for bait. Not *me.*

Wait a minute. This guy's name was Ronan? Screwing my eyebrows down, I glared at my friend.

How did you know that, Calvin?

Cal shrugged and, as if reading my mind, said, "He told me."

Ah, right. Cal beat me to the counter. *Ronan* told Cal his name, but he won't say *two words* to ME.

Asshole.

I took a deep breath, but before I could speak, *Ronan* headed over to the bait tanks in the next room. Walking with Cal. Who touched him. On the arm. It was then I noticed that our visitor was barefoot.

"Ahhh, *Cal?*" He turned around, and I motioned with an eye roll toward Ronan's feet. Cal waved it off and took him over to get the bait.

Oookay, then. The king of footwear enforcement just gave this guy a pass.

Maybe this *Ronan* guy affected Cal the same way he affected me. I grimaced at the thought. Cal had never said it out loud, but I suspected he was gay—so no worries—*right?*

I went cold, and the earth and I had a directional disagreement. My eyes burned as I wrestled with brimming tears. Oh. My. God. Is Ronan *gay*? It would explain so many things. I resisted the urge to flee and busied myself behind the counter instead, my eyes closing on the tears I refused to shed.

I shot furtive looks at them as they paused by the bait tanks. There were murmurs, but I had no idea what they discussed. Cal was being awfully friendly over there. He gave Ronan a t-shirt, so at least Cal solved the *no shirt, no shoes* problem.

I deflated like a week-old balloon. Letting out the breath I'd been choking on, I closed my eyes. Ronan was gay. *How did I not see it before?* I couldn't wait to hear what Cal had to say for himself. I wrestled with the urge to go over and butt in like a schoolgirl with a crush. Every time I looked, I caught Ronan staring back at me.

At least he's consistent. All eyes, no information.

His luminescent green eyes drew me in, and I couldn't stop peeking their way. Tears pushed harder against my lids, and I looked away.

Oh my god, now Cal is whispering in his ear? What the hell, Cal!

I dashed the sweat from my red face as they approached the checkout. Letting out a quiet *pfffft* to myself, I mentally face-palmed and concentrated again on what I was doing. Which was what exactly? Oh yes, rearranging the staff pen holder. By color.

What the hell, Eddi? What are you, twelve?

Stop it. Don't be selfish, Eddi. It's fine. So Ronan was gay. Cal deserved to be happy, too. There were more fish in the sea for me. I retreated to the racks, smashing a bunch of t-shirts in a disorganized heap and muttering to myself. When I glanced up again, Cal put something in the cash register. I almost laughed out loud.

Where did you get the money, Ronan? Out of your ass?

I couldn't stand it. No more playing it cool. Mr.. Green Eyes was about to leave, so I sidled over.

"See ya round," Cal said to our visitor. Anxiety punched into my chest as Ronan headed for the door, a small pail of bait under one muscular arm.

Ronan turned around, and I saw the shirt Cal gave him. It was pink, and on the front, it said "Master Baiter" with a cartoon fish. I looked at Cal, who smiled and shrugged. Ronan seemed none the wiser.

Gah! Ronan was leaving, and I never got a chance to talk to him. I must have been out of my mind because I opened my mouth, pointed at his purchase, and blurted, "What's that? Your afternoon *snack?*"

Behind me, Cal snorted. Ronan slowly turned towards us, his glorious green eyes sparkling with mischief. He reached into the pail, pulled out a wiggly little minnow, and popped it into his mouth. Slowly chewing the poor thing, his eyes crinkled, and he winked. At me. Then, without so much as a word, he opened the door, strolled out, and disappeared around the corner.

As the door tinkled shut behind him, the shop went silent. I looked at Cal, my mouth hanging open. He laughed.

"Smooth, girl. *Real smooth.*"

CHAPTER 6

A week went by with no sign of my green-eyed visitor. Cal and I were okay again, but it was touch and go. Cal swore that Ronan wasn't gay, but when I pressed him, he said, "Trust me, Eddi, I'd know." He felt terrible for trying to get a rise out of me that day in the shop.

"I had no idea you cared so much. I'm sorry, Ed."

"That makes two of us." I said. And just like that, we were solid again.

Putting Ronan out of my mind wasn't easy. Cal joked that I should get laid and suggested we hit the Brass Rail, a local hangout. After days of teasing, he let it drop. I had no idea how this Ronan guy could so profoundly affect me. I'd run into him three times and never exchanged a word.

Stop thinking about him, you obsessive dummy.

Jamming my hands through my silvery hair, I put my delusions aside and focused on my job. James had a charter for me tonight. A group of three guys booked a night fishing trip past the reef to try some deep drops.

Nerves tickled my belly all afternoon. Anchoring in one hundred feet of water could be tricky. If the steel triangular tips lodged in the coral, it was a bitch to get out, and the idea of damaging the reef made me cringe. Driving in circles with an anchor ball usually worked but added to my stress, even though we fished in regulated areas.

Showing up early to stock the live well with bait, I filled the cooler with ice and put some drinks in for the trip. Preparations didn't help with the nervous flutter in my gut, and when my clients showed up at sunset, their vibe turned my flutters into anxious fists.

They were unfriendly, and it immediately struck me that they didn't give their names. I received a bland "hello" as everyone shook my hand, then climbed aboard. I showed them where to sit, and they plunked themselves down, speaking in low whispers.

With a shrug, I pulled the dock lines off the cleats, backed out, and turned the *Wanderlust* toward the reef. The sun had already slipped below the horizon. As peaches and pinks filled the sky, I looked at my passengers, surprised by their utter lack of enthusiasm.

In a last-minute fit of nerves, I almost returned to my slip to bring Cal for backup. Ultimately, I continued on, determined to manage on my own. I relied on my friend far too much. It was time to put on the big girl panties.

The *Wanderlust* took thirty minutes to reach the reef. Judging by the rocky start, it would be a long trip out. At least the sky streaked a gorgeous magenta, lifting my spirits. In the failing light, the water was eerily dark against the burgundy sky.

Night fishing was productive, and the stern of the Wanderlust was well-lit for handling tangles. This was my first night trip, and I tried to relax, hoping my customers would lighten up once we got our lines in the water.

Strangely subdued, none of the men seemed interested in fishing. Clients usually chatted and asked questions. The charter may be an office bonding experience, with co-workers forced to participate. It happened. I shrugged. *Not my monkeys.*

There was still no reaction as we approached the reef. My guests seemed impatient, and the gray-haired guy kept looking at his watch. I tapped my foot, checked the horizon a million times, listened to the radio, and glanced sideways at my guests. They stared back at me, their expressions blank.

To pass the time, I made up names for them. I dubbed the tall, skinny one with long blonde hair "Twitch" because he couldn't sit still. His hands were always moving, rubbing his ear, raking through his hair, and scratching his chest. I would keep an eye on that one.

The other two barely spoke to Twitch, and when they did, it was harsh. My old Yamaha outboard was loud and drowned their conversations, but their expressions said it all. Who booked a fishing charter with people they disliked?

Oh, and "Norman Bates" was here, too. The guy was a dead ringer for the actor on the Hitchcock thriller *Psycho*—right down to the strange stare and quietly *menacing* speech pattern. I swear I heard sinister background music every time he spoke. When our eyes met, I squirmed.

Quiet and crisply attired, "Hannibal" watched the ocean slide by with hooded eyes, smiling and humming softly to himself. The tips of his fingers tapped together, a thin smile on his lips.

Hannibal's smile was unpleasant. The ice-cold expression was like peering into the eyes of a monster. Every time I spoke, his head turned toward me so slowly that I half expected it to keep going all the way around. No wonder captains didn't like bananas on their boats.

Unnerved by it all, I did what any good captain would do. I focused on my driving and ignored the horror show going on behind me.

When they whispered amongst themselves, I swore I heard the occasional growl, but if I glanced back, the men looked away. This trip became stranger by the minute, and my shallow breaths added to a light-headed feeling.

In a moment of near histrionics, I thought about slipping *The Doors* into my CD player and blasting *People are Strange.* Thankfully, I kept the urge under wraps.

I made several attempts at pleasant conversation. "So, where are you all from?"

Hannibal continued to stare, but Norman Bates, to my surprise, answered. "Nowhere you've heard of," he said.

Well, that killed three seconds. Only five million more to go.

"Have you men ever fished before?" They all shook their heads except for Twitch, who tapped his leg harder.

"So what do you do for work, Hannibal?" I cringed, hoping he didn't notice the slip.

"I beg your pardon?"

"Do you work on Sanibel—you know, the Island?" I held back a nervous giggle.

Nice save, Eddi. Only 250 miles away on the opposite coast of Florida.

Hannibal gave me a strange look, but after a few seconds, he answered. "Pharmaceuticals. We work in medical testing—*and distribution.*" He grinned.

All attempts to draw my guests into conversation failed. The urge to talk incessantly and fill the silence forced me to bite down on the tip of my tongue. I should have turned tail and taken the *Wanderlust* and my three serial killers back to the Marina before the sun disappeared completely. But Cal and I booked tickets for the Yankee Freedom trip to the Tortugas. I needed the money.

As we approached our fishing coordinates, I relaxed into my routine. The structure on the ocean floor in this location produced fish, but sharks were a problem. If you didn't reel fast enough, guests caught themselves a trophy fish head.

Visitors to the Keys loved seeing sea monsters, and this far out, we always spotted big predators following fish to the boat. Hammerheads, Bull Sharks, and monster Barracuda were gasp-worthy spectacles as they flashed out of the inky depths beneath the boat.

Dropping anchor upwind, I cast a look over my shoulder. Hannibal Lecter rechecked his watch, and Norman Bates gave his squirmy co-worker dirty looks for biting his nails and incessantly bouncing his skinny leg. Wait until Cal heard about this trio.

I ran through my usual *pre-fishing* speech, but no one listened. I gave up and concentrated on getting the anchor set, then went to the stern and began setting up the first rod.

In hindsight, I should have acted on my instincts from the very beginning. I should have asked Cal to come. Now, I would pay the price. Because when I turned around, my heart stopped. The menacing vibe hadn't been my imagination. Hannibal raised a gun and pointed it straight at me.

***

"I'm sure you are a little curious, my dear, but would you be so kind?" With a flick of his gun hand, Hannibal stepped aside and indicated the cuddy cabin beneath the bow.

My stomach fell into my feet. He had a gun. The *Wanderlust* was being hijacked. *By Hannibal fucking Lecter.*

I glanced toward the radio, but Hannibal frowned and said, "That's a really bad idea." He reached over and fished behind the radio, gathered up a handful of wires, and yanked.

"Do what we say, and you won't get hurt."

I almost laughed out loud at the cliche. I'm pretty sure my mouth hung open, but with imminent danger and pending bullet wounds aside, I was pretty damn calm. I stood frozen, holding a fishing rod in one hand, and a wriggling baitfish in the other.

I didn't comply fast enough because Bates stepped forward and, slapping the bait out of my hand, tossed the rod overboard. Out of habit, I grabbed for the rod as it went over only to find my wrist in an ice-cold vice.

Bates jerked me around to face him, his glittering eyes close enough that I smelled his breath. It was pretty disgusting, to be honest.

"Forgot to brush, did we?"

The words were out before I could stop myself, and in a flash, I sailed across the deck and crashed into the shutters of the cabin below. A sickening pain lanced my side as the shutters cracked under the force of my impact.

Before I registered the pain in my ribs, a hand around my throat lifted me and pinned me against the helm, the plastic molding digging into my back. It was Twitch, his deathly grip squeezing my neck. I couldn't breathe.

I CAN'T BREATHE!!

I struggled, kicking with all I had and prying at the fingers around my neck, but they wouldn't budge. I landed a few good kicks to Twitch's legs, punching his face a few times, but he grunted and squeezed harder. The longer he choked off my air, the harder I thrashed against his hold.

Desperate to pull air into my burning lungs, I gave one last buck with my entire body, but it was no use. My air was gone, slipping away with the last of my strength.

My mouth opened and closed like a fish; my legs hung limp against the helm; my half-closed eyes saw nothing. As my eyes closed, I thought of Ronan. A bitter laugh pushed against the hand taking my life, but all that came out were bubbles.

Oddly enough, I wasn't afraid. I was sad I would never find out where Ronan kept his wallet.

***

I lay on the ground, staring into a robin-egg-blue sky. My hands waved in front of my eyes, and they were tiny, the little nails cute and perfect. I giggled while something flew in loops over my head. Whatever it was, it darted quickly, left, then right. I squealed with laughter, screeching at the thing and clapping my hands.

"Stop teasing her, Ezen," laughed a kind female voice. Whatever entertained me stopped, and although I couldn't see the thing, it hovered above me, a faint stain against the clouds. Then it blinked out of existence, the saturated blue sky empty again. I clapped my chubby little hands, screaming for more.

The images flitted and flirted, the random, short bursts of recognizable things flashing, as dreams often do. There was the frustrating sensation of the world out of focus, like a window sheeting with rain that blurred my view.

My tiny fingers clutched the soft muslin of her tunic. A golden cage of fine webbing tamed her shimmering black tresses, but her face was pale and still. I asked the silver-haired man beside me if she died, and he cried her name. *"Ariya."*

I never saw the woman again. She had been loving, kind, and quick with a smile. It hurt, being without her. Instead, silver eyes watched, a fierce smile on a drawn face.

The dream skidded sideways, and I crouched near a forest, holding a knife. Something burned. I smelled it. From the shoulders up, a female figure peered over the grass, her face filled with terror, her mouth open in a scream. Someone grabbed her brown hair, and a red line appeared on her throat.

In my dream, I saw her clearly this time. Her mouth didn't move, but her eyes held mine. *"Run, Edaline!"*

CHAPTER 7

An odd sensation woke me—that strange haze when you were half awake and background noises seemed clear, but voices had a distant quality. One voice sounded odd. Deep, and guttural. When I thought of my dream, my stomach pitched.

As I slowly adjusted to the blackness surrounding me, I knew it wasn't the dream that made my head throb and my stomach churn. I lay in the bow cabin, sprawled on the padded bench. The attack forced its way back into my reality, and I blanched.

My eyes were useless in the black hole of the cabin, but my ears focused on the sounds around me. My captors were at the stern, talking. My throat burned, and my ribs brought tears whenever I took a deep breath, but I was alive.

I jolted upright, instantly regretting it and easing back down onto the cushions. I would display some severe bruises tomorrow. Would there be a tomorrow? I wasn't stupid. I had landed in some serious shit, right up to my eyebrows this time. I tried not to think too hard.

One step at a time, Eddi. Relax. Think. Breathe.

Who were these people, and why did they want the *Wanderlust?* I mentally kicked myself for not listening to my instincts. How on earth did James not notice these guys were sketchy as hell? My mind raced frantically between blame, fear, and resignation.

Am I going to die out here?

I looked at my watch. It was midnight. We'd left at dusk, and it was a three-hour charter, so James would be worried by now. Did he try the radio? I usually checked in around supper time. James would notice, *right?*

They destroyed the radio. Shit.

I searched my joggers for my cell phone, but it was gone.

They're not stupid, Eddi. Goodbye, Pixel.

My thoughts raced. Would Cal come looking for me? Sometimes, tours ran late, but we always called in if that happened, especially at night. I had to think this through, but my ribs throbbed, right along with my head and neck, making it hard to concentrate.

The sound of a diesel motor coming up from behind, followed by a slight bump against the hull, and I knew we had company. More talking—something about the *north*—more footsteps, and a few minutes later, I heard the other boat putter away, then throttle forward—an inboard diesel motor.

My nausea ebbed, so I chanced sitting up. The darkness in the cabin didn't help, and my head swam, but I managed to hold down my lunch.

Slowly, so I didn't alert the hijackers, I padded over to the shutters and looked to see what happened on the deck. Visible under the canopy light, my kidnappers stood in the stern as Hannibal opened a leather messenger bag. Twitch sat on a cooler against the wall with his sleeve rolled up. The rubber tourniquet above his bicep turned my stomach, and I stifled the urge to vomit. Pulling away from the broken shutters, I covered my mouth.

I should have known. The Keys had issues with drug trafficking because of their proximity to the Caribbean. There was water access from every direction. Why was I surprised?

Getting out of this situation in one piece didn't look promising. There was no way they were letting me go. I choked down the urge to cry and looked back through the broken shutters in time to see Hannibal pull a thimble-sized vial of clear liquid out of the satchel.

He poked the seal with a tiny syringe and drew out a few drops of the contents. It looked like an insulin syringe, making me wonder if Twitch was diabetic.

I rolled my eyes at the absurd thought. Ya, Eddi. That's why they kidnapped you and stole a thirty thousand dollar boat—to deal in the illegal insulin trade.

I watched as Hannibal found a vein and injected our twitchy friend, and that was when I knew. This was NOT insulin.

Tipping his head back, Twitch's body changed from jittery to wet rag in *seconds.* This was some potent shit he sampled because a look of euphoria smoothed over his features. With a slack-jawed smile, his head lolled to the side, his arm dropping to hang beside him.

Hannibal handed Bates the injection kit, and they both stood back. With excited, strangely greedy looks, they watched Twitch flying with the pink elephants.

His head rolled back against the wall, and his eyes tracked slowly back and forth as if dreaming with his eyes open. A serene smile plastered his face. The guy was so high that he gradually slipped from his seat, his body rolling until he lay in an awkward heap, face down on the floor. Twitch was blissed out, and the dynamic duo loved it.

His hands grasped at nothing, and he moaned, long and low. It was a strangely erotic sound. But when he began to pant and grind his hips firmly into the deck, my skin prickled. Whatever was in that vial was the mother of all roofies, and Twitch was in some sort of pornographic *la la land.*

The stillness broke when the other two scumbags looked at each other. The gleam in their eyes made my stomach pitch.

"The quality is unbelievable," Hannibal said with a twisted smile. He rubbed his hands together. "Let Hex know. We need to get moving on distribution." He paced back and forth, his steps brisk.

"This shit is costing us a small fortune. We need to ramp up production to bolster the wild—" Hannibal's voice trailed off as he muttered to Bates in the shadows of the stern deck light. I didn't need to see or hear more to know these assholes were deep into some pretty bad shit.

"What about the girl?" Bates asked.

Hannibal looked up from packing his satchel.

"We need to get moving. Hex doesn't need to know about our little side trip. Kill the girl and throw her overboard."

Bates looked across the deck, focusing on the helm, and paused. "Where are the Keys?"

My chest tightened, and my blood turned to ice. I had nothing to defend myself with. My mind scrambled for a solution, but there was no time. I had the keys. And Bates was coming for us both.

I had a nervous habit of pulling the keys from the ignition when I wasn't driving. We usually had little kids on board, and they got into things. Heat flushed my skin. I tried to see through the darkness of the cabin, and my ears buzzed in the absence of light or sound. I couldn't see!

THINK, Eddi!!

Then I remembered. I held my throbbing ribs and reached over, using my hands to find the shelf in the dark. A small cubby hole under the electronics might save my life.

Feeling around inside, I fished out a standard orange flare gun. It was pitch black in here, and I couldn't see past my nose. But I had a weapon. *Sort of.*

I didn't have time to plan anything clever. Anything was better than sitting here and letting death come for me. In the end, I did what any desperate person would do. I took the fight to my enemy.

Standing up, I ignored the searing pain in my ribs, lifted my leg on my good side, and kicked the shutters off their hinges.

I'd love to say that I was a rock star and yelled something witty as I took out the bad guys. In reality, I hobbled out of the cabin, took aim, and fired a flare at them while screaming at the top of my lungs.

My two intended targets didn't flinch as the glowing orange ball sizzled past them, their eyes tracking it as it disappeared over the ocean. When the smoke cleared, the only sound was the water gently lapping at the hull.

Then, in a strangely choreographed way, they both turned to face me. Lifting his gun, Hannibal smiled.

Oh. Shit.

What happened next was a visceral reaction to being kidnapped, beaten up, and threatened with death. With superhuman precision, I hurled the flare gun at Hannibal's head. The Gods must have smiled at me because my aim was true.

The orange plastic gun hit him square in the face. As he staggered backward in shock, blood dripping from his forehead, Hannibal dropped his weapon. It tumbled through the air, bounced off the side rail, and, with a satisfying splash, went overboard.

Without thinking twice, I turned and threw myself over the other side.

Unfortunately, the water was as black as pitch, and I became disoriented when I came up for air. With expert precision, I cracked my head dead center on the motor's prop.

Seeing stars, I grabbed onto the Yamaha outboard and huddled behind it with my hand on my head, waiting for the pain to subside. I pulled my hand away because it felt slippery. Yep, I bled like I'd sprung a leak. Blood dripped down my chin and puddled in the dark water.

I cursed my luck. It was like a bad movie. I floated in a pool of blood in a shark-infested ocean. But I knew something important. Human blood didn't attract sharks. They couldn't care less about anything but fish blood.

Coming to my senses, I made a decision and started swimming. To where I had no idea, but away from the *Wanderlust* was a good start. Brought up short when something sharp pierced the front of my thigh, I bellowed with pain, rage, and fear. Dragged backward toward the boat, I shrieked at the top of my lungs; they gaffed me. Snagged like a prized marlin.

I didn't dare struggle, and all the fight left me. It was bad enough that I bled from my head and leg. I didn't need to make things worse. Tapping out of this nightmare, my muscles went limp.

Hauled up by the ankles, my head slammed against the railing when they pulled me onto the boat. I was unceremoniously dumped on the deck, then kicked in the side with a wet splat as someone's foot connected. I tried to scream, but there was no breath to give it substance.

I was out of screams and out of fucks to give. I was done being strong. I lay on the deck, sobbing and gasping for air. There was no point sorting out what to do now because I already knew. They would kill me.

Twitch lay on the deck beside me, still partying at a brothel in the land of Oz. On his back, a monstrous arousal tented his pants. His lips moved with licking motions as his hands massaged at nothing.

Through the pain and disgust, I knew something dark and deadly was at work. Someone needed to sound the alarm. Do something. Stop this, whatever *this* was. But it wouldn't be me.

Foggy and stunned, I turned my head in defeat and looked up at the hard top above me. *Huh.* Where did the crack up there come from? I would have to tell James about it.

Two menacing faces drifted into view above me. Hannibal's eyes were black, with no whites. The strange thought barely registered when another kick landed, this time on the side of my head. Everything went black.

Someone spoke, but with the buzzing in my ears, I couldn't understand them.

"Where—Keys?" It was Bates.

Yes, I know we're in the Keys, you dumbass.

Wait. Was I thinking it, or saying it? I put my hand to my mouth. Nope, my lips weren't moving. Definitely thinking it, then. I giggled.

With a cough, blood spewed from my mouth. I knew because it splattered my hand, which still hovered over my lips. At least my eyes still worked.

Someone yelled, "I *said*, GIVE me the KEYS to the BOAT, you *BITCH!*" Bates was in my face this time, so close I smelled his breath.

If I get out of this alive, I'm getting you a toothbrush, you fucking psychopath.

I raised my hand and shot him the finger.

Keys. Are you talking about the ones I tossed while I was overboard? I laughed and spit blood in his face in a fit of panic-induced rebellion.

My eyes ached to close, but I forced them open to watch as Bates, his expression glittering with hatred, stuck out his tongue and licked my blood from his lip. He gave me a bone-chilling smile.

I knew what was coming—so I smiled at him—because the small shred of power I stole back was worth it. My head snapped back, and a ferocious snarl came from my attacker.

"Quit horsing around and check her pockets," Hannibal snapped. Rough hands practically ripped my pockets, and I moaned when the jostling hurt my ribs.

Bates shook his head at Hannibal. I saw it clearly, but it was as if peering through one of those spy glass thingies from an old movie.

Bates stopped searching my pockets and dropped me back on the floor.

"Ooof."

Another kick. I didn't even feel it this time.

"Never mind," Hannibal said. "I'll call Hex. The guys can't have gotten far. We need to hurry. Deal with her already."

When I saw the wheels turning in a pair of sadistic eyes, I went numb. Bates grabbed me by the arms and lifted me. My ribs screamed, but the banging in my head was far worse.

"I have something extra special, just for you, princess. Something slow. Something terrifying." Bates leaned close, his eyes flicking red as he added, "Something *fun*."

He pulled my hands behind my back, and I heard the sound of a zip tie as my wrists crushed together. I tried to object, but all that came out were drooly sounds.

God, I was tired. I faded out for a moment, but the odd sensation of cold sludge running down the inside of my joggers brought me around. It took me a moment to realize it was chum. Ice cold and reeking, the bait slid down my leg like a fishy milkshake.

I struggled, which earned me a backhand across the face. My throbbing head flopped forward, and the thought of gushy chum made me gag. Norman growled and held me away, avoiding the puke before it splashed on his shoes.

I didn't have enough sense to be afraid as I watched him lean over and pick up the football-sized Bonito from my cutting board. Grabbing some fishing line, Bates ran it through the gills and tied it around my waist.

Dragging me to the side of the boat—which wasn't easy, as I couldn't stand—Bates chuckled with delight. When my head flopped forward, and I saw the fat fish hanging from my waist, I snorted. I was so fucked.

"Tadaa!" Bates chirped. "I even accessorized for you. You can thank me later." Then he tipped me over the side.

When I hit the water, it was head first, and the salt made the cuts all over my face sting like a mother. That was enough of a shock that my thoughts cleared for a moment or two.

I tried twisting my hands loose but couldn't feel them and quickly gave up. I wiggled around to get some of the chum from my pants. I kicked and twisted, pushing myself through the water enough to wash it from my joggers. It was useless.

My hands tied behind my back made it hard to keep my head above water, so eventually, I laid back and took deep breaths, concentrating on floating face up.

What a stupid way to die.

As I tired and my attempts grew feeble, I was still close enough to the *Wanderlust* to hear a boat arrive and then leave again. I thought they would burn my beautiful boat, but when I lifted my head and looked back, she was anchored and bobbing gently on the flat sea.

When they disappeared from view, I tried to head back to my boat. I could cut the zip ties if I made it to the motor. But I was too tired, and the current steadily carried me south. It was too late. Soon, my beautiful boat disappeared from view.

CHAPTER 8

I didn't know how long I bobbed along under the constellations. As my core temperature dropped, I slipped in and out of reality. People thought you couldn't get hypothermia in warm water. They were wrong.

My world narrowed to drifting on the Gulf Stream, staring up at the Milky Way and wondering why I always wound up alone. Every day, a gnawing desolation lived beneath my skin. But tonight, as I swirled under the stars, an endless void of misery swallowed me whole. I wasn't a rock, standing solid on my own and damned the consequences. I was an unwanted, wasted life, washing out to sea on a raft of despair.

For a while, I stared at the back of my eyelids, beyond caring. The pain disappeared when I stopped shivering; then I felt nothing. It was heaven.

Somewhere along my route, I managed to get my joggers off. Using the gentle current and my toes, I slowly worked them down far enough to kick them off with the last of my strength. Now it was me and the ten-pound Bonito floating below, tethered to my waist like shark bait.

Cal won't find you. No one will. You're done. Let it go.

I felt strangely at peace. The vastness of the deep, dark ocean spreading below no longer scared me. Sometimes, accepting things can set you free.

Eventually, I felt what I had been waiting for. The water beneath me rose up, pushed from below by something big. A hard fin brushed down my bare leg. I must have been in shock because instead of panicking, I relaxed. In calm acceptance, I floated and waited. I may have prayed a bit, too.

I thought about when Cal and I cleaned fish at the marina. We threw the carcasses into the water because customers loved watching sharks come in to feed. We tracked how long it took them to find their snacks, the bloody water like a beacon to their sensors. It never took long. Twenty minutes, tops.

Sometimes, we got one shark, but often, it was more. Bulls, Lemons, Black Tips. They were all the same when it came to eating. They were careful.

The smaller sharks would make several quick, darting passes before nervously grabbing the leftovers. The big ones were braver and moved slower. Just one or two passes, then they'd have it. Sharks are careful. They check to see if it's safe to eat before snacking. Sharks are wonderful, really—Nature's cleanup crew.

There it was a second time, only this time, I felt the surge, then a swirl of water, and it had me in its mouth. Intense pressure squeezed my hip, but I felt no pain as it clamped on tight.

It released me just as quickly. A few minutes passed, and I waited, drifting in shock, unable to care. The sensation was surreal.

Another surge, but this time, I felt the fishing line around my waist go tight, and the shark pulled me under. Something snapped, and I coughed up seawater when I bobbed back to the surface.

In a haze of jumbled thoughts, I vaguely recognized my stroke of good luck. The Bonito was gone.

***

I dreamed that I was lost. Terrible things happened in the dream. Impressions flickered through my mind like an old Charlie Chaplin movie. A gun. Red eyes. A vicious predator, hurting me. I faced off against so much hatred and violence, and I was all alone. It was bad. So, so bad.

Then, in my dream, he came, appearing out of the water beside me. His green eyes glowed with a gentle light. Ronan was here, and I wasn't afraid anymore. His large, gentle hand lifted my head above the water.

Finally, for the first time, I heard his voice, and it made me cry. It was lilting and musical, and I couldn't help but smile through the tears. I knew it would be perfect.

"Shhh. I'm here, don't cry. You're safe now. It's over. I've got you."

I cried harder. I couldn't stop. All the strength that kept me going until this moment slipped away. I was broken.

"You did so well. You are brave and fierce, little Barracuda." He smiled down at me. He had such a beautiful smile.

Dream Ronan was strong and incredibly sexy and teased me by swimming around me under the water.

"Come back!" I cried. He kissed my wrists, and they were finally free. Free to soak in the heat radiating from his body.

He reached out, and when he pulled me into a hug with his powerful arms, I stuck myself to him like Velcro and soaked it all in. My hands shook uncontrollably, so it was hard to hang on.

Stupid hands!

An inferno against my skin chased away the numbing cold. This dream got better all the time. But my savior looked worried. Why was he looking at me like that?

"By the Gods, Eddi. Your face! What happened to you?" I tried to lift my hand to feel it, but his arms wrapped me so tightly that I couldn't move.

"You are too cold! We must hurry. They are close." Tucking me under his chin and holding me against his hot, hard chest, we swam.

I giggled at the sensation tickling my bare skin as I sprawled on a smooth, rolling pillow. The water swirled by, reminding me of standing on the shore, letting the tide push around my legs.

The energy coming from his warm body gave me a tremendous rush. It soaked through my skin and mingled with my blood. Tingles swept over my body, and I relaxed into the heady sensation, my mind wandering.

Can you fall asleep in a dream?

"Almost there. Stay with me, Edaline." Dream Ronan gave me a gentle shake, and I grumbled.

"Am I dead?" I whispered. "I'm so cold." I shivered, and his arms tightened.

"You're dreaming. When you wake up, you will be well."

Dizzy, weak, and slurring a bit, I chided, *"I don't think so, Mr. Sexy Pants.* This is my death dream. How do you come back from death?"

Ronan hugged me close and whispered in my ear, *"Magic, Edaline."*

My name on his lips made me smile, and I wriggled even closer. This dream was *terrific*! I was drunk on whatever came from him in thick, pulsing waves. I wanted more. I wanted closer.

I pressed my cracked lips to his neck and felt his pulse tapping beneath them. The urge to grind against him overwhelmed me, and I rubbed myself on his thigh. I stuck out my tongue and tasted his salty skin.

Ronan chuckled. *"Not so fast, Eddi. You are badly injured. Soon, you will be with your friends. I promise."* Ronan pressed a gentle kiss to my forehead.

I was flying. In my dream, Ronan told me things. It came from far away and inside of me at the same time.

"I am so sorry, Eddi."

Dream Ronan was very sweet.

"Sorry for what?" I asked, snuggling into his chest. I didn't care, I wanted closer. He was so warm and *wonderful*.

"I was too slow. You are bleeding. The shark was hungry tonight."

I wanted this dream to last forever. It was so freaking good.

Lost in Ronan's warm embrace, I barely registered the mad flapping of sails and familiar voices. There was some tugging and jerking, which made me mad and slappy. Ronan's arms loosened, and the intoxicating heat disappeared. I cried out and grabbed for him, but strong, thick fingers pulled me away.

In the distance, I heard Cal's voice, and then he held me. I couldn't see him, but I knew Ronan kept his promise.

Finally, the tears came, and it was one of those crying dreams where you woke up with your face wet with big, sloppy tears.

Cal cradled me on his lap to stop the bouncing and tucked me into something soft that kept out the wind. I relaxed, and in my friend's carefully folded cocoon, my dream faded into the darkness of a bottomless sleep.

CHAPTER 9

The sun shone through a window, and I heard quiet voices nearby. I had a sheet pulled up under my arms so tight that I felt like a burrito. I felt like crap, and my ribs ached, but when I lifted my fingers to my lips, they were smooth and supple. Huh.

Beside the bed, Cal slouched in an uncomfortable-looking chair. His chin was on his chest, and he was snoring softly. My heart grew two sizes bigger. I may not have a real family, but I had at least one champion.

As I waited for him to wake, the trauma from the attack last night drifted back, and my stomach pitched. My head was packed full of cotton, and I was parched. I reached for the cup of water and bendy straw conveniently left by my bed. As I sipped, I slowly allowed the details of last night to filter back in.

I had so many questions. How did I get here? It looked like Fisherman's Hospital, judging by the color of the walls and the bed I was in. Where did they find me? How did they find me?

And *Dream* Ronan? I smiled at the memory of it. He couldn't have been there, could he? I blushed with embarrassment at the thought of Ronan seeing me without pants.

I heard Cal stirring, and when I looked, he was straightening in his chair, his red puffy eyes flitting over me, checking to see if I was ok. He looked at me, and his eyes went wide.

"You're awake! Thank the Gods in Heaven. You scared the crap out of me!"

Jumping up, he came to the bed and pulled me into a gentle hug.

"I'm so sorry this happened to you," he said, his voice anguished.

"It's all been like a bad dream. Like I'll wake up, and it never happened," I said as I smoothed my hands over the sheets. "I'm lucky to be alive, aren't I? I keep wondering how I'm still alive." My voice broke with a sob.

"Do you want to talk about it?" Cal asked carefully. I could tell he didn't want to upset me. I could also see he was desperate to know what happened to me out there on the reef.

I didn't know where to start. How do you talk about something you'd rather bury and never think about again?

I took a deep breath and started with some simple questions. That was nice and safe.

"I'm so confused, Cal. How did I get to the hospital? How did you find me?"

I scrunched my face in distress and confusion and suddenly realized it wasn't very sore. I reached up with my fingers, where I remembered cuts and huge bruises. I could feel a stitch or two and a tender spot, but it felt ok.

With a gasp, I brought my hand to the top of my head. I could feel the line of a scabbed-over gash.

"No staples," I said. Now I was baffled.

"What do you mean?" Cal asked, looking worried.

"Last night. I cut my head on the motor. I know I did. It hurt like a bitch, and I bled like a fountain. I REMEMBER IT. Right before they *gaffed* me!"

Tears welled in my eyes again, and I turned to Cal, who looked stricken.

"Those fuckers GAFFED me!"

The look on Cal's face said it all. Shock, anxiety, and fear were followed closely by anger. He needed some answers too. Cal sat down on the bed and took my hand. It felt like I had an anchor rope to hold.

"We almost lost you, *Eddi*. You were BLUE! What would I have done if you died!? I can't do it without you." The last was more sobs than words, and tears rimmed his lids.

"It's ok, Cal. I'm here. You saved me. I don't know how you found me, but you came for me. I was so scared. I floated for so long. There was a SHARK. Oh my God, the *shark!*"

The room spun, so I settled back on the pillows. We sat quietly for a while, and Cal couldn't stop twisting his fingers together in anxiety.

Finally, I asked, "Is the *Wanderlust* ok? Did they catch the bastards that did this?" I felt tears prickling at my lids, but I rubbed them away. There would be lots of time to bring back the horrors of my ordeal. All in good time.

"I want to know everything, Cal. I NEED to know. Start at the beginning." At the concerned look on his face, I added, "Please. Tell me."

I saw a battle raging behind his eyes. He wanted to protect me from the stress of it all but fill me in on what happened last night. He knew I wouldn't quit, so he told me everything.

"I was in the bait shop, cleaning the tanks. I closed up and just hung out, playing games on my phone. I waited for you because I picked up some Dion's Chicken."

I smiled. My favorite. So damn crispy.

"At first, you were just late. Then you didn't come back." He looked at me, the panic reflected in his eyes. At the break in his voice, my heart melted. He had waited for me with my favorite snack. God, I loved him.

"I tried to call out to the reef, but there was no answer on the radio, and I got worried. Bert said he saw you go and that there were strange guys with you. I tried to call James, but he didn't pick up!"

That was odd. James always came back to the marina when the night charters returned to help with everything. Night trips sucked if you had to clean up alone.

"I totally panicked because I knew something bad was happening. I didn't know what to do!" I could see that I wasn't the only one who was traumatized.

"Is James ok? Did you find him? Does he know about what happened?" Something definitely wasn't jiving.

Cal looked at me, and I saw that hesitation again. "He knows now. We found him after you were pulled out of the water. Brian went looking and said he was sitting on his couch at home with the TV going. His phone was off, and he was out to lunch." Cal was furious. "He was groggy, and had absolutely NO idea you were out at the reef."

Cal looked as confused as I felt. A slither of apprehension rolled down my spine. That was so unlike James. Davy Jones Locker was his *baby*. It usually ran like a well-oiled machine because he was such a stickler for safety. How could he not remember I was on a charter? He set that trip up himself!

"To answer your other question, the *Wanderlust* is right where you left it, or at least it was until this morning. I wanted to help retrieve her, but the Sheriff's Marine Unit was taking over. Besides, I didn't want to leave you. I wanted to be here when you woke up." He gave me a watery smile. "I'm so glad you're ok."

Small mercies. At least my boat was safe and not somewhere being stripped down for parts. I loved that damn boat.

"Anyway, when you didn't come back, we went out to the reef and found the boat, but there was no sign of you or your clients. The current was heading south, so we started searching in that direction." Cal's eyes were wide, and he kept rubbing his neck.

"We got SO lucky. You don't know about him, but I have a friend who flies—a drone, I mean." He gave me a wry smile.

"He was home, and he came to the reef with me, and we got up just south of your boat and started searching. He has great night vision." He bit his lip. "Cameras. You know, like a FLIR? They read heat signatures?"

I nodded. That made sense.

"It took a while, but he found you. Thank the Gods he found you! You were halfway to Sombrero Lighthouse, for fuck sake. You were so cold he almost missed you. We lost you several times before finally getting a solid fix on you. If we hadn't had help—" He paused, looking flustered.

I was barely listening to him. I just realized he meant that I was so far gone I wasn't showing on the FLIR. I blanched.

"You were in bad shape when we plucked you out of the water. I was so scared—" His voice broke again, and I reached for his hand.

"Cal, it's ok." He gave me a watery smile. "Thank you for saving me." We sat there, holding hands until it was safe to continue.

"Look, I know this is going to sound strange, but was RONAN with you?" I asked.

Cal gave me an odd look. "No, why do you ask?" I could see Cal was humoring me. I was still a bit messed up.

"Because I had the weirdest dream. I must have been hallucinating. In my dream, he saved me. He swam with me and brought me to you." Cal was looking at me strangely, so I let it go.

"Ah, never mind. I was pretty out of it, I guess."

I looked around the hospital room, and I could see out the window. It was a brilliant day, and the ocean was putting on a minty show that lifted my spirits. I lay back on the pillows, and Cal sat on my bed, looking down at me with obvious exhaustion.

"Can you believe all this?" I took a deep breath. "I mean, what the hell, right? How does something like this even happen? It doesn't make sense."

Cal looked at me, gave me a sad smile, and asked, "Are you feeling well enough to tell me what happened? I need to hear. If you need more time, that's ok too. But if you can manage, you should start at the beginning. Tell me everything."

CHAPTER 10

With short breaks, reliving every scary moment of the *night from hell took a while*. I started with the weird vibe from the clients and how I wanted to turn around. When I got to the drug part, Cal was so angry he ground his teeth.

He gave me a weak smile about my bad aim with the flare gun. When I began rehashing their beating, his face screwed up, and Cal appeared torn between wanting to cry and killing someone.

I told him about the chum, the shark, and the strange dream about Ronan. He chuckled at my red face when I mentioned licking his neck.

"I don't blame you, girl! I would too," he laughed. "He's got some serious hots going on, that boy."

Not long after, the police came and took my statement, which took a lifetime. At least, that's what it felt like. They were kind to me but, at the same time, very thorough.

Cal mentioned that the cops towed the *Wanderlust* to the County Sheriff's Marine Unit for fingerprinting. Impressed that they were all over this thing, I was still a little bummed at them taking my boat

The police were most concerned about my assault, taking pictures of all my cuts and bruises, which were much better than I imagined. They cataloged the bite wound on my hip, now neatly stitched. Based on the bite pattern, they figured it was a Lemon Shark. That explained why I was still here. Lemon Sharks were like the Keanu Reeves of the ocean. They look dangerous but are pussy cats under most circumstances. Things might have ended differently had it been a Bull or a Tiger, which are more aggressive—especially the big ones.

The gaff wound was still pretty gross, but the Doctor said it didn't need stitches. It already had a large, bulging scab over the puncture wound. The doctor prescribed antibiotics and told me to return if there was any heat or redness.

My run-in with the motor was the biggest surprise. I must have overimagined things because the head wound was tiny. The doctor said I was in shock when it happened, and head wounds always appeared much worse than they were.

The trauma to my face was significant, but the bruises were already turning that ugly banana brown, and the cuts were closing over. The Doctor put my quick recovery down to good health and the vigor of youth.

Everyone was good to me, and the nurse gave me the card of a local psychologist who would help with the wounds I couldn't see.

When the doctor said I could go home, I wasn't thrilled. I felt safe here. But beds were in high demand. It was time to face the music. Bending over to tie my shoes, I sucked in a breath and had to call the nurse. My ribs missed the memo about the whole *vigor of youth* thing.

After Cal picked me up, loaded me into a taxi, and deposited me in my own bed, I slept like a log. Knowing I was nervous about being alone, Cal offered to stay over. He slept on my couch, and I woke up at some point to the sound of him snoring like a gremlin in the living room. Apparently, I was in charge of protection if we had unwanted visitors. I sighed and turned onto my side, grimacing at the tug on my sore ribs. I couldn't believe it was over.

***

In a few days, I was back to work. It was odd how quickly I healed, but I shrugged it off. Things were weird enough without borrowing trouble.

Getting back to work was necessary, with bills to pay and no time to laze about. But I felt good. The stiffness and bruising were gone; within a week, even the cuts healed.

The only things still on the mend were my shattered nerves. Everywhere I went, I jumped at shadows and became one of those cowards who wouldn't go out alone. I wasn't fond of *scared* Eddi. She was weak and dependent. I tried to make the best of it. I just needed time.

Cal was amazing. He went through the same thing in reverse, constantly checking on me and going out of his way to help. We licked our wounds together. I always knew we were close friends, but the traumatic events brought us that much closer.

Ronan appeared more often but always at a distance. Usually out on the ocean, but I saw him at my bus stop once. He would wave or nod but never came over to talk.

One day, I saw him across the channel at the State Park beach while I fished around the Island. At first, I thought he might swim across to chat. He stood in the surf up to his thighs and watched me but made no move to close the short distance. When I looked back over, he was gone. The guy was a freaking ghost.

It started to annoy me. Whenever Ronan appeared, I scratched the back of my neck where it tingled and ignored my lady bits doing their happy dance. The guy burrowed in under my skin, and was constantly in my thoughts. And still, he never said a word to me.

My god, I'm turning into an overstimulated spinster.

I don't know if it was the crazy dream I had that put romantic notions in my head, but I was disappointed in his lack of interest. I read too much into things, I guess. I vowed I wouldn't spend another minute obsessing about him.

It was my first shift at the Crazy Conch since the accident, and Ada heard about my injuries. She made a considerable fuss, looking me over and hugging me tight. I felt ridiculous but was honored that Ada cared so much.

"I'll take extra tables today, hun," she offered. "It doesn't feel right making you work so hard your first shift back."

I told her not to worry about it, but she insisted. To be honest, I was glad. It wasn't anything physical. I was fine that way. It was the *recovery on the inside* part that I found challenging. I knew the brutal assault changed me. I was more fearful and hesitant about everything. I hated feeling vulnerable and looking over my shoulder all the time.

I had that card for the psychologist, the one that the doctor gave me. I could call, but I was stubborn and knew I wouldn't. I didn't want to discuss it with strangers, so I used my anxiety exercises. I had a lot of practice with those.

Breathe. Get the coffee pot. Fill it up. You can do it.

Coping was my middle name. Edaline Coping Gin.

I didn't have a name when they picked me up off the highway, so when the authorities gave me a choice for my ID, in a bitter moment, I chose Gin for a last name. I'd read somewhere that it was Japanese for *silver*, like my hair. I wasn't fond of my counselor, so I let her think I meant the booze. Now, I was stuck with it, but it had grown on me. I skipped the middle name altogether.

About halfway through my shift, I popped back into the dining room with a heavy tray of orders and almost dropped the whole thing. *Ronan* sat down to eat, and he was in my section. Of two tables. What were the chances?

I almost laughed when I saw he wore the shirt Cal had given him. He must have been too cool to care. At least Pink went well with his fancy green eyes and dive skins.

Someone needs to update your wardrobe, buddy.

I wasn't surprised. After all, it was the Keys where *relaxed beach bum* was a dress code. If it dried quickly, it was perfect; if it had a marine theme, even better.

Delivering the food to my other table, thankfully without dropping it, I watched him. Or, we watched each other—quite obviously. I finished up with my table's order, which wasn't awkward *at all*.

He hadn't taken his eyes off me and smiled when I came to his table. I pulled out my pad and pencil.

"Hello, Ronan. What can I get for you? The specials are on the board over there." I pointed, but he didn't say a word; he stared at me like I was the prey of the day.

Here we go again.

He scowled at me, sighed, and pulled out a menu from the center holder. Opening it, he ran his finger down the column and pointed at one of the pictures. I looked at where he pointed.

"Clubhouse and fries—got it."

Heat flared along the back of my neck, and I felt my scalp tighten. My pen cracked in my fingers, and I was ready to rush back to the kitchen when I heard a chair scrape across the floor. Turning my head, I watched someone sit down. A beautiful girl with the face of an angel. Sitting with Ronan. In my section.

As she looked up at me, I frowned. The long blonde hair flowing off her shoulders in silky waves and her glorious hazel eyes captured my full attention. Her radiant complexion gave her a trifecta of classically stunning features, and tears puddled behind my eyes.

No dive skins for this beauty queen. No, she was in an exotic-looking pair of tiger-striped Capris with an incredibly detailed brown, tan, and white pattern and a cute spaghetti strap top in a color that matched her eyes.

I'd like to say I was cool about things, but that would be a lie. I tried, though. At first, the only obvious sign that they rocked my boat was when I leaned back and looked under the table. Both were barefoot, and I laughed out loud.

Startled by my rude behavior, I looked to explain they needed shoes to be in the diner. At the look on the blonde's face, I zipped it.

Her look of complete and utter hatred was as plain as the less-than-perfect nose on my face. It made her pretty face into something ugly. She was as beautiful as Ronan on the outside. Inside? Not so much.

She was probably his girlfriend and was not impressed by me ogling her boyfriend.

My face flamed, and I snapped out of the embarrassing staring match with a visible judder. Ronan sat with a stunning blonde chick. Not talking to me. Again.

I looked down my nose at the blonde, probably on holiday before her next Victoria's Secret gig. "And what can I get you?"

She didn't answer, her victorious expression greedily flicking over my icy stare. I thought my head would explode. I wanted to drop my pen, scream out loud, grab her by the hair, drag her out the glass front door, and shove her into oncoming traffic. Instead, I slowly and deliberately turned to look at Ronan. He held up two fingers.

"Two clubhouse and fries. Got it. NO problem," I snapped.

My face must have shot flames into the air, because as I turned to walk away, I thought I heard Ronan say, *"Eddi, wait."*

I turned to look at him, but he was staring—at *her*. Like he stared at ME. I sucked in a breath at the sudden blades slicing my insides to ribbons.

How pathetic was I? Jealous of some uppity bimbo coming in here today, taking that one tiny piece of him that was mine. It wasn't much, but I had to share it. With *HER*.

It was right there that I could have let Karen out, but she would have painted the dining room in blood. So I shoved that bitch back down to the basement, forced a smile, and walked into the kitchen on wooden legs.

The swinging door hit the wall so hard that wood splintered. A moment later, Ada came blasting through the injured door and rushed over to where I leaned on the serving counter, taking deep breaths.

"Are you ok, honey? Who is that guy?" She sounded worried. She must have seen my face, which was probably bright red.

I let my head hang between my arms. "Nobody, Ada. I don't even know him." At that moment, under the weight of all that had happened, I shrank. I was less. I looked at Ada and shook my head.

"I can't. I'm sorry." Without thinking about it or saying another word, I took off my apron and headed to the door. I could have sworn that when I passed Bert, smoking by the dishwasher, I saw a sympathetic look cross his face. I didn't even bust him for smoking. I pasted on a flat smile, marched out the ratty screen door, and headed home.

That night, I couldn't sleep. I tossed and turned and thought about the crazy things happening in my life. Kidnapped and beaten to a pulp by three psychos and left for dead? Check! Have your finger almost removed by a bloodthirsty parrot? Check! Obsessing and horn-dogging over someone who wasn't interested in me? *Check!*

Someone with a *girlfriend*. A freakishly gorgeous girlfriend that looked amazing on his arm. She would make pretty green-eyed babies. *With him.*

Don't be so dramatic—dumb, dumb, dumb—Edaline.

I cried all day. I watched TV until midnight. I ate some M&Ms, read a book, and pulled out Buzz. But I just COULD. NOT. SLEEP.

You need to relax. Give yourself time to heal. Stay away from men. Especially that one.

No matter how hard I tried, I couldn't pull myself out of the tailspin. In total frustration, I thought about heading down to work. There were invoices James asked me to check over. I could get those done and start work a little early.

I looked at the clock. It was 5:00 am. Ok, a lot early. Whatever. Sleeping was definitely out of the question.

I threw off my sheets and started up the coffee machine. After I had my second cup, there was zero chance of going back to bed. So I put on my clothes, trotted down the stairs, grabbed the door handle, and stepped outside.

It was pitch black out there, and I froze. I always thought I was strong, but this was impossible. I couldn't force myself into the darkness alone. Not yet. I wasn't ready.

I looked over my shoulder at the mess my insomnia had made and pictured wimping out and going back to my pillow. Frig that. I was NOT going to let fear be a ball and chain that brought me up short every time I hit the end of it.

With a deep breath, I walked—no, I *ran* to my bike, grabbed it, and pedaled as fast as possible. I panted with exertion when I got to the Marina.

To be honest, I was also pretty damn proud of myself. My first nighttime adventure outside the safe walls of my apartment. It was a baby step, but it was progress.

When I went to lock my bike up, I noticed Cal's was here too, and I breathed a huge sigh of relief. As I walked to the doors, I thought about all the shit he had done to me over the years.

We had a lifetime of practical jokes between us. We were due for a good laugh, and I decided it was payback time.

So instead of throwing open the doors and yelling, "Lucy, I'm Home!" I opened them gently and slowly so the bells wouldn't go off. I held it until it shut, then tiptoed through the brightly lit dive shop.

Cal usually stocked bait in the mornings, so I padded softly to the wide doorway connecting the two shops. The lights were off. I heard the humming of the pumps, and it looked safe, but I hesitated. Just as I was about to step through to find the switch, the light behind me shone on something moving, and I froze.

As my eyes adjusted to the darkened room, I scanned for what caught my eye. As I stood there, something large and white pushed up over the side of the crab tank in the middle of the room.

What the f—?

It pulled itself over the side of the big white tub and slowly lowered itself toward the ground using its long arms. It couldn't reach, so it had to let go. With a soft wet *plop*, it dropped the last six inches. I let out a slow, calming breath, realizing I'd been holding it.

It's a freaking octopus, you ninny.

A weird white one but just an Octopus. I put my hand to my chest and realized my heart thumped a mile a minute.

Relax, Eddi. You wimp. Now you're afraid of a little Octopus.

It wasn't that little, actually. It was about the size of a basketball, with long, thick arms. The hundreds of little suckers were a light pink color. It was cute, in a weird way, and was pretty big for an Octopus.

I was about to head in to see if I could catch it and put it back when it's skin started to sparkle. And then, it began to glow in the strangest way.

My mind panicked at what I saw. *Not* natural. Definitely *not natural!* ANNND I was right back to shock and terror because it began to glow like a disco ball.

Then, like a scene from some sort of bad science fiction flick, it grew. It stretched up and got wider. Up, up it went, stretching taller and thinner and taking on substance. There was a sudden pulse of light so intense it made a snapping sound, forcing me to squint my eyes. When I opened them, the light faded.

There wasn't an octopus in a puddle on the floor anymore. There was a person. He was standing there, his bare butt cheeks towards me. Slowly stretching his hands up, he gave a big yawn, and turned around. It was CAL.

CHAPTER 11

I looked at Cal; he looked at me, and we both opened our mouths and screamed. It was hard to tell whose scream was more impressive. Dimly, I registered the scene before me. My friend stood in front of me with his junk out. Oh, by the way, he was a fucking octopus.

Cal stopped screaming, looked down, and with a yelp, covered himself with both hands. His chest heaved, and his eyes rolled in his head frightened marbles.

I had a different reaction. I slammed my mouth shut and promptly fell on my ass. I crab-walked backward faster than an actual crab and bumped into a rack behind me.

Assorted packages and equipment rained down, and with a gasp, I reached out, grabbed a pole spear from the floor, and pointed it at my best friend. A deadly weapon. Pointed. At my best friend.

"Stay right there!" I shrieked.

When Cal put his hands out in a placating gesture, I closed my eyes because now his junk was on display. Cal covered himself with one hand, shooting wild looks around the bait shop. He finally settled on a dip net, which didn't help much.

"Eddi, wait! I can explain!" Cal pleaded.

I don't know where my mind went right then. It skipped and hopped through the years—yes *years*—of shared memories with this ... *thing!*

Like a ball in a roulette wheel, my thoughts came to rest in a really odd place, and I snarled at him.

"FUCKING CALAMARI!?"

Cal disappeared around the corner, but a few seconds later, he was back with his shorts on. His muscular pale chest glowed in the light from the Dive Shop. My whole world came crashing down around my ears.

Eight? No nine years we had worked together. Nine years of *LIES*. I couldn't process what I had seen. It did *not* compute.

With the spear pointed at him, I pushed to my feet. Cal looked like he might cry, and a momentary flicker of sympathy panged in my chest. I didn't know what to say or do, or how to even *begin* thinking about what I just saw. Talking? Definitely out of the question.

It was too much. I threw the spear on the floor, turned, and ran. And for the second time in twenty four hours, I bailed on a job.

***

I sat on the couch for a long time, staring into space. Over and over in my head, I recalled the events of our many happy years together. And I shed lots of tears.

"Cal is an OCTOPUS."

Maybe if I said it enough times, it wouldn't seem so ridiculous.

Eventually, I called Patsy and apologized for leaving yesterday. Patsy was so kind it made me cry again. She understood that I needed more time.

Then I called James. I told him I was still having trouble with *things* and needed a few days. He told me to take all the time I needed.

I felt terrible. Walking off a job wasn't something I had ever done. But this was different, and my brain decided to punch out for the day. After taking something for the raging headache I was now *thoroughly* enjoying, I closed my curtains against the sun and fell asleep on the couch. I slept like I hadn't done so for weeks.

I woke up before lunch the next day. I never slept late, and certainly not for twenty four hours straight. I guess shock would do that to a girl. I sat on my couch and stared at the black screen of my tv for most of the day.

My pathetic attraction to Ronan was the least of my worries in a bizarre twist of fateful events. I couldn't understand what was going on. What did I just see? I mean, come on! An octopus?

In my head, I ran through the gamut of explanations of what it could have been. I put alien in the *no* pile, and science experiment gone wrong, mutation, and creature from the Mariana Trench in the maybe pile.

At the moment, I was going with *psychological trauma due to kidnapping* in the *most likely* pile. But that couldn't be right because Cal had said, "I can explain." So how could I have imagined it? He confirmed that *"it"* happened.

That was as far as I got before I burst into tears. I poked around the apartment for the rest of the day but didn't spend my time doing laundry or cleaning the fridge. Oh, no, no, no. I sat on my phone researching octopuses. Octopi? Whatever. I performed an obsessive string of Google searches on *octopus man* and *octopus hybrids* that took two and a half hours.

I gave up when my thumbs started to ache. The truth was I used Google to avoid thinking about the situation. I was a cephalopod expert now, at least.

Some cephalopods flew through the air for distances of up to one hundred and sixty-five feet. Which reminded me of the time I dropped a crab down the back of Cal's pants. I laughed. Not quite that far, but close. That made me smile—and then cry some more. I was a mess.

Looking at the clock, I saw it was five p.m. I opened the fridge, but I had a half carton of milk, some cheese in a can, and enough margarine to butter one slice of bread. Ever hopeful, I looked through the crumpled bags on the counter, but canned cheese and two moldy end crusts would not a sandwich make.

I was ravenous and knew it was time to *deal*. I flung open the curtains and enjoyed a quick eyeful of the ocean at the end of our street.

Bike. Pedal. Shop. You can do it, Eddi.

I grabbed my purse, slipped down the stairs, hopped on my bike, and headed for groceries.

As I rolled down the street behind Publix, I noticed Bill sitting in a nice new chair. One of his many friends must have brought it for him. I pulled in, sat my bike on the kickstand, and went to sit on the grass beside him. The shade was lovely.

Bill was a wise and incredibly optimistic homeless man who stayed in the area. Pushing seventy, with pure white hair, his suntanned face always smiled. We all loved him and would stop to drop off essentials or food, and spend a bit of our day chatting with him. One visit and you knew, despite being homeless, Bill's soul glowed brighter than the Florida sun.

Dang. I didn't even have a bottle of water to give him. Bill combed his fingers through his hair and fished a soda from his cart. He stretched out his arm and tried to hand it to me.

"No, Bill, I can't take that. It's yours!"

He smiled, and his tanned face lit up. "Take it," he said with a gentle smile. "I want you to have it. You look like you need it."

I didn't want to insult him, so I popped the lid from the warm soda. "Thank you, Bill."

"Simple pleasures," he said and tipped his can at me.

We sat and talked for a while, chatting about the weather and the local gossip. Bill considered taking a trip. It humbled me to hear a man with absolutely nothing material in his life planning a trip. To Oregon. Like, thirty four hundred miles. Knowing Bill, he would do it twice.

"So, lovely girl, what is troubling you today?"

I don't know why, but my traumatic goings on came pouring out of me. I told him about the assault, about being strung out on a stranger, and about Cal. I skipped over the whole *Cal was an Octopus* thing and instead went with *my best friend lied to me for almost a decade.*

Bill listened patiently and then asked me if I loved my friend before the bad things happened.

"More than anything," I said.

Bill thought it over and asked, "Did he ever hurt you in all those years?"

I didn't hesitate. "No, never." I brushed away a tear.

Bill smiled, in that kind way of his, and said, "Will you miss him if you never go back to being friends?"

I started to cry, and Bill put a hand on my shoulder.

"I've been to many places in my life, and I've met some good people, some bad people, and everything in between. I learned that for real peace in my life, I had to trust in my Maker to keep my path straight and true. I realized somewhere along the way that if you are positive and kind, you draw good, kind people to you."

Bill looked up at the clouds with a smile. "You always bring me cold water or a tasty treat, and once, you even brought me an ice cream cone."

I laughed through my tears at that. The ice cream hadn't been a great idea. Very messy at ninety degrees.

"I think you're a very kind young lady, so your friend Cal must be kind too, especially if you've been friends for so long. I would trust in your Maker to make things right. Maybe if you do that, things will work out for you."

Bill always blew me away. I got up, hugged him, and thanked him for the chat. Then, I headed home.

CHAPTER 12

After I got home, took a shower, and got my shit together, I called the marina, leaving a message for Cal. It was now or never. I waited for a return call, but none came. I didn't know whether to be angry or relieved. After waiting fifteen minutes, I got up and brushed my teeth. I got in my pyjamas and was ready to pop some popcorn and hit the couch when there was a knock on the door.

Shoving away the ghostly flash of fear, I straightened my shoulders, and opened the door. *It was Cal.*

I waved him in, giving him lots of room to pass me. He went to his favorite chair, and I sat on the chair furthest from his. His eyes went from hopeful to sad.

"Listen, Cal. I'm not sure I can handle it, but I'm ready to hear what you have to say. Just stay right over there, ok?"

It was an impossible thing for me to comprehend, let alone accept. My best friend sat across the room from me, and I couldn't even look at him.

Cal took a deep breath. "I'm so sorry, Eddi. I never wanted to scare you like that. It shouldn't have happened that way." He twisted his fingers in distress. It was his worst habit, but now all I saw were tentacles.

Oh my god. Can I do this?

My mind flipped back and forth between hearing him out, running like hell, or moving to North Carolina.

"Ok. Let's start there, Cal. Why didn't you tell me?"

Cal's breath hitched, and he stared at his feet. "All these years, I wanted to tell you, but I didn't know how. I was afraid to lose you." He licked his lips. "And it's not that simple. We aren't *allowed* to expose our kind. It's just not done. It's dangerous."

I raised my eyebrows at that. It sounded like an excuse to me.

"Humans don't have a great track record when it comes to caring for the planet, you know? If they knew about us? Imagine what could happen; what they might do to us if they knew we were here."

At the skeptical look on my face, he frowned. "We call ourselves *Others,* and that's what we need to stay. Separate and living in peace. We have that right. Just like you do."

I thought about that, and it blew my mind to weigh the potential repercussions. And then I realized what he had just said.

"Wait a minute. We? *US!?"*

Cal rubbed his neck. "There are more like me. And there are other species as well. I'm sorry, Ed. It's pretty big. Bigger than you know."

His Adam's apple bobbed, his eyes wide. He was scared what I would think once I knew the truth. He was right to be, because I was freaking out right now.

"What exactly are you?" I whispered.

"We're what's called "shifters." It means we can shift forms, in my case, from octopus to human, and vice versa."

At the incredulous look on my face, he rushed on.

"There are other types of shifters, too. But we are pretty spread out. We don't reproduce very easily, so our overall numbers are small. Well, compared to humans."

That made me feel a little better. "What other kinds are there?"

"Let me see…." Cal rubbed his hands down his thighs.

"Well, there are so many kinds; it's too long a list, but the most common ones are wolves."

I froze, and my eyes went wide. "You mean wolves, as in werewolves?"

He laughed and rolled his eyes. "No, wolf shifters are *not* werewolves. Like me, they can shift between human and animal forms. They stick to themselves even more than we do. Then, there are a lot of different predators that can shift, like Jaguars, Bears, Crocodiles, Gorillas—" Cal counted on his fingers.

"Gorillas!? You're shitting me now, right?" I couldn't believe what I was hearing.

Cal shook his head. "I know it sounds nuts, but my friend's cousin Tessa is engaged to an Ape Shifter up in Hollow Cove, just outside New York. He's the Sheriff."

Cal smiled a genuine smile. This was going much better now, both of us relaxing. It was helping me choke down the large chunks of crazy. I was still stuck on the Gorilla part, and some sick part of me wondered if he was hot.

"There are lots of nonpredators, too. Octopus—" he pointed at himself— "Beaver, Horse. I even met a turtle shifter once." At the expression on my face, he laughed.

"He didn't do much, just sat around all day eating lettuce."

"REALLY?"

Cal grinned. "No, I'm kidding. He wasn't going to win any races or anything, but he was pretty much a normal guy. He was a Librarian."

Despite the stress of this *tinfoil hat* conversation, I had to smile.

"Okay. Let's move on to the fun stuff. So explain to me how you can do … *that*." I wiggled my finger with a flourish as I said it.

"Well, that's harder to explain. None of us know how it all got started. There are all kinds of ancient myths and folklore and many stories handed down among Native Americans. Some of us appear in ancient art. So we've been around pretty much the whole time, I guess. Most species learn to shift naturally at puberty. It just … *happens*."

Cal gave me a soggy smile. "We keep to ourselves, keep a low profile, and live our lives as peacefully as we can."

As he struggled with how much to tell me, Cal let out a long, slow breath. As if a giant weight lifted from his shoulders while he spoke.

"Ok, so let me get this straight. There are many different types of shifters, and you're all pretty normal and do human stuff when you're not dancing with your *beast*—or whatever you turn into. And you what, shift during the full moon?"

Cal laughed. "Not quite. We can shift whenever we want, as long as we don't reveal ourselves when we take our animal form."

"Or what?" I asked. "You get in trouble with the boss?" I giggled, then stopped when I saw his face. "Oh. There's a boss. Right."

Cal laughed. "Something like that. Our society is well governed, but it's very spread out. Each area has its own *Enforcer*. They're in charge of discipline and keeping the Sovereign informed if there are issues. I guess technically, you could call them the Sovereign's police force. That's a really simplified description of how it's set up, though."

My head reeled, but I kept going. I had to hear him out. Plus, now I was *really* curious.

"So there's a King?" I pictured a royal chicken sitting on his throne of straw, with a crown and a scepter.

Cal said, "A Sovereign, not a King. Someone needs to do all the paperwork." He smiled, and I knew he was teasing me, trying to get us back to somewhere sane. "I'm not all that well-versed on the system, but there's a council for the entire country, and our area has a representative. Each representative is called a Sovereign.

"So what's to stop predatory shifters from ignoring the higher-ups and going on a killing spree?" The image of a Giant Gorilla wearing a sheriff's badge ripping my arms off popped into my head. I shivered.

"The Enforcer. They're very powerful. There's no court system where you can get off the hook. It's simple. Reveal yourself, and—" Cal made a slicing motion across his neck.

I paled. "But Cal, you revealed yourself to *ME!* Holy crap. I mean, it was an accident, sure, but it still happened! What's going to happen to you?"

My stomach churned. Now that the shock of Cal's revelation had worn off, my protective instincts were back, and I worried for my friend.

"It's ok, Eddi. There won't be any fallout. I met with the Enforcer, and told him what happened. He knows everything that goes on here, at least among our kind. He's familiar with how close we've been all these years. He couldn't believe you didn't find out before now. But if it goes any further, and you tell someone, it won't end well. *For either of us."*

I frowned. That didn't sound very good, and I liked my head right where it was, thanks.

"Wait a minute! So even though I'm human, they'll let you off the hook? Just like that? What happened to the 'reveal and die' rule?" I asked, making air quotes with my fingers.

"That's the thing," Cal said. "They've been watching you. They're pretty sure you're not human."

CHAPTER 13

After a colorful blast of swearing and lots and lots of pacing, I turned to him.

"Ok, that's seriously fucked up, Cal. And not very funny."

"I'm not kidding! They don't talk to me about these things, so I'm reading between the lines a bit. They know you're something. They just don't know *what.*"

"Nope, nope, nope. You're so wrong. Never once have I ever wanted to change into…" I slid my fingers into my silver hair… "a Polar Bear, an Arctic Fox, or a Beluga Whale. I mean, come on, Cal! I'd know by now, wouldn't I? I'm twenty-six years old!"

Scratching the bridge of his nose, Cal said, "I hate to add more to your plate, but there's more than just shifters out there. There's what we shifters call *Immortalis*. They think you might be one of those."

"What the fuck, Cal!" My mind reeled, about to capsize again. Not only had he revealed a new plain of existence to me, but now I might be *part of it.*

I jumped up from the couch and went to stand by the window. My mind raced. And then I thought about my past. The empty void in my mind that should have been filled with memories, but wasn't. The dreams, the visions, and the unwavering sense that I missed something that should be obvious. I looked out at the distant ocean, where the seabirds hung suspended on the air currents. This was too much.

"I want to throw fits and say *that's the most ridiculous thing I've ever heard,* but it's not, is it Cal?" He gave me a look of sympathy, warily watching my reaction.

Turning to face him, I embraced the crazy and stepped into the shit storm coming my way.

"What is an Immortalis, Cal? We may as well sink the boat, right? I'm obviously not waking up from this fucking nightmare *anytime soon.*"

Before yesterday morning, the world was a nice normal place. This afternoon, my next stop was the Twilight Zone.

"Shifters are not very high up on the food chain, as they say. They are rooted in history and Nature. Immortalis—they're the children of the Immortal Gods."

Of course they are.

"It's all much more complicated, of course, but the gist is that at some point, the Gods of old dallied with the *Others*, and the results were nearly immortal offspring. Their lifespans are extensive, but not forever. Only Gods are true Immortals and live forever."

He looked at me for confirmation that I wasn't melting down, then looking down at his twisting fingers, he continued.

"Well, that's not entirely correct. *Vampires* live forever, too, as long as they don't misbehave. Sometimes, they break the rules and take too much blood, or maybe one will snap and be brought down by the Enforcer—"

Cal must have noticed the deafening silence in the room. He looked up to see me staring at him with a horrified look on my face.

"There are *vampires—?*" It came out as a whisper, but one look at his face, and I knew he spoke the truth.

I turned away, but my eyes weren't looking at the view. *Others. Immortalis. Vampires. Immortals.* What the fuck was next in this quagmire of crazy? And how did I end up in the middle of it?

"So what type of Immortalis am I, Cal?"

There. A nice easy question. Maybe it would be a simple answer.

"I'm not sure he knows, Eddi. I mean, the Enforcer is pretty tight-lipped about things. That type of intelligence is dangerous stuff. He's an ancient Immortalis, so he's playing the game. In our world, information is currency and things are political as hell. He may know, but he's not saying."

At my defeated look and with a sad smile, he added, "Eddi, if I knew, I would tell you. I swear I would, even if it put me in danger. No one wants you to struggle. It's a strange world, and the rules are different. There are many things in play, and I'm sorry I can't say more."

Cal looked down at his twisting fingers and licked his lips. His stricken expression broke my heart. I tried hard to wrap my head around everything, and in a hidden corner of my mind, I felt a sense of relief. As if a piece of a puzzle snicked into place.

"You're still my best friend, Cal. Maybe if we do the *let's freak Eddi out* in small doses, it will help?"

Cal let out a long, slow breath. "I can tell you more later if you want. All you need to know is that you're safe. Shifters are safe. The Enforcer makes sure of that. Anything bad is dealt with right away."

Snapping his fingers, Cal added, "There is some news, actually. The Enforcer thinks your attackers were some of ours. He's hunting them as we speak. He won't give up until he finds them."

I was too mentally exhausted to react to that little tidbit. I teetered on the edge, and we both knew it.

"Later, yes that would be good." I took a deep breath and turned to face him. "There's one more thing." I hesitated, then went for it. "I want to see you change. I mean right here, right now, in front of me. So I can watch and really see it this time. When I'm not having a freaking *heart attack*."

Cal turned red, and I remembered the eyeful of octo-penis I got yesterday. I couldn't help it. I started to laugh. Hard.

"*Riiiight*. The *'Cal's octopus has a ninth leg'* thing." Cal turned even redder.

"Ok, I know it's probably rude of me to ask and awkward for you, but I want to see this beast of yours again. I need to understand this thing you do. Plus, part of me still thinks I imagined it."

At the look on his face, I asked, "Is that alright? They won't chop your head off?"

Cal looked at me with a grin. "No, it's all good. And no head-chopping, promise. You already know about me, so the damage is done. It's just weird, changing in front of someone I've known ..." he trailed off.

"You know me better than that, Cal. You knew the minute you got here I would ask." I plunked down on the vinyl chair he had been sitting in and said, "Ok, let's see it, Octoboy. You can change back after. In the bathroom."

Then it occurred to me. "Wait, you don't need water, do you?"

"No. But I can't stay out for long, or it'll hurt like hell. And if I'm out of the water in octopus form for over half an hour, I might suffocate."

I cringed. I wasn't so sure I wanted to see it again. I didn't want to hurt him.

But after Cal reassured me, he looked around, sat on the tile floor, and looked straight at me. His expression was a mixture of pride and embarrassment, but I saw him take a deep breath, and it happened. He changed so fast it made me jump.

It must have seemed longer the first time because shock paralyzed my brain. This time, it was over in seconds. After that same brilliant, snapping flash of light, when the spots faded, he was there.

Cal's clothes lay in a puddle around him. His octopus sat there, with his legs curled neatly around his bulbous body. I stared. I mean the full-on, take it all in, see all the details sort of stare. His octopus mesmerized me.

Cal, or *Cal the octopus,* lifted one long arm and, with the long skinny tip, gave me a little wave.

Cal gave me a tentacle wave.

"Very funny, Cal."

I'm pretty sure Cal smiled because his eyes narrowed. That snapped me out of my shock, and I shook my head.

"I'm sorry, Cal, I know I'm staring, but *HOLY SHIT!*"

Cal used his tentacles and pulled himself free of his clothes in a weird, arm-over-arm crawling motion. Flicking his long, flexible tentacles ahead of him and tapping his suckers to the floor, he pulled himself towards me. The round discs made a cute little popping noise as he pulled his body forward. It was a surprisingly smooth action and quicker than I thought it would be.

He didn't come too close in case he freaked me out. But when he stopped a few feet before me, I made out the fine details of his animal. Even though it made sense, I was still surprised by his creamy white color. I'd have to ask him about that when he could speak again.

"Wait a minute. You can't talk like this, right?" His bulbous, ok, I'm going to say it, really bizarre head made what I could loosely describe as a NO movement.

I watched the breathing tube on the side of his head as it opened and closed. It made me a little nervous, wondering if he could breathe. I tried to hurry and look my fill so he could change back.

His pebbled skin had varying shades of white and off-white. No wonder he needed that stupid hat, I thought. His eyes were pretty and very interesting—luminous, flecked with a tan and ringed with blue. Huh. That explained Cal's light blue eye color. His goat-like pupil, horizontal and pill-shaped, watched my every move.

I stood up, and Cal scrambled back a few pushes.

My heart melted. Even with this whirlwind tearing things up around us, Cal was still my friend. And he was afraid of me. I crouched. "I won't hurt you, Cal. I promise." I don't know why, but big, blobby tears hit my lids and kept right on going.

I leaned forward, slowly reached out, and touched his pale skin. I watched flickering patches come to life under my fingers as if trying to change color. What blew my mind was the soft feel of his skin— like slippery velvet. I gasped.

"You're beautiful, Cal." Tears poured down my face and dripped from my chin. Seeing him like this moved me in a way I couldn't explain.

Cal sat very quietly, unmoving except to breathe. Then, oh so slowly, one of his long arms reached up, and the long, slender tip wrapped around my hand. At that moment, I knew. Everything would be just fine.

CHAPTER 14

The next day, my steps felt lighter, and my chin tipped higher. I'd finally pulled anchor and sailed right out of the funk holding me under for days. I celebrated by working. I did a morning shift at The Crazy Conch and an afternoon shift at Davy Jones Locker and rocked them both. Dispensing a friendly wave to Bert, I skipped making ugly faces at his parrot on my way to the bike rack. Life was good.

I got home and cleaned my apartment like a demon, not stopping until everything shone. By suppertime, I had a glass of sweet tea in my hand and was ready for some sunset action.

My landlord was a generous soul and, to my delight, offered me access to a special place. I climbed a wooden ladder in the hallway outside my apartment and popped out above it on the Widow's Walk.

The wooden deck was small, about ten feet long and wide, with a three-foot-high railing. At the end of each day, relaxing up here was heavenly. It gave me a fantastic view of the ocean from the breezy deck. I wasn't pining for my husband to return from the sea, or watching for wrecks. Still, the platform injected some nostalgia into my sunsets and star-gazing sessions.

Nothing could spoil my mood today. Being on the island's eastern side, we didn't get the spectacular sunsets of the Gulf side. But the Atlantic still offered a sweet view in the evening, streaks of magenta and tangerine flaring as the sun disappeared.

As I relaxed and drank my sweet tea, I watched the boats on the ocean and breathed in the fresh salty air. Below on the street, couples walked their dogs as they enjoyed the cool evening. The palms swayed in the slight ocean breeze, their rustling sounds reaching me on my perch. Seabirds rode the air currents above, their calls adding to the essence of living by the sea.

Someone marched up the street from the ocean, their purposeful steps looking familiar. As they came closer, my hand tightened on my glass. Green dive skins. No shirt. Dark hair. I heard a record scratch as someone pulled the plug on my dreamy evening, and every muscle in my neck tensed.

Assuming Ronan would walk right by, I was surprised when he reached the apartment, stopped, looked up at me, and treated me to a stunning smile.

CRAP. Now what?

I hesitated, but unlike his girlfriend, I wasn't a toxic bitch. I gave him a polite wave.

Ronan didn't continue on his way. No, of course not—why not mess with me a bit more? Before enough time passed to call his gaze *staring*, I slammed my drink on the small table, descended the ladder, and stomped down the stairs to the street. I forgot my promise not to let this guy under my skin. He walked into MY space and brought the drama to ME. Twice. It was showtime.

When he saw me charge through the street-level door, he turned to give me a megawatt smile.

"What. Do. You. WANT?" My molars ground together, my words coming out as a snarl.

He frowned. Then the rug came right out from under me because Ronan licked his lips, cleared his throat, and said in a strange, gravelly voice, "Good evening, Eddi."

I barely concealed my shock. The guy actually spoke. To ME. A whole sentence. I almost slapped myself for getting excited about it.

"How are you today?" he asked. His tongue felt along his top lip, and I struggled to keep my eyes from following it.

He spoke with an awkward, halting rhythm. And his voice? Sandpaper-covered marbles was a perfect description. How strange. And not at all what I expected. I guess that cleared up the whole *dream Ronan* thing. That version was harps playing and Angels singing.

Going along with the casual pleasantries, I replied, "Fine. And you?"

"Just lovely," he said, his lips curling into an enormous smile.

Where was he going with this? Your pickup material needs work, buddy.

"Nice day… Nice day…." he started, then stopped, appearing troubled.

I frowned and glanced around to see what could be wrong. "Pardon?"

Ronan looked at me and said, clearly this time, "Nice day, is it?" His gaze turned inward as if thinking hard.

I gaped, staring as I tried to figure out what he was going on about. He tried again.

"Nice day, is not it?" Sweat beaded on his face, and there was more frowning.

Ok. This conversation was bizarre. Ronan looked nervous. Why did he look nervous?

He screwed up his face, then grinned and belted out, "It's a nice day!"

If anything, his voice sounded worse, as if he'd swallowed some rocks while trying to form his words. I resisted the urge to clear my own throat.

My mind whizzed like a runaway train. *What the actual f—*

And then it hit me. Ronan had a speech issue—an impairment or something. Holy Crap. I stared at him, wide-eyed, as a tsunami of regret washed over me.

I'm sorry—so, so sorry—ran on repeat through my thoughts. I'd been a complete ass to this poor guy.

"It's alright, Ronan. I know what you meant. Are you alone?" I glanced down the street for the blonde harpy, just in case, but he was alone.

Ronan looked at me, the wheels turning in his head as a myriad of expressions flitted across his face.

"Alone. Yes." He smiled and seemed relieved to get over his verbal hiccup. In the face of his obvious issues, my anger blew away like a ship at sea. Heat wafted over my skin as I turned a bright shade of pink. I was a bitch.

"*Uhhh*, would you like some sweet tea?"

He cocked his head in that cute way of his, thought about it, and said, "Yes. That would be FINE." His charming smile made me feel even worse.

I waved him in, brought him up the stairs, and showed him the ladder. With a gentlemanly flourish, he motioned for me to go first. Ronan appeared thrilled with how things panned out. A little flower budding in my chest bloomed under his attention.

He wants to spend time with me.

Torn between overwhelming elation and mentally punching myself in the face, I kept quiet and climbed the ladder. When Ronan's hand brushed my thigh, heat flashed up my spine. *Oh boy.*

I thought he was handsome before, but when Ronan climbed from that hatch and stood tall, it took my breath away. With the colorful evening sky as a backdrop and the wind tugging at his dark hair, I lost the ability to function.

Everything between his muscular thighs and intoxicating eyes was spectacular. His abs were something girls dreamed about, the six little cushions lined up and begging to be touched before trying out the feel of his gorgeous, perfectly symmetrical pectorals. Even his nipples were perfect, the tiny buds speaking to me at a visceral level. And the sexy look on his incredibly beautiful face? Well, the entire package made my vagina wake up and struggle for freedom.

CRAP. Now I was the one staring and unable to put two words together. And then, I remembered. The girlfriend.

He's got a girlfriend, you tramp. Stand down.

I gave the V queen a mental kick and shoved her back into her crate. Turning, I showed my guest the table and motioned for him to take Cal's seat.

"I'll be right back."

Nodding, Ronan settled down in the plastic chair, taking in the view with great interest.

Dashing down the ladder, I nearly ripped off the apartment door, then filled a glass with tea in such a hurry that it sloshed all over the counter. As I raced one-handed up the ladder, somehow without spilling a drop, I dreamed up methods of self-punishment for being so rotten to him. Being bitchy to a guy with a disability—*Gah!*

Flopping into my chair, I watched while Ronan took a sip of his drink. In an oddly formal manner, he smiled and said, "Thank you. This is pleasant."

Ok, he sounded a bit like he just graduated from Mrs. Holmes Finishing School, but who cared? When you were gorgeous, you got away with stuff. Maybe he underwent rigorous speech therapy?

"I'm so sorry, Ronan. I haven't been very nice to you. I had no idea." Lowering my eyes, I fidgeted. "The truth is, I thought you were deliberately trying to goad me."

At his look of confusion, I added, "I thought you were teasing me. *Making fun of me.*"

He smiled, his eyes lighting up. "You have very small breasts for a chubby girl."

My mouth fell open, and I'm pretty sure I felt my chin hit my knees. A my expression, Ronan rushed on.

"Your vagina smells from here! Do you wash it?"

I sat there, staring, as my mind tried deciphering what had just come out of his mouth.

Ronan set his tea down, smoothed his hands over his dive leggings, and said, "Would you like to fuck?"

Maybe they should have called it the Spinster's Walk. Because I'm pretty sure my vagina put up a *"Closed until further notice"* sign.

CHAPTER 15

My carefully constructed mantra of *positive thinking, positive life* crumbled into microscopic dust. With an icy glare, I snarled through clenched teeth.

"WHAT DID YOU JUST SAY?"

Ronan hesitated. I guess it was the waves of fury pouring from me. Smart man.

"You? Me? Fuck?" he asked.

No hesitation. My ice tea hit his face hard enough to shoot up his nostrils and make him choke. We both jumped up. I hate to admit it, but giving him a shove over the edge and buying myself a shovel briefly crossed my mind. I wanted to shout, but I had neighbors.

Ronan was the first to speak. "What is problem, Eddi?"

I growled. When he caught the expression on my face, Ronan stepped back and put his hands up defensively.

"I'll tell you what's wrong, you asshat. You come up here with your flowery words, and drink my tea, and then you *insult me?* I don't care if you have a speech impediment. You've crossed the line into the next UNIVERSE. You're done. GET. *OUT.*"

Ronan seemed confused. Then he looked panicky, and the words began tumbling from his mouth. I think my murderous expression made him fear for his life.

"No good at language! Bad speaking! Learning Now! *Learning!*" He raised his hands as I took a menacing step toward him.

"What do you mean, *learning?*" I hissed.

"Learn now. Not know before. Learn *now!*"

Ronan's wide eyes pinned me with such desperation that I reeled in my crazy.

I plunked down on my chair. I tried to take a sip of my tea, saw it was empty, and grabbed Ronan's instead. As I chugged it, I shot him a sideways look, but his expression of absolute misery brought me up short.

"What?" I snapped. There wasn't any real bite in it. This guy tired me out.

"Beautiful," he drawled. At my grimace, he tried again, slowly.

"Eddi, you are beautiful." He gave me such a sweet look that the last of my anger slipped away, and frustrated tears threatened to take its place.

"Oh, for heaven's sake!" I swore under my breath. Now, he was being all cute. How do you smack down someone showing their belly?

"Ok, I'll bite. You're learning to speak. NOW? You're an adult!"

How does that even *happen?* And how did he learn those nasty phrases? What kind of school teaches that sort of crap?

Then a light clicked on in the attic of my brain, and I asked him suspiciously, "Who? Who is teaching you to speak, Ronan?"

He grimaced. "Tara. Tara is teach me to speech."

He looked genuinely remorseful, so I dialed it right back. "The girl from the restaurant." I sighed. "Blonde hair. Bad attitude."

At his nod, I asked, "How long have you been learning to speak?" I couldn't fathom how a grown person couldn't talk. What, did he take a vow of silence or something? I glanced at him again, my eyes drinking in his sheer perfection, and noticed the iced tea beaded on his belly. I had the urge to lick it off.

Nope, definitely not a monk.

Ronan spoke again, his halting phrases making more sense now.

"Learning since day with..." He struggled to find the word, and then, using his hand, he mimed something arcing out of the water.

Dolphin. He's miming a dolphin.

"Wait. What!? You've been trying to learn to speak since *the day* we *met!?*"

Ronan nodded again. "Try other way first. Too hard."

I was so confused. All this time. I thought my hottie from the island was ignoring and deliberately taunting me. Now I find out he wasn't able to speak. He was learning. *To talk.*

I felt like an absolute heel. I looked at Ronan, swirled his iced tea, and took the last sip.

"Well, Ronan, I hope you aren't very fond of your teacher because we will have a little chat when I see her again. It seems she was playing a little trick on you. To get at me."

Then, a sudden thought interrupted the drama unfolding on my little rooftop oasis.

"Are you and Tara together?"

Ronan cocked his head, so I tried again.

"Boyfriend and girlfriend?"

Ronan seemed confused by the words. I sighed.

"Are you having sex? Are you a couple?"

His head cocked the other way. Honestly, he really needed to work on his vocabulary.

"Ronan, are you and Tara *fucking?*" A bit harsh, but that one did the trick.

Ronan laughed and with a warm smile, shook his head.

As I hauled in a deep breath, the massive knot of tension slowly uncoiled in my stomach. I wasn't a poacher, not in any sense. I let it all out and looked at Ronan.

Studying my expression closely, Ronan inched over to the table. As if testing the safety of the situation, he hesitated—.

I gave him a warm smile. "It's ok. We're good." I put my hand over my face. "I thought you had a speech impediment, for crying out loud!" I split my fingers and peeked at him before dropping my hand into my lap.

"I thought you were some sort of slimeball there for a minute. It wouldn't be the first time I'd met a handsome guy and found out he was an a—" I sighed.

He rolled the words on his lips. "Handsome? Slimeball?" The question in his eyes made my lips curl up.

"It's a guy with a really bad attitude toward women."

Ronan cocked his head.

"A guy who treats women badly and only wants them around so they can"—I remembered his vocabulary—"so they can *fuck*."

The words felt harsh on my lips. I would kill that hateful cow when I saw her again.

Ronan still looked confused, so I tried again.

"They were bad things to say to me, Ronan. *Really bad*."

I swore I heard the thoughts whisking through his mind. The precise moment that Ronan realized his *teacher* set him up was obvious. A kaleidoscope of expressions bloomed over his face, and he frowned, then slowly closed the distance between us. When he stood before me, a hair too close, I resisted the urge to lean away.

Bending down and lifting his hand to cradle my neck, he ran a thumb over my pulse and said, "I alone most of day. Not good at people things. Tara is friend. *Friend.*"

Placing his lips gently on mine, he kissed me. The brush of his thumb, the tease of his soft lips; my breath hitched as glorious warmth spread through me. Drawing back slightly, Ronan explored me with those beautiful eyes and whispered, *"Eddi is beautiful."*

His sweet breath whispered over my lips, and a zip of arousal dashed to join the heat swirling between my thighs. He tasted salty. Like the sea.

Ronan studied my face, but he didn't pull away. The ethereal moment bloomed with a life of its own, our heat twining in a subtle embrace.

"That was very nice," I whispered. "You are definitely *not* a slimeball."

He gave me a glorious smile.

Desperate for some elbow room in this suddenly intimate moment, I laughed and said, "Very gentlemanly."

Ronan obviously knew what that meant because he beamed. It was all the encouragement he needed. Pulling me to my feet, gently but deliberately, his eyes never left mine. I was drawn into a powerful current where struggling was futile. With the playful ocean breeze licking our heated skin, the moment became surreal.

"*Beautiful*," he whispered.

I looked into his soft, sexy eyes and melted. It wasn't Ronan who closed the gap. It was me. Our lips met, and as if meant to be together, they danced.

Ronan pulled me closer, and I went, digging into his arms and raising my hands to run them over his firm, deliciously warm chest. I had wanted to touch him so badly, to explore the tantalizing display of muscles for so long.

They didn't disappoint. Firm and supple beneath my fingers, their tanned contours invited my hands to wander over every inch. My thumb found his perfect nipple, and he twitched, his throaty chuckle slicking my core with heat.

Large, gentle hands explored my body, making my pulse flutter—but his breathy huffs on my lips made it *race*. His firm confident touch smoothed over me, every sweeping caress spreading tingles as Ronan's mouth explored mine. Our lips slid and pressed, our tongues dipped, and the sensations that arose sent my mind into a sensual tailspin.

Oh my God, *his lips!* They nipped and teased as they skated over mine. When they nibbled along the line of my chin to trace down the curve of my neck, I moaned.

A tingling heat flared up my spine, then back down again as Ronan turned his attention to my throat, his breath coming in soft puffs that tickled my collarbone. I didn't care about anything except getting *more* and pushed against him.

When he dropped a squeezing hand to my buttocks, I melted, his urgent fingers molding me against his hips. I couldn't open my eyes. I burned for him, the ache in my core lighting up every nerve as I ground against his thigh.

A dim awareness tugged at my consciousness. We were twined together on top of the world; anyone could see us. I didn't care. I was wild for Ronan's touch; his wandering hands and probing tongue stirred flames that licked at the apex of my thighs. A thick ridge of arousal prodded my hip; my clit throbbed in response.

Raising my hands to slide fingers into his soft hair, I felt Ronan shudder, his soft, sexy rumble sparking every nerve ending beneath my pebbled skin.

I couldn't stand it. He felt incredible, and I was ready to risk it all. I had to get closer. I slid my hands down his chest and across his abs, my thumbs finding that beautiful V muscle that made me drool whenever I saw it. No wonder they called it the Adonis belt.

Running my thumbs along the grooves in awe, my thighs clenched when his hips thrust forward in response to my touch. When my fingers took a tour of his incredible washboard stomach, it tightened in response. Dimly aware of his heavy breaths blasting the top of my head, I kept going.

Slowly, I slid my hand down to the bulge that had been throbbing against my tummy, and feeling it under my hand flared new life into my sopping core. My touch explored the outline of his arousal, now unmistakable through his dive skins.

His hips pulling tight to my hand, Ronan dropped his head into my neck and groaned, sending shivers across my shoulders. I was high as a kite on the erotic sensations, and so was he, judging by the quick pants blasting my neck.

"*Eddi—*" he groaned, his voice muffled against my throat. His hands shook as he tried to ease me away. But I was on fire and slipped my hand to access what I wanted so desperately. When my fingers reached his waistband, Ronan's head jerked up. Together, still riding a lusty stampede of sensation, we both looked down.

Confused, my fingers probing and searching, I struggled to find a way past the waistband of his dive tights. There was none.

I reared back, and Ronan shot me a panicked look.

Agitated, I reached again and tried to pry them open. I ran my finger along the thick ridge at the seam but couldn't find the edge. Ronan grabbed for my fingers, but I shook him off. I tried again, but they wouldn't budge, and I sobbed. Those fucking pants defied me, and mocked my frantic efforts.

My heated blood slowly turned to ice; they weren't diving skins.

The thick, soft and supple layer was something I'd seen so many times before. That elaborate, perfectly symmetrical pattern slowly fading at the waistband and raising to a slight ridge over his hips—wasn't material. It was a seamless covering of tiny, glittering scales. And they were *real*.

My mind swerved, and my vision went out of focus. The force driving my very existence skidded across the center line and crashed.

***

I dreamed, and it was not a good dream. A slender tower of a man grabbed me by my hair, and held me in the air, my legs kicking uselessly. He laughed, and it was a deep, booming laugh, with a hiss on each end that made it sound like pure evil had slithered up from Hell itself.

Another voice—behind me this time. Why did I never see who spoke? It made me angry.

"Let her go, Hex. Hurt her, and I will erase your bloodline from this world."

The voice, a man's voice. It was so familiar. White eyes, but the dream wouldn't let me see. I wanted to see!

The pain was bad, and I stopped struggling against the fist in my hair. Tears poured down my face.

A nauseating blur shoved me into a clearing near a forest. Darkness. Terror. Someone, no, *something* landed in my lap. A head, the soft flesh of its neck slumping as it came to rest, looking up at me.

I screamed.

Silver hair. Loud, banging sounds. Metal on metal. White eyes. Desperation. Pain. Like a dervish, things spun and dipped in my dream. A crazy dance, where the music was grunts and bellows.

"Fire! There's a fire!" I screamed, but the faces ignored me.

"Run, Edaline!"

CHAPTER 16

When I awoke, my skull jackhammered the contents of my stomach onto the rug beside my bed. Laying back, I wiped my mouth. My nausea settled, and my mind went to the dream.

It was so violent and bloody. The nightmares always seemed so *real*. I shuddered at the vivid image of the dismembered head in my lap. Were the dreams a knee-jerk reaction to anxiety? Because it had been a doozy couple of weeks. The last thing I needed was the standard post-dream raging migraine.

Why can't I remember? What is wrong with me?

I did my exercises. *Breathe in, relax, you're fine. You're in bed. You're safe.*

My stomach settled. After being sure it would stay that way, I staggered to the bathroom to find some aspirin. Taking them with ice-cold water, I padded over to the couch, and lay down with my arm over my eyes.

As I sank into the darkness of the room, I allowed myself to go there. Back to my evening with him. Back to the pants. The ones that clearly demonstrated my life had become some sort of magical mystery tour, and I was powerless to stop it.

I thought about how he looked up there on the deck. The incredible, mind-blowing kisses, the connection. The longing to touch him, and feel his skin beneath my hands. The sensory delights of his hands on me.

But it was all a silly fantasy, wasn't it? And I never guessed. How could I not see it coming?

I moaned and rolled over, and stuffing my face into the cushion, I cried. About the dream, the kidnapping—the freaking parrot almost biting my finger off. But most of all, I cried about Ronan. All those silly schoolgirl fantasies of what it would be like. What *we* could be. Together.

I eventually had to stop because bawling like a two-year-old didn't help the headache, and my throbbing noggin was threatening cataclysmic escalation. So I got a cold cloth for my face and tried to settle down.

I must have fallen asleep because it was still dark outside when I woke to a knock on the door. I looked at my watch—six am. I thought of ignoring it and nursing my wounds a bit longer, but eventually, I got up and answered. It was Cal.

He didn't wait to be invited. He took one look at my baggy red eyes and marched right in, just like the good old days. He grabbed my hand and hauled me to the couch.

"We need to talk. You don't look so good." His tone was soft, his eyes probing mine.

I slumped in my seat. "Gee, thanks, Cal. Must we? My coping meter isn't working right now. I had a bad night."

"Yes, I heard."

My head whipped around so fast it sent a stab of pain through my eye. I winced. "What do you mean, you *heard?*"

"Ronan came by the marina and told me you were upset. He was worried. He wanted me to stop by and look in on you." Cal gave me a sympathetic smile. "He was a little wound up himself."

The fog cleared, and I realized I didn't get to my bed by magic carpet. Ronan must have carried me down the ladder. Then, with a sudden comprehension, I wheeled on Cal.

"You son of a bitch! Did you KNOW!?"

At the look on his face, I shrieked, "*CAL!* You knew! Oh my God, you knew," I sobbed, my head splitting like a stick of firewood.

"What is he?" I demanded. "You know! What does he turn into, a fucking *FROG?*" That sent me into another cascade of tears, and my head into a crushing vice of agony.

I had finally arrived at the end of my rope and was too sluggish to punch him. At this point, I was too sick to care. I slumped back on the couch and covered my eyes with my hands, choking down more head-splitting sobs.

Cal leaned forward, his hands gently peeling my fingers from my face.

"I wanted to tell you—you know I did. I tried to help. You know the rules. Even if you're potentially involved in all this, it's still not my place to tell you about him. What he's all about. What he is."

I looked at him, and the compassion in his eyes said it all. He hurt for me, his brows pulled down between troubled eyes. With a sudden comprehension of Cal's situation, my anger toward him sizzled out like a wet fire. It wasn't about Cal, it was about Ronan. The what ifs, the what could have beens.

"That day at the shop. You knew him then, didn't you?"

Cal nodded. "I've known about him for a while. He wanted you to know his name, and I that's why he visited us at the shop. I can't be sure, but his kind has interaction rules, too."

At the look of absolute misery on my face, he reached out and hugged me. "For what it's worth, Ed, I'm really, really sorry."

"Did he talk to you that day at the shop? He can't even string two sentences together. How in the world were you chatting back there in the bait room?"

He shook his head. "I'm sorry, Edster. I can't get involved with what is going on between you two. I'm here because I care about you, and was worried. Are you going to be alright?"

I spat out a sarcastic laugh. "Do I have a choice? I mean, it's not like I can lie down and take a break. Life marches on, and I have to make the rent."

Of course, I started to cry again, which made my headache roar to life like a chemical fire. Cal shoved himself over and pulled me into his arms, grabbed the blanket from the back of the sofa, and pulled it over us. With my red, tear-stained face on his shoulder, we cuddled together.

***

When Cal left, I showered and dressed for my shift at the diner. I managed to get through the day, and Ada brought me out of my funk by forcing Bert to clean up a plate of grits he'd chucked that missed the garbage. Hands on her hips, she gave him a tongue lashing that made me smile on the inside.

"Listen to me, you shiftless oversized bean bag. Do I look like a MAID to you? Clean up your mess before I rub your nose in it!" It made my day, Ada, with her pink hair and perfect manicure, giving it to the hairy throw pillow with both barrels. *Priceless.*

At Davy Jones, I was lucky enough that Cal was on my shift. In between customers, we chatted about our upcoming trip while working on all the little tasks that made the shop run smoothly.

Cal did his best to cheer me up. Today we cleaned shelves. It helped me take my mind off of everything.

"So Cal. I keep meaning to ask. Why were you in the crab tank that day?" This could go either way, and Cal knew it, giving me a cautious look. He scrubbed the shelf and thought for a while before answering. We were still a little uncomfortable talking about his big surprise, but we were finding our way.

"I'm an unnatural color, so every time I'm in the ocean, I'm a sitting duck—a beacon to predators. I need to eat, so I snack on the bait crab and sometimes the minnows. Then I curl up in the corner of the tank and sleep. Although I prefer to sleep in the tank with the fish, not the crabs," he joked.

At my expression, he added, "I run a tab at the shop, and square up on payday." He laughed. "James thinks I'm big into fishing for Trophy *Permit.*"

"My roommate doesn't know. He thinks I work the night shift a lot. I still need a place to keep my stuff, and on my days off, while Edward is at work, I stay at the apartment. In the kitchen sink." He waggled his white brows for effect, and I couldn't help it. I burst out laughing at the image of Cal curled up in his kitchen sink.

My smile faded. "Wait. If you enter the ocean in your animal form, are you in danger?" I bit my lip, my eyes huge. "How terrifying is it to be on the wrong end of the food chain?"

"Being white sucks. It's not a great genetic variation to live with. A handicap, really. My kind should have died out for obvious reasons." Cal shrugged. "If I didn't have a job here at the bait shop, I might become a snack for something."

Moray eels lived in the coral under our docks. Octopus was their food of choice. It made me shiver to think of the danger he'd be in. I reached over and grabbed Cal by the arm.

"Cal, my God! Tell me you won't go out there!"

He laughed. "Don't worry. I am heavy into 'survival of the smartest.' I keep myself safe. Remember, I can stay in human form for quite a while. I don't have to sleep in the water every night, but I prefer it."

I rubbed my arms, heaving a sigh. "Geez Louise, there's a lot more to this whole shifter thing than I thought."

Cal shrugged and said, "The worst thing is the sun. It's tough on me, no matter which form I take."

His crazy hat. Yep, things made more sense all the time. The things he did, and his mannerisms, made me wonder how I could have been so blind all these years. How did I not notice that Cal was ... *different?*

I frowned. If he told me sooner, I would have headed for the hills. Change was terrifying to me, especially with my history. I had hated chaos for as long as I could remember. I reached out and put my hand on Cal's shoulder.

"I'm so glad you told me, and that you can be honest with me now. No matter what, I'm in your corner, Octo-boy."

We finished up and sold the last of the crabs to a local fisherman. I teased Cal that he would have to come to my place for dinner, which earned me an eye roll. At least the listing boat we were both on had finally righted itself.

I offered to close up, so Cal left at four thirty to head to The Fishery for happy hour. Our conversation must have made him hungry, and he wanted to grab some Stone Crab claws. I would have joined him, but Captain Brian was out on a Sunset Cruise, and someone had to hang back to help him. It was a *free drinks* deal, so there were always tipsy customers needing a hand off the boat.

Plus—hello, *tips*. Big ones. The thought made me smile.

I was in the back room, organizing things to lock up for the night, when the door jingled. I came up front to serve the customer, shocked to see the girl from the restaurant. The blonde. *Ronan's* blonde. *TARA.*

She browsed the racks of ladies' rash guards, then saw me at the till. Her eyes narrowed, the sly look she gave me making my ear tips burn.

"Can I help you?" My tone was pleasant, but my expression ... wasn't.

She thought about it, and for a moment, I thought we were going with *let's ignore Eddi* again. And then she spoke. Her voice was a devilish purr that made my hackles rise.

"I just thought I'd come to meet the girl who thinks it's ok to poach in another girl's territory. *My territory.*" There was a menacing edge to her voice, and I raised my eyebrows.

She kept slipping around and through the circular clothes racks, almost like she was on the hunt, and they were her cover. She kept looking at the tags and making unpleasant faces before flinging them on top of the rack in a heap.

"I'm sorry? What do you mean by that, exactly?" I furrowed my brows and frowned.

Who does this snide bitch think she is?

"Oh, you know, following Ronan, mooning over him, hoping you can convince him to tangle with you. Don't you think it comes off as a little—*desperate?*"

Ok, *now* I was mad. According to Ronan, she wasn't his girlfriend. Maybe I'd march her right out the door by the hair and be done with it. James didn't need the thirty bucks *that* bad.

"Listen here, *sweetheart*. I don't know how you got it into your head that I would discuss my romantic interests with you. But I can tell you right now. It's not *ME* that's been showing interest. So, if you're having problems with your *relationship,* you should discuss that with Ronan, because he doesn't seem aware it exists.*"*

That comment must have hit the bullseye because anger flashed over her face. She recovered quickly. Picking up a t-shirt, Tara held it up to her shoulders to modeled it in the mirror on the wall.

Tara smirked. "I guess Ronan spends so much time *fucking me* that we don't have *time* to talk about it. I'm here to give you a public service announcement. I have a problem with you making moon *eyes* at him like a lovesick cow. I want you to know I'm onto you," she said, putting the shirt back on the rack.

I threw my head back and laughed. "That reeks of insecure and slightly toxic, don't you think? I'm not a *relationship* expert, but if Ronan cared about you, you wouldn't be here right now, *would you?"*

Now, it was her turn to be angry. She threw the shirt on top of the rack and marched up to the counter. Her frown was so big it looked like an upside-down U, and I did a double take.

What the hell?

But when I looked again, her mouth was normal. I shook it off. I would have to ask Cal about *this* one.

The blonde nutter was talking. "I'm only going to say this once, and you'd be smart to listen. I didn't spend years building my life here so some penniless *orphan* could swoop in and ruin everything."

Ok, the orphan thing stung a bit. Bitch.

Tara got herself under control and smoothed her hands down her pretty striped capris before continuing.

"Ronan and I are meant to be together. We are a perfect fit. You're not *like US,* and you don't fit in. So nothing you can do or say will mess this up for me." She turned and stomped out of the shop, the bell tinkling hard as she left.

Well, that was weird.

I felt a little sorry for her. I finally found someone who had a Ronan addiction worse than mine. But her barb had hit home. I was definitely NOT like them, and it was getting more apparent every day. I tried to ignore her digs, and finished tidying up.

When I was ready for Brian's eventual return, I ventured outside to sit on the picnic table by the Tiki. It was a perfect evening, and the no-see-ums were busy elsewhere. I relaxed and watched the evening sky change colors as the day slipped away.

As I waited, my skin prickled, and I felt eyes on me. I knew who it was before I even looked. I think a part of me had hoped he would come.

Ronan stepped out of the thick stand of Palms down by the beach. I got up and headed down the rise to where he stood, watching me. I took my time, figuring out how to go approach the *Ronan is Other* conversation.

I would like to say I dreaded the confrontation, but the truth was, I still reeled from last night and was too numb to care. Better to get it over with.

As I got closer, I saw his expression. Ronan drank me in, and yet there was hesitation in his eyes. In my fanciful imaginings, this would be a quick talk, and we would go our separate ways.

He had other plans. When I was most of the way there, Ronan made some sort of internal decision, and I got one helluva surprise. He took three giant steps toward me, and before I could react, grabbed my wrist.

Startled, I pulled back, but Ronan was a man possessed. He dragged me down the beach to the water, his face set in stone. Wait a minute. *Was he ... angry?*

"What the fuck!" I yelped.

I struggled, skiing behind him as he dragged me with brute strength. Pulling for all I was worth and hissing obscenities between my teeth, I was helpless to resist. I don't know why, but I thought he would stop near the water's edge. He didn't.

He kept going, splashing through the shallows and right up to his waist. When he stopped, I was dripping wet, squirming, and ready to get serious with my fingernails.

Dragging me front and center, Ronan wrapped his hands around my forearms and brought his face close to mine. His eyes found mine, and that familiar, intense stare drilled into me.

Like a deer in the headlights, I went still. I watched the jade, teal, and minty flecks of his irises dance in the reflections from the water. I was drawn in, suddenly floating free in my own mind. And that's when I felt it. A whisper of something down my backbone. Something soft, and subtle.

Ronan broke the stare and gave me a frustrated look. I tried to turn away and head to shore, ready to call Cal for backup. But before I took a step, he yanked me back to him, and this time, when his eyes found mine, they sparkled with a brilliant intensity.

I turned to stone. I couldn't move. My instincts told me to relax.

He's not going to hurt you.

Before I could change my mind and go into full-on panic mode, something popped in my eardrum. At first, it was a faint ringing noise, like tinnitus. Then, as plain as if lips were actually involved, I heard him speak.

"Eddi! Eddi! By the Gods, why can't you hear me?"

He said a few colorful swear words, and I pulled back a little and scrunched my shoulders. What the—? He's talking. In my head. No, *now he's SWEARING* in my head.

Somehow, I knew what to do. Like I had been trying to hear him for weeks and failing miserably, with no idea why. Like I bought a vacuum, and I thought it was broken, only to have someone finally give me the manual.

"You really shouldn't swear," I snarled. "And that last word?" Shaking my head and closing my eyes, I *pushed*. *"That one isn't fit for a lady's ears, Ronan."*

My words sounded loud in my head, but at the startled look on his face, I knew. I had spoken without my voice. Yes, busting him for swearing were the first words out of my— *mind?*

I concentrated hard and tried again.

"Ronan, I can hear you. I don't know how, but I can!" I was in awe at the sound of my own voice in my head. It had a bit of an echo, which was strange. How in the world was this possible? I wasn't talking. I was thinking. And he heard me loud and clear.

His grip on me tightened, and Ronan dropped his head between his arms in relief. I couldn't see his face, but I felt the tension leave his body. My whole world changed when he looked up, and his eyes met mine. Things would never be the same again.

His eyes searched my face, and he spoke in my head. Wait. Projected in my head? What the hell do you call something like that?

"I'm so sorry, Eddi. Sorry for everything. There are things I need to tell you. Things you need to know. And then, if you want me to, I'll leave you alone."

Still a little stunned by the mind-speak thing and the beautiful, lilting quality of Ronan's voice in my head, I nodded.

I wanted to hear him out. Of course I did. But I was also giddy with the need to explore this amazing new *thing*. It blew my mind that we could, what, *communicate through telepathy?* It was fantastic!

Then I remembered I was in the ocean up to my waist, and I frowned. Maybe I didn't want to hear him out. I wanted to hide from what he would say. I wasn't ready. I felt the familiar coil of panic rising from my guts.

Relax Eddi. You'll get answers now. Just wait.

Ronan plunged on. *"I've been trying so hard to get you to hear me. I tried so many times, but I couldn't get through. At first, I thought it was because you were on land. But you couldn't hear me the day we met, and we were both in the water."*

"Wait—the first day? Is *THAT* what all the crazy staring was about? You were trying to *talk to me?*"

An embarrassed look swept across his face, and he hesitated.

"*Yes, for the most part. It wasn't my finest moment, let's just say that. You were mad about the dolphins, and I heard your thoughts while I played with them. I didn't like being told what to do. I may have misbehaved a little.*"

My mind was too busy getting a speeding ticket to think very clearly, but it was all starting to make sense. Well, most of it.

"*You made a huge impression on me, I'll say that. It buzzes a little when I speak to you here.*" I pointed to my temple. "This *mind-speak thing is incredible!*"

Giddy at the thoughts tickling around in my skull, it must have shown on my face.

Ronan gave me a proud look, and I heard him say, "*It's how we communicate, where I'm from.*"

Unfortunately, the shock of my new trick was wearing off, and his words brought me crashing back to reality. There was still the little matter of *what he was* and how things would play out—*for us.*

I sighed, and the tears I'd been fighting since yesterday nearly choked me. I pulled myself up a little straighter. I didn't want someone to paddle by and think two crazy people were standing in the ocean staring at each other.

So I said out loud, "Ronan, I appreciate you wanting to show me that I haven't been losing my mind these last few weeks. I'm guessing all the weird feelings and attraction on my end were you trying to communicate?"

He shrugged, but he looked worried. "*Something like that. I knew you couldn't hear me, and nothing I tried worked. I decided that it was time to learn your language. My kind, we don't use speech. It's not natural for us.*"

He glared at the water and said, "*Well, I didn't speak, although most of my kind learn to do so. I had no use for it.*" He looked into my eyes, and a warm glow appeared. "*Until you.*"

My skin flushed, and that stupid flower in my chest grew so fast it almost choked me.

"So that's the issue, isn't it Ronan?" I tried to decide how to phrase it without it sounding bad. "Your kind is not *my* kind. I'm human, Ronan, and you're …" I waved my arms around, then pointed down. "Whatever *that* is! You're obviously not human!"

Some of the hurt and confusion came rushing back, and tears threatened. I made up my mind, right then and there. "It's not going to happen. I'm sorry. It's one thing to have Cal in my life, *as a friend*. But this is too much."

Ronan's chin tightened, and his brows pulled together.

"*I'm not sorry that I came to you, Eddi. When we met by the island, you were so fierce, and very protective of the things around you. After I calmed down, I knew you just wanted good things for my friends. When you threw the tiny fish at me…*" He chuckled. "*I wanted to see more. To know more. About you.*"

"The minnows I threw at you? I felt terrible about that! *That's* what made you want to know me?"

"Yes, the small fish you were using to catch bigger fish. It is a big thing with humans, yes? You like to eat fish, just like us."

"Forget about that, Ronan. Listen, I appreciate that you went to all the trouble to learn to speak for me. It's amazing, really. Above and beyond, and I'm very flattered. But it won't—no, it *can't* work, even if I wanted to do whatever *this is*. With you."

I shrugged my arms out of his grip, and his hands dropped away. I started walking to shore, then turned back momentarily. He was still there, and the look on his face almost made me change my mind. With the distance between us, I finally had the courage to ask.

"What are you?" I whispered.

"I don't need to tell you that, Eddi. You already know."

And with barely a ripple, he turned and slipped beneath the surface. The round swirl of water in his wake revealed what I knew was there. A giant, glittering green tail that with one powerful push, took him away from me.

CHAPTER 17

My heart was in pieces. Cal tried to talk me out of my misery, but like any girl who tasted the dizzying heights of romance, it was a hard tumble when things didn't work out. Of course, my romance didn't include dizzying heights—a step stool, maybe. A few hot kisses and world-class groping weren't much to pine over.

I kept telling myself I never really knew Ronan, but it didn't help. I swerved back and forth between gut-wrenching misery and red-hot anger at the guy. Creature. Whatever. How could he do that? He knew the score. He knew we could never be together! And then the tears would start.

Poor Cal. I'd given him a rough couple of weeks. It was so bad that even *I* hated listening to myself. On the bright side, on one of my angry, *"I'm fine, screw Ronan"* days, I agreed to take out a Charter for the first time since the night from hell.

I was thrilled to have my boat back. Well, James' boat. But she felt like mine. We'd been through hell together and survived. Girl power and all that jazz. The police hadn't found anything, so they released her. James and Brian brought the *Wanderlust* back from Stock Island, where the Marine Unit worked. The investigation stalled. No fingerprints, no matching mug shots, and no trail to follow. It was time to move forward.

Cal came along on my first charter, and I felt an unrealistic terror for hours before the tour. As soon as the smiling, happy family climbed aboard the *Wanderlust*, I fell right back into the comfortable role of captain.

Of course, I had to put up with Cal, who shouted "Captain, my captain" every time he was on the bow. He tried to cheer me up, and for the most part, it worked.

Cal and I had fun on the charters. When the kids reeled in a whopper, their smiling faces went a long way toward healing me. The world wasn't always a horrifying place. I needed to remember that.

I held back tears whenever they asked to take a photo with me and their fish. It was too big a reminder that I didn't have a family. Or a romantic relationship. Nope, that one splashed in and out of my life so fast it broke the line.

On Thursday night, we sold out of crab again, so I went with Cal to Happy Hour at The Fishery. We sat in the overhead Tiki bar, which was open on all four sides. Looking over the water, we enjoyed a clear view of the horizon. I loved watching the fishing boats coming in with their catch while enjoying a rum punch.

It was a fabulous place for cheap happy hour drinks and stone crab claws, Cal's favorite. We enjoyed the festivities and raised a glass for their complimentary sunset toast. After a few rums, poor Cal was poked and pawed by an overly loud Eddi, and I needed to use the ladies' room below. I wanted fries at the concession stand and waited for my order when a sultry voice whispered in my ear.

"Hello, Eddi." I recoiled and wheeled around. *Tara*. I resisted the urge to slap her silly and, in a surprisingly steady voice, said, "Hello, Tara." Her expression was venomous.

I glanced over her shoulder, and a forest fire swept across my face and shoulders when I saw Ronan sitting at a nearby table. His expression was unconcerned, and his eyes didn't flicker when they met mine. The tight line of his lips said it all. He could care less.

Breath in Eddi. Get your fries. You're fine.

Controlling my breathing, I looked at Tara, who loved every minute of this encounter. She may as well have rubbed her hands together.

Casting a sickly sweet smile at Ronan, Tara turned to me and said, "I don't usually go for sloppy seconds, but seeing as you two never actually hooked up, I didn't think you'd mind me *looking after things*. I must say, you missed the boat. He's divine. All that muscle."

Somewhere in the deepest recesses of my soul, I found the ability to keep my face neutral.

It's ok, Eddi. She's a bitch. Stay calm. Don't let her win. Breathe.

Completely ignoring Tara's barb, I picked up my tray of fries, turned, and deliberately walked over to Ronan. It took every ounce of courage, but somehow, I pulled off *confident* and *completely unaffected* on my way there.

Ronan watched my approach, his eyes locked on mine. His bland expression almost made me falter. I looked up at the Tiki. Cal had eyes on the situation, his gaze darting back and forth between us.

Hang onto your HAT, Cal. This might get bumpy.

"Hello, Ronan. Good to see you," I said with a convincing smile. Inside me, the cold hand of regret twined itself around my heart and yanked.

Tara, who had trailed me from the concession, sat beside Ronan and slid her arm over his shoulders in a possessive cuddle. He didn't pull away; our gazes locked. I died inside, but my face revealed nothing.

There was a pregnant pause, and Ronan said, "You as well, Eddi. I see Cal is here. Please give him my warm regards." He smiled with empty eyes.

My blood chilled at his perfect diction. Somehow, I pulled it together and continued.

"Well, you certainly seem to have mastered the art of speech. I'm very happy for you. My compliments to you both."

Tara, a wicked smile on her face, piped up. "Oh, he and I work *very* hard *every* day. You might even say he's my favorite student. He's *come* a long way. You know what they say. Practice makes *perfect!*" Her smug look shot a flash of bile into my throat.

Ronan didn't respond to either of us. He looked up to where Cal sat, and their eyes met.

I turned to Tara and said, "I meant to chat with you about that. At first, I didn't know you could speak at all, let alone well enough to teach."

She shot me a suspicious look at my overly pleasant tone.

I smiled, my eyes cold. "You don't work, so you have no money, and language tutors aren't cheap. I asked myself, how did you become so proficient? You're very talented with your tongue, so I guess you must be pretty good at wrapping it around something other than words."

Tara didn't like that, not one little bit.

Amateur. That wasn't even a good shot.

Tara's skin went white, and I saw a flash of reddish brown stripes, some big, some small, as they whispered across her face before disappearing.

"At least I'm not a *cock tease*, Edaline," she spat.

I should have expected the blowback. What I didn't expect was the dizzying pain that tore through me. Ronan told her my name. She knew about the night on the Widow's Walk. Now he had perfect diction, and he was sitting there, letting her paw him over.

It was clear they had been spending plenty of time together. I couldn't catch my breath and thought I might pass out. I would have packed it in right there and slunk from the concession with my tail between my legs, but something inside me snapped. I was done being the victim.

"You're right, Tara. Ronan deserves *much* better than me," I said. Tara smiled, sensing a victory. Ronan's attention snapped to my face, his eyes boring into me.

My eyes locked with Ronan's. "But I honestly thought he would have better taste than to spend his valuable time with a vindictive little tramp with a *'fuck me I'm available'* sign around her neck."

That was all it took. Tara's eyes shot open. Her face flushed red and white stripes again. But this time, her lips turned down and kept going down, down, down until she sported a fishy moue. Her hair stood up, straightening to spikes that jutted at the sides.

My eyes bugged out for a second or two because she went full-on fish in front of a crowd. Lurching to his feet, Ronan took this moment to get involved.

"Tara, cut it out! Do you have a death wish? Stop that right now!" he hissed, his tone quiet but deadly serious.

Tara reeled it in, but it was too late. I suspected she had an animal; now, I knew what it was. This bitch was mine. I pushed a quiet laugh through my clenched teeth.

"You're a Lionfish? That makes perfect sense, doesn't it? The most beautiful fish in the ocean. Ironically, also full of a toxic poison that injures anyone it touches. Oh, this is rich!" Her face went red, and her teeth ground. I covered my mouth with my hand and laughed.

"It fits, doesn't it? Trashing your environment wherever you go, killing everyone by out-competing them. I bet you have *lots* of friends! Your impact at the reef is *so* bad that the FWC has declared an open season on your kind. You're so fucking toxic that even the *Conservationists* want you dead!"

I laughed, and I laughed. I must have gone off the rails because, through the tears, I saw Cal bolt to his feet and rush for the stairs. Ronan stood rigid beside Tara and looked ready for anything.

But Tara. Oh my god. If she was mad before, she was going full-on *nuclear* right now. Cal almost made it in time. He was too late.

Tara stood up, her body vibrating, the hatred rolling from her in a seismic rage. Her index finger morphed into a long, flat needle—and she struck. Too fast to track, her barb slammed into my neck, and the burn of toxic venom pulsed through my blood like a high-speed train.

Cal caught me as I fell. Ronan launched himself at Tara, pulling her away.

People gathered and stared. A few clustered around us as I thrashed in pain on the deck, a high-pitched keening sound coming from my tightening throat.

It hurt. By the Gods, it hurt. My vision went white with pain. I heard Cal, to the rescue as usual. He told people to stay back, that I had epilepsy, and everything would be fine. He scooped me up and took me out of there.

***

Cal bolted. I knew Lionfish Venom was bad news, but the panic rolling from him was so thick I tasted it. I couldn't talk. All I could do was choke and gag as my windpipe closed off.

Feet pounded the pavement, and I knew Cal was taking me to Fisherman's again. In a stroke of good fortune, the hospital was at the end of the street. No matter how fast he ran, it didn't seem fast enough.

I tried to hold still, but instinctively, I struggled with the need to breathe. I started slapping and kicking and clawing at my throat. Cal tightened his death grip and ran faster. At some point, starved for oxygen, I lost consciousness.

CHAPTER 18

I woke up to beeping machines. My throat burned, a long tube rubbing the tender inner lining. As the choking sensation returned, I panicked and clawed at my face. I heard pounding steps and a door, and suddenly, gentle hands held me down.

Someone asked me to cough, and the tube slid from my throat, causing more choking and gagging. Then it was out, and my mumbled groans were the only sound in the room other than beeping.

My throat felt like someone had taken sandpaper to the insides, and my head swam. I had two IVs in my hand, and I guessed it was a catheter coming out of my unmentionables. The electrodes on my chest left me wondering who had won the concession stand round.

The nurse took my blood pressure and left. I was alone and fell back into a restless sleep. I dreamed of monsters, swords, and blood. In this dream, I flew. I couldn't see my hands, but I saw the knife I slammed into someone's forehead.

I woke up with a gasp to beautiful green eyes flicking over my face. I would love to say I was unaffected by my visitor, but that was a lie. The traitorous little flower in my chest bloomed at the sight of him.

Ronan wore a navy rash guard stretched across his bulging chest. His skins were a muted, dry-looking green; he appeared exhausted.

"You could have died," he said, and hearing his smooth, baritone voice made me sigh. To say it had a heavenly quality would be an insult. The deep, husky purr incited an involuntary reaction, and I mentally punched myself.

Swallowing with a wince, I tried to speak, but my throat was so dry and sore that nothing came out. Ronan brought water over and helped me sip out of a straw with shaking hands.

I tried projecting my words to him. With a firm mental *push*, I was successful.

"It's not your fault." Geepers, I thought. This mind-speak thing could come in handy.

When I finished drinking, Ronan stood up, taking the cup with him. He pulled his chair next to the bed, and I noticed his pale face and hooded eyelids.

"What happened to Tara?" I wasn't sure I wanted to know, but it seemed like the thing to ask under the circumstances.

"She is gone." Ronan frowned and looked out the window. I glanced past him to see the ocean putting on that intense turquoise show I loved.

"Gone? Do you mean dead?" I felt a flash of dread. *"I never wanted it to come to this. I don't know what got into me. I had some drinks before I saw you. I'm so sorry, Ronan."*

"No, she's not dead. She's gone back to the sea. If she is smart, she will stay there," he said, his jaw tight.

"I'm glad to hear that. I don't want to look over my shoulder for the next five years."

Ronan smiled at my little joke, then looked down at his hands. "This is my fault. I shouldn't have rubbed salt in your wounds." He tipped his head back and took the kink out of his neck. He looked like he'd done ten rounds with a bus.

"I have no claim on you, Ronan. You can see who you want. But I'm not going to lie. It's hard for me to see you together."

He leaned in, bringing me that glorious water again. "I wanted to talk to you so badly that I trusted her too much. Tara taught me to speak more clearly. To exercise my throat muscles." Looking concerned about his word choice, he saw my smile and continued. "I did not realize how much she wanted it to be *more*."

"You are doing a great job and are speaking so well now. It's truly miraculous how fast you learned." I tried not to think about Tara, spending time with him. Laughing with him. I reeled it in and focused on Ronan.

"I should have known better. I should have walked away. I'm sorry, Ronan."

When the door opened and the doctor came in with a nurse in tow, Ronan sat back in his chair, politely sliding it out of the way. I saw his feet. He wore matching water shoes. I smiled at the sight. An image of a glorious green tail flipped through my mind, but the doctor started speaking, forcing me to concentrate on his words.

"Well, my dear. You gave us quite a scare. How you managed to get such a severe Lionfish sting on your throat is a mystery. Any other spot and you would have escaped with just an epi-pen and some medication. But I must tell you, you are fortunate your young friend can run like the wind and got you here so quickly. You were in full-blown anaphylaxis when admitted yesterday."

Yesterday? Good grief. I looked at the clock on my wall. *Sixteen hours!*

"How bad was it?" I rasped. The doctor gave me a fatherly look. "We had to do an emergency intubation. It wasn't looking good for a while because your heart started to act up. When that happens, these types of things can turn deadly."

He turned to Ronan. "But you must have wanted to see your young beau here because you immediately responded to the treatment when he showed up. You turned a corner and have improved quickly. Like *magic*." He gave me a wink.

"You'll be out of the ICU soon. Once we know you are stable, you can go home. Get some rest, dear. And be thankful it wasn't worse." He patted my shoulder and nodded to Ronan before leaving.

Ronan pulled his chair back over and leaned in to give me another sip of water. He looked at me, his tired green eyes dull when I searched his face. Did I miss something? The mattress dipped under his heavy frame as Ronan sat on the edge of my bed, the water in his hands. He looked ... *sad*.

"This emergency of mine doesn't change anything, Ronan. You don't have to stay with me. It would probably be better if you didn't. I'm sure Cal will come and get me." A war raged behind his eyes, but he kept his thoughts to himself.

"I know you feel bad about Tara's attack. But trust me. It wasn't your fault. I asked for it. I should have let her be toxic without me."

This telepathy thing was getting easier by the minute. My throat certainly appreciated it.

Ronan turned his head. He looked at the water in his hands. There was a long silence before he spoke.

"When I was younger, I lost my mother. She was an extraordinary soul. She was kind to everyone and very protective of the *Shoal* and all Syreni." At the confused look on my face, he said, "The *Shoal* is our home, and we call ourselves Syreni."

He stopped for a minute, his eyes lost, focusing on the past. "When she died, I became angry. I was spiteful and hard to manage. When everyone else was growing up, spending time on land and learning to speak, I did not go. I hated humans."

At the pain on his face, I reached out to take his hand, and squeezed.

Ronan continued, "I had no need to speak. I had the ocean. It was all that I needed. It was everything to me. But then I saw you, and it was a good day." He gave me a sad smile.

"I need to tell you something important," he said. "Then you will understand everything."

I gave him an encouraging smile, and waited.

"When I was younger, Syreni began disappearing, one at a time. Males, and a few females. It happened once, perhaps twice a year. There would be no trace of them, even though we searched the shallows and the deep waters." He looked up, his lips a tight line. His hand gripped mine hard enough to hurt.

"Then my mother must have found something. Somehow, she learned what was happening and tried to stop it. One day, she left and never came back."

He dropped his chin to his chest. "We looked everywhere but found no trace of her. She was gone. I looked far longer than anyone else but found nothing."

"Then I discovered someone who was on shore near the harbor the day she disappeared. They saw her get off a boat in Boot Key Harbor." He gave me a wistful smile. "She had long, beautiful red hair that was hard to forget."

The pain in his eyes took my breath away. "Her name was Oriana. It means *'Heavenly Sunrise'* in our language." I never saw her again. She was taken, Eddi. By humans. Humans killed my mother."

I gasped, and my heart broke into a million pieces. I didn't know what to say.

"Ronan, I'm sorry. I have no words." I pushed my words to him and tried to convey emotion—a mental hug. It must have worked because he gave me a soft smile.

"That's not all. After she disappeared, we stopped losing our folk. Whatever she did, somehow she put an end to it." His eyes glistened, his words choked with emotion.

"A few months ago, it happened again. In the last few months, we have lost five more Syreni. Whoever was after us is back, and they're taking our people. I need to find out who, and why. And I need to learn what happened to my mother."

After his revelation, Ronan released a huge breath, his mouth relaxing. I got the distinct feeling that Syreni didn't reveal secrets lightly. Sharing this bit of his past with me was a big deal.

He talked with me for quite a while. I told him what I knew about my past while he listened intently. I was surprised he remembered seeing me sleeping by the mangroves down at the end of Sombrero Beach. I guess my hair was hard to forget ,too.

Ronan explained that his people lived in hidden tunnels running through the thick ancient coral under the Islands. He had one brother and one sister, and neither liked Tara, which made me smile.

He also told me that honor was important to Syreni. If you weren't acting in the best interests of the *Shoal*, you were considered selfish—a *"lesser."* The Syreni were a thriving race scattered along the Florida Keys and into the Caribbean and Gulf of Mexico.

I was soon exhausted, and Ronan looked parched. As he rose to leave, I tackled the elephant in the room.

"I'm not sure where this leaves us, Ronan. I don't know what to do."

"Do what you must, little Barracuda."

The door clicked shut behind him.

CHAPTER 19

When Cal came for me that evening, to say he was happy to see me was the understatement of the year. He crushed me in a hug, and I returned it. He always soothed my mental aches, and I was a lucky girl to have him.

When he pulled back to look at me and opened his mouth to give me crap, I whispered hoarsely, *"NO, NO, and NO."* He looked at me like a disappointed father, and I laughed.

It killed me to speak out loud, but I did my best. "We aren't going to dwell on it. I know it was terrifying. I'm a terrible friend—who almost gets killed a lot. I'm sorry."

Cal kept nodding. He couldn't yell because I sounded like shit, and you can't scream at injured people. It's a rule.

"What do you say we blow this joint, Ed? I'm sick of negative energy. Time to pump up the positive in our lives. Just promise me you'll try a little harder not to die."

I tried to answer, but it came out as a croak. Ouch.

"Cal—thank you. For saving me. Again. I didn't know you could run that fast." I grinned and punched his arm.

My throat threw a fit at all the talking, so I let him chatter away while I changed in the bathroom. With a playful giggle, he said, "I thought I'd go fishing today. I have a craving for some *Lionfish.*"

We both laughed, and he held my hand all the way to the parking lot.

***

Life was good again. I went back to work soon after, and other than a raw throat, I had no ill effects from my tangle with Terribly Toxic Tara. That was Cal's nickname for her. I loved it.

I also loved that there was no sign of her, and I tried to put yet another physical attack behind me. This time, I had borrowed trouble. I vowed to work on that. Other than another dream a few days later, I moved forward.

This dream was similar to the others, but there was no violence this time. Just snippets of the man and woman together and a sense of affection. In one part of the dream, the woman called the man *Ezen* again. I heard it more clearly this time. The E was hard like eel, or easy. I had no idea if these dreams meant anything. They were always the same. I may never know, but at least this was a happy dream. Just before the dream ended, the sky turned stormy. I was in a meadow, and fear filled my heart.

"There's a storm coming, Imara. We must be ready." A bird flew high in the dark clouds above, floating on the currents, with a long feline tail waving behind it.

Without warning, the bird's face was pushed into mine, its brilliant yellow eye filling my vision, making me jump. "Run, Edaline." Its whispered words tickled across my senses as the dream faded away.

I didn't feel frightened when I woke up this time. I felt powerful. At least I didn't end up with a migraine.

***

I may have put Tara's attack behind me, but Ronan was another matter altogether. I didn't see him much, but when I did, it was always a positive experience, and we were never alone. I thought it was by design, but whether that was his work or Cal's was hard to say.

Maybe Ronan was letting me adjust to his revelation. Or maybe Cal was busting his butt and not allowing him close. When I asked him, Cal evaded.

I saw Ronan at the island one day, but Cal had come with me, so it was a casual visit. It was one of those perfect days with cloudless skies and flat, crystal-clear water.

I did some fishing from my kayak while we chatted. Ronan lounged in my favorite swimming spot, and I had difficulty not staring at him. That magnificent physique of his made it hard not to gawk. I saw his smirk when he caught me staring, and I hastily looked away. Of course, to make it worse, water kept pooling in his belly button while he floated, and it kept distracting me. Buzz would be busy tonight.

Ronan was nervous about showing his tail, keeping it down where I couldn't see it. I knew he was in Syreni form because when his tail moved, the water swirled. I suspected he wanted to desensitize me to its presence without freaking me out. He was clever, because there was plenty of distance between us at this point, the intimacy we had shared buried under circumstances.

So on this bright blue day, we relaxed into the holding pattern we had going on and enjoyed our time together. Cal slipped into his pale Octopus form and scuttled off to find a snack. There were plenty of stone crabs around the Island, and he was a pro at getting them out from under their rocky hideaways without getting pinched. He told me it always tasted better when you hunted your dinner. And like any good Keys fisherman, he only took one claw and released the angry crustacean to thrive and grow a new one for next year.

Of course, I worried the whole time he was gone. Ronan laughed at the expression on my face and told me not to worry. He would help if Cal tangled with anything he couldn't manage. The day went splendidly, with everything nice and neutral between us.

As we waited for Cal to return, Ronan opened up again. It turned out he could walk on land for quite a while. It had more to do with proximity than time. Something about natural residual energy in the coral foundation under the islands. If he tried to leave the Keys and got too far from the coral, his time on land would be shorter, and over an extended period, it could be lethal.

Evidently, to change back and forth from legs to fins, his process was almost like Cal's but without the light show. Syreni weren't shifters. They were Immortalis. Their alternate forms were not separate, like a shifter, they were merely hidden.

And that's as far as the conversation went because I wasn't ready to deal. Not yet. Ronan didn't need to know I might belong to that gene pool, and Cal, as always, kept my confidence.

I heard a tremendous splash, and Ronan surged out of the water, the wake he created rocking my kayak and almost dumping me. Cal had found a crab and thought it would be funny to goose Ronan. I enjoyed a laugh while Ronan rubbed his butt and growled at Cal. It was a lovely afternoon, and my tank felt full for the first time in forever.

***

A few days later, I was at the Island by myself, fishing, swimming, and relaxing. Did I hope Ronan would show up? Of course I did. I had it more or less under control behavior-wise, but lusting after him was a work in progress.

They say that once you kiss someone, you exchange pheromones, and it causes a bond to form. I wondered if that was why I longed to push friendship aside and get right to the good stuff.

I kept a set of snorkel gear in my kayak, and today, I felt like exploring. I drifted up and down the drop-off, marveling at the beautiful things below. A multitude of sea creatures went about their lives; it was like swimming in a tropical aquarium.

It was a clear day, and I saw the bottom everywhere except the center of the channel, where the current churned up the silt. Below me, a piece of debris half buried in the sea floor held a cluster of tiny fish.

I held my breath, dove down, and got a surprise. A cluster of Cocoa Damselfish darted around the structure, having a turf fight. I watched in fascination, bobbing to the surface to breathe through my snorkel a few times. They glowed, the bright purple and yellow color flashing as they fought. It was hard not to smile when they ducked into their holes to watch me from safety. They were one of my favorite tropical fish, and watching them lifted my spirits.

I floated face down along the surface, taking a last look at the world below, when something eased out of the depths of the channel. At first, I thought it was a manatee because it was moving along the bottom, its tail undulating. But it was Ronan. A thrill tickled my neck at seeing him in his element. But it was strange, too.

He stopped below me, looked at the damselfish and smiled up at me, his voice whispering between my ears.

"They are my favorite. So feisty." Ronan rose to the surface, his large, graceful tail giving one slow wave before he bobbed up beside me.

"Where is Cal today?" There wasn't a trace of gravel in his voice. It was deep and rich, the rumble hitting me in all the right places.

"He's at work. It's my day off." There was an awkward silence as we hovered over the drop-off. Salty droplets glistened on his face, and his eyes held mine, shining with curiosity.

As we hovered in the turquoise water, mere feet apart, I broke the silence. "I have to say, you speaking to me out loud is still a bit strange."

Ronan laughed, and its low pitch vibrated enough to tickle behind my ear. "I am glad I learned. It makes things much easier when I walk on land."

Before his luxurious voice made me do something stupid, I pointed to my kayak, bobbing in the shallows. "We can hang out if you like. I'm done fishing. I want to relax before heading back to the marina."

Ronan took my hand, pulling me along as we swam to the island. I stowed my snorkel gear in the kayak before flopping beside Ronan in our sandy swim hole. He stretched out, his tanned torso drawing my eye as it shimmered beneath the water. We didn't talk, content to watch the horizon in comfortable silence. And then I asked him something that surprised even me.

"Can I see your tail?"

CHAPTER 20

Ronan's head whipped around, his eyes shooting wide. His entire body went still.

Nervous at his expression, I backpedaled. "Never mind. I don't want to invade your privacy. I know it's rude that I asked, and I'm sor—"

There was a tail in my face. The intricate details of it rippled just beneath the water's surface, and I stared. Ronan's eyes drilled into me with a strangely erotic expression. For one long, awkward moment, I was unsure. Then I reached my fingers out to smooth over the shimmering skin of his sparkling emerald tail.

It wasn't what I expected. Unlike the skin at Ronan's waist, his tail was firm and had no scales. The texture was slippery, like a dolphin's, but it was broader and thicker, with a rubbery feel. It wasn't perfect, either; tiny pieces were missing. It wasn't frilly. It was practical. Masculine. Breathtaking.

Combined with his tail, Ronan was massive, at least ten feet long from top to bottom. His bulk was impressive, and I could understand how a group of Syreni males would be intimidating.

The color was darkest on the fin, where it was a green-black. It lightened to dark chartreuse toward his hips, the delicate patterns that covered it were like everything in nature—too intricate to describe. The colorful scales wove together seamlessly, tiny in places and bigger in others. I already knew, at his waist, they were too small to see.

His tail was beautiful in a way that boggled my mind. I ran my finger over his fin in wonder and breathed out a soft "*wow.*" I looked up.

Ronan had gone completely still, watching me with a strange expression—like a cat before pouncing on a mouse. He lowered his eyes and turned away, his beautiful tail sinking back under the water.

The spell broken, I cleared my throat. "It's beautiful, Ronan. Truly, it's the most magnificent thing I've ever seen."

He slanted me a sad smile.

I knew the smart thing would have been to let it rest and head home, but I didn't want that. I wanted *him*. Without thinking, I closed the distance between us and reached for him.

His hand came up and grabbed my wrist. "*Eddi*. No. You don't want this." His low voice was a growly, intensely male drawl that gave me shivers and tightened my nipples.

I ignored him. I didn't want to hear what he had to say. Sick of holding back, sick of being careful, today, I just wanted to *be*.

I pulled my wrist from his grip and kissed him. Ronan stilled against my advances, his muscles tight, his expression hesitant. I forged on, probing his mouth with an eager tongue, feeling like I might fall right in after it. When I grabbed his cheeks in both hands, at last, he kissed me back.

Our tongues dipped and plunged, the wet slide of our kisses spurring him on. Ronan slipped his hand under my top to play with my tightening breasts, each thumbing pinch shooting an electric sizzle of heated pressure to my nub. Heavy pants filled the air in the sandy pool where we floated, locked in clinging exploration.

With a sudden splash, Ronan flipped onto his back, pulling me onto his belly. And then we were swimming.

I don't know what came over me. My lips devoured his salty skin, my nibbling caresses working up and down his neck, along his jaw, then going back for deep plunging kisses that made my toes curl. I couldn't get close enough.

Ronan held me tightly in his arms, swimming lazily on his back. Floating out to sea on his wet, gently undulating body did crazy things to my throbbing sex. Crazy, wet things.

My hands were everywhere, and I rubbed against him, aching for pressure against my swollen clit. Ronan's erection pulsed beneath me, and not stopping to think, I ground along the hard ridge of him, slipping my feet into the water and behind his tail and pulling him closer.

Water splashed, and he groaned, tightening his arms. I needed more. I *wanted* more.

Pulling back slightly, I reached down and ran my fingers over his hard length. His tail vibrated with tiny tremors, and he had trouble swimming. I smiled. It was hot as hell and pleased me to steal his control.

Ronan gazed at me with hooded eyes, the desire I saw there adding to the pressure already throbbing through my core. Encouraged, I rubbed the smooth skin over his erection, palming and squeezing. He grunted with a spastic jerk, a long, low moan easing over his lips. With a slipping sensation, his turgid shaft swelled into my hand.

He was hard and velvety, his swollen arousal jerking in my grip. Ronan groaned, long and low, then shuddered, the tanned skin of his chest pebbling and his nipples tightening to nibs. When I took one in my mouth, his body pulled as tight as his clenched jaw.

We got into a situation because he was so involved in what I was doing that he stopped swimming. I giggled when we sank and the ocean splashed over my shoulders. Ronan gave a few lazy strokes of his tail, and we were back on top of the almost flat sea, moving again in that slow, undulating rhythm.

I never let go of his hard length, keeping up my firm strokes. His neck straining, Ronan's head tipped back, his eyes closed, and funny little sounds came from his mouth. I pulled away slightly, and he tightened one arm and dropped the other to give me room. I had to see it. I needed to see.

Still massaging him, I looked down. His penis looked human. It was beautiful. Long and thick, the intense pressure formed a sexy ridge from base to tip. His shaft pulsed, the hard length of it curving from between his hips like a human male unzipped and being pleasured through his pants. It was unbelievably sexy, and I loved it.

A fiery warmth coursed through me at the sight of him, the hot, insistent pulse between my legs begging for more. Aching for pressure. Hungry. For him.

With that little hurdle behind me, I tackled him.

Before I could do more, Ronan pulled my hand back to his neck, his mouth devouring me in a searing kiss. I grumbled, but when I felt his long, nimble fingers dip into my shorts, I lifted my hips to give him better access.

Around and around, with wet circles over my nub, his finger dipped into me, pressing on that wondrous knot inside that made me gasp. In and out, slowly, firmly, his fingers teased my slick core. I rocked my hips and threw off his timing, and we sank again.

Grinning and giggling like two clumsy teens, we got back up on plane. I was through waiting.

I wasted no time and grabbed his throbbing length in my hand. Gripping it firmly, I turned back to him and ran my teeth under his jaw, nipping and sucking and giving him deep, probing kisses while I stroked him in long, sweeping motions.

With a gasp, Ronan stretched his neck and tensed, his breath coming in short bursts. He was so hot, and hard, it made me wild. I ran my thumb around the tip, and it was slippery. Smiling as I swirled my thumb, I lubricated the head of his cock to the sound of strangled hisses. Grunting and bucking his hips, Ronan nearly tossed me from my comfortable perch.

My pussy was as wet as the sea splashing over my thighs, and when I looked into his beautiful face, and he opened his eyes, they were soft and filled with desire ... *for me*. When he saw my expression, Ronan's eyes shot wide. I licked my lips, tasting the salt there, and grinned.

He grabbed my waist as if to stop me, then froze, his eyes flashing a brilliant green. Slipping my swim shorts to the side, I pressed myself against the head of his slippery shaft. The sounds coming from his parted lips were erotic as hell, and I wiggled and squirmed, pressing downward.

He groaned, a rumbling vibration powering from his throat and sending a tingling heat to my aching sex. The sounds, the sensations, his hands squeezing my buttocks—they drove me over the edge.

The desire snapping between us had a life of its own, and when I slowly sank onto his straining cock, he grabbed my hips and, after a brief hesitation, slid himself home. I met him, grinding down in earnest, his hips thrusting into me with slow, sweeping strokes.

My eyes drifted closed, and I dropped my head under his chin. His length sliding in and out of me in a steady, delicious rhythm, rubbed against all the right places. My chin tightened, my breaths stuttering as I opened my legs and welcomed him into me. I hooked my feet behind his thighs, and pulled him closer on every thrust.

"Ronan," I gasped. His lips explored mine as he kept a perfect rhythm of firm, gentle strokes. Tingles curled outward from the base of my spine, and his lips dropped to my neck. The tempo built, the need rising between us, the exquisite pressure of his cock massaging and stretching me—it was all too much.

"Oh my GOD, Ronan!" I cried. Lost on an ocean of feeling and need, I didn't startle when I felt two tiny, sharp pricks on my neck. I almost pulled back, but my body swam through a pool of intense, drowning pleasure.

I had no control and dropped my head to his chest with a shaky sigh. My neck wouldn't hold it up anymore.

A clenching tightness overwhelmed my pussy. Ronan slicked in and out in perfect harmony with these new, incredible sensations as they curled and dipped through my drenched vagina. I couldn't stop, and my hips mashed down on his, my breath coming in panting huffs.

A mind-blowing euphoria swept through me, my body screaming to come. With a throaty growl, Ronan's hips slammed into mine, and a tingling explosion raced from my tailbone to my shoulders as I sailed over the edge. Ronan thrust in plunging strokes, then threw his head back, and followed me into the bliss that sucked us under.

Panting, my wool-filled head soaking in the aftermath, I tipped back and tried to lock eyes with Ronan. His expression was distant, a look of blissful serenity clouding his face. Soft green irises slowly tracked me, and he gave me a drunken smile.

I tensed. I tried to focus my eyes, but things were hazy. Two pointed teeth, where his canines should be, slowly came into focus.

They were barely visible, peeking out from under his top lip. And hanging from each of those razor-sharp points was a single, clear drop of liquid. They dripped, and tracing across his bottom lip, the beads disappeared into his mouth.

My mind picked up speed. What was that? Not knowing made me panic. I found the strength to move and started to scrabble around on top of Ronan, trying to climb off. But we were in the ocean.

Pulling myself from the Utopic haze, I desperately tried to escape. Ronan, still lazily swimming under me, a serene smile on his face, seemed completely unaware of my panic.

Looking round wildly I saw the distant shore. We were a long way out. My frantic breaths came faster. *I had to get to shore!*

I slithered into the ocean, and Ronan tried pulling me back. Struggling wildly, I kicked against his hold and scratched him.

Suddenly I was free and swimming as fast as I could. Something come up beneath me, a giant wall of water pushing up from the ocean below, and I screamed. A pair of strong arms grabbed me, and Ronan pulled me against his hard chest.

I struggled, but I couldn't break free. It was like being caught in a vice. Roaring in fear and frustration, my fingers grabbed at nothing because my arms were locked to my sides. I couldn't move. I couldn't breathe.

"Shhh. I'm here, I've got you." I frowned at the musical sound of the voice in my head.

"It's alright, little Barracuda. I will take us to shore. Just relax. It's going to be fine. There are no sharks here, I promise." Ronan had me firmly in his arms.

My mind bolted and raced back to the night from hell. Clear, tiny drops. Drops from a vial. Lips licking at nothing. Hips grinding. And then, scenes from that horrible night stretched before me with a gut-wrenching focus.

The black ocean. The shark. The feeling of helplessly waiting to die. *My little Barracuda.* That's what Ronan called me in the dream.

He was there. I tried to process it. My dream wasn't a dream at all. He was fucking *there!* The night I almost died. The night they almost killed me.

I sobbed as it all came rushing back. Images no longer buried flashed through my mind like a Rolodex of trauma. Hannibal. The vial. Twitch, grinding into the floor. The needle. Tiny drops of clear, horrible liquid. A drug that took you away on a hazy cloud of bliss. Two pricks. Two drips from a pair of razor-sharp teeth. Trailing across his lips, and into his mouth.

I wiggled a hand free and felt the side of my neck. It was sore and swollen. There they were, two tiny bumps.

He bit me. He bit me!

I panicked. I couldn't move. *TOO TIGHT!* I struggled. I roared. I tried to flee. Ronan, his movements jerky as he held me tight, stopped swimming. He pulled us both upright and gently shook me. He was afraid. I felt it on the ocean breeze.

"Eddi! What is it? Why are you screaming? I don't understand. Tell me! I can help, but you have to tell me." His words reached me. I heard the caring in his musical voice.

I stopped struggling, and panting hard, looked into his face with wide eyes. His eyes were clear. His teeth looked normal. Just when I started to get control of myself, he smiled.

And there they were. Two tiny, razor-sharp fangs.

I went stiff and turned cold. I couldn't speak or move. My lips were numb. My head fell back because my neck went offline. I was frozen with terror.

"What's wrong, Eddi? Please tell me. I don't understand!" Ronan frantically searched my face, his brows screwed together in a frown.

My eyes found his beautiful face, and something shattered inside me. Completely immobilized, I could only manage a tiny whisper from my mind to his.

"Cal. Get Cal."

In one swift move, he scooped me up, plunged ahead, and swam as fast as he could.

CHAPTER 21

"Are you out of your EVER-LOVING MIND?!"

I heard Cal. I had been awake for a while and knew he was in my apartment. He kept popping in to check on me, but I pretended I was still asleep. I wasn't ready to talk just yet. I lay there and tried to piece together what happened. My mind was clear now.

Whatever Ronan had done to me was over. I slept it off and felt fine. That didn't mean everything was alright.

I had pieced it all together after I filtered through the memories. I needed to tell Ronan. No matter what happened, I owed him that much.

A choking sob nearly gave away that I wasn't asleep. Every time I thought about the beautiful thing I had experienced with Ronan, a sense of longing and loss flooded through me. I didn't regret it. Well, not all of it.

"What were you thinking, Ronan?" Cal's voice was loud and razor-sharp.

"Keep your voice down, Cal. You'll wake her up," Ronan snarled.

"Ronan! How in the *fuck* did you think it was a good idea to have SEX with her? She doesn't need any more trauma right now. She's barely over what those fucking monsters did to her!"

I heard Ronan sigh. "I must talk to her, Cal. I need to explain."

"Explain what, exactly? That you had interspecies *sex* with her, and she doesn't even know everything yet? You didn't tell her, did you? My God, *Ronan!* You have to tell her!"

"I need to see her." Ronan spoke through his clenched teeth, his words a tight hiss.

"No. Absolutely not. You've done enough. *You fucking bastard.*"

Cal was losing it. Time to get up.

I climbed out of bed and looked in the mirror. I had on a cute, super skimpy pair of boy-short pajamas. Cal's favorite because they had little cartoon crabs. My ass hung out of the bottoms, so that was a *yup* to wearing a robe.

I opened the door. The arguing stopped, and two guilty faces peered at me. I padded over and poured myself a coffee. My friend the octopus. Barista extraordinaire.

"Thanks for making the coffee, Cal." I took a sip. Java was exactly what I needed.

Cal shuffled his feet and jerked his head at Ronan. "He made it."

Slowly, I turned to look at Ronan. I didn't know whether to laugh at the image of him making coffee or cry at how handsome he looked in the light from the window. Bare-chested and in skins, as usual.

The look on his face made my chest tighten. That was a grocery cart full of feelings, right there. Remorse, hope, fear, longing. The anger, I assumed, was for Cal.

"Can we sit down?" My jaw cracked on a yawn as I moved over to Cal's chair. They could take the couch.

Ronan and Cal both sat down, one at each end of the sofa. The crunched brows and laser eyes they lobbed back and forth almost made me laugh. Almost. I took another sip of my coffee, and the morning ritual soothed me.

"I'm not sure exactly what happened out there this afternoon. It *was* this afternoon, right?" The clock in the kitchen said 8 pm.

"Yes," Cal snapped. "You've been out for three hours." The look he gave Ronan was scalpel-sharp.

"I want to know what happened. I don't think it was just a panic attack. It was worse than usual. I couldn't control it." I raised an eyebrow at Ronan, who flushed red.

"Cal, I'm sorry if I scared you. Again. I know I promised. But at least death wasn't on the table this time." I looked at Ronan. "It wasn't, right?" He shook his head no and looked down at his bare feet, his hands rubbing his thighs.

Cal looked at me with that expression a friend uses when you do something dumb, but they forgive you anyway. "Maybe this *asshole* will fill us all in on what happened," he complained, glaring at Ronan.

I looked over, seeing only the top of Ronan's head. "I know we need to talk about what happened, and I would normally ask Cal to leave and give us some privacy. But there's something I discovered today when I was with you, Ronan. And Cal needs to hear it. I have some answers for you. Is that alright?"

Ronan lifted his head to look at me. He nodded.

"Can you tell me about the bite? What is it, exactly?"

He shot a furtive look at Cal. "It is a *private* Syreni custom. We don't discuss it with OTHERS. It is for mates to share." He rolled his shoulders and his neck cracked, his eyes drilling into Cal's.

"Syreni customs are not discussed outside the *Shoal*. So Cal needs to keep his *beak* shut." Cal growled at him.

"Go on," I urged. "I'm sure you can trust Cal. Right Cal?" He nodded, his eyes hard.

Boy, I was doing great. Not sure where it was coming from, this adulting. But ok.

Ronan sent Cal a sizzling look that promised pain. "When Syreni tangle and it is very pleasurable, the male has small fangs that appear. He releases a special *nectar* that makes things very intense for both partners. It is an honor to share it with our *mate*."

"So tangle means *sex?*" I asked. God how I would get through this awkward tea party was beyond me.

"Yes, that is the human word. Tangle means sex. The fangs are only down for a short time, and then they recede." Ronan kept glancing at Cal, his leg bouncing slightly.

Cal looked torn between fuming and being grossed out by Ronan's *sex* talk.

"There is also a form that Syreni use for fighting. When a male Syreni is ANGRY," another sizzling look at Cal, "the fangs grow, and the *nectar* is more concentrated. It becomes useful as a weapon. Then we call it *MORS*."

He lifted his chin and looked at me. "When males are fighting, and it gets very thick, it is *death*. We use it to defend the *Shoal*."

I sighed. He just revealed a Syreni secret that Cal didn't know. One that explained so much.

"Ok. So are the effects of *nectar* long-lasting?" Things got awkward when Ronan looked at me with a smoldering expression.

"How long it lasts depends on many things. But usually, it takes two or three hours. It is always strongest at the first bite."

At the word bite, he clamped his lips together, and in my mind, he hissed, *"I'm sorry I hurt you, Eddi."*

I almost cried at the remorse that filtered through his projected apology.

"You didn't hurt me, Ronan. It was very pleasurable." My expression warmed at the memory of our tryst, while Cal looked like he wanted to pour acid into his ears.

I looked out the window. I saw the seabirds floating over the aquamarine water, and it gave me strength. "There's something I need to tell you, *both* of you. And you aren't going to like it."

I had their full attention when I said, "I know what happened to your people, Ronan. The ones who were taken."

I shoved down all my thoughts about the panic attack and focused on the important subject. My severe reaction to Ronan's secretions could wait.

"Someone, I'm not sure who, but they are horrible people—are distributing drugs. A *new* drug. It has the same effects as your nectar, Ronan." When I looked over, his expression had frozen.

"The night I was taken, the hijackers had a sample on the boat. It was clear, like nectar. And the effects were the same. A blissful feeling, and strong sexual urges." I blushed, and Cal looked away. I focused on Ronan.

"I told Cal, but you and I weren't really…" I thought about the right word, "friends, yet. So you wouldn't have known the details from the night I was kidnapped."

I watched Ronan's face and the thoughts and feelings warring there.

"How would they get our *nectar*? I don't understand. Males must be aroused to produce it. A Syreni male would not be aroused if he was held captive. It makes no sense."

"Your missing people. Are they all males?"

Ronan thought about it and nodded. "Except for my mother. There is talk of others females disappearing two decades ago, but it was another *Shoal*. I do not know the details. Right now, we are losing males. "

I turned to my friend, who listened carefully, but refused to look at Ronan.

"Cal, what do you think? Can you tell the Enforcer? I mean, we don't know much, but this information may help the Syreni. If they are collecting and selling the nectar, and it catches on, Ronan's people won't be safe. They'll never be safe. And who knows what it will do to humans?"

Cal jumped to his feet and headed for the door. He looked over his shoulder and said to Ronan, "Stay away from her. I mean it."

The door slammed behind him. I was shocked at how fiercely he protected me. We would have to talk about it. I needed to know what rattled him. It wasn't like Cal to be so aggressive.

I looked at Ronan. He sat on the sofa, quietly watching me. He made no move to leave.

Nerves tightened my skin. This would be hard, but I was awake now and plunged right in.

"Ronan, I don't know what to say. I'm trying to wrap my head around it. Why did you bite me, without warning me what would happen?"

Ronan rose and came to kneel by my chair. He took my hand.

"I tried to stop the *tangling*, at first. But you were *ready,* and very determined." He smiled, but at the troubled look on my face, he forged ahead.

"I didn't want to stop, either. Then I got carried away. You are so …" He looked inside himself. "You are who … " Ronan frowned and went silent for a moment or two, weighing his words.

"You are *very* important to me, Eddi. When we tangled, it felt right." He paused, his jaw tightening.

"It happened because we were both ready. I am not sorry I bit you. I'm only sorry that I didn't explain it to you first."

I bit my lip. How could I blame him for any of this? He came from the ocean. He didn't know human customs. I decided to sidestep the whole sex thing for now. *It's complicated* was a grand understatement in our case.

"Ronan, I want to tell you how bad I feel about having a fit while on the ocean with you. Sometimes I have problems with stress. I get panic attacks." Ronan tipped his head to the side, listening.

"It was a bit of everything, you know? The bite, the amazing sex, remembering what happened to me that night. It was pretty crazy, coming all at once, and I guess I got a helluva buzz from your *nectar*."

I smiled at the word. "I couldn't control it. Normally, when I get stressed, I feel it coming, and I can talk myself down. I'm sorry. It's very embarrassing that you saw me like that."

Ronan put his hand on my shoulder and gently massaged the crook of my neck with his thumb. It felt both intense and comforting. But I had more to say, and it was time to get it all out on the table.

"I also need to thank you. All this time, I had no idea that you were the one to find me on the reef the night I almost died. Something you said today made me realize I wasn't dreaming that night. It was you who saved me, wasn't it?"

Ronan gave me a generous smile. "I helped look for you. Everyone was frantic after they found your boat. I was close to finding you when they saw the flicker of your heat. Your signature kept disappearing, so they traveled in circles, searching and praying it wasn't too late."

He squeezed my hand. "I sensed you from a long way. Even through the water, your magic shone for me. It brought me straight to you. Once we were together, I brought you closer and Cal took you out quickly."

He glared at the sky outside my window. "You were close to death. They almost killed you. I will use MORS and kill them when I find them," he growled.

"I'm sorry, Eddi. I wanted to tell you the truth, but everyone thought it best that you believe it was a dream. You didn't know about the *Others,* then."

I huffed. "Yes a lot has gone on these last few weeks. You've got that right. I can barely believe it, even now, how much things have changed."

Tears threatened, but I pushed them back. "Ronan, you saved my life. How I treated you was horrible. I'm really sorry. I seem to be saying that way too often these days, but please know, I will *always* be grateful."

Ronan looked like he would lean in and kiss me. I tensed, and he noticed. When he looked me right in the eye, my stomach fluttered. He was so close that I smelled the ocean on his skin. I wanted to reach for him, but things were so confusing that I stopped myself. When in doubt, do nothing.

He saw the conflict on my face. Ronan stood up and, with a sigh, walked towards the door. Before he left, he turned to face me.

"I must hunt for these men. I must stop them." He stared at his hand on the doorknob, and then at me.

"What will you do now?" He meant our connection, whatever that was.

"I don't know, Ronan. I really don't. Let's start with finding your people. Now that we know what's happening, we can start looking for them." I smiled. "Small steps, right?"

Ronan shook his head. "No, Eddi. It's too dangerous. These men have no problem killing to get what they want. You have already been on the sharp end of their spear. I will find them. Then, I will kill them. If they were involved in my mother's death? I will kill them very slowly."

The look of murder on his face was clear to see, his emotions rampaging beneath his skin.

Killing. The word turned my stomach. I looked at Ronan and wondered if this was common in their world. Even with my terrible start in life, killing was so far from my list of solutions that Ronan blurting it out was jarring. Judging by the look on his face, I wouldn't want to be there when he found the bastards.

After he left, I remembered what I meant to ask him. Something he said. "Your Magic was shining for me … "

What did he mean by that? I needed to ask him before I forgot.

***

I saw Cal the next morning at work, and he gave me the cold shoulder. He was polite, and helped me when needed, but he didn't smile the entire shift.

It was an awkward day, even more so when we closed up shop. I finally got to ask my questions when we locked the door.

"Cal, are you going to tell me what's wrong? I'm sorry about yesterday. It was a mistake. I'm sorry you ended up involved in our … *issues."*

He swung around to me, but his look wasn't anger. It was fear.

"A mistake? Giving back a twenty instead of a five is a mistake! Unprotected sex with another species? With a *Syreni?* It's not a mistake Eddi. It's a disaster!"

Leave it to Cal to put it right out there. We were at the Tiki, and the wooden shutters slammed as we closed up. I feared for the hinges.

"What the hell will you do if you get pregnant?"

I cringed at his words. "It's too late now, Cal. We shouldn't have gone so far, and I guess in my mind, I thought he… *I thought I…"*

I didn't know how to say this without sounding dumb. "I didn't think about it, ok? I didn't think we were compatible, in that way."

Cal gave me the look. The one that said *you can't possibly be that dense.*

"Relax Cal. Maybe it's like donkeys and horses?" Ok, that came out sounding dumber than I thought it would.

Cal went wild. "You know they still have babies, *right Eddi?* Sterile babies, but there are still *BABIES!"*

"I know. It was a really a dumb thing to do. We got carried away, and you know I've been crazy about him since the first day I met him. The attraction is almost unbearable sometimes. I don't know what came over me. But it's too late. It's done."

Cal sighed, some of the anger leaving him like a deflating balloon.

"Look, Eddi. I don't know how involved I should get. But I'm *so* worried about you. You're dealing with things that you don't know about. Things that we *Others* learn from childhood."

I felt the prickle of nerves on the back of my neck. I didn't know what he was lining up to shoot my way, but I knew I wouldn't like it.

"There are some things you don't know about our world, Eddi. Lots of things. The *Others*, the Syreni, we all have many adaptations that allow us to thrive. Syreni? They have things that…" He looked stressed. "Shit! I don't know how to put this. If I should even…" Cal trailed off, biting his lip.

With the way he struggled with this, the more I was sure I didn't want to know about it.

"Just say it, Cal. I know it's coming from a good place. Then I can deal with it, once I know what *IT* is."

Cal slumped his shoulders and sat down on a Tiki stool.

"Syreni can influence people with a pheromone. They can attract them. It's an adaptation from long ago. To catch people and eat them."

"They EAT people? Are you kidding me right now!?" I bellowed.

Cal looked around to see if anyone listened as he jumped up and guided me onto his stool. He sat me down and started pacing.

"No! Not *NOW!* A long time ago, Ed. Thousands of years! His eyes were wide. "I'm making this worse. Let me try again." He took a deep breath to collect his thoughts.

"The Sovereigns have ruled for over five thousand years. When they first came to power, it was for the greater good. Things were pretty bad, with no rules and no consequences. They brought things under control. Made the world a safer place."

I nodded to him.

"Since then, all the really bad stuff has been outlawed. It helps keep our existence secret and everything running smoothly. I shouldn't have even mentioned it because the eating thing wasn't my point. It's ancient history."

"So what is your point, exactly, Cal?" Frowning, I tapped my fingers on crossed arms. "Why are you telling me this?"

With a look of total defeat, Cal blurted, "They have a special pheromone to attract people, Ed. Don't you get it? It's still a part of the Syreni culture, even now. But now it's not for catching people to eat them. It's to *mate*."

He paused, watching my face, then continued, "Our world isn't all rainbows and unicorns, Eddi. It can be very harsh."

I was still processing this whole speech of his when it hit me. Why Cal was so upset. I'm sure my face went as white as my hair.

"That first day we met. By the Island. When I got so…" I paused. "Oh, my god. When I was horny as hell!? That was *him!?*"

Cal nodded. Then the waterworks started. Instead of looking relieved, Cal's face went dark, and his lips turned down. No one liked to be the destroyer of romantic fantasies, but here we were.

"Do you think this whole thing was some fucking *luring game* for him? That I'm completely off base about him having *actual* feelings?" I didn't need to ask. I knew it was true.

"Oh my God, Cal. Was this about *fucking* for him? *This whole time!*"

The waterworks came in earnest now. Cal did his best to comfort me, telling me he didn't know for sure, that he wanted me to be aware, and that he and Ronan had argued at the apartment about him telling me. I sobbed into his shoulder for ten minutes before coming up for air.

"I'm such a fool. I fell for it, hook, line, and sinker. He must think it's hilarious. And Tara! Bloody Hell!" I blew my nose on the paper towel Cal gave me.

"I suppose she got the last laugh, didn't she?" I blew my nose again. The waterworks were over. We were moving into self-blame now.

"I guess on some level, I always knew." I gave a hiccuping sob. "I even remember telling you how confused I felt about it the day I met him."

Cal shook his head and said, "I would have told you right then and there, but you didn't know about the *Others*. What could I have said? Oh, be careful, that's a Syreni. They shoot microscopic mists of love juice so they can trick you into sleeping with them."

When he saw my face crumpling and the tears returning, he reached down and put his arms around me.

"I'm sorry. That was supposed to make you smile." He frowned and hugged me.

With a huge, sputtering sigh, I said, "It's ok. It must have been hard for you to watch without being able to say something. I'm glad you told me. If he cared, he would have told me himself, wouldn't he?" With a wet sob, I said, "I think that's the hardest part."

Cal hugged me and mentally propped me up at least twice more before I was ready to head home. I was a high-maintenance friend right now, and I knew it, but I was so glad to have a shoulder to cry on.

When I stood to head home, Cal rubbed my shoulder. "You have certainly had a hellish couple of weeks, girl. Let's just hope everything settles down soon. You've given me enough heart attacks for the month."

I gave him a watery smile, and we headed home for the night.

The next week passed uneventfully, with no sign of Ronan, and Cal hadn't heard anything through his sea critter contacts. I felt more confident and started taking Charters on my own again. James said to trust my instincts and bring Cal along for help if I ever needed him. But there were no issues, of course. Things were back to normal. My small charters were business as usual, and I was thrilled to be back at the reef with the *Wanderlust*.

James let me Captain some of the family snorkel trips with a new hire named Evan as my divemaster. It was fun. Evan was a spicy, dark-haired guy with a quick wit and good humor. He never stopped moving, and I rarely needed to step in because he was good at his job. I loved to tease him about how he herded his sunburned *goslings* on and off the boat like a mother goose.

Even though Captains keep their eyes on the horizon and watch their swimmers, I knew I was subconsciously watching for *him*. I couldn't help myself. Ronan may have been in it for a quick lay, but I had been in it for more. So here I was, pining for an oversexed Syreni who could have any girl at any time. All he had to do was turn on the love juice.

Cal said I should date, but I had no interest. I was happy to fall back into my celibacy mode and look for peace and quiet. A quick roll in the sand held no appeal for me.

Several days later, I sat on my captain's chair, watching Evan chatting up the customers, when I heard a voice. It wouldn't have caught my attention, but it was *in my head*.

I listened carefully. It was on the port side, opposite the swimmers. I was shocked to see a Lionfish right up at the boat. I knew right away that it was Tara. She swam small circles at the waterline below where I sat.

I knew I shouldn't engage and that she was dangerous, but I couldn't resist.

"What can I do for you, Tara?" I was a bit rusty at *mind-speak* but she answered. And she didn't waste any time on small talk.

"He's missing. Ronan is missing." Her high-pitched voice sounded anxious. Frantic.

Hot fear flashed through me. *"How long?"*

"For the last five days, he's been a no-show back at the Shoal. No one has seen him. Is he with you?"

I felt a little bad for her. Maybe she drank the Kool-Aid too.

"No, he isn't. And I haven't seen him for a week." I saw her fishy smile at my admission, and made a mental note to remember she was a Lionfish. Poisonous until you pulled their fins out.

"Where was he last seen?" I asked her. Tara flopped around down there in some sort of fishy distress.

"Out at Coffin's Patch. He searched up and down the reef, watching for suspicious boats and talking to Others. He scoured the reef all day and night, questioning everyone. He was so determined. Didn't he tell you?"

Jealousy burned a hole in my chest.

Stop. Just stop, Edaline.

I ignored her efforts to bait me. Evan popped up beside me, and, looking over the side, said, "Crap, a Lionfish. Should I call the snorkelers back in?"

I looked over my shoulder at the swimmers and frowned.

"No, it's fine. But I'll report it so they can let the local spear fisherman know where to hunt."

After he left, I looked back, but she was gone.

CHAPTER 22

~ RONAN ~

The sun poked through the clouds overhead, and the watery ceiling far above rippled in a wavy mirror of reflection. I swam along the buttress of the reef, looking for the scorpionfish *"Viggo."* The predatorial reef-dweller sent word of information for me, and I was anxious to collect it.

The clouds of tropical reef fish parted as I swam through their school, the brilliant colors causing a smile. Small tropicals couldn't shift forms, and being simple creatures, they couldn't communicate. They were a vital part of my world, and Eddi loved them as much as I did.

The thought of her lusty response to our tangling made my sex twitch, and I let out a bubbly chuckle. She was an exotic, wary creature. I looked forward to tearing down her walls and seeing more of her captivating soul. Thoughts of her warmed me as I swam.

There. Near the ocean floor. The bulbous gray head and tiny tail blended perfectly with the coral. Resting on an overhang, Viggo used his effective camouflage to ambush prey. I only spotted him due to his faint magical signature. All *Others* glowed faintly, making them visible to my Syreni eyes. This ocean predator was a shifter.

His beady eyes rolled up at me as I turned and swam down to where he perched. His pectoral fins and the decorative skin flaps covering his body waved gently in the current, mimicking coral. When he spotted me, Viggo went more still, if that was possible. I thought he might flee, so I sent my thoughts to him.

"You sent for me? Do you have information to share, Viggo?"

The scorpionfish flicked his eyes back and forth as if deciding whether to run, then answered, his voice thick and froggy in my head.

"A boat comes to the reef and anchors here every night. It sits for a time. Another vessel comes. Then, they both leave. Last night, they threw a body into the water. After they left, I went to see it. It was a tall, skinny male with blonde hair. He was alive at first."

My heart leapt in triumph. *Finally*, a solid lead.

"What else, Viggo? There is more to this story. Tell me everything you know."

His eyes darted back and forth before answering, his fins becoming stiff and unmoving.

"When I got there, the human made strange movements with his hips and hands. They were not swimming motions. He licked his lips and squeezed his hands. His eyes did not see. He did not care that he breathed water. He died quickly. The boats both left soon after."

I should have felt bad about the human death, but in my heart, I knew this man was up to no good. So, despite the loss of life, my spirits lifted at the apparent link to our stolen nectar. Viggo's description mirrored the effects of the drug.

"Why did you not report this sooner to the Shoal Elders? You know it is required. What are you not telling me?"

With a saucy look, Viggo said, *"I didn't care about one more boat parked above me. It was not unusual. The death was last night. There was no time to report it. And the body is still here. And now, so are you."* He gave me a fishy smile.

I could not believe my stroke of good fortune. I glared at the scorpionfish for his insolence but was eager to see this dead male and uncover his secrets.

"Show me."

The disgruntled predator wriggled off his perch and, with a flick of his tiny tail, propelled his portly head and torso down the reef to where a body lay hidden under the coral. Jammed in far enough to remain hidden, it was in a terrible state.

I drifted closer to see—a tall, thin blonde male, his eyes already removed by hungry reef fish. His state of decay was advanced. Something was off.

I narrowed my eyes at Viggo, who sat on the coral, silently watching me.

"Who put this body here? This male was not killed last night. Why are you lying?"

Viggo gave me a fishy shrug. "Last night, a week ago, it's unimportant to me. I'm hungry. Get on with things so I can return to my hunt."

The desire to choke the life from him raced through me, but scorpionfish venom was dangerous. I would deal with him later. Turning back, I investigated the corpse.

After trying unsuccessfully to pull the body out, I managed to get enough room to feel around in his pockets. There was nothing in them, so I reached under the jagged shelf and ran my fingers along his legs, looking for what snagged him on the coral.

"I'll ask one more time, Viggo. Who put this body here? You are already in enough trouble. Answer me, and I will go easier on you."

There was no answer from the scorpionfish, who was doing his *"I am coral, nothing to see here"* routine. Motionless, he hunted while waiting, his fins floating and swaying on the current.

Frustrated by the situation but desperate to learn more, I wedged my arm under the ledge so far that my shoulder rubbed on it. My fingers searched, finding something metallic. Too late, I tried to pull away.

With a forceful clack, something clamped around my wrist. I jerked my hand back as something sharp pierced my skin. Pulling hard, I struggled against the painful hold. Slowly, inch by inch, I worked my arm out enough to see what held me firm.

A metal cuff, firmly clamped around my ruined wrist, glimmered in the filtered light from above. Strong chain ran from the cuff and disappeared under the ledge, the body still firmly wedged inside. On the inside of the shackle, pointed barbs pierced my skin and were now deeply embedded in my wrist. Searing pain licked up my arm.

I began to struggle in earnest, my tail thrashing as I tried to break free. The chain was unbreakable. Blood from my wrist wounds began floating in little red clouds as the barbs dug deeper. With my free hand, I clawed at the painful band, but the strange metal burned my fingers when I touched it.

Powerful strokes of my tail stirred up silt from the ocean floor, creating a cloud around me. It was no use. There was no escaping the shackle and chain.

My entire arm prickled with a fiery heat, and I stopped struggling to look down at my hand. Strands of black ran from my fingers to my shoulder like an eerie network of putrid veins. *Demon magic.*

I snarled at Viggo, whose bulbous eye watched intently from where he lay on the coral beside me. He still hunted. I was a fool, trapped through the treachery of one of our own.

"You are a traitor, and a vicious death is coming for you when I get free, Viggo."

A numb sensation began in my jaw, quickly strobing down my neck and shoulders before racing down my spine. My tail froze, a numbness seizing it in an icy fist. Immobile, the only freedom was my ability to breathe.

Viggo snorted. *"The other five were just as dumb as you, Ronan. I will enjoy watching them cart you away. I think in this case, the only vicious death might be your own."*

As my paralyzed body gently bobbed on the end of the chain, I watched the scorpionfish spring his trap, gulping down a fish when it wandered too close. The last thing I heard before I slipped into oblivion was his quiet, fishy chuckle.

CHAPTER 23

Tara. Say the name, and my hackles rose as I relived what she did to me. I may have wanted to report *Terribly Toxic Tara* to the *"REEF"* organization, but I didn't. I wasn't that cruel. But as soon as I returned to Davy Jones, I found Cal and filled him in.

"We have to do *something!* We don't know how far those monsters will go if they have him. What are they doing to him!?" Ronan was missing for almost a week, and the possibilities made me sick. I'd had trouble sleeping every night, constantly worrying about him. He didn't deserve such a cruel fate.

Cal told me the Enforcer was chasing down information, but with no leads on the men who hurt me, he had come up empty-handed.

Tracking someone who steals boats to do their deals on the open water was virtually impossible. It was too big an area to police, and the traffickers knew it. At night, most local fishermen headed home to family, so there weren't many witnesses along the reef. How they'd captured a perfectly healthy Syreni was anyone's guess.

Desperate to help, I spent a few days this week back at the police station. I needed to keep busy, so I asked if I could take another look at their mug book to see if it jogged my memory.

After spending hours and hours going through photos, I found nothing. Searching through image after image of the dregs of society depressed me. The faces in there were a grim reminder that humans could be monsters, too.

Cal checked with friends in the Lower Keys—the human friends of his roommate. Most Keys residents frequented local hangouts, which often had a Happy Hour. That meant cheap drinks, food and a band. Cal asked his acquaintances to listen for anything suspicious like a new drug on the scene or people acting strangely. It was the best we could do.

The next day, Cal met me at my place after work to watch a movie. The longer Ronan was missing, the more anxious I became. I was winding up for another anxiety attack.

"You've got to stay calm, Ed. You can't keep going this way. He's strong. Whatever is going on, he'll be ok." Cal tried to be positive but he didn't believe his own words. I saw it on his face. I'd seen the monsters in action. That was all the proof I needed that we must act fast.

"I've been going over and over it in my head." I looked at Cal and tossed him the chip bag. We watched Star Trek, as I'd sworn off Rom-Coms until we found Ronan.

"There are some things that seem odd to me. Like why would Hannibal try to take the *Wanderlust*? It makes no sense. Why not just *buy* a boat? Don't drug dealers have lots of money?"

"That's the thing," Cal said, chewing his nails. "James couldn't remember the clients, but I asked him to check the receipts. No money came in for that booking, Eddi. They didn't pay a dime."

I thought about that for a bit. "Do you think those creeps hit James with the drug? I mean, Brian said he was out to lunch when they found him, right?"

Cal shook his head. "No, it didn't affect him the way you described. It was like a big piece of his memory was missing, and he was totally whacked for a while. Like, lights on, no one is home."

"What could mess with his memories? Do shifters have that power?"

"Whoever it is, I don't think they're *Other*." Cal stood, going to stare out the window into the night. "Shifters don't have any tricks except shifting. Some have enhanced strength, but that's about it. And it wouldn't matter because we'd know who acted out. It's a small community. Any shifters coming in from other areas must report in as they arrive. The Enforcer ensures that everyone complies, or else."

I'd never asked because it would bring up an uncomfortable subject, but I had to. "Do *Immortalis* have those types of abilities? Because it would be a great fit for criminals. Talents like that would come in handy."

Cal shrugged. "There are too many kinds, to be sure, but vampires manipulate memory, and they are one of the most common factions. The damn things reproduce like rabbits, too." He looked over when I didn't speak and saw the look on my face.

"You aren't kidding, are you? Was there a vampire here? *At work?"*

Cal nodded, his eyes soft. "It's a lot, I know. I'm not supposed to tell you anything. But it's a definite possibility."

Quickly, I moved on to our other options. "I suppose they could be human, but there was something strange about those guys. They gave me the creeps. I doubt they were human."

Cal was as frustrated as me. Spending all night guessing wasn't helping. I knew my friend wasn't happy with Ronan, but he was a softie and cared about everyone. And he knew the implications if this drug made it onto the street.

"We don't have enough information." I paused the movie because neither of us watched it anyway.

"I don't know what else to say, Eddi. The Enforcer knows all the details but doesn't share much with me. He knew about James' condition after those men hijacked you, so I'm sure he would have chased down any leads there."

We sat in uncomfortable silence for a while, each of us racking our brains. We bounced theories around for a while, then tried to return to our movie, but neither of us could settle down. Eventually, we called it a night, and Cal headed home.

We had struck a big fat zero, but everything changed at work the next afternoon. Cal's friend from the Lower Keys popped in because he saw something, and being in town to run errands, dropped by the marina. Cal cornered me when he got a chance.

"This might be it, Ed. I can't believe it! So, Jax tells me that he was at the Big Pine Tiki Bar yesterday and saw a girl getting screwed right in front of the bar—*in plain view.*"

I looked skeptical, but he rushed on. "Yah, Yah, I know, it's the Keys; weird things happen. But this pair was so messed up they had to call the cops and an ambulance. My friend described their behavior. It was too odd to be normal. It so sounded like the effects of *nectar*."

It was a small lead, but at least it was something. Was it just another drunk couple sowing their wild oats in paradise? It could also be a drug commonly available to humans these days. And even if it was *our* drug, these people could have picked it up anywhere along the Keys.

After mulling it over, I figured this lead was safe enough for us to check out. The chances were slim that we would find anything. Going to poke around Big Pine Key wouldn't hurt. I did NOT want to run into these guys again, but the need to find Ronan nibbled away at me. I pushed my fears aside.

"So, Cal, wanna help me stake out a tiki bar tonight?"

Cal smiled. "Hang on, I'll get my hat."

***

The tiki had a special event tonight with an All-You-Can-Eat Crawfish deal, one of Cal's *favorites*. Big Pine was an hour by bus, so after closing, we went without changing clothes. Yes, we were both the whitest *and* the lamest heroes on the planet. Cal and Eddi, saving the world one bus ride at a time.

We both loved Crawfish, so when we arrived late, and there were leftovers, we were thrilled. Because of the spice, Cal got wicked heartburn afterward, so he popped Tums like crazy during our snack. I teased him, of course.

Anxiety rode me hard, so to pass the time, we finished our snacks, listened to the music, and I peppered him with questions to take my mind off everything.

"I don't have a mate because octopuses only mate once and then die," Cal said.

I spit out my drink, wiped my mouth, and hissed, *"WHAT!?"*

He nodded. "I mean, we aren't *exactly* octopuses, but we share most of their traits."

Great. Now I had to avoid the *"he mates and he dies"* conversation I accidentally started. I didn't want to spoil the evening, but inside, I freaked. My friend would never find love. The little flower in my chest sagged.

I focused on the band and the burning lips that made my eyes water. Suspicious activities being precisely zero, I figured we would strike out tonight anyway, so I relaxed and tried to have a good time.

"So you're celibate, you can squirt ink, rip off dive masks, *and* bite people really, really hard? Those are some awesome superpowers, buddy."

"Yep!" He popped the "p" and tossed our last crawfish in his mouth. "I have three hearts, too." My jaw dropped open. "Only in octopus form, though, which is a good thing. It might be hard to explain at a hospital," he laughed, wiggling his eyebrows at me. "It also explains my kind, caring disposition."

I had to smile when he made a heart over his chest. I appreciated the distraction.

During a break for the band, Cal headed across the parking lot to the gas station next door to get some Tums. He'd already popped half a roll and needed more already. When Cal returned, I knew something was up. His face was white.

"Eddi, you're not going to believe this. I was at the gas station getting my stuff, and a guy walked in. When I saw him, I got a really weird vibe, so I hung around looking at magazines. When he came by me, he looked *exactly* like Hannibal Lecter—from the movie. Just like you described! It was such a creepy resemblance that I had prickles up the back of my neck when he looked at me."

Cal was so excited he squirmed. "Guess what he bought? *Six bottles* of rubbing alcohol! I mean, that screams suspicious activity, don't you think?"

I was excited for a nanosecond before my stomach revolted. "What should we do?" My leg jumped in place, my fingernails clenching into my palms. We had to find Ronan!

Cal looked around the bar, his brows furrowed. "We've got to hurry, or we'll miss him. If you can get a good look and it's your guy, we'll follow him."

Walking through the bar and out the far door as casually as we could, I looked over at the gas station. He wasn't there. There wasn't much we could do now. So plopped onto the bench outside the tiki bar and waited for the bus. Excitement drained from with a disappointed hiss.

We weren't waiting long before someone walked across the parking lot behind us, and the tiny hairs lifted on the back of my neck. It was Hannibal. My back was to him, thankfully. I'm not sure where he came from, but when he walked around the corner of the bar, we followed, always keeping something between us.

The tiki was the first of a string of businesses along this stretch of Highway 1, so we hung back and walked down the sidewalk, holding hands to blend in. It was dark, and we weren't alone, couples strolling hand in hand between the shops. We blended in, and Hannibal didn't notice us. He turned the corner at the end of the plaza and headed down a side street.

Most of the residential streets in the Keys dead-ended at the Atlantic, and many backed onto canals leading to the sea. An abandoned marina squatted halfway down Cobia Lane, its broken windows dark and lifeless. Sure enough, it backed onto a canal.

Cal and I walked along the opposite side of the street, and as we came within sight of the building, the metal door slammed shut. We kept going, and after we passed the shop, we stopped and melted into the bushes.

The marina butted against a vacant lot, and we followed the edge of the bush line between the two. Hunkered down in the brush, we saw everything, even the back of the building where it met the canal.

Our vantage point was miserable. The No-See-Ums enjoyed my skin, and I scratched like mad. Cal sweated freely, his hand constantly brushing his forehead. The humid night air sent trickles of moisture down my back.

"What are we going to do?" I hissed. "We can't call the police, because if there are Syreni in there…" Ronan's skins would pass casual observation, but close inspection or police interrogation? Not a chance.

The main building was enormous. It was solid but tattered on the outside, with peeling paint and pieces of tin hanging as if shedding an ancient skin. The numerous outer storage buildings and short docks looked ready to fall into the water. The sprawling business had been successful at one time—another Hurricane victim, judging by the damage and debris scattered around the building.

"If these guys are in there handling narcotics, I'm sure they'll have surveillance cameras," Cal whispered. "We can't get close, or they'll see us. So we sit tight."

His eyes were wide, and his teeth biting his lips as he darted looks around the creepy place. I was about two streets past terrified. But we had a location, and like hell was I letting it slip through my fingers.

"We have to do something! How do we get help?" I couldn't stand it. Ronan could be in that building. We didn't think this through. Neither of us expected to find anything tonight. I guess we forgot how trouble followed us around.

"If I can get back to the marina, I can contact the Enforcer. We have a way to communicate." At the look on my face, Cal added, "I can't reveal that. Sorry Ed."

Right. *No information available.* As usual. I didn't care about that right now because anxiety nipped at my belly, and staying calm was my focus.

We went over our options. I hadn't replaced my Pixel phone since the night from hell, and Cal didn't carry one because he had no one to call. James had gone down to visit a friend for a cruise in Key West harbor and wouldn't be back until late, so we couldn't even bum a phone at the bar to call him for a ride. Cal's roommate, Edward, worked nights. We were out of options.

Chewing his lips Cal looked back towards the bar. "With Fantasy Fest going on in Key West, a cab will take forever, and the bus comes hourly at this time of night. It won't be quick enough. God, we are lame, aren't we?"

"Maybe I can try hitchhiking and keep walking as I thumb for a ride. If I can't get a lift, I'll change form and swim from the Spanish Harbour bridge. It's not far down the road."

He looked at me, his expression guarded. "It's fifteen miles to Davy Jones, but I can probably make it in half an hour if I don't take breaks. I'll get the Enforcer. He's swift, so we can make it back in no time. I mean, I'm pretty fast myself. I can knock the distance off in short bursts."

"NO, Cal, you can't! It's dark. The ocean at night? No way. No freaking way." Panic rose to clog my throat.

"It's our best chance, Eddi. You know it is. I'll be careful and avoid the bridges where the sharks like to cruise."

Hot tears pushed against my lids. If I didn't let him go, I risked Ronan. "Cal, I'm scared. What if something happens to you?"

"I'll be fine, Eddi. I'll try hitching first. And hey, I'm tough! Remember the ink and the biting? I'm strong. And I have EIGHT, count 'em, *EIGHT* arms!" He wiggled his ten fingers at me and winked.

Then he remembered who he came with and frowned. "If I leave you here, you *have* to stay back. Watch to see if they leave. That's it, no more. *I mean it!"*

I promised, then looked back at the marina, barely visible through the grass and the bushes. "Make sure you check at the bar first, Cal. Ask around. Someone MUST be heading to Marathon." He didn't answer, and fear blinded me, the thought of losing my best friend chilling skin.

"We can find another wa—" I turned, but he was already gone.

CHAPTER 24

Moving closer to the marina parking lot, I crouched behind a pile of rusted-out oil drums in the tall grass, waiting for Cal and struggling not to panic.

What if a shark attacked? The ocean was dark, and everything hunted at night. Squirrels did laps in my stomach at the thought of him out there all alone. A half-hour in the black ocean. A white octopus standing out like a beacon. Terror sent icy tendrils of panic over my skin, and I struggled to breathe.

Ten minutes turned into what felt like ten hours. I would die before Cal returned. I was sure of it. I shook my head. It was too late now, and I had to stop thinking about it, or I'd have another panic attack. I had to trust he could make the swim. *I couldn't lose him, too!*

Grim reality set in. I was alone. I had to deal with it. I slowed my breathing and watched the building from my hiding place, wiping sweat from my chin.

Nothing moved around the building except for the insects buzzing across my skin. My wait was an unpleasant, itchy experience.

A while after Cal left, a powder blue BMW pulled up and parked by the front doors of the old marina office. A tall, slim blonde climbed out, dressed to kill, wearing a dark, fitted dress. She opened the heavy marina door and disappeared inside.

What was going on in there? That chick looked like she was going to a party for crying out loud. I hunched down, waiting for what seemed like forever. Breathing helped, but my nerves got the better of me. I jittered my leg and bit my nails.

Breathe. Ronan's Fine. Cal's Fine. It's alright, Eddi.

I thought about leaving the safety of the tall grass and moving closer, but before I could act on the impulse, a dark shape moved behind me. I gasped, and a vise-like hand clamped over my mouth from behind. My scream went nowhere, the hand so tight over my mouth that no sound escaped. Lifted off the ground, I kicked and screamed through the suffocating hold. Barely able to breathe, I panicked.

Kicking like a mule, my attacker carried me through the heavy metal door and into the shop end of the marina. I almost passed out, the sudden rise of choking fear sending me into a mental frenzy. I fought to stay awake. I needed to stay awake.

I must have lost that fight because my head filled with air, and my eyes refused to focus. When the room stopped spinning, through the haze, I watched gloved hands tie me to a chair in the shop, a greasy floor beneath my feet slippery with grit.

Tied by the arms and the legs to an old office chair, the vinyl peeling from the armrests pinched at my skin. The wheels squeaked, and my chair slowly turned until I was face-to-face with my captor. He smiled that vicious smile I knew so well.

Norman fucking Bates. He leaned down to look at me like a lizard eyeing his prey.

"What have we here?" His eyes, so close to mine, were menacing. "Well, if it isn't our little captain from the boat! I guess I should have been more thorough, *hmm?*"

Bates crouched to finish the tape on my ankle and said, "What, did you think we wouldn't have cameras everywhere? *Silly* little girl."

Of course, I'm always a complete idiot when scared. So, instead of laying low, I tried to head-butt him when he came up from tying my feet. My head rocked back with a snap when he punched me. The back of my neck burned with the strain, and my cheek didn't just sting, it throbbed. Damn, he was strong.

Stunned, I slowly raised my head. He growled at me. How odd. He sounded like an enraged dog, but when I looked at Bates, his lips were closed. I squinted. He growled louder. I pulled my head back, trying to focus. When my captor looked over his shoulder, I saw where the growling originated.

RONAN! My heart jumped in my chest, but I stifled a cry when I saw what they had done to him. I knew these guys were twisted, but I had underestimated them.

Naked from the waist up, Ronan was in skin form, his feet bare. Thick leather cuffs shackled his wrists and ankles, the old vinyl dentist's chair rocking on its wheels as he fought. Firmly buckled down and angled backward, Ronan raged against his bonds. The sight of the leather muzzle firmly cinched over his face sent a painful jolt through me. Bates must have been careful to secure him well because his wild struggles rocked the chair at its base.

"Shut the hell up, you fucking *FISH!*" The man walked over to Ronan and bent down to eye level. Ronan snarled, saliva trickling through the small openings in the leather mask. Bates stared into his eyes, taunting him, then slowly turned his head to follow Ronan's gaze.

"Oooh this is good! We have your latest strumpet here, do we? This will be so much more fun than I anticipated." With a smug look, Bates turned to me and said, "Your timing is impeccable. I'm excited to show you the fun things we've been doing since our last visit."

Before he could say anything more, Hannibal walked into the shop from a side office. He gave Bates a pointed look and said, "Stop provoking him. He's already been far too much trouble, and we have work to do. Come here and help me."

Glaring dark eyes glanced at where I still struggled, the bastard looking like he was denied a toy. With a quiet snarl, he followed his instructions.

On a table near the dentist's chair, Hannibal sorted through a cluster of tubes and straps. Ronan's eyes focused on me, and the shame I saw there made my anxiety spike.

They'd muzzled him. *A freaking muzzle!* He'd obviously given them a rough time, and in some small way, his defiance gave me hope.

At first glance, he looked alright. There were no marks or obvious signs of trauma, except for a ring around one wrist that looked like a burn or scabbed-over wound.

Physically unharmed, Ronan's snarls said things had happened. *Bad things.* His eyes pleaded as if desperate for me to understand something.

"Ronan, what's wrong? What are they doing to you?" I pushed it to him with my mind, but he lowered his gaze and didn't answer. His arms quivered, and sweat beaded along his skin, his chest heaving like he'd run a marathon.

Hannibal set a mess of tubes out on the table, and they both began organizing the tubes and clips. Several of the contraptions lay in a pile next to clear retainers, similar to the ones the orthodontist used.

Assembling one of the fittings, Bates held it up, and that was when I understood what they were up to. Hannibal planned to put one of those things into Ronan's mouth! I laughed under my breath.

Good luck with that, boys. I'm pretty sure someone's going to lose a finger today.

Ronan's eyes darted between me and Hannibal as he became increasingly agitated. His breath came through the leather holes in raspy snorts as if he had trouble breathing in the mask. Oh, Gods, what had they been doing to him?

"Hang on, Ronan. Cal's getting help!" I sent the thought out to him as firmly as I could. Ronan looked up but wouldn't answer. It made no sense. Why wasn't he answering me? Maybe he was out of the water too long.

Looking at Hannibal I said,, "Good luck getting that thing in his mouth. I don't think he's feeling cooperative today." I shot Bates a defiant look, and for a minute, I worried he might retaliate. But then he smiled at me. A confident, happy smile. That's when I knew I wasn't getting the whole picture. My blood ran cold.

Hannibal ignored me, and his gaze lifted to the back of the shop, where five male Syreni crouched in a large cage. They watched me, their stares intense. A muscular male with long sandy hair darted glances between Ronan and me, his brow furrowed. His eyes glittered green from the darkness before he blinked and turned away.

"Ok, almost ready. We need to hustle," Hannibal snapped. "We only have a few hours to collect all of these Syreni."

Were they going to do this to *all* of them? How in the hell would they manage it? Ronan was already fighting them, and the Syreni in the back cage were massive brutes. They sure as shit weren't going to stand still to have their *nectar* collected. I had missed something vital. Hannibal and Bates were too confident.

A growing unease curled in my gut. I sure hoped Cal was on the way because things were not looking good. A sense of impending doom filled me as my chest constricted. Shame dulled Ronan's downcast eyes. What the fuck was going on here?

"Go get her," Hannibal said. "She's in the office."

Bates headed for the door and smiled back at me before saying, "I'm so glad you came tonight. You're going to get a real kick out of this."

My eyes darted to Ronan, who had gone still. He'd stopped struggling, his body vibrating with fine trembles. His eyes shot wide, and he darted a wild look at me.

"*What is going on, Ronan!?*" I screamed at him in my head. I don't know if he could hear me, but it didn't matter. He wouldn't look at me. He was looking at the door.

When it opened, my eyes snapped to the door and a woman stepped out. The woman from the parking lot. Taking her time, she strutted into the shop. She looked like she stepped out of a Vogue Ad, from her platinum blonde tresses to the little black dress and ruby lipstick.

She swaggered across the shop floor, her heels clicking on the cement, and stopped before Ronan. He was motionless and watched her with a strange expression slithering behind his eyes. She turned her pretty face to me. When she spoke, she addressed Ronan but looked straight at me.

She enjoyed my distress, *the bitch*. The hungry look in her eyes put a sour taste in my mouth.

"Just relax, sweetheart. You loved it all those other times, remember? It feels wonderful for me, too. You know I won't hurt you. You're my favorite. So delicious." She licked her lips, and after she finished checking me out, she turned back to Ronan.

Leaning down, she put her hands on his arms, then swayed closer and gently nuzzled along the underside of his jaw. "Just imagine it's you and me, with no one else watching," she whispered to him.

Ronan's entire body tightened. His eyes shot me a look that was both confused and panicked. There was something strange about him.

Then I saw it. His pupils dilated, flashing as the green irises shrunk to a thin ring. He looked at me but didn't *see* me.

On a sob, I began struggling against my bonds again and choked out, "Ronan! Fight her! I don't know what she's doing to you, but fight her!"

Bates just chuckled. When I turned my head toward him, I saw the fucker had a tent in his pants. With a sick grin, he looked at me and rubbed his bulge while making kissy faces.

"You sick *fuck!*" I screamed at him. "You're going to die for this!" Norman strolled to the table, picked up a roll of tape, and returned, promptly taping my mouth shut.

"Don't spoil my fun, darling, or I'll tape it over your nose, too." He grinned and walked back to where he had been standing.

"Hurry up," Bates said to the blonde. "We haven't got all night."

I was so confused. What was happening? What was she going to do to Ronan?

And then I felt it. In fact, *I saw it*. An almost imperceptible mist began to lift from the blonde, floating on the air currents. I watched in horror as the scene unfolded.

It started from her body and began to spread. One long thin strand broke off and started towards Bates, and he jumped back a few steps. "Watch it, whore," he snarled.

The mist slowly wafted over Ronan, whose eyes had gone hazy. And then I heard him, just a slight murmur in my mind. *"I'm so sorry, Eddi. Please, look away. Don't watch! I don't want you to see."*

And then, the mist reached his face, his eyes going soft and filling with desire. There was no green. Only the black of his dilated pupils showed against the whites. He let out a quiet, breathy moan and slowly turned his head away from me.

"RONAN!" I leaned forward and screamed as loud as possible through the tape, sheer terror icing my skin. I rocked and heaved in that damn chair, the wheels squeaking madly with my efforts, but it was useless. No amount of struggling would break the ties.

Ronan relaxed and tilted his head back onto the headrest, his jaw slack. Weakly, he tried to turn his head away from the advancing cloud, but it kept coming.

Slowly, it crept over his body until it surrounded him. Barely visible, it hovered, caressing his skin, licking over his chest, drifting around his ears, and slipping into his widened nostrils.

Ronan's breaths started to huff through the muzzle in soft pants mixed with short, breathy moans. He no longer fought what was happening. His tense body slumped, and his hands, which had been tightly clutching the chair, slowly kneaded the arms. Occasional twitches in his ankles were the only sign of tension before a long, relaxed sigh came through the mouth of the mask.

Who was this bitch? And what was she doing to Ronan!?

Oh my God, Ronan. My heart cracked, and I sobbed, tears streaming down my face.

Bates noticed. He looked at me with a sick grin. *"Succubus,"* he whispered with a dramatic flare, giving me some *jazz hands*. He burst out in malicious chuckles before turning back to watch. The sick bastard enjoyed the show.

So far, the blonde hadn't laid a hand on him, but Ronan had an enormous erection that threatened to burst through his skins. I watched in mounting horror as inside, my guts turned to lead.

I glanced at the Succubus. Her lips were slightly parted, and she looked—*hungry*. It's the only way I could describe it. I had no idea what a Succubus was, but she was a predator. That much was clear.

Hannibal spoke, his voice breaking through the erotic chorus of Ronan's pleasured sighs.

"I think it's safe now. Layla, if you would?" Hannibal motioned to the contraption he had put together while she toyed with her prey. Layla looked up from where she leaned over Ronan's squirming form and frowned at Hannibal as if angry at his interruption.

Ronan's head lolled back, his bulge monstrous, and every once in a while, he flexed his hips as if searching for friction. I couldn't see his eyes, but I knew Ronan was lost in some sort of lust-filled haze. And it wasn't coming from his *nectar*. It was coming from that God damned *shit* rolling from the blonde in waves.

Tears poured down my cheeks, my glistening eyes watching in disbelief. I looked at the cage near the back of the shop.

The other Syreni males had turned their backs and were gathered as far from the action as possible. I imagined they knew all about what would happen.

The Succubus took a small step back from Ronan's chair and looked over at Hannibal, who was busy setting up more contraptions. The other Syreni were next.

"I won't work with restraints, Malus. I have standards. Take them off," she said, with a moue of distaste. My eyes shot to Hannibal. Malus? His name is *Malus*? I'd remember that, you son of a bitch.

Malus nodded to the Succubus, who leaned over and whispered something to Ronan before dipping her tongue into his ear. He slumped, and as easy as that, she removed the restraints and discarded his muzzle on the floor.

Ronan's head rolled my way, and I saw his eyes. Ronan was blind to his surroundings. A lazy, erotic smile played on his moist lips, his two slender fangs exposed and dripping.

Oh God, No—RONAN! Tears rolled freely down my cheeks. This couldn't be happening. *Where is Cal? Oh my God, Cal, hurry!*

Groggy, Ronan lifted his head, sharing a slanted look with the Succubus. His eyes soaked with desire, Ronan reached for her, but the blonde easily redirected him, his weak arm falling back to the armrest.

Malus handed the tube contraption to her, and she fitted it on Ronan's face. She slid the retainer over his fangs, now fully distended and dripping freely. She leaned in, whispering how big, strong, and powerful he was before fitting the tubes and harness over his ears. She set the vials Malus handed her into a rack on the back of the chair and connected a tube to the first vial with an IV needle. Ronan never moved.

"Very good darling," Malus said. "Could you pull back your magic on this side? I need to get closer to see if the collector is working."

The mist moved. Layla had complete control over whatever she pumped across Ronan's skin.

Hannibal checked the unit carefully, then looked at the nearly empty vial with a frown. He moved away from her.

"A bit more, my dear. He's resisting."

The Succubus focused her gaze on Ronan and, with a ravenous smile, leaned closer to his lips. She reached down with one hand, sliding it up the enormous bulge beneath his skins, and blew lightly into his nostrils. Ronan jerked, a groan forced from his lips, then clenching his hands on the armrest, he thrust his hips with a lunging stab. The chair creaked under the sudden movement, and she giggled in delight.

"Whoopsie! There it is... *Ohhh*, you are such a long, throbbing fellow, aren't you? And so *tasty.*"

Layla licked her lips and wrapped her manicured hand around Ronan's pulsing erection, and began stroking up and down, slowly and firmly, gathering the glistening drops that beaded on the tip. A silly, intoxicated grin plastered across her mouth, Layla enjoyed this as much as Ronan.

I threw my head back and screamed, but it was muffled by the tape over my mouth. I felt sick. Tears poured down my face. I was helpless to do anything.

The Succubus gave a few more gentle strokes up and down his engorged rod and breathed into his nostrils again. Ronan lunged, holding his straining hips off the chair, trying to get closer to the pressure of her hand. I looked at the vial, and saw a thin stream of clear liquid jetting into it.

They had won. These fucking, disgusting animals had what they were after. They'd taken something beautiful and polluted it with greed. And they didn't even have to fight Ronan to get it.

Layla called out to Malus as she stroked Ronan, his penis bulging with veins as it pulsed and jerked in her grip.

"You'll want to get a second vial ready, Malus, because he's not resisting *now.*" She turned her head and smirked at me.

I would rip her head off with my bare hands.

Bates followed her look and turning to me, he shrugged and said, "It's perfect really. She feeds, he comes, and we make money. *Everybody wins.*"

***

At this point, whatever mutual feeding deal she had going on with Ronan created some blowback because Layla slowly and steadily lost control of herself. I don't think anyone noticed because Malus was busy setting up for the next collection, and Bates was—I didn't want to look.

Layla squeezed and rubbed her thighs together, and her face morphed into a greedy scowl, almost as if she wasn't getting enough of what she desired. She stroked him harder and harder, spitting long trails of drool over her hand for lubrication. Then with a lusty moan, she leaned forward and licked the corner of Ronan's mouth.

Ronan was lost, his heavy-lidded, unseeing eyes staring from his tight face, his head lolling as he pumped into her hand. Clumsily, he tried to return her kiss.

Their lips clashed around the extractor, and that was when all hell broke loose. She must have accidentally gotten a mouthful of *nectar* because, with an inhuman-sounding snarl, she *snapped.*

The mist wafting from her skin began pouring off in waves, thickening until it scented the air with musk. It coated Ronan so heavily that it beaded on his skin. Finally, the roiling cloud shot outward with an explosive force, catching Bates and Malus dead on.

Several things happened at once. The Succubus put both hands on Ronan, jerking and twisting his slippery cock, then pounced, slathering the tip with her tongue. Ronan, his head thrashing back and forth, howled in ecstasy, grabbing onto the arms of the chair. He climaxed, his hips stabbing upwards in uncontrollable spasms. The only thing holding the chair upright was the Succubus, who was latched onto him, her eyes glowing candy apple red.

Layla was out of control. With wild abandon, she lifted her face up and tried to catch the thick white jets of cum out of the air like it was popcorn and she didn't want to miss a single drop. She didn't stop there. With a wet plunge, her mouth swallowed Ronan's spurting cock right to the base. Her throat worked as she twisted her head, trying to jam it deeper.

Her nails had lengthened into sharp talons that burrowed into Ronan, blood rolling down his glittering green thighs. He whined and yelped in excitement, his neck straining as his hips thrust wildly. He was having a full-on orgasmic seizure, and the chair rocked beneath him, the bolts clacking and squeaking with the strain.

The second vial, already full, overflowed, but Malus stood frozen, woozy eyes glazed over as if he had taken a huge hit of crack and was riding the wave. He swayed on his feet, his shaking hand slowly lifting to the bulge in his pants.

Out of the corner of my eye, I saw Bates stagger into dense cloud around Ronan, change to a third vial, and beat a hasty retreat. Once he was at a safe distance, Bates fumbled with his zipper, pulled out his dick, and grabbed it with both hands, his head back and hips thrusting with gleeful anticipation.

I was the only sane one left in the shop. Or the only one far enough away to be unaffected by the bitch's lust cloud, or whatever the fuck it was.

Well, except for the Syreni. They watched the chaos from the far corner with shocked looks on their faces. Apparently, this wasn't standard operating procedure.

Somehow, Malus managed to get a grip on himself. He stumbled to the door and, after getting a few gulps of fresh air, staggered back to do damage control, his hand fisted over his bulge.

He stalked over to Layla, his face thunderous, and yanked her up by the hair, tearing her puckered lips from Ronan's streaming cock. She snarled at him, striking out with her claws and trying to pull his hand out of her hair.

"This stuff is priceless, you *stupid, selfish bitch!*" he roared. "If you think your pathetic, uncontrollable appetite will *cost me*, you're sadly mistaken." He shoved her away, tearing out a handful of her hair, but she caught herself and stood up, breathing hard.

A few seconds later, she had gathered her wits, fixed her hair, and smoothed her dress down. With one manicured finger, she wiped the corner of her mouth.

"Then you might want to check on your little lab rat there," she said. "Because I may have gone a little overboard with my feeding. I think I broke him."

And with that, she turned around and marched for the door, her heels clicking as she left.

Every eye in the building shot to Ronan. His engorged organ was hard against his belly, the veins bulging. Clouded a deep pinkish purple, and hopping in fits and bursts, cum still dripped from the tip. His eyes were closed, his head back and hanging off to the side. The liquid streaming from his teeth overflowed the third bottle and now trickled down the back of the chair. Bates jumped forward, scrabbling around, trying to hook up a fourth.

I yelled through the tape over my mouth, sobbing and screaming obscenities at the monsters who would do this to him.

Ronan's mouth was slack, and his face flushed. Little rapturous sighs fluttered over his slightly parted, shockingly white lips.

He's in shock. Oh dear gods above, she killed him.

The mist slowly drifted away, and Bates sidestepped it as he hooked up a fifth vial on the extraction rig. He smiled and shot me a contemptuous, slightly glazed grimace. Then he spoke to Malus, who fussed over his equipment.

"He's not looking so good, is he? Oh well. Not to worry. There's plenty more *fish* in the sea." Bates hooked up the sixth vial.

Ronan, his body slack, slowly turned a grayish color. His beautiful skins were dull, and his breathing was shallow. He was dying.

Helpless to do anything, screaming in frustration, I struggled to free myself.

Cal, where are you!?

I was frantic. My eyes darted around the shop, looking for something, anything, to free myself. Terror iced my veins when I thought about Cal. Did he make it back to Davy Jones to get help? Was he coming back, or was he attacked along the way?

I sobbed. I struggled. I glanced at Ronan, seeing his life slip away. I tried to guess how long I'd been in this shit storm, but I had no idea.

"Pity," Bates said, examining the sixth vial. "Not much coming now. I guess we drained him dry." He sighed and disconnected the tube.

Malus packed up his satchel, putting the vials into a padded plastic box and sliding them into a center pocket.

"Hex should be satisfied with this amount for now. It's amazing really. We seem to get much more when Layla loses control like that. Maybe we're onto something?" Malus chuckled. "Well, as they say, some of the greatest discoveries are accidents."

I froze. Hex. Where had I heard that name? My eyes shot to Ronan. He was ashen, and I watched as his flaccid penis slipped back into his skins. Was he dead?

Oh my God, Ronan! Hang on. Help is coming.

Bates heard my sobs and, at my horrified expression, strutted over to taunt me. He pulled off my tape, and I screamed with rage, spewing saliva on his face. He grabbed a handful of my hair and yanked, bringing his face close to mine. I saw my spit track down his cheek, tainted pink with blood.

"None of that *Edaline*, or I'll put you down slowly, instead of making it quick."

He knew my name? "How do you know my name?" I didn't expect an answer.

Bates glanced at Malus, who was listening as he packed up. "Let's just say, we knew your father. Very well, in fact. We had *dealings*." He chuckled to himself.

Smiling at me, and forming a little pout with his mouth, Bates chided, "You ought to be smarter than getting mixed up with a *Syreni man-whore,* Edaline."

I pulled all the saliva I could out of my mouth and spat it at him. I was off my meds, but I didn't care. I would kill him. If I got my hands out of these bindings, I would kill him. And I would enjoy it.

He wiped his face and growled through clenched teeth, "You're going to regret that, you little *Djinn mutt."* He looked at Malus, who was heading for the door with his satchel.

"Can I kill her now?" Bates begged, turning his head to wink at me. He reached down, and fisted his bulge, mouthing, "*Fun times ahead, bitch.*"

With a disinterested wave of his hand, Malus looked over his shoulder and said, "Fine, fine. But do a better job this time."

Malus opened the door, but before he stepped out, he halted and looked skyward. With a curse, he pulled back into the building and slammed the heavy metal door shut.

Whirling around to Bates, he hissed, "He's here. Take the vials and use the alley. I'll handle Gideon. For *good* this time." Shoving the leather satchel towards him, he bit out, "Meet me at the cannery later."

Bates, who eyed the ceiling with a worried frown, grabbed the bag and headed for the door. He seemed anxious to leave.

"And Cain?" Malus rumbled, giving his partner a menacing look. "If you take off with those vials, you won't like what happens when I find you. And not one drop better be missing when I get there." Hannibal's voice was like a throat full of marbles.

Cain nodded, making a beeline for the door like the hounds of hell were hot on his heels. Even in my current situation, I had to laugh at the irony of his real name.

Where are you going, Cain? What's your rush? Something scary out there, tough guy?

Stalking to the shop's center, Malus turned towards me, but he glared up at the tall ceiling. His eyes were shot through with black, with no white visible—just like on the boat.

What is with his freaking eyes?

His breath came in raspy snorts, a rumbling echo issuing from his chest. Lifting his arms out to the side, he clenched his shoulders and screamed. Before my eyes, he transformed.

Erupting with wet snapping noises that made me gag, Hannibal's clothing hung in tatters in seconds, his growth quickly shedding what was left. This was no longer the creepy man that had made my life a living hell. He threw his head back and released a roar that shook the rusted metal rafters. What started as a man had ended as a monster.

The smell rolling from him was disgusting and made my eyes water. Hannibal's skin was now gray, his face coarse and ugly. When he looked at me, I cringed. He was a ten-foot-tall linebacker monstrosity.

Mottled, dead-looking skin covered the ponderous frame, the eyes glittering black orbs that bulged from his face. The head was oddly undersized compared to the body, as if from two different creatures.

Unlike the skull, the two horns curling from his head were massive. The thick rack was a shiny black, and after sweeping backward from the sides of the tiny head, they did a U-turn, ending in razor-sharp points just above his two, beady red eyes.

Covering Malus's hips and legs was something like alligator skin, and the feet were cloven hooves. The power rolling from him terrified me.

I didn't know much about Cal's world, but I'm certain Malus had come straight from hell.

My pulse ran wild. We were in some deep shit right now. I glanced at Ronan's unconscious form, which dangled from the chair. We were fully exposed. Being strapped to a chair in the middle of what was about to go down was guaranteed suicide.

Something cold and slimy touched my hand, and I screamed.

CHAPTER 25

"Shhh, Eddi, it's Cal! Hang on. I'll get you free." Tentacles wriggled over my wrists, but I was too happy to care how weird it felt.

"Cal?" I sobbed with relief. *"Oh my God, Cal, I thought you were dead!"* I slashed my thoughts to him as quickly as I could. *"I didn't know you could mind-speak!"*

Cal ignored me, pulling at my bindings with his suckers.

"Cal, it's Ronan. They did terrible things to him. I think he's dying!" I felt tiny tentacle tips working their way under the ropes and prying hard. The air whistled in and out of Cal's breathing tube, and my panic tilted off the charts when I thought of him being unable to breathe.

"Shh. Hold on. It's alright, Eddi, I saw him. We'll get to him as soon as I free you. Stay calm, and try not to move."

Cal's squishy legs probed and pulled like mad, and his sharp cusses slashed through my mind.

"They're too tight. I'll have to use my beak. I'm sorry, but this is going to feel strange. Just HOLD STILL."

A spongy mass of suckers wrapped around my hands and half of my arms, pulling on me as he got into position. Then, something gnawed on the ropes. I held my hands as far apart as possible to help him. Something hard and pointy scraped across my wrists, and I tried not to think about his beak slicing me open by mistake.

My eyes darted around the room. The hulking giant that had been Hannibal waited for whatever was outside, a grin on his thin, ugly lips. He chuckled to himself, the sound like someone gargling with rock salt. Whatever was outside better be big.

Malus snorted, a loud hollow sound, and his hooves raised dust as he stomped around the shop, searching for something, a weapon to roll some heads, no doubt.

Then I heard it. It was big. As in, *really* big.

WINGS. Colossal wings, judging by the heavy thumps at each long stroke. With a sound like sails snapping tight in the wind, it hovered somewhere above the rooftop. A piercing screech blasted through the building, the pitch so intense that my ears rang. I cowered in the chair.

"It's ok, Eddi, it's the Enforcer. I've almost got you free. Hold still!"

Malus stared at the roof as he lumbered back and forth across the shop, now dragging a heavy chain, the three-inch links clanking together. With bulging arms he tore off a hunk to make it shorter, testing it with a heavy flick.

The sound of shearing metal rent the air, debris raining down as an enormous winged beast crashed through the roof. My heart stopped.

The bird from my dream!

This was *not* a bird. Its massive wings slapped the air with noisy strokes, the wind they generated blowing rocks and gravel off the floor and into my face. It dove into the shop, its body so heavy that the ground shook on landing, its thick feline tail slashing angrily.

Fur and feathers covered the tiger-striped legs, and enormous black talons clicked on the concrete as it stalked toward Malus. The newcomer stood eight feet tall at the shoulder and twice that at the tips of its long, thin ears. These swept back against its head, the feathered points tight against his skull. Up front, he was all bird, but from the neck back, he was tiger-like, and he was furious.

Heavy feathers ran from the sharp beak and regal head to the V of his chest. A heavy mane of narrow pin feathers clacked when his head shook. The shoulders, a blend of tiger and bird, were bound in thick muscle.

Avoiding the chain sizzling through the air, the Enforcer launched straight up, his wings powering him out of range before dropping nimbly back to the ground.

The rear feet landed first with a muffled thump, but the forelegs were ready to tear, the thick claws fully extended. He ripped into Malus, opening slashes across his chest before jumping backward. The magnificent beast shook its head and bellowed its rage at the monster.

Snapping his wings tightly to his sides, he raced forward and struck, the razor beak tearing out a hunk of flesh. On spring-loaded legs, he easily avoided the chain a second and a third time before taking to the air. He landed on a beam in the rafters above, and large glassy eyes tracked his opponent from beneath deeply furrowed brows.

Malus snarled and crouched to meet the next attack.

My ropes fell away, and Cal answered my unspoken question.

"It's a Gryphon, and he's with us." Cal glanced past me, and his goat-like eyes went wide. There was a ferocious roar, and something heavy whizzed over our heads.

"Eddi! LOOK OUT!"

Instinctively, I ducked, and a second massive anchor shot past before crashing into the side of the building with a tremendous bang.

"RUN!" Cal's panicked screech rang in my head, making me wince. I darted after him, shocked to see him scrambling across the floor, arm over arm, suckers popping so fast they sounded like music. I stumbled at the sight but regained my feet and joined him as we dove behind a heavy metal bench, panting from the sprint.

A flash briefly lit the dark corner, and Cal was back in human form. Wide-eyed, we watched the battle unfold before us.

All hell broke loose in the center of the shop, but in our panic, we'd forgotten something. Eyes bugging, I rounded on Cal. "Ronan!"

Leaving the safety of the corner, we ducked along the wall, coming up behind the chair where Ronan lay sprawled, his skin a sickly gray. Keeping an eye on the fight, we pulled his arms over our shoulders and lifted him. He was solid muscle, and I felt every ounce. The scent of his skin brought tears to my eyes, the smell of the sea faint, a rancid odor taking its place.

Dragging him back to the dark corner, we lay him down gently. We were helpless to do anything but protect him from the battle. Cal popped up to look over the bench at Malus and hissed, "Lesser Demon." If that was a Lesser demon, I sure as hell didn't want to meet a Greater Demon.

Malus was in rough shape. Blood poured, and V-shaped wounds peppered his chest, but he paid no attention to the injuries. Again and again, the thick chain whipped through the air, making the Gryphon leap and flap to stay out of range.

The winged beast launched into the air using its powerful hindquarters, trying, again and again, to find an opening and drive Malus to the ground. When he sailed overhead, the knife-like beak and claws snatched at the demon's thick gray arms, trying to find purchase.

Malus finally caught one of the Gryphon's front legs and pulled down with his powerful shoulders. A meaty fist repeatedly pounded at his feathered head, but the Gryphon arched his neck and ripped at the monster with his hind feet, avoiding a lethal blow. Blood streamed from Malus' chest, the Gryphon with only a few feathers missing. Hope bloomed in my chest.

Wings pounding the air, the Enforcer lifted the demon from the ground. Slowly but surely, they rose to the ceiling in a twisting blur of swinging arms and flapping wings. The uproar deafened me, and I covered my ears against the ear-piercing bawls and roars.

The winged beast curled his spine as he reached the roof, bringing his hindquarters forward. Razor-sharp claws sunk into the monster's chest and raked downwards with a mighty thrust.

A horrific scream filled the shop, and with a wet, tearing sound, the Malus' stomach ripped open. The strands of the demon's guts fell out in a wet mess, tangling around his wildly kicking legs. The Gryphon let go, and Malus hurtled to the ground.

With a booming crash, the cement floor exploded under the impact. Malus tried to crawl out of the crater he'd made, but in a flash, the Gryphon slammed into him with a triumphant squawk. Clouds of dust flew under the impact.

The demon struggled to rise but collapsed under the sheer weight of the feathered beast. His beaked mouth opening wide, the Gryphon clamped down on the demon's head and with a tremendous yank, ripped it off.

The leaking mess still hung from his mouth when he turned toward us, Malus' horns swinging and nearly taking out an eye. The Enforcer's golden stare glittered victoriously, and for a second, it crossed my mind that he might eat the dripping head. I could have sworn he smiled and gave me a wink before he spat it out on the floor.

CHAPTER 26

Cal and I lifted Ronan as best we could, trying not to hurt him. He was near death, his breathing weak and shallow. We half lifted, half dragged him to the center of the shop.

I looked over at the gaping hole in the floor, startled to see nothing but a pile of ashes. A sulfurous stench filled the air, but I would ask Cal about that later. I wanted to get out of here and help Ronan.

I still reeled from the violence of the battle, the depraved things I had witnessed sending sickly fingers to claw at my stomach. I felt numb, and nausea spiked when I kneeled beside Ronan. I took his head in my lap.

Seeing my slightly green face, Cal said, "Hold on, Eddi. We'll get him some help." He looked down at himself and turned red, mumbling something about overspray. I refused to follow his gaze because I knew he was still naked from changing forms.

Cradling Ronan's head in my lap, I watched his color fade to a deathly pale, his lips turning a whitish blue. Lifeless and in shock, he hovered near death. Terror and stress made me reel, the events of tonight crashing in all at once.

"Cal, he's going to die! We have to help him!"

The Gryphon prowled to the far end of the shop and peered into the cages there. I jerked when I heard a metallic crunch, the sharp squeaks and clangs of tearing cages echoing through the building. Cal nodded towards the Syreni, who clambered from their mangled prison.

"He's Syreni, Ed. They'll know how to take care of him. We need to get him back into the ocean, for starters."

The Gryphon quickly freed the Syreni, who were all alive but shaky. Their skins were dry and patchy. Strong arms carried an unconscious male with his legs dragging behind him. Being kept from the ocean must have been a special kind of torture, but what had been done to them was far worse.

They were large and rugged males, some with long hair. Like Ronan, they were lean and fit with handsome faces, but the group offered fierce looks as they passed. Some had been here for a while, and my heart went out to them.

Two broke off from the group and came to us. Scowling at me with tight lips, the long-haired male reached for Ronan. I put my hand out and touched his arm to stop him.

"Where are you taking him?" Hysteria bubbled up. I was a stranger to them. I had no power here.

The Syreni looked down at my hand on his arm and then at Cal. His eyes narrowed. I don't know if Cal said something to the Syreni, but I let go at the dark look on his face.

The males took Ronan's muscular arms and lifted him, his head dangling. I wanted to stop them, but I knew I couldn't interfere. Pushing past me, they hauled him out of the building. Tears threatened, but I held them back. Cal took my hand and squeezed it.

"Don't worry, Eddi. They'll help him. There's a canal behind the marina that goes straight to the ocean. He's better off in his element, trust me."

Cal was right, of course. Yet desperate helplessness filled me as the last Syreni stepped into the darkness outside the door. I had only myself to blame. I set myself up for heartbreak. An outsider with no rights to Ronan, the painful pangs of loneliness made my little flower sag.

Cal rummaged around and found a pair of dark green cotton coveralls. The name Sue on the pocket was perfect, but they were eight inches too short. Leave it to Cal to make me smile even when things got rough.

The Gryphon approached us, the only sign of injury a slash on his back leg and a few missing feathers. I was relieved. The fight had been terrifying to watch.

He gazed at me, blinking his large, shiny eyes of the deepest yellow I'd ever seen. When he spoke in my head, his voice was low and throaty.

"You did well to find him the Syreni so quickly. You and Cal saved their lives. You are remarkably courageous, Edaline."

What could I say to that? I didn't feel brave. My eyes stung from all the crying I had done in the last hour, for heaven's sake.

I was in complete awe of the majestic creature towering before me. His intimidating aura made my knees weak, but I wasn't afraid. I did, however, have a giddy inclination to bow. I heard a throaty chuckle and jerked to look at Cal, who stared at the Gryphon with a tight expression.

"Well done, Cal. I am proud of your courage. Your ride home will come by sea, so be patient. Wait on the docks. Take care of Edaline, and I will come to you soon. There are things to plan. This demon is not the end of it, of that I am certain."

The Gryphon bunched his rear legs, leaned back, and sprung into the air. With a few powerful strokes of his wings, his massive body punched through the mangled roof and shot into the night sky. I saw stars twinkling through the giant hole he'd left in the metal.

Shell-shocked, we made our way outside and found a crumbling dock on the canal behind the building. The ocean peeked at us from the end of the canal, the moon riding high and lighting everything with a brilliant glow. Tonight, it was nature's streetlight.

While we waited, I had questions.

I asked Cal how no one heard the deafening racket and came to investigate. It seemed that Immortalis of all kinds, including the Gryphons, could "glamor" things. That meant they could smother sound and hide things from view. They could also alter appearances, even themselves—very handy when trying to hide from the human race.

Cal beat me to my next question.

"His name is Gideon." He told me about Lesser Demons and Succubi, and I told him the horrifying details of what the bastards had done to Ronan. Some of those I kept to myself. It wasn't fair to Ronan to share *everything*.

Cal wasn't sure about who would pick us up, but we didn't wait long. As we sat at the end of the canal, watching the stars and doing our best to decompress, a boat approached. My heart swelled when I saw it was the *Wanderlust*.

When the boat pulled up, James was at the helm. Cal grabbed the bow, and we both hopped on. James smiled, his long sandy hair fluttering in the evening breeze.

"I heard you guys needed a lift. Sorry I took so long." He laughed at Cal's outfit and shook his head. "Do I even want to know?" We left it at that. James was so used to us by now that he didn't bat an eye.

Cal and I flopped back in the two rear-facing chairs, and James spun the boat, heading for home. I sent Cal a questioning look, afraid to come out and ask if James knew about their world. Cal just shrugged.

Another topic for later. Oh, goody. I would have to put my foot down with Cal and get more information about the universe currently sucking me in—preferably before it killed me.

The ride home was uneventful, but the salty breeze on my face and the stars above us calmed me down. The colorful Milky Way freckled the night sky and held a unique appeal tonight. We had come out on top of something evil, and the wind in my face felt wonderful.

My hands still trembled, and I wasn't sure why or how to stop it. Cal watched me, and when I looked at him, he mouthed *"adrenalin"* and gave me a reassuring look.

We helped James tie off the boat when we got to the Marina. I begged Cal to stay the night at my place because I was anxious and afraid to be alone. I'm not sure Cal wanted to be alone either because he agreed to stay without hesitation.

James gave us a ride home, stowing the bikes in the back of his truck. We were both exhausted when we closed the apartment door behind us.

After I showered away some of the horror, I fixed Cal a snack. We had a good laugh because all I had were goldfish crackers. The laughter was strained, though. My head swam with exhaustion and Cal wasn't much better.

Poor Cal looked done in. He had changed too many times and swam so far tonight that he was badly in need of a recharge. I used the last of my salt to make him comfy in my tub. I wouldn't let him go home, and he sure as hell wasn't going to the ocean. No, I wasn't letting him out of my sight again. Like, ever.

***

An excruciating week passed, the minutes taking hours. Cal finally heard from Gideon. Ronan was on the mend, but it had been a close call. It was taking a long time for him to regain his strength. Those filthy bastards had almost killed him. I would find them and return the favor. Somehow.

We heard the other Syreni were in better shape than Ronan. They overheard a lot of valuable information while captive, so Gideon gathered details. The males confirmed an uptick in collections in the days before we rescued them. Something was brewing in Key West. The details weren't clear, but it had something to do with *nectar*, and it wasn't good. I didn't want to know, to be honest. I wanted my nice, boring life back.

Ronan had gotten no closure about his mother. We suspected Malus and his crew had killed her, but we had no evidence. Were humans involved? Why would they take her? She was female and had no nectar. Maybe they made a mistake and killed her for *convenience*. We may never know.

As the days came and went, I tried to stop thinking about him. The incident in Big Pine reminded me that I had no claim on Ronan. The void between us was cavernous and growing larger. Nothing had changed between us. Physical attraction is not enough to make a lasting foundation for a relationship. Then there was the whole *living on a different plane of existence* thing. How could I forget about that?

Oh, right. Because I was still hopelessly attracted to him, sometimes to the point of distraction. In the back of my mind, I wondered if it was real or a by-product of his Syreni magic.

Over and over again, I had to remind myself there was NO *us*. There was nothing ordinary about any of our time together. No walks to the park, movie nights, or time merely getting to know each other. Those were human things. I was curious to know what Syreni did for courtship. It wasn't like he could take me home to meet his family.

Every time I dwelled on it, I'd call Cal, and we'd do something fun. Our camping trip to the Dry Tortugas was coming up in two weeks, so there was a lot to plan. It gave me something to look forward to.

Knowing Bates—*Cain*—was still out there gave me some tense moments. Gideon sent someone to stake out the cannery in Key West. Cal let it slip one day; there was no sign of Cain *or* the drugs. The Enforcer was still working on the new leads, but I wouldn't be in the loop if they found anything. I had to let it go.

The night it all happened, Cain said he knew my father. They had "some dealings." It could mean anything. I wanted to believe that my father was a good person. Wishful thinking, maybe, but it was all I had. It was sad that any mention of my father caused so much excitement—he could be a horrible individual. What sort of being hung around with demons?

The only positive outcome was that we now knew the name of the drug ring's leader. *Hex.* It even *sounded* creepy. How this monster figured into my dreams was a mystery. I realized now they were more than dreams or my wild imagination. Did I even *want* to know the truth?

I hadn't forgotten Cain's comment about being a *Djinn mutt*. Cal looked into it, but there wasn't much hope. He knew someone with a connection in Savannah that might be able to help. Apparently *Djinn* were a rare type of Immortalis. And if Cain wasn't messing with me, then I was half Djinn, half—*what?* I may never know. It's not like I could go to Ancestry and do a search.

I did have a little chuckle when I thought about the name I'd picked out all those years ago. Maybe my subconscious tried to ring my bell. Gin and *Djinn*. You pronounce them exactly the same. I shook my head. It was too big a coincidence.

Sadly, I had no powers. I was plain old me. I was too embarrassed to admit to Cal that I had stared into my bathroom mirror a few times and tried to *will* myself invisible.

A few weeks passed, and I was down in the dumps. When I got my monthly visitor, I heaved a sigh of relief, then promptly burst into tears. *Stupid, stupid Eddi.*

I still went out to the Island occasionally, but it was hard to enjoy myself when I spent my time scanning the horizon for a certain someone. So I stayed away, at least for now.

***

One afternoon, I was on the docks cleaning the *Wanderlust*. It was a lovely day, and the sun shone in a cloudless sky. The boat was clean as a whistle, with everything detailed and the polish wiped off. I finished the last piece of chrome on the bow railing and felt the boat bob from someone coming aboard. Before I could get up, I heard a familiar voice.

"Hello, Eddi."

My face flamed. It was the moment I had anticipated with excitement and dread for four weeks. I turned, my hands shaking, and Ronan stood on the stern deck.

Bare-chested, his skins dripped with seawater, his lips curling into a smile as he stared at me. My eyes drank in the sight of him, and I felt true joy when I saw the power radiating from every pore of his body. I devoured him from head to toe until I was satisfied. Ronan had recovered. He would be fine, and the weight of the world slipped from my shoulders.

"You're dripping on my clean deck," I said with a smile. Ronan looked down at the puddle he made and then at the railing, where a piece of seaweed fluttered in the breeze. He looked back at me, and I could have cried at his beautiful smile.

"I'm sorry. Do you want me to clean it up?" He held out his hand for my rag.

"It's fine." I put down the cloth and edged along the walk around, hopping down beside him.

"How are you doing?" My eyes searched his face, and my heart ached at the sight of his beautiful features. "You look well. We were all worried about you, Ronan."

That's it, nice and safe Eddi. Keep it up. Breathe. You're doing great.

"I am well, and so are my people. We can never repay you for saving our lives. You and Cal did a tremendous thing for the *Shoal*."

Ronan held out a hand, and when he opened it, there, gleaming in lustrous perfection, was a giant pearl. It was magnificent, larger than a marble but irregular in shape. Soft pinks and creams in a myriad of hues swirled together, glowing with a lovely finish. I made a happy sound of appreciation at its beauty and looked at Ronan in wonder.

"We wanted to show our gratitude. This seemed like a good way." His eyes searched mine as if wanting to say more. Breaking the silence, Ronan took a step forward and placed it in my hand. His fingers slid over mine, shooting a tendril of excitement through me at his touch.

I shook my head. I knew I should return the gift, but that was out of the question. This wasn't just from Ronan. I didn't want to offend the *Shoal*. That's what I told myself, anyway.

"It's absolutely beautiful, Ronan. Thank you so much."

I looked up at him, and his expression completely undid me. A month of work to forget him, gone in a blink. I took a deep breath and forged on.

"You don't owe me anything, Ronan. Cal and I made some guesses. We got lucky. We found our way to the right place at the right time." I took a deep breath and added, "I'm glad you're ok, and can get back to your normal life now."

He cocked his head with a questioning look, and I lied—to both of us.

"I did it because it was the right thing to do."

Ronan looked confused. "Tara told me that she came to you at the reef. I know you and Cal searched for me. Lucky or not, you saved my life. *All of our lives.* That is worth at least a pearl."

A sliver of jealousy needled me when he mentioned Tara, but over a month of separation helped tame the green-eyed beast. When I looked down at the pearl in my hand, it was all I could do to keep the tears from flying free.

Ronan's eyes flicked over my face. "I found it for you myself. Its colors are detailed and complex, just like yours." He stepped closer. "I missed seeing you, Eddi."

A whisper of sadness flickered over his face. He must have come to a decision because he picked up my hand, his thumb stroking the back.

"We need to talk," he said. "There are things I need to tell you. Things you should know now that I am healed enough to see you again."

When I pulled my hand from him, he frowned. This was it. This was the moment I had been dreading.

"No, you don't, *really.*"

I felt like a bitch, but I already knew what he was about to say. He cocked his head at me again.

"No explanations are required, Ronan. Cal told me about your *hidden talents*." My ears flamed. "Your *seduction* skills."

Ronan growled. "Cal had no right to interfere. It's our story, not his. He should have kept out of this—"

Anger flashed through me. "Well, at least he *told* me, didn't he? He's my best friend. He worries about me. That's what friends *do*. They *talk*. They work things out." A month of dwelling on the entire mess made me lash out.

"You knew what your *abilities* could do to me the whole time, and yet you continued like it was no big deal. *'I'll tell her later.'* Is that what you thought? You would tell me when YOU were ready?"

Ronan's eyes blazed. "I planned to talk to you. *Today*. But yes, in the beginning, I was—*concerned*." He ground his teeth, then added, "I couldn't tell you because I had no voice! I was trying to find a way. Then we tangled… *unexpectedly*."

He tried to smile at me but frowned when he saw my expression. "Then I was taken, and there was no time left—"

At my skeptical look, Ronan's face flashed with frustration. His chin tightened, his hands clenching into fists ... and I knew why. So I brought that damn elephant onto the boat, knowing it would sink us.

My voice quiet, I asked, "The first day we met, by the Island. Did you use your power on me? To make me want you?"

Ronan answered quickly. "Yes. But I had my reasons."

At the horrified look on my face, he rushed on. "Eddi, I'm sorry. I was angry that day. I started to tell you about it once…"

I cut him off. "Did you use your powers on me any other time?"

With a pleading look, Ronan said, "Yes, but it was the night you were hurt. I tried to make you *warm*. It's a side effect of our lure." Visibly agitated now, his hand plucked at his ear. He wouldn't look at me.

I forged ahead. "Anything else? Did you use it that night on the Widow's Walk? Or the day we—*tangled*?" I crossed my arms, but it was to cover my trembling hands. My heart was filled with holes and sinking fast.

Listen to him. Let him speak. He deserves that much.

Ronan shook his head and looked insulted. "NO, I did not. *I would not*. It's not right to use our power that way."

I almost cried out in relief. But I wasn't done yet.

"People make mistakes, Ronan. I get it. I am relieved that you didn't manipulate me for … *that*. But I have another question. And I want you to be completely honest."

He shot me a wary look.

"Let's say someone gets a dose or two of your special *'panty remover.'* Are there long-lasting effects? For instance, could they form a strong bond with you? Become *infatuated?*"

My legs joined my hands in frightened trembling. Because I already knew the answer. I felt the smooth pearl tucked into my fist. It was the symbol of a stolen future.

"Yes. It can be that way ... for humans." He frowned and looked out at the ocean, visible at the end of our channel. "Eddi, I'm sorry. I was angry the day I met you. I tried to tell you about it—several times." He looked back at me, his eyes pleading.

"I misbehaved that first day because I was angry with you for trying to interfere with the dolphins. I'm always alone, and it's a fun game we play. I don't—I *didn't* like humans, and I lashed out when you got pushy. I would take it back if I could."

Tears bloomed on my eyelids. "Don't you see, Ronan? You can *never* take it back. I will *never* know if my feelings for you are *real*. You took away my choice. Surely you understand about *choice*—after what *happened* to you?"

His face paled under his tan. Ronan had recovered physically but was far from over the invisible wounds of his ordeal.

I took a deep breath. "The Syreni have their customs, and I know nothing about them. Not one thing. And the *nectar*? Ok, it's involuntary. You can't help yourself."

He frowned but stayed quiet.

"Is that what's wrong with Tara? Did you use your powers on her? Hit her with nectar a few times?" I didn't try to hide the jealousy that gnawed at me again.

Ronan jerked, then raised his voice for the first time. "I have *never* used my powers on Tara. She has NO excuse for her bad behavior. Surely by now you know this!"

I sighed, some of my anxiety washing away at his words. In their wake, tears threatened to fall. "It's all too much for me, Ronan. Syreni are so far outside of my comfort zone, with the fangs, the *nectar*, and now the pheromone lure. I'd never know if what I felt was real or a drug-induced illusion. Do you understand what I'm saying?"

He didn't answer. His brows lowered, and his teeth clamped together between rock-hard jaws.

I couldn't stop my bitter laugh. "A relationship between us is so far from reality that it might as well be on Mars." I looked up at Ronan, and the expression on his face brought me up short. His eyes glowed a brilliant, angry green, brighter than I'd ever seen before.

Coldly, quietly, he said, "You're right, Eddi. You know nothing about Syreni customs. They are precious and beautiful. If they are enjoyed with love and care, it is a wondrous thing."

He turned his back to me and looked out over the water, taking in the blue skies and the palm trees swaying in the breeze. The ocean was beautiful today, more blue than a robin's egg. Without looking at me, he continued.

"You should be honored by our customs, not suspicious ... not ... *disgusted*. What I shared with you was the *Syreni* way."

There was a long silence, then he turned back to me. "You are very wrong about one thing. What those bastards did to me wasn't the same as what happened to you, Eddi. Not even fucking close."

He paused. I had never seen him angry at me. The little flower in my chest withered under his quiet anger.

"I am not—no, I *WILL* not apologize for what I am. For *who* I am. I should have told you sooner. But it's not like we got the best start, is it?" His eyes blazed into mine. "I did try to tell you. You simply weren't listening."

His eyes turned to ice chips, and I faltered. But my back was up, and "shoot first" Eddi didn't want to hear. She was stubborn that way.

"You had plenty of time to tell me, Ronan. We spent time together. If you had shared this information with me, I may have *trusted* you. Without trust, there's nothing."

This wasn't going well, the confrontation taking on a life of its own. But Ronan wasn't finished yet, either.

"You will *never* value Syreni customs, *Eddi,* because you are a *human.* You like things cut and dried, fit into neat little boxes. That is not the Syreni way. *I will never* be that way."

He hopped up onto the edge of the boat and looked out over the water. "I am sorry that you feel this way. You have made things very clear to me. Thank you for saving my life."

As he hovered over the bay, his muscles tensing to jump, I knew. This was it. I wanted to take everything back and throw things in reverse to see him smile at me again.

Ronan paused as if to add something, then sighed. "Goodbye, Eddi."

He dove into the water, leaving a footprint of round eddies from his magnificent tail. I followed the little round swirls all the way down the channel and out to sea.

Tears roared into my eyes like wet horsemen of the apocalypse. I didn't want to leave it this way. Was I too hasty? Maybe it was for the best. Suddenly, I wasn't so sure.

I heard footsteps pad down the dock, and Cal climbed aboard. He put his arm around me, pulling me in for a hug.

"That didn't go very well, now, did it?" He looked down at me with a sad smile.

"No." I laughed, then burst into tears.

CHAPTER 27

As far as days go, this one had been disastrous. Ronan was gone. It was done, and that little flower in my chest gave up and died. Cal was there to comfort me, of course. One of these days, he would trade me in. But not today.

There *was* one good thing that happened. And it happened that evening. I got the surprise of my life, and it was a doozy.

I sat with Cal after hours, wasting our tip money on beer. Cal had run across the Highway and picked some up at the gas station. Yes, I drowned my sorrows, although it was more like rinsing them off since he brought back light beer.

We decided to call it a wrap around eleven and head home. We'd been sitting in the dark for hours, watching the ocean and discussing our trip. And Ronan, naturally.

We closed the Tiki, and Cal looked up at the darkened sky.

"The Enforcer. He's coming." At the expression on his face, I looked up, too, my chest tightening with a sliver of fear as my legs began to tremble.

The slow, heavy strokes of enormous wings announced his arrival. I heard the sound of sails flapping, but there was no breeze. Looking up, I saw nothing coming, yet the sounds were sharp and clear. Where had I heard that noise before? It was so familiar…

And then, after all this time, it hit me. The *night from hell.* The flapping of sails. Strong thick fingers pulling me from Ronan's arms.

My skin peppered with goosebumps. I wasn't rescued by *just* Cal and Ronan that night on the reef. I didn't have *two* rescuers—*I had three.* One with night vision. One who could fly.

I turned to Cal, who watched me intently. My eyes narrowed, and as if he read my mind, Cal gave me a sheepish grin.

With a heavy thump, the Gryphon blinked into view before us, the ground vibrating as he landed. I jumped at his sudden appearance.

Where the hell did he come from?

He was magnificent. His large golden eyes glittered, giving off a faint light from beneath feathery furrowed brows. He stalked towards us, his taloned feet and huge cat paws working together in a dignified strut, his tiger's tail held high with an arrogant wave. His long, thin, feathery ears lifted from beside his head, which swiveled on a powerful neck and shoulders. As if checking for danger, he took in everything around him as he came.

I smiled at the black stripes down his tawny sides and hindquarters, his dusty orange feline body a muscular backdrop for the pattern. Weird. I'd have to ask Cal about the stripes later.

"It is because my mother was promiscuous and favored Tigers to Lions." In my head, his voice was a deep throaty rumble that was almost a purr.

I flinched. I guess I thought THAT too loud. *Oh boy.*

He nodded his great eagle head, and I flinched—again. Great. He heard everything going on in my noodle. Like, *everything.*

"If I am close enough, and things are calm, I feel emotions too." His wings stretched high and, with a quick snapping ruffle, settled against his back.

"Good to know," I said. I heard Cal's quiet chuckles beside me. Turning my head so the Gryphon couldn't see, I mouthed *"oh my god"* with my eyes wide.

"I have news." Gideon rumbled, his long tail flicking at the tip with irritation.

"The drug is surfacing in the Lower Keys. Based on what the Syreni males told us, they have a stockpile of nectar. They've been collecting it. Something nasty is brewing."

He turned his glittering eyes on me, and I felt a breeze on my skin. *Huh.*

"You are in grave peril, Edaline. They know who you are. They will come for you."

"Wait. *What!?* What do you mean by *'they'?* Why would they want *ME?*" Fear pricked my skin.

Ignoring my questions, Gideon turned to Cal.

"The answer is in Key West. We need to convince James to take the Wanderlust there. We will start in Garrison Bight."

I frowned, my anger rising. Here we go again. Ignore Eddi. Don't answer her questions. Just drop a bombshell and walk away. *Not this time, flyboy.*

"Hold it right there!" I hissed. "No one tells me ANYTHING. Now I'm in some sort of danger, and do you clue me in? *Nooo,* just ignore Eddi. She doesn't need to know." I shoved my hands on my hips, and snapped, *"That stops NOW."*

I stomped my foot, and ok, it was childish, but I was *ticked.*

In a flash the Gryphon was on me, the space so tight that I had to lean back. One of his massive paws pressed down on my foot, the long talon pricking my ankle. His eyes glittered, close enough that the bright yellow cast a faint glow over my face. I swallowed. Twice.

"You would do well to remember that there are RULES for us ALL, Edaline."

I was done being the weakling in a little boat bobbing towards the waterfall and certain death. My comfortable life was in shambles, my heart shattered into pieces, the little flower there crumbling to dust. So I risked it all. I went for it—*loud.*

"*NO.* You don't get to do that to me. Not this time. I'm not a *BABY* and I'm not sitting in any fucking *CORNERS*! Kill me now, *ENFORCER.* Because I'm not waiting for death to sneak up on me in some sort of colossal blindside."

Cal gasped. *"Eddi! No!"*

I was so angry I was out of breath. Gideon's eyes, so close to mine, tried to intimidate me, flickering as he weighed out how the next few seconds would go down. It took a moment, perhaps two. But it felt like a lifetime.

And then, decision made, the Gryphon rocked back onto his haunches and sat down, his tail flicking quietly on the ground. He lifted one massive paw and began grooming it with his curved beak. Finally, he put it down.

"You will follow orders. You will do as you're told. And you will never, EVER reveal us. Do you understand?" His giant regal head swiveled to look at me, and chills rushed over my shoulders and spine.

I heard the huff of breath Cal let out, and I followed suit. I nodded to the Enforcer. But of course, I was still stressed and wasn't done flirting with death.

"So how does that work exactly? You can't really strut around downtown Key West like... *that?* I mean, ya, there's the whole "Key Weird" thing, but a three-thousand pound Gryphon might be a hard sell."

Gideon smiled. In a bird-like way, the very corners of his lips tipped up. The outer edges of his feathers started to glow—faintly at first, and then brighter and brighter, until it was like staring into the sun. I put my hand up and closed my eyes, and when the burn subsided, I opened them, spots dancing.

And there, in all of his chubby, balding glory, his nasty parrot on his shoulder, *was Bert*.

EPILOGUE

Prowling through the nighttime revelers, Cain kept to the shadows. It was tempting to slip into an alley and take a teeny little sip from one of them. So easy, a nip and a suck, and erase their memories. They'd return to stumbling around and think the booze made them groggy. Easy peasy.

But these sodders were all shit-faced, and Hex would have his head for showing up drunk. Fucking cretins in this town. It became harder and harder to find one that wasn't wasted, especially at night.

Welcome to Key West. *You can't drink all day if you don't start in the morning.*

A few blocks later, Cain slipped into the narrow alley between the houses in front of the old factory. It was a good spot because it was close to the Pier, and the jammed-in houses helped with soundproofing.

Not that any of the screaming ever leaked out of his "workspace." The wards and glamors on the building were top-notch. It must have cost the boss a pretty penny. Witches weren't cheap, and they'd had to bring this one all the way from Savannah.

The door clanged behind him, and as it clicked shut, his enhanced hearing picked up a pathetic sobbing that made his dick jump. Ahhh, Little Red Riding Whore was sad tonight. She probably still smarted from when he harvested her eggs yesterday.

That would teach her to sacrifice herself for her people. Good thing she was unaware Hex didn't stick to the bargain. By the time the poor creature figured it out, it would be too late. The thought amused him to no end.

Ah well, the blood of a Martyr had turned out to be pretty sweet. Maybe he'd drink from her again today. She seemed like she could use a pick-me-up and enjoyed it well enough yesterday. He snickered to himself as he entered the hall.

Cain was happy tonight. When he showed up two days ago, Hex had been thrilled to see so much of the drug in one batch. Unfortunately, the reverse was true about Malus disappearing, and Cain almost lost his head. At least Hex knew who won the fight in Big Pine.

Ah, Malus was a wanker, and way too soft. Hex moved Cain up the ladder immediately and now he gave all the *fun* orders. And if the boss didn't know about a few of his more heinous proclivities? No harm, no foul. Or, no harm, and *an eensy bit* of foul. *Hmmm, ok.* Harm and lots of foul. He snickered to himself.

Walking down the stairs into the basement of the old Cigar Factory, he practically skipped. Cain took the time to draw in a deep breath and enjoy the aroma of fine cigars permeating the ancient bricks. They lined the first of many rooms in the historic factory. People didn't know what they had lost when this place finally shut down.

He sighed, then perked up. Maybe Hex would let him paint the walls in blood. That was also a smell that appealed to him. He chuckled when he thought about the colorful little room at the end of the hall. So red.

Turning into the first doorway, he found Eric elbow-deep into dosing and packaging the goodies. It hadn't been easy to find someone to stabilize the potency of *"GUSH."* Such a snazzy name for Hex's narcotic masterpiece. When Eric finished packaging the doses, there would be an awful lot of happy, horny customers running around the Keys.

Cain had found a dead ringer to finish the R&D of their latest marvel. Eric went to Yale and graduated with… well, with a drug problem. One that worked really well with this little enterprise. He supplied Eric with *party* favors, and the junkie found a way to put the fuck juice into an easily dosed form.

Last night, Eric had a breakthrough and was ready to process the nectar into microdots. The little bastard was clever. Thank God he still functioned, although Cain wasn't sure how.

Eric looked up with a hazy wobble, giving him a stupid frat boy smile. Someone really should clue the boy in that when the job was done, Cain would drain him dry and throw his body into the Florida Straits. The guy was too happy all the time.

"How's it going, *Errric!?*"

The dummy smiled and put down his tools to shove the *snuff bullet* up his nose for another shot of white candy. Eric raised his brows and huffed the load, then gave Cain a wasted smile.

"It's going great, and I've got it stable. The first few dots we sold were too strong, but I fixed it. It's tedious, but I can get the dose small enough if I use the microlitre syringe. Man, this stuff is strong! It will go a lot further now." Eric sniffed, and a trickle of blood traced down his lip.

Excited, he added, "I tried one of the new batches of microdots yesterday with a cute little blonde at a party I went to. She sucked me dry for fucking *hours*. It was amazing, man. That shit is going to sell like hotcakes."

Cain wanted to say, *"Blah blah blah, let me know how long I'll have to listen to your prattle before I can tear you to pieces and feed you to the sharks."*

Instead, he said, "Well, that's simply wonderful, Eric. Keep up the good work. When you finish, I'll reward you with a private sunset cruise on my boat."

Eric didn't notice the twinkle in his eye. Cain smiled with his mouth shut because tiny fangs had appeared at the sight of Eric's bloody nose, and all these thoughts of killing the boy made him hard.

"Toodles!" Cain waved goodbye to Eric and pranced down the hall to their *guest room*. He opened the door into what he liked to call *the honeymoon suite*. His eyes drank in the wretched figure huddled in the tank. Ohhhh, she looked perky today! Fun, fun, fun.

"Hello, beautiful!" Cain gave the resident red-headed slut a happy wave. She didn't look at him, turning around in her tank and sinking to the bottom. Listless, she flicked her tail and stared at the wall.

"Well, you're not very much fun today, snookums. Turn around. I want to see your beautiful face!" She ignored him, so he asked her again using compulsion.

"Turn. Around."

Slowly, resisting every inch of the way, she rotated to face him. Her long tail twitched with anger as her stunning green eyes glared at him, a feverish hatred burning like wildfire in their depths.

"OOO—*OUCH*! Don't you love me anymore? You liked me just fine yesterday! That's quite an about-face, Oriana."

He clapped his hands. "So what do we want for our snack tonight—fish, or fish?"

THE BLOOD TIDES

BOOK TWO
THE TIDES SERIES

PENELOPE AUSTIN

This book is a work of fiction.
Any references to historical events, real
people, or real locations are used fictiously.
Other names, characters, places, and
Incidents are the product of the author's
imagination, and any resemblance to actual
events locations, or persons living or
dead, is entirely coincidental.

THE BLOOD TIDES
Book Two
Of the Tides Series
Copyright © 2023
by Penelope Austin
All rights reserved.

No portion of this book may be reproduced
in any form without written permission
from the publisher or author.

DEDICATION & THANKS

My husband, once again, has been
so supportive during the writing of
this book, even if it meant fast food
and air fryer meals. I love you!

Thank you, Susan, for once again making
time to read through and give suggestions
and funny additions that really added to the
flavor and flow of the story. You're the best!

Again, thanks to the people and creatures
of the Florida Keys. Every tidbit in this book
was taken directly from our experiences there.
It's like no other place on earth, and someday,
I'll live there with my hubby and the dogs.
(or even just a little vacation would be nice)

PROLOGUE

THE OLD CIGAR FACTORY
KEY WEST

"For the love of God Oriana, hold still! Eric, tighten the loop already!"

An enormous green Syreni tail flopped over the top of the massive aquarium, soaking my new cream suit and tie with a surge of seawater.

The wet rope made a hard sound as it tightened around the base of Oriana's fin, Eric struggling to get the opposite end fed through the overhead pulley. The entire wooden platform wobbled beneath his frantic movements, tapping against the ancient red bricks of the historic factory.

Momentarily elated, I hooted like I was offshore fishing and bagged a monster Marlin. "That's the way. Tighter, man!" I threw my head back and laughed, taking a deep breath of the fine smell of Cuban cigars that still permeated the cool underground room.

Eric hauled until his muscles shook, fighting against the thick tail as it slapped and sloshed, drenching him from head to toe. Eventually, the thrashing slowed, the lift motor straining as my helper raised our prize partway out of the tank. Breathing hard, his drug-wasted muscles trembled by the time gravity pulled Oriana tight to the inside of the aquarium. Pausing to catch his breath, Eric's hand reached out to gently stroke the delicate scales in an attempt to soothe her.

Frowning at the soft-hearted fool, I bent over and peered through the glass at the red-headed pain in the ass giving all the trouble. Bubbles poured from her nose as she hung upside down under the water, a murderous look meeting my gaze. At my smirk, her eyes flashed a poisonous green.

"You're a feisty one, Oriana. But why you insist on struggling after all these years is beyond me. I always thought Syreni were clever, but perhaps I was wrong."

I motioned to Eric and he hit the button on the hoist, lifting the female Syreni out of the water and dragging her stiff, resisting form up and over the platform. I sidestepped the puddles and bent down again to peer at her upside-down face.

"There, now. That wasn't so hard, was it? Now behave yourself, and we can extract those eggs of yours and get you back where you belong." I clapped my hands together in delight. "I may even have a roommate for you soon. She's ferocious, too."

The words were no sooner out of my mouth than she snarled and twisted her body, flinging her head up to catch me right between the legs. My vision went white as I fell to my knees, Eric yelping in horror as he activated the hoist to pull her into the air. Wheezing, I clamped my hands over my privates. After a brief recovery, I rolled myself to my knees, my eyes glowing with a fury bright enough to light the entire platform with a crimson hue.

"You BITCH!" I glared at Eric, who whimpered in terror as motionless, he waited for me to gain control of myself.

I dug deep into my mind and blasted Oriana with a wave of compulsion that made her eyes water. Gradually, they turned soft and compliant.

With a groan, I rose and stumbled closer, nodding to my helper to lower her onto the table beside us. As she touched down and settled onto her back, I smiled. Reaching out, I stroked her cheek and tutted.

"You're mine until I say otherwise, my little anchovy. And if you do that again, you'll be very, very sorry." I leaned close and breathed in the salty scent that perfumed her skin. "Just wait until you meet all your new children. The cross produced something more powerful than even we anticipated."

Her eyes glazed over as her body relaxed, and I nodded to Eric to bring the kit. As he wiped the sweat from his face with a tired sigh, I chuckled.

"Yes, yes, it would be far easier if I just compelled her from the beginning. But this was so much more fun, don't you think?"

God, I loved being a vampire.

CHAPTER 1

"You're BERT? You've got to be kidding me!"

I stared at the last of the shiny motes drifting magically off into the night. My annoying co-worker glared back at me, his balding parrot, Mr. Darcy, riding shotgun on one chubby shoulder. My brain struggled to register the explosive transformation that just blew my doors off.

Moments ago, a tank-sized Gryphon stood on my foot and threatened me. I looked down, the marks from his six-inch talons still dotting my skin. I wasn't imagining it, then. Gideon was Bert.

I turned to glare at Cal, who was suddenly fascinated with the Tiki Hut next to us, refusing to look my way. "You knew!? CAL! This whole time, you *knew* about this, and you didn't say anything!?" He looked at me, his pale eyes filled with sorrow.

Right. He didn't have a choice.

Bert scratched the ratty blue and gold macaw, his eyes twinkling above a sarcastic smirk that said it all. Gideon—or should I say, *Bert,* was enjoying his bombshell, the jerk.

A mental short circuit left me speechless. I looked down the slope behind the marina, vaguely registering the boats bobbing in the darkness. My eyes found the derelict liveaboard that belonged to Bert. I was surprised that it hadn't sunk by now. The boat fit the man, I'd give it that.

Bert cleared his throat and Gideon's silky smooth drawl clashed with the potato dumpling visual. I snapped out of my funk as he spoke.

"I cannot wander around the Florida Keys in my Gryphon form, Edaline. Bert is the ideal Glamour. It allows me to do my job undetected. He is *necessary*." Turning the snuggle his parrot, he added, " And Mr. Darcy occasionally joins my Gryphon for little adventures."

I blanched as the implications hit home. I constantly bickered and argued with Bert, who was the cook at my second job. For the better part of a year, I had been pissing off a paranormal cop and didn't know it. Thanks a bunch, Cal.

I pulled myself together, eyeballing the chain-smoking traitor with a whole new perspective. "So let me get this straight. You had the choice of ANY body you could dream up, and you chose a balding guy who needs a motorized shopping cart at Publix? Shouldn't you have, I don't know, chosen something that would get you *laid?"*

Bert ignored my question, as usual. Smelling a secret, I narrowed my eyes at him. "Wait a minute. You're immortal. Bert isn't your real form." I cocked my head as understanding dawned, then laughed at the giddy thought that popped into my head.

"You really look like Chris Hemsworth, don't you?"

Dead silence. Sweat trickled down my back in the heat, and I heard something plop into the water down near the docks.

"I get it. You're messing with me right now. A little payback for mouthing off at you for withholding information, right?" I pointed at him, my eyes narrowing. "None of this changes the fact that you're putting me in danger by keeping secrets. If someone is after me, you need to give me details. NOW."

Bert growled, the hollow sound bubbling from deep within his chest as his eyes flashed yellow. The deadly Gryphon was still in there, and if I was smart, I would watch my mouth. Like that ever happened.

"I mean it. Either you start giving me the information I need, or I'm tapping out. I'm not going to stand for your smoke and mirrors crap anymore. Cal may not have a choice, but *I DO*."

Crickets. Nothing moved except for Mr. Darcy, who turned and jabbed his sharp beak toward me. With a muffled shriek, I stuffed my hand into my shorts pocket. The flying buzz-saw almost chewed my finger off a few weeks ago. The next chance I got, I was finding a taxidermist. Maybe he'd include the Gryphon at a discount.

Bert laughed, and I slapped my hand over my eyes. Right. How could I have forgotten the whole mind-reading thing so soon?

"My brain is off limits, you got it? Stay out of my head, Gideon!"

Wiping the tears from his eyes, Bert spoke, this time in his gurgly smoker's rattle. As usual, he completely ignored me.

"Edaline, remember my warning. Do what you're told, and don't reveal the *Others* to humans. I think I've been very clear about the penalty."

Until I stood up to the Gryphon a moment ago, Cal wasn't allowed to share information with me about the *Others*. "Animals that can turn into people" was a taboo subject that needed a warning label. *Expose the Others or their hidden world to humans, and the Enforcer would—*

"Take my head off! Go ahead. I don't care!" I ignored Cal, his slashing hands and bulging eyes warning me from behind Bert. "It doesn't really matter now, does it? Because if it's not you, some other Immortalis demon will snatch me off the street for a bedtime snack. What difference does it make who kills me first?"

Bert turned to glare at Cal. I wasn't supposed to know anything about Immortals, but my best friend had given me the Cole's notes on their history. Apparently, the Gods had shagged a bunch of paranormals called *Others*, and now we had Gryphons and Dragons and other mind-blowing creatures roaming around in disguise, living quiet lives for the rest of eternity. No one asked me if I wanted a heads-up on the bizarre world surrounding me. I didn't.

Unfortunately, I walked in on Cal at work one day and found him shifting from Octopus to human, which threw me for the mother of all loops. I got over it. Then, a drool-worthy Syreni male stole my heart before dropping a bombshell that destroyed me. I would get over that, too.

In a while. Maybe. Hopefully. I felt a stab of pain at the thought of Ronan's beautiful tail and rubbed my chest.

I looked Bert up and down, grimacing at his Michelin man curves. "I guess Chris Hemsworth is a bit of a stretch." I snapped my fingers. "I know—Danny Devito!"

That made Cal chuckle. He bit his lip as he cautiously watched the exchange. He knew me. I was winding up for another clash with the eagle-tiger monstrosity. Not lion—tiger. Our Gryphon Enforcer broke the mold for pretty much everything.

Bert's eyes sparkled, a tiny smile tugging the corner of his mouth. "I am many things, Edaline. This body is but one of them. You must be vigilant if you want to see my birth form."

Mr. Darcy rolled his ratty head in for another scratch, but before I could say anything further, someone flipped a switch. Bert's expression hardened and he turned to Cal, who stood up straighter.

"You can fill Eddi in on things as needed. I'm sure I don't have to remind you of the rules. I'm counting on you to protect her with your life."

Then he looked at me and snapped, "Behave yourself, Edaline."

On that ominous note, Bert turned and flumped back to the ratty old Ranger tugboat currently uglifying the last slip in our marina.

I had a thought and turned to Cal. "Holy crap! Is Bert's piece of shit glamoured too?"

Grinning, Cal shook his head. "I don't know, Eddi. Maybe you should ask him?"

I gave my best friend a dirty look and a slap. "We're going to have a little chat about you keeping secrets—"

The look on his face made me wince. I pulled him in for a hug and whispered in his ear, "You owe me dinner, Octoboy."

* * *

Cal and I worked together at Davy Jones Locker, a busy marina in the Florida Keys. The sport fishing was world-class, and offshore fishing trips topped the bucket list for visitors. After being homeless, getting my captain's license was a proud moment. Now, I made extra cash doing private fishing charters on the *Wanderlust*, a perfectly maintained 1994 Grady White Explorer. The 24' beauty belonged to James, the handsome, sandy-haired owner of the marina, but she felt like mine.

As Cal and I locked up the dive shop, I looked at my watch—almost midnight. I swallowed hard and tried to control my breathing. Nighttime and I had a bit of an issue ever since I was attacked and thrown overboard by a demon and his sidekicks. I swallowed down a surge of anxiety and unlocked my bike. I didn't need to pile more of my issues onto Cal.

"Well Cal, I'd love to hang out with you and recover from Gideon's fun and games, but I have to hit the hay. I've got a shift at the diner tomorrow." Cal's white hair glowed under the parking lot security light as he straddled his Schwinn. Before he took off, he gave me some news that ramped up my anxiety even further.

"I meant to tell you. I finally got the phone number for that mystic in Savannah—the one I told you about. She might be able to help us dig up your past."

My hands tightened on the handlebars. He'd found the contact we were looking for. I cringed. Lately, I had been wondering if my past shouldn't stay buried.

A few weeks ago, I would have jumped at the chance to learn more. Hell, I'd been searching for ten freaking years to figure out who I was. But life was good now, and my brush with death had changed me.

His eyes wandered over my expression, and Cal's mouth turned down at the corners. "You still want to keep looking, don't you?"

"I guess. But to be completely honest, I'm nervous about it. The more we dig, the more trouble seems to find me. Sometimes, I'm not sure I need to remember my childhood." I looked at Cal, my expression soft. "I'm good now. We're good together. Maybe my past should stay right where it is. I want to move on with my life. Get back to that nice peaceful rhythm we had until now."

Deep down, I knew it was wishful thinking. I needed to get answers before my new reality full of monsters dragged me under. I just learned the hard way that I could be half Djinn, a powerful and mysterious form of Immortalis. Like that wasn't going to stir up any trouble for me.

Nope, I wasn't going there tonight. Tomorrow. I'd think about it tomorrow when I wasn't riding my bike home at midnight.

I sighed. "You're right, Cal. And I appreciate your help. Yes. We'll keep going. I need to know the truth. Let's do it." The look of happiness on his face made me squirm. "It's pretty bad when the whole *Bert is a Gryphon* thing is small potatoes compared to the other weird shit that's been happening to us."

Cal laughed and waved goodbye, pedaling into the darkness. I gave him the *I'm watching you* fingers and headed home on my bike. Most people on a budget used bicycles to get around the Keys. Cal and I were no exception. We were the lamest heroes on the planet. That was the running joke after we hopped on a bus to go and save a handful of Syreni warriors a few weeks ago.

My bike light barely illuminated the blackness around me as I hurried home. Constantly glancing over my shoulder and scanning the brush near the side of the road was my new normal. Getting caught in the middle of a Gryphon versus Demon death match would make anyone jumpy.

***

THE BLACK CAT CLUB
~ SABRINA ~

I felt beautiful this evening in my glittery pink cocktail dress. It emphasized my shiny blonde hair that I had twisted into a messy updo. A matching pink shade of lipstick highlighted my plump, kissable lips and made my features pop. Tonight, I was getting laid, and that was final.

A hot new party drug was here in Key West, and Fanny and I lucked out tonight, snagging an invite to an exclusive nightclub. The venue was private, so the adventurous and entitled could let their hair down and take the latest party favors for a spin. The word around town was that *Gush* gave you a pleasant, horny buzz with no after-effects.

The party at this club was a private affair of roughly eighty people. Most were wealthy College kids whose blue-blooded good looks were part of their family inheritance. Fanny was already preening under the interest of one, a beautiful guy with great hair.

Go, Fanny!

Never, ever look needy, I told myself. Own it, work it, and be confident. That was my mantra. The best way to hook a rich guy was to act as if you deserved him.

Rick, the fashionable guy chatting up Fanny, grabbed a small packet off a tray making the rounds. An exotic waitress with a black bob and runway legs smiled back at him, then headed for the next table.

Shouting over the music, he yelled, "Do you want to try some?"

I nodded, and Fanny held out her hand. I looked at the little black microdot and frowned.

"It's not very big, is it?" I don't think Rick heard me over the music, but he was smiling, holding his drink to toast before popping the goods in his mouth. Fanny and I chased ours with a swig of wine, and we clinked glasses—party *time!*

Rushing into the mob, it wasn't long before we were sweating, laughing, and having a great time, the techno beat throbbing through the oak floor and making me giddy. The DJ was fantastic, and the floorboards bounced, colorful lasers adding excitement. When Tiësto came on, the thrashing mob went wild.

Someone brushed up against me from behind, and when I looked back, it was a devilishly handsome blonde dude with bulging guns. I checked him out and decided he was squeezable, his muscular body almost as pretty as his face.

Putting his arm around my shoulders, he leaned in, and in a deep, provocative voice, he rumbled into my ear, "That pink dress would look much better on the floor."

I couldn't help it. I laughed. *That line deserves three buzzers, buddy.*

I looked at Fanny, but she was locking lips with Rick. Shrugging, I hooked up with the muscular hottie for a dance or two.

Danny was from Ohio, but that's all I heard because the thumping music drowned everything. Chatting was out of the question.

Danny pulled me in close and started nibbling along my jaw. I relaxed into it, but in the back of my mind, I was a little disappointed that after all the hype, *Gush* was turning out to be a dud, at least for me. I felt nothing but the usual wine buzz.

On the other hand, Danny was well on his way, judging by the impressive bulge poking against his zipper. I smiled as he led me through the dancers to a dark alcove below the balcony.

Here we go. Showtime.

There were booths here, and I could see crowds of people sprawled on the tables and benches in various stages of undress.

I giggled at the girl doing a handstand while a guy held her ass and buried his face in her muff. Full marks for originality—canyon yodeling with a flourish.

I should have been shocked by the display, but I shrugged it off and ground my thighs together. Damn, that visual made my kitten slippery. I giggled and sipped my wine.

Danny pulled me into his arms and leaned us against the wall. I figured, why the hell not, so I snuggled in, and we tongue-wrestled for a bit.

I came up for air and realized my shoe was missing. Dammit.

"Can you hold this for me?"

I handed my drink to Danny, and the glass slipped through my numb fingers. Looking down, I was mesmerized, watching it roll around and around between our feet before coming to rest against Danny's foot. It didn't break, so I bent down to pick it up.

That's when it hit me.

The powerful pulse that clenched my pussy was somewhere between "O" and *shiiiitttt*, my thong instantly drenched.

I stood up and looked at Danny. His eyes were unfocused, and slack-jawed lust oozed from him.

Someone jostled my arm and turning around, a lightning bolt of arousal pulsed through me.

A sparkling ball chandelier lit the soft curves of a ravishing brunette who lay face down on a pedestal table.

An athletic guy with intricate tats and an impressive erection stroked in and out of her artfully trimmed pussy. Eyes closed, his head hung forward in a euphoric daze while his strong hands pinned her hips for deeper penetration.

Her peachy pink lips were busy. A second partner with blown pupils held her firmly by the hair while he thrust into her mouth. The slick sounds from the trio made me reach down and grab my throbbing vagina.

With hazy eyes, I searched the dance floor for Fanny, but she was lost somewhere in a sea of enthusiastic bodies writhing in heaps throughout the club.

Desire flooded my body at the incredible sight, but a vague sensation of cool air on my thighs made me look down. A pair of masculine hands kneaded my bare hips, and my pretty pink dress was hitched around my waist.

Something prodded against my slippery core from behind and filled with a blazing need, I spread my legs and leaned forward, closing my eyes.

"*Danny,*" I whispered with a shuddering sigh of invitation.

His forehead flopped onto my shoulder, and pushing inside me with a groan, Danny pulled me close with shaking hands. A shudder wracked his body as he began driving into me with deep, sloppy thrusts.

Right here in a room full of people, I was banging a total stranger. I couldn't have cared less because I needed the stabbing fullness like I needed to breathe.

There was no more music and no more dancing. The room was quiet, except for the wet sounds of *Gush* working its magic.

I trembled on weak legs, and pleasure exploded from every pore. I welcomed the sensory overload and slipped away on a riptide of bliss.

***

MONROE COUNTY SHERIFF'S OFFICE
~ DEPUTY JAKE MILLER ~

Down at the Sheriff's office, all hell was breaking loose. Every squad car was out on calls, thanks to a new street drug flooding Key West in time for the weekend. The situation was bad enough to call in backup from the Upper Keys.

This drug was strange. It sounded fabulous to potential users, but there were huge issues.

People who took it didn't care if they dropped their pants in the middle of a shopping mall full of families.

Users were completely unaware of their surroundings. A couple fell off a rooftop patio tonight, their frenzied lovemaking against the railing ending badly. It was the first of many hospitalizations for a boutique roofie they called *Gush*.

The effect was pretty standard among users: a senseless night where the single-minded focus was chasing the big "O."

Officers were exhausted after struggling to subdue people high on the drug. Fighting over sexual partners had already caused one stab wound, a few broken noses, and several missing teeth. The pace of arrests was unsustainable. It often took twenty minutes or more to get zip ties on the hands and feet of the bucking, kicking nymphos.

He swore. If he had to shoehorn one more sweaty, sex-crazed idiot into his squad car tonight, he was calling in sick tomorrow.

CHAPTER 2

~ RONAN ~

As I swam along the reef, I ground my teeth together, my rumbling growls shoving bubbles up my nose. All I could think about was *her*.

I proved myself repeatedly. Learned to speak. Saved her. *Tangled*. Still, I couldn't convince that damned human female that I cared for her.

Teasing Eddi with my pheromone lure the day we met was a mistake. I was angry at her bossy attitude and lashed out. I tried to explain it to her, but she wouldn't listen. My hot-headed behavior had cost me—again. Gods, I hated humans. When would I learn to stay away from them?

She was right about me. I could have confessed much sooner. But I was afraid to lose what we had started. Cursing, I tipped my head back to stare at the watery ceiling. She'd never trust me again. It was over.

I frowned, scrubbing my hand over my face. I was done with suspicious, judgemental humans. Scanning the azure blue panorama surrounding me, I couldn't help but smile. Choreographed schools of colorful fish drifted this way and that along the reef. The coral waved in the ocean currents as the myriad of living creatures went about the business of daily survival. I would return to my quiet life here and forget about the human that briefly wriggled herself under my skin.

Sucking water through my lips to run over my inner gill plate, I gradually assimilated extra oxygen from the surrounding ocean. Slowly, the tension in my shoulders faded away. My home was a watery paradise and the only place where humans weren't comfortable. Down here, I was free from their drama.

I heard a squeak, and flinching, I looked up. Hovering inches above my head were three tubular snouts, their tips almost touching. Six dark, round, curious eyes met mine.

Their aerodynamic bodies inverted in the water column, the motionless dolphins drifted with me in the current. My eyes followed the sleek gray contours ending in tails much like my own. I looked for their pod, but the three bachelors had broken off to find me.

Being discovered at their game excited them, and they whistled, their clicks and trills reaching my ears in a cacophony that told me what they wanted.

"Not today, friends. I am busy hunting." My telepathic words meant nothing to them. Dolphins were uncomplicated creatures motivated by simple things.

Their tapered bodies rotated to get a better look at my face. They understood natural cues: the movement of my fingers, the tension in my tail, the noises I made. But most important of all—did I have a snack?

I raised my hand to trail my fingers along their rubbery skin and shook my head at them. Slowly, they righted themselves and moved off down the reef, chattering to each other in a happy chorus. As they faded from view, I smiled. Eddi would have loved to meet them.

I shook my head, releasing another bubbly growl. The human was beautiful and clever, but she would never understand my world. Like everyone else, she thought Syreni were vulgar. Edaline was a barnacle that I must pry from my brain.

My muscular green tail swept under me as I straightened, and tension punched through my shoulders. Thinking about humans was a waste of time. I must focus on what was essential—finding the monsters who killed my mother. She had been missing for ten agonizing years, and I was determined to find justice for her.

Thoughts of her beautiful red hair and smiling face snapped me back to the task at hand. I was hunting a *Lesser*, a low-life traitor to the *Shoal*. Bacchus was helping—if that's what you call annoying the hell out of me.

I turned in time to see him shoot past. With his powerful tail, he slapped me on the back of the head, his sudden wake teasing my dark hair.

"Wake up, Ronan. Your silver-haired wet dream will get you killed one day."

Bacchus grinned as he swam around me in wild circles, telepathically sharing his smart-ass comments. My younger brother's festive mood was trying my patience today. How fitting that our mother named him after the god of drink.

We had recently recovered from horrible abuse by an evil force of demons. Bacchus and I, and a few other males, were captured to extract our *Nectar*. The Syreni erototoxin was a sacred gift shared only between mates. Having it stripped from our canines by force had been a waking nightmare. Since then, no one has traveled alone.

In the Atlantic near the reef, we were hunting the scorpionfish Viggo, a double-crossing shifter. Working for the demons, he had trapped and milked us like cattle, earning himself a slow, painful death.

Once he was dead, I would hunt down his boss, Cain, and rip his throat out with my fangs. Eddi believed Cain and the demons, not humans, killed my mother. If that were true, I was wrong for hating landwalkers for so long.

I had no idea why Viggo would team up with our enemies to do such a thing, but I would find out. And when I finished with him, he'd squawk like a begging Pelican and reveal their plans before I killed him. My gums throbbed at the thought.

I shifted my short sword to the other hand. Dangerously sharp, the double-edged gladius was a valuable weapon for underwater combat. Meant for stabbing, the sharp tapered point would keep Viggo from getting close enough to sting me. Scorpionfish were ugly predators, and their venom was dangerous.

Swimming to my side, my brother searched my scowling face with his luminescent green eyes and frowned.

"Maybe Viggo is hiding offshore at the humps," he said.

"I don't think so. The humps are too deep for his kind. And it's a long way to shore if he wants to shift and meet with his new friends."

Bacchus swung his weapon, a homemade mace, onto his shoulder. *"I'd love to poke some holes in that bastard."*

I looked around the section of the reef we had checked. *"Viggo is not out here. We'd have seen his aura by now."*

Viggo was a stealth predator, and his exceptional camouflage made him hard to spot in the coral. Being *Other* meant that he emitted a subtle glow visible to Syreni eyes. We had that going for us, at least.

I felt my fangs recede as I looked toward Marathon. *"He may be hiding in the mangroves along the shore and hiding his clothing somewhere. Viggo has been land-walking if he got himself hooked up with the demons that took us and hurt Eddi."*

One night, Cain and his crew attacked the female that haunted my thoughts. Hijacking her boat, they beat Edaline half to death and cast her overboard. I shuddered at the image of her pale, lifeless body, floating near death in the cold, dark ocean, her hands tied behind her back.

The leather-wrapped handle of my short sword creaked under my fist, and a low rumble rattled my throat. I rubbed my thumb along the golden crossguard, silently thanking the pirates that had lost it to the sea. Soon, it would serve its intended purpose.

Bacchus went still, his eyes wide. *"Whoa, easy there. I don't know what you're thinking, but your fangs are showing, brother."*

I sucked in more oxygen to calm myself, giving him a grim nod. My fangs sank back into my gums. *"I'll be fine. Relax."*

His sandy locks suspended on the currents, my brother floated beside me. A noble face and brawny shoulders drew females to him. They loved his long tresses and playful manner, but their constant gibbering about his bright blue-green tail gave me a headache.

There was only one Syreni who pained me more than my dashing brother. Tabitha, our sister, often joined us for our misadventures. She and Bacchus loved a good fight, being fierce like our strong-willed mother, Oriana.

Thoughts of my mother's glowing green eyes made my heart ache. Bacchus and I weren't taking any chances with a female of the *Shoal*, especially our sister. Fearing her wrath, we snuck away before Tabitha could follow. No doubt she was furious and throwing fits. She was probably tearing up our chambers and planning her revenge. I would worry about that later.

"Viggo trapped me on the reef at Coffin's Patch, directly offshore from Curry Hammock. The maze of mangrove trails and sheltered bays in the state park would be the perfect place to hide."

Bacchus nodded. *"He could use the bathhouses, and no one would notice him. That park is close to Marathon and on a bus route. It would be easy for him to travel from there. I have no* doubt he's getting paid." He shook his head and frowned. *"Buses are for peasants. What I wouldn't give for a Ferrari."*

He stopped swimming and shouldered his weapon. The mace was a section of mast from an old sailboat, heavily studded with nails. Our kind don't mess around when there's trouble. Anyone who mistakenly attacked a Syreni soon learned it was a terrible idea.

If our weapons didn't kill you, get us mad enough, and Syreni teeth would do the job. Our canines extended to deadly fangs in the right conditions, and the Nectar thickened to a toxic concentration. We called it *MORS,* which meant death.

Stifled for centuries under Sovereign rule, *MORS* was the dark, dangerous side of a Syreni and something to avoid at all costs. No one wanted an enraged madman on the loose, ripping out throats. There were strict rules about exposing the *Shoal* to humans. It was the only way to live in peace.

A gleam crept into my brother's eyes as we worked our way toward the shore.

"So, Ronan, tell me about the pretty gray-eyed girl. The one with the silver hair. What's the story?"

Bacchus tilted his head and rolled, looking under a coral shelf.

"She seemed like a huge fan of yours when she saved your ass from the Nectar thieves."

His hand darted into a gap in the reef, and he pulled out a spiny lobster by the antennae, its thrashing tail churning the water.

"I thought I would have a battle on my hands to get you away from her and back into the ocean," he chuckled. The lobster crackled as he tore it in two.

"She was pretty tough, facing off against those demons. She looked as if she would puke when Gideon ripped the head off that lesser demon, though." He took a big bite of his lobster, the crunches sounding hollow underwater. Smiling around his mouthful, he offered me half of the delicacy.

I frowned and shook my head, declining his gift.

"It's none of your concern, Bacchus. Leave her be. She's nothing to me."

Bubbles rolled from my brother's mouth when he laughed, then started choking.

"I know you, Ronan. You're as moody as a female before her moon cycle. You want this girl for more than a tangle."

"Butt out, brother. It's complicated. I have better things to do than convince a human female that I'm not an eel."

Bacchus leaned over and laughed so hard that he had to hold his muscular stomach. A bright cloud of bubbles surrounded him, and I felt like reaching through it and choking him.

"Wow, Ronan. That was quite a speech. What will you do, swim back to your dolphins and other sea pets?"

He held the lobster to me again, waving it under my nose. He was insistent, so I took it from his hand.

"Toughen up, brother. If you like this girl, send her a bit of lure and take her for a ride under a palm tree." Bacchus waggled his eyebrows at me, his teeth crunching on the thin carapace of his snack.

I snarled. *"I'm not like you, Bacchus. Playing with humans is not entertaining to me. This girl was special."* I looked out at the sandy sea floor and vibrant mounds of coral around me. *"She IS special. I cared for her."*

Bacchus shrugged. *"That's a surprise, considering how much you hate humans."* He picked his teeth with the tip of a lobster leg and chuckled. *"Well, if you get bored, let me know. I can encourage one of my Syreni girls your way. Some of them tangle with me to get a shot at you anyway. Not that I mind, of course. I'm not as fussy as you."*

Our kind thrived with a modest population. We lived on the Atlantic side of the Keys, our home a network of tunnels running through the thick ancient coral that ran under the islands of Marathon.

Syreni always stayed close to the 180-mile archipelago. The further we traveled from the natural magic of the coral, the weaker we became. Not that we'd want to leave paradise. No one willingly left the Florida Keys.

Bacchus snapped his fingers. *"Better yet, why don't you tangle with the lionfish constantly waving her fins at you? Her name is Tara, right? She's made it clear that you're her type. And she's got a nasty streak. She could be fun!"*

Bacchus flipped himself upside down and floated in front of my face.

"She'll make you forget the nice, boring one," he drawled, reaching to punch my shoulder. Before I could retaliate, he rolled and took off like a shot toward shore.

My brother, the partier. I knew nothing about this thing—*Ferrari?* But it was bad news. He probably saw it on one of his frequent trips to learn about the human world. Our mother should have named him *Lothario*.

Reaching down, I left half of the lobster under the coral for someone hungry. I followed Bacchus, my mind stubbornly drifting back to the beautiful girl with the fierce disposition. It would be hard to forget her.

CHAPTER 3

As I headed to the Crazy Conch to work the lunch rush, thoughts of Ronan plagued me. I had dark circles today because last night, sleep was elusive, his emerald green eyes haunting my thoughts.

I smiled, remembering Ronan taking offense when I called him a mermaid.

"Mermaids are fairy tales. Syreni are *real*," he'd said.

I was desolate this morning. I'd never hear Ronan's irritated growls or see his charming smiles again. The thought of another girl running her hands over his sculpted body was killing me.

I'd still be exploring what we started if I hadn't learned about the pheromone lure he dosed me with the day we met. Sure, it was a mistake he later apologized for, but their lure permanently affected humans. I'd never know whether or not my feelings for him were real. And judging by how much I'd lusted after him, I was already hooked and needed to steer clear.

It didn't matter now because we'd ended things yesterday. Letting him swim away was one of the hardest things I'd ever done. I would never see the Syreni again.

He was so angry. I bet I'm already in ancient history. It made me grind my teeth to think about that shifter bitch, Tara, getting her lionfish barbs into him. She'd love it, seeing as she's chased him forever.

Giving myself a mental shake, I vowed to accept that being miserable was part of moving on. Like it or not, Ronan was under my skin, the stubborn memories burrowing in for a long, torturous ride.

At least our timing was perfect. My boss, James, planned on moving the *Wanderlust* from Marathon to Key West in a few days. Someone convinced him that we needed to branch out and do more charters, and Key West swarmed with tourists every day.

Cal and I purchased tickets to camp at Fort Jefferson on the Dry Tortugas. As soon as we returned from our camping trip, I'd be running fishing trips on the *Wanderlust* from a slip in Garrison Bight on the west side of town. The ferry to the Tortugas departed from a terminal down the road from Garrison Bight, so it worked out perfectly.

Gideon letting us take our holiday rather than throwing us straight into danger was a huge surprise. I huffed out a laugh. I needed shares in Xanax because the Enforcer would be the death of my mental health. And if the stockpile of Syreni *Nectar* was in Key West, trouble would surely follow—and so would my panic attacks.

Cain will be there, too.

I shuddered as I pulled up to the restaurant. I took a deep breath and locked my bike, heading inside. Patsy was here today, which lifted my spirits.

She owned the diner and was a great boss, partly because we rarely saw her. Ada and I were good at our jobs, so she let us soldier on without her most of the time.

"Hey, Patsy! It's good to see you. How have you been?"

I grabbed my apron and started prepping for the shift, and she looked up from her food inventory to smile at me.

Her short, dark, wavy curls always made me think of Patsy Cline. My boss was a terrible singer, but she rocked things in the fitness department.

Wiry and strong and moving with efficiency, it was always a bonus when she helped us out on the floor and in the kitchen.

I didn't know much about her home life. I asked her once what she did away from the diner, and she told me she liked puzzles and genealogy. It must be nice to be semi-retired in the Florida Keys.

Today, she felt chatty and brought up the hijacking. A trio of monsters tried to steal the *Wanderlust* six weeks ago. I was still recovering after the night from hell when they stuffed my pants with chum and threw me overboard.

Patsy's eyes glittered with anger. "I've been thinking about you a lot, Eddi. Those assholes almost killed you. I can't believe it! A sweet young thing like you shouldn't be fighting bad guys. Do the police have any leads on the men who attacked you?"

Goosebumps peppered my arms.

"Unfortunately not. It's a dead end. I'm afraid the Sheriff's office couldn't find anything. No fingerprints or mugshots match in the database. I spent forever going over the photos. It's like those guys are ghosts."

I couldn't tell Patsy that Gideon had decapitated their crew leader, Malus, after he almost killed Ronan. Or that Malus was a vicious *lesser Demon*, and his boss *Hex* was still at large.

Sharing that information was a huge no-no; the Enforcer would have my head for exposing the *Others. Literally.*

Patsy wouldn't believe me anyway, and I liked my head right where it was.

"Well, be careful, Eddi. There are way too many people down here nowadays. You just never know who the bad guys are anymore."

She squeezed my hand and left through the back door, giving Ada a wink on her way out.

I turned to my favorite partner in crime.

"Ada, I can take the dining room. I don't mind. You take a break until it gets busy."

We were back near the dishwasher area, and Ada rubbed her sore feet again. A sixty-something whirlwind, Ada was one tough cookie, but her feet took a pounding.

Patsy made us a nice little nook to sit in the tiny kitchen during downtime and installed security cameras in both rooms for our safety. It was a thoughtful gesture.

Ada's pink curls bounced as she shoved her foot back into her shoe, washed her hands, and plopped down on our break chair.

"That would be lovely, Ed. Thank you so much. It was a crazy morning, and I think someone slapped my insoles with a two-by-four."

Ada lounged back in the chair, and I brought her a coffee. The brilliant smile she gave me was all the thanks I needed.

Our part-time cook, Miguel, worked with Ada this morning in our retro diner. Seeing Miguel made me wonder what *Bert* did on his days off.

I closed my eyes and pushed that thought right out of my brain. It said so much about my current situation when I could process the Bert-Gideon drama like it was no big deal.

Hey Eddi! Your friend is an Octopus, the cook is a Gryphon, and your boyfriend has a tail!

I grimaced because thinking of Ronan's handsome green tail made me miserable again. I was part of a strange new world, and it was time to toughen up and get with the program.

The door chimed, and I waved Ada back to her chair before taking the order. When I saw who it was, my instincts went into overdrive.

This guy was odd, and at first glance, my intuition screamed *Shifter*. I'd bet my life on it.

He was short and fat, with legs too skinny for his top-heavy body. The stained blue coveralls that pulled against their buttons had the reek of sun-cured garbage rolling from them. Was he a trash collector for the county?

"What can I get for you, sir?"

I had my poker face on, but it was hard to maintain. His stench assaulted me and turned my stomach.

Jabba the Hut sat and stared, immediately getting my hackles up. He had big lips and was one of those guys who constantly licked them.

Yuck.

Looking at the menu, he ordered, his voice sounding as if there was a frog in it—like an *actual* frog, croaking from inside his throat.

"Give me a Shrimp Po'Boy and some grits. Clamato. Not tomato juice."

I was startled by his rudeness, but ok.

"Sure, coming right up."

I'd have to be careful using that phrase right now. This guy smelled like death, and it just might.

Guys from Monroe Waste Collection had been here many times over the years and had never reeked like that. Something wasn't right.

While I waited at the counter for Miguel to plate his order, my creepy customer sat back in the chair and watched me like a hawk. As if that wasn't odd enough, he was unnaturally still and only moved his eyes as he tracked my movements.

This guy was off the charts spooky, and after all the shit I'd been through lately, I almost called the marina to have Cal come over. But that was silly because Ada and Miguel were here, and even with her perfect manicure and makeup, Ada was fierce when provoked. I was safe, at least for now.

I brought his order to the table, but before I could set it down and high-tail it back to the kitchen, he spoke to me in his croaky voice.

"I've been looking for a guy and heard youse two were an item."

At my surprised look, he smiled, his beady little eyes giving me the chills.

"Tall, muscular, dark hair, green eyes? Thinks pretty highly of himself?" he muttered, a smug look on his ugly puss.

Whoa, *what?!* Did this guy just insult my boyfriend? Ok, not my *boyfriend*, but still. The rude asshole.

I plunked the plate down harder than necessary, and some grits slid onto the table.

"OK, listen here. He's *not* my boyfriend, but that's none of your business, right?"

With a chilling smile, he said, "Well, I have a message if you see him. Tell him *Viggo* sends his regards and needs to get hold of him again soon." He gave a throaty chuckle. "Last time I seen him, he was pretty tied up."

I stood there, staring at him with my mouth open. *What. The. Fuck.*

This guy wasn't at the condemned marina where the demon had collected the Syreni *Nectar*. Was he involved somehow?

"Do I know you?" I asked.

He sneered, and I saw a mouth full of small, sharp teeth.

"No, ma'am, not yet. But you will soon." He laughed, and it sounded like short little croaks.

And with that, he tucked into his lunch, gulping down big mouthfuls of food. The man was an absolute pig and made Bert look like Mr. Clean.

I turned and stormed back to the kitchen, telling Ada about our odd customer. She peeked through the door and agreed.

"That guy looks like he belongs on a wanted poster," she said. "Maybe we should call the cops?"

"And what, they arrest him for reckless body odor?"

Ada laughed, which helped ease some of the tension in my gut. It's too bad Patsy just left. She would get a kick out of this stinker.

I couldn't tell Ada why this guy showing up at the restaurant worried me. None of my friends knew about the paranormal world around us, and I needed to keep it that way.

When I went back out front, Viggo was gone. His plate was there, and looking down at it, I swore he'd licked it clean. I moved the dish and saw slimy tongue marks on the Formica table where I'd sloshed the grits. They were gone.

I felt like sanitizing his money as I picked it up. All quarters and a ten-cent tip. What a jerk.

The rest of the day was long and busy, but Ada and I made a great team out front, and Miguel was a rock star at the grill. We served crowds of customers, finishing our shift around 4 pm, footsore and needing showers.

I helped Ada and Miguel clean and lock up, and then we all headed home.

Miguel was a short, muscular Cuban who could roll some heads if needed. With a smirk, he told me to call him if I had trouble with the stinky *hombre*. He was a Mariel Boatlift baby, and once you've crossed the Florida Straits in cloth diapers and a glorified dingy, nothing scared you.

Actually, when Ada was angry, it scared him. The thought made me laugh.

If I pedaled a little quicker than usual on the way home, I had a good reason. That Viggo guy reminded me how dangerous my world had become. I would never be safe until Gideon took down the monsters hell-bent on dragging the Syreni into the human drug trade.

My mind went to the psycho that was still at large. *Cain*. A dead ringer for Norman Bates, the bastard had a sick fascination with torturing me. I'd already had two run-ins with him that nearly killed me, and I wasn't itching for a third. The Knight could deal with that sadistic freak on his own.

Making it home without an issue, I whipped up a quick meal of tossed salad and broiled chicken breast.

After tidying the dishes, I made a sweet tea and climbed the ladder to the Widow's Walk above my apartment.

It was painful to sit up here and take in the view, knowing this was where I had first kissed Ronan. It was also where I discovered he wasn't human.

That will teach you to try and put your hands down a hot guy's pants, Eddi.

I blew my bangs up with a heavy sigh. I wondered how much longer I'd pine over Ronan. Tears burned my eyes, threatening to spill over, but I took a few deep breaths and buried everything under the dead little flower in my chest.

I lingered and enjoyed the view from the lofty deck, relaxing as I watched the seabirds drifting on the air currents. The pretty pinks and purples of the Atlantic sunset were good for your soul.

As I picked up my empty glass, I heard the sound of flapping sails high above me. I looked up, but there was no sign of Gideon.

I knew he had just passed overhead. Knowing the deadly Gryphon was out there, watching over us all, was a comfort.

CHAPTER 4

When I saw Cal at work the next day, he had called his Savannah contact. We could make an appointment in two weeks if we wanted to take a trip to the most haunted city in America.

"A witch named Sybil? Really?" I rolled my eyes at him.

Her shop, *Witches Brew*, sounded pretty hokey to me. And this witch wasn't cheap. At $85 an hour, I'd need to dig deep to afford the answers I sought.

"I know you've got a stash in your undie drawer," Cal teased. "You asked, the Octopus delivered. I know you're dying to learn more about your past."

"I do want to know. I do. But forking over so much money on a potential fruitcake makes me nervous. You've seen the *"mystics"* at events around here. Let's just say I'm a skeptic. And Savannah is so far away!"

I didn't say it out loud, but my mind still resisted the notion that I was something other than human. I didn't feel special. And I liked my life the way it was. I'd gotten used to it being just Cal and me against the world.

It would have been nice to learn what caused my horrifying dreams. Both the Gryphon and *Hex* had appeared in them, making me wonder. Were they memories?

The fire, the violence, and the silver-haired man seemed so real. Who were the two women, and why did one have a golden hairpiece? Did I want to know what it all represented?

My nightmares stopped after Gideon killed the lesser demon, Malus, and my life returned to normal. Hopefully, I wouldn't wake up with more vomit-inducing migraines now that the dreams were gone. I worried that a trip to Savannah would stir things up again.

In the end, finances saved me—not mine, but Cal's roommate Edward. He called Davy Jones to tell us his boss asked him to work overtime for the next month, and he needed the money.

"That sucks. I was excited to see Savannah. I even had my eye on a ghost tour." Cal hated it when his plans went south.

"You tried, and I appreciate it. It's fine, Cal. Our camping trip to the Dry Tortugas was expensive, and we're already pushing the timeline. Another trip to Savannah would have been tough to manage. My answers can wait. I'm ok with it, honestly."

Cal pulled me in for a hug. "We'll figure it out, Edster, don't worry. You deserve to know who you are. And WHAT you are."

The next day, James and Cal loaded the *Wanderlust* onto a trailer to move it to Key West. Gideon—or *Bert* must have influenced James to move the boat, although I'm unsure how. Hoarding information like it was solid gold was typical for the Gryphon, and he considered me part of his fold now. So, like Cal, I was expected to do my part, even though I didn't have the bigger picture.

It made sense. Being stationed in Key West would mean more feet on the ground. Cal and I would help Gideon snoop around downtown searching for Cain. Find him, and we would uncover the surplus of Nectar and stop its distribution. The drug had already surfaced in the Lower Keys and caused severe problems.

Using common sense, posing as tourists would be relatively safe. And who knows, we could find something useful.

I wasn't thrilled about sticking my neck out again, but I was loyal to James. And honestly, I'd go to ensure no one messed with my boat.

As far as we knew, James wasn't aware of the *Others or that* a vampire messed with his mind the night Cain and Malus hijacked the *Wanderlust*. Cal and I knew what we were up against. Working in Key West would be safer for us. Gideon told us to lay low and observe. No more following people and ending up in a jam like the night we saved Ronan. I kept telling myself everything would be fine, but I didn't believe it.

Cal and I stood by the launch and watched James pull the Grady-White up the ramp, trailing seawater as he turned onto Highway 1. It felt strange watching her go.

Cal turned to me with a wistful smile. "Are you going to miss me while you're gone?"

I rolled my eyes. "You're going to be there four days a week, Cal. I won't have time to miss you."

He's such a nut.

Cal grinned and listed how he planned to pimp out the living quarters for our stay in Key West.

"Cal, you realize the cuddy cabin is the size of a large closet, right? There will be no *pimping*."

Cal frowned. "Not even an ice maker? It's Key West. I want Rum Punches! Don't be such a downer, *KAREN*. And I'm bringing my laptop so that we can watch chick flicks."

I laughed. "You know, that's a great idea. And I know what you're doing. Thanks for trying to cheer me up. You're a good friend, Cal."

***

After months of planning and gathering gear, Cal and I were in Key West. We would lug everything onto the Yankee Freedom Ferry bright and early tomorrow.

After the 70-mile boat ride to the middle of the Gulf of Mexico, we'd enjoy camping on an Island surrounded by a turquoise ocean and cobalt blue skies—two days and nights of sun, sand, and stars. The Dry Tortugas were the end of the line in the United States, and we were thrilled to experience it.

The *Wanderlust* was in Garrison Bight, and the Kayak and camping gear stowed on board until we left in the morning. James planned to upgrade the boat with newer twin outboards so she'd be ready by the time we returned from our trip. He already had charters lined up for me. Everything had worked out perfectly.

It was funny how a holiday could lift your spirits. Cal and I were on a giddy high, touring Duval Street the afternoon before our trip. The street was famous in Key West for a reason.

We walked past a bar called "The Garden of Eden," stopping to chat with the girl at the door. Or, the guy, as I soon realized. It took me a minute because he was prettier than most girls. The Drag Queens in Key West had a striking flair for perfection.

I giggled at her shirt that said "Queen" in sequined letters. When she caught me looking at her boobs, she gave me a gracious smile and handed me a card for a free drink. Most of the bars and businesses on Duval had someone at the door to coax in potential customers.

"Sugar, you need to come up to the second floor!" she told me. "We have a special tonight. If you go topless, you get a free drink!"

She handed Cal a card and ran her eyes up and down his lean, muscular frame with appreciation.

"And honey, if YOU come up, I will buy you a second drink *myself*." Cal turned eight shades of red.

Laughing, I pulled the brim of Cal's sun hat.

"Thanks for the invite, but my friend here is Amish. Carnal knowledge isn't on the curriculum." My poor friend was so red I thought I saw heat wafting from his ears.

"Well, if you change your mind, come see me, kiddos! My name is Taffy."

She gave Cal a little pat down the arm before sashaying over to charm the next party.

Key West was a busy place, with bicycles being the main form of transportation. There were pink golf carts, mopeds, and a Trolley. Crowds of people enjoyed the shops, bars, memorabilia, and restaurants. Palm trees added to the Island vibe, and parts of Old Town still had the original bricks from a bygone era. It was fabulous, and we had a wonderful time.

Cal turned and grabbed my hand, looking up the street. *"T-shirts!"* he shouted, dragging me to a shop he'd noticed a few doors down. Cal was a tee-shirt freak. He loved looking for island-themed shirts and tried to find ones with clever slogans to wear at work.

"You're such a great shopper, Cal." He had pawed through a bargain rack and found a shirt. Raising my eyebrows, I said, "Sorry, Ladies, I like Guys?"

"What?" he grinned. "You remember the whole 'if I mate, I die,' right? This shirt will keep me from disappointing the drunk girls. Of course, you'll have to help me fend off the guys," he said, his eyelashes fluttering for effect.

I wondered what other goodies he'd found in the t-shirt store.

The afternoon was non-stop shopping and wolfing down plenty of treats. We waved to people on the Conch train and told people *it's pronounced KONK, not conch!* We had so much fun.

We even stopped in to get our Conch Republic passports. Key West was entertaining. I hadn't visited in a while, so I had forgotten how much fun you could have just walking down the street.

As evening approached, we headed to the harbor at Mallory Square to watch the Sunset Celebration. Everyone gathered there to see the sun dip below the horizon, which was always spectacular. Key West was as far south as you could get, and with the ocean as a backdrop, there was no prettier place to be at sunset.

The sailboats were out for their evening cruises, crossing in front of the glowing red sphere as it slowly sank out of sight. It brought tears to my eyes whenever I experienced a sunset here, and judging by the orange faces crowding the pier, I wasn't alone. For a brief moment, the sheer beauty brought the world into balance. You could always count on the sun in Florida.

All around us, the buskers were doing their thing, putting on a show for tips. Artists, magicians, and unusual talents peddled their wares to tourists. Tonight, a tightrope walker and a sword swallower entertained the crowd.

My favorite was The Catman. With subtle jokes and batshit crazy antics, he had a talent for engaging the crowd. It was impressive that he had his cats so well trained, and his merch was adorable. Cal bought me a T-shirt.

The Catman always set up in front of The Bistro patio. Tonight was busier than usual, thanks to a convention of—*witches?* Yep, it was wall-to-wall Halloween.

Witch hats, wands, colorful wigs, and funny shoes with silver buckles adorned the partygoers as if a contest existed to see who could look the witchiest. I laughed at the woman with a giant fake spider glued into her pink wig.

It looked like a blast, and judging by the racket, the refreshments were flowing. As we passed the end of the patio, a table of rowdy women caught my eye.

Decked out with every witch-themed trinket available, they drank hard, toasted, and did shots. One had green skin and a fake wart glued to her nose; another wore just the nose, the six-inch rubber proboscis dangling above her lip. She had stuck a nose ring in the end, which was hilarious.

But a slender, dark-haired girl wearing a monstrous witch's hat captured my attention at their table. The brim covered her shoulders, and the long corkscrew tip curled in on itself, ending with a twisted crook. But it wasn't the hat that caught my eye. A vibrant blue, the brunette's eyes followed us, her mouth catching flies. That wasn't odd at all.

I motioned to Cal, who glanced at the table, but the brunette returned to whooping it up with her friends. I must have imagined it.

Cal shrugged and threw his arm around my shoulders, his grin infectious. I narrowly avoided his knuckle rub by bolting to the booth selling made-while-you-wait guacamole & warm chips.

CHAPTER 5

We sat on the wall, relaxing under the palms and enjoying the cool night air while snacking on our delicious treat. Live music filtered out of the Cuban eatery. Taking in the purple-orange glow of the darkening sky, with happy music tickling the senses, made me cherish this time away from the rigors of work.

Our quiet spot under the palms was so pleasant I could have stayed there all night. The trees above us whispered in the salty breeze, and I reached for Cal's hand. It was the perfect night, the delicious smell of Cuban cigars making my nostrils flare in appreciation.

As Cal and I discussed heading back to the *Wanderlust,* I felt eyes on me. Tensing, I saw the brunette from the Bistro standing a few yards away. This time, she held the monstrous hat in her hands, and I noticed a wand glowing in the pocket of her floral sundress.

We locked eyes, and she stepped closer. Her hands fussed with the big black brim, but her wide eyes focused on me.

"I need to speak with you."

She followed us. I knew she was watching!

Still, there was something so non-threatening about this girl that I didn't feel the need for caution.

"Can I help you?" I looked at Cal, but he was eyeing our visitor. I'm not sure if he was alarmed or admiring her cute dress.

She took another step forward. "I saw you on the pier. Sorry to bother you, but I have some important information."

I raised my eyebrows, feeling tension creep up my neck.

"*Uhh...* What sort of information?"

Cal didn't acknowledge what I said. He was too busy studying the girl.

"We should start with names, I think. You are?" he asked.

Holding out her hand, she said, "Sorry, I'm Phoebe."

Cal ignored the gesture, his light eyes skittering over her features.

I shot him a stern look and held out my hand. "I'm Eddi."

Phoebe smiled, and the tension in the air dissolved. "I need to speak with both of you about a rogue—she lowered her voice to a whisper—*vampire.*"

Well, that was unexpected. I looked at Cal, sitting up straight and all ears. Phoebe hesitated, waiting as a group of people with drinks in their hands passed by.

"Talking about this in the open is a bad idea. We need to go somewhere private. There have been some nasty characters roaming around the last few nights."

Her wide eyes darted around the pier as if looking for someone. "If you are game, we can go to my rental. It's not far."

At the look on my face, she flashed a smile. "It's right in the middle of a busy area, Eddi. Someone would hear you screaming."

I wasn't too keen on this little twist, but for some reason, Cal was unconcerned. Phoebe must have passed his inspection.

Nodding, Cal stood up and grabbed my hand, pulling me along as she led us around the outside of the eatery patio.

I was ready to panic and sent him my thoughts.

"Cal, what if it's a trap? I'm not sure about this..."

He looked at me, his eyes calm.

"Old Town is a busy place, Eddi. I don't get bad vibes from her. Do you?"

I shook my head and decided to trust his instincts for now. But I was ready to run if the shit hit the fan.

As we passed Pepe's patio, people danced and enjoyed the live Cuban music. Everyone looked so happy that stopping to enjoy the pleasant evening was tempting. But Cal was on a mission and dragged me behind him.

Phoebe cut through a charming square filled with bronze busts celebrating the founders of Key West. Each one was on a pedestal scattered throughout the brick courtyard. I wanted to stop and read the plaques, but Cal was hell-bent on following Phoebe.

I realized then that I didn't want to know what she had to say. Was keeping things simple during my holiday too much to ask? A few days of peace and quiet would be lovely.

Phoebe led us down a small side street full of people. When she got to a little red door, she unlocked it, and we jogged up a set of stairs. At the top, she let us into the tiniest apartment I'd ever seen. She motioned us to a red leather loveseat that filled the small living room.

"It's eensy, but it was the right price," she said. "I'm on holiday for the month and have two weeks left."

She dropped her witch paraphernalia onto the kitchenette counter and pulled open the space-saver fridge.

"Would you like some sweet tea?" she asked.

Cal nodded, and soon, we sat around a miniature coffee table, with Phoebe taking the leather barrel chair across from us.

She didn't waste time.

"There's no point in beating around the bush. I'm a witch."

My mouth dropped open, and I stared at her. Cal frowned, his fingers twisting together. He glanced at the door, and my pulse spiked.

Phoebe laughed. "I get it. You don't believe me because of all the witchified tourists down at Mallory Square." She rolled her eyes.

"I'm from Augusta, Georgia, but my friends are part of a would-be witch chapter in Tennessee. We met here for the convention, so I've been hanging around with them while they're in town. It's a good time, but they are human. I am a witch. *A real witch."*

She wiggled her fingers for effect and giggled. I smelled alcohol wafting from her and wondered if she was messing with us.

Her eyes locked on Cal, who looked ready to bolt. She smoothed her skirt.

"Relax, Cal. I'm a ward witch," she sighed. "Witches rank somewhere between Immortalis and *Other* on the paranormal scale. There's too much to lose if we're discovered. Remember Salem? Don't worry about me. I play for the same team as you two."

Now, I was curious. "I don't know much about witches. How did you know we were *Other?*"

Phoebe's gaze flicked between Cal and me. "When you walked by the patio tonight, I saw your glow. I knew what you were, so I followed you."

Cal and I looked at each other in surprise.

Phoebe took a sip of her drink. "I was surprised to see Others in the Keys. I haven't seen many since I left the mainland. But Eddi, I had to check you out when I saw your aura. You're a Djinn, aren't you?"

I didn't answer. How in the world did she know that?

"Uhhh...I have an *aura?*"

Phoebe removed her witch shoes and put her feet on the coffee table.

"Yep." She popped the "p" and grinned.

Putting her glass on the side table, she said, "Here's the deal. I knew a Djinn once, and he was a lot like you."

She circled her finger in my direction. "Oliver had the same light show thing going on. It was like nothing I'd ever seen. It wasn't a glow like the *Others*. It was more of a vibration that was so rapid that it gave off a light—like a beacon. You have the same shine that he did."

She looked me up and down while I fidgeted.

"There's something about you that reminds me of him. I don't know if it's the silver hair—his was the same—or the way your aura moves in waves. I hope you don't mind me cornering you, but I couldn't resist learning more about you."

I looked at Cal, who was listening intently. His face was a mask.

"Where's your friend now?" I asked.

She frowned. "That's the thing. I don't know. Oliver disappeared about eight years ago. We were close, and I miss him. His disappearance hit me hard."

Her eyes misted, and she covered the awkward moment by finishing her iced tea.

"The cops said he pulled up stakes and left, but that's not true. I have no idea what happened to him. And when I saw you—I guess I just wanted to talk."

"I'm sorry about your friend, Phoebe. I won't be much help, I'm afraid. I know nothing about my background, and was hoping you might know something. Do you mind sharing what you know about Djinn?"

"Just a sec," she said.

She got up and brought us another drink: two fingers of scotch. I took a sip and coughed, and Cal laughed at me.

She took a deep breath and gave me a game smile. "Ask away."

I peppered her for almost an hour. She was a wealth of first-hand knowledge and didn't balk at my curiosity.

She told me that most Djinn could dematerialize and move quickly from place to place. The color of the mist they traveled in varied between Djinn families. A talented Djinn could disappear entirely and remain undetected for quite some time.

Djinn were known to have strange-colored eyes and were an emotional bunch. Some were so sensitive that they lost control, slipping into a dark state that could be quite dangerous.

Phoebe's friend Oliver could walk through walls and slip into other people's bodies. She said it tickled, so I assume Oliver gave her a personal tour of that skill. I didn't want to know the details.

Some Djinn could mimic animals. Oliver turned into a polar bear one night and scared the crap out of her when she came home to find the gigantic white creature sitting on her couch.

"I swear to God," she laughed. "A polar bear. On my couch. The bastard didn't let on until he chased me through the kitchen and out the back door."

She grabbed a Kleenex from behind her and wiped her eyes.

"I'm sorry. I shouldn't drink. It makes me miss him terribly. He was ... special to me."

Poor Phoebe. I think Oliver may have been more than a friend.

"Do you think I'm full Djinn? Can you tell by my aura?"

She gave me another once over. "Hard to tell. Yours looks like Oliver's, and you have those shocking gray eyes, so it fits a Djinn's characteristics."

She swirled her drink and looked at me, her expression intense. The frown on her face made my shoulders tense.

"There is one important thing you must know about Djinn, Eddi. They're the proverbial Genie in a bottle—an Arabian Knights myth. But like everything, there's a shred of truth to their story. A powerful Djinn can deliver your heart's desire. But you must enslave them to wring it from them. And it's not pretty. We're talking slavery here."

My eyes shot wide, and I swallowed. Great, just great. If Phoebe was right, I was in greater danger than I realized.

I took a long sip of my whiskey and coughed. I licked the fiery liquid from my lips.

"How do you enslave a Djinn?"

"I'm not sure," she said. "Oliver wouldn't tell me." She cocked her head. "I guess it's a well-kept secret because I've never heard the finer details."

We sat in awkward silence, the only sounds coming from outside the window as party-goers enjoyed the night.

"Listen, sorry to change the subject, but the aura-Djinn thing wasn't the only reason I followed you and dragged you up here. Some bizarre shit has been happening around the apartment the last few nights."

She looked toward the window. "I like to people-watch. One night, I spotted a vampire selling drugs to humans on the corner. I don't know what that drug is, but it's messing people up. There are a lot of stories going around town."

"How did you know the guy was a vampire?" I asked.

"Vampire's eyes glow red, but most humans don't see it unless the vamp is pissed off. In my case, I can see it all the time; it doesn't matter if they are angry. My witch powers allow me to see it regardless. The guy I've been watching is a vamp, no mistake." She raised her glass in a toast. "Here's to seeing them coming."

Cal saw me blanch and took over the questions. Phoebe described the dealer, and he sounded exactly like Cain. It all fit, and as she talked, I realized he must have been the vampire that messed with James the night the *Wanderlust* was hijacked.

A vampire almost killed me. A freaking vampire!

My heart stuttered, and the room took on a foggy haze. Tipping from my chair, I was halfway to the ground when Cal grabbed my shoulder and put his arm around me for support.

"Deep breaths, Eddi. You're ok. I'm here," he whispered in my ear.

Phoebe looked concerned, but I waved a trembling hand at her.

"It's ok. I get panic attacks when I'm stressed, and I've had run-ins with this—vampire. He tried to kill me. Twice."

She frowned and sat up in her chair. "That's nuts. What the hell is going on in this town? Vampires don't usually flaunt their powers and run amok, killing indiscriminately. They're too afraid of retribution. How is he getting away with it?"

* * *

CAIN

I screwed down the lid on the cryo container. The tall, slim canister was heavy with dry ice to keep the embryos viable until they reached their destination. It was time to work on the next batch of eggs that Oriana generously donated.

Okay, that I forced her to donate.

With a smile and a signature, FedEx would transport the very thing that would destroy this great country. The endless possibilities of our new product line made me giddy.

Hex and I would toast the end when these little eggers had their date with Dad. "Soon" was a relative term for a vampire. I would live forever, and so would Hex. Being immortal was so dull.

Hex had entertained us over the years, planning crazy things and watching the chips fall. I'd had the fun of tagging along as a minion.

The game was intense this time, Hex promoting me when Malus bit the dust. Now, I ordered people around—so much more fun than being a pee-on.

Our latest masterpiece of mayhem was some of Hex's finest work. It was an intricate web of treachery that would culminate in the country's fall and trigger our rise to power.

But we were patient demons. There was plenty of time to relax and enjoy the dramatic unfurling of our marvelous scheme. And later, we would spend all that incredibly green money.

I poked the form lying unconscious across the table before me. I'd watched him for ten minutes, trying to decide whether I wanted a sip.

"Wake up, Eric! Tick Tock!"

Hair smashed from his restless snooze, Eric lifted his head and rubbed his eyes. A tiny smear of blood decorated his upper lip, and white powder frosted his nose. It looked like a tasty little beignet.

My lip curled with distaste. Posh Universities turned out plenty of addicts, but they had such a short shelf life. Ours was already tipping over the edge. I'd have to keep an eye on his little substance problem, possibly even detox him before his retirement party.

I had plans for Eric when he finished tweaking *Gush*. No sense in wasting any O-negative by killing him outright. I loved playing with my food. Arterial spray already decorated the back room at the cigar factory—a fun reminder of my last recruit.

I loved the historic building, which smelled of fine cigars and the salt water from Oriana's tank. Here we were, five minutes from the pier, and Gideon had no clue where to find us.

Sybil, the witch from Savannah, did a fantastic job when Hex brought her down to Key West. The wards were impenetrable, the cloaking sheer perfection. Even if Gideon and his lackeys got close, they'd never find our lab. I thoroughly enjoyed driving the Sovereign's toy soldier insane.

Hex had been digging around and was confident the Sovereign for the Southern states lived in the Keys. If we could figure out their location, that would add a whole new dimension to our game. It was a shame that Malus had to miss the final act.

The Lesser Demon was incompetent, but I'd missed the old lunatic since Gideon took his head and sent him back to Hell. The last laugh would be at the expense of that bastard

Enforcer. My clever trap awaited, and I would have a Gryphon mount for Malus—if he made it back from Hell.

Eric's eyes were wide as he watched me muse about my enemies. My pupils must be glowing red again. I smiled and let my fangs show.

It no longer mattered if Eric knew the truth. You had a serious drug problem when your drug supplier was a monster, and you stuck around anyway. The cocaine was free, and Eric understood that as long as he did his job, he'd get to keep his pulse.

With hazy, bulging eyes, Eric finally got it together from his little nap. It was quite a dilemma he'd snorted himself into, and he knew it. I could tell by how fast he scrambled to his feet and reached for the cryo container.

"Contact the courier, Eric. It's time to schedule a pickup."

Brown had certainly nailed their slogan. *Customer First. People Led. Innovation Driven.*

I chuckled to myself. Soon, we could add "Insanity" to the end of that tagline.

CHAPTER 6

Phoebe's eyes were wide, her knuckles white on the highball glass.

"Wow, that sounds like a pretty messed up situation."

Cal and I told the witch about Hex and Cain and the terrible things happening in the Keys.

"I had no idea who the Enforcer was for Key West, so when I saw you guys, I figured it was my best shot at reporting the rogue."

Cal sipped his whiskey, the ice clinking in his glass. "You did the right thing by coming to us. The Enforcer is aware of the situation if it makes you feel better. I'll pass on your information, though."

Casting a grim look my way, Cal said, "Eddi and I didn't know Cain was a vampire."

"Well, I'm glad to help. I'm not a combat witch. I'm more of a 'ward' nerd."

Phoebe saw the confused look on my face. "Wards are my family specialty. We cast strong protection spells that keep unwanted guests out. A well-trained witch can create a virtually impenetrable shield around something. An outstanding spell caster can cloak things so well that even the best Immortalis can't see or hear through it."

So that's how Cain and Hex avoided Gideon for so long.

"Unfortunately, there isn't a lot I can do to help you guys because I leave to go home soon." Phoebe's eyes sparkled. "But I CAN do some wards for you while I'm here."

I looked at her, my eyes wide. The thought hadn't even occurred to me. It's not like we had a witch on retainer.

"Wow, Phoebe! That would be amazing—a total game-changer. What sort of wards can you do? I know zilch about wards."

"I learned from the best. My father was top-notch." Phoebe ticked them off on her fingers. "I can cast 'Nothing to see here' aversion wards. Sound muffling wards. Sound amplifying wards. Security trespass wards. And my personal favorite, Protection wards. I can set a ward so powerful that it will knock those bad boys on their rear ends. I guarantee you, there will be smoke coming from their ears," she said with a vicious smirk.

I looked at Cal, and he nodded with a huge smile.

"I don't know if I can afford you, but I need one of your favorite wards," I said, my eyes bright.

She nodded and swirled the ice in her drink. "Honey, for you, I'll do one for free. I hate vampires, especially ones that have gone rogue. It's the least I can do."

She laughed and slapped her knee. "I wish I could be here to see some vertical hair."

After exchanging contact information, Phoebe went to the window to check the street. She motioned us over.

"I always check before going out. Look. There's one of the dealers now. Right there, on the corner."

I looked down the street and felt terror slice through me.

It was Cain.

As if he felt me watching, he turned and looked up at the window, giving me a happy smile of recognition and a nerdy wave. Panic tickled the base of my neck at the look on his face. I yanked myself back from the window.

I sucked in slow, calming breaths. Cal had never seen Cain but knew his description. When he looked down the street, he paled and grabbed Phoebe's elbow.

"We can't let him get in here. He's after Eddi."

Phoebe was remarkably calm. "Then it's a good thing you're with me because this place is warded up the ass.—a regular Fort Knox."

It seemed our Phoebe had some teeth. I knew I liked her for a reason.

***

We headed back to our boat about an hour or so later. Cain hadn't bothered us, but he watched our window for a few minutes before disappearing. I guess he had bigger fish to fry. We had suspected that Cain and his crew were here. Now we had confirmation.

I was terrified to leave Phoebe's place. We had zero protection from that monster and were sitting ducks on the *Wanderlust*. Marina security wouldn't be able to do a thing if Cain made a move.

Phoebe could do the ward at noon tomorrow because the sun's power would maximize its strength. She suggested we stay the night, but the Yankee Freedom Ferry to the Tortugas left early. It was unlikely that Cain would follow us offshore, so a tropical island was the safest place for us right now.

As we figured out how to get back to the *Wanderlust* safely, I did find out how Cal contacted the Knight. Bert had a cell phone—it was that simple. I had my phone to keep in touch with James, so Cal called Bert. *Gideon?*

Whatever. Bert was on his boat and picked up on the third ring.

Cal told him the situation, and Gideon left Marathon immediately. It would take an hour, but when he arrived, he would scour the streets from above and watch the boat for the night.

We headed back to the marina, and being so late, we stuck to the well-lit areas. I was nervous about Cain, but talking helped.

I asked Cal, "Why didn't we call Bert the night we saved Ronan? It would have been safer than swimming around a dark ocean."

Cal laughed. "Bert carries a phone, but he forgets it and is unreliable about picking up. Gideon can't carry a cell phone in his Gryphon form. He's tried, but once he shifts, it's impossible." Cal wiggled his fingers and grinned. "No opposable thumbs. And a fanny pack would look ridiculous."

"When I need him, we have a system that works well. When Gideon goes patrolling at night, if I have a problem, I head to his boat. When I cross the threshold, it triggers his ward, which recognizes my physical signature. No matter where the Enforcer travels, he senses the disturbance. If the wards trip, either he's being invaded, or it's me—and it's an emergency."

I rolled my eyes. "It's stupid that Gideon doesn't have a cell phone. I'm going to figure out a holster or something."

Cal winked at me.

"If you figure it out, let me know. I want to be there when you convince Gideon to wear it," he laughed.

"It's not fair, Cal. You help him so much and don't get anything for your trouble. Wouldn't you be happier if you could *call* him when there's a problem?"

"You're forgetting something. The Knight can't talk in Gryphon form. And shifting back and forth isn't always possible."

I grumbled as we walked. I would make the sack of feathers wear a cell phone if it was the last thing I did.

The nervous chatter continued on the way back to the *Wanderlust*. It was a long walk to Garrison Bight because we'd left our bikes in Marathon. We kept our eyes open for signs of trouble, but things were quiet.

We headed down Fleming Street. It was picturesque and had no bars. Several people walked their dogs, so we weren't alone, but there were no rowdy crowds. The quaint little houses and palm trees were like stepping back in time, and the trip home went by quickly.

We were almost there when we walked up to a commotion. A crowd had gathered around a well-kept shotgun house, and as we approached, we tried to make sense of the scene. A white stone wall surrounded the front yard, and everyone watched something over the barrier. The barking, moaning, and screaming that rang through the air made my nerves jangle.

Cal and I looked at each other and knew what it was before we arrived. As we looked over the fence, our suspicions were confirmed.

A woman and two men were on the front lawn, locked in a heated sexual encounter. On its own, it could just be another night of partying in Key West. But the angry little Pomeranian tearing into their naked legs and getting no reaction made it clear this was no ordinary situation.

The homeowner screamed at the trio, the dog, and into a cell phone. The entire time he was trying to grab the snapping dog, there was no response from the lovers.

They were utterly unconcerned about anything except getting their rocks off, and when the woman lifted her head, her eyes were unfocused. Judging by the torn-up grass and the bite marks on their legs, the threesome had been putting on a show for quite some time.

We looked at each other, and Cal mouthed, *"Nectar?"*

I nodded. "Look at their eyes. They're completely off their gourds."

Cal's face paled. It would have been humorous if it wasn't so messed up.

Of course, none of the other spectators knew the reality of what was going on. But we did, and judging by the number of sirens we heard during our walk, this wasn't an isolated incident.

We had happened along just in time for the Cavalry to show up. Two officers jumped out of a squad car and, running through the front gate, tried to break up the orgy. Unfortunately for the homeowner, dispatch had sent Snoop Dog, with his partner Pee Wee Herman for backup. This arrest would be interesting.

As the two skinny officers teamed up to pry the offenders apart, they got nowhere fast. Sweat rolled from the cops as they hauled one of the guys from the pile together.

Going with the "one train wreck at a time" method, they dragged Casanova away by the arms and legs, working him toward the cruiser. He struggled wildly, waving an impressive, fully erect flagpole. Judging by the looks on their faces, the officers weren't happy about being so close to the guy's babymaker. Eventually, he broke loose and scrambled right back to the orgy.

Wisely, the officers gave up and called for backup. Snoop was sweating so hard that his shirt soaked through, but Pee Wee patted his pockets and pulled out a phone to take pictures.

Another police car arrived, and two enormous officers jumped out. A pair of athletic female cops joined the fray with a third cruiser. Ultimately, it took all six to get the partiers stowed in the back of the three vehicles.

Everyone's festive mood changed when they saw the three blissed-out prisoners throwing themselves against the windows, trying to get back together. The unhappy cops pulled out more restraints and started over, eventually trussing up their prisoners like butt-naked turkeys. We left after twenty minutes, and they still weren't finished.

I couldn't watch any more. It was too disturbing. I overheard one of the officers refer to a drug called *Gush*. It had to be the Syreni Nectar, a disaster waiting to happen. Things were already getting ugly if the sirens we heard were any indication.

It was well past midnight when I crawled into bed on the *Wanderlust*. Cal and I were wiped out and had to be up at six a.m. to make the early loading time at the Ferry.

I was still worried about Cain, but thankfully, Gideon was here. I heard Cal talking to him on the dock outside my window. I didn't catch what was said, but Gideon's heavy tread calmed me. We'd be safe as long as he was near.

CHAPTER 7

~ RONAN ~

For three days, Bacchus and I searched the mangroves and shallow coves around Curry Hammock. I was determined to find Viggo, but we'd been swimming in circles so far.

The State Park was popular, and humans were everywhere. Although it wasn't easy, we stayed clear of the swimmers and kayakers. We were ocean dwellers, but we weren't stupid. One misstep and we invited unwanted attention.

Early the second morning, a human caught me modeling my Syreni tail as I swam along the shoreline. While passing a sandy break in the mangroves, I saw a six-year-old boy watching me from the shade. His eyes were huge as he stood in the water up to his ankles, a fishing pole in his hand. A look of wonder swept over his face as he stared at my impressive green fin—on full display.

Crashing sounds from the mangroves alerted me, so I quickly changed forms. And not a moment too soon because we had company. I stood up in the waist-deep water, trying not to look guilty.

A red-faced mother came charging through the gap in the bushes and grabbed the little boy's arm. A suspicious look and a motherly snarl came my way, so I smiled to soothe her. She glared back, then turned to her son.

"Connor, what have I told you about running off? Your father said he would take you fishing after breakfast." Her voice was sharp, her eyes blazing with fear-laced anger.

"Mommy, that man has a ginormous green tail!" Connor waved his arms, his face flushed with excitement as he tried to pull his mother toward me.

I went stiff, and the hair on my neck stood up. This was precisely the reason I hated landwalking.

She needed to see there was no tail. Nervous about how this unfolded, I started towards the shore. The angry mother inspected my sparkling emerald dive skins as my muscular legs came into view above the water. Turning, she snapped at her son.

"What have I told you about making up stories, Connor?"

She sent death rays my way while she chastised the boy. Mothers had great instincts, and her eyes followed the contours of my legs as if noticing something wasn't quite right.

I fidgeted, my pulse rising as I approached, moving slowly. It was too late to turn back now. My heart was in my mouth as the gap narrowed, the mother watching me too closely.

I was ready to use my lure to gain control of her thoughts when she relaxed, tugged on Connor's hand, and dragged him from the water. He argued with her as they walked down the trail through the brush, their voices fading through the shrubs.

It was a near miss, and my pulse slowly returned to normal.

Bacchus appeared beside me in the shallows, his legs brightly patterned with blue and green scales that shimmered as he approached, the water splashing over his solid thighs.

When we changed to our leg form, our scales shrunk until they formed smooth, intricate patterns. They resembled a type of human clothing for water sports called dive skins. As long as no one looked too closely, we walked on land without issue.

Eddi got too close once. I shut my eyes at the memory of her fainting on the widow's walk. We had so little time together, but I remembered the details of every moment. I recalled the sensation of her exploring my body with her hands and lips, and I squirmed. Gods, I missed her.

"Ronan, snap out of it. We've got to keep going if we want to catch Viggo." Bacchus laughed at the sweat beading my torso and the bulge under my skins.

I wasn't ashamed. Syreni didn't hide their bodies under clothing; physical reactions were natural. We preferred bare chests, and it was so hot in the Keys that being shirtless meant we blended in. We kept a stash of garments on shore when we planned to landwalk or enter buildings.

I smiled to myself. Cal gave me a T-shirt. It was a unique shade of pink with a picture of a person fishing. He explained that "Master Baiter" meant I had excellent fishing skills. It was a kind gesture, especially since he didn't like me hanging around Eddi. It was puzzling that she got upset every time I wore it. Maybe she was jealous.

My brother broke up the train of my thoughts.

"By the Gods, Ronan, you're a disaster. Look at the boot lip on you. How is it that you're always on my case for taking chances and going to shore, and yet here you are, having such a close call in your tail form? You just caused that poor kid a world of grief from his mother."

"Stuff it, Bacchus." I looked at him with a frown. "Did you find anything?"

Bacchus shook his head. "There's a mangrove thicket in the middle of the next bay. It's the only spot we haven't checked."

He sounded tired and frustrated. That made two of us. We both itched for action. It was hard to understand why we found no sign of the Scorpionfish after such a thorough search.

We couldn't give up now. I nodded to my brother, and we swam to the next cove in skin form in case we ran into more humans. There was no sense in taking unnecessary risks this close to land.

A broad mangrove tussock sat by itself in the quiet bay. It had enough mud and sand pushed in around the roots that vegetation had begun to spring up. Soon, it would be a new island, thanks to the natural action of the tides.

It was rough climbing over the arched roots, but Bacchus managed with some annoyed grunts. When he got to the center, he looked back at me and grimaced.

"Viggo was here. But he didn't leave clothes. He left a body."

I joined him, balancing on the thick curved roots and trying not to break them. Mangroves were critical to the ecosystem here in the Keys, protecting many small creatures.

I climbed to where my brother was balancing and saw the body. Cradled in the middle of the thicket, away from prying eyes, was the well-decayed form of a young male. Wearing a sweat-stained undershirt and a pair of blue underwear, the lad was bare otherwise.

Bacchus took the unpleasant job of rummaging under the body and came up with a wallet and a cell phone. There was no money inside the wallet—only a plastic card with his picture. The effects of decomposition made identification difficult, but it was his image on the card.

Bacchus breathed through his mouth as he wiped his hand on his leg.

"It's his identification. Young humans must carry these if they want to get into bars to drink alcohol refreshments."

I was not interested in learning how Bacchus knew about human bars and refreshments. I assumed it was from one of his many trips to shore: my brother, the risk taker.

The dead boy's wallet held another card with a symbol Bacchus had seen on trucks that traveled the streets picking up human garbage. This man had worked for waste collection services.

His body stunk with decay, the eye-watering stench made worse by the molten sun. I tried not to look at his decomposing face. Without touching his body, we looked him over carefully. Around his ankles were eight or nine black puncture marks surrounded by swollen red flesh.

The wounds on his ankles were typical of scorpionfish stings. The toxins in the venom reacted with tissues that swelled at an alarming rate. The pain was intolerable. This kid had no chance with so many stings on both ankles. After taking his clothing and money, Viggo dragged him up there to get him out of sight, and he died from shock.

Bacchus looked at me, his eyes blazing. "Let's take this identification to someone who can read. It may give us clues that lead to Viggo."

I knew someone who could look at it, but I wouldn't risk seeing *her*.

"I don't know anyone except Tara, and that means a long swim home and more delays."

Bacchus saw my expression and gave me a wicked smile. My discomfort amused him. He wasn't stupid, and I wouldn't get off the hook so easily.

"That silver-haired beauty of yours isn't far from here. We can visit the marina and get some answers from her. She'll tell us."

He winked at me, and I resisted the urge to punch him in the face. He knew I was avoiding Eddi.

"Oh, come on! Don't be such a crustacean, Ronan. She doesn't know I'm your brother, so I'll do it. You won't have to go in."

When I frowned, he added, "I'll behave. I Promise!"

The sparkle in his eye said otherwise.

***

We changed to our tail form and concealed ourselves by using Hawk Channel. The deep trench followed the mainland and was often cloudy. With our muscular tails, the short trip to Davy Jones Locker was effortless.

Bacchus chattered away in my head, droning on about the marina's name.

"If I owned a marina, I wouldn't name it after a metal box you lock stuff in. It makes no sense! I'd name it something cool, like Feelin' Nauti."

He laughed bubbles and turned to swim on his side, staring at me. I ignored him and picked up the pace.

"Or how about Wet Dreams Marina? That would be more fun!"

I ignored his prattling and grumbled to myself instead. What if I saw Eddi? I was torn between wanting to march to the office to confront her and swimming out to sea without looking back.

I obsessed about never seeing her smile again or learning new things about her life on land. She was the only human I ever spoke to, and I was miserable without her. I needed to stay away from people. Yet here I was, swimming right to her doorstep.

What if she was right? I foolishly dosed her with my lure; did it cause an unnatural attraction to me? I'd *never* used my lure on anyone—ever. But I had always hated humans, and her bossing me around the day we met angered me. I regretted the childish way I lashed out. I should have told her about my misdeeds before we tangled. I didn't, and now she hated me for it. What if she saw me at the marina?

"Ronan, are you listening to me? We need to talk to the owner and see if he'll change the name to Test Tackle! Good one, right?"

For so long, I watched Edaline from a distance and ached to talk to her. Tara taught me to speak so I could converse with Eddi, but that didn't turn out well. Lionfish are notoriously aggressive, and Tara nearly killed her in a fit of jealousy. I sighed. I should have asked an angelfish for help.

Speaking had been difficult for me. While other young Syreni journeyed to shore to learn the human language, I stayed behind, nursing my hatred for humans. Getting to know Eddi changed everything.

I heard Bacchus going on about names for the marina, and I had to smile. At least I had my crazy brother for company.

Once we arrived at Davy Jones, Bacchus jogged up the hill to the office. I scanned the docks, searching for Eddi.

Brian, the other charter boat Captain, cleaned the catch for his customers. A few people washed their boats and enjoyed the sunshine. But there was no sign of Eddi or Cal, which was odd.

There were pretty palm trees in the cove, and a cooling breeze came from the mouth of the channel. I sat on Eddi's favorite coral rock in my skins form, with my elbows on my thighs, and waited for Bacchus. I wanted to catch a glimpse of her, but I also felt like turning tail and swimming for it. I settled for feeling ill.

Bacchus returned and plunked down on the sand next to me.

"Your *friends* aren't here, but a pretty blonde-haired guy helped me."

At the look on my face, he said, "Oh, chill out, Ronan, it was fine. He didn't suspect a thing. He told me this was a sanitation worker's ID with an address in Marathon. He looked up the name on something he called 'Net,' which made no sense to me. Anyway, the worker was recently reported missing."

I rubbed my thighs, the scales soft and pliable under my hands. I couldn't believe that Viggo killed a human, and it was the two of us sitting here with targets on our backs. Humans weren't stupid, and if the police tried to question us—

"Bacchus, what if he thinks you are involved? Did the blonde man seem suspicious?"

"Relax, brother. I can handle humans."

I gave him a skeptical look.

"You have so little faith in me, Ronan. I know what I'm doing."

I glared, and Bacchus sighed.

"Look, the ID was soaking wet from our swim here, so I told him I found it in the water while snorkeling at the park. I gave him a very general description of where we found it. Nice and cool. Relax, brother."

I growled at him, and my eyes darted around the marina. Where was Eddi?

"My god, Ronan, settle down. It'll all work out. It should be easy for them to find the body once they check the bay. I pointed them in the right direction. The rest is up to them. That body was getting pretty ripe, so it shouldn't take them long to find him."

I looked out at the water, my lips tight. Now that I was here, I wanted to see her. Why had I agreed to this ridiculous trip?

"The blonde guy wanted me to stay and talk to the police when they arrived, but I slipped away. I gave him a fake name, one I heard on the TV box thing. By the way, if anyone asks, I'm Abu Garcia," he said with a snort.

My head snapped around to him.

"Bacchus! What did you do?"

"Take it easy, Ronan. They'll locate the poor guy soon enough and see the scorpionfish stings, and we'll be off the hook. They'll never find us anyway, right?"

Bacchus had it all figured out. I was impressed, but he spent much more time on land than I did, so he was clever about human ways. Sadly, this little side trip hadn't helped locate Viggo.

I couldn't stop myself from asking about her.

"Was Eddi there?"

Thankfully, Bacchus took pity on me.

"Nope! I knew you'd ask, so I checked with the blonde guy. He gave me a strange look and said he couldn't give out personal information without permission. Man, these humans. So worried about minor details!"

He popped a baitfish into his mouth and chewed.

"Wait! Where'd you get *THAT?*" I hissed.

He opened his hand, and a few minnows wriggled in his large palm.

"These? Oh, they had a whole tank of them near the cash. I figured they were freebies for customers. You know, like those nuts you get at bars."

Groaning, I put my hand over my face. Sometimes my brother was an absolute dolt.

Bacchus held out his hand. "Want one?"

CHAPTER 8

I woke to darkness and the sound of waves gently lapping at the boat's hull. Cal was snoring, and the light from the marina coming through the cabin window threw shadows across his peaceful face.

I thought about our talk with Phoebe last night. I knew so little about the world of the *Others*, and everything I learned about my origins took another chunk of my confidence. I was torn between wanting to know more and the fear it generated. Gideon still withheld information; I was sure of it. But arguing with a creature that could tear my head off wasn't wise.

I sighed and checked my watch. Too bad Cal's not a morning person because he would hate me in about ten seconds. With a wicked grin, I jumped up, jostling Cal awake.

"Holy Crap, Cal! We have to get moving, or we'll miss the Ferry!" I jumped out of the bunk and started throwing clothes on.

Cal politely rolled over to face the hull and mumbled, "It's still pitch black out, Edaline. Go back to bed. We have plenty of time."

Cal's grumpy morning persona brought out the worst in me. I answered him with a pounce that caused a storm of cursing. He pulled the covers over his head and kicked at me, but I didn't give up, eventually pulling him free of the blankets.

"Get up, sleepy head! We have to get ready. Our ride will be here in thirty minutes, and we still have to lug everything up to the end of the dock!" I loved driving him nuts in the morning.

I was up and through the shuttered door before he could retaliate. I was pleasantly surprised by how much room we had in the cuddy cabin. It wasn't big, but it was enough, especially since we were always outside. This Key West gig might double as a fun mini vacation.

Cal stumbled up the step onto the stern deck, his hair messy and his clothes rumpled. With a groan and a big stretch, he looked into the darkness. The only light was the marina office near the parking lot and a few boats that winked over the calm, dark water. I loved the smell of the ocean in the morning.

"You're nuts, you know that, right?" Yawning, Cal looked over the equipment piled neatly around the stern. Even packing light, we took up almost every square inch of deck space.

His expression was priceless as he surveyed the mountain of gear we had to move. I'd have to get him some coffee, stat. Luckily, the marina opened early, and I could scoot up and get massive cups of extra bold to kick start our day.

Our slip was far from the parking lot, but somehow, Cal and I piled it in the driveway before our lift came. James' fisherman friend lived in Key West and kindly offered to move everything to the Ferry. Being the wee hours, it was a huge favor from someone we barely knew. Lucky for us, these were his regular work hours.

A hearty thank you was in order as he helped unload the truck at the Yankee Freedom dock. Getting it all onto the Ferry was quite a fuss, but the crew provided a wheelbarrow to move everything. By the time they called passengers on board, we were all set.

Our trip was finally happening, and Cal and I were in high spirits. The Ferry had a shower for guests, and we planned to use it this morning. I was always hungry, so the provided snacks were a blessing.

The ferry ride was slightly over two hours long, but the ocean never disappoints. We saw dolphins and a few sea turtles as we powered through the cyan-blue water, so the time flew by.

As the Ferry pulled up to the Island, Fort Jefferson looked peculiar, sitting alone on a spit of sand in the middle of nowhere. I couldn't wait to explore the fort after the Ferry left with day trippers. Only a few campers stayed over, so some private nights lay ahead.

After we docked and hauled our kit to the camping area, Cal and I hurried to set up the site. We had some pre-soaked briquets to cook our dinner this evening. Our carefully planned meals meant we had something fresh tonight, then freeze-dried meals afterward. Ice melted quickly in the Florida heat, and non-perishable foods after day one were essential.

We booked two days and nights, so we lugged a lot of water along. Packing for the trip was an exercise in streamlining, but planning it was all part of the fun.

I set up the Cobra for two paddlers to kayak this afternoon. But first, we took a guided tour of Fort Jefferson. It had an exciting history, and the tour was free along with your Ferry ticket, so why not?

Cal and I trailed behind the crowd, listening but taking things at our own pace. The brick-lined arched hallways curved around the Fort, but on this side, the Gulf of Mexico glowed a vibrant cerulean blue through the huge unfinished cannon holes. It was spectacular.

Later, Cal and I paddled around Garden Key, which surrounded the Fort. We brought our fishing rods and tried for fresh fish as we paddled around the circumference.

It was a beautiful day with no clouds and almost no breeze, which was great for paddling. Cal hooked into a nice Mangrove Snapper as we headed around the point. It was a four-pound fish and took us for quite a tour before Cal got it to the boat.

Cal wasn't a fisherman, so he went bananas whenever he caught something. He wrapped the line several times around the kayak before getting his fish on board. I laughed so hard that I almost dumped us into the Gulf. At least we had fresh snapper for dinner.

I hooked a massive Crevalle Jack, and for a few minutes, I thought we might make the three-mile jaunt across the ocean to Loggerhead Key. Cal, his eyes wide, back-paddled while yelling 'Reel, reel, REEEL!"

I managed with lots of huffing and puffing, and then it was Cal's turn to tease. As I reached out to lift the heavy fish into the boat, there was a clothes-drenching splash as a five-foot Hammerhead surged up from under the kayak. It grabbed my fish from under my nose, nearly giving me a coronary. All I had left were lips and cheeks because the hungry bugger took the rest. I was lucky he didn't take my hand, too.

As my pulse returned to normal, I looked around us and admired the surreal scene. "Can you believe we're finally here, Cal?"

I looked around us at the sparkling water. The blend of azure and aquamarine continued forever before meeting the cobalt sky at the horizon. There were so many shades of blue that our surroundings looked like a painting.

"I mean, look at it. We're a speck out here. It blows your mind if you stop to think about it. We're all just guests in the ocean, aren't we?"

Cal smiled. "Ya, unless you're a shark. Then you take what you want because no one will argue," he joked.

After kayaking, we swam in the crystal clear waters on the sandy beach in front of Fort Jefferson. It was a heavenly first day at the Tortugas.

Later, Cal cleaned his fish, and I scolded him when he forgot about the humans around us. He had the fish heart halfway to his mouth, intending to have himself a little snack. When Cal relaxed, so did his Octopus.

The day flew by, and the spectacular streaks of violet faded to a night sky frosted with stars. Campfires weren't allowed, so Cal had ordered an ingenious new gadget called *Campfire in a Can*. It's a soy-based wax that gave off a tall flame and would last for both nights if we didn't overdo it.

We sat back together and enjoyed the fire while gazing at the sky. What a show it was, far from the pollution of humans. I've never seen anything so breathtaking. It made me feel like a speck in a universe of possibilities.

Cal made me a drink, and it seemed like the perfect time to ask him what he and Gideon discussed outside the boat last night.

Cal shook his head. "It's worse than we thought, and *Gush* is a huge problem in town. We only saw the tip of the iceberg on our way home. Gideon cloaked his Gryphon form and watched everything unfold from the rooftops. He overheard some terrifying conversations. It's not looking good."

"He cloaks himself. Of course, he does." I rolled my eyes at Cal. "That explains a lot. Like how he scared the crap out of me at the marina a few nights ago."

"Thank goodness he has that power because he can track what's happening around Key West."

Cal paused for a sip of his drink, his eyes fearful. He knew something, and I watched him weighing how much to tell me. He was still keeping secrets. I thought we were past that little issue.

"Gideon told me it caused a complete shit show in town last night. The police didn't have nearly enough manpower. Several humans had severe reactions to it. Scores of people wound up in the hospital overnight—someone even fell off a roof!"

"Gods, that's terrible! I wondered when I heard all those sirens. And the arrest we saw was pretty intense."

"Gideon said there were at least eighteen calls last night, maybe more. This drug is not safe for humans. And even worse, it appears to have addictive properties. He says some users were out on the street desperate for more as soon as their buzz wore off."

Cal looked up at the sky and the carpet of stars glittering so far away from our reality. He turned, his expression serious and stiff.

"It makes me think back to your reaction when Ronan—the time you— reacted to it." He looked embarrassed. "Do you think your issue that day was similar to what we are seeing here in Key West?"

"Ya, well, as embarrassing as that question is, Cal, no. I don't think so. I didn't react like that. I didn't want more and was aware of what I was doing the whole time, even though I panicked. I'm not 100% human, so it makes sense that it wouldn't affect me the same way. I've thought about it a lot. It was the buzz from the Nectar and the shock of remembering *the night from hell* and making the connection to the Syreni abductions."

I stared at him for a moment, searching his face. "What aren't you telling me?"

"Gideon confirmed that he watched Cain dealing the drug all over town. They're pushing it. Hard."

I thought about it for a minute, and it made sense. "It explains why Cain didn't stick around to grab us after we left Phoebe's, I guess."

Cal nodded. "There's more. Gideon followed him, staying back and hoping he could find their base of operations."

The look on his face told me there was a bomb coming. I braced for the worst.

"Cain met up with a guy named Viggo. He matched the description of the stinker that came to your diner. Right down to the voice and the smell. He was still wearing the same coveralls."

Dammit. I knew the creep was connected!

"Who is he, and why is he hanging around Marathon while the rest of them are here in Key West? It doesn't make any sense."

"Gideon said Viggo helped capture the Syreni from the reef near us—at Coffins Patch. The dude is a scorpionfish shifter and worked for Cain and Malus. I have to wonder, why would he do that?"

I didn't hide my frustration, and Cal rubbed my shoulder.

"*Others* don't usually cause any trouble. There has to be a reason why he turned on the Shoal. Why he became *Lesser*."

We dropped the subject before it ruined our lovely evening. There would be time to deal with all that crap when we returned. I looked over at Cal, and I could see something else was troubling him. I sighed.

"Spill it, Octo-boy."

He looked at me and chuckled. "I guess there's no harm in telling you." Cal turned and handed me another drink from the cooler.

"Gideon saw someone else when he was patrolling Key West. Ronan is there, and he's not alone. The Syreni are in town, and they aren't happy. They're looking for revenge."

***

CAIN

These humans think they're infallible—going to church, living by rules, and no killing, lying, or stealing. They're just as depraved as the rest of us bad guys. I laughed softly to myself and focused on the scene at the bar.

It was a beautiful hotel, and I fit right in with my tailored cream three-piece suit and navy tie. Key West had some splendid hotels. Polished wood, brass fittings, beautiful furniture, top-of-the-line everything. I could get used to this if Hex kept picking up the tab.

But right now, I have a big fish to catch and fry. And Sophia was the bait.

She was a vixen, our little Sophia. Panther shifters were petite, but Sophia had a boatload of sex appeal packed into a miniature package. She had athletic legs, a squeezable bootie, and luscious bubbles that threatened to pop out of her top in a way that looked classy, not tacky.

And Warren was taking the bait. He'd already sent his security detail to their rooms across the hall from his own.

Leaning in, Warren whispered something in Sophia's ear and put his hand on her arm, absentmindedly running it up and down her smooth skin.

I had to adjust myself because watching her flirt gave me a boner. I chuckled to myself and ordered another Glenfiddich single malt. The show was about to heat up.

He kissed her neck, and I wondered what his wife would think if she saw him now.

Warren, Warren. Shame on you. Two kids and a house in the burbs, but so far from home, you'll go for it just to exercise the snake in his pants. No one will know, right? Tsk, tsk.

He'd find out soon enough that his behavior was a recipe for disaster.

Sophia picked up her purse, and Warren rose to guide her out of the lounge—party time. Room 608 would hold a few surprises for our National Security Advisor. He really needed to take security more seriously.

I smiled his way as he passed, but he looked bored and ignored me.

The bigger they are, the harder they come, Warren.

A chuckle bubbled over my lips as I swilled down the last of my drink and manipulated the bartender with a twist of compulsion. I got a two-fanged discount today. Well, every day. Compulsion is a handy thing.

I let myself into our room just down the hall and motioned for Emma and Charles to prepare for the second phase of our brilliant plan.

I sat in front of the laptop in the corner and brought up the live feed. Warren and Sophia were having a little lip time. Perfect. I pressed record for some full color and 4K resolution. You gotta love technology. The sound coming through from the hidden mics was immaculate. Crisp, clear sound is an extortion essential—sounds really make the movie, and the sloppier, the better.

Watching the monitor, I thoroughly enjoyed Sophia's show and could appreciate a consummate professional. She pulled out the two doses of *Gush* and showed them to Warren.

***

WARREN

"What is it?" Warren asked. "I've never heard of it before."

Sophia gave him a kittenish smile and held up the pair of microdots in her palm. "It's very trendy here. Everyone's using it. It amplifies the sensations and will blow your mind," she purred.

Warren must have had a few scotches because he didn't question the party favor. With a cocky smirk, he shrugged and tossed both microdots, chasing them with a sip from the drink he had just poured.

Warren went to the oversized plush chair in the corner, undid his tie, and shrugged off his suit jacket, laying both out neatly on the dresser. As he sat down, Sophia said, "I'm going to take a quick shower. Do you mind?"

Warren gave her a disinterested wave, kicked off his shoes, and grabbed his scotch and the newspaper, shaking it out to read while enjoying his drink.

A few minutes later, he was warm, so he unbuttoned his shirt and opened it. After a minute, he adjusted the growing bulge pressing against his fitted pants.

Warren's eyes glazed over in no time at all, a crooked smile twisting his lips. Standing unsteadily, he grabbed the chair to balance and removed all his clothes except for his black socks. He sat back down, his hips squirming to get comfortable. His turgid erection sprang against his belly, taking on a life of its own as Warren read the paper.

Sophia popped her head out of the bathroom door. She looked at his socks and smiled. "You ok out there?"

Warren looked up, his features slack. His eyes were unfocused, but he finally recognized her and gave her another crooked grin. Using the tips of his fingers, he beckoned her to join him.

Sophia looked fantastic, her long golden hair wet and slicked back, her freshly applied black cherry luster shine lipstick making her pouty lips pop. She sauntered over, knotting her robe as if to tease him.

Warren's lids were heavy as he took in the show, his mouth hanging open as she approached. He reached up and pulled Sophia into his lap, parting her robe and cupping a breast in his hand. He massaged it, looking at it like a masterpiece in an art gallery.

"Fucking gorgeous," he mumbled, then opened his mouth wide to take in a nipple, sucking and tonguing it before spreading her robe and repeating his ministrations with the other.

Sophia squirmed in his lap, a mischievous smile on her face. Warren's head fell back, and spreading his legs, he groaned.

Sophia swung around to straddle him, and putting her hands on his shoulders, she gave him a sloppy kiss. Rubbing her pussy up and down his shaft and kneading his shoulders, she moved her lips to nibble his jawline.

Without warning, Warren stood, his eyes wide and unfocused, almost dropping Sophia onto her ass. Always the sexy kitten, she landed on her feet without missing a beat.

His eyes hungry, his breathing labored, Warren turned and sat his date on the window table, his giant erection surging like a divining rod looking for moisture. Grabbing Sophia by the knees, he shoved them apart, finding her entrance and sliding his shiny pink head into her.

Slippery and delighted, his engorged rod punched into her with explosive thrusts; the wet sounds added to his ardor. It wasn't close enough, so he leaned forward and braced his arms on the table, pumping harder.

Sophia's eyes closed in bliss, but he didn't see that. He was too busy in his head. The grunts and barks made it clear he was enjoying his two doses of *Gush*.

Rock hard and balls tight, Warren gave a deep-throated shout and came with a mighty jerk. On legs so weak that he lost his balance, Warren fell on his ass, his cock jetting an impressive amount of happiness. He sat there on the carpet in blissful confusion, and that's when the door to the room opened.

Charles and Emma quietly slipped through it wearing matching navy robes, enjoying the erotic scene as they closed the door. Charles' eyes sparked, and he smiled and dropped his covering.

He was jaw-droppingly handsome with a trim, muscular build, his dark, wavy curls shining in the light from the wall sconce. Charles was a classic beauty, his body GQ material, but Emma was spectacular.

Tall, with short black hair worn in a bob just below her ears, her long neck and matching arms and legs were runway material.

The pair prowled toward Warren, who gaped at Sophia as she sat back on the table, rubbing her slit at his eye level. Warren enjoyed the show, licking his lips and fondling himself.

Charles got there first, and Warren looked up at him, slack-jawed and oblivious. Charles smiled back, reaching out and running his fingers through Warren's hair.

"Hello, Warren. I'm Charlie," he said, leaning forward to give Warren a long, slow kiss while he fisted himself with matching strokes. Warren's face reflected the twin red halos of his new partner's eyes.

Charles stood back up and held his turgid member in Warren's face.

"It would feel so good if you sucked it for me, Warren. It's fun. And when you're done, I'll return the favor. It's my specialty. You'll love it."

Warren hesitated, then struggling to his knees, he grabbed Charles by the ass cheeks and swallowed him down.

Warren had probably never given head in his entire life, but you'd never know it by the zest with which he tackled the job. He choked and slobbered as he tackled Charles' cock like a pro.

Grabbing Warren's hair and thrusting his hips in delight, Charles' glowing red eyes shared a lusty smile with Sophia as she did up the buckles for Emma's strap-on. Soon, the room was awash with the sounds of panting, moaning, and *Gush*.

***

CAIN

I pulled Sophia's face off my spent pole and stood, letting her tuck me in and zip me up. Leaning in, I watched Charles and Emma working on our newest pawn. Emma brandished Warren's leather belt before cracking it across his bare ass. I giggled at the raised red welts before applauding with slow claps.

"Perfect," I said to Sophia. "You Panther shifters take your work seriously, I have to say." I grinned and let the recording run.

Looking at my watch, I figured Warren could go another hour or so, and then we'd let him sleep. I had to be back before the sun poked its asshole face over the horizon, but Warren and I would have lots of time to chat before then.

I'd make sure he knew who owned his ass. Warren was the winner here, really. He bagged a mind-blowing threesome with gorgeous, talented lovers, and our brand-new product line obtained a champion with the National Security Council. Warren simply convinced the VIPS at the White House that our latest creation would keep America safe, and we all won. Easy Peasy.

Gush was just the beginning and an incredible source of entertainment. The drug income was the financial boost required for something momentous. A spectacle guaranteeing immeasurable wealth and the wedge we'd been seeking to topple the country—absolute power over it all. The anticipation was killing me.

I wouldn't mention to Warren that he would crave another dose of *Gush* by tomorrow, then on the weekend, and every day after that. We'll make sure he gets what he deserves.

"I think I enjoyed that as much as you did, Sophia. I just love this job, don't you?"

CHAPTER 9

"Bacchus, why must you always be such a pain in the ass?"

It was late, and we were walking on the main street of downtown Key West. The dark hadn't slowed the partying, and the streets teemed with revelers.

I'd just saved him from an aggressive human female who insisted she wanted him, *and now*.

It had taken us half a day to swim from our home reef near Marathon, mainly because Bacchus insisted we stop and chat up a few Syreni females we met along the way. He insisted it wasn't polite to blast through their *Shoal* and not stop to say hello.

I sighed and rubbed my neck, my jaw cracking with a yawn. Bacchus got his way on the trip down, but did he listen to me when we arrived in Key West? Of course not. We could have been laid out on the beach relaxing and catching a nap. But no, he wanted to see Old Town and enjoy the ruckus.

It's not like we'd never been this far south because we had—as young Syreni boys who weren't allowed out of sight of our intelligent parents.

That is how we found ourselves in a bar where the humans were either topless or completely naked. We were on the second floor, and the windows were open to the fresh night air.

A balcony ran around the building, which I admit was pleasant. Being up high was unusual for us, being water creatures, so I enjoyed looking down at something for a change. The streets below were crawling with inebriated humans, so we were temporarily safe from exposure.

The "clothing optional" theme of the bar was a perfect fit for us. People loved our bare chests and thought the colorful dive skins were "pretty." I couldn't relax, but the alcohol was flowing freely, so it was unlikely anyone would notice we weren't exactly human.

Bacchus was thrilled when he got his way, and as usual, I was babysitting. And now, one fetching and entirely naked female wouldn't take no for an answer.

At first, Bacchus let her paw him over, grinning from ear to ear. I stomped on his barefoot when I saw his growing arousal. He got the hint and tried to extract himself from her Octopus-like arms.

That was when the trouble started. The woman, her expression crazed, gave up on pawing him over, and climbed his muscular body, shoving her ample breasts in his face. His smothered voice was amused, but that changed when Bacchus realized he couldn't breathe under her ample bosom.

At his muffled shouts for assistance, I laughed.

"You'll have to get out of this one yourself, brother."

Bacchus staggered under the load and couldn't see where he was going. His blue-green skins were visible, but her writhing body covered his torso, her arms wrapped tightly around his head. Frantically pulling at the arms around his neck while being peppered with kisses on his head, he made quite a spectacle.

The attractive woman must have liked his scent because she rubbed her face into his long sandy locks. Her long brown hair fell in waves over both of them, and I was certain Bacchus was running low on oxygen.

He staggered backward and fell onto a table, spilling some drinks. That's when I decided to intervene. As amusing as this dilemma was, I didn't need any trouble tonight.

I grabbed the woman's arms and pulled them off his neck using all my strength. Bacchus reached down and worked on her legs, and finally, we got her detached. She was incredibly strong and driven like a wild thing to have him.

"Settle yourself, woman!" Bacchus snarled at her.

He dropped her legs back to the floor, and I let go of her arms. That turned out to be a terrible mistake. She launched herself at him again, scrambling up his body and swinging her legs over his shoulders.

With a face full of pussy, Bacchus struggled to keep his feet. The woman hung onto his hair, grinding herself on him, her head thrown back in delight.

I couldn't help it. I doubled over and laughed so hard my sides hurt.

Bacchus grabbed her thighs, frantically chasing both equilibrium and breathing room. The load was so top-heavy that my poor brother lost his battle with gravity and toppled backward onto the floor.

Two sour-faced, burly men rushed over, grabbing the woman and pulling her off Bacchus.

I was no help because a sudden cramp from laughing so hard had me bent double, holding my sides and gasping for air.

Bacchus clambered to his feet. He was breathless, his long hair was a mess, and he had a few scratches across his chest.

With a thunderous expression, Bacchus marched over to where I was standing and punched me—*hard*.

"Ow!" I howled. "Settle down, Bacchus! I can't help it; that was hilarious. You know, it's the first time I ever saw a woman get the better of you."

Bacchus bent over, his hands on his thighs and his breath coming in bursts, his nostrils flaring to take in air. Slowly, his face went from bright red to his standard, tanned color.

"You're an ass, Ronan. That woman almost suffocated me!"

We both looked to where the two muscle-bound humans were doing their best to subdue the woman. One straddled her torso while the other put thick zip ties on her wrists and ankles.

When they stood up, the woman went wild. Her dazed eyes found Bacchus, and she started working herself across the floor in our direction. The woman wanted him, and no one would stop her.

"Look at her eyes, Ronan. There's something wrong with her," Bacchus whispered.

He was right. The woman's eyes were glazed over as if seeing but not understanding. She was in a lustful, uncaring state. An alarm bell went off in my head.

"Bacchus! That woman has taken *Nectar*. Do you see it?"

Bacchus nodded, his expression grim. "Our females don't behave like that with *Nectar*. I don't understand. What's going on?"

I thought back to the day that Eddi and I tangled, and I shared a love bite with her. She reacted strongly to my *Nectar* and had a panic attack. The reaction was so intense that it scared me.

I looked at Bacchus, my face grim.

"I think this human is reacting to a dose of our stolen Nectar, brother. I've seen something like it before. Humans don't respond the same way as Syreni females."

His eyes darting back and forth between the door and the woman, Bacchus shifted his weight. The woman wasn't giving up, even with the two burly males trying to get a hold of her. She was like a woman possessed.

Giving me a wild look, Bacchus bolted for the stairs.

***

"I don't understand. Why would humans want Syreni *Nectar*?"

Bacchus, visibly rattled, panted as we walked down the long, busy street heading toward the beach. Our dramatic expedition cured Bacchus of his desire to dip a fin in the human world, at least for tonight.

"People are peculiar," I growled. "They are never happy to just 'be.' They always want more, and that includes more pleasure. Humans are willing to pay money for this sort of thing."

Deep down, I knew this wasn't wholly true, and it was my bitterness talking. Eddi hadn't been like that at all. And if I was being honest, most humans were decent folk.

Bacchus was looking around at the drunk people passing us on the street. He couldn't seem to decide if he was amused or distressed. As we passed a colorful and rowdy bar, I got worried when his eyes lit up.

"Let's get a drink, Ronan!"

I rolled my eyes and grumbled, "We don't have money, Bacchus. How would you pay for a drink, even if I agreed to go in with you?"

We had stopped in front of a noisy bar with a gigantic light made from green bottles. The cold air blasting from the entryway was refreshing, so I stepped closer to cool off.

That was all the encouragement Bacchus needed, and pushing past me, he marched right up to a pretty red-haired female near the door. She had a white veil on her head.

I'll never understand human fashion.

"Buy me a drink, pretty lady?" Bacchus gave her his most charming smile.

The girl scanned his beautiful face, heavily muscled body, and long, flowing hair.

Turning to her friends, she yelled, "This hot guy wants me to buy him a drink!"

As if it were a signal, her eight friends held their drinks high in the air and screamed at the top of their lungs, their eyes squinched shut.

That was how, two hours later, I had my hands full hauling my intoxicated brother back to the beach. All nine of them bought Bacchus a drink. They kept yelling "strip, strip" and trying to stick bills in his skins, but when that failed, they stuck them to his sweaty torso. I watched from the doorway the whole time, worried that my crazy ass brother would expose us. At least a lady with a tray offered me a glass of water with a yellow thing floating in it.

I do have to admit, it was funny to watch Bacchus in his element.

I'd never tried a drop of human alcoholic beverages, and looking at my brother, I was glad. As we staggered along the sidewalk with his heavy arm over my shoulder, I struggled to keep him upright.

Bacchus was singing a bawdy Syreni song about spreading a human's legs and licking her happy place. It's a good thing humans didn't understand Syreni. I was lucky that his pretty little school of guppies didn't follow us.

When we returned to the beach, I laid a chuckling Bacchus down on the sand. Checking that our weapons were still where we left them under the mangroves, I heaved a sigh of relief. There was no one around, and things were as I left them.

Looking down at his starry-eyed expression, I said, "Bacchus, you realize you look ridiculous, right? What would Mother say?"

Bacchus looked up at me, and his face crumpled. He burst into tears and started sobbing like a child.

I groaned and looked down at him. I was fond of him, and it hurt to see him missing our mother. He never spoke of her, and I often wondered if he remembered her kindness and fiery red hair.

"She loved you, brother, and was proud of you."

That made him cry harder, curling up and putting his hands over his face.

Oh, for heaven's sake. His sobs were due to the alcohol he consumed. Typically, my brother was tough as nails.

"Stop being such a baby, Bacchus. Be thankful our sister isn't here. Tabitha would be kicking your ass right now."

There was no answer. I looked down and saw that my brother was out like a light. Syreni and liquor didn't mix, it seemed. Sitting down on the sand, I remained watchful. I knew we could pick up the trail again in the morning. We were close, and I wasn't giving up.

We had tracked Viggo to Key West through a stroke of good fortune. As I sat on the sand, watching Bacchus snore, I reflected on our lucky break at Davy Jones Locker this morning.

***

Back on the beach at the marina, we were enjoying the fish snacks that Bacchus had pilfered as we tried to decide our next move. A family paddled back to shore on their rented kayaks, dragging them onto the beach beside where we sat.

The little boy loudly complained that his mother wouldn't let him talk to the "frogman" this morning.

The frogman comment caught my attention.

While the mother went to the office, she left her teenage daughter on guard duty. I gave them both a casual smile.

"You met a frogman? That sounds interesting. What makes you think this man was a frog?"

The little boy seemed relieved that *somebody* was listening to him.

"Because he had a huge head and skinny legs. And he talked like this—" The little boy imitated the man's strange voice, and my chin dropped. It was a nearly perfect imitation of Viggo.

"Plus, when I talked to him, one of those ugly black Palm bug things landed on his arm. And he ate it!" He made a face and stuck out his tongue.

His sister was concerned about the conversation and looked nervously toward the marina office. But the little boy was smiling and happy to tell me his story.

"Do you know where the frog man went?" I noticed the mother coming back down the hill from the office. I was out of time.

"Key West! He told me that if I went with him behind that building over there, he would take me to Key West today and pay for me to ride on a jet boat! He even said he would let me drive."

His mother arrived and took the little boy's hand. I smiled at her, but she didn't return it. With a worried frown, she hustled her two children away from us and marched them up to the parking lot.

I didn't blame her. A monster almost took her son today, and she knew it. My skin prickled, and I felt my skin heat as my gums throbbed. I'd get that slimy bastard if it was the last thing I did.

I turned to Bacchus, who was chewing on the last minnow.

"We're going to Key West."

Bacchus smiled, popped the last snack in his mouth, and rubbed his hands together.

***

So here I was, twelve hours later, listening to my brother's soft snores.

We must find Viggo. I would kill him slowly. Maybe even slower for the little boy.

The *Lesser* was here, somewhere. I could sense it. I would have my revenge.

Instinct stabbed my brain, and I leapt to my feet and dove for the mangrove beside me. In a split second, I came up with my short sword and swung it around, the point coming to rest at the throat of a Gryphon the size of an elephant.

"Hello, Ronan. I see your reflexes are back to normal," Gideon chuckled.

I dropped the tip of my sword and tossed it back in its hiding spot. The Gryphon looked at Bacchus, who counted seashells in a deep slumber.

"You've been busy tonight," Gideon said, swinging his great eagle head back to me. His golden eyes glowed a brilliant yellow in the darkness, the tip of his feline tail flicking back and forth. The Gryphon was nervous about something.

"We're looking for Viggo. If you know where he is, tell me now, Gideon."

"The scorpionfish that trapped you at the reef?"

I snarled. "Yes, and you won't stop my sword, Gideon."

"No, I don't imagine I will. You would be doing us all a favor. I'm not here to see you about that. I need you to do something for me."

"I'm listening." Gideon never asked for favors. It was beneath him.

"Eddi is here in Key West. I need you to stay away from her while you are in town." Gideon turned his regal head to look at me, and his shining eyes blinked. My heart soared at the news.

She's here. She's in Key West.

I shook my head. "Eddi means nothing to me. I don't wish to see her while I'm here. I'm here for Syreni business, nothing more."

Gideon lowered his head and gave a long, slow laugh, his glowing eyes never leaving my face.

"I know what is in your heart, Syreni. You cannot deceive me. Eddi is going through a rough time right now. You need to give her some space."

My heart stumbled at his words. "What's wrong with Eddi? Is she injured?"

Gideon turned his head and looked over at Bacchus again. I heard my brother's grumbling snores and wished he was awake.

"In a manner of speaking. But do not concern yourself. I am watching over Eddi. In the meantime, do not engage with her. She needs peace right now."

And with that, the beast rose to his full 15 feet and spread his wings. His four tiger-like legs bunched beneath his great mass, his talons open. Then he thrust, launching himself into the air with so much power that I could feel it through my bare feet. The flying sand hit me in the face.

I rubbed my eyes. As I watched the Gryphon rocket into the sky and disappear, my heart ached for the girl I could never call my own.

CHAPTER 10

Looking up at the billions of stars in the night sky, I listened to Cal snoring softly in the tent behind me. I couldn't sleep.

I should have been exhausted, but I felt energized about camping under the stars surrounded by the Gulf of Mexico. Maybe it was easier for me to function this far from my responsibilities because I didn't *have* to do anything.

I struggled from my camp chair; my muscles were stiff from so much kayaking today. Deciding I wasn't ready to crawl into a hot tent to try and sleep, I opted to take a walk instead. Snuffing out our campfire in a can, I quietly tidied up the campsite.

I wound up in the fort, my legs carrying me there as if they had a travel plan. I looked in through the doorway. It was dark and a little creepy, but I wasn't afraid. It was the first time in a long time that I hadn't been scared of being alone in a dark place. This island was magical, and I felt at peace for the first time in a long time.

Quietly, I padded around the outer hallway of the historic building, occasionally stopping to take in the beautiful seascape through gaps in the wall.

Navigation was a piece of cake, thanks to the full moon tonight. The ocean was putting on a show, and the brick cannon holes were the perfect vantage point over the moonlit water.

During one of these pauses to take in the fresh, salty air, I heard someone crying. I strained to hear the subtle noises.

I looked around me, but seeing no one, I cocked my head. The silence was deafening, and the echo in the hallways made pinpointing the sound challenging.

I followed my ears and tiptoed to a canon hole three arches down.

There.

As I peeked around the corner, I saw a faint glow on the brick sill overlooking the ocean. I might not have seen the tiny creature if the moonlight wasn't angled just right.

It was a small, almost translucent humanoid form, and whatever it was, it was sobbing with its hands covering its face.

I wasn't sure what to do. Was I dreaming? I looked at my hands and touched the brick wall beside me. No, this was very real. Whatever it was, it looked feminine.

I stepped out from behind the brick column. The creature looked up, was startled, and blinked out of existence.

Flinching at her sudden disappearance, I cautiously moved into the open space where she had been sitting in the moonlight.

Looking around me, I whispered, "I know you're still here."

I really didn't. I was totally guessing. I had no idea what the creature was, but I desperately wanted to find out. I'd never seen anything like it, and surprisingly, I wasn't afraid.

I tried again. "I'm not going to hurt you. I just want to talk."

Silence.

"Why are you so sad?"

I looked up at the ceiling and around the entire brick alcove, trying to see where it had gone. I saw nothing but dark corners and the arched hallway that I knew was empty.

Sighing, I sat down on the ledge and looked out over the ocean, which sparkled in the moonlight like a million tiny lights floating on the water.

I had no idea how to get the creature to show itself, so I started chattering in a soothing voice. Like I would if I were trying to catch a frightened animal.

"It's a shame. I would have loved to help you. I'm Eddi. I'm part *Djinn*. I get sad sometimes, too. I don't even remember my father. Or my mother," I said softly, my tone bitter.

It worked. A tiny voice came from the darkness behind me, but I didn't look. I didn't want to scare the tiny thing away again.

"A Djinn...?" I heard the odd sound of whispering leaves. "I've never met one of those before."

I kept looking out over the water, but every ounce of my focus was behind me.

"Why were you crying?" I asked the creature.

There was a long pause before it answered.

"They took my friend away. Now I'm all alone. I have no one."

In a hushed voice, I replied, "I know exactly how that feels. I've been alone since I lost my family."

I paused, but hearing nothing, I added, "Well, except for Cal. He's my family now. He's an Octopus shifter." I laughed. "He's here now, but he's sleeping."

I almost fell out of the window when a glowing blue Barbie doll appeared in my face. Jumping, I let out a shriek. Falling out of the window was a momentary possibility.

"By the *Gods*! Don't do that! You scared the life out of me!"

With a tinkling laugh, the doll-sized creature moved to hover before me, unaffected by the water fifty feet below. Her hands were clasped behind her back as the little thing hung there.

I was surprised to see her happy expression.

"You know an Octopus shifter? How exciting!" Her wings vibrated with a gentle flutter, like a dragonfly.

My mouth was open, and my eyes flicked eagerly over her delicate features. How incredible!

The blue glowing thing smiled at me. "I had an Octopus friend once."

Then she frowned. "August ate him. August was an eel. He's not around anymore. Cleatus took care of him for me," she tittered.

The tiny creature drifted down and landed on the bricks beside me.

"Who is Cleatus?" I asked her.

Her face fell, and the tiniest tear tracked down her cheek.

"He was my friend. They took him away."

I thought she would start crying again, but in an instant, her face brightened.

"Tell me about your Octopus friend. I *love* shifters!" She was so excited that she threw her hands up and wiggled them.

I looked down and finally saw her clearly. She was very petite, delicate, and about 8 inches tall. Her chin was sharp, and her almond-shaped eyes were on the same slant as two tiny, pointed ears. She gave off a faint, shimmery glow that made her appear translucent.

A soft, downy material covered all her girly bits from thigh to midriff before splitting to cover the tiniest suggestion of breasts. Finely detailed eyebrows were the same silver as her hair, which was medium-length and a bit wild. Unsurprisingly, her legs and feet were bare.

But it was her wings that inspired my attention. They were transparent with slight veins throughout, and the three sets moved in unison. The intricate details of this fascinating being had me mesmerized.

She was looking at me impatiently, tapping her foot.

"Looked your fill?" She snipped.

I laughed and snapped back to the moment. "Octopus shifter, right! Sorry."

I told her about Cal and how I discovered his secret one morning when I accidentally caught him shifting back into his human form.

That amused her to no end. "I bet you were surprised!" Her laughter was like tiny bells chiming.

This wild, miniature being was suddenly happy to talk—and quite possibly a little manic-depressive. Following the things moods was a rollercoaster ride.

She cocked her head and ruffled her wings, making that unusual fluttering sound again. Taking advantage of the brief pause in her antics, I went for it.

"Who are you?" I asked. Asking *what* she was seemed too harsh. I didn't want her to disappear again.

"I'm Miri!" Proudly, she added, "It means 'of the sea' in my tongue."

"That's a beautiful name. But why were you crying? You seem like such a happy little creature."

She glared at me and said, "I am not a *creature*! I'm a *sea sprite*."

She went from angry to miserable in a flash and began to cry again.

"They took him away, and I'll never see him again."

I quickly flipped back through our bizarre conversation and asked, "Do you mean this Cleatus fellow?"

She wiped the tears from her eyes and nodded. "Cleatus was a crocodile shifter. I was here all alone, and one day, he showed up after a storm. He stayed for fourteen winters to keep me company."

"Sometimes, he would shift to two legs and walk around the island with me at night." Her face brightened at the memories. "He was very handsome. He let me ride on his shoulder!"

She clasped her hands in front of her chest and closed her eyes. I think Miri might have had a little crush on this crocodile of hers.

Then the tears started again.

"Six years ago, the men in brown came and took him away. He was always well-behaved. The humans loved seeing him. Whenever the boat came, he would come out, and sometimes he would swim with the people. Every day, they brought him snacks and fed him when the men in brown weren't looking."

She was miserable, with tears pouring down her cheeks. "Everyone loved Cleatus. I don't understand!" She stomped her foot, and just like that, she was angry again.

"The men in brown caught him and trussed him up with ropes. They even taped his mouth shut! They roasted him over a fire and ate him!" She wailed in anguish.

I frowned. "Miri, did you physically *see* them roast him over a fire?"

That didn't sound right to me. It was obvious the little fairy thing meant the park rangers.

"No...." She hesitated, then added, "But they loaded him on a plane. I think they took him to the mainland and ate him there," she wailed. "What other reason would they have for tying him up and taking him away?"

I could think of a few. I laughed, and Miri gave me a dirty look.

"I don't know if you'll believe me, Miri, but I am 100% sure they did *not* eat Cleatus. If I had to guess, I'd say he's in the Everglades right now and having relations with a cute girl crocodile."

She looked at me suspiciously, so I added, "Trust me on this. They did not hurt your friend. They helped him. He's probably thrilled."

At her horrified look, I added, "And missing you terribly, I'm sure!"

She gave a huge sigh and seemed to accept my suggestion. Looking around our little nook, she sat down with a plunk.

"Who will I talk to now? It's so lonely here."

I looked at the forlorn Sea Sprite and felt terrible for her. What would it be like to have so many people surrounding you but no friends? Or have nothing to live for except the daily grind of feeding yourself and sleeping? My heart went out to the lonely little thing.

"I'll tell you what, Miri. I have an idea, but I must talk to my friend Cal first. Can you meet me back here tonight?"

She nodded with excitement and giggled furiously before buzzing up into the air. She did two laps around my head and shot off into the night.

As I watched her disappear, my shoulders sagged. Engaging as she was, the chatty sea monkey had worn me out. Exhausted, I made my way back to the tent. I had no trouble sleeping this time.

***

"No," Cal said with a scowl. "Don't even go there, Eddi, because we are not taking a sea sprite back to Key West with us."

At the expression on my face, he added, "This is not a sea turtle or a bird that's got itself into a fishing line, Eddi. She's a pesty, annoying chatterbox pain in the ass. My god, didn't you notice that she never shut up? Up and down, happy then sad, laughing then crying—exhausting!"

I laughed out loud at that comment. "Yes, I did notice. I had trouble sleeping, but a little Sprite time tired me out."

Cal wasn't amused.

"Oh, come on, Cal. She snuck onto the Yankee Freedom, fell asleep, and wound up here. Now, she doesn't want to leave because she thinks Cleatus will return. I can make her see sense. If she stays here, she could wind up pelican food! We need to help her."

Cal groaned and rolled his eyes at me. He'd seen this look before.

"Come on, you saved me, remember? Let me save her. We'll take her back to the mainland, find her people, and hook her back up with them. Easy peasy. She has to have relatives or something, right?"

Cal gave me a suffering look. "Eddi, it's obvious that you know nothing about sea sprites. They don't have families. Their sire finds a mate, and the couple quickly raises a nest full of the little suckers. Then, one day, the parents get tired of all the chatter and bail. When the little monsters realize mom and dad aren't returning, they quickly give up waiting and go their separate ways."

He finished his speech, and at my horrified look, he slowly shook his head.

"Tell me you'll think about it," I said.

Cal just threw his hands up and walked away, heading for the park facilities. I smiled. That was one way to win a dispute.

For our last day at the park, we opted to kayak out to Loggerhead Key and go swimming and snorkeling. The patch reef just offshore there was terrific. After paddling back, we made dinner and enjoyed the endless stars one last time.

I didn't want to bug Cal about Miri, but I did plan to confront him about his love life. I had so many questions about his fatal flaw.

Cal had informed me one night that Octopuses die right after their first and last mating. We'd brought a few canned cocktails to enjoy on our last night here, so it felt like the right time to bring up the subject.

"So you can never have sex?" Okay, that was a bit blunt.

Cal looked uncomfortable. "I don't know, to be honest. I just avoid it because I don't want to find out *the hard way*," he said with a wry smile.

At my horrified look, he explained, "It has something to do with a gland attached to the eye of an Octopus. Mating triggers the maturity of the gland, which causes a quick decline, and within weeks, that's it. Game over."

I swallowed my drink in a rush and choked. The tragic words made me wish I had never initiated the conversation.

Cal patted me on the back.

"That's for the Octopus *animal,* of course. Octopus shifters are very rare, especially white Octopuses. There are so few of us around that no one can be certain that mating is fatal. I know our lifespan is short because I've never heard of an Octopus shifter living longer than fifty."

My heart broke for him, and my protective instincts surged. "We have to find out, Cal! We *will* find out. I want you to be happy, and if there's a way for you to have a relationship without kicking the bucket, we'll find it. *I'll* find it."

Cal looked at me like I was a complete idiot. He took another sip of his drink, his expression stiff.

"Why on earth would I even try, Eddi? It's not like I miss it because I've never had sex. I'm fine, honest!"

"That's so unfair, Cal. You can't die a virgin! I can't believe you're not upset about this. It's a disaster!"

He laughed and said, "This conversation just officially got weird."

Cal took a sip from his drink, and with a big sigh, he stretched his legs and put his hands behind his head. He mulled something over as he took in the stars.

"It's ok, Eddi. Don't worry about me, honestly. I don't need a sexual relationship to be happy. I have you." He turned to look at me. "I don't need anything else."

Tears threatened, because my best friend had given up hope. I could see it on his face. He was resigned to settling. Of all the people I'd ever met, Cal deserved to be loved more than any of them.

It dawned on me that Gideon probably had some answers. That's it, then. I would drive him up the wall until he told me. Cal might have convinced himself that a loveless life was fine, but I was on it.

Feeling better now that I had the beginning of a plan, I told him, "Uh, so *Cal,* I promised Miri I would meet her tonight." Cal looked cross and shook his head.

"Oh, come on!" I begged. "Just come and meet her. What will it hurt?"

CHAPTER 11

It was late as my brother and I scoured the Key West shoreline. Methodically, we explored the sea bed, checking every nook and cranny that looked like a place where Viggo might park himself for a snack.

Scorpionfish are night hunters, so if Viggo was hungry, this would be the time to find him. It was our best chance to look for the faint shimmer that would make him easier to spot. I knew there was a good chance he was still on land, but we wanted to check along the shoreline first.

At least, that's what I told myself. If I were honest, I eagerly scanned the mooring areas for Eddi's boat, the *Wanderlust*. Finding her was more challenging than I expected as we drifted in and out of the harbors around the Island.

There were hundreds of boats of every shape and size, and many were liveaboards. Luckily, Bacchus hadn't noticed what I was up to.

As we passed an expansive pier, we popped our heads out of the water and stopped to watch two lovers wrapped in each other's arms. They were enjoying more than just the night breeze at the moment.

Seeing me staring, Bacchus poked me with his homemade mace and pointed at the sexy action on the pier.

"Did you tangle with the human, brother?" He grinned and stuck his tongue out at me, wiggling the tip. "How do landwalkers taste down there, anyway? I've always wondered. Was she salty or sweet?"

I was close enough that he didn't notice me move until, with a splash, my short sword was under his chin. The gilt handle reflected the light of the pier, and the hard light glittering in my green eyes reflected on his face.

He raised his hands above his head. "Ok, ok, it's too soon to joke, got it! Don't get your tail in a knot!"

I lowered my sword and continued while Bacchus grumbled about his *hangry* brother needing a tangle.

Rounding the point, we found an entrance to another marina, this one well-protected from the open ocean. We cruised around the bight, taking in the crowded rows of vessels of every shape and size moored beside strange floating houses.

And that was when I saw her boat. The *Wanderlust* bobbed gently on the water, tucked away in the furthest corner.

As we drew closer, I heard the ocean rippling against the hull, but the boat was otherwise silent. The only sign of life was a light glowing through the curtains in a small bow cabin. Given the late hour, it must have been a security light.

I thought of Eddi's beautiful, bright hair and her gentle smile. She was probably sleeping. I pictured her wearing the cute pajamas with cartoon crabs, and blood rushed to my groin. I'd had to dress her in them the day she reacted to my Nectar. The day we tangled.

I almost moaned at the memory but got control of those useless thoughts. Why was I punishing myself? She had made her position clear.

I should have left and focused on finding Viggo, but I was powerless to do anything but swim toward her boat. She was here, just out of reach. If I got close enough, I would catch a hint of her unique citrus and summer breeze scent.

I didn't want to be seen, so I swam carefully, leaving no wake to alert anyone to my presence.

Gideon said she was hurting and not to disturb her. Hinting at injury or telling a Syreni "no" would surely yank on our protective instincts and bring out our legendary stubborn streak. Now, I was anxious to know what was wrong with Eddi.

I paused, frowning. That meddling Gryphon. What was he playing at?

I looked the boat over carefully but saw no sign of trouble. I did notice there were two newer outboards where there used to be one. The *Wanderlust* had received an upgrade.

I smiled, knowing how much Eddi would love that.

The closer I got, the stranger I felt. I knew I wanted to go closer, but my mind told me no; go the other way. How odd.

Gritting my teeth, I pushed forward, a sharp pain sizzling across my skin when I was ten feet from the hull.

Bacchus bobbed to the surface between me and the boat, his sloppy waves ruining my attempts at stealth. With a hiss and a splash of his tail, he almost bowled me over in his haste to escape the strange sensation.

"Holy mother of jellyfish!" he snarled, grabbing his chest. With a gasp, he switched to telepathy.

"Do you feel the wards on that boat? Don't touch it. It'll kick you like a mule."

"Wards? What do you mean, wards?"

My lack of knowledge about the human world annoyed me, and I grumbled with frustration. Eddi was so close, but I would never get past this ward thing to see her.

Bacchus lifted both hands and wiggled all ten fingers at me. *"Witchy mojo, brother. It's a type of protection spell. No one is getting on that boat unless the owner wants them there. Someone with money has hired a witch. A good one, judging by the strength of that ward."*

He must have seen the yearning on my face because Bacchus shot me a suspicious look.

"Ronan, where have you brought me? Whose boat is that?" He pursed his lips in sudden understanding. *"My God, you're so pitiful, Ronan. Just tangle with her and get it out of your system already."*

I ignored him and moved closer, feeling the stabbing prickles from the top of my head to the tip of my muscular tail.

I saw another small light on the stern, but it wasn't a boat light. It was blue.

"What is *that?* Do you see it? At the stern." I grabbed Bacchus and, pulling him closer, I pointed. He resisted, clearly not wanting unnecessary pain.

He shook his head at me and shrugged. We drifted around the boat to the stern, and the light moved.

With a flash, it was in my face, and hovering a hair's breadth from my eye was the tip of a tiny plastic sword. I froze, not wanting to lose my vision.

"Who goes there?" Shouted the little minx. I could see it now. It was a Sea Sprite.

Bacchus laughed as I tried to swat it away. "She sure got the drop on you, didn't she, brother? Bested by a Sea Sprite."

With all the racket the blue disaster made, stealth was out the window.

I scowled and hissed, "What are you doing on Eddi's boat?"

Zipping back and forth between Bacchus and me while waving her plastic sword, she kicked out with her feet. Her aim was outstanding, and she caught Bacchus on the nose. I almost laughed out loud when he covered it with his hand.

"Who are you to ask me questions? I'm the Queen's guard. State your business!" she hollered.

The Queen? "I'm here to see Eddi. Keep your voice down before someone hears you."

Bacchus floated on his back, his arms behind his head and a malicious grin on his face. His tail hovered below the surface, making little ripples. Winking at me, I realized he planned to swat her with his tail. I shook my head. He enjoyed this far too much.

The little sea sprite buzzed in circles around my head, hurling obscenities that gave me a headache. I waited, and when she flew a hair too close, I snatched her out of the air and snarled into her face.

She shrieked so loudly that I had to squint my eyes.

"Unhand me, you *asshole!*" She struggled, frantic to free herself.

I hated sea sprites. So fucking annoying. With an evil smirk, I raised my hand and opened my mouth as if the nymph was a tasty treat. As the sprite caterwauled in earnest, I heard a familiar voice. One I had been longing to hear. A voice that was music to my ears.

"RONAN! What the *fuck* are you doing to Miri!?" Her silver hair ruffled in the ocean breeze, and her eyes glittered with anger.

I smiled. Eddi was magnificent.

Bacchus took off so fast that there was a ripple where he'd been lounging.

Looking up at Eddi with a playful grin, I slowly lowered my arm.

"LET. HER. GO."

I opened my hand, releasing the annoying insect, who darted up and clung to Eddi's shoulder. It stuck its middle finger up and growled at me. What that meant was a mystery, but the sprite was furious. And so was Eddi.

I could see Cal standing behind Edaline. He mouthed at me, "Eat it next time," but he was smiling. I don't think he meant it.

I finally found my voice.

"Hello, Eddi. I was just in the area and saw your boat. I didn't know the Sprite was with you. I'll let you get back to what you were doing. Sorry to disturb you."

I turned to go, hoping she would stop me. She didn't. Feeling like a fool, I dove, my tail slapping the surface in annoyance.

That was a half-baked idea, Ronan.

I berated myself all the way across the bight, where I caught up to Bacchus.

I found him waiting on the far side of the marina on a cement pier, lounging on a comfortable-looking bench. He laughed at me as I pulled myself from the water, where I effortlessly changed into skins form.

"Did you kiss and make up?" he teased. "I don't think she was too happy when you almost ate her pet."

"Zip it, Bacchus. You know I was playing games. I was trying to scare the miniature devil spawn."

I looked up to see the moon, full and gloriously bright. I turned to my brother, who was enjoying the feeling of it on his face. His eyes were closed, and his hands were behind his head. He'd braided his wet hair and secured it with a woven piece of seaweed.

"Why does she have a sprite guarding her boat? And why does she have it warded?" I turned and poked my brother, who was unconcerned. Bacchus answered without opening his eyes.

"She's afraid of something," he mumbled. "It must be dangerous because that Octopus shifter she's hanging around with would be tough in a fight." He yawned and crossed his legs at the ankle.

I looked back at the boat, and the lights blinked out. A gut-wrenching loneliness tugged at my heart. "Bacchus, do you remember when mother and father brought us here? We were so young."

There was no answer. "Where in the world did she find a witch? Why is she in Key West?" I heard a soft snore and knew Bacchus had drifted off.

A feeling of despair overwhelmed me, and frustration roiled my guts. I had no idea how Eddi spent her days or why she was hurting. What was frightening her?

I felt an urgent desire to protect her from harm. Bacchus was right; I did have it bad for her, and it was eating me alive.

I settled myself on the bench. I couldn't enjoy Eddi's company or talk to her, but I could stay here and watch over the boat tonight. Whatever was worrying her might show up. Then I would kill it.

CHAPTER 12

Seeing Ronan again had been difficult. It took my breath away, and I ached at seeing him. As he teased Miri, his laughing eyes glowing like an ethereal shamrock in the darkness hit my lonely heart like a bus. It was hard to conceal my happiness to see him again.

I knew he was just teasing Miri. I wanted to squeeze the life out of her myself sometimes. Cal was pretty close to hiring a boat to go and dump her back on the Tortugas.

Out of sheer desperation, this afternoon, I devised a plan to help with Miri's constant chatter.

"We need a guard, Miri. Would you like to help?" I asked.

She was over the moon. "I'd be a great soldier in your army! What do you need me to guard, Exalted One?"

I rolled my eyes. I was going to kill Cal, who thought telling Miri I was a monarch in the human world would be funny.

"We have some bad people after us, Miri, and I need you to watch and sound the alarm if we have visitors. Do you think you can do that without being seen?"

She humphed. "Of course I can, silly."

Seeing Cal's expression, she tried again. "My most precious Queen! As you know, I'm incredibly fast and acrobatic and wear invisibility like a second skin!" She popped in and out a few times to prove her point, with a different ferocious expression and fighting pose each time. It was hard not to laugh at her antics.

"Well then, I am appointing you my Queen's guard, Miri. Just stay out of sight because the harbor is busy, and we can't let anyone see you, right?"

Cal rolled his eyes, and I sent him a dirty look. I knew he was jealous of Miri. She was my constant companion since we smuggled her back to Key West in our empty cooler bag.

"If they see me, it's off with my head!" Miri mimed a throat slice.

She thought the decapitation part was funny, but it was entirely possible if she screwed this up. I'm not sure the reclusive sprite fully understood the laws of the *Others*.

We were sitting on the boat, relaxing after our trip. Cal mixed a few rum punches for a sunset toast to celebrate a perfect weekend away. Plucking one of the plastic swords out of my drink, I ate the candied fruit with a flourish and held it out to Miri.

"Here you go. Use this. If anyone gives you trouble, you'll have a weapon." Cal's eyes sparkled as he sipped his drink.

Miri zipped over, grabbing the little blue sword out of my hand. "It matches my skin! It's amaaazing!" she shrieked. She did a few quick circles, brandishing her sword with a ferocious scowl, then blinked out of sight.

"You're a genius, Ed. That was a brilliant workaround. You realize that getting peace and quiet will be a constant struggle with her, right?"

I snorted into my drink. "Yes, but there's something even worse that hasn't occurred to you yet. How do we know the blue monster is watching the boat and not sitting on the step spying on every word we say?"

Cal laughed, and we clinked our plastic cups.

Propping ourselves up with cushions, we settled in for an evening of reminiscing about our trip. It was unforgettable, and I was so glad we got the opportunity to go.

When Miri's screeching pierced the silence, Cal and I jumped off the bunk in a panic and scrambled to the stern deck.

It was Ronan, and he was threatening to eat my guard. I caught a glimpse of another Syreni ducking away under the dark water.

I almost laughed at Ronan's antics. I'd forgotten he had a playful side. I had the irresistible urge to jump into the water for a joyful reunion.

Then, the memories rushed in, pushing an unbearable tsunami of hurt, followed closely by anger.

How could he? Whenever I got a little breathing room and started to get over him, he popped back into my life. Was he trying to make this more challenging?

A civil war raged inside of me. I was still angry with Ronan, but deep down, I wanted him to stay. Getting close to him would relieve the constant feeling of loss that dogged my steps.

I managed to reel my emotions back in. What the hell was wrong with me?

"Sorry to disturb you." Ronan was speaking the whole time that I wrestled with my emotions. His beautiful voice reminded me of how rough he had sounded when first learning to talk. It felt like ages ago.

Cal watched me as I stood by the bow, tracking the round swirls from Ronan's tail as he swam away. My face must have said it all because he put his arm around me.

"What do you say we head up and get a drink at Schooners? It's early yet, and it doesn't close until three in the morning. I'll even spring for a taxi so we can have a nice little end to our vacation?" He kissed the top of my head and gave me an encouraging squeeze.

Cal was just trying to make me feel better. He should write a manual, "Standard Care and Handling for Mixed up Half Djinn Orphans."

I sighed. "That's not a bad idea. We'll leave Miri here to *guard the boat*. I gave him a sarcastic look, and he giggled.

"I must admit, it keeps her out of our hair." He leaned forward until his face was right in mine. "I miss our quiet times together," he whispered, waggling his eyebrows.

I gave him a shove, and he grinned. Mission accomplished.

We gathered our sandals and some money for drinks, and I finger-combed my short hair with a quick mirror check. Satisfied that I looked presentable, Cal and I climbed out of the cuddy and hopped onto the dock, warning Miri to stay out of sight for the next few hours.

As we stepped over the rail onto the dock, something moved in the shadows of the mangroves.

Not something. *Someone.* I stifled the urge to scream.

I tugged on Cal's shorts and sent a mental shout—*thug from the diner!*

I hadn't projected thoughts in a while, so I was rusty, but Cal heard my warning because his head whipped around, and registering the intruder, he froze.

Viggo was even uglier than I remembered. This time, small flaps of skin hung from his face and down his arms, waving like fins and dripping seawater. Some of the broader flaps had spines on the tips.

Are those fins?

Cal nodded.

A grotesque caricature of a man, the little bumps, lumps, and floppy bits turned my stomach. I finally registered what I was seeing skulking in the mangroves. The scorpionfish was mid-shift.

Viggo stepped from the shadows and finished his change, mincing toward us in all his big-headed, skinny-legged glory. Even entirely shifted, his humanoid form was hideous. I kept my eyes up because something freaky dangled between his legs.

"Hello, kids." His dark, bulbous eyes rolled back and forth between Cal and me, and every muscle in my body tensed, screaming for me to *run.*

"I've been waiting to bend your ear, girl. You're hard to track down." His fat tongue shot out, and he licked his lips.

Ambling toward us, Viggo stopped a few steps away. The reeking stench wafting toward us made me nauseous. I wanted to scramble back onto the boat and drag Cal behind the wards. But Cal was furious and wouldn't budge as he braced to defend me. I grabbed his wrist and was about to use force when Viggo looked up at the black sky above.

"Where's the Gryphon? I know he watches you two like a hawk." He smirked at the simile, unsheathing a long, thin stiletto from behind his back.

"Will he come swooping down here and make me pay for what I did to all those Syreni womanizers? I hope so!" He frogged, pointing the tip of the knife at us.

"After what Ronan did to my cousin Tara, he deserves to pay a heavy price. She was mine before he came along, and look what he did to her. He never appreciated her. And that two-timing prick never did figure out that lion and scorpionfish are family. He'll be awfully confused when I gut you."

"Tara's his cousin, and—oh my God, Cal, be careful. They're not right in the head."

I watched Viggo creep closer, ready to dive for cover.

"Get back on the boat with me! Please, CAL!"

Viggo's eyes swiveled and focused on me as if he could hear my frantic pleas. Cal shoved me further behind him.

"You are a yummy thing, aren't you? No wonder the Syreni man-slut likes you so much. You come trolling around the reef, spreading your legs and stealing him from Tara. They were the perfect match. Everything was fine until you messed everything up for her, you bitch." He spat out the curse, his eyes bright with hatred.

It was all twaddle, but Cal wouldn't budge, and I wasn't leaving him. I had to do something. So, I tried empathy.

"Maybe Tara can get some help. Being addicted to Syreni *Nectar* doesn't have to ruin her life. I struggle with it, too. If I can shake the attraction, so can Tara. Please, don't do this!"

Viggo gave a froggy chuckle and lifted the knife, focusing intently on the tip, turning it in the moonlight to enjoy the shine of his blade.

"My cousin's venom addled your brain, didn't it, Princess? I can see you're a bit touched. Syreni Nectar doesn't cause addiction in anyone except humans," he snorted. "And those weaklings deserve it. Half of Key West is addicted already, and soon, they'll all be buggered."

My breath hitched at his words. *Gush* was addictive, and Cain and his gang knew it all along. I heard Cal gasp, and I felt sick at the revelation.

Viggo's face brightened. "We'll be working on more of those Syreni bucks as soon as I can catch a few. We're running low on *Nectar*."

Viggo ran his repulsive eyes over my face, thinking out loud.

"Maybe I have the perfect bait right here? Or maybe I'll finish you so Tara can have her lover back. Decisions, decisions."

His head bounced like a bobblehead as he snickered. "So here's the thing. My boss doesn't like how you've interfered with operations. I told them it was time to off you both, but everyone complained, *'No, Viggo, you must wait. We need them.'"*

His fat mouth curled up in a nasty grin. "I've decided I'm not waiting any longer. Starting with you."

Without warning, Viggo's hand shot out as he sprang forward. In a motion too fast to follow, the bastard grabbed my arm and, with inhuman strength, yanked me away from Cal. Hauling me to his chest, his fat hands flipped me around, and in one sweeping motion, there was a knife to my throat. I sucked in a sharp breath but didn't dare to move.

There was a blinding flash of light, and the furious white Octopus that appeared didn't miss a beat. I felt two fat, sucker-filled tentacles grab both ankles while another shot up to wrap Viggo's knife-hand. With a mighty yank, Cal pulled me straight down. I landed on my butt at Viggo's feet, and Cal was on him in a blink.

I didn't even mind the squishy suckers when he used my torso as a launch pad because, in an instant, he was over me and clinging to Viggo's shoulders, two of his thick arms wrestling for the knife.

A sparkling blue tornado streaked from the bow to join Cal, stabbing Viggo in the arms with her plastic sword and then swerving out of range. It didn't break the skin, but it must have hurt like a bugger because Viggo started screaming in weird, froggy croaks that sounded like a distressed pufferfish.

Clearing my rattled brain, I scrambled to my feet but could only watch, helpless, as Viggo staggered across the dock, an Octopus wrapped around his shoulders. I couldn't get close.

Eight arms had a choke hold on Viggo, two grappling for the knife, the other six pulling at his arms, legs, and face. The suckers stretched and yanked at Viggo's skin everywhere they touched, pulling it to the breaking point.

The two thick arms around his legs easily tripped the top-heavy shifter, and he flopped over onto his back. In a furious tangle of arms, the Octopus wrapped himself around Viggos' head, blocking his breathing and stifling his terrified shouts.

Cal's suckers ripped at Viggo's face, tiny splits leaking blood as he torqued and heaved on the skin. Never piss off an Octopus.

Cal's parrot-like beak tore at Viggo's throat, whose muffled shrieks reached a fevered pitch as blood began to trickle down his neck. Cal was winning this fight and, in a few seconds, had overpowered the scorpionfish shifter.

I froze in shock as I watched it unfold, but Miri buzzed Viggo, screeching with rage as she stabbed exposed skin. She would have done some severe damage if she had a real weapon.

But Viggo wasn't going down easily. Somehow, he made a partial change, prickly skin flaps appearing across his arms and torso. Waving and flapping, the pointed barbs on the tips dripped a clear fluid. Seeing the victorious look in his eyes, I shouted to Cal. I was too late.

The enraged Octopus flinched and, with a spastic jerk, went limp, his pale arms falling away one by one. When the last one plopped down on the dock, Viggo was free.

Panting like he'd run a marathon, the scorpionfish kicked Cal's limp form off his body and struggled to stand.

I scrambled forward to protect my friend, but with a vicious snarl, Viggo knocked me away and rammed his knife straight through Cal.

Pulling the blade out with a sickening squoosh, Viggo turned toward me. Blood trickled from the tip of the wicked edge, and a gloating expression tracked me as I crawled to Cal's limp body.

The gut-wrenching scream that tore from my chest should have woken the dead. But we were beside the boat, and Phoebe's ward dampened all sound. I would get no help this way. Impulsively, I attacked.

Launching myself at our attacker, I had no plan, but death was coming for him. I could barely see through the white-hot rage clouding my vision. I was light as air, then whole again as I found my feet.

But before I could take a step, someone beat me to it.

Viggo, knife raised to slash at me, looked up and froze. His eyes widened, and his mouth gaped, an unnatural stillness seizing his body.

From behind him, a tapered log filled with nails swept out of the darkness, catching Viggo in the side of the head with a sickening crunch. The prongs stuck in the shifter's skull with a hollow sound as the tip of a sword burst into view through his chest before quickly disappearing.

Viggo's shocked mouth opened in an "O," his eyes wide and unseeing.

My face went numb, barely registering the violence, when the sword reappeared, this time arcing in from the side. It sliced through his neck with a wet sound, and Viggo's head slid sideways.

His ugly mug still wore an "O" as it tumbled to the dock with a thump. Knees crumpling, the fat body fell, revealing Viggo's executioners.

With white knuckles, Ronan gripped a shining short sword, Viggo's blood still sheeting along its length. Beside him was the powerful Syreni male from the marina, his long hair dripping with seawater. His mace was stuck—in Viggo's detached head.

Ronan's flashing eyes glittered as they searched me for injuries. Both Syreni were splattered with blood, their chests heaving. Puddles formed around their feet, the seawater stained pink with Viggo's blood.

The Syreni with the mace lifted his weapon and shook it, unable to free it from Viggo's detached skull. When that was unsuccessful, he placed a bare foot on the rolling head, repeatedly jerking the log as he pried the nails loose. The hollow tearing sounds made me gag.

My knees wobbled, and I fell to the dock, crawling to Cal. The Octopus was still, his long tentacles in a heap. The siphon tube on his mantle fluttered weakly, and he was no longer a beautiful translucent white.

My friend, the person I loved more than life, was deathly blue. His goat-like eyes were dull and unmoving under his hooded lids.

"CAL!" My hands flitted over his body, looking for the wound.

Cold panic sluiced through me. "Oh my God, no, no, *NO!* Cal, hang on!"

Wild with fear, I looked around to see Ronan land on his knees beside me.

"RONAN!" I sobbed. "Help him! He's DYING!"

Tears poured down my face, Ronan's form a blur through the cascade.

Gently, I rolled Cal over and found blood and air bubbling from a long, thin slit. Droplets of red spray flecked his velvety white skin, now covered in swollen red welts.

I switched into crisis mode as an eerie calm descended over me.

"CAL, you have to shift back! Can you hear me? You need a hospital but can't go unless you *shift!"*

Even as I said it, I knew it wouldn't happen. My world was about to shatter.

"He can't shift this close to death," Ronan said softly. "There is not enough strength left to make his change."

A sob tore from my throat, my terrified eyes finding Ronan's. He looked resigned, and I knew we were too late.

"Help me. PLEASE! I can't lose him." I choked on my tears, but Ronan looked calm.

Carefully lifting Cal away from me, Ronan settled cross-legged on the dock's wooden planks and pulled my friend gently into his lap. With one knee bent, he cradled the deathly pale Octopus close.

Ronan looked at me, and I could see it in his eyes. It was a mortal wound. My friend, the one thing that mattered most in the world to me, wasn't going to make it.

I felt like someone was crushing my chest because I could barely breathe. I reached out, touching my ice-cold friend.

Ronan gently moved my hand aside and pulled Cal closer to his belly.

"I can help," he said. "But you have to be ready. I won't be able to do it all myself. He will need much more when I finish."

Ronan's eyes searched my face, and I saw a faint glow in their depths.

I looked up and hissed, "Miri, you know that black thing I carry around all the time? You need to go and find it and bring it to me. QUICKLY!"

Her face ashen, Miri turned and was gone in a burst of blue motes.

Ronan hunched over Cal's body, whose tentacles were flopped on the dock. Ronan bent until his forehead touched Cal's velvety skin.

Something was happening. I couldn't understand what I was seeing, so I watched, muffling my sobs with my hand over my mouth.

A soft seafoam glow slipped over Ronan's body, slowly spreading to Cal's Octopus form. It became brighter and brighter, increasing intensity until it changed from mint to white. Finally, the light began to pulse like a heartbeat, a throbbing heat reaching me where I knelt.

The long-haired Syreni standing behind Ronan lifted one of Cal's stray tentacles and draped it across Ronan's neck, then carefully picked the rest up one by one, tucking them around his glowing form. Stepping back, he gave me a sympathetic smile.

I saw something black waving in front of my face. Miri had bought my phone.

I scrolled quickly down the contacts and found the one that said Outrageous Asshole. With a silent prayer, I hit call. There was no answer.

Bert didn't pick up, and I sagged in defeat. Cal needed to shift; a hospital was our only hope.

I looked back, and Ronan was still glowing, but it was faint. Groggily, he lifted his head, and his half-closed eyes found mine. He smiled, his eyes rolled back, and his arms went slack. He would have tipped over, but the long-haired Syreni reached down and steadied him.

"Easy there, brother. I'm here."

Ronan tried to open his eyes and gave me a weak smile.

"I did my best," he said. "For you, I will always do my best." Then his head flopped forward, and he passed out.

I gasped and would have freaked out, but the long-haired male gave him a fond smile and laid him down on the dock. Cal, still tucked in Ronan's lap, was no longer blue.

It took me a second to see it, and hope bloomed in my chest. I reached out to hold one of his tentacles. No longer ice cold, Cal's body radiated warmth.

The slender tip of one rubbery leg slowly lifted and wrapped around my wrist. Snot mixed with tears as I choked in relief. With a weak pulse of light, Cal appeared, his hand still squeezing my wrist.

He tried to speak, but I shushed him, gently kissing his pale cheek. He wasn't strong enough to open his eyes, and blood seeped from a wound a few inches below his throat. He was trying to swallow. Picking up my phone, I frantically dialed 911 with one hand.

"We're trying to get you some help, Cal. Just hold on, ok?" I choked back a sob. "I love you, Cal. With all of my heart, I do. Don't die on me. I can't live without you. Do you hear me?" His hand squeezed my wrist.

Those words were barely out of my mouth when, with a loud crack, the dock bounced so hard I had to put a hand down to balance. Booming thumps thundered down the boards, shaking me with each step.

Gideon materialized over us, his eagle head snaking down to scan Cal's still form.

"I felt your fear so strongly I tasted it, Edaline. I came as quickly as I could."

Almost incoherent, I blurted, "Hospital — due east across the bay—the chopper pad! Oh my God, Gideon, *hurry...!*"

My voice trailed off. Gideon was fast, but Cal was going blue again.

Gideon squatted on his haunches and pulled Cal to his feathered chest. His claws sheathed, the Gryphon looked skyward and spread his monstrous wings, Cal's arms and legs swinging lifelessly in his grip.

Gideon shot upward into the darkness with a tremendous thrust, blinking out of sight as his wings took him east.

I turned to look at the long-haired male Syreni, who smiled at me as he squatted over Ronan's unconscious form.

On the dock, my phone chattered away, a tinny voice saying, "911, what is your emergency?"

With a tremendous, gut-wrenching hurl, I blanched and emptied my stomach into the ocean.

CHAPTER 13

"I need your blood, hurry!"

The long-haired Syreni stood before me, Ronan unconscious and dangling from his arms.

"Bacchus. Pleased to meet you too," he teased. "I'm Ronan's brother. And the blood is for—?"

I didn't have time for this.

"To get you past the ward. Unless you want a new hairstyle when it blasts you two into the Gulf of Mexico."

A drop of their blood smeared on the hull with a few words, and it was done.

Bacchus lifted Ronan like he weighed nothing, carrying him over the railing and laying him on the cabin bunk below.

At my wild eyed expression, Bachus sighed. "Ronan is fine. He's out cold because healing drains him." After reassuring me that Ronan would wake up once he rested, the Syreni sat on the stern deck and put his feet up.

"He's fine. Go and see your friend before you have a stroke. I'll watch Ronan. Promise."

I was torn, but I had to trust the calm confidence of Ronan's brother and get to Cal.

I left Miri guarding the boat and called a cab. I was in a full-on panic and needed to get to my friend before I lost it completely. Not knowing the details was killing me.

It was midnight on a Friday, with doctors and nurses calmly managing the chaos of a packed emergency room. As I waited for information, my heart in my throat, a regular flow of people came through the doors in police custody. Zip ties restrained their hands and feet, and their grunts and moans grated on my last nerve.

Gush had been well received in town, and my blood ran cold at the chaos it had created. Are they all addicted to the drug?

I couldn't think about it right now.

The *Gushers* clogged the system, and I had trouble getting a nurse to help me. Cal wasn't checked in through the Emergency department. I convinced them I was family, so they allowed me into the ICU.

On the elevator, I heard two orderlies talking in hushed tones about a fat, balding man who showed up an hour ago on the helicopter platform, butt naked. He caused quite a stir, mainly because he was holding an equally nude male in critical condition with a stab wound to the upper chest. The chubby fellow had disappeared before the police could question him.

"I'm sure he did," I mumbled under my breath. It was the only smile I had in me tonight.

Gideon must have hauled ass across the bay because it sounded like Cal was here mere minutes after leaving the boat. We'd done our best. He was in the capable hands of the medical team, and the relief was overwhelming.

I learned that they had operated to close the deep wound. Cal was barely out of surgery, so I couldn't see him.

When I stopped at the ICU desk, the nurse took one look at my deathly pallor and tear-stained face and let me sit outside Cal's room. She was terrific, giving me a kind look and promising to keep me posted as soon as I could go in to see him. Knowing he was just a few feet away calmed me somewhat.

It was an hour before I got the okay for a short visit. I stepped into Cal's room and froze in shock. Tubes and monitors ran everywhere, and my vision blurred. The nurse saw my face, grabbed me, and hooked her foot under the corner chair to pull it close. She held my shoulder while I put my head between my legs, then went to get me a drink of water.

Cal hovered at death's door, and here I was, adding to the problem. I was so pathetic.

I kept my head down for a while longer. The nurse left when my color improved. As the door snicked shut, I heard a faint voice in my head.

"You need to toughen up, Eddi."

I shot to my feet and almost fell flat on my face. Grabbing the table, I worked my way over to Cal's bed.

He had an oxygen mask over his mouth, and his eyes were hooded as if someone had scrambled his brains. But he smiled at me. At the dopey look on his face, my waterworks started again.

"Shhhh, it's ok. I'm ok. Stop crying. I hate it when you cry." His voice was so faint in my mind that I could barely hear it, but it was there.

Stress was riding me hard. I longed to hug my friend, but that was a no-no, so I held his hand instead. In whispers, I told him Viggo was dead and that he was safe here. He gave me a groggy smile when I told him Ronan and Bacchus would stay with me and not to worry. I didn't share any gory details, of course.

He briefly widened his eyes when I told him how he got to the hospital.

"Gideon never gives anyone a lift. I feel special." His soft laugh made him wince.

"Just rest," I said in a soothing voice. "We'll have plenty of time to catch up later. The nurses will let me stay for a while, but if they kick me out, I'll return in the morning."

Cal nodded slightly and closed his eyes.

A nurse came in, adding a bag to the assortment on his pole before nodding to me. She motioned that I had five minutes, then left.

I let out a long, slow breath to try and relax. I could see Cal was back to his "normal" shade of pale, much darker than the scary blue shade I never wanted to see again.

I squeezed his hand, and before I left, I told him how much I loved him.

"You were so brave, Cal. You've got to stop rescuing me. You're making me feel like a high-maintenance woman."

He smiled, but whatever the nurse gave him worked, and he quickly faded out.

When his breathing was soft and regular, I left as quietly as possible, taking one last peek before softly clicking the door shut. My head swam as weakness and nausea battled for top billing, and I leaned against the wall outside his room.

When my nerves settled down, I stopped at the nurse's station, and luckily, the doctor had arrived to grab a chart.

"That young man is lucky," she said. "A penetrating stab wound is usually a guarded prognosis. I would also love to know how he ended up with scorpion fish stings all over his torso."

She gave me a pointed look over the rim of her glasses.

I chewed my lip and shrugged. "I wasn't with Cal when it happened."

I saw the suspicion in her eyes and wondered how many shifters she'd treated over the years without knowing it.

"Strangely enough, the wound had already started healing from the inside out. It shouldn't be possible to heal that quickly. I've never seen anything like it in thirty years of practicing medicine."

The doctor searched my face, watching for my reaction.

I gave her a warm smile. "Thank you for saving Cal's life, Dr.—" I looked for a name tag—"Rosenblum."

That wasn't a lie. I was more grateful than she could ever imagine.

The doctor shrugged. "Calvin should be sitting up by tomorrow, but he'll be here at least another day for observation and wound treatment." She nodded to me and, picking up her clipboard, headed to her next patient.

It was three a.m., and Key West was still hopping, so my taxi took half an hour to arrive. I waited on a bench by the hospital doors and let the warm breeze from the ocean calm me.

I thought about the night Ronan saved me from death's door as I bobbed along on the gulf stream. And the time Tara, the lionfish shifter, poisoned me with a toxic stab to the throat.

Both times, Ronan was there. Looking like a bus ran him over. Tired and weak. My sudden improvement when he was near. My head wound from the boat prop that healed in hours. It all made sense to me now.

"Magic," Ronan had said. At the time, I thought he was teasing me.

And now I knew his secret. Ronan had quietly used his power to heal me every single time. He had never said a word or asked for any thanks. The implications blew my doors off.

I had underestimated him. I had judged him and found him wanting. The magnitude of what he'd done for me...? I was a complete jerk. He was a much better person than me and wasn't human. I didn't deserve HIM.

Our issues were far more complicated than being a good or bad person, but relationships are never cut and dry. Now, I was second-guessing every decision I had ever made where Ronan was concerned.

Is it possible that he was telling the truth all this time and my feelings for him were real? Because his actions didn't seem like someone after a quick *tangle*.

Did it even matter anymore? In typical Edaline fashion, I screwed it all up. I wanted to punch myself for my sheer stupidity.

When the cab dropped me off at the docks, I hurried down the long jetty to the *Wanderlust*. After what happened tonight, I was terrified of shadows again, but that wasn't the reason for my haste.

I passed a spot halfway down the jetty with a gaping hole and several broken boards. Gideon must have landed there.

When I got to my slip, I saw everything was sparkling, and the dock rinsed clean of blood. There were eight deep punctures in the deck boards where Gideon had taken off with Cal, but you wouldn't notice them if you weren't looking.

I scrambled over the railing of the *Wanderlust* and opened the door to the cuddy cabin. I held my breath, but when the light filtering through the windows revealed an empty bunk, I blew it out with a swear.

My heart did a high dive into my shoes because, deep down, I'd hoped he would be waiting. I wanted to hold him and thank him for saving Cal's life. Most of all, I wanted to tell him I was sorry.

Tired and aching, my eyes gave up the fight to control the tears. I felt raw. I stripped down to my undies and crept into bed to nurse my bruised soul.

"Man, you sure cry a lot, don't you?" I jumped, then turned to see Miri peering out of the darkness in the corner.

"Whoops. Sorry, Queen Edaline. I forgot. Can I assist you in some way, my Liege?"

I gave her a wet smile. "Yes, Miri, you can. I release you from your royal servitude. Never again, please. I'm not a Queen, and I don't deserve your respect. That's how you can help me."

Looking around the cabin, I saw that Miri had made herself a small bed in the cubby hole under the helm—the exact spot that once held an orange flare gun.

"Ok," Miri said, rolling over and pulling the little tea towel over herself. It was the one with the cute sea shells on it.

"I'm not royalty, Miri. I don't help people. I hurt them."

***

I'm not sure how long I slept, but at some point during the night, I heard a quiet thump as someone climbed aboard. But I trusted the wards and was too emotionally exhausted to give two shits. The shutter doors to the cabin slowly opened, and I turned to look. Ronan.

We stared at each other, the silence pressing down on us. I nodded toward the little cubby hole where Miri was sleeping.

Looking over his shoulder, Ronan shook his head with a wry smile. Then he turned to look at me again, a question in his eyes.

I reached out my hand, and he smiled, climbing into the bunk with me. He lay down on his side and looked into my face, his eyes glowing like polished emeralds. He took in my tired, puffy eyes and gave me one of his heartbreakingly beautiful smiles.

"Cal's going to be okay," I whispered. And damn if the tears didn't start again.

I wiped my burning eyes with the pillow slip and looked at Ronan, drinking in his warm, kind expression.

"You saved him."

He nodded, inspecting the details of my face like he'd waited a lifetime to be this close to me again.

"You saved me too. Twice."

Once again, he nodded, his intense eyes locked on my glistening ones. He reached up and combed my bangs with his fingers.

Moving his hand down, Ronan wiped the tears from my cheek with his thumb. Then, putting his arms around me, he pulled me to his chest, tucking me neatly under his chin. With a deep, contented sigh, he snuggled into the covers beside me, his voice whispering in my mind.

"I'd save you a thousand times, Edaline."

***

I awoke to the sun filtering through the portholes. I was alone in bed if you didn't count the angry-looking Sea Sprite sitting on the pillow beside me, her legs crossed and her foot tapping.

"Oh, I see you're awake, *your whoreness.*"

Sarcasm was on tap this morning. I yawned so hard that tears sprouted from the corners of my eyes.

"What's up, Miri?" I prayed that she got to the point more quickly than usual. I wanted coffee, a bite to eat, and a shower, in that order. Then I would go and see Cal.

My heart lurched at the thought of him alone in that bed with all those tubes and monitors.

"You had a Syreni in your bed last night, you shameless trollop!" She spat that last part out with a wet hiss, and some of it got on my face. *Eww.*

"What century were you born in, Miri? The eighteen hundreds? No one says trollop anymore. Technically, it's my boat, so what I say goes. But ok. I'll bite. What's your point?"

"The same Syreni who tried to eat me?"

I laughed. "Miri, he wouldn't have eaten you. He was just teasing you."

She gave me the Sea Sprite death stare.

"Besides, nothing happened, and I like him. You know, the way you liked Cleatus. I'm only human," I said with a wink.

She put her hand to her face, her finger tapping her lips. "*Well...* Cleatus WAS pretty hot, but we never 'did it.' I did have dirty thoughts about him, though. And I would have done wanton things to him if we weren't physically incompatible."

I grimaced at the image and tried to un-hear her words.

Miri shrugged. "Ok. I can accept you as a shameless strumpet if you accept the same from me. Let's get coffee!"

I was still stuck on the "if you can accept the same from me" part when I felt the boat bump again.

I thought it was Ronan, so I whipped my clothing on, vowing to change the undies after breakfast. A giddy laugh rose from my chest.

It wasn't Ronan I saw when I bolted onto the stern deck. It was Bacchus. He held up two cups of coffee and gave me a warm smile.

"Ronan will be here soon. Cappuccino?"

I liked him already. Grabbing the cup and sitting back in my captain's chair, I sipped the delicious, rich brew. I closed my eyes and gave a lusty moan of appreciation.

"Mmmm, oh my word, Bacchus, this is amazing."

I licked the whipped cream off my lips with a moan, and when I opened my eyes, he was staring at me with his mouth open. Then, reaching over to the chair beside him, he quickly grabbed my dolphin beach towel and threw it over his lap.

I turned fourteen shades of red and hid my grin behind another sip of the delightful brew.

"Sorry. It's been a while since I've tangled," Bacchus stammered, his face molten. "I could have, though. Last night. With nine girls." He crammed his lips together and stopped talking.

"Nine, huh? Wow. That's impressive." I smirked into my coffee.

"There was a tenth, but that was a different bar. And she was high as a kite on *Nectar.*"

He looked at my worried expression and fidgeted in his patio chair.

Bacchus bit his top lip. "She wouldn't count, right? You don't get points if the girl isn't sober."

I raised my eyebrows at him, and Bacchus started tapping his bare foot.

"Sometimes humans confuse me with their damn scoring system," he growled, then quit talking and pretended to watch the boats coming and going from the harbor. He glanced at me several times, but thankfully, the conversation came to a screeching halt. I shook my head and smiled into my cappuccino.

"Where did you see the girl high on Nectar, Bacchus? They're calling it *Gush* now, by the way."

"Ronan and I went to a nude bar, and I met her there. I didn't think much of it at first because, you know, *nude*. I didn't expect her to go wild, so I didn't discourage her behavior until she climbed me like a coconut palm."

The handsome Syreni explained what happened in great detail, and I'm sorry to say I couldn't keep a straight face. Picturing Ronan at a nude bar was hilarious. I bet he drank water and kept edging toward the door.

As I sipped my coffee, I asked him, "How long do you think it takes Nectar users to return to their senses? Humans are having horrible reactions to this stuff. People affected by it were packed into the hospital last night."

Bacchus shrugged. "I have no idea. But the well-muscled guys at the door couldn't control the crazed woman."

I frowned, thinking about Cal. "Gideon must stop Hex before the whole thing blows up and your *Shoal* is exposed. Or even worse, they start retaking Syreni males."

Bacchus growled. "Well, there's one less *asshole* to cause trouble. Viggo is feeding the fish right now. I wish we could have made him suffer more before killing him."

"*Wait*. So the ugly shifter from last night is the one who trapped you and Ronan out at Coffin's Patch? He was in our diner a few days ago. He told me to give Ronan a message—that he'd see him again soon."

"They're obviously planning on catching more Syreni to keep their supply going. Ronan and I will warn the *Shoal*. But we are already taking precautions. No one goes anywhere alone."

Bacchus took a giant swig of his cappuccino. His eyes went wide, and leaping out of his seat, he spewed it over the railing into the bight.

"How do you drink this *cacas*? It's so bitter!" He made a face, opening his mouth and sticking out his tongue. Looking into his cup, he dumped that over the rail as well.

Movement caught my eye. Ronan was jogging down the landing. His glowing green skins shimmered in the sunlight, his tanned, chiseled body a head-turning delight. I smiled when I saw the other female captains shooting him appreciative looks. He caused quite a stir, but Ronan had no idea of his effect on women.

"Good morning, Eddi," he said, giving me a broad smile as he bounced over the railing. He had something in his hand.

"This is for you." He held out a chain.

My eyes went wide, and my hands started shaking.

"It is proof of my *praesidium*." He gave me a solemn look, and when I glanced at Bacchus, his eyes were wide.

"I'm not sure what that means, Ronan."

Ronan leaned closer, his voice quiet. "A vow of protection."

I opened my hand. It was the beautiful pearl he had given me for saving his life. It dangled on the end of a solid yet delicate chain, tucked safely into an ornate filigree cage of gold. Just above the pearl was a slim golden rectangle designed to accept the chain. A sparkling emerald glittered inside the rectangle. It matched Ronan's eyes.

Speechless, I looked up at him. My mouth moved like a fish, opening and closing.

"How did you find my pearl? I hid it in the cabin."

I liked to have it with me because I was a sentimental fool. Whenever I was alone, I would take it out and stare at it, running my fingers over its smooth, irregular shape and thinking of Ronan.

"I felt it when you were sleeping. If a Syreni gifts something of the sea to someone special, a sliver of their magic goes with it. It gives off a small signature that our senses can detect if we are close. I felt its hiding place."

"It's breathtaking, Ronan." *Someone special.* I looked into his glorious green eyes and felt warm tingles across my shoulders. Then I stared at the pearl and ran my fingers around the gold filigree cage.

"How did you get the chain so quickly?"

Ronan took it from my trembling hands and hung it around my neck, doing up the clasp for me. He was so close that I smelled the sunshine and salty breezes on his warm skin.

Pulling back, he admired where it nestled just below my throat.

"I stopped at a jewelry shop and got lucky. The little cages are popular, and they had many. I liked this one best." He grinned, his eyes sparkling in the sun. "It matches my eyes, so you'll never forget me now." He winked.

I felt his eyes on me as I stared down at the pearl, the pinks and creams glowing in the sun. I was speechless.

"I brought the jeweler an enormous bag of pearls I collected in the Gulf. He seemed very happy. He gave me paper money as well as this chain."

Looking at my cup, he added, "I know you like it, so I sent Bacchus for coffee."

When I didn't speak, Ronan started to fidget.

"Do you like the necklace? I can get another if it is not to your tastes."

I picked it up off my throat and looked at it again, the emerald winking at me.

Having fought back the rising tears enough to speak normally, I said, "It's perfect, Ronan."

"I asked the jeweler to ensure it was strong enough to take some abuse. I don't imagine it will have a peaceful life around your neck."

CHAPTER 14

Cal was sitting up and looking much better. He was still weak as a kitten, but his color returned to its pale version of normal. He would be in the hospital for at least two days.

When the police questioned him, he told them the stabbing had happened downtown and that a strange man had come to his rescue. It wasn't a stretch to say he didn't remember because his recollection was, in fact, hazy at best.

Cal told them he couldn't describe his assailant because he wore a mask, although he gave them Viggo's body type. The police knew there was more, but Cal was tight-lipped, so eventually, they gave up. There wasn't much they could do about his silence. They pressed him on the scorpionfish toxin, but he played dumb.

James was harder to convince. When he called me for a charter update, I told him what happened to Cal. He showed up at the hospital an hour later. He was so distraught about Cal's injuries that James threatened to scrap the Key West charters and return the *Wanderlust* to Davy Jones Locker. Cal convinced him it was a "wrong place, wrong time" scenario.

I'll never forget the gray look on James' face when he left the hospital room, his lips pressed into a hard line. He looked like the weight of the world sat on his shoulders.

"He doesn't believe us, does he?"

I was biting my nails, worried that James would change his mind and pull the plug on our Key West location.

"He'll settle down. He knows we tend to get into ridiculous situations, right?"

Cal picked at the sheets on his bed, his expression tight. He sighed. "Not to change the subject, but how are you managing with the *Wanderlust*?" Cal hated being unable to protect me. Why he worried was beyond me, considering he was in the hospital recovering from a near-fatal knife wound.

"I'm fine, so stop fussing, Cal. The wards are rock solid, and Miri is keeping me company. She's an absolute pit bull when it comes to watching for strangers. I couldn't have a better guard. Her chatter drives me nuts, especially when she's invisible. It's like she thinks I can't hear her in that form. The other day, I had to lecture her because she growled—out loud—at someone walking by. The strange look they gave me was comical, but still."

Cal laughed, then winced. "I'm not going to say I told you so. But I did. Just saying."

I visited him when I could, bringing him a bag of salt and canned mackerel from the grocery store. I even popped into a pet store and got a package of dried mealworms so he had some protein to snack on. It was meant for iguanas, so I banked lots of future joke material when Cal decided they were the bomb.

I threw myself into work, taking out as many charters as possible. Garrison Bight was busy, so I had to keep my eyes peeled. Plenty of boats in the marina were rentals, and only some credit card captains knew how to handle them properly. Some days it was close calls and bumper cars getting out of the harbor.

Soon, I had a good fishing spot for yellowtail snapper, and customers returned to the dock smiling and holding up their fish for photos. Captains live for catching fish and making people happy.

Ronan and Bacchus watched over me every evening. I noticed them the first night that Cal was in the hospital, sitting on the wooden bench on the pier across from the *Wanderlust*. I brought them food and drinks and picked their brains on how the search was going. Ronan was taking the whole *vow of protection* thing seriously.

Key West was a small island, and the lack of a solid lead was hard to understand. The Syreni focused on finding Cain, determined to wipe out the monster responsible for holding their males hostage and stealing their nectar.

I worried about the brothers. I tried to help the search after work every day, even stopping by to see Phoebe. I wondered if her corner got regular dealer traffic, but Phoebe hadn't seen anyone suspicious since the night we met.

There was no sign of Gideon, although Ronan mentioned they met with him several times to coordinate the search. Everyone worked in pairs for safety.

A pair of Key Deer shifters spotted Cain one night by the market. They trailed him, but being slightly over four feet tall in their shifted form, they lost him in the crowds.

So far, between the Syreni, the Gryphon, and the four *Others* living on the island, they had come up empty-handed. Cain's wards were exceptional because there were no other sightings.

The night before Cal left the hospital, I clashed with Miri. The little blue pill made the boat feel claustrophobic because she was constantly into my things. I didn't blame her. She was bored, and the 24' deck didn't give her much room to entertain herself.

Things came to a head when I found her pulling out all my *"ooh—pretty"* underwear and spreading it all over the cabin. I bit my tongue and packed everything back in my bag, but I would strangle her if I didn't get a break soon.

After work, I showered, put on cute shorts and a tank, and walked around the Garrison Bight docks. The vast network of slips quickly filled with crab and shrimp fishermen returning from their day and Fishing Charters showing off their catch. I enjoyed the fresh ocean breeze in relative safety as I walked along the wooden planks.

I took my time, enjoying the hustle and bustle of the docks. Before I knew it, the sky was a Van Gogh painting of mandarin and magenta, the first stars popping into view on the distant horizon.

Walking along the jetty, I admired the assortment of million-dollar yachts, colorful cigar boats, and well-fitted fishing vessels. There were terrific houseboats, too, done up like floating mansions. One had a huge covered deck with an enormous happy face smiling skyward.

I drooled over a multi-million-dollar Spectre AB 100 yacht. Italian-made and lightning-fast, the blood-red hull sported a detailed graphic of a *Black Widow*. Very cool. I heard these were some of the fastest yachts on the ocean. Even at a hundred feet of length, at full speed, they could stop and turn on a dime. I was drooling and would have given anything to see inside.

Looking at the exterior living space gave me goosebumps, with plush couches and polished wood floors on the outer deck. A set of curved stairs led to a world-class living space above, where darkened glass windows allowed privacy.

I was in the wrong tax bracket. People with boats like that lived in a cutthroat world of financial games, which gave me some comfort. It wasn't me. I was plain and simple, like my boat. I shouldn't even be looking.

As I came to the end of the bight, the blazing tension of my reality snaked back into my mind. Almost losing Cal had shredded my nerves. If I thought about it too much, I fell into a nasty slump, so I tried to think positively and keep busy today.

With a heavy sigh, I turned to head back to the *Wanderlust*.

Something caught my eye. I looked across the small street that curved past the end of the bight and noticed a Bar perched on the street corner. It looked like a local hangout. A neon blue, pink, and green sign glowed with a welcoming invitation.

"You're in the right place," I read aloud, laughing.

Feeling rebellious after my spat with Miri, I crossed the street and stepped up, opening the door. My mind dove back into the pleasant hum of its extended holiday.

The sign had a palm tree, so it must be the right place, right?

I was thrilled to find the tail end of a great Happy Hour. I pulled up a stool and ordered three of their house cocktails just under the wire. Specials are rarely a full pour, an excellent excuse to stockpile. At least, that's what I told myself.

I was spacing out, enjoying the lack of annoying chatter, and slurping my fruity drinks when a tall, athletic guy pulled up a stool. He smiled at me and ordered a whiskey sour.

Right away, the soft brown eyes and shiny dark curls struck me. Handsome, and that five-o'clock shadow would feel wonderful on my thighs. I looked at my drink, and guilt slashed through me when I pictured Ronan's handsome face.

Whoa! I should go easy on these.

He smiled, and we exchanged pleasantries. His name was Charles, but his friends called him Charlie.

I laughed and made off-color jokes that would have been embarrassing if I hadn't felt so buzzed after that first drink. I smirked at the handsome gentleman behind the bar wiping glasses. He gave me a blank look.

Maybe the bartender thinks I'm cute and gave me a full pour.

I'm not a drinker, but for some reason, I didn't care today. I guzzled the last drink and ordered another. Giddy at my freedom, I lived life large. Throwing caution to the winds, I ordered number five.

I turned and, with a bit of work, focused out the window. Across the bight, I could see the Wanderlust bobbing at her slip. I was so close to my boat that it felt safe to let my hair down. Besides, Cal would be back tomorrow, and I'd have to *behave*.

I was probably slurring my words and shooting six guns of horrible jokes, but I didn't care. This illegally handsome guy laughed at all of them, which was hot as hell. Ronan always laughed at my jokes. Thinking of him sent a stab of guilt through my chest, but the handsome dude reached out and touched my arm, and I shrugged it off.

The longer we chatted, the more my heart fluttered at his charming smile. Those brown eyes were mesmerizing. With a long pull on my cocktail, I realized I wasn't following what he was saying, and I snorted, spilling my drink.

"Sorry, can you say that again? I'm having some retention issues at the moment." I burst out laughing and almost fell off my stool.

Charlie smiled, and at his pleasant, understanding expression, I felt the irresistible urge to bend over and stick my tongue down his throat.

I shook my head because Charles was speaking.

"You're fine, Eddi. I'm the same way. When things stress me out, a nice drink in the air conditioning can take the edge off." He tipped his drink against mine, and I put my hand out to touch his arm, missing entirely.

I decided that six was my limit and ordered one more drink. Charles was pouring on the charm, and chatting with a plain old human was nice for a change.

I couldn't stop looking at his handsome face and wanting to run my fingers through those curls. Damn, this guy was making my little soldier clamor for a big canon. I clamped my thighs together, but the raging girly boner was distracting as hell.

Charlie leaned over and whispered in my ear. "You are so lovely," he said, and I felt his whisper slither down my spine and knock my soldier's helmet askew.

"WHOA," I said. I felt out of breath from the intensity of what was happening in my shorts. "You're pretty intense, Charles."

The flirting continued for a few minutes until I realized my poor lady purse couldn't decide if it wanted heavy petting or a trip to Tinkle Town to drain the tanks.

"Excuse me, but I need the ladies' room." I chugged down the last of number six and got up. I had to grab the bar to balance, and Charlie smiled again. Damn, if his expression didn't unleash a tsunami in my shorts. Clenching my legs tight in case of premature tinkling, I laughed out loud. On unsteady legs, I headed for the bathroom.

"Take your time," Charlie said. "I'll wait for you, pretty lady."

I broke a world record getting to the can, and after relieving myself, I stood in a stall trying to catch my breath. What was wrong with me? I didn't even know this guy. I felt woozy, horny, and a little out of breath. I thought of Ronan and burst into tears. It was time to split.

I splashed my face and opened the bathroom door, and Charlie was there.

'Are you ok?" he asked, leaning in.

I looked up, and his beautiful brown eyes were dancing with humor. He couldn't be all bad. He couldn't help it if he was too hot for his own good.

Irresistibly drawn to him, I reached up and touched his face. His stubble felt terrific under my fingers. He spoke, and his voice throbbed with a sex appeal that matched the pulse in my shorts.

"Let's go somewhere a little more private," he purred, running a hand up the back of my thigh and softly squeezing my butt. "I can help you with your little problem."

He smiled at me and reached forward to massage me through my shorts.

My hips shot forward, and I swear something dribbled down my leg. God, I was randier than hell, and the lust pumping through my veins made sweat trickle down the small of my back on its way to the ground.

We stepped out the back door into the small staff parking lot. The next thing I knew, his tongue was down my throat, and I was unzipping his pants. I was so fucking aroused right now that I thought I might come without any help from my handsome stranger.

Somewhere in my fevered mind, I knew something was wrong.

Who was this guy? Where's Ronan?

I turned my head to try and see the Wanderlust, desperate for some coherent thoughts, but Charles pulled my chin back with a gentle hand and gazed into my eyes.

Ah, fuck it. I didn't care. All I cared about was getting some release. I lifted my leg and, pushing into Charles' hand, kissed him harder. His fingers slipped past my panties and tested the waters down south. I was all for it, my loud moans feeling strange in my throat.

Something sharp was stabbing at my ass cheeks. Wait, my shorts were down. How did they get down to my knees?

I looked up at the dark angel before me, who was unzipped and pushing his shorts down his hips. His impressive erection popped free, and he gave me a luscious smile, putting my hand around his cock. Kneading my bare bottom with skillful hands, he pulled a breathless groan through my tingling lips. My nub was throbbing, and I needed him to get into my business, and now.

Ouch! Something stabbed me in the ass again. I reached back to rub my bare butt, and again, something pricked the back of my hand.

"HEY, now!" I opened my eyes to see Charlie frowning. His eyes were darting around, making me dizzy for a second. I let go of his neck.

"Fuck off!" He hissed. Ooooh, Charlie was ma-ad.

Hey, is he mad at me?

"Hey, asshole!" I slurred. "Don't talk to me like that!" Frowning, I reached down and pulled his fingers from my traitorous pussy.

Looking down at the back of my hand, I saw blood trickling from a little puncture there. I was so confused.

Why am I out here with this guy?

My head felt like it was full of cotton, and I looked at Charlie suspiciously. He gave me a crooked smile. And just like that, I was ready to go again. Holy jumping jelly beans, my panties were on *fire*.

I reached up to kiss him again, but something blue slapped his face with a fluttering smack. I tried to focus, and what I saw sobered me, the heat in my veins fading away with a hiss.

Charlie had a tiny blue sword buried in his eyeball right to the hilt.

I fell backward in shock, landing on my bare ass. Scrambling to get up, I yanked up my shorts and backed away from the sexy stranger. I was panting so hard I could barely breathe.

Charlie's mouth was wide open, and a strange muffled sound reached my ears. I tried to understand what was happening, but my cognition department had closed for the day.

Gods! I bent over and groaned because my pussy was blazing with such a breathtaking heat that it was all I could do to pull myself upright. The pain of it helped bring things into focus. I stood up, my mind clearing.

Like that, I heard the racket before me as if I had pulled out a set of earplugs.

Charlie was screeching and clutching his eye with one hand while waving the other at whatever was buzzing around him. The blue thing paused to hover, a vicious look on its face. Wait. Was it trying to pull the sword out of his eye?

What the–?

Miri! It was Miri, and now she had her feet on his head, pulling his hair with tiny clenched fists. Charlie was trying to grab her out of his curls, and the one eye I could see was glaring with rage. Red flashed in his pupil, and then it was gone.

With a lunge and a lucky grab, Charlie had her. He had a hold of my Sea Sprite, and she was screaming!

I didn't know who, or what, this fucker was, but he was hurting Miri.

Fear for her narrowed my focus, and a black rage ignited somewhere in my brain. My head felt like it was going to explode as I rushed him. I wanted to kill him, but my sane half opted for standard self-defense, and I kicked him as hard as I could in the neuticles.

His breath shot out of his mouth like an airbag going off, and he doubled over, releasing Miri. Tears were streaming from his eyes, and the guttural words blasting out of his clenched teeth were not human.

Nope, not human, and that glowing red eye looked *pissed*. Uh oh.

Free from his crushing grip, Miri fluttered almost to the ground before catching herself. Then she hovered before me, bobbing erratically.

My hearing wasn't working well, but I read the gestures and got the hint, so we hit the bricks together. Miri popped out of sight, and I hobbled out of the parking lot and onto the side street, buttoning my shorts as I half ran, half waddled. My poor vagina was paying me back for the whole "Let's do Happy Hour" decision.

I looked around, and for a minute, I couldn't remember where I was. I rubbed my forehead in confusion, but Miri popped in momentarily and pointed, her lips moving in her terrified face. My eyes lazily tracked her finger, and I saw the Wanderlust. Relief flooded through me.

Piecing things together as I hobbled, I realized I had narrowly avoided unprotected sex. With a total stranger. In a parking lot!

I'm not a drinker, and I'm not promiscuous. Realizing that the asshole must have roofied me, I almost turned around to go and kick him in the nads again. But my common sense was coming back online, and Miri looked a little worse for wear, barely able to hover.

As we headed down the Bight, I stopped to catch my breath, ducking between the towering crab traps for privacy. I wanted to get a good look at Miri's injuries.

The liquor made me feel warm and winded, and my pussy was complicating things by roaring with arousal. I didn't know whether to grab a fire extinguisher or my vibrator.

Miri landed on an overturned bucket. Twisted at an awkward angle, one of her wings didn't work correctly. Panting like a dog, it was unclear whether she was angry or scared. I leaned my butt against a stack of traps and bent over, putting my hands on my knees, trying to catch my breath.

"Are you alright?" I huffed. "Oh my god, Miri, thank God you showed up when you did. I was about to *f*—"

I didn't finish that sentence because the look on her face said it all.

"Yes, you were. And you're welcome. I can't have my Queen shagging some guy in a dirty alley. Not on *my* watch!"

Miri looked down at where I was rubbing my crotch with the palm of my hand, and she smiled, then covered her mouth with her hand to stifle a giggle.

"I'm fine, in case you're wondering," I grumbled.

She looked over her shoulder at her crumpled wing, trying to smooth it out. "This will take a few days to heal, dammit."

I looked her over between deep nostril breaths.

"Oh my god, *Miri*. Your wing! It's broken!"

The finely laced membranes were intact except for one, bent in half and somewhat mangled.

Seeing my anguished face, she grinned.

"Talk about going *nuclear on the nads*! He won't walk right for a month," she tittered. "Seeing you kick that Incubus in the oysters was worth a tattered wing!"

It was like turning the mothership, but my brain was finally catching up if you didn't count being intoxicated.

"Incubus? Don't you mean *Succubus?*"

I went pale at the memory of the bitch that almost drained Ronan to death.

"No, silly. Succubus are females. Incubus are *males,* and they use sex to feed off the energy of *females."* She crossed her arms and gave me a dirty glare. "Females *dumb enough* to follow them into dark alleys, that is. What were you *thinking*?"

Things were making more sense now. I looked at Miri and felt terrible for ditching her at the boat.

"Ok, an Incubus. This world of yours needs an instruction manual. And for the record, it was a parking lot."

Miri rolled her eyes at me.

"I'm sorry, alright? I didn't know! He walked in and sat beside me, and the next thing I knew, you were stabbing him in the eye!"

I put my hands over my face, my eyes misting over. What the fuck just happened? I almost—and Ronan. Oh my god. I almost cheated on my Syreni. I burst into tears.

I felt Miri land on my shoulder. She patted my hair with one tiny hand until I stopped sobbing.

"It's ok, toots. There's no stopping them. Once they latch on, the only thing that can save you is ... well, *ME!*" She giggled and took a bow.

I stood up, having caught my breath. "Thank God you showed up. Thank you, Miri. I can't say it enough. You're a lifesaver." I wiped my eyes and shuddered a sigh.

Miri beamed, then frowned. "You shouldn't have gone alone, Eddi. And now I lost my sword. Gadzooks!"

Her little pout chased away the clouds, and I grinned, waggling my eyebrows. She glared at my expression.

"Don't worry, my little swashbuckler. I brought you some swag!" I opened my bag and pulled out a little blue sword and a pretty pink parasol. "I saved these for you."

The truth is, I'd ordered a pina colada so I could surprise her with the trinkets.

Miri clapped her hands with delight, and tucking the sword into her tiny leather belt, she grabbed the parasol and started fluttering around with it.

And just like that, she was back to normal as if nothing ever happened. My Sprite was emotionally unbalanced.

Still, I had to laugh at the bang-up Mary Poppins impression she had going on.

CHAPTER 15

As we headed back to the *Wanderlust*, Miri remained invisible but came to sit on my shoulder. I was still randier than a dog in heat, and the constant rubbing from walking made it worse. Miri must have understood female *problems* because she kept giggling at my obvious distress.

"That will teach you to keep your hands out of a strange man's pants!" She started humming the theme from Jaws, and I resisted the urge to make her fly back to the boat without me. She'd learned how to run the laptop, the brat.

"You should find someone to scratch that itch," she said. "If you don't, it will take you weeks to recover."

With a twinkle in her eye, Miri motioned to the little pier across the Marina from our boat. "Maybe they can help?"

I looked where she was pointing. Ronan and Bacchus sat on the bench, staring over at the *Wanderlust*.

I laughed at the absurdity of it all, and when they turned at the sound, their shock was apparent. Yes, they'd been guarding an empty boat. I'd have to tease them after I wasn't walking like I needed a pickle party.

I walked down the pier toward them, trying not to let my discomfort show.

"Great security skills, guys. Too bad you missed the Incubus." I was laughing, but it must have been the booze because they didn't think it was funny. They were up off the bench in a flash, their faces thunderous.

"Where!?" Ronan's fangs peeked out from under his top lip. Bacchus eagerly searched for something behind the bench, popping up with his log full of nails. I chuckled at his attempt at discretion as he ran back to us, holding the weapon beside his leg. He looked like a dog ready to chase a stick.

I hadn't thought this through. If I had, I would have realized the whole *getting roofied* thing wouldn't go over well with two Syreni who recently suffered a similar experience. This night had been bad enough; I didn't want them rushing to my defense and one of them getting hurt or, God forbid, killing someone.

"Whoa, whoa, down boys. It's fine, Ronan. Miri came to my rescue. I'm ok, it was a close call, but she got me out of there."

It didn't help. Between the brothers' stiff and silent staring contest, complete with rumbling snarls, I knew they spoke privately to each other. The sounds coming from Ronan's throat made me nervous, and I decided an angry Syreni was terrifying.

I flopped down on the bench, Miri landing beside me. We exchanged a look. Informing them hadn't been a good plan, it seemed. Bacchus broke from Ronan, tipped his head to me, and took off at a jog in the direction I'd come.

"Is that wise?" I shot a worried look at his brother as he disappeared into the night.

Ronan bit out, "Any Incubus with half a brain in his head will run for his life from an angry Syreni. Their magic doesn't work on *males*. If Bacchus finds him, that Demon won't feed for a month."

I poked Ronan and gave him a silly smile.

"Well, I may have already taken care of that problem. I kicked him in the man sponges, so he'll go hungry for a while." I slapped my hand over my mouth and giggled.

Ronan cocked his head at me.

"I see you're still feeling the effects of the alcohol, Eddi. Among other things."

Buzzed out of my tree, but more urgently, horny as hell, the throbbing in my vag reached epic proportions. It made me crazy.

Miri piped up. "That leech won't be seeing so well for a while, either. I stuck him right in the eye with my sword. I rammed him so hard, it went all the way in!"

Ronan laughed. "I owe you an apology for teasing you the other day, Miri. It's a miracle you happened along when you did. Thank you for watching out for Edaline."

I looked at the sprite and frowned. "Just how DID you end up being there, Miri?" Fortunately she showed up, but we had to be so careful no one saw her.

"I was with you the whole time, dummy. You didn't have a clue, though." Miri frowned and put her hands on her hips.

"I couldn't very well do anything after he latched onto you, could I? I kept quiet and watched for an opening. I'm scarred for life now, thanks." She mimed putting her fingers down her throat, and Ronan frowned and looked at me.

Miri grumbled, "I tried to get into the bathroom with you, but the door was too quick. Then I thought you'd wise up when he lured you outside, but you fell for it hook, line, and sinker."

She inspected her nails, then at my ashamed look, she relented. "I'll give you a pass this time since you didn't know he was an Incubus. Just don't let it happen again. It's *humiliating.*"

Ronan didn't like what he was hearing, and with a murderous expression, he thumped down beside me on the bench, glaring in the direction his brother went.

"Are you alright, Eddi? As he inspected me, Ronan's eyes glittered with malice in the darkness. "I know what it feels like to try and shake off their magic." When I squirmed, his look softened.

"Are you in pain ... down there*?"* He didn't look the slightest bit embarrassed as he gave me a visual inspection of the awkward kind.

Alas, my inhibitions had flown with the fourth cocktail, so my mouth opened, and stupidity ran out.

"God, it's uncomfortable! I need to find Buzz to help me out."

Ronan looked confused, then with a growl, he snapped, "You don't need this male, Buzz." He thumped his pectorals, reminding me of a gorilla.

"I will help your release if it is needed."

I snorted, but he didn't like that, judging by the hurt look sweeping his face.

"Ronan, Buzz isn't a man. It's a—" *How did I put this so he'd understand?*

"It's a pet name for my vibrating *TOY*. One I use, you know, down *there. For ... womanly ... pleasure.*"

Gods, how was I having this conversation with a straight face? Oh, right. Still tipsy.

Ronan seemed relieved he wouldn't have to kill some guy named Buzz. And oh, goody, the fangs were gone. That was a good sign.

"I know how difficult it is, Eddi. There was a reason why you didn't see me for a month after the Succubus attacked me. I healed from the physical trauma quickly. It was the sexual distress that was the problem. I know how you feel right now, trust me."

"Whoa! You were like this for a MONTH? That must have been hard." I giggled again.

Oh my God, shut up, Eddi.

Ronan gave me a strained look. "It was terrible. Even after I regained my strength, I couldn't go anywhere because I was always—" He sighed.

"I needed a release every few hours at first. I spent two weeks just trying to manage the uncontrollable need."

A searing bolt of jealousy blasted through me, the alcohol making me bold.

"Who the fuck is she? Was it *TARA?* I'm going to pull her fins out!"

Blushing red, Ronan laughed. "I'd rather keep my fins, thank you very much."

"What? *Ohhh, sorry.*" I was embarrassed for him, but inside, I did a happy dance.

Ronan looked away, his face an adorable shade of maroon.

"It was horrible. I was raw from all the 'overhandling' while I recovered. Succubi magic can be dangerous. All five of us were in a mess, but it was worse for me because I received a near-fatal dose."

Ronan looked uncomfortable, staring down at his toes like they fascinated him. He frowned and fidgeted, shooting me sideways looks, then gazing across the bay at the Wanderlust. A stricken look marred his handsome face.

Then it dawned on me. He knew I was there and witnessed the Succubus attack. He'd hidden it until now, but his humiliation was on full display. Pain shot through my chest. My proud Syreni, ashamed. I'd put that night behind me, but Ronan still carried it with him.

I swallowed, my face flushing with regret. I had been so tough on him. How difficult was it for him to come and see me that day on the Wanderlust, knowing what I had witnessed? And then I dumped him. My god, I'm an asshole.

My heart ached for him, and reaching up, I ran my fingers through his hair. He pushed his head into my hand and closed his eyes. The sweet gesture of affection warmed my heart, and goosebumps flashed across my skin.

Unfortunately, it also woke up the pantie pirate. I yelped and threw my knees up, grabbing onto my crotch. I couldn't help it. My skin beaded with sweat, and I cursed a blue streak.

"Oh my god, Ronan, it's excruciating." I was making faces and rubbing myself, but I didn't care. My dignity had bailed a while ago.

I tried to sit up but ground my throbbing core into the bench at the sensation. I crossed my legs to stop myself, but a moan slipped out at the friction between my vag and the slats.

Ronan, to his credit, didn't seem weirded out at all. He knew what I was going through.

"How bad is it? Have the stabbing pains started yet?"

My head snapped around. "What do you mean, *stabbing pain?*"

I was not into pain, especially down *there*.

"Is it ok if I touch you?" Ronan moved a little closer to me and took my hand.

"Define *touch*," I said, raising an eyebrow.

Ronan exhaled, and his expression showed genuine concern.

"I know this sounds wrong, but I can make it feel better, Eddi. I can help you release the energy, and the pain will ease."

There was passion and kindness in his eyes. I also saw a hopeful look.

Yes, I just bet you can "help" Ronan.

Ah, what the hell. In for a penny, in for a pound, and all that. I'm not Sandra Dee, and my penis fly trap begged for sustenance. And I was supposed to be easing up on the poor guy, right?

"I almost sullied myself in a parking lot with a stranger. What difference will it make?" I said with a snort. And then I saw his face. His mouth tight, Ronan turned his head away, staring out into the night. Right, I did it again.

Eddi, you don't deserve him and need your butt kicked.

"Yes. I mean, YES! I'd be honored if you'd help me." I grabbed his chin and turned his face back to mine.

Our eyes met, and for a moment, we were silent. His eyes searched mine, and I smiled. Something raw ignited between us.

Our lips crashed together in a flash, his kiss lighting me up like the fourth of July. Wanting him and not having him brought forth a monumental reckoning, and not just in my pants. Hidden under a pile of ash in my chest, a tiny dormant seed swelled, sprouted, and flowered with a shockwave of joy.

Our tongues were getting creative, and our breathing came out in sucking gasps, but my hands? They grabbed at him like a Black Friday shopper when the doors opened.

"UUUHHHH *HEM*. This little scene is entertaining as hell, but aren't you two forgetting something?"

Tearing my lips from Ronan's, I looked up, gasping for air.

Miri was on the bench behind me. Crossing her arms and tapping her toe, she frowned at us, raising one delicate eyebrow.

Ronan and I broke apart, and he hung his head on my shoulder and groaned. I joined the chorus.

"Miri, unless you want to witness something that will make your eyes bleed, you should head back to the boat."

I looked at Ronan.

"Ronan is *helping me*...."

We grinned at each other and burst out laughing.

Miri was gone, a sparkling blue comet sizzling across the water.

"I'll bet he is, you *tramp!*" Her shouts echoed across the water as she fled.

And then Ronan's lips were on mine again.

My vagina was about to explode, but Ronan was on it. Whether it was my soaking wet shorts or the heady scent of my arousal that made him hurry, I don't know, but he didn't waste any time.

My buttons popped and the pretty peach-colored shorts were off in a flash.

The night air was a blessed relief on my flaming pheneuter for a second or two. Ronan slid off the bench onto his knees, gently guiding my knees over his shoulders. The look he gave me made my pussy flush to a whole new moisture level. And then his tongue worked divine magic that made me clench my knees and butt cheeks in a synchronized spasm.

I grabbed the back of his head and sobbed in delight. I was oblivious to the pain in my ass, compliments of the wooden slats on the bench. Uncaring about the branding that would mark me tomorrow, I threw my head back and writhed under his frontal assault. I pushed against his mouth, chasing some friction.

"NNNGGGGGHHHH," was all I had to say about his warm, busy tongue.

Ronan lapped and licked and nibbled, diving in deep and then circling, the timing steady and even and perfect. At some point, a slippery finger joined the fun, sliding in and out into all the right places.

My sexy Syreni knew exactly where to focus his attention to make my hips surge. I lasted about three minutes, then nearly ripped out two handfuls of his hair as I came. The yowl that left my throat probably turned heads in Georgia.

Panting in a rather unladylike way, my quivering arms flopped lifelessly onto the bench, all the air out of my balloon. Ronan raised his head to give me an erotic, smug smile. If he hadn't just rung my bell with a clang, I probably would have shoved his face back down there for dessert.

Ronan rested his head on my lap, his warm hands rubbing over my hips in a soothing caress.

"Does that feel better?" he murmured.

I opened my mouth, emitting a dry little croak. I licked my lips, and, clearing my throat I sighed, *"Does it ever."*

I was surprised when things didn't get awkward. Being with Ronan felt as easy as breathing, and the natural feel of it choked me up.

Ronan helped me stand because the awkward position had stiffened my back. He pulled on my shorts because my hands were shaking and my arms weren't working properly. Zipping me up, he grinned.

"Let me help you back to the boat, Eddi."

I thought he was teasing, but when I went to take a step, I almost did a faceplant.

"What the hell is wrong with my legs?" I yelped.

Ronan gave me a gentle smile. "It's a side effect of Incubus magic. It generates a release so powerful that it temporarily numbs the core muscles. You'll be fine by morning. I don't think he had you in his thrall long enough to do any long-term damage.

"My god, Ronan. I had no idea. You must have gone through hell!"

I turned to look at him. His beautiful eyes were luminescent, looking at me as if I were the only thing in the universe that mattered. With a spasm of bittersweet remorse, I burst into tears.

Taking me by the shoulders, he pulled me close while I sobbed into his chest. He was warm, and the firm, soft skin under my cheek was comforting.

"Shhh, it's ok, Edaline. Emotion is another side effect of Incubus magic. You'll be ok soon. I've got you. Let me walk you back to the boat."

Taking my hand to steady me, he guided me down the docks. At one point, he slipped an arm around my shoulders and pressed a kiss into my hair. The gesture made me cry again.

We finally made it back, and Ronan climbed in first, putting his hands around my waist and lifting me over the railing like I weighed nothing.

I stiffened. His eyes searched mine, looking for the source of my suddenly tense expression. When I gave him a nervous look, he asked, "What's wrong, Eddi?"

"I have to pee! Like, really bad. Can you give me a second?"

Ronan chuckled but helped me to the shuttered door of the cabin and waited politely outside, ready to help if I fell on my face. I was appalled at myself for underestimating his kind, caring side. I was getting a serious wake-up call tonight.

Ronan stayed with me, and twice more, he helped ease the stress of a ridiculous level of arousal. At one point, I thought of firing up Cal's ice maker, but the bed was already wet enough.

I would never admit it to anyone, but the second time was just for fun. I think Ronan suspected, judging by the grin on his face when he came up for air.

Spending the night with him was magical. I woke once, staring at his sleeping face like a lovesick kitten. I marveled at the tendrils of a growing connection curling around my heart. For this brief moment, I was content.

In my mind, an irrational fear gnawed at my foolish pleasure. I cared about him deeply. I could no longer deny it. But in my life, happiness was never permanent. Deep down, I was afraid.

CHAPTER 16

Cal grinned as I helped him onto the *Wanderlust*, and finding his sun hat, I plunked it firmly on his head, pulling the string under his chin. I mothered him, and he loved every second of being the recipient this time around.

I learned today that shifter bodies heal quickly, and Cal was recovering at warp speed—something about their godly bloodlines boosting metabolism.

He was still weak, and I'm sure he hid lingering fears from the trauma. Time heals all wounds, as they say. And Viggo was now fish food, which helped.

The sun was high in the azure blue sky, the ocean was at its turquoise best, and people were out and about at the marina, so Miri stayed hidden. I could hear her hovering in front of Cal, her fluttery wings giving her away.

"Did you miss me, Miri?" Cal teased.

"You're joking, right? Now I'll have to choke down large doses of your sappy good nature every single day." Miri had been annoying me all morning, rattling about Cal finally leaving the hospital. I think she missed him.

Turning the stereo on at the helm, Cal laughed at her, then went to the stern to sit on his favorite bench seat. Relaxing on the cushions, he sighed and reached for a bottle of sunscreen from a cubby hole. Smiling to himself and humming to the music, he started slathering it over his pale skin.

"Thanks for picking me up, Ed. I really missed this. Getting time in salt water these last few days has been tricky. The nurse found me in the tub room that first time, with the water up to my stitches, and she lost her marbles. She told me I might pass out and drown," he said with a wry smile.

"Thanks for bringing me those Epsom salts, by the way. It really helped."

Even when he was healthy, Cal couldn't be away from water for more than two days. When badly injured, he couldn't breathe well in his human form without a daily saltwater dunk. Being stuck in the hospital must have been horrible for him.

"I need to get into the ocean. Could you take me out to a sandbar so I can shift? It'll be fun. We can get some quality time together and catch up."

Guitars and Tiki Bars came on the radio, and he smiled, stretching his arms out along the back of the bench and crossing his ankles.

"You're in luck, Octo-boy, because I know someone who needs to get in the ocean too. *ME*."

I went down in the cabin to ensure everything was secure, then came up and checked the tide chart.

My only trip today was in the afternoon, which worked perfectly. Miri was so excited that she popped into view for an instant but, at my shocked look, blinked back out. "Miri, be careful!" I hissed. I looked around, but no one was near the boat.

I fired up the Yamaha motors and felt a little thrill when I heard their smooth rumble. James had outdone himself with these 300 four-strokes. Even used, I'm sure they cost a fortune.

I pulled the bow and stern lines from the cleats and pushed off. Cal was grinning from ear to ear and tipped his head back to feel the sun. The breeze tickled my face and lifted my bangs as I settled into my chair.

Spinning the wooden captain's wheel, I steered the *Wanderlust* into the open channel. I heard a giggle before me, and I knew Miri was sitting at the helm. She sounded as happy as I felt.

Once on the open water, I eased the throttles forward so I didn't jostle my invalid. Glancing over my shoulder at Cal, our eyes met, and my heart swelled at the look of joy on his face.

We had rough seas around Key West a few days ago, so instead of fishing, I took my customers snorkeling off one of the small islands not far from shore. Plenty of sandbars were out there, and I'd found a good spot between some small mangrove islands where we could swim away from prying eyes.

With the tide coming in, I had enough depth to anchor the Wanderlust close to the sand bar safely. There were plenty of things to see along the sandy bottom, so I was glad I brought my snorkel gear.

As I pulled in, the calm water looked delightful, the sheltered cove the perfect spot for Cal's first swim since the stabbing. The horizon was visible in narrow gaps between the fledgling islands of mangroves, the ocean meeting the cloud-dotted sky in an artist's palette of blue. The view was spectacular.

I set the anchor and jumped the railing into the waist-deep water. Helping Cal off the boat, I eased him into the ocean beside me. He stiffened, so I gave him a bear hug.

"It's my turn to take care of you, Cal. Just be a good boy and humor my mothering side for five minutes, okay?"

He smiled at me and hugged me back, and in a flash of light, I saw his white Octopus form sink to the bottom and crawl away. Clearly visible under the sparkling seawater, he crawled over the washboard of sand.

It used to freak me out when he switched forms because I had no idea about Others. It was amazing how a brush with death changed people. I focused on all the positives in our friendship these days, tossing the rest away.

As I watched him creep into the shade of the mangroves, I plucked his sun hat from where it floated and threw it over the railing onto the *Wanderlust*. With a grin, I fished his shorts from the water and hung them on the railing. Poor Cal was so white he'd fry without his big sun hat; my face would fry if he lost his shorts.

There wasn't just shade under those mangroves. There was also a forest of curved, thick roots sheltering a smorgasbord of tasty sea critters hiding from predators. Watching Cal hunt for his lunch was a welcome return to normal for me. I prayed our comfortable old life was just around the corner.

Out of nowhere, a splash and a tidal wave of water rolling past nearly knocked me down and startled me out of my thoughts. I whirled around to defend myself.

I had to stifle a snarl because behind the mini tsunami was an enormous Gryphon who snapped into view and flopped down in the shallows.

"Hello, Gideon. Is it mandatory that you scare the life out of me every time you visit?"

Gideon rumbled, shaking his dripping, eagle-like head. Sticking his long feline tail out of the water, I noticed as it waved in the air that it looked more tiger than lion. That made sense to me because didn't lions hate water?

Gideon gave me the Gryphon version of a shrug. Then I heard him speak in my mind.

"Promiscuous mother, remember? Favored tigers to lions?" His throaty laugh sounded like air bubbles in a drain.

"I thought now was a good time to check in on Cal. How is he doing?"

Gideon's eyes scanned our shallow hideaway, and seeing Cal under the mangroves, he relaxed into the water.

"He's good, Gideon. Really good. He'll be fine soon. He's moving around under his own steam, but the doctor said he couldn't do any sudden twisting or lifting for a while. Cal tells me that being *Other* amplified his healing."

Gideon turned his head and looked at me, and as direct as always, he said, *"I understand an Incubus attacked you."*

"Yes, it was pretty embarrassing, honestly. Miri saved me. I'm fine now." I turned fifty shades of red, remembering Ronan's "assistance."

"Ah, yes. Ronan 'assisted' you. Needing a release after an Incubus attack can be quite a problem."

Taking pity on my red face, Gideon added, *"You aren't the first one to have those issues after being exposed to their magic."*

DAMMIT. Why did I always forget that Gideon read minds? I slapped my hand over my face, trying not to give him a flashcard of memories from my tryst on the bench with Ronan. I must have failed miserably because Gideon started to laugh, making a deep booming noise in my head.

"I'm glad I amuse you, GRYPHON. Thanks for popping around long enough to embarrass the hell out of me. Let's never do it again, alright?"

Like a car swerving across a four-lane highway, I blurted, "Why didn't you tell us that Cain was a vampire?"

I may never be alone again with this gigantic wanna-be cop. It was now or never.

Gideon's golden eyes drilled into mine, his bus-sized frame rigid. He reminded me of a dog that was considering eating your face.

Slowly, he stood, the water sluicing from his feathers and coat. Lowering his head, Gideon narrowed his large eyes, took two steps toward me, and stopped, his tail stiff. Head down, eyes boring into mine; he looked ready to pounce.

I swallowed—*hard*. I'd decided that this was a bad idea and was about to start babbling like an idiot when he spoke.

"You did not need that information. It was irrelevant."

His voice slipped quietly through my mind, the blunt finality of his words shooting me down in flames.

Gideon flopped down again with a splash, causing another surge that made the *Wanderlust* dance on her anchor rope.

I rubbed the back of my neck, more than a little freaked out about his aggressive display. Maybe Cal was right, and I was pushing my luck with the big bad bird kitty.

"When were you going to tell me? A vampire almost killed me, and a demon nearly killed Ronan. We're on your side. Why don't you tell us anything? We're supposed to be helping!"

He rolled on his side, lifting one wing and preening it with his sharp beak. I watched his tongue—forked, how *weird*— running up and down the feather.

"You ARE helping, Edaline. What have you been up to in Key West?"

Gideon turned to stare at me with those golden eyes, and I saw an intense glow in their depths, reaching out to me and calling to me. I answered a bit too quickly.

"I met a witch named Phoebe, and she did some kick-ass wards for the Wanderlust."

I slapped my hand over my mouth, realizing I'd just thrown Phoebe under the bus. I felt violated by his intrusion into my brain. I couldn't help myself. I had a death wish because my voice was snarly when I lashed out at him.

"Gideon, stay the FUCK out of my head!"

My voice was overly shrill, and I knew I should tone it down with the Enforcer. But I was getting riled up, and Cal wasn't here to stomp on my foot.

The Gryphon surged from the shallows, seawater pouring from him in sheets.

"You are Immortalis. I am the Enforcer. As your Knight, let me make this very clear, Edaline. YOU answer to ME."

He tilted his head and growled, the feline noise sounding odd out of his eagle throat.

I needed to settle down before things got any uglier. It was a good thing Cal wasn't listening because he didn't deserve the stress right now.

I couldn't stop, though. Not now. I had to get answers, and I was confident that Gideon had them, every single one tucked away to be pulled out like currency when he needed them.

"You know more than you're telling, Gryphon. You know everything, don't you? Except where to find Hex and Cain, of course," I snapped.

"You knew Ronan was in Key West hunting for Viggo, didn't you?"

He didn't answer, so I switched to telepathy, my eyes on fire.

"Maybe you should look in the mirror, Gideon, to see who's responsible for Cal's brush with death."

Gideon surged toward me, water flying, my insolence the final straw. But before he reached me, he hesitated, shutting down and turning toward the mangroves. The waves eddied around my calves as I swallowed, my eyes following his stare.

"Speak of the Devil." The long tiger tail flicked, and he glanced at me, his eyes briefly narrowing.

Seeing Ronan walk toward me through the shallows, with dripping hair and his bronze torso sugared with sand, my anger melted away like butter in a hot pan. I couldn't decide whether to slap myself or clap my hands like a toddler.

Jeepers, get it together, Eddi.

Then I remembered Gideon standing in the water before me, picking up every pervy thought racing through my noodle. He looked over his shoulder at me, and I swear, he winked.

Ronan walked straight to me, Bacchus pausing by Gideon and flopping down in the water. Beneath the ripples, a long blue-green tail unfurled. Wow, these guys could change forms *fast.* Impressive.

I smiled at Ronan, who gave me a lusty grin and reached out to inspect my necklace.

"It looks beautiful on you, Eddi."

I blushed. "Thank you, Ronan. It was a lovely gift."

I slipped down in the water and pulled him down beside me. His tanned chest was beaded with salt water, and with him being so close, I itched to reach out and touch him. I couldn't help thinking back to last ni—

I looked up to see Gideon watching me.

"Oh, will you *stop?"* Can't a girl have some privacy?"

Bacchus burst out laughing. "There's no such thing as privacy near a Gryphon, Eddi. It's why they make excellent Enforcers."

I blew up my bangs in frustration. "Ya ya, I get it. So what's the news? Has anyone found any leads on Cain or his crew?"

No one had heard anything. It was highly unusual, considering Gideon constantly cloaked himself, watching everything as he moved across the rooftops. Gideon's voice rumbled through my mind. From their expressions, I knew everyone heard his thoughts.

"Wild parties are going on seven days a week now. The drug is spreading like wildfire. The human police cannot manage the issue and called reinforcements from the Upper Keys and the mainland. It's not good news."

Gideon rolled over, and another wave rolled past.

I had to ask. "To the human Police, it's just another drug, right? Why do you care what happens to humans? How would *Gush* alert anyone to the *Others*?"

Bacchus shrugged. "Humans may not be strong, but they are smart. Maybe they will look at the drug too closely. They will hunt for the source if they discover it is a natural substance. If humans find out about *Others*, we'll all pay for it in ways you can't imagine."

Ronan held my hand, but he looked at the beautiful horizon through a break in the mangroves. He turned towards me, his face grim. "If Hex and Cain sell their stockpile of stolen Nectar quickly, they will be aggressively searching for more. From what Viggo said to you the night we killed him, they are already doing so."

Ronan turned to the Gryphon. "It sounds like they're planning to get humans hooked on *Gush*. If they do, who knows how big this could get."

"None of those things are good for our people, nor is it good for humans. We may not have an obligation to help them, but by getting rid of Hex, everyone wins."

Bacchus shook his head. "I still can't believe our Nectar is becoming such a monstrous issue. Leave it to humans to find a way to use it for the buzz."

His lips tipped up at the corners, and Ronan shot me a sideways look. I blushed, remembering the day we tangled and shared a love bite. I reacted strongly, but not to his Nectar. He still doesn't know I'm not entirely human. I needed to rectify that as soon as possible.

Gideon's voice in my head startled me. *"There is other news you all must hear. I have proof that the Incubus that attacked Eddi works for Hex's drug ring. He targeted you, Edaline. It was deliberate."*

At my shocked look, he added, *"Bert can come and go because he is not memorable. He hears things that others might not."*

Huh. I never thought about it like that. That sloppy garden gnome Glamour of his might be a good idea after all.

"I'm thousands of years old, Edaline. The hunt for Hex is not my first rodeo."

Glaring at his snark, I said, "If Charles was after me, they must know where I'm staying. That bar is a few hundred yards from the *Wanderlust*. Are you suggesting they're watching me?" Goosebumps ran up my arms. "That's a bit freaky, Gideon. I'm not thrilled about being the bait. Thanks, but no thanks."

"I am aware, Edaline. Ronan and Bacchus watch the boat at night, and I also have Others on duty. You will never see them, but they report to me. If Hex or Cain make a move, I will know."

I looked over at Bacchus and almost jumped out of my skin. A long, thin tentacle rose into the air behind him, and when it was above his head, it shot forward and wrapped around his neck. With a yank, it pulled him back under the water. His tail splashing wildly, Bacchus surfaced, but there was no sign of Cal. I laughed, remembering his comment about his octopus being fast.

Looking around our private oasis, I realized it was too quiet. Someone was missing. "Has anyone seen Miri?" A bright light flashed under the water behind me, and Cal returned to human form. Wiping the salt water out of his eyes, I saw his pupils were still horizontal black pills, like a goat.

"I thought she was on the boat?" he asked, grabbing his shorts from where I hung them on the railing.

I looked around and saw no sign of Miri, and my nerves started jangling. Rising from our sandbar party, I looked over the boat railing and called her name. There was no answer.

Panic choked me up, and I slapped my hand over my forehead, my eyes darting around the sandbar. Where was she?

Even Cal looked worried. "When was the last time you saw her?"

"When we left the bight. She was invisible, but I heard her laughing. She was sitting on the helm, giggling like a teenager." I climbed aboard the *Wanderlust* and went down to look in the cabin. Opening the shutter doors, I got the surprise of my life.

Miri was in the middle of the bunk in her birthday suit. But she wasn't alone because there were a matching pair of blue moons down there. And to say I'd caught her and the male sea sprite in a compromising position would be an understatement.

CHAPTER 17

"You said you would accept my trampy behavior!" Miri screeched. "Remember the night I listened to you go two rounds with the Syreni?"

My face flamed. Was Miri awake for that? *Oh boy.*

Ronan appeared at my shoulder, quickly turning away from the visual.

"I'll help Cal," he choked, scrambling over to the railing to lift him onto the boat. What a fiasco.

"I'll give you five seconds to 'disappear him.' I'll talk to YOU back at the dock, OK?"

Miri nodded, and she and her blue stud disappeared. But not before he winked at me and mimed a phone at his ear.

Rolling my eyes, I turned to help get Cal settled. The party was over.

Way to go, Miri.

Bacchus waited for Ronan in deeper water, rubbing at the sucker marks on his neck and shooting impatient looks at the *Wanderlust*. Ronan came up behind me and slid his hands up and down my arms. Pulling me back to his chest, he whispered, "Can we get together later?"

His deep, rumbling drawl in my ear made goosebumps skitter down my arms, and I shivered. Ronan chuckled, running his warm hands up and down and chasing them away.

"I would love to get food for you, Edaline. There is a place that serves raw meat from creatures of the sea, and it's close to your boat. Have you seen it? I keep overhearing humans say that it is wonderful."

My eyes lit up. I'd often walked past the Sushi joint and considered going there with Cal. I loved seafood.

"That would be amazing, Ronan. But I have to clean up the *Wanderlust* after my Charter and grab a shower."

I looked into his gorgeous green eyes. I couldn't believe we would spend some time together doing something as mundane as eating. It would be amazing.

"I'll meet you at our bench when I finish work, OK? It's on the way." I almost reached around and kissed him, but Cal was there, and the Gryphon stood in the water beside the boat, watching intently.

No, not watching. Listening. In my *head.*

"YOU PERVERT," I thought-screamed at him.

The Gryphon shook his regal head and saturated neck feathers. His enormous wings thumped as they snapped open, extending to let the sea breeze dry them. I'd never noticed the enormity of those monstrous flappers, Gideon's wingspan almost as long as my boat. It made sense that lifting a 3000-pound Gryphon took some power.

With a hop and a few determined strokes of his wings, Gideon lifted above the Grady-White, his sopping wet tail swinging so close that I jerked my face out of the way. Then Gideon streaked skyward, blinking out of sight. He must have seen me shoot him the finger because I heard his chuckle flutter through my mind as he disappeared.

Ronan hopped over the railing on the deep side of the boat, slipping under the water and changing forms with a flash of green. His tail left a wake on the surface as he swam to Bacchus. Then they were gone into the shimmering cerulean blue of the gulf.

Under the shade of the canopy, Cal relaxed in the seat beside me. The sun was getting hot, and the salt itched as it dried on my skin. It was time to get back. I had to get ready for my afternoon trip.

I fired up the motors, which grumbled to life. Man, I loved that sound.

Cal turned up the radio, and the tropical rhythm of *Key Lime Pie* drifted through the helm. I smiled at Cal, and he smiled back.

The trim whined as I lowered the motors, then easing the throttles forward, I turned us out to open water. Listening to the island vibe of Kenny Chesney, we headed across the Gulf to Garrison Bight and our responsibilities.

***

It was the longest shift of my life. The people were terrific, the kids were adorable, and we caught many fish. But all I could think about was returning to the marina, changing, and spending time with Ronan. It felt like Christmas Eve.

We'd come so far, with many ups and downs, and now I would enjoy a good old-fashioned date with him. It would be strange, but I knew it would be amazing.

With all that I'd learned about my place in this new world and Ronan showing me his rock-solid character, I was no longer worried about him being Syreni. Hell, I was at least part Djinn, so how could I judge?

Tonight, I would tell him I wasn't human. The idea of broaching the subject made my nerves jitter, but Ronan cared about me. It would be fine—I hoped.

Cal showed up when I docked, lending a hand to passengers and helping me filet the catch. It was a big haul, so we both stunk like fish when we finished. As we hosed off the boat, the glowing red sun slowly descended to the horizon.

"Are you running up to have a shower? I know you've got a hot date tonight," he said, his eyes twinkling.

At my worried frown, he said, "I can finish up here, Eddi."

Cleaning the deck was a simple job, so I agreed. I felt very protective of my friend these days, but dragging hoses wasn't strenuous and wouldn't get him into too much trouble.

"You'll hang out on board after you're done, right? Promise me you'll stay behind the wards tonight, so I don't have to worry while I'm out."

Cal laughed. "Sure, but can I have a shower first?"

I threw my rag at him, ducked into the cabin to grab my toiletries and towel, and headed to the main building. Miri was on guard duty and followed, invisible, but I heard her wings humming all the way to the showers.

Liveaboard customers had full use of a shower house and laundry near the office. It was well thought out and made things simple for those staying long-term. The amenities were basic. Four stalls with curtains and a dressing room with a slatted bench and sinks along the wall. It was spotless, and the water was always hot. Nothing was better than a hot shower to scrub the smell of fish from your skin.

The showers were empty. I would enjoy some privacy tonight. Miri opted to sit outside and enjoy the sunset. Putting my things on the wooden slats of the bench, I grabbed my toiletry bag and stepped into the stall. It was heavenly, and I enjoyed a thorough sudsing, getting off the sweat, salt, and scales from the day's adventures. When I rinsed off, it felt so good that I took a little extra time to feel the hot water on my face and revel in being clean.

I might have heard him coming if I hadn't been enjoying myself so much.

***

CAIN

Watching the silver-haired minx enter the showers; lust surged through me. Something about this Djinn half-breed aroused me to a painful level.

To say I was thrilled was an understatement. I'd patiently awaited Hex's nod to add Edaline to my collection of distressed damsels. Dragging my heels and *"waiting for the right time"* had gotten stale. Finally, I would have satisfaction. My fangs were just as enthusiastic, and I had to be careful not to smile whenever someone walked past the Tiki hut where I waited, biding my time.

I finished my drink, and the waitress approached me when I stood. One look from me and her brains scrambled for cover.

"I'm sorry," she mumbled in confusion. "I didn't think you'd paid." She rubbed her forehead and staggered back toward the till.

It was so easy. Being ancient, all you needed were a few tricks up your sleeve, and getting what you wanted was a piece of cake. It's boring as hell after a while. I wondered if that was why I enjoyed killing so much; it helped break up the monotony.

Invisible, the sea sprite sat on a bench by the doors. Vampires were blessed with powerful vision, and shards of her opaque form allowed me to track her. I didn't have to wait long. A second shadow joined hers, the pair eventually wandering off into the shrubs behind the building.

I walked through the bathhouse door and slipped into the women's section. As I was about to turn the corner and duck inside, a man appeared, headed for the men's showers.

The short, portly gent wore flip-flops and bathing trunks and held a bar of soap and a towel. He looked at me, startled, then opened his mouth to tell me I was going the wrong way.

One intense look from me, and he had a stupid smile pasted on his face. Robotically, he turned away, unsteadily wandering back the way he came. I laughed at him, wondering if the wife would complain about his stinky pits tonight.

Stepping into the shower area, I heard her humming away with nauseating happiness, warm water splashing around the two adorable feet visible beneath the curtain.

Pink nail polish? *Hmm.* She'd look better in red.

I sauntered over to her pile of clothing, picking it up and looking at each piece: rags. I would dress her in something much finer—something from Bergdorf Goodman.

There was no time to waste dreaming about all the fun we'd have. I walked to the vixen's stall and pulled the curtain back with a quick yank.

Her eyes widened, and she pulled her hands over her privates, trying to hide. That was disappointing. I always thought she'd be more of a fighter. *Ah,* there it is. I always wondered if her eyes blazed a solid white when angry. I gave her a triumphant smile.

"You're mine now, Edaline. Relax, and you might enjoy this."

I saw her hand go back and laughed as I recalled her pitiful ignorance about the speed of a vampire. I ducked, and the shampoo bottle whizzed past my head, followed quickly by everything she was hoarding in there, one item after another. Every one missed, and I popped up and smiled at her with a mouth full of fangs.

She opened her mouth to scream, and I pounced. I didn't even need to move my feet.

Her mouth froze open, and a bewildered look crossed her face. Slowly, she closed her mouth, and the glowing white of her irises sputtered out. Her eyes took on a stoned look, and her jaw went slack. Finally, her arms dropped to her side, and she swayed a little on her feet.

Easy peasy. I reached up and brushed Edaline's cheek with my thumb. She didn't flinch. She was tantalizing, and I couldn't resist.

I opened my fingers, cradled her neck with my hand, and pulled her to me for a long, slow kiss.

She tasted like victory.

I pulled back and looked over her beautiful features: the perfect nose, the defined cheeks, the chiseled jaw. I loved her dark eyebrows; they set off her shimmering silver hair. Slicked back, they highlighted her exotic face. A beautiful golden pendant caged a cream-colored pearl dangling above her breasts. *Magnificent.*

I felt my sex throb and the thought briefly crossed my mind that Hex would never know if I shared some pleasure with the alluring vixen under my thrall.

With a sigh, I got my head on straight. I didn't need it ripped from my shoulders tonight because if Hex found out I'd double-dipped, that's how things would roll. *Literally.*

I tilted my head, looking into those beautiful gray eyes. I wouldn't lose my head for a taste, though. It was how we collected our samples without so much as a whimper.

I leaned in and breathed into her ear, whispering a few intoxicating words of suggestion. She turned her head for me and tilted her chin.

What a rush, having her in the palm of my hand. That Syreni man-whore would lose his mind if he knew I was tasting her right under his nose.

My fangs were fully distended, the razor-sharp points dripping with an erototoxin, the funnest weapon ever.

I leaned in and, oh so gently, closed my mouth over the delicate curve of her neck. With a confident squeeze, I pierced her skin.

Her artery ruptured under my fangs, and blood flooded my mouth. The taste was sublime. A sigh fluttered across her lips, and for the briefest of moments, I was lost.

Grabbing her shoulders with both hands, I pulled her to me, uncaring that her wet, naked torso soaked my expensive cream suit. The fine cotton-linen blend soaked up the water droplets like a sponge, infusing me with her delicious aroma.

With long, deep pulls, I celebrated the flavor and power that came with each jet of her blood into my salivating mouth. I drank, and the high was instantaneous.

Thankfully, common sense knocked on my skull, and I pulled back, releasing her bruised neck. I pressed my forehead to her temple, sucking in deep breaths as the shock hit me. It had been hundreds of years since I'd come so close to losing control.

I buried my face in the crook of her neck, breathing deeply. She smelled of citrus and summer breezes. I moaned and nuzzled her jaw, licking the wounds on her neck closed and trying not to think about the tent in my trousers.

For an instant, I was angry that I couldn't have her and that Hex was calling all the shots. Telling me what I could do and who I could do it with.

I heard the slow thump of her heart as I cuddled into her neck. The beats stuttered, then raced, catching me off guard. Pulling back, I examined her expression with groggy eyes. Deep furrows darkened her brow, and the look on her face was no longer one of pleasure. After releasing her from my bite, I'd made an error. I'd forgotten to hold the thrall.

She turned her head and stiffened, focusing her hazy eyes on my face. They shot wide, and her mouth opened to scream.

With a heavy-handed push, I hit her with a compulsion, quickly subduing her.

That was too close. My soon-to-be hostage was stronger than I expected.

GET. DRESSED.

Part of me wanted to tell her to bend over so I could get a better look, but some do-gooder human may come prancing in here and call the police. When I got her home, there'd be plenty of time for a bird's eye view.

She walked unsteadily to her clothing and dressed herself. I felt her resistance and smiled.

"I'm more experienced than you, my dear, so don't waste your energy. You'll need it where you're going."

As we strolled like lovers out of the lavatory, she held my arm and smiled into my face. Unwilling, of course. My prisoner mentally kicked me in the groin at every step, but I was stronger than she. Her ferocity made our battle of wills that much more enjoyable, and I smiled at the nails digging into my arm.

I gave a pleasant nod as we passed a couple in colorful tropical clothing, reveling in the knowledge that I forced her to do my bidding, and no one had a clue.

Edaline was seething inside, and her rage tasted like spicy jalapenos on my tongue. She would slice me open the moment I let my guard down. The fight in her was intoxicating.

But I never lose control. Never. And the sooner Edaline figured that out, the better it would go for her.

CHAPTER 18

Goosebumps woke me up, with shivers racking my body and something hard poking me in the ribs. Not a speck of light pierced the suffocating blackness that closed me in. Dressed in shorts and a tank, and minus my shoes, I felt completely exposed.

I tried to lick my parched lips, but my tongue felt like a wad of cotton. I must have been sleeping with my mouth open again.

Wait, did I sleep?

Where was I? Confused, I rolled my head, trying to see something—anything—in the black void surrounding me. My neck felt bruised when I moved. I lifted my hand and pressed down, feeling the tender spot beneath my ear.

I padded my hands over the ground around me. Bricks. I was lying on bricks. I raised my hands above my head, and found bricks there as well. Panic licked at the base of my spine, but I swallowed it down.

Panic gets you dead, Eddi. Where had I heard that?

I closed my eyes, then opened them again. There was no difference. I pulled myself into a sitting position. Except for feeling muddled, and that throbbing bruise on my neck, I was unharmed.

What is this place? How did I get here?

I wasn't dreaming. My situation felt all too real. I closed my eyes and concentrated, grabbing at the wisps of memories that flitted just out of reach. And then, like a hardball to the head, it came to me.

The eyes. Cain yanking back the shower curtain. Being forced to do everything he asked and hating every miserable moment. The fury I felt at having to cooperate. The searing desire—I gasped, and my fingers flew to the bruise.

He drank my blood! That fucking piece of shit drank my blood.

Fangs. I remember the long, white fangs and the pain as they pierced my skin.

Oh my God. I enjoyed it.

The thought made me physically ill. I leaned over and heaved, the bitter taste of bile making me all too aware that my stomach was empty.

I wiped the back of my hand across my mouth, the darkness closing in and making nausea simmer in my guts, even though I was hungry.

RONAN. I was supposed to meet him for dinner! We had a date, and I didn't get there. Despair crushed me at the loss of my freedom, being forced to do Cain's bidding, and missing my first chance to spend time with *him*.

Only after my stomach settled did I remember my conversation with Phoebe. Cain was a Vampire.

"FUUUCK!!!"

I screamed at the blackness around me, all the anticipation, disappointment, and fury giving me extra volume. When I had no more air left in my lungs, I slammed my mouth shut, and dropping my head on my knees, I sobbed.

I don't know how long I sat like that, but it was long enough for my ass to go numb. I heard nothing except the occasional muffled sound of a voice, and once, footsteps passed the room.

Using those sounds, I figured out where the door was, eventually getting brave and rising to feel my way around the wall. Sure enough, it was there.

A handle. I wiggled it, but of course, it was locked.

I explored the room, my eyes open and my head tilted back like I was blind. At this moment, I *was* blind, and my heart went out to anyone forced to experience this day in and day out.

But I *would* see again at some point. And when I did, I'd kill the bastard who did this to me.

The room was completely empty, which didn't offer much help. I ventured across the center of the room. Hands out and waving in front of me, I found a table.

The fact that there was something other than bricks in this godforsaken black hole excited me. How ridiculous. I blamed my lowered standards on being kidnapped and held hostage by a madman who drank blood.

It took me a while to explore the strange table, but eventually I discovered it was a raised hospital bed with stirrups, like the ones they use for pelvic examinations on women.

I wasn't stupid, and the implications chilled me to the bone. Then, I recalled a distant memory; a kernel of brilliance lodged somewhere in my brain.

"Find something, Eddi. Anything. Then use it as a weapon."

After a thorough examination of the table, I hurried back to the wall and sat down, leaning against it.

I must have jinxed myself by exploring and daring to dream of escape, because the door opened and someone threw a switch. I had company. The light that flooded the room blinded me, and I shrank back and covered my eyes, dots dancing at the sudden change.

"Well, well, she's finally awake. Look at you, all tuckered out. Did exploring tire you, Edaline?"

It was Cain. I blinked until my vision returned and there he was. Tall, slender, with dark hair and expressionless black eyes, he oozed a demonic glee as he stared down at me.

"I hope you slept well," he said, coming around the table to stand in front of me.

I ignored him, refusing to answer. Wary and watchful, I tracked his progress across the room. If he tried to drink my blood again, I would fight as hard as I could.

"STAND UP. COME HERE."

The power streaming from him blasted my skin like sandpaper, and I scrambled to my feet, going to stand before him. Angry hisses seethed through my clenched teeth. I wasn't in a daze this time. I was completely aware of each miserable step.

Every muscle that strained against his pull scalded like a son of a bitch. I gritted my teeth and tried to resist, but the white-hot burn was too much. All that pain, and I accomplished nothing. I was standing in front of him, powerless and hurting like hell. I held my chin up and used my eyes to tell him he was going to die.

Cain's eyes glittered as he roared with laughter, slapping his thigh. "I've seen that look so many times before, yet it never gets old." Grinning, he snapped his fingers and did a little tap dance, his cream tailored suit making him look like he stepped out of a 1960s musical.

"I'm so happy you're finally here, Edaline."

He walked around the table, stopping to feel the foot pedals of the stirrups.

"You must be wondering why I brought you home with me."

I tried not to be obvious, but now that the lights were on, my eyes catalogued everything in the room. It was a short list.

The surveillance camera up in the corner was how he watched me, the sick bastard. The wooden door was painted charcoal gray. A piece of weather stripping ran across the bottom of the door. That was it. The room was completely empty, the white brick walls barren.

"I'm not supposed to tell you anything, my dear, but you must be so bored in here." He turned, and with a flourish and a bow, he motioned to the white-painted brick around me. "You aren't just my esteemed guest here. You're going to give me something—and you're going to love it."

He smirked, and reaching out his hand, he ran his thumb along my jaw.

I was screaming with rage and fear in my mind, and being unable to release it into the atmosphere made me choke. I couldn't ask what he wanted from me, because he'd taken my speech.

"OH, my! Look at those brilliant white eyes. You're more Djinn than I realized, my dear. It's a shame you haven't learned how to use your powers. The plethora of possibilities at your fingertips is mind-boggling. The mischief you could enjoy! Why, even Galahad has come to realize the fun we have on the job!"

Brittle eyes turned on me. "I can't believe Gideon hasn't enlisted someone to train you yet. He's not very smart, that Gryphon."

Cain shook his head. "I guess he hasn't realized the progress we've made with our groundbreaking procedure."

I filed away everything he was saying, but my eyes cast darting glances around the room. It was empty besides the table, devoid of clues to my whereabouts or anything to help me escape.

Even the maternity table, which was an ancient gurney style, had nothing under it, just metal legs on rollers.

Cain stood in the corner, looking up at the camera.

"You know, Malus was the one who decided it was your boat we would borrow that night. He was curious and wondered if you'd discovered your powers yet." He turned his head to give me a dark look. "Hex told us to stay away from you."

He shook his head, and in a squeaky voice, he said, "Still no powers yet. Poor, poor Edaline. So lost, and no one to guide her."

Cain turned to me, his eyes hard. "It's a good thing Hex never found out I lost my temper and tossed you overboard. You were being saved for a rainy day, and I would have mucked up the entire plan if you died that night."

He slunk back over to stand before me, and tilting his head, he grinned.

"I'm glad that rainy day has finally come. I've wanted to get my hands on you for so long. Now you'll see what you've been missing all these years."

It's a good thing Cain was so busy entertaining himself that he didn't notice something was missing from one of the stirrups on the table. When I had blindly surveyed the room, it was the only thing I found that remotely resembled a weapon.

A metal L-shaped handle with a 2" threaded bolt clung to my skin inside the waistband of my shorts. When I got a chance, he would get some Miri-inspired eye damage. The possibilities kept me sane as he forced me to stand motionless while he gloated.

"Ahh, I see your clever brain ticking away, looking to hurt me and escape. There is no way out, Edaline. Don't try it. The boss wouldn't like it if I damaged you."

He headed to the door, his back to me, and I felt the compulsion that held me slacken. I waited, knowing he was baiting me into showing my hand.

Cain paused at the door and looked over his shoulder.

"You're a shrewd one, Eddi. But you're not as smart as you think." He spoke to someone out of sight in the hallway, someone I hadn't realized was standing there listening.

"Bring our supplies, Eric. It's too late to start this morning, so I'll need them tonight, after I've rested. Be sure and bring both hormones, and the ultrasound, please."

And with that, he left through the only door leading out of my prison.

***

Time passed slowly in the darkness. I started by gnashing my teeth and thinking up wild plans to escape. Then I gloated, knowing my friends would rescue me, and kill his sorry ass. My hope surged.

After a bit more reflection, I realized there was a reason we hadn't found these bastards yet. It had to be an amazing ward to avoid detection all this time.

Somehow, Cain had erased my memory of the walk here, but I sensed that this place wasn't far from the marina. My friends could be ten feet away and wouldn't know where to find me. All my optimism fled, leaving me in a sorry mess.

After hours of highs and lows, I deteriorated into a depressed, sobbing disaster.

To reduce my mounting anxiety, I did the only thing I could—I worked on the gurney handle. I spent most of the day with my hand under my leg, quietly, slowly, with almost imperceptible movement, sharpening it on the brick.

I knew he was watching. I could feel his eyes on me. So I waited, and slowly but surely, grinding, grinding, grinding, I tapered the threaded bolt into something slightly sharper.

I don't know how long I sat there, my tool keeping me occupied, but I was hungry and dying of thirst. I slept, and when I woke, I stayed where I lay on my side, and under my chest, I scrape, scrape, scraped the bolt.

I heard a noise, and my eyes snapped to the door.

It swung open and slammed against the wall, and from the light of the hallway, I saw someone standing on the threshold. Even in silhouette, I knew it was a male.

His disheveled hair was shoulder length, and as he leaned over, the light shone through the entrance. He was blonde.

He must have been high as a kite on something, because he was holding onto the door jamb on wobbling legs. Breathing through his mouth, he took loud sucking breaths.

"I'm sorry," he said. "I wish I could help you." I thought I heard a sob. "If I do anything, he'll rip me to pieces."

He let go of the door jamb and tried to stand up straight. His legs gave out, and he toppled, grabbing the door handle to right himself, narrowly missing falling to the ground.

I was on my feet in a flash, the gurney handle hidden in my hand. My eyes had adjusted, and I could see well enough to shove this guy out of my way and run for it. He held up a hand as he pulled himself together.

"Don't do it. He's outside, and he's fast. You won't make it."

He sobbed again as he staggered back a step to close the door. Before it shut, I heard him say quietly, "I just wanted you to know I'm sorry. For all of it."

And then it was just me and the inky blackness.

***

RONAN

I was close to losing control of myself. My breathing was ragged, my chest constricted as if a kraken had me in its tentacled grip. Where did she go? I couldn't breathe, and my fangs were threatening to pop through my gums.

Something had happened to her.

After Bacchus and I had finished our daily hunt for Cain, I had been on my way across the docks when I saw her leave for her shower. I waited at our bench, but when she didn't come back, I went looking for her. I found Cal cleaning the *Wanderlust*.

Cal dropped what he was doing, and we immediately went to the shower house. Eddi wasn't there. Miri, who had been keeping watch, was a blubbering mess when she revealed her error. She'd left her post to tangle with the wretched male she favored, and could tell us nothing. I wanted to kill her.

I couldn't be trusted to speak without growling, so Cal questioned the cleaning staff, but we didn't get anywhere with that. It wasn't until we went to the office and Cal threatened to call the police that we convinced the office manager to check the security tapes. I did not know there was such a thing, but I was glad for it. There was a camera in the courtyard by the showers, and it didn't take long to find evidence of her fate.

Eddi entered, and a short time later, Cain followed. Not long after that, they left together, Eddi looking up at him with a smile on her face.

The snarl that tore from my throat made the manager push her chair back in terror. Cal covered for me, telling her that we were engaged to be married and that Eddi was cheating on me with another man. I wanted to kill him for the insult, but I held in my rage and let him handle things.

The woman on duty immediately felt sympathy for me. My foot still throbbed from where Cal ground into it to keep me quiet while he dug for more information.

Another camera at the gate showed them both leaving the marina, turning right onto one of the roads that led to Old Town.

I wanted to rip the monitor from the wall, but Cal whispered in my ear, "If they throw you in jail, it will be over for you in so many ways. You won't be able to help Eddi. So get it together, ok?"

He was right. I needed to stay calm. But Cain had Eddi, and no one knew how to find them. Terror ate at me, and my frantic mind wondered what that sick bastard was doing to her while we were caught in a riptide, going nowhere fast.

Soon, Cal had everyone gathered at the *Wanderlust*, including Gideon. He looked like the Bert creature that Eddi hated with such a passion.

Gideon suggested that since Cain had been seen on the streets around Mallory Square several times in the past few weeks, that was the place to start our search.

Bacchus put his hand on my shoulder. "Stay calm, Ronan. We will find her."

I stared out at the ocean and watched the seabirds, desperately trying to think of a way forward. My thoughts drifting, I recalled the night we searched for her in the ocean. The night that Cain tried to kill her.

I had helped search for Eddi and followed the soft glow of energy that was distinctively hers. I could see it from afar.

I groaned and rubbed my eyes. If she was being held inside a building, that wouldn't work. Then something occurred to me, and I sucked in a sharp breath. Hope surged.

I looked at Cal and grabbed his arm. "I know a way." Three pairs of eyes turned to face me.

"The necklace. I felt it in the cabin below. The chance is slim, but it is possible. If I can get close to her location, I may be able to sense the pearl."

When I saw their expressions, I knew they didn't believe me. I didn't need them. I would find her myself. I stood and motioned to Bacchus.

"I won't sit here and wait for him to kill her. Cal, I need another t-shirt."

Angry, I stomped down into the cabin, and rummaging around, came up with an empty knapsack. I ransacked Cal's clothing and found a T-shirt to cover my brother's chest.

Cal frowned when he saw it.

"You need a different shirt," he said. When I asked him why, he explained that it read, "*Key West, where the Cocks Run Free.*"

I ignored him. I didn't care what it said. I needed to find Eddi.

It was skin tight on Bacchus, and one of the sleeves ripped when he flexed his shoulder. It didn't fit as well as my pink Master Baiter shirt.

Bacchus and I wasted no time stuffing our weapons into the knapsack. It wasn't a great fit, and the ornate handle of the short sword stuck out a few inches.

The wooden handle of the homemade mace was two feet longer than the sword, and being part of an old mast, it looked far too suspicious. Cal was worried it would attract attention.

"Here, try this." He handed us a beach towel, and when I wrapped it around the handle, it didn't look as obvious.

Bert, speaking with Gideon's voice, held up his hand.

"Ronan, I'm not going to stop you. But know this. If you expose the *Shoal* or the *Others*, I won't have a choice about the penalty. You know it is death."

I nodded and pulled on the knapsack. I didn't care about any of that. I needed to find Eddi.

Bert wasn't finished. "I'll take the rooftops and search Key West again. If I see anything, I'll find you. Be careful, Ronan. If you go stomping around town with that look on your face, you won't get far before the human police detain you."

The Bert creature climbed out of the boat, huffing with exertion, and headed off down the jetty.

Cal, his face white, looked at us. "I'm coming with you."

I wanted to argue, because if anything happened to him, Eddi would never forgive me. He was still weak from his injuries.

Cal disappeared into the cabin and came back with a filet knife. It was long and sharp, with a wicked point. He might need it before the night was over.

Bacchus glowered at him, and I knew he wanted to deny Cal's participation in our hunt.

Cal became angry with both of us.

"What? Don't look at me like that. I know how to handle a knife. I won't pull my stitches, I promise. Just hang on one more second."

He felt around in the tackle box near the back of the boat and pulled out a leather sheath. Sliding the filet knife home, he tucked it into the waistband of his shorts.

"I have as much right as you to search for her. She's my friend too. I can't live without her," he choked.

I thought he would cry, and I felt his pain.

The flying blue pain in the fins came zipping around the corner, shrieking at the top of her lungs. She wanted to come too.

I looked at Cal, and snarled. He turned white, and calmly explained to the Sea Sprite that we were going to need to focus all our attention on finding the pearl, and she would be a distraction.

Miri threw a fit.

Cal convinced her that she could use her invisibility to look up and down the blocks closest to the marina. I suspected Cain was not in this area, but it never hurt to look. It was the perfect solution.

Bacchus and I climbed out of the boat and started down the dock, but when Cal didn't follow, we looked back. He was still standing on the *Wanderlust*.

Bacchus rolled his eyes and grumbled, then jogged back and lifted him onto the platform like he weighed nothing.

"We aren't going to need a pram for you, are we, Cal?"

At Cal's downtrodden expression, Bacchus chucked him on the arm.

"Just kidding. Let's go kill a vampire."

CHAPTER 19

RONAN

Old Town was loud for a Monday night, although I wasn't sure it was ever quiet in Key West. It would be difficult to hear the pearl's song with all the human noise.

I felt a momentary loss of hope. But Eddi needed me. I would find her. I had to find her.

My heart was in my mouth as the three of us strolled up and down the streets of Old Town, attempting to look casual as we stopped at every corner. At each pause, I closed my eyes and pulled my chin to my chest to concentrate. Every attempt failed, wasted plenty of time, and frustrated me to no end. Time and again, I wrestled with myself, pulling patience from nowhere by remembering something my mother once told me.

"Ronan, patience is the most important thing for a young Syreni to master. Without patience, you cannot hunt. Without hunting, you won't eat. And without eating, you will die. Remember, patience will save your life, every single day."

I shook my head, and once again, we moved halfway down the block to try again.

On and on, corner after corner, I hung my head. Cal and Baccus would stand close, trying to keep people from bumping into me. It was the hardest thing I had ever done—looking inward, trying to feel the music of Eddi's pearl.

By midnight, we had checked all the main blocks closest to Mallory Square and the Pier. These were the places that Cain had been seen many times.

Humans made strange noises at us when we went past the bars. Cal said they were "cat calls." I would ask him later what that meant.

Key West was a town full of strange people, especially at night. Bacchus and I walking down the street in tights and dumb T-shirts did not register as odd, even carrying a lumpy knapsack with a towel hanging from it.

I was growing tired, but I was as determined as the moment we started. I must find her. It was the only outcome I could accept.

The only area we hadn't checked was the block by a museum for shipwrecks, so we headed there next.

I struggled to keep my thoughts positive, and Cal looked nauseous. Bacchus was all business tonight, the girls holding no interest for him. I think Eddi had grown on him since they met.

I was born to hunt, and so was my brother. Being patient and methodical, and walking for hours did not concern me in the slightest. I would not lose my female.

Cal said we were on Caroline Street south of Duval, and as his words faded away, I felt something tug on my mind. I stopped, peering down a side street with a tightly packed row of houses. The road was gravel and so narrow that it was more of an alleyway, the lack of street lights casting it in shadow.

"What is down there, Cal?"

He looked past me, trying to remember. Cal was not familiar with Key West.

"A bar at the end, and a couple of historic buildings that were renovated and turned into offices, I think. Nothing much. Why?"

I didn't answer. The tugging was like faint music, and it called to me.

I turned and walked slowly down the street, my head cocked and swiveling left and right, searching for the quiet song of the pearl.

Three steps. Stop. Listen. Feel. Then another three steps. It took a fair amount of time to work my way down the street. When I got to the far end, the whispering notes were faint.

Grumbling, I turned and looked back the way we'd come.

"Something is there."

Bacchus and Cal followed my stare, and Bacchus shrugged, turning to follow me back the way we came. Halfway down the lane, the subtle notes called to me as they whispered in my ear. This had to be it.

I stopped and melted into some brush along the side of the path, with Cal and Bacchus following. The humid heat of the night air closed in, and sweat trickled down my spine. Cal scratched and itched as the bugs gathered in the dark stillness of our hiding place. I looked across the lane, and pointed.

"I feel something. There."

Bacchus and Cal followed my gaze. Nothing seemed odd about the two shotgun houses that were so close together that even a car couldn't fit between them.

"There?" Cal asked.

I nodded, my face tight and my weight shifting back and forth as I rose to the balls of my feet. I was ready to bolt into danger, but I held firm. I had learned over the years that going into something wild always had the worst possible outcome.

"I can feel the pearl. It's very faint, but I can feel it. She is there."

Bacchus pulled our weapons from the knapsack and unwrapped them, laying everything out of sight in the thick weeds beside us.

Nothing moved as we stood watching for a few more minutes. It was so dark behind the two houses that nothing was visible—no swing sets, bicycles, or even a line to dry clothing. It was a black void.

I couldn't wait any longer. I stepped out of the bushes, crossed the alley, and headed between the houses.

"Ronan, come back!" Cal hissed, unsheathing his knife. My Octopus friend was scared but ready to fight.

I jogged into the shadowed gap, then stopped, holding out my hand. Something nasty was in front of me. I reached forward, and when heat seared my palm, I hissed and jerked it away.

I looked over my shoulder toward our hiding spot, then turned and trotted back.

"Ward," I said. "A strong, *painful* ward."

He and Bacchus looked at each other, and the smile they shared made me shiver with excitement and reach for my gladius.

***

Cain didn't return for quite some time. The room was dark and cold, and I was at the end of my rope. I'd been working through a plan in my mind, but it was total rubbish, and I knew it. At least it passed the time and helped take the edge off the rage that was building inside of me.

After what felt like a lifetime, the light flickered on and would have burned my retinas had my eyes been open. I covered them as the door swung wide.

"Hello, Edaline," Cain said, rubbing his hands together. "Thank you for your patience. Let the fun begin!"

I heard tinkling glass, and the wasted guy—what was his name, Eric?—followed Cain through the door. He didn't seem totally out to lunch this time, but something was wrong with him. With his eyes down, Eric pushed a cart with an assortment of glass vials and a tall white container with a handle. A styrofoam box was on the bottom shelf of the cart. The label was clear.

Dry Ice? What the hell?

Cain snapped his fingers at me. "Did you hear me?" he bit out.

GET UP. GET ON THE TABLE.

The compulsion punched deep into my abdomen, and I gritted my teeth against it. My face turned red with the pain, but I resisted for as long as I could.

Eric looked at me, and his red-rimmed eyes popped open in shock.

"I said, GET ON THE TABLE."

Gritting my teeth, I dug deep, burrowing into my soul to find the strength to fight him. My foot moved forward in compliance, so I strained my neck and clenched my teeth harder, resisting with everything I had. It felt like boiling water replaced my blood, but I hung on for Father, for Imara, and for Ronan.

Fuck you, Cain.

"You bitch! I said, GET ON THE TABLE, RIGHT FUCKING NOW!"

He snarled, and the boiling water in my veins turned to lava. I fell to my knees, tears pouring from my eyes at the blast of pain in my head. Every muscle in my body clamped down as if in the grip of molten steel.

I laughed, and tears trickled down my face. Resisting his probing, evil mind unleashed a brain-melting agony in every cell under my skin.

Crawling toward him against my battered will, I threw myself to the ground. A scream of anguish tore from my throat as he doubled down on his compulsion.

Writhing in a heap on the brick floor, I covered my head. Every time my hand went down to pull myself forward, I bit down hard on my tongue, the pain briefly snapping me out of Cain's thrall.

Panting, I opened my eyes and looked up. I saw Eric, his bulging eyes darting back and forth toward the door. And then Cain was there above me, bending over with a ferocious scowl on his face.

"Oh, for the love of all that is holy." Cain reached down to grab my arm, intending to drag me to my feet.

With every ounce of strength I had left in my pain-wracked body, I swung my arm up and drove the screw into his temple. My aim was true, and it punched through bone and lodged in his skull.

Glass crashed to the floor, and I heard the sound of running footsteps.

Eric, you wimp.

His eyes rolling, Cain toppled over, landing face down on the ground, blood splattering his cream colored suit.

I was up in a flash, staggering around the puddle of broken glass. Snatching up the neck of a broken bottle, I jumped over the worst of the glass and pushed past the cart blocking the doorway, running for my life. My bare feet left bloodied footprints as I bolted for freedom.

The hallway led to a large room with blackout curtains on every window.

What the fuck?

Door—door…..*there!* I pelted across the room and had my hand on the knob when someone grabbed my wrist and jerked me around.

"For the love of God, just die already!" I screamed at him.

Cain looked at me with the handle still stuck in his temple, hanging down like he had one antler. I stifled the urge to laugh.

It was the shock talking, and I had to keep my wits about me.

Panic gets you dead.

Remembering my makeshift weapon, I swung my arm in an arc, catching the vampire in the throat with the broken bottle in my hand. All of my strength was behind the swing, and as it punched through his skin, I gave it a hard twist. Pulsing spurts jettisoned through the air, the streams painting us both a grisly color.

Cain twisted his upper body, the broken bottle pulling free and clinking to the ground. With a face of stone, his eyes glowed a deep crimson behind the pupils. Cain was on the roof of a flaming penthouse of fury.

He wrapped his hand around mine and squeezed until I screamed. The delicate bones in my hand crunched, and I went to my knees, wailing in agony. Desperate but determined, I opened my eyes and stared into the face of a stone-cold killer.

"You're going to pay for that," he said in a calm, quiet voice.

Blood from his wounds flooded his neck and chest. Oblivious to his grave injuries, Cain continued crushing my hand while I sobbed, screamed, and clawed at him with the other.

Slowly, he reached up and pulled the metal handle from his temple. The sickening crunch of his skull made me gag as bile flooded my mouth.

He pulled me to my feet by the hand without releasing any pressure, and smiled at the unintelligible noises coming from my mouth.

With his free hand, Cain grabbed my hair and pulled my head to the side, his fangs extending so close to my face that I heard the wet sounds they made as they slid through his gums. Through my tears, I looked into his eyes, but I couldn't move.

"This will be worth my punishment," he said. Then he struck.

I experienced a moment of sheer terror, then an erotic sensation flooded my legs and arms, and I moaned. My knees went weak, so he held me up by my crushed hand. I felt no pain, just a heady desire that went straight to my core. I knew he wouldn't hold back this time, but I had no reason to care.

Mouthful after mouthful, he drank me down, his bubbly moans mixing with mine. Slowly, life drained from my body.

My legs no longer worked, and when he let go of my crushed hand to hold me up with both his arms, I felt like a Raggedy Ann doll.

I laughed softly, tears pouring down my face. I wasn't crying because it hurt; I cried because it felt so damn good.

With life stealing swallows, Cain drank. His blood loss, or perhaps his stolen high, made him wobbly. He sank to his knees, pulling us both into a bloody heap.

For a brief moment, I was free and flopped helplessly onto the cold floor. But with a mindless snarl, Cain grabbed me and dragged my limp form across his chest, latching onto the opposite side of my throat to finish what he started.

On and on he drank, his body spooning me, his lips slipping and sliding on the blood covering both of us. Sometimes he sucked, and sometimes he chewed and lapped. I heard the sounds, but I felt nothing except a euphoric high.

I knew this was the end for me. My life didn't flash before my eyes. But as the last of it whispered away, I saw a pair of glowing emerald eyes and felt profound sorrow.

***

RONAN

I knew she was close. I could feel it. The melodic whispers from the pearl were faint, but I was certain. Eddi was somewhere in the darkness behind those human houses, and I was going to get her out and kill the bastard that took her.

As we whispered and argued, trying to form a plan, my heart raced. My Syreni instincts urged me on, whispering, *"Hurry, hurry, or you'll be too late."*

"How do we get past the wards?" I asked Cal.

"I have no idea. Phoebe is staying a few blocks from here, but it won't be quick enough, and we can't be sure she's at her rental. She and her friends might be out on the town."

I felt like choking him, but I knew Cal was right.

"If we go monster truck on that ward, will it break?" Bacchus asked.

"No idea," Cal snapped. "We could try, but that would let everyone know we're here. Eddi was right. We need a cell phone for that *fucking* Gryphon!"

Something caught my eye, and I focused on the darkness between the houses. Something was moving back there.

I grabbed Cal's arm, and everyone looked where I pointed.

A sickly blonde male staggered from between the two buildings. Looking wildly up and down the street, he headed toward Old Town.

The human didn't make it two steps before Bacchus had his hand over his mouth, dragging him to where Cal and I waited in the bushes.

"Nod that you'll stay quiet, or I'll snap your neck right here," Bacchus hissed.

Nodding, his red eyes bulging, the wretched character held his hands up and mumbled something through the hand over his mouth. Bacchus lifted it, and the blabbering started.

"I'm sorry; I didn't know he would hurt a girl. Please let me go," he sobbed.

I looked him in the eye, then grabbed him by the bottom half of his face and asked, "Is she in there? The silver-haired girl! Do you have her in there?"

Terrified, he nodded. "Cain has her. She stabbed him, and I ran. I didn't see what happened after that. Please help me, or he'll tear me to shreds."

I glanced at Bacchus and Cal, then shoved my face so close to the human that he yelped.

"Can you get us past the wards? If you can, we will let you go."

He choked back a sob and nodded, an odd smell from his mouth reaching my nostrils. This human was ill.

Bacchus lifted him under his arm like a surfboard, and everyone dashed across the small alley and ducked between the houses.

Cal sliced all of us with his slender blade, and while the ailing human chanted unusual words, I focused on his bloodshot eyes. Blood trickled from his nose, and he breathed from his mouth. I didn't understand what was wrong with him, but it was clear he had gotten into something deadly.

He worked quickly, and I felt a prickling sensation as the wards dropped.

"Where is she?" I demanded. The young man pointed into the darkness behind the house.

"Show me, then go," I snarled, desperation making my gums ache.

We followed him between the houses and down a path of stepping stones before crossing a small backyard. As we crept through the darkness, it became evident that the black void was not made by the shadows of trees. The inky curtain was magically designed to keep prying eyes away from something secret.

"There." The young man pointed, but I saw nothing.

I took another step, and a door appeared, tucked into a cement porch with two walls and a short roof.

Bacchus dropped the human, who bolted for the alley as the three of us charged at the door. In my frenzy to get to Eddi, I yanked so hard that I ripped it from the hinges.

I'm accustomed to seeing the life and death that play out on the reef daily, but nothing prepared me for what I saw when the barrier fell away.

The white brick of the room contrasted sharply with the bright red splashes on the wall. In a heap on the floor in front of me was Eddi.

She was crimson from head to toe, and lying on something that used to be white but was now a glistening red rag. The coppery tang of blood assaulted my nostrils.

My sword clanged on the bricks as I fell to my knees, my hands wide, afraid to touch her until I discovered where she was hurt.

As I reached for her hand, something moved. A pair of long legs in white pants stretched out from beneath her, and a torso lifted eerily from the ground, a blood covered face smiling into mine.

Bloody fangs and glowing red eyes filled my vision. Before I could jump to my feet, a long arm snaked out and clamped onto my throat. Under the crushing weight of Cain's grip, my windpipe collapsed.

Frantic for air, I reached up with both hands, my fingers struggling for purchase on his slick red hands. But he was strong. Strong from drinking blood. Eddi's blood.

I couldn't speak, but my eyes rolled downward as I choked, taking in Eddi's lifeless body. He drank from her. He killed her.

Rage blasted through me, and the heat of a thousand suns turned my blood to fire and my eyes a molten yellow. I saw the brightness of it reflected across Cain's face as he choked the life from me.

My blazing eyes blinded the vampire, and he shrank back, his hold momentarily loosening.

I surged to my feet and would have torn his head off with my bare hands if he hadn't scrabbled backward, his blood-soaked jacket slipping through my fingers.

But I was not alone. The roar that erupted from Bacchus made the hair on my arms stand up.

Cal landed beside me on his knees, sobbing as he picked up Eddi's lifeless hand.

Unsteady on my feet, I caught my breath as my windpipe healed, my eyes pouring with tears from the strangulation. As they cleared, I saw Bacchus swinging his mace and missing; the vampire was moving so fast that he was a blur.

Cain swept around Bacchus, and with a mad cackle, he sliced through his T-shirt with the broken neck of a bottle. Bacchus ignored it and kept swinging, trying to peg the bastard.

My throat healed in moments, and I straightened, my burning rage giving me strength. With glowing eyes and my distended fangs dripping a toxic death, I clenched my hands into fists and bellowed at my prey.

The vamp stopped harassing Bacchus and looked my way. With a theatrical little skip, Cain chirped, "Gotta run!"

He was a red and white blur as he blasted by me and out the door. As he swept past, I looked down and saw my shirt was torn, blood pouring from a gash across my ribcage.

Bacchus bolted after him, but I grabbed his arm. "Not now; Eddi needs help. We must get her help!"

Cal was on it. The clever shifter had Eddi's phone with him and was calling for human help. Giving someone our general location, we were to meet them on the corner.

I cradled her head in my lap, but Eddi wasn't moving. She was deathly white, with two neat holes on one side of her neck. I gently turned her head and gasped. The opposite side looked like he'd been gnawing on her, her neck a complete mess. No blood oozed from her wounds.

I threw my head back and howled in anguish.

"Ronan, you have to keep it together. We've got to get her down to the corner, or they'll miss us." Cal was sobbing and rubbing Eddi's hand.

I gathered my beautiful female into my arms, unable to control my sobs. As carefully as I could, I jogged out the door and across the yard, following Cal to the corner. We found a spot on the grass and laid her down, with Cal kneeling at her head and holding his hand to the underside of her jaw.

I twined my fingers with hers, and as I crouched over her, I sent her pulses of my healing energy. I had to be careful. In my panic, I could share too much and make things worse.

Slowly and steadily, I transferred my life force. It made no difference. She was barely breathing, and the feeling of her cold hands made tears drip from my face.

"Keep going, Ronan." Cal sobbed. "I still have a faint pulse. We're not too late. We have to keep trying!"

I did what I could, pumping every last bit of energy I had into her. I must have passed out because I woke up when Bacchus dropped me in the bushes.

"Easy, brother. It's ok, help is here."

I looked out of the brush he'd dumped me in and saw lights and humans running around doing something to Eddi. Someone held a clear bag of fluid above her, and they had silver paddles that whined. Eddi bounced when they put them on her bare chest, a snapping sound making my rage flare.

Furious that they were hurting her, I tried to get up, but Bacchus pushed me down.

"NO, Ronan. You have to stay here. Cal is with her. He won't let anything bad happen. They are healing her." His eyes wide, Bacchus darted glances between the bustle around Eddi and my numb face.

Too weak to rise, I fell back and watched. In moments, they had Eddi's lifeless body loaded and drove away with flashing lights and a loud wailing noise.

I rolled my head and looked up at Bacchus. "Is it good that they are making all that racket?"

Bacchus smiled, but his face was grim. "I think it means she's not dead," he said, biting his lip.

I let my arms fall to the dried leaves and rubbish beneath me and whimpered.

"I can't live without her, Bacchus."

"I know, brother. I know."

CHAPTER 20

I floated in a cold, gray place. I sensed things moving around me and registered that there were sounds. But they didn't reach my ears; they were soft and subtle whispers on my skin. Exhausted, I longed to let everything go, feeling sure it would be *sublime*.

A searing pain blasted through me, my body suddenly on fire. Every nerve screaming, I lifted with the involuntary spasm across my chest. Again, it raged through me. Then, *AGAIN*.

As the heat subsided, a black hole appeared before me. A mere speck in the distance, it was a moving dot in the endless gray surrounding me. Growing as it came closer, it darted towards me, faster and faster, until, with a thump, the inky blackness swallowed me whole.

And then, in the darkness, a light appeared. Something was on fire. I smelled diesel.

I remembered.

***

THE BALD MOUNTAINS, TENNESSEE

I looked at the door, and Imara hissed, "Stay inside, Eddi. Do NOT go out that door. I mean it."

It was dark, and I was terrified. My father instructed my Guardian to keep me inside, no matter what happened. I wanted to ignore her and charge out to be by his side.

"Never back down from a fight when it's the right thing to do, Edaline."

I can't recall how often he said it to me, but the thought brought tears to my eyes.

Here I was, hiding behind a curtain, forced to stay out of it. I begged Imara to let me go outside and help him. Teenage Djinn were as stubborn as human youths, and I was right on the edge of ignoring her and following my heart.

But Imara wasn't having it. She knew it was dangerous and futile; deep down, I did too. If I went out there, the consequences would be grave.

I pulled back the floral chintz curtains she'd made for our modest log home and wanted to laugh at how feminine they looked. Imara was a lot of things, but girly wasn't one of them.

We'd been so excited about moving into Father's wilderness cabin because we would finally be together—be a family again, in the loose sense of the word. Imara wasn't my mother, but she'd been with me so long that it felt that way.

The naturally beautiful meadow surrounding the cabin was high in the Bald Mountains of Tennessee, far from the nearest road. Father felt we'd be safe here, and last year, Imara and I came up on weekends to help him finish it.

Before we joined him, my clever father hired a talented witch from the city to ward the ever-loving hell out of the solid log structure.

"You'll be safe behind the walls, Edaline. No one can get past these wards."

We were about to find out if he was right.

Looking outside, I saw him, his bright silver hair glowing in the darkness. Feeling my gaze, he turned his head, the cold frosting his breath. Our eyes met, the silver of his irises sparkling through the darkness, giving me strength.

He would handle this. My father was a skilled fighter. I knew because he taught me. I smiled, remembering the bruises and the sore muscles as he taught me everything, never holding back because I was a girl.

In the inky black of the surrounding meadow, I caught the outlines of two figures just out of sight. Father spoke with them, their angry voices filtering back through the log walls between us.

Tall for a Djinn, Father had lean muscles without an ounce of fat. It was February, and for colder seasons, he favored a black leather tunic that hugged his torso with matching leather leggings.

Heavy use had molded them to his form. He barely felt the occasional hit I scored during practice fights with our wooden swords. My Guardian always grumbled that he never let her clean them. He'd say, "Imara, warriors don't hang their fighting leathers on the line with the Sunday wash," making her laugh.

Black was his favorite color. Father said it showed off his hair, and I always laughed at how he said it like he had any sense of style. My dad had as much fashion sense as a turtle. And he may have looked dangerous, but his heart was all kitten.

Looking at him now, trying to protect me, I could see I was wrong. My father had the heart of a lion. I held back the curtain, biting my lip as my blood raced, my ears roaring with an elevated pulse.

"Who are they, Imara? What do they want?"

My eyes flicked back and forth between my father and the intruders. I heard Imara behind me, donning her black guardian clothing. She wore lightweight, fitted pants and a waterproof cloak, fastened at the neck with a gold medallion embossed with an owl. As she looked for the key to the cellar, her cursing grated on my shot nerves.

"Edaline, come here. It's time. We must get into the tunnel. Your father will keep them busy long enough for us to escape."

I shook my head. "No, I'm not leaving him!"

I heard a noise. Something was happening outside.

Through the curtains, I saw my father had drawn his sword from its sheath, permanently strapped across his back these days.

Father never relaxed. He put on a grand show as if it were common practice always to be heavily armed.

"You never know when you'll need some firewood, Edaline." How he said it with a straight face, I'll never know.

My eyes stung as I watched him take his fighting stance, and I thought again about running to his side. He was so alone. He needed me!

From over my head, Imara looked out the window and gasped. With a snarl, she said, "Edaline, we have to go. *NOW*."

She took my hand and pulled me toward the trap door to the cellar, now open in the middle of the living room floor.

I wasn't having it and struggled in her grip. Frustrated, she yanked me to face her, lifting her hand as if to slap me.

"Your father has worked your whole life to keep you safe, and if you go out there, you'll undo everything he's fought for. Grow up and *GET IN THE CELLAR*."

I started to cry, and with a resigned sigh, she hugged me close. The strain of leaving Father was written on Imara's face, and it dawned on me that I wasn't the only one feeling like a traitor.

I followed her down the ladder into the space beneath the thick wooden floors of the living area. An ample space, strengthened by massive log walls, was sparsely furnished with sensible chairs and a small leather couch. On hot summer days, I used to relax there, teasing my father that I always wanted a place of my own with air conditioning.

My eyes flicked over my father's prized possession, possibly for the last time. A carved piece of marble rested on a shelf, a stylized Arabic scrawl framing the image of a lion crushing a jackal. It was my father's family crest. The word was "justice."

But we weren't stopping here tonight. Imara reached up and closed the trap door, which had a carpet over it that flipped back into place if you closed it quickly enough. I knew because we'd both practiced the move until we got it right every time. Turning the key in the lock, my Guardian slid a heavy board through the metal brackets to secure it from below.

Through a dark doorway at the back of the room, we headed down a tunnel carved through the rocky soil, the damp air tickling my flaming cheeks. The tunnel was wide enough for one person to stand, and I marveled at Father's handiwork. Even a speedy Djinn would have had a hard time with all the rock constantly pushing up through the soil in the Tennessee Mountains.

The tunnel led us from the underground room and under the meadow, coming out into the forest a few hundred feet downslope from the cabin. From the weapons stashed inside the hidden entrance, Imara grabbed the 308 Browning rifle, threw two clips in the pockets of her cloak, and handed me my Bowie knife.

These weren't toys for us. Imara was an apprentice Knight of the Sovereigns, and both she and my father had taught me to fight. I knew how to use everything in our storage locker.

My father had picked out the Bowie knife for me. If I got lost in the woods or had to defend myself, it was a practical choice for any situation.

The beautiful 16" Damascus steel blade had a delicate handle of elkhorn and walnut, customized to a perfect fit for my small hands. When he gave it to me, he joked, "It's pretty and sharp, just like you, Edaline, so it must be a good fit."

Cracking the door that led into a moonlit forest, her breath huffing with frost, Imara peered around the woods before deciding it was safe. We quickly and quietly slipped through, grabbing a knapsack full of supplies on the way out.

I wore my favorite jean jacket and a fleece turtleneck to keep off the February chill. It was fresh from the line and smelled of wildflowers and mountain breezes. I shivered in the cold, and sheathing my knife, I stuck my bare hands in my pockets, cursing the oversight of forgetting gloves.

Imara motioned for me to hurry, and we jogged down the hill, following the path that would bring us to the creek. From there, we'd grab the canoe and paddle into the current. The stream would take us down to Madcap and from there to Bumpus Cove. The creek ended close to Clark's Creek Road, and after a half-hour hike, we would find the car Father left hidden in the brush, with money and supplies.

Father perfected the evacuation route long before we moved in. On a sunny day in May, Imara packed a picnic lunch for the three of us, and we did a dry run. Exploring the river together was a fun afternoon, provided you weren't running for your life.

Father may have been sweet on Imara, but I never knew for certain. If there was any romance, they kept it well hidden. He still spoke of my mother, a vague image from my early childhood. I never learned what happened to her; I may never know.

My father once told me that the name *Ezen* meant a free spirit—someone who loved adventure, excitement, and independence. He was all that and a great father, too, letting me run amok through the meadows and forests around the home he'd built.

I'd always considered his meticulous preparations a game, but there was nothing fun about tonight. When we laughed and picnicked that day in May, I never anticipated the searing pain of abandoning my father to fight alone. That wasn't part of my training.

We were halfway down the hill when I heard the first ring of steel on steel and angry shouts echoing through the forest. Imara stopped, and from the look on her face, her heart was breaking alongside mine.

I followed her gaze and saw the flames. The cabin was burning. After careful consideration, meticulous preparations, and rock-solid wards, all it took was a match and some accelerant. I sobbed into my hand at the sight as we turned, resuming our flight downhill.

We were almost to the creek when a figure stepped out of the forest. We skidded to a halt, and I swear my heart stopped.

Standing before us was a hulking monolith of a man with hands the size of barrels. His skin was a dull gray, his flat face at odds with a bulbous nose. He turned his head, and his glittering eyes looked me over. With two thudding steps, he was on us.

Imara didn't waste any time, the lever action of the Browning clacking as she unloaded her clip at the monster, released the catch, and slammed a fresh clip home.

I held up the Bowie, taking the stance my father taught me—one leg forward, my center of gravity low. With a saber grip on the knife, I lifted my other arm, closing my fist and turning it toward my face to protect tendons and blood vessels. It was good for a surprise punch, too. My training snapped into focus, and I relaxed into the stance like a pro.

Imara's bullets didn't slow the colossus down, sparking and zinging into the bushes like he was made of stone. And when he reached down and wrapped one big hand around me, I realized he *was* made of stone.

Viscous strikes of my knife did nothing, scraping over the hard skin of his hand as I stabbed at him. My angry screams rang through the forest as he lifted me.

Kicking my feet to no avail, I switched to a reverse grip, using both hands for more power. My knife skittered off with each jarring strike, barely scratching the giant's skin.

Irritated by my efforts, he squeezed his fist hard enough that, with a grunt, I dropped the knife. It tumbled to the ground, and reaching down, the giant retrieved it and tucked it into his waistband.

He scooped up Imara, who was still shooting, aiming at his legs to avoid hitting me. She blasted off two more rounds just before he grabbed her.

And just like that, we were finished.

We were nibbling ants to the two-legged mountain, who lifted us and casually walked back up the hill. Still tucked into a tattered waistband, I heard my knife scrape against his stony skin with every step.

I twisted my neck to see Imara struggling, her long brown hair out of its tidy bun and floating on the breeze as we swung through the forest. Her eyes blazed with determination, hardening my resolve. I screamed and renewed my struggles to free myself from his iron grip.

I wouldn't stop fighting. Dad needed me. In my heart, I was relieved to go back. I never wanted to leave him in the first place.

Kicking, screaming, and hammering on those fingers had no effect whatsoever. The giant simply grunted with annoyance and walked a little faster, leaving me with aching hands for my efforts.

As he strode into the meadow, I smelled diesel and saw the cabin engulfed in a raging firestorm that licked the sky. The inferno seared my skin, and a sob tore from my lips at seeing our home disappear before my eyes. Tears poured as I turned my head, frantically looking for Father. The fight had drifted to the forest's edge to avoid the blistering heat.

My father still danced, his sword out, sweat pouring from his face. Two attackers circled him, the trio parrying and stabbing, but Father's skill kept them back, even though they harried him from both sides.

He was as fast as light, his form flitting back and forth from wispy to solid, but I could see he was tiring. Our eyes met when he looked at the approaching monstrosity, shock and defeat flitting across his face. Briefly, he lost focus.

In a flash, one of his assailants landed a blow, the short sword sliding through his thigh. My scream joined Father's as he fell to his knees.

He was determined not to fail us, so without missing a beat, he refocused and sprung to his feet, almost taking off his attacker's head.

Father wasn't the only one who noticed the giant approaching. A figure broke away from the fight and sauntered over, his tall, lean body reeking of confidence and swagger.

The smile he gave me raised goosebumps along my arms.

"I'll take it from here, Saxum."

The giant's arms swung forward, and he dropped us in a pile of tangled limbs before stepping back.

Imara didn't waste any time. She shoved me behind her, wheeling to face this new threat. She pulled a needle-sharp stiletto from her cloak and prepared to defend me.

"Oh, isn't that cute? Imara, you made a wonderful mother figure, didn't you?"

"Keep your hands off her, Cain, you blood-sucking piece of shit."

Imara sounded ferocious, but I recognized the thread of fear in her voice.

My neck swiveled in desperation as I looked for something to arm myself. I glanced toward the giant, who still had my bowie knife tucked into his waistband.

In a moment of clarity, I remembered Father hounding me, "Never panic, Eddi. Panic gets you dead."

Whipping back around, I watched the man Imara called Cain, who was in front of us now. He eyed me like you would an intriguing piece of art in an exhibit.

Head cocked, he smiled and said, "You've raised her well, Guardian. She's a strong, healthy child. That will be most helpful."

Cain straightened, clapped his hands in delight, and said, "Well, Imara, I hate to say it, but you've outlived your usefulness." He turned to the giant.

"Saxum? Kill her." Then he sprinted away, his long legs returning him to the fight still raging with my father.

Faster than I expected, the giant lurched forward. In one smooth motion, he pulled my knife from his waist, grabbed Imara by the hair, and lifted her, slashing the blade across her throat.

"*Noooooo!*" I screamed my heartbreak to the stars, watching Imara's blood sheet from the gash in her throat. Imara took her last breath as my grief echoed across the dark meadow. Her voice whispered from far away, echoing quietly in my mind.

"I'm so sorry. I never meant for this to happen. Run, Edaline."

She fell forward, her lifeblood draining into the tall grass that swayed around her motionless form. Frozen in horror, I stared at the black cloak barely visible beneath the grass curtain.

But grief would have to wait. The giant turned toward me, his malicious eyes locking on mine. I ran.

Not away, as instructed. Never away. Never again.

I ran straight at that fucking giant, who shouted in surprise as I launched myself over his grasping hands.

Raising his arms too late, he staggered back in shock as I slammed into his chest, my momentum focused high above his center. My meager weight hit him, and somehow it was enough to tip the scales and push his great mass onto his heels. Slowly, like a tree falling in the forest, he toppled.

As the giant fell, I was still moving. I tore the Bowie from his loosened grip, and with a flip of my wrist, I turned it, and with every ounce of strength in my arms, I jammed it between his two shocked eyes.

Luck was with me. The area above his nose was softer than the rest, just as I had hoped.

With the hilt clutched in both hands, my weight and the thunderous impact of the ground combined to force the knife home. The giant gave a jerk and lay still, the handle protruding from his brow.

Panting, my mind numb to the horror of what I'd done, I scrambled to my feet. I had to stand on the stone man's head and use two hands and both my knees, but I pried the knife out of his skull. I stopped to catch my breath.

My muscles throbbed with an energy I didn't understand. There was no fear, and escape was off the table. My course was set; my only focus was on my father and helping him defeat these bastards. Jumping to the ground, I headed straight into the fray.

We'd practiced this many times, Father and I. Scrambling behind him, I covered his flank. He was a master—whirling, slashing, retreating. I danced behind his organized attacks, the distance perfect to protect him but not get in his way.

His look of surprise switched to pride, and I felt intense love for him at that moment. We could do this. All those hours we'd worked on this technique came into focus. I wouldn't fail him when it counted most. I couldn't stop to think about Imara. So, I fell into our routine and let it guide me.

Dad focused on Cain, the freak that ordered Imara killed, and I concentrated on the other fighter—the ugly one. He was short and wiry like a monkey, his arms long and his legs bowed.

Nails as long as my pinky tipped his fingers and toes; his hairy torso was naked from the waist up. Monkey man was clumsy but fast as a sneeze, and he knew how to use the short sword he held.

With his reach longer than mine, I had to keep moving to stay out of his grasp. I may have trained hard, but I was no match for this creature. I knew I'd have to outsmart him.

Focused and buzzing with energy, I watched for my chance to strike—and it appeared.

He lunged forward, trying to skewer me with a thrust, but aimed too high. I dropped to the ground, rolled once, and stopped under his elbows. Striking upwards, I drove my knife into his diaphragm, then yanked it out, rolling away before he could react.

I was too slow. The short sword sliced down and stabbed through my jean jacket, pinning me to the ground. I heaved backward and dug in my heels, trying to tear myself free as I swiped wildly with my knife.

His long-fingered hand shot out, trapping my wrist and clamping down until I screamed. As I stared into his ugly, chimp-like face, he smiled at me and squeezed harder. My knife slipped from my limp fingers, sticking into the soft earth.

I glanced at his stomach, expecting to see blood pouring freely from the wound I gave him. As I watched, the ugly gash closed, and the streaks of blood dried on his skin.

Seeing the focus of my stare, the chimp-like thing cackled.

Struggling to free myself, I aimed for his crotch with my booted foot, but with unbelievable balance, he stuck out a leg and stepped on my ankle, gripping it with his monkey toes, then quickly repeating the process with the other.

Pinned and powerless under the crushing weight, I scratched and tore at him with my free hand.

Ignoring my feeble attempts, Monkey Man reached into a back pocket and pulled out a pair of handcuffs.

What the—?

With a gleeful chuckle, he tried to slap the cuff on my wrist. If he got those things on me, it was game over. I punched and scratched at him with my free hand, bucking for all I was worth, finally gripping his face and gouging my thumb into his eye.

He screeched in anger and reared back, but before he reached for me again, something shiny arced through the air behind him.

A red line appeared on his throat, and his mouth opened in shock. Then, as if in slow motion, his head slid forward from his neck and tumbled into my lap.

I screamed at the surprised face staring back at me. Someone grabbed the short sword that pinned my jacket to the ground and yanked it out. I was free.

Father! His eyes focused on Cain, father extended his hand and flicked his strong fingers. I grabbed tight as he pulled up, setting me on my feet. Then he was gone, his attention never leaving the fight before him as he spun. His ethereal form blinked from hazy to solid and back again like a flickering black-and-white film. He was magnificent, and I felt a surge of hope because the odds were in our favor now.

Father stabbed, then blinked out of sight, coming up behind his opponent, swiping, then blinking back in front of me. It would have been the perfect strategy, except Cain was faster than he looked.

There was a brief moment when the fighting paused, and the duo caught their breath. Heaving in great gulps of air, Cain was holding his side.

Father had a few slices on his face, and his upper thigh was dark with a creeping stain of wetness. I saw the injury happen. How he fought through the pain was a mystery. His face glistened with sweat, Father was barely out of breath.

Cain straightened and spoke, his voice having a smooth, elegant timbre that grated along my nerves.

"Ezen, give her up. You know Hex won't take no for an answer, and I don't want to kill you."

"You'll not take my daughter, Cain. Not as long as I draw breath. Leave now, or I'll slice your heart from your chest and burn it to ashes so you never rise again."

Cain was a silhouette against the cabin's flames, and recovering, he stood tall and held up his sword.

"Well, Ezen—you can try." Then he disappeared, a streak of color trailing him as he attacked.

I felt the air move as Cain popped up behind me, and then his hand was in my hair, and like I weighed nothing, he lifted me off the ground.

But silver hair and a pair of glowing white eyes were faster, and as my feet left the ground, Father's sword appeared, stretching past my face and out of view, the point somewhere behind me. I knew without looking that the tip was at Cain's throat, ready to take his head off.

But Father couldn't act.

I felt the cold bite of steel on the opposite side of my neck, and blood dripped from where Cain's blade nicked me. The trickle felt like a bug crawling toward my collar, and I wanted to dash it away with a scream.

Deadlocked, Cain and Father stilled. Their heavy breathing was loud in the silence.

I stopped screaming and kicking for fear of losing my head. The strain on my scalp blinded me, tears pouring down my face from the pain of being held up by my hair.

"Let her go, Hex." Father's eyes never left Cain's, his focus somewhere else. Confused, my eyes flicked wildly around the clearing, but it was empty.

And then I saw who he spoke to because a third person walked out of the shadows, and I followed their approach from over Dad's shoulder.

No, not a person. A monster.

CHAPTER 21

It sauntered into the flickering light from the inferno on four legs, a dark brown stain against the blackness of the night. The beast's eyes glowed red in a body oozing with malice.

Oval, hairless, and wrinkled, its vaguely humanoid face extended into a short muzzle that protruded below two glowing red eyes. Wet slits sniffed the night air as it strode forward. A cage of long, thin teeth set into powerful jaws met with a click when its mouth closed. But as it came, it gaped its maw with a malevolent grimace, strings of saliva trailing from its lips.

Its grotesque face was framed with a mane of short, stiff fur and small triangular ears tipped with black tufts. They swiveled as it approached, listening.

Small and terrifying, the head hung low on a short neck that blended into thick, mountainous shoulders corded with muscle that flexed as it stalked forward. The stout, almost hairless front legs ended in thick cat-like feet tipped by five fat claws.

While the front half was vaguely feline, the back was a strange blend of lizard and insect. A narrow waist tapered to long slender hips, the rear legs oddly iguana-like except for being upright and standing on sharp triangular toes.

From front to back, short, stiff fur blended to scaly skin, then into an armored carapace shielding the loins and hind legs. The entire hair-raising monstrosity ended in a long, segmented scorpion tail that curled over its back, the needle-like stinger dripping with a clear, viscous fluid.

It snarled, and I wet my pants.

"Hello, Ezen," it purred, its voice sharp and soft at the same time, with a hiss on each end, like a serpent.

"Let her go, Hex. Hurt her, and I will destroy you and erase your bloodline from this world."

Father's face was so close to mine that I saw the cream flecks in his glowing white eyes. He didn't look at me, focusing instead on his sword tip at Cain's throat. But I could hear him in my head.

"When it happens, RUN. Don't look back. I will find you, I promise. Run as fast as you can, and then dig deeper. You can move more swiftly than you ever imagined if you reach for it." His eyes flicked to mine briefly, and I felt a numbing sadness trickle through our connection.

"I love you, Edaline."

The monster chuckled, a strangely hollow sound.

"Let her go? I don't think you're in much of a position to bargain right now, are you, Ezen?"

Its voice was so strange, high pitched with a cat-like purr when it wasn't hissing.

What is that thing?

It strolled closer, its face nonchalant, as if it had all day. The scorpion tail curled over its back and waved like a cat's, the forward-facing barb swinging left and right as it moved. Elephant-sized but with feline grace, the monster's black carapace shimmered in the firelight, clicking as it walked. Partially cloaked by the night, it looked fearsome and invincible.

The thing looked at Cain and said, "Put her down, Vampire. We can't have you damaging such important goods, can we?"

Cain lowered his arm until my feet touched down, but he didn't let go.

So here we stood, the four of us on the meadow's edge, locked in a stalemate.

My father's arm trembled ever so slightly, the cost of extending it taking a toll. Cain saw it, too, and chuckled in my ear.

"Lower your sword, Ezen, or I'll change my mind and take her head," Cain gloated, confident that his victory was assured. I thought he would follow through, and I closed my eyes for a moment.

But then I heard something strange. From somewhere over the forest behind us, it came on the night breeze. The flapping of sails, closing fast.

The monster paused, looking up into the night sky, its cat-human face frowning.

"Gideon," it hissed. "That Gryphon bastard is here."

I'd seen him before, this Gryphon creature. He'd come to visit my father. I saw him from a distance when I was at the creek. By the time I'd run up the hill, he was flying away. Father wouldn't tell me what he wanted.

And now, he was coming, and his name was Gideon. It must be good for us because our attackers looked tense. Hope surged in my chest.

I wanted to turn my head but didn't dare, with two swords as bookends to my neck. So I moved my eyes, searching for the Gryphon over the dark forest, its edges illuminated by the crackling fire of the cabin. I couldn't see him, but I heard the slow slaps of his wings pushing a hard wind.

And then, silence.

My eyes snapped to the approaching monster, its red orbs locked on my face. "You're mine, Princess," it hissed. It crouched, its scorpion tail lashing as it searched the sky. Then, it sprinted toward us, closing the gap with alarming speed. With an athletic, crablike scramble, it gathered its limbs to leap.

I was lucky I didn't lose my head because out of the darkness, Gideon suddenly appeared. His enormous wings snapped open as he blinked into view a split second before impact.

Glowing yellow eyes locked on the target, his four taloned paws rocked forward, the gigantic claws outstretched and ready to tear. With a shriek that made me cringe, he punched into the monster from behind with a tremendous crunch of feathers and bone.

They tumbled along the ground, wings, claws, and the scorpion tail tangled together as they rolled. Ferocious snarls and piercing screeches created an eardrum-shattering crescendo that startled everyone into action.

Father recovered first, and from behind me, a masculine ear tumbled down my chest, leaving a streak of blood.

There was a pained yelp, and Cain's sword disappeared, his hand no longer in my hair. In a flash of movement, my father pushed me down, skewered Cain on his sword, and leapt over me.

"RUN, EDALINE, RUN!"

Father's voice shot through me like a thunderbolt, jarring me to action.

I didn't want to flee. By the Gods, I wanted to stay and fight. But my father hadn't only spoken in my mind a few moments ago. He'd spoken in my heart. He made me FEEL how desperately he wanted me to live. My warm, fun-loving, dedicated Djinn father would fight to his last dying breath to see me free.

So I got up, and I ran. I ran so fast and dug so deep that, at one point, I felt like my feet were no longer hitting the earth. My arms, which moments ago had been furiously pumping the air as I ran, were suddenly weightless.

I had no idea what was happening, but I plunged deep into my soul, and from the shadowy depths, I pulled on a force I didn't understand and pushed on.

I was lighter than air, and the ground whizzed past, now ten feet below me. I was moving faster than I'd ever been, dizzy from the sensation of being weightless. Excitement seared my veins, and for a moment, I lost myself to the thrill of it, eagerly pushing for more.

I did it! I was flying just like my father, my body no longer solid, the feeling of hurtling above the ground indescribable.

I didn't get far, though, because as I saw the woody trunks of the inviting forest, something slammed into the ground in front of me.

The monster stood there in all its terrifying glory, red eyes glowing, blood dribbling from talon marks on its ugly face.

I mentally braced, an impact imminent. With my arms and legs flailing wildly for balance, I managed to skid to a halt twenty feet from the beast. The creature stepped toward me, and I froze in terror, my now solid body tingling from the abrupt transformation.

"You're getting to be quite a pain in the ass, Edaline," it hissed. "I'm starting to wonder if you're worth my time."

Head low, eyes locked on me, it took another step and then another. I tasted blind terror for the first time, my tongue coated with acrid bitterness.

Out of nowhere, three thousand pounds of angry Gryphon slammed into the thing and flattened it. The ground shook, dust rising in a cloud from the impact.

Without hesitation, Gideon rose, and with his feline legs pumping, he bounded toward me. With an enormous leap, he scooped me up and launched off the ground with one thrust of his powerful hindquarters.

My neck burned with the force of the sudden vertical trajectory, his enormous feathered wings snapping out. Loud, frantic thrusts rent the air in a brave effort to ascend before the thing recovered.

My hair whipped into my face as I gripped his thickly furred leg with both arms. I looked back to see the creature rise; with a terrifying howl it streaked toward us, launching into the air to intercept.

But the Gryphon was fast, and dipping one wing, he swerved out of reach, and we were safely airborne.

A chilling numbness spread through my hands and lips. Looking down, I watched the raging thing below as it ripped up bowling ball-sized chunks of sod with unbridled fury. Having just stared death in the face and survived, I closed my eyes and succumbed to the shock.

As we rose over the treetops, Gideon curled his front legs, tucking me snugly to his feathered chest. The wind whipped downy fur into my mouth, and he held me so tightly I could barely turn my head. I could just make out the blazing cabin as we swept past, but Father was gone, the meadow empty.

"Where are you taking me?" I asked. Gideon answered in my mind.

"Somewhere safe. Somewhere they can't find you."

The desolation of losing my father sucked me under, and my exhausted body relaxed into his crushing hold. I closed my eyes at the sudden knowledge that I feared heights, and my stomach pitched.

"What was that thing? That Hex creature?" My lips trembled as I spoke.

The Gryphon's voice was a low rumble between my ears.

"A Manticore. The monkey-like beast was an Amomongo and a Stone Giant also lay in the clearing. You are as brave as your pedigree would suggest, Edaline."

I didn't know what he was talking about, but I'd find out. And then I'd search for my father so we could return and bury Imara.

Tears bathed my face, but the shock made me mindless, shielding me and lending time to process the night's events.

We flew for what felt like hours, the Gryphon's massive wings gliding through the air as the wind whistled past. We coasted for an eternity, and then he stroked the darkness again, riding the currents that held us aloft.

I kept my eyes tightly closed most of the way, turning my face into his downy chest so the wind didn't tear my eyes from my head. He smelled like a spring breeze, this bird-tiger creature. I was cold, but the Gryphon was a furnace that warmed me wherever we touched.

At last, my savior touched down somewhere near a big city. I knew because I briefly opened my eyes to see a carpet of lights in the distance.

Our landing was awkward, and he dropped me as we touched down. I clambered up to scold him, my stiff muscles protesting madly. When I turned around, I sucked in a shocked breath. He was bleeding from cuts and gouges scattered across his body.

How did he fly us this far? A gaping tear crossed one shoulder, with a matted patch of dried blood and feathers below it. A hunk of flesh was missing from a deep bite in his neck, the wound packed with dirt and feathers. Angry skin showed in patches across his chest and back, and when he stepped forward, he limped. The Gryphon was a mess.

"You're hurt," I said. "You should have said something."

"It's fine," he rumbled. *"I'm hard to kill."*

He looked me over and, satisfied that the blood on my jacket was someone else's, gazed into my eyes.

"There are things you don't know, Edaline. Vile forces at work that would make you a slave, using you for their depraved schemes. I can't let that happen."

"What do you mean? I don't understand."

I didn't like where this was going, my ire rising now that I was on the ground and fully awake.

"You'll feel nothing, I promise. When you wake up, you can start over. Be someone else. Someone new. This country is a big place, Edaline. They'll never find you if you disappear without a trace."

"Wait a minute, you overgrown parrot! What do you mean I won't feel a thing? Where is my father!?"

Those glowing yellow eyes softened, and inside of me, something cracked. The certain knowledge that he was gone and couldn't possibly have survived the Manticore alone brought me to my knees.

"I'm sorry, Edaline. There's no other way. It's for your own good."

I jerked my head up, suspicious now and ready to fight. But his face was already in mine, and I couldn't move.

I was frozen. I wanted to scream, but I couldn't open my mouth. All I could do was breathe, so I did, biding my time, waiting for the beast to make a mistake.

His eyes glowed a brighter gold, and moving his face close enough to touch, the glow flared until all I could see was a blinding cream-colored light. I couldn't close my eyes, and they stung with the brightness of it.

"One day, when it's time, I will lift this shield from your mind. Your day for revenge will come, Edaline. In the meantime, be patient. Live your life. Be happy."

Blind to all but the words in my mind, a fizzing sensation tickled through me all the way to my fingernails.

And then, I tumbled, down, down, into a giant black hole of nothingness.

CHAPTER 22

The beeping was first. Then, I registered the groggy haze clouding my mind. Then came the stuporous thought that jarred me awake.

Here we go again.

I tried to blink, but my crusted-over eyes didn't cooperate. Blinking hard enough to crack them open, I sighed with relief, then registered a dark head resting on the edge of my bed. My tired stare followed a muscular neck and bunched shoulders down a strong back covered in a pink tee shirt. A chair pulled up to the edge of the mattress held a sight for sore eyes. Ronan.

Numb from my horrifying experience, a vague awareness of emotion overcame me. Glad to see him—happy Ronan was alive—the muffled thoughts came as if through a thick cotton barrier.

Then I remembered—*everything*. My mind reeled from the mental face punch of every lost memory slipping back into its place like a sassy child who was late for class. There was no doubt. It was real. I recalled everything in vivid detail, but I couldn't face it. Not yet.

I closed my eyes and drifted back to sleep.

When I awoke, my dark-haired Syreni was there. This time, he was sitting up. His luminescent eyes created a soft green glow that lit his face and cast some light in the shadowy room.

A nurse took that moment to pop in, looked at Ronan, and pursed her lips. Seeing I was awake, she came to my bedside and smiled. "You must be quite a catch, my dear, because this young man has refused to leave."

She smiled, checked my assorted gadgets, and said, "I'll be right back. I have a new bag of electrolytes for you. The doctor will be in shortly to go over your condition." She shook her head. "You have an incredible capacity to heal, my dear."

As she left the room, I looked at Ronan, expecting my usual joy at seeing him. Instead, I felt dead inside—shattered.

With a tender smile, he reached for my hand. Ronan's relief was evident; taking my fingers in a warm grip, he spoke to me with his mind.

"Edaline. You..."

There was a pause.

"I was so scared."

Tears sprang to his eyes. I never knew emotion could move through a telepathic link, but the heartbreak that surged from him made me gasp. I squeezed his hand.

Turning to look at the dark windows, I noticed street lights reflected in the glass. For once, I was too tired to use my lips to talk, so I joined Ronan in my cotton-stuffed head.

"Was I out for long?"

"Yes. One full day. Bacchus and I have been here the whole time. He has taken a dip in the ocean, but he'll be back soon. He needs to rejuvenate."

Ronan rubbed his thumbs over my fingers, then pulled them to his lips, kissing them gently.

"You should rest, Edaline. For some reason, my magic isn't working to heal you. I'm afraid you'll have to heal naturally this time."

My head whipped toward him, and I frowned at the dizziness that swept through me.

"Is that so? I thought you were unconscious when I woke earlier. You were sleeping here?"

He smiled and said, "Yes, I couldn't leave you, and they didn't have enough orderlies to kick me out."

I smiled at him and felt the numbness in my mind begin to clear. He was here. My proud, strong Syreni male was here, and he had protected me the whole time I was unconscious. The thought made my eyes rim with tears again.

And that's why you shouldn't think about anything yet, Eddi.

"I'm sorry I'm not the best company, Ronan. I feel drained—like I haven't slept in a year. Where's Cal?"

He wasn't here, which was odd. I felt panic rise, but I tamped it down.

You've been a wimp for too long, girl. Pull it together, for crying out loud.

"Cal had to go back to Davy Jones Locker. He didn't want to leave, but he had to. Someone named Evan is sick."

That made sense. We had a skeleton crew on the best of days, but Evan was never sick. It must be the flu.

"Cal gave me this." Ronan held up my cell phone. "He wanted you to text him as soon as you can manage it. He's worried sick, as I am sure you can imagine."

I laughed and decided to "test" Cal. I powered up the phone. It was at ninety percent; someone changed my lock screen.

It said, **"Get up, you lazy ass!"**

I smiled and sent him a quick text.

"Alive and well. Sorry about scaring you again. Come and see me when you can. I miss you."

I looked at Ronan, who seemed confused. I guess technology wasn't a Syreni thing. My phone dinged immediately.

"You scared the living shit out of me! Again. I can come tomorrow after work, and then I have two days off to spend with you. You owe me breakfast."

There was an emoji of a shrimp, a fish, an egg, a big mouth, and an octopus. I smiled at that because Cal was fond of incredibly gross seafood omelets. The smell of fish and eggs always made me gag. He knew it too, the bugger.

In the silence of my room, Ronan watched me, a sad, distant look in his eyes. I was doing it again. Letting the best thing that ever happened to me drift away while I focused on everything else. I put my phone down on the side table.

"Thank you for saving me, Ronan. I want to hear everything when I'm not so tired, starting with how you found me."

The warmth returned to his glorious green eyes. Ronan leaned forward and picked up the pearl necklace still hanging from my throat. It must have been covered in blood, but someone had cleaned every crevice, and it was glowing in the light of the headboard lamp.

"The pearl led me to you. We scoured the streets until, finally, it sang to me. It was very faint, but I heard it. I knew it was you."

I looked at his face and his misty eyes. Reaching out, I beckoned him closer. When he leaned toward me, I slid my hand around his neck and pulled him close, looked into his eyes, and whispered in his mind, *"Get in here with me right now. I want to see the look on that nurse's face when she comes in, and you're actually IN my bed this time."*

And that was how Bacchus must have found us when he returned from his swim, the strong scent of *Lost Cherry* ladies' perfume wafting from his skin. Ronan sprawled on my covers, and the pair of us twined together, sound asleep.

***

HEX

His screaming was giving me a headache.

Incensed by his grievous misdeed, I smiled at the blood dripping from my fingers as Cain writhed on the ground in agony, begging for his life. It was a little hard to hear him because the blood bubbling from the holes in his gums made the words almost unintelligible.

I opened my bloodied hand and, looking down, pictured the inch-long fangs polished and added to my necklace of horrors. I would have smiled, but I still rode the high of a scorching rage.

"What makes you think I won't end you for nearly killing her?"

I dropped the fangs in the empty cup on my leather patio chair and crossed my legs, feigning nonchalance.

Cain pulled himself to his knees, his chin trembling from the pain.

"You need me. I bested the Djinn *Ezen* in a fight, and I know all of them, their personalities, who they care about—what they fear!"

"Hmm. A bit light, *CAIN*. What else can you offer that might persuade me? And don't forget, I'm still angry that you left Malus to die at Gideon's hands."

"And where is Viggo? I need that ugly little bastard to catch more Syreni, and he's gone. Under your distracted eye, this entire operation is going to *shit*."

Cain was panting in distress, the blood streaming from his mouth. I watched in fascination as the bubbles rolled down his chin, clumping together before dropping off to stain his cream suit. It made me peckish.

But I was angrier than I was hungry, and the vampire's sniveling was getting old. I sighed and took a sip of my wine.

Galahad was far more reliable and trustworthy enough to handle the child. It would have toppled countless years of careful planning if Cain had killed Edaline with his disgusting blood lust.

Cain must have seen the decision in my eyes because his pleading became frantic.

"I'm fast, and I have compulsion. I can stop the Enforcer before any plan he hatches can get off the ground!"

I rose from my lounger and stalked toward him. A few more steps, and I could move on from this near disaster.

"Please, Hex! I promise it will never happen again. I lost control. I'm sorry! You don't have time to train someone else, and besides, who would you promote? Charles? Layla? They're hacks!"

He was desperate now, throwing his co-workers under the bus. With a tsk tsk, I shook my head.

"You compromised the operations house. You alerted the police to a fanatic on the loose—a *vampire* fanatic. And you almost killed the ONE thing we have that can close the only weak link in our plans."

I paused, then added, "*And* you let her get away."

I looked down at him. He was pathetic, bloodstains splattering his expensive suit like a Jackson Pollock painting.

The intoxicating fear wafting upwards from his bootlicking position excited my inner beast, and my control dissolved, prompting an involuntary shift.

Reaching down, I slid my cracking fingers around his neck and lifted him off the ground, raking my lengthening claws across his throat for effect. As my shoulders sprouted fur and swelled, I lifted him with a mighty yank, making him scream anew.

Bringing my face close to his, I let the change take me so he could see the ice-pick fangs that would devour him and hear the chattering hiss of my voice.

His feet dangling, I rose to my full height, his tall, slim frame squirming like a worm on a hook.

I scented the urine tracking down his leg, the smell turning foul when I brought my scorpion tail around and held the toxic tip a hair's breadth from his ear.

"You have three seconds to convince me."

Cain blubbered and whined, and then out popped the sentence I'd hoped to hear from the scheming bloodsucker.

"I have someone on the inside!" he screeched.

***

It was another twenty-four hours before they let me out of the hospital. I had an impressive assortment of bags hanging from the pole next to my bed, and I didn't pee for most of my stay. The doctor wanted to ensure I had no heart or kidney problems from losing so much blood.

My room was a swinging door of people coming and going. Phoebe was first, and later, James dropped by. Ada and Miguel came separately because the restaurant was hopping. Even Patsy visited after Ada told her what had happened.

The door of my room swung open, slamming on the wall, and Patsy bustled in with an armload of flowers and bags. She pulled a vase out of one bag and, rushing to the bathroom, filled it, then quickly arranged the flowers. Patsy set the expensive-looking bouquet on my roller table.

Plunking down, she popped the tab on a can of fruit juice and, inserting a bendy straw, handed it to me.

"Well, hello to you too, Patsy," I said with a grin. My boss. She's crazy.

"My God, Edaline!" Patsy clucked. "You do have a way of getting yourself into trouble, don't you?"

She reached out and swept my bangs from my face, giving me a caring smile.

"I've got something else for you." Leaning back, she plucked a Get Well Soon card from her purse and handed it to me.

"Thank you so much," I said, reading it out loud. "Laughter is the best Medicine." I flipped it open. "Unless you have diarrhea."

I giggled and put the card next to her lovely flowers. "I'm sorry I haven't been at the restaurant these last few weeks. I should have stayed in Marathon." At her smirk, I said, "I know, I know. I'm a walking disaster, right?"

Patsy snorted. "No, but you seem a magnet for horrible people."

We chatted for a while, and when Patsy asked about my accident, I was vague and told her that someone attacked me. At the look on my face, she dropped the subject.

She clapped her hands and said, "Enough about your penchant for seeking an early death. What do you think of my new shade of nail polish?" Giggling, she held out her hand. Painted a luxurious shade of dark red, her nails glimmered with sheer perfection.

"Maybe when you leave this place, I will take you for a makeover you'll never forget," she said, looking at my ratty nails. She tsked. "It might take a while." She rolled her eyes at me and laughed.

Patsy stayed for a pleasant visit, catching me up on what was happening at the Crazy Conch. As she left, she gave me a finger wave and told me to keep her posted.

It felt great to be loved. Everyone brought cards, snacks, and helpful smiles. I was still weak, so no one stayed long. Secretly, I was glad for the distraction.

Gideon deliberately withholding my history was a topic that stayed padlocked in a closet inside my mind. There would be plenty of time for that later.

Bacchus and Ronan were my constant companions, taking turns so they could get enough ocean time. It was also a clever way to avoid annoying me with their helicopter behavior. I appreciated the guard routine, though, because I wasn't ready to stand on my own two feet yet.

Miri came too, and I was happy to see her. I think out of everyone, the sprite was the most distressed by my abduction. She failed as my guard—her words.

Popping out of Cal's messenger bag, Miri zoomed from the end of the bed and splatted right under my chin, grabbing my neck and digging in for a good cry.

With much hiccuping and sniffling, she came up for air. "You won't get away from me again," she whimpered. "I'm going to be all over you like blue on rice."

I laughed. Clearly, the pesty thing had been playing with the laptop again.

"How's your sea stallion doing, Miri?" I expected laughter or joking, but instead, I got tears. Lots and lots of tears. Cal was behind her, shaking his head, bugging his eyes, and mouthing, *no, no, no!*

Miri's face crumpled. "It's all my fault," she wailed. "If I hadn't left with Ryker, I would have seen Cain and raised the alarm. It's all my fault! You almost *DIED!*"

The wails and shrieks continued while I cradled her under my chin for quite some time. Eventually, she stopped crying long enough to pat my chest dry with a tissue and swerve into the angry lane.

"I told him he'd have to find another gorgeous Sea Sprite to jottle."

Then she tumbled back into an ear-splitting yowl.

I looked at Cal and mouthed, *"What the fuck is jottle?"* Then, widening my eyes, I implored him for help. He sent me a quick mind-o-gram.

"She's been like this ever since you were taken. I don't know what to do. It's excruciating. I can't decide if I want to let her cry on my shoulder or choke the life out of her."

"Miri, calm down. It wasn't your fault. Sshhhh….." I winced when the volume went up instead of down.

"I'm not upset with you, Miri. Everyone makes mistakes. And I thought you and your little fella were cute. He can come around—" I caught the look on Cal's face "—occasionally. When it's not busy."

Cal gave me a wry look and mouthed, *"You sucker."*

Miri's little face popped up just in front of my nose. She was so close she was blurry.

"Really? Can he come over?" She buzzed up by the head of the bed, sounding incredibly happy. I was unsure what I just agreed to, but at least she wasn't crying anymore.

Eventually, the revolving door slowed; it was just Ronan, Cal, and me. Bacchus was off swimming or chasing girls. I wasn't sure if I bought his *dip in the ocean to rejuvenate* story. The ladykiller smelled like perfume every time he came back to the hospital.

The three of us chatted about everything except—*that*. My friends still had no idea what happened to me. I don't know why, but I couldn't talk about it.

I needed mental rest, and for now, they humored me. Eventually, the whole house of cards would tumble, and it wouldn't be pretty.

We did talk about *Gush*. The boys told me it was still creating a nightmare for the Sheriff, and a task force was put in place to tackle the problem. It was getting dicey for Gideon, who was busy trying to do damage control and keep the truth from bubbling to the surface.

The police came to question me at the hospital. I was lucky that when Cain drained me dry, he was sloppy about it and made a real mess of one side of my neck. It was a bad enough injury that I blamed the extreme blood loss on a crazy vampire wannabe attacking me while I waited on the corner and making a mess with his human teeth.

The story was a tough sell. The officers peppered me with questions: where was I, how did I meet him, why was I waiting on the corner, could I give a description, and so on.

I answered them as vaguely as possible, then managed to get some breathing room by pretending I felt woozy.

Ronan disappeared when the police arrived at the hospital, and neither he nor Bacchus were visible at the scene, so they were off the hook.

Unfortunately, they grilled Cal mercilessly when they caught up to him back in Marathon.

After years of masquerading as a human, Cal was a master of deception. He convinced the police that my attacker hit him from behind, knocking him unconscious before going after me. Luckily, there were no street cameras down Caroline, so eventually, they had no choice but to accept it.

Somehow, the newspaper learned of the attack and tried to interview me in my hospital room by sneaking in at the end of visiting hours. At one look from Ronan, the reporter made tracks.

With the whole *Gush* insanity running them ragged, the authorities were less resistant to the idea of nutters running around town thinking they were vampires. I breathed a sigh of relief when things finally settled down, and I was left alone.

The day came when the hospital released me, and having the sun on my face was glorious. My color was back to normal, and I felt stronger.

Returning to the bight was a relief after the hospital, and I was desperate to hit the ocean. I refused to think about what happened and wanted my life to return to normal immediately, if not sooner. I knew I wasn't acting reasonably, but I didn't care. Some days, it was ok to be batshit crazy.

Unfortunately, James was determined to pull the plug on my stay in Key West.

"You're coming home to Marathon, Edaline, and that's final. There's too much shit going on in this town, and it's no longer safe. I'm sorry. You understand, don't you?"

"I understand, James. I don't want anything to happen to the *Wanderlust*, either."

James frowned. "Eddi, this has nothing whatsoever to do with the boat. I don't care about the Grady-White."

He ran his hand through his sandy hair and looked over at Cal, standing quietly at the stern.

"I care about you. Both of you."

Accepting his decision and running home to lick my wounds in private crossed my mind. I wanted to hide from the evil beasts that did this to me.

But if I gave in to fear, they would get off scot-free. My father was dead, and Cal, Ronan, and I had all suffered at their hands. They would pay for it if it was the last thing I did.

Ronan was right. Sometimes, revenge was justified. Gideon had said something similar the night he took my memories. Ever since my past came flooding back, I felt like a different person. A tougher person.

So I took a deep breath and lied through my teeth.

"James, I know you want me home safe and sound. But I like it here. A lot of fun stuff is happening in town, and I met a new friend. Things run smoothly when Cal is here four days a week, and you have Evan back at Davy Jones. He's doing fine, isn't he? He was a good divemaster for me."

James nodded. "Yes, he's a hard worker and getting his Captain's license. But Eddi, I worry about you down here. Look at you! It was too close this time. I would never forgive myself if you got hurt again."

"How about this, James? I'll come home for a week or two. I'll heal up, take some time to get over this incident, and then come back and start up with charters again."

James shook his head.

"You can leave the *Wanderlust* here and return for large groups while I'm gone. That will make it worth the drive from Marathon. I'll come back good as new and ready to make you some money."

Frowning, James turned to look across the bight. He was thinking it over, so I added, "I get bored doing the same tours repeatedly. This is fun. It's different. *Please?*"

I got my way. The whole time I was pushing James, I kept wondering why I was being such a dumbass. Staying here with all the chaos and danger was beyond stupid.

But then I remembered my father and how hard he fought for me. It was time they paid for what they'd done. It was time to break free and end their reign of terror.

CHAPTER 23

It was evening, and I was on the *Wanderlust* as the sun streaked the skies with a blazing display. I was packing my things for home, the walls of my cozy cabin glowing a bright mandarin from the light coming through the portholes.

I wouldn't be gone long, but I would miss Key West. Somehow, living here had grown on me, and I loved the town's quirky vibe. I was glad that we'd be coming back soon.

James was our chauffeur tonight, returning to take out my Tuesday and Thursday charters. I joked that he had to pay for the motor upgrade somehow. He didn't laugh, his expression more like eating a lemon.

As I packed, Gideon stood guard on a rooftop nearby while Cal and Ronan helped one of the Gryphon's shifters scour the town one last time before we left.

The legwork so far had been extensive, and coming up empty-handed was infuriating. Where were the bastards hiding?

I still hadn't come face to face with the Gryphon since the kidnapping. I considered that a plus for now.

"Thank God I don't have to deal with him," I mumbled as I zipped up my suitcase.

I spoke too soon. A thump on the dock and heavy footfalls padding toward the boat told me Gideon was here.

I peered sideways through the porthole window, startled to see his big cat half visible beside the boat. Gideon sunned himself like a cat with his feline paws tucked under and his tail gently tapping the boards where he lay. It was strange that he wasn't cloaked. What was he doing?

I tiptoed over to the shuttered door and peeked through. I saw the Gryphon's eagle half from here.

Slowly, he stretched his feathered neck over the boat railing. His face was right outside the door, but he was preternaturally still. Gideon folded his long, narrow ears alongside his head, the tufts lifting in the breeze, but that was the only thing that moved.

It was time to face the beast that had saved me, only to drop me off on the highway like a bag of unwanted puppies. With my game face on, I stepped through the shutter door.

"How are you feeling, Edaline?" His voice boomed in my face.

Even seeing it coming, I jumped.

"I'm fine, Gideon. James will be here soon." I looked around nervously and said, "Quite a few people are still around. I'd be careful if I were you."

He seemed disappointed by my reaction and cocked his head at my words. I felt him probing around in my mind.

"So, Gideon, are you staying in Key West while Cal and I go home to Marathon? Mr. Darcy must be missing you by now."

"I will remain for a day or two. We will watch Cain's house to see if anyone comes back. It is unlikely, but we must be meticulous."

I didn't want him digging around in my head and discovering that my memories had returned. So I talked about the weather, the hospital food, and my suspicions about Ronan's brother being a bit of a lady's man. I kept hoping he'd leave before someone happened by and saw a massive Gryphon lying on the dock beside my boat.

I knew he was puzzled over my sudden chatty streak, so I blocked him by thinking about Mr. Potato Head with his glasses and mustache face.

Bite on that, you intrusive bastard.

Gideon cocked his head and blinked. *"We need to talk, Edaline. I must know the details of your attack."* He stood, shaking his wings out with a feathery ruffle.

I glanced around the harbor, but we were still alone. Why was he standing there in plain view?

The giant bird-tiger flicked his tail, his eyes watchful. Gideon was clever. He knew something was up, and eventually, I'd hear about it.

"I'll tell you when I'm ready, Gideon. I need some time, OK? Don't push."

I felt a paralyzing tension rise in my guts, so I beat a hasty retreat into the cabin, slamming the shutter door in his face. I heaved a relieved sigh when I heard the dock bounce again and the sound of his wings thumping away above the *Wanderlust*.

My stomach churned; a confrontation with him was not an option. I felt sick about my past and how things had unfolded in that meadow. I needed time to process what he had done.

My pulse was racing, and I wondered how long it would be before I felt normal again. I was brushing off my near death, shoving it into a corner of my mind to fester, and I knew it wasn't wise. But I was used to hiding my feelings.

I had one close friend, and I couldn't bring myself to tell him the details of my trauma. What was wrong with me?

I grabbed my bag and sunglasses, wondering how long I could hold Gideon off. It would help that he stayed in Key West for at least a few days.

I heard footsteps and James' gentle voice as he said, "Are you ready, Edaline?"

Boy, was I ever.

***

When Phoebe visited me in the hospital, I had asked if she would ward my apartment and Cal's for good measure. She was happy to help, gave us a meager price for her work, and drove the hour to Marathon to meet Cal at my place. A robust set of protection wards were in place well before we arrived home.

Miri had remained on board the *Wanderlust*, promising to stay away when James was there for his trips. It worked out perfectly. As much as it pained me to say it, getting a break from her was a huge relief.

It was the best feeling in the world when I climbed the stairs and opened the door to the familiar scents and sounds of my personal space. I hadn't realized how much I missed it.

I looked over at the little kitchen table and saw an envelope. It was from Phoebe.

Inside was a card with a cartoon of someone in a hospital gown dragging a pole with an IV of wine. It said, "They say laughter is the best medicine, but have you tried Zinfandel?"

I had to smile. At least there was one good thing that happened in Key West.

***

"I'm coming with you."

Cal stood on the little beach at Davy Jones as I launched my kayak. He glanced at Evan, who was scrubbing the deck of Captain Brian's charter boat, to make sure he couldn't hear us. Evan looked up and responded with a wave, his short brown hair and dry shorts almost blending in with his lean, bronzed torso.

"Cal, it's ok. I'm fine. It's been almost a week! Besides, you know Ronan will pop out of the channel when he figures out where I am.

Ronan and I spent a few hours together every day doing what he called *human* things. He was terrified to let me out of sight, and he needed an excuse to guard me.

Gideon had returned from Key West and was hovering more than usual. I fixed his wagon when I rigged up a holster for Bert's phone. I ensured Cal was with me to run defense on the "picking my brains" thing. Gideon was not impressed.

I knew Hex and Cain were out there. They would be gunning for me after my escape. Sure, I was terrified of the monsters that hunted me, and I'd be a fool to think this was over.

But I was tired of running and being afraid. No more drowning under the pain of loss, abuse, and the constant fear of attack from a force I didn't fully understand.

My memories did not return alone. With them came all the knowledge and training my father had given me up on the mountain. The courage that had helped me stand tall by my father's side was elbowing its way to the surface, shoving out all the insecurity and fear of the last ten years. I was becoming myself again.

Today, I wanted to get out and relax—no talking, no thinking. I wanted to see the turquoise ocean and enjoy my favorite island haunt. I was ready to face this battle head-on, starting today.

"Eddi, I don't like you going alone. Don't fight me on this. I'm coming, and that's final."

"No, you're not. You're staying at work so that James doesn't fire your ass, and I'll be back in an hour or two. Let me do this, Cal. It's important to me."

Cal wasn't happy, but in the end, I won the battle.

I let the tide take my kayak, and as I drifted under the bridge to the Atlantic side, I felt like I was breathing for the first time since Cain stole my freedom.

With a happy smile, I paddled past a sandy tidal pool and came across a baby lemon shark stranded in the shallow water. The tide was low today, and the poor thing became frantic when I got close. It threw itself against the thick clumps of sea grass walling the pool, desperate to escape me. The water would rise again in a few hours, but the lemon shark didn't know that.

I shivered, and my skin prickled as my mind snapped back to being trapped in a cold, dark room at the mercy of a psychotic vampire.

Shaking off the terrifying memories, I back-paddled to give him space. I wondered what sharks would think about their reputation with the human race. We weren't that different when it came to basic instincts.

I paddled a couple hundred yards offshore to the long sandbar stretching toward the park, stopping to swim in the center of the enormous cerulean playground. It was an extreme low tide today, and in places, large patches of sand stuck out of the shallow water. I always laughed at how strange it looked to have a beach in the middle of the ocean.

The crystal clear water was incredible. I floated my kayak into the kiddie pool depths and plopped down next to it, sipping my can of iced tea. Holding my hand out just below the surface, I marveled at the clarity of the seawater. I turned my hand back and forth, looking at all the scrapes from working outside on my boat.

I turned and did the same with the other hand. The hand that Cain had crushed. It responded to Ronan's healing magic and was almost normal now. I lifted my fingers to my neck, the scab healing quickly as well. I had been very lucky.

I examined the two crooked fingers that he couldn't fix. The nail bed of each finger had a dark blue stripe, and I would lose them both, eventually.

I snatched a breath as my chest tightened and closed my eyes.

Breathe. In. Out. You're fine.

I sat quietly, almost jumping out of my skin when a spotted eagle ray coasted past. It was so close that the two-and-a-half-foot wingspan almost touched my leg. I froze so I didn't scare it away.

Every beautiful ring of white on its black skin was plain to see, and its cat-like eyes darted glances toward me as it sailed along, looking for a meal. Instinctively knowing it was being watched, with a flip of its tail, the wing-like fins carried it away to safer waters.

The glowing blue ocean surrounding the Keys carried on as far as the eye could see, blending into darker water near the horizon. I floated and looked up at the incredible sky and the tufts of clouds slowly drifting across it. I felt at peace, and my nerves slowly calmed as I soaked in the tranquility of my happy place.

I was glad I had sunglasses. The sun was hotter than Hades, and my skin prickled under its assault. Before heading to the island, I slathered on more SPF 60 waterproof sunscreen. Every Floridian knows a second-degree burn sucks.

As I approached the island, I passed a couple as they left. They smiled and waved, their fishing poles poking from kayak rod holders, making me wish I hadn't been so lazy today. A fish taco for dinner would have been amazing.

I hung out at my little swimming hole, alternating between sitting on my Cobra to dry off and flopping back in the water when I got too hot. I hadn't seen anyone in a while, so I jumped when I turned around and Gideon was there.

"Hello, Edaline."

I don't know why, but his intrusion into my perfect day made me hot under the collar.

"Why the hell do you always find it necessary to make me jump out of my skin? Does it tickle your funny bone? Because I've had just about enough of your games, *Gideon*."

If he was surprised by my lashing out, he didn't show it. The Gryphon flopped in the water and sank until only his feathered neck and head stuck out. I saw the tips of his impressive wings folded under the surface, occasionally poking out as he settled in. He turned his head, and I saw he was panting, his short, forked tongue fluttering.

"I was hot. I'm sorry. I didn't mean to scare you."

He cocked his head, his eyes glowing as they stared into my face.

"Why have you been avoiding me, Edaline?"

Ignoring him, I pulled up an image of Mr. Potato Head again.

"What is this potato creature you keep showing me? And why does he change features every time?"

"None of your business, you big hairy Albatross."

Gideon jerked so hard that the ripples from his hefty frame made small waves.

His glowing yellow eyes narrowed, and he went still, staring into my eyes without blinking.

"Don't try your mind fuckery on me, bird. I'm onto you."

"Edaline. What aren't you telling me?"

One leg cocked, I put my hand on my chin, my index finger tapping my lips. "Hmmm, let me see." I dropped my hand. "NONE of your business."

I was making him angry. His long feline tail curled high out of the water, the Q-tip end tipping forward and swinging back and forth.

I shivered at the memory of the scorpion tail on the Manticore, then snapped my mind shut like a steel trap.

Gideon dropped his tail with a splash.

"*I see.*"

That was all he said before turning his head and rolling over onto his other side.

I dropped down onto my knees until the water covered my shoulders. We stared at each other.

Well, he was staring. I was glaring.

"You did the tail thing on purpose."

Gideon chuckled, the deep rumble echoing in my head.

I wasn't giving him an inch, so as I enjoyed the cooling water, I doubled down and thought of Mr. and Mrs. Potato Head going at it, making baby spuds, and dealing with diapers, formula, and babysitters.

I thought about Mrs. Potato Head hoeing her garden. She smiled when the trampy Yukon Gold from next door hopped the fence and pulled off his plastic shorts with a flourish. When Mrs. P reached into her apron and slapped on her hooded eyes and "O" shaped lips, Yukon sprouted. She bent over and *su—*"

"*Edaline, stop it. We need to talk.*"

"Ok, I'll talk. I need to know about Cal. He said he can't mate because he'll die. Is that true?"

Gideon startled, pulling his head back, then cocking it. He didn't answer.

"I know you have the information, Gideon. So tell me. Is he destined to be lonely forever?" There was dead silence. Gideon looked out across the water, and then he turned to me.

"*Cal's lineage is obscure. There is not much information available. I do not have answers; I have presumptions.*"

I stared. The bird-tiger knew something.

"Well, what are these 'presumptions' you have, Gideon?"

"*I cannot say, in case I am wrong. But there is someone who would have solid answers. When we finish with Hex and Cain, I will tell you what I know.*"

I gawked at him. Finally, after all this time, I got a straight answer about something. Well, almost an answer. I was on a roll.

"Ok, I'm going to hold you to that. So, while we're bonding here, where's the cell phone I rigged up for you?" I looked at his monstrous paws visible under the crystal-clear water, minus a harness strapped to his leg.

"I don't see it. Why aren't you wearing it, Gideon?"

"*I forgot it at home.*"

I growled in frustration. "How will it work the next time I get kidnapped, and no one can contact you, hmm? Wear the phone, *Gideon!*"

"*I can't answer it in my Gryphon form.*"

"That's bullshit, and you know it. I rigged it up so you can hit any key with that long pointy thing on your face, and it will answer. Then all you have to do is listen carefully while we frantically scream what's happening and where to find us so you can save the day."

"The band is too tight. It hurts my leg."

"Then adjust it, you moron. It's not rocket science. It's VELCRO!" By now, my face was crimson, and my blood pressure spiked. Why did this asshole get me so angry?

Gideon was quiet for a while, his shining eyes scanning my face. I heard a sigh in my mind.

"Edaline, this isn't about Cal, Velcro, or that potato creature you keep showing me. It's about the night that your father d—"

My eyes shot open, and I jumped to my feet. At the top of my lungs, I shrieked, "Shut it. Don't you say one more word, you bastard!"

A raging inferno of heat flared through me, and I grabbed my paddle, tossed my gear onto my kayak, and pushed off into the current. I let the brisk tide sweep me away from the mythical mouthpiece.

CHAPTER 24

"You said WHAT? How do you get away with that, Eddi? If I said that to him, he'd cut my head off and feed me to the sharks."

I hadn't told Cal or Ronan what happened while hovering between life and death. They had no idea my memories were back, although they suspected something had changed in me. I would tell them when I was ready and not before.

For the last ten years, I had fanned the tiniest spark of hope that my father might still be alive somewhere, looking for me. Now that I knew the truth about what transpired that night in the meadow, I had a crushing certainty that he died that night in the meadow.

The naive, blissfully ignorant basket case was gone. Every day, I felt confidence and a deep-seated anger growing alongside my restored memories. Secretly, I wondered if Ronan would care for the real Eddi—the one that could stand on her own two feet.

My first day back to work was a relief. The routine of biking to the marina, serving customers, and joking with Cal was a breath of fresh air after moping in my apartment for days. I was glad to be back where I felt at ease.

I headed for my hunk of coral to sit and eat lunch, my gaze drifting to see what was happening around the marina this afternoon.

Captain Brian was leaving for a charter, a bachelor party on board. Evan was the first mate today, his white teeth gleaming in his darkly tanned face as he smiled. The High Society idled past me down the channel, and Brian waved. His sunglasses were propped on his head, showing off his white raccoon eyes and making me grin.

I watched as they cleared the channel and entered the colorful ocean, the three powerful outboards churning as Brian throttled forward and turned along his GPS coordinates.

Good luck today, Brian.

Cal rinsed life jackets at the nearby wash rack, and James tinkered on a boat motor in the shade. Another day in the life at Davy Jones Locker.

I smiled and looked to see if the Troll had another barbeque going with his man-eating parrot while enjoying his derelict monstrosity. He wasn't, and I got a big surprise. Bert's boat was gone.

That's odd.

I scanned the slips, looking for his eyesore, then wondered, did Bert win the lottery? Because instead of the beat-up Ranger Tugboat tainting the end slip, there was a brand new navy blue Ranger R27 Luxury Edition Tugboat.

It was so clean it sparkled. It had all the bells and whistles—satellite, solar panels, covered decks, curved glass windshield, overhead atrium, and stainless steel ... *everything*.

I stood up and headed over to investigate. As I got closer, I saw it had air conditioning and was pushed through its glamorous, fun-filled life by two matching white 300-horsepower four-stroke Yamahas, each worth more than most people's vehicles.

Those would look amazing on the Wanderlust.

I kept walking. When I was almost there, a strapping man in his thirties came out of the swanky teak and leather living quarters and fired up the fancy schmancy barbecue on the stern deck.

A built-in grill. Sweet.

The owner was a big boy, maybe six-three, and his sandy blonde hair was gorgeous—medium length and with a soft wave. His profile was spectacular, with a chiseled jaw and bare, tanned shoulders sporting muscles for days.

Ronan was a heart-breaking hottie, but this guy had the symmetrical perfection you expected of a marble statue at the Louvre. It was hard to resist a peek at his sculpted butt—*HOLY SHIT.*

He stared at me, his mesmerizing hazel eyes curious. Was that—yep, he had a small cleft in his chin. Blushing, I decided retreat was no longer an option, so I walked the rest of the way as if I wasn't busted.

"Hello," I said with a red-faced smile. The handsome stranger didn't respond, but he did raise his eyebrows.

"I'm Edaline. I work at the Bait Shop and noticed you're new here. I wanted to say hi. Welcome to Davy Jones Locker."

His mouth dropped open. I got a clear look at the bronze highlights dancing in his hair, and sinfully, I wondered what it would feel like to run my fingers through it.

"You want to run your fingers through my hair?" he asked, his voice sharp with surprise.

I slapped my hand over my mouth.

Did I just say that out loud? Shit, I think I did.

I shook my head and looked at Adonis. I figured that was as good a name as any because this guy was a God among mortals.

I realized I was staring; he stared back, and the conversation died before it got off the ground.

Wow, Awkward.

"I'm sorry," I stammered. "I usually avoid this end of the docks because the piece of junk that usually sits here is such an eyesore."

The guy put down his barbecue flipper and, turning toward me, frowned. In a deep, familiar voice that was almost a purr, he spoke.

"Hello, Edaline. I see there's something else you haven't told me." Mr. Darcy flew out of the glassed living quarters, landed on his shoulder, and began preening his sandy locks. Even the damn parrot looked perfect, not a feather out of place; there was a shine to the blues and golds that made my eyes hurt.

I gawked. I tried to speak and choked. My mouth hung open, and I said, *"Ahhh..."*

All in that order. It took me a minute to finish one loop around the NASCAR track in my brain and put it all together. I slapped both hands over my mouth and laughed into them.

"It was a *Glamour?* Oh my GOD, that piece of crap was never real!?"

I bent over and laughed so hard I couldn't stop. Tears streamed down my face, and my guts started hurting, but still, I couldn't stop. I was drunk on the laughter; I stood up, and Bert—no, *Gideon in his birth form*—was laughing too. That set me off again.

I took a momentary break and forced out, "I'm happy to see you have a shot at getting laid in this lifetime," then doubled over in choking laughter again.

Cal heard the commotion and came over from the wash station.

"What's up, Edaline? Are you ok? Why are you laughing?" He looked at Gideon and back at me, clearly confused.

I turned to Cal, my eyes pouring sparkling tears of sunshine, my face red from the lack of air.

"Bert's piece of shit boat—*and BERT*—they're beautiful! Like the Gods have come down and waved magical stardust on everything, and now the pumpkin is a carriage!" I wheeze-coughed, having trouble pulling in air, and Cal looked even more confused.

"Edaline, what are you talking about? It's still ugly, and Bert—Cal looked at Gideon—well, he's still *Bert*. Are you ok?"

I stood up straight, looked at Cal, then glanced at Gideon. It dawned on me.

Cal can't see through Gideon's Glamor. But I can. What the —?

Gideon answered my unspoken question with a voice that perfectly matched his God-like physique. "Edaline, I think dancing with death has brought out a few changes in you. Or so it seems. Starting with seeing through Glamors."

He gave me a "we'll be having a chat" look and returned to flipping his burgers, shaking his head.

Cal handed me the towel he had around his neck, and I wiped my eyes, still laughing a bit but trying hard to reel it in.

My throat raw, I looked at Gideon and said, "Well, on the bright side, working with you will be more fun now!"

And then I started laughing again.

***

The "Gideon is beautiful" hysterics lifted my spirits, and returning to my normal routine, even for a week, made me feel like myself again.

I revisited every memory from that night on the mountain. In the safety of my warded apartment, under the covers of my comfortable bed, I relived the hellish scene moment by agonizing moment. I cried and sobbed, punched my pillow, and let my anger and sorrow wash over me until I reached an agonized acceptance. I had waited ten years to experience it and let it come.

As the days passed, and I became more accustomed to the hole in my past suddenly filled with a living nightmare, I slowly came to terms with my new reality.

Our break in Marathon was nearing an end, and I decided it was time to share my story with the guys. I'd invited them to my warded apartment for a quiet night on the Widow's Walk. It was time to spill the beans.

Ronan hauled a new plastic patio chair up the ladder he'd picked out himself. It was pink.

"I like pink," he said when he pulled it off the shelf at the Big K. When Cal laughingly explained that it wasn't a GUY color, Ronan frowned and jammed it awkwardly in the cart.

I love a man who was in touch with his feminine side. Also, one who knew what he wanted, which apparently was ME.

We lounged on the elevated deck, enjoying the last rays of the sun. I told them everything. What happened with Cain, how I tried to defend myself and escape, and the rough-looking addict who, it turns out, saved my life.

It was a lengthy, painful retelling, and by the time I finished, it was black as pitch on our tiny rooftop oasis. Cal lit a Citronella candle, which was nice. It gave us enough light to enjoy our sweet tea and relax.

I tipped my head back and let the salty ocean breezes blow away the last two weeks of tension. Somehow, it was easier to tell my tale in the dark. And surprisingly, getting it out in the open eased my mind.

Halfway through, Ronan pulled his chair beside me and grabbed my hand, tucking it against his belly. I looked at Cal, wondering what I'd see, but he smiled at the kind gesture. My friend had accepted Ronan into the fold. How ironic that an octopus was the best friend a girl could ever hope for—even though he sometimes sided with Gideon.

"So what now, Ed? Is Gideon going to hear these details? He's the Enforcer. He needs to know everything. You're putting yourself in danger by giving him a hard time and withholding vital information."

Cal's hands were twisting in his lap again. A nervous habit that always reminded me of his Octopus. My friend was concerned about how things were going between me and the big furry feather bag. He cautioned me, time and again, that one day I'd cross the line, and Gideon wouldn't have a choice. He would be forced to put me in my place, even if he liked me.

"Eddi, If you push him too far, he'll come down on you."

"Let him," I said. "I don't care."

***

Ronan had given me plenty of space ever since Key West, and after a week, I still couldn't bring myself to cross that line in the sand between us. I hadn't a clue what was holding me back.

Sure, he'd helped me relieve the physical stress of the Incubus attack, and I'll admit, Ronan was a world-class pearl diver, but that was all we'd shared. The giant space between us was back, and neither knew how to cross it. I cut myself some slack.

Having a near-death experience gives you a free pass for a week. It was a new rule I made up since I'd had so many of them these last few months. It was hard to fathom why horrible things kept happening to me. Being a Djinn, I was born into it, I guess.

There were still so many unanswered questions. Why was Hex targeting me? What was on that cart that Cain brought into the room before I escaped?

Gideon knew. But as always, that was a dead end. I ground my molars together, my hands clenching. I needed to find out the entire story. I would get answers, one way or another.

Today, Bacchus and Ronan were my watchdogs. I was no longer allowed much freedom; for now, I was okay with it. I paddled to the Island for a swim and a snorkel. I was heading back to Key West in the morning, and Cal would come with me.

As we lounged in the swimming hole at the island, Bacchus had my sunscreen. Pulling the flip cap up, he sniffed it and made a face. "What's your plan once you get back to Key West?"

"I honestly don't know, Bacchus. Cal will help get the Charters going again. We'll always try to stay together and keep looking for signs of where they're hiding their operation. It's a small island. I know we'll find them."

Ronan growled. "He found *you,* Eddi. Let's not forget that."

"I understand you're worried. But in my heart, I know I have to keep moving forward. My father died because of these bastards. Surely, you understand the need for closure?"

It was a touchy subject. Ronan still felt responsible for his mother's death. He would never stop looking for justice. He turned away and dropped out of the conversation, gazing at the sparkling ocean.

I licked my lips, trying to decide if I wanted to set things straight with Ronan. In the end, I went there.

"Ronan, the first day we met—the day you used your lure on me. It didn't stick. And I'm not addicted to your *Nectar*, either."

His head whipped around. "How do you know this?"

I looked at Bacchus, glad he was here to help diffuse this tricky conversation.

"Because I'm not fully human. I recently found out I'm half Djinn."

There was silence, so I looked up, and two sets of emerald eyes stared at me with a stiffness that made me nervous.

"What? Is that a bad thing? It just means I'm not human, so I'm not as affected by your lure, right? Viggo told me only humans get addicted. I'm fine. What I felt for you was—"

I glanced at Bacchus, then turned to Ronan, who watched me intently.

"They were real feelings. I wanted to let you know, in case you still felt bad about using your lure on me."

Bacchus burst out laughing. "Eddi, Syreni don't feel bad about using lures or Nectar. We live for that shit," he held his stomach, his deep snorts sounding ridiculous.

Ronan gave him a searing glare, then looked at me. His eyes searched my face, but he appeared relieved.

"Don't listen to Bacchus. He may love messing with humans and Syreni girls, but I'm not like that. You're a Djinn?"

"Well, half Djinn. At least, I think so. Gideon's not saying, and I keep trying, but I don't seem to have any powers." I rolled my eyes. "That's pretty much par for the course for me, right? I'm a dud."

Ronan pulled himself closer, and under the water, he took my hand and spoke in my mind.

"I'm so relieved to hear this news, Eddi. Thank you for telling me."

Bacchus wiped his eyes, his laughter trailing off. We talked about Djinn for a time, but the Syreni didn't know much about them either. Ronan kept staring into my face as if trying to understand this new side of me.

Bacchus was unconcerned as if he met a Djinn every day.

"Not to change the subject, but Tabitha wants to return to Key West with us." He looked at Ronan, who was still seething at his disrespectful comments. "Big Brother won't let her."

I looked at Ronan. "Who is Tabitha?"

"She's my younger sister." He grinned at me and gave me a playful poke under the water. "You'd probably get along well. She's always getting into trouble as well."

"Ronan is mad because she beats him at *Bellum* sometimes."

I looked at Ronan for an explanation.

"Fighting," he said. "We train weekly to protect the Shoal, and she never stops trying to best me."

He gave me an intense look. "I would love to show you the Shoal sometime, but I don't know how we would do that. The entrances to the tunnels are underwater."

I smiled. "Well then, it's good that I'm a certified diver, Ronan." I reached out to rub his tanned, muscular shoulder.

"I'd like nothing better than to see where you live."

***

As James' truck headed south on Highway 1, I had a lump in my throat and determination in my heart. Going back was harder than I thought, but once I hit the lively streets and spent a bit of time shopping and seeing the sights, I felt better.

Cal was with me, which was a blessing. This time, the plan was daylight adventures only because Vampires couldn't tolerate the sun. No one was to go anywhere alone, and Ronan, Bacchus, and Gideon would resume their neighborhood watch.

"Don't guard an empty boat this time, guys." Miri cackled. She was still bragging about saving me that night while the "dumb" Syreni missed everything.

The wards on the Wanderlust would protect us, and Gideon was already in Key West. It was as safe as we could manage.

Even if it wasn't enough, I didn't care. I was done running. I dealt with a rising tide of fury, and Cal was becoming worried I would do something stupid. My octopus friend was my constant shadow.

The Gryphon had visited the widow's walk the night before we left Marathon. I was enjoying my last sunset in Marathon, surrounded by the glowing sky and sipping a sweet tea when I heard his wings. I braced for an inquisition.

He landed directly behind me with a gentle bump and a rustle of feathers that sounded loud to my ears.

How he managed the landing was a mystery because the rooftop terrace barely held the table and three chairs. I looked over my shoulder and saw that he was sitting, his wings clenched tightly to his sides.

"I wouldn't move too quickly if I were you. I don't think the building codes have Gryphons in mind."

It was harder for him to scare me now that I could see him coming, but hearing his six-inch talons clicking on the wooden floor behind my back made me shudder.

Gideon was quiet at first, and I felt the whispers of him fishing through my mind, still trying to get the answers he wanted.

Mr. Potato Head, now divorced, had his pirate hat on. He and Miss Idaho, in her pageant swimsuit, did naughty things in his new infinity pool. Neither were taking questions at this time.

Sadly, Gideon interrupted my fun.

"Enough, Edaline. It's time. I know you've remembered some of what happened that night on Bald Mountain. I can't do my job if you don't tell me all the details of your abduction. I must insist, and if you don't tell me, I'll drag it out of you. I cannot keep everyone safe otherwise."

He meant business, so with a huge sigh, I laid it all on the table. Front to back, top to bottom, memories, Giants and Manticores, the blood bath with Cain, the guy who inadvertently saved me, the works. I spilled.

"Satisfied?" I turned away to watch the seabirds out over the water.

"No, not really. There are tasks that I must perform that I don't like, Edaline. That was one of them. It's no coincidence that I'm here with you in the Keys. You realize that, don't you?"

I looked at him, and his yellow eyes glowed. He blinked.

"I had thought of that, yes. But I wasn't sure you had a heart, Gideon."

He ignored my barb, and it was quiet for a moment, and then I asked him something that had festered ever since my memories returned.

"Why did I have a Guardian? And where is my birth mother? I can't remember much before the night they killed Father."

Gideon scraped Cal and Ronan's chairs to the side as he carefully eased himself onto his belly, his massive feathered head at eye level as I sat in my chair. It was like having iced tea with a sphinx.

Gideon sighed. He was so close that I smelled the ocean breeze on his feathers—and the bonito he had for lunch. Yep, definitely too close.

"The Sovereign appointed the Guardian to protect you when your mother died. Imara was with you since you were five. Most children don't recall much of their early childhood. You must remember snippets, do you not?"

"Not much. I remember living in a big city and my father being gone a lot. There was a school, and I remember one teacher, but I can't recall my mother's face." I looked at him. "That's strange, isn't it?"

Another lengthy silence. Right, no answer for that either. I resisted the urge to slap it out of him.

"Edaline, it's important that you know—your father was very dedicated to you. Ezen contacted the Sovereign Council when he realized the people he worked for plotted something terrible. They were after you, Edaline."

"Let me guess, that's all you can tell me, isn't that about right?" I crossed my arms in frustration and watched as twilight fell over the ocean. Gideon ignored my question, his eyes glowing as he stared into my face.

"What happened to my mother, Gideon? Tell me." I turned to look at him, my eyes wet with unshed tears. *"Please."*

He looked away as if deciding how much to say. Then he lowered his head and said, *"She was assassinated."*

My eyes shot open. Not cancer, a car accident, or dying in childbirth, thank the Gods for small mercies—*assassinated.*

"Tell me, Gideon. I need to know! You can't drop a bomb like that and leave me hanging."

The monstrous Gryphon eased himself to his feet and opened his wings. He held them there for a moment, letting the ocean breeze lift them, ruffling the small feathers on the underside. He flicked his long tail, and it knocked over Ronan's pink chair.

"I cannot. It is not time. I have specific instructions on this. I am sorry, Edaline."

I wanted to punch and kick and scream at him. But I knew it would be wasted energy. I would figure it out myself. I didn't need him.

"Edaline, be careful in Key West. Hex and Cain are still there and running out of Nectar. That will make them very dangerous. They weren't just after the Syreni for their Nectar, Edaline. Stay together, and I will watch over you as much as I am able."

He crouched, and the Widow's Walk made a sound of protest. Gideon slanted a wide-eyed look my way, then, with a gentle hop, used muscular strokes of his wings to lift himself daintily from the deck.

Thanks to the unknown power I'd acquired, there was no blinking out of sight. Gideon's glamor no longer worked on me. I followed his progress as he rose to the currents high above and, with a few powerful strokes, disappeared into the gloaming.

At least he couldn't scare me half to death anymore like he had so many times in the past.

The evening I left Key West, and he visited me at the boat, Gideon was unaware I saw through his Glamor. He'd lain in wait for me, planning to scare me—for kicks. For some strange reason, that made me smile.

CHAPTER 25

~ DEPUTY JAKE MILLER ~

It was his third call of the night, and he was exhausted. His partner, Frank, was behind the squad car, upchucking the two burritos he had for dinner. One of the *Gushers* had kicked him in the groin hard enough to make him see stars.

He looked at the rear window of his cruiser and watched the blood trickle down the inside of the glass. Their detainee had smashed his forehead repeatedly until they opened the door to restrain him. The twenty-minute struggle had ended with a taser that stunned him long enough to truss him up in zip ties and cram him back into the cage.

The flashing lights gave him a headache, the hissing and popping of radios from ten cruisers adding to the throb at his temples. Patting his breast pocket, he found the travel packet of pain relief and ripped it open, popping two Advil to tame the beast attempting escape from his head.

He heard a whistle and looked up. His supervisor was waving him over, so he jogged across the street. Seven of Monroe County's finest were already milling in front of the bar, checking their tasers, with more arriving in a steady stream.

Shattered, the outer doors of the famous club hung by the hinges. Known for his height, Jake had an unobstructed view inside the club as he looked over the heads of his co-workers. The visual made his skin crawl.

Everywhere he looked, there were naked bodies, their writhing forms reminding him of a ball of worms in a bait can. There had to be close to a hundred bodies squirming on the floor of that bar, and every one of them was high on *Gush*.

The moaning and grunting were irritating enough to send his headache into the white pain stage. He rubbed his temples as it hit home that the next hour would be a living hell.

He heard a booming crash that made him jump, then stared through the flickering shadows on the other side of the broken doors. A couple, now deathly still, were pinned under the modern-looking jukebox they'd been fucking against.

His supervisor had just called for backup and several ambulances, and the coroner already loaded one of the four bodies at the the scene. Suffocation and fighting were the main culprits tonight; it looked like a jukebox would go on that list.

The officers shared concerned glances, the shuffling sounds of their heavily booted feet growing louder. There weren't enough squad cars or jail cells in the Keys to hold that many thrashing detainees and the local hospital struggled with the injured from other calls. The only saving grace was that this bar wasn't in Old Town, where access and crowd control would have been difficult, if not impossible.

He wanted to turn around, walk to his car, process his arrest, and go home to be with his wife. But that wasn't going to happen. Not tonight, and at the rate they were going, not any night in the foreseeable future.

The cluster of nineteen officers moved in closer, their nods and grim faces signaling that it was time to begin clearing the bar. He took a deep breath and hoped that his balls wouldn't suffer the same fate as his partner's tonight.

***

If you've never gone into a bar at Happy Hour with two Syreni warriors, a Sea Sprite, and an Octopus shifter, you've never lived. Yes, we were a terrible joke tonight.

I was surprised to find out my best friend had an aversion to drunken crowds. Cal gawked at the milling faces, trying to avoid being touched by the crowds of revelers jostling around him, drinks in hand.

Bacchus smiled and danced with clusters of girls as we passed them, every enthusiastic group raising their glass in the air and screaming as he passed. Bacchus was eating it up.

Rejuvenating in the ocean, my ass.

As we worked our way through the bar, I smiled back at Ronan. He looked around with a frown on his pretty face, like he was a secret service agent sent here to protect me, Cal, and his distracted brother. I don't think Bacchus needed any help in the defense department, so perhaps Ronan was working on damage control when it came to his carousing brother.

We made our way to a tall table, and our waitress was fast, getting us a round of drinks in no time. Ronan was drinking ice water, the party pooper. Cal was drinking clamatos, and I was into the rum punches. Bacchus was drinking whatever his harem of girlfriends bought for him.

"Do Syreni have a high tolerance for alcohol?" I shouted over the noise.

Ronan shook his head. "No, those guppies are going to lead Bacchus right in over his head. I'll probably have to drag him home later."

I laughed at the guppy thing, then reached into my messenger bag where Miri was waiting. She wanted to drink tonight, so I gave her the little cup of punch I'd dunked out of my glass. She snapped her fingers.

"Oh, sorry, I forgot." I handed her the pineapple hunk from my drink, and she smiled up at me, the juice running down her arms as she lifted it.

I wonder how she's planning on eating that.

I had brought her an even bigger treat from Marathon. While biking past a yard sale last week, I saw something that made me put down my kickstand and look closer.

The woman was selling an adorable Barbie Dream Camper. Sucker that I am, I bought it for Miri. She loved it, and now it was on the *Wanderlust* taking up prime real estate.

"What a beautiful thing!" Miri had buzzed around, getting underfoot as I set it up, jamming it under the passenger seat while grumbling about my lack of foresight.

"Don't you want me to have my own place?" Miri threw her arms in the air and twirled, screaming at the top of her lungs.

"Just remember it's got no curtains, ok? No prancing around naked." I looked up and down the darkened marina, but it was late, and no one was around. "And keep it down before someone sees you."

That was yesterday. Miri had rifled through all the kit that came with the camper and found some neat things, each eliciting an ear-piercing shriek.

Tonight, the clever sprite brought a little cup from the china set. She loved it because the size fit her hand perfectly. She decided to dress up, but we got the Slutty Barbie set because the sparkly white dress barely covered her tiny ass cheeks. I cut two slits for her wings and, according to Miri, would pick up my Best Mom award later.

Something poked my arm. The miniature headache jabbed me with her sword and held up her cup.

"Slow down there, sea monster. I need you snappy if there's a problem tonight."

She blinked out of sight, and a few seconds later, there was a ripple as something dipped into a drink on our table. I ignored it because what the heck? We all needed a night out, annoying sea creatures included.

"So, Ronan. How does it feel to be a tourist having a night on the town?" I sipped my punch and gave him a coy look over my glass.

"It was a great idea, coming to Old Town. We're close to the boat and can watch the streets if we sit near the window. More eyes mean more chances of seeing something."

He leaned close to my ear and whispered, "Best of all, I get to spend time with you, "off the clock."

Ignoring the aftershocks in my shorts, I leaned back and looked into his handsome face. The smile he gave me was intense, and I loved it. It was the closest thing we could manage to a first date, and I thoroughly enjoyed spending time with him.

"Where'd you learn that phrase?"

"I watched Cal's laptop while you were in the hospital. I learn a lot about human culture by watching game shows." At my disbelief, he added, "Tara taught me how to use a few human devices."

I frowned at the mention of the jealous lionfish that had taught Ronan to speak. Seeing my expression, he gave me a soft smile and squeezed my thigh.

We visited six bars along Duval, alert for anything unusual, then headed back to the boat at dusk. We had to drag Bacchus away from his guppies, who threw a hissy fit when he left.

"Oh, come on, Ronan. They loved my muscles. We need to go back!" He did an about-face, staggering at his sudden change in direction, his eyes rolling.

Ronan slammed his shoulder into his brother's belly, and grabbing his thighs, he tossed Bacchus over his shoulder. Miri watched over the zipper of the messenger bag and howled at the sight of the muscular blue buttocks next to Ronan's face.

"Bottoms up!" she giggled.

We made it back to the boat, where Ronan unceremoniously dropped an unconscious Bacchus on the floor of the stern deck. His arm flopped out, his knuckles cracking on the toe rail. Ronan laughed, then bent down to pick up his brother's hand. He roared with laughter when he saw blood and the fish hook stuck through his brother's fleshy palm. Ronan tucked the hand over his lipstick-covered belly while Bacchus snoozed on. Brotherly love, Syreni style.

Looking tired, Miri went to her RV, which rattled as she stomped around, searching for the little tea towel blanket and sponge pillow I'd made. The RV windows were big enough that I could see everything she was up to in there. I'd have to get on those curtains.

Heaving a sigh of relief, Cal flopped on the bench in the stern.

"I'm beat, but I won't be able to sleep. You guys take the cabin. I'll keep watch." I tried to argue, but he waved me off, giving me a sly smile.

I felt guilty as I handed him a blanket and pillow, nervously checking him over for skin color and any signs of discomfort from his brush with death. All his systems appeared to function correctly, so my motherly instincts shut the door and turned off the lights.

I turned around, and Ronan was standing behind me, looking uncertain. He looked at Cal, who was already reading something on my phone. He glanced at Miri's RV, which was now quiet. She must have gone to her toy bed.

Then he gazed at me, his eyes searching my face. I grabbed his hand and pulled him into the cabin below deck.

***

Closing the shuttered doors, I turned around, suddenly unsure of what I was doing. All night, I'd imagined this moment, and now that it was here, I felt awkward.

Our night on the bench was different because I was high on Incubus magic, and it wasn't about romance; it was about relief. And the first time we *tangled*, I was naive and knew so little about him. Since then, so many things came between us. Was I doing the right thing?

He looked so sweet, standing there in his pink mermaid shirt. My heart swelled at the wide-eyed look on his face. He was nervous, too. Somehow, the knowledge soothed me. Shadows filled the cabin, the only light filtering in from the portholes on each side of the bow. I felt brave in the darkness. I could do this. I wanted this.

Ronan's eyes darted around the tiny space, his weight shifting subtly on his bare feet. He looked everywhere but at me, then saw the shoebox full of Barbie dresses lying on the bunk. They were the ones Miri and I had searched through earlier.

"You treat her well. Not many would tolerate a Sea Sprite. She's lucky to have you. I'm sorry I teased her that ni—"

I surprised him by reaching out and smoothing my hand over his cheek, pulling his face toward me. He stilled, and in our quiet, darkened nest, his emerald eyes revealed many emotions.

Worry. Fatigue. Affection. A hopeful yearning for what might happen next.

I slid my hand into Ronan's hair, and happiness joined the mosh pit of feelings whisking across his face. I smiled at him and breathed, "I've missed you so much."

His breath hitched, and closing those beautiful eyes, he leaned into my hand.

At that moment, while the world was spinning out of control outside our door, I felt happy. Being with him felt *right*.

With a groan, Ronan pulled me close and wrapped his arms around me, his hand gently caressing the ridge of my shoulders. I snuggled my face under his chin and kissed the hollow below his neck, my hand spreading open and smoothing over the hard contours of his chest. He growled; the hollow rumble sounded like an avalanche beneath my ear.

"If you keep holding me like this, I may not want to leave," he murmured.

I leaned back, giving him a wicked grin. "You aren't going anywhere, buster."

A brilliant smile flashed across his face, and I felt the lingering tension in his solid frame melt away.

Taking hold of the hem of his T-shirt, I whispered, "Lift your arms."

He stilled, and I nodded at the pretty pink mermaid staring back at me from his chest. Although it had a slice through it, Ronan refused to throw the silly thing away.

"We need to take that off. It's distracting," I said, nibbling on my smile.

Ronan lifted his arms, and I pulled it over his tousled hair, then leaned in, breathing in his masculine scent. He smelled like salt and sunshine.

"Eddi, are you drunk?" he asked, a cautious look in his eyes.

"Uh-uh," I said, shaking my head. "I only had three drinks, and I spread them out. I'm just appreciating your wonderful qualities tonight."

The smoldering look he gave me made my toes curl.

Bared to the evening air, his firm, tanned chest, and mesmerizing six-pack looked incredible. And they were all mine. I slid my hands over him, feeling every ridge along the smooth surface of his tanned skin. He shivered, goosebumps flushing across his glorious body.

I smiled at him and pulled my tee over my head.

Ronan didn't react other than a subtle widening of his eyes, his pupils expanding into the liquid green of his irises. He reached for me, and with one warm, firm hand, he cradled my neck, brushing his thumb along my throat.

Pulling me in for a kiss, Ronan sighed as his lips parted mine, and I welcomed the wet slide of his tongue. His breath dusted across my cheeks, the tickling sensation sparking a tingle across my shoulders.

Our mouths tangled in a slippery dance, the plunging sweeps of his tongue peppered with moans. Being so close and sharing such intimate sensations lit up my brain, making me frantic to get closer still—to push past his solid frame and wiggle right into the very heart of him.

Soft panting filled the stillness of the cabin, the erotic soundtrack lending a subtle background to our explorations. Ronan released my lips and nibbled down my neck, his hands smoothing across my shoulders and down the dip of my back. He flicked the clasp of my bra with a skill that made me grin against his skin. And then he was easing the dull ache in my breasts with his tongue, his warm hands cupping me, his thumbs tracing the rounded contours of my nipples.

"By the gods, Eddi. I can't stand it," Ronan whispered with a muffled groan.

With a tug, my pretty pink shorts disappeared, his masculine hands sliding down to take their place. The muscles in his shoulders flexed under my grip as Ronan eased himself onto his knees, his large palms smoothing over the rounded cheeks of my ass, kneading, squeezing. Trailing his lips across my flat belly, Ronan teasingly worked his way down until a wet tongue slid into me. I groaned, my legs parting to welcome the touch.

The tip of his tongue slid up the length of my moist slit, making my legs shake, before plunging deep inside. My fingers slid into Ronan's hair, clenching tight as his probing, stroking tongue ripped a groan from my throat. He was relentless, his hands pulling me closer as he rolled his tongue around my clit, turning my legs to jello.

"Stop....! I'm going to fall!" I rasped, my head rolling forward, my rubbery legs threatening to give way.

Ronan looked up, meeting my hooded gaze. He smiled at the expression of hazy arousal on my face, and I wobbled. He stood and wrapped an arm around me, nudging my arms up to his shoulders and dropping his lips into the crook of my neck. He kissed and nibbled while his hand slid down to part my slick channel, his fingers slipping in and out with gentle caresses.

I groaned and pushed into his hand, grabbing his shoulders. My forehead flopped forward to rest on his chest as he pulled back to look down at what he was doing to me. His strong arm held me tight as he slowly, gently circled his fingers around my throbbing nub. An inhuman strength lifted me, the tips of my toes barely touching the floor as I writhed against his slippery assault. Between the fingers sliding in and out and the lazy circles around my sopping clit until I came undone.

Sensation overwhelmed me, and I stifled a squeak, breaking his hold. Out of breath, I huffed a laugh against his chest, and he lifted his head to look into my eyes. Ronan's lust-filled gaze sent another shot of arousal straight to my belly.

His arousal pressed against me, the bulge under his skins shadowed with a thick outline. He growled, and I swear I felt it all the way to my toes.

With a hazy grin, Ronan turned and sank onto the bunk, pulling me onto his muscular lap. Leaning back, he took in my disheveled hair and glistening skin, smiling into my flushed face.

"I've wanted you for so long," he murmured, his deep voice vibrating in the quiet cabin. He massaged my butt cheeks, pulling me tighter into his lap.

Looking into his questioning eyes, I whispered, *"Me too."* I wanted to see him, take him in my hands, and watch his reaction; I would bury him in the affection dying to pour from me.

Pressing his torso back onto the mattress, I reached down to explore his length, palming the stiff arousal pushing against his glittering skin. With one firm stroke of my hand over the butter-soft scales, his erection slid free, throbbing against my hand.

His penis was beautiful, shaped as a human male's would be; he wanted me. Seeing him like this, thick, hard, and exposed for my pleasure, was an instant high. I grasped him firmly, running my hand up and down, exploring his shaft's turgid thickness. Leaning forward, I licked a bead of moisture from the tip.

Ronan grunted, his head flopping back onto the covers, his thighs arching beneath me. I stroked my hand up and down, the spastic sounds from his lips intensifying the ache between my thighs. I couldn't stand it any longer. Pressing him onto the mattress, I inched forward and straddled his rock-hard arousal; his hand shot up to grip my wrist.

Green eyes watched me in the darkness, his body tight and still. For a moment, I thought he would say no. I gave him a smug smile and reached over my head, pulling a condom from the cargo netting above. My evil side had talked me into buying them last week, the hussy.

Ronan had never seen one before because his eyes went wide.

"Shh. It's ok. It's to keep the babies away," I said, giggling.

Ronan watched as I rolled it over his massive erection. With sudden comprehension, he relaxed, his expression morphing from concerned to emboldened and then to a slack-jawed hunger. He reached for me.

I climbed his body, and after sharing a deep, probing kiss, I pushed my hips back. Finding his throbbing penis, I rubbed myself up and down the thick length of it. Ronan's eyes closed, and he moaned, his clenched hands gripping my biceps. His legs quivered, and I smiled to myself, the heady sensation of control making me feel powerful.

Seating the slick tip of his arousal into position, I slowly pressed down, easing myself over his thick, stiff cock. A guttural snarl tore from his lips, and his eyes shot open, shocking green and churning with desire. Slowly, I sheathed his granite length, the full stretch of his penetration a sublime tease to my wet channel.

Ronan squirmed beneath me, but I held his chest down with one hand and made him lie still while I destroyed him inch by tantalizing inch, raising my hips between every gentle stab of fullness. I couldn't help my soft moan of pleasure as I gazed down at his tortured expression.

Ronan's eyes clamped shut as if in pain, his Adam's apple bobbing below his clenched jaw. I stifled a grin at the tension on his face and cuddled down onto his torso. Closing my eyes, I massaged him with slow strokes, up and down, the precise swings of my hips deliberate.

Groaning, Ronan reached up to put his hands on my ass, pulling me closer as I teased more erotic sounds from his throat. I kept up a persistent, slippery rhythm as warm, darting tingles played at the base of my spine.

Growing impatient, Ronan yanked my face down to his, kissing me fiercely, his eager hips thrusting up to meet me. With a wicked smile, I flipped my ankles and held his legs down, my eyes laughing at his frowny face.

Ronan pulled me close and grumbled in my ear, "You've had your fun, puella."

With a surge of his powerful thighs, he bucked, bouncing my head off the roof. I squealed as he laughed, and in one swift movement, flipped us so that I was on the bottom, his heavy body caging me in.

Looking down at me with his chin tucked, his bright eyes roamed across my pink cheeks. The only sounds in the room were our breathless pants, and Ronan smiled. Then, he kissed me.

Stroking long and deep, his hips controlling the angle of each wet thrust, he pushed me along on a ribbon of pleasure. Gently, firmly, and steadily, he slid in and out, his turgid length prodding all the right places. I opened my thighs in invitation, my hands pulling on his bulky shoulders as his smooth stabs made my clit ache with need.

I felt passion and desire, but there was something else—something deep, binding, and solid. Emotion bubbled up like champagne, and I almost sobbed from the intensity of it.

Dragging his swollen lips from mine, Ronan found my pulse—and hesitated. He rumbled, the sound shooting straight to my core as his heavy breaths blasted my neck. I knew what he was asking.

"Yes," I moaned.

Forming a seal on the sensitive skin of my throat, he bit me, his hips thrusting deep. Two needle-sharp points pierced my skin, holding me still while his plunging length arced into me and Nectar flooded my bloodstream.

An earth-shattering orgasm rolled through me, a detonation exploding outward from our connection. Ronan's hips ground me into the mattress, his neck and shoulders tight under my hands, every muscle in his body straining. The low keening moan that tore from his throat pushed us both out to sea on a wave of pleasure—a surge of jolting spasms that finally, peacefully, ebbed away.

Ronan curled in around me, panting hard and licking the bite on my neck. I felt his Syreni Nectar dancing through my body. Tingling waves of euphoria trickled into my fingers and toes, every part of me coming alive with swirling eddies of bliss. It was an incredible cocktail of feelings; affection for my lover, a powerful sense of connection, and lingering aftershocks that circled my pussy and felt—*wonderful.*

Ronan relaxed his arms, embracing, yet somehow not crushing me with his heavy frame. Our heads were together, Ronan's buried in the crook of my shoulder.

I reached up and ran my fingers through his hair, feeling bursts of warm air against my neck. His hips juddered, the tiny strokes giving me a final, gentle massage. I cradled him close and let out a deep sigh of satisfaction.

Moments, or maybe years later, Ronan lifted his hand to my face, and turned it toward him. He smiled at me, his two luminescent green eyes glowing softly in the darkness. They fluttered closed as he placed a sweet kiss on my lips and snuggled in closer.

I smiled, hoping for a long, blissful night.

***

Bacchus laughed at me when I crawled out of the cabin, sticking my head out to see who was around. The morning was fresh and sunny, a light breeze helping to cool the burning cheeks I was currently sporting.

Of course, Cal wasn't letting me off the hook.

"We're here, you can do your walk of shame, and we're going to love it. Your hair, by the way, is directionally confused. You might want to comb it."

Ronan's head popped up behind me, and I smiled at the random thought that his pink T-shirt went well with his eyes.

The look he gave me made my heart sing. His hands found my hips, and he leaned down, whispered, "Where do you think you're going, Edaline?"

I giggled at the throaty rumble in my ear, a shiver shooting across my shoulders. Reluctantly, I stepped away from our love nest and his vibrant warmth and jumped onto the deck, clapping my hands together.

"Who bought coffee?" I asked, trying to hide my embarrassment and looking around expectantly. Three pairs of eyes looked back, with Miri's rolling as she mimed gagging.

Cal stood up, a sparkle in his eyes. He was enjoying this.

"We thought it would be nice to hit that little place by the end of the dock. The one with Cuban bread?"

Well, I was up for that, and I turned around to glance at Ronan, who was all smiles. He nodded, and I grabbed my messenger bag, watching the others clamber onto the dock. Miri wriggled into my satchel and immediately started going through my things.

"Hey. What did I tell you about that?" I grumbled. "Stay out of my Tic Tacs, you little bugger."

The walk was lovely, with the morning sun sparkling on the water and the heat not yet uncomfortable. Mornings in the Keys are always the best time of the day, with salty air, cool breezes, and the sun not yet high enough to fry unprotected skin.

The bight was already busy, with boats of every shape and size coming and going. It was surprisingly noisy in a good way. Boat motors, snatches of people's music playing quietly, and fragments of conversation and laughter floated on the breeze.

I breathed deeply, and all of my tension whispered away. Ronan strolled beside me, and when I glanced over, he smiled at me—the kind of smile that got my knickers in a knot.

"Stop that!" I tried to pinch him, but he grabbed my hand and laughed.

Ronan leaned over and whispered in my ear. "That was fun last night. Let's do it again soon." He pressed a little kiss under my ear, which made me crunch my neck. I shot him a happy smile. I had the extra sunny, morning-after aura, and it must have been pretty sappy because Bacchus turned around and rolled his eyes at us.

Everyone chatted as we strolled down the pier, and Miri chirped from my messenger bag, bugging Bacchus about his exploits from the night before.

The restaurant served standard Key West fare. Butted against the ocean, it was practical, plain but immaculate, with a magnificent view. It was one of the "about to fall into the ocean" businesses that gave the Keys a downhome vibe.

We were lucky enough to get a table on the dockside patio. Thank goodness it was in the shade because the sun was quickly building up a head of steam.

While we waited for our order, I breathed in the wonderful smell of Cuban bread, certain that it floated down from heaven. My hand was tucked into Ronan's, as if he couldn't bear to let me go.

An impressive selection of boats slipped past on their way in and out of the harbor. Boat-watching was something I relished. It was the hustle and bustle of a typical morning here in Garrison Bight, and I loved it.

When our food came, I had to laugh at the slender White Heron that landed on the railing beside us in all his long-legged splendor, waiting for a snack. The wind played with the long feathers on his head, and his golden eyes were intense. It made me think of Gideon, and I wondered where he was this morning.

Miri must have been hot in my bag because I felt her climb out, and judging by the muted grumbles, she plunked herself down near the middle of the table. The waitress gave me an odd look when I put a smidge of everything from my plate onto my saucer, and I heard Miri laugh after she left.

Sitting down with such a mixture of species was odd, but our party of five felt natural now. Bacchus entertained everyone with his silliness, and Cal took it all in, watching, thinking, and dissecting. He had his floppy sun hat on, and I smiled as memories of our adventures with that thing on his head flitted through my mind.

As I finished breakfast, I looked up in time to see James walk by, headed for the *Wanderlust*.

"Cal, James is here. Look." I pointed my knife and said, "Maybe we can catch him, and he can come to eat with us?"

Cal frowned. "That's strange. He told me he had a big charter today at Davy Jones. He said we wouldn't see him until tomorrow. I hope everything is ok."

James was too far away to catch his attention without disturbing everyone, so Cal grabbed my phone to text him, letting him know where we were.

We watched in silence as he strolled toward our slip, his face smiling and his shoulder-length sandy brown hair lifting on the breeze. He looked carefree and every bit the Keys business owner. Relaxed casual, with a look of purpose about him.

My eyes followed him, watching to see if he checked his phone. But he stopped when he was halfway down the docks, then turned around and slowly walked back. When he was in front of a big red Spectre yacht, he stopped and stared at it.

"I remember that yacht," I said. "The Black Widow. It's been here a while, but I never see anyone on board."

I looked at Cal, a nervous jitter starting in my stomach. "I stopped to look at it on my way to the bar; the night the Incubus attacked me." James was still too far away to get his attention, so I watched him, hoping he'd look our way so I could wave.

At first, I thought he was just admiring it. It was a spectacular, smaller version of a superyacht with a reputation for being speedy and maneuverable. Everything was three levels of luxury, with smoked glass windows for privacy around the main deck.

"If James knows someone on that vessel, I'm in," I joked.

A tall man wearing black gloves and carrying an umbrella came down the curved stairway. He waved James on board, and it occurred to me the guy looked familiar. When he turned, my heart stuttered.

Cain!?

Looking ill, Cal watched as his face slowly turned white, his brows creasing. I wasn't the only one freaking out.

"Eddi, give me your phone." I fished around and handed it over, and he flipped through my contacts.

"Hottie from Hell?" Cal rolled his eyes and hit the call button.

Ronan stared at me. "What's wrong, Eddi?"

"James just climbed aboard the Black Widow, and Cain is on it."

Ronan's eyes shot to the boat. "The big red one?"

I nodded.

I looked around the table, but everyone's eyes were on Cal.

I shook my head. "Why is James meeting Cain in Key West, and more importantly, who else is on that boat?"

How could James be involved in this nightmare?

"I don't know," Cal said, listening to the call ring through. "I've never known James to hang out with anyone who owned a luxury yacht before, and Cain? That's impossible to explain away."

I leaned over to listen in at Cal's ear. After five or six rings, I heard a click as someone answered. No one spoke on the other end of the line.

"Gideon, it's Cal. We're at the Cuban Cafe down on the docks. James just boarded the red Spectre Yacht that's been sitting at this end of the slip for weeks. Cain was the one to let him on board. Something is up, and it's not good. Can you meet us here?"

Cal listened, and there was a long pause before I heard the snapping sound of wings and a sharp wind buffeted the microphone. Gideon was coming.

I can't believe the arrogant feather pillow answered.

"What do we do, Cal?"

"What can we do? It's not like we can rush the stairs and demand to know what's happening." He thought about it and added, "I've got to hand it to you, Ed. The velcro holster was a great idea."

With a wan smile, I glanced across the harbor at the blood-red yacht. My heart was in my mouth. We had their location. Was it right under our noses this entire time?

We waited ten minutes before Gideon strode around the corner in his birth form. I knew he wasn't wearing a Glamor because of Miri's soft "WOW" in my ear. At least the Sprite had good taste.

Gideon blended in, wearing Khaki shorts and a white linen shirt with a stand collar. He looked like every other tourist on the street if you considered an ethereal God-like beauty normal. But Gideon was all business this morning, his jaw set like steel, his fists clenched in his pockets. He had a rectangular box clamped under one arm.

When he got to the patio, he surprised me by passing our table to sit alone. I felt a surge of anxiety and sent him my thoughts.

"What the hell are we going to do now, Gideon?"

"For starters, stop staring at me, all of you. They have eyes on you, I'm sure."

Gideon was reading the menu, and when the waitress came, he ordered breakfast.

Cal relayed to him, mentally, what we'd seen. He never looked up, but I glanced over, and his face was furious. Gideon's birth form did *terrifying* as well as his creature form.

I looked at the *Black Widow*. Something was happening. Without staring, I watched as two figures descended the stairs dockside. Gideon saw it, too, because he glanced toward the Spectre from behind his menu.

It was James. Cain briefly clasped a gloved hand on his shoulder before they parted, with James stepping onto the pier and heading back toward Old Town. Cain jogged back up the steps onto the Spectre.

Gideon's face was like granite. He looked down at his breakfast and asked, "*Bacchus, Ronan, are your weapons close?*"

The brothers must have answered because a savage gleam of anticipation appeared in their eyes.

"*Perfect. After we finish here, I will follow you to the Wanderlust and Glamor them. We can't have you running around the docks with weapons in full view.*"

My Gods. They were excited, but I felt like puking.

While pretending to eat, Gideon reviewed his thoughts about who was on that vessel and cautioned us that we couldn't be sure if James was involved. He stared off in the distance for some time, finally relaying the semblance of a plan.

"*I should tell you, we are alone in this endeavor. The four shifters that were assisting me here in Key West are dead. I found them in an alleyway in the middle of the night.*"

The five of us looked at each other, and my eyes bugged out of my head. Dead. Four shifters, just like that. What did I get myself into?

Seeing me squirm in my chair, Ronan reached out to squeeze my thigh. His look was grim, and I knew he wanted me to leave.

I shook my head at him. I couldn't. This was my fight, too.

I watched Gideon place the rectangular box on his table from the corner of my eye.

"*I have something for you, Eddi. After I leave, you can open it—discreetly.*"

I tried not to look, but it was hard. He had a box. For me. Curiosity was killing me, and not looking at his table was tough.

A fleeting look of sorrow dashed across Gideon's face, pushing my irritation aside. Now I was *really* curious.

As we parted ways, Ronan leaned in and softly whispered in my ear.

"If there is trouble, I'm taking you out of there. If the time comes, don't argue with me. I won't risk you again, *little Barracuda.*"

Before I could complain about his bossy male attitude, he and Bacchus rose and headed for our slip. A few minutes later, Gideon followed.

"Aren't you going to look?" Miri whispered impatiently. I felt her foot kicking my wrist.

Nonchalant, I stood and picked up the box from the nearby table. I brought it back and waited a few minutes before peeking inside.

I sucked in a breath, pain shooting through my chest.

It was my knife. The beautiful Damascus Bowie Knife with the custom elkhorn and walnut handle. My father had it made for my fourteenth birthday.

Nestled beside my knife was a sheath of mahogany-stained leather. It was a Huckleberry holster designed to hold a knife securely at your hip. It had a thin strap around the waist and diagonally across the chest, so the minimalist design was comfortable to wear.

I didn't have to take it out to examine it. I knew about this holster. I admired it at a knife shop on Duval a week ago.

I watched Gideon casually stroll along the pier, checking out all the boats and slowly working toward the *Wanderlust*.

The Gryphon must have felt my reaction.

"I returned to the cabin after we parted that night ten years ago. I found it stuck in the dirt."

I snorted. *"Convenient choice of words. 'Parted' sounds so much better than 'dumped you off like an unwanted pet on the side of the road,' doesn't it?"*

"Edaline, not now. The knife and holster are already Glamored, but put them on somewhere that won't attract attention."

I didn't need to see him up close to hear the thread of sadness in his telepathic voice. For once, I felt bad for giving him attitude.

"Thank you, Gideon. I can't tell you what it means to have my knife back after all these years. The holster is beautiful."

I looked back into the box, and tears sprang to my eyes as memories flooded through me. My father teaching me the different knife holds. The day we made a straw-stuffed scarecrow to practice putting weight into my strikes. Seeing my knife after all these years was bittersweet, and the memories painful.

The tears could wait. This was about my father and Ronan's mother. It was about Hex and Cain, and James' possible involvement; not to mention what the drug was doing to Key West. It wasn't about me.

Gideon had a plan, and it was a good one. Of course, they're always good until all hell breaks loose and things go to shit.

***

~ ORIANA ~

Key West was a pretty town with many palm trees and sandy beaches. The people here were unusual, but it was a fun diversion. She smiled at the memories that flooded back to her.

Oriana had visited many moons ago with her two rambunctious offspring and their doting sire, Daniil. She smiled at the image of her boys' tiny tail fins as they splashed and played on the beach under the strawberry moon.

She had been carrying a third babe in her belly at the time. Three days after her return to their *Shoal* near Marathon, she had produced a female.

The live birth was uncomplicated despite the taxing trip home. Oriana remembered the pride in her heart as the beautiful blue and gold tail unfurled and her daughter opened her glittering green eyes. Female births were rare on the *Shoal*, so this momentous occasion was a cause for celebration.

Pain lanced through her as she thought of her slender blonde child, who must now be fully grown. She had been as beautiful as a southern sunset, her love of life radiating like the beacon of a lighthouse.

Not long after that trip, Daniil died tragically in a monstrous tangle of fishing line, another needless Syreni death that haunted her today.

Being the eldest and yet too young, Ronan had become the dominant male, his shoulders taking the weight of responsibility without complaint. His younger brother Bacchus had a wild and untamed heart, but Ronan would see that his brother was well-raised.

Her eldest never mentioned his father; his sensitive nature preferred to bury the pain of his loss. She worried about Ronan and wondered how he was managing to—*NO*.

She shook her head, and bubbles rose from her parted lips. Thoughts of the world outside were foolish if she wished to remain sane while in captivity.

Turning her face towards the brick wall behind her tank, she brought her hands to her eyes as if to wipe the tears away. It was an empty gesture, given the salt water surrounding her. With a deep sigh, she looked up at the mesh clamped tightly over her prison, and vowed never to give up. One day, she would be free.

Until that day, her offspring would have a good life because of her sacrifice. They were strong because she had raised them to be. It caused her immeasurable pain—and no small amount of hope—that they were living free, although she wasn't there to see it.

Oriana hadn't seen the sun or felt the ocean breezes in ten long years. And for what? Her eggs were now in the hands of monsters, out in the world wreaking God only knew what kind of havoc. The sword of her sacrifice had three edges.

The *Shoal* was full of Syreni introverts who would rather hide than confront head-on the disappearance of their bulls. When her male friend Sirus went missing, she decided someone needed to step up, so she struck out on her own to search for answers.

The strapping male Syreni had disappeared at Boot Key, so Oriana spent day after day watching the rows of bobbing sailboats as she lay in wait. Then, one night, her patience was rewarded.

A vampire, and what she suspected was a Demon, crossed Boot Key harbor in a large dinghy. With evil intent glittering in their eyes, they disappeared into the enormous mangrove island across the bay.

She followed the pair through the extensive watery trails, and when they pulled a dead Syreni from their vicious trap, she learned the truth. Outraged, she showed herself.

Thinking too quickly, she struck a bargain that was doomed to failure. At the time, it seemed like the best choice. Why she believed their promises was something she questioned to this day, often wondering if the vampire had a hand in her compliance.

As it turned out, her selfless deal was foolish and one-sided, their prison stronger than she had anticipated. Her face flamed with shame at the misstep she had made so many years ago.

With a flick of her tail, she spun and, using her buoyancy, rose near the surface to swim in lazy circles around the cramped cistern. Today, she would recite the names of all the fish on the reef and, if she had time, the sharks and mollusks as well.

As she swam, her mind drifted. The monsters who enslaved her had promised that her people would remain untouched if she donated her embryos. She snarled and ground her teeth. They had recently resumed preying on the Syreni males, proof of their devilish lies reaching her last month.

Eric. She didn't know whether to pity or hate him. The Vampire's pet junkie fed her and did Cain's bidding, yet was her only source of information from the outside world. Sometimes, when the vampire wasn't here, he read to her.

Her swimming slowed, her heart plummeting at the futility of it all. How did one stop an evil of this magnitude from inside a cage? Ten excruciating years with no chance of escape and none likely to present itself anytime soon. Cain was too careful.

She squared her shoulders and bubbled a sigh. She must not give up. She was of ancient blood, the same Syreni line that founded the *Shoal*. Clamping her lips tightly together, she resumed her exercise.

She heard footsteps, and with a sweep of her large green tail fin, she settled herself in the bottom corner, facing away from the door. She briefly turned her eyes up, worried that the waves bouncing at the surface would give her away.

Luckily, the door was locked, and Cain was distracted as he burst through it. He didn't see the disturbance in her tank. Perhaps today would be the day. She turned her head down and closed her eyes, the tiniest of smiles playing at the corner of her lips.

CHAPTER 26

It was done. There was no time for second thoughts or running for the hills. Everyone was where they needed to be, and Miri was out in the line of fire, doing her best to help.

Cal and I were still sitting at the cafe, with a clear view of the Black Widow, an untouched Tres Leches on the table between us.

My stomach was in knots, but Cal? He was beside himself and trying not to show it. His fingers had twisted a napkin into knots, and he'd been rubbing his thumb up and down the handle of his spoon forcefully enough to bend it.

Cal came across as this mellow dude who wouldn't hurt a fly. I'd seen him in action, though. His Octopus was no joke.

As we waited, I mentally kicked myself.

"Why didn't I get a weird vibe from the Spectre the first time I saw it? I mean, come on! It's red. And the name? *Black Widow?*"

Cal frowned. "It's likely warded up the butt, Ed. 'Nothing to see here' is part of how wards work. There could be a huge party and an orchestra on that thing, and you wouldn't know it."

I was worried about Miri. What if they couldn't see her but heard her wings fluttering? She'd been so brave, flying off without a second thought about her safety. I never bit my nails, but I was chewing like mad.

Finally, she was back, her not-so-subtle wing sounds announcing her arrival.

"Holy Shark's teeth, that was fun!" I heard Miri panting, breathless but unafraid.

"The vampire you described is there alright. He's standing under the overhang across the room from a dark-haired guy in a suit who looks pissed. Oh, and there are two women, one with short black hair that looks like a model, and the other is a blonde with big boobs. A real Playboy centerfold type of chickie."

"One other female is sitting alone. I think you'll want to watch out for her. Her expression is weird, and she has a nasty vibe."

There was a pause, and Miri added, "There's something else there, too. I can't see it, but I can feel it. I don't know what it is, but I hope it didn't notice me. It made my skin crawl, so I boogied out of there when I felt it coming my way. It's something very dark, Eddi. It's bad news."

Cal and I exchanged fearful looks, and then we dialed Gideon. The phone picked up, and Cal explained what Miri had seen.

There was a long pause, and finally, Gideon spoke.

"They are known to me. It's likely a trap, but we may not have another opportunity. We're moving forward. Be careful."

There was no turning back. It was time.

***

"Hurry up, Gideon. We're going to be too late." Ronan growled.

The Gryphon ignored him and backed up another few feet until the thick fur of his tiger-striped legs mashed against the far ledge of the roof. Bacchus and Ronan stood by the slight ridge overlooking the street, their backs to Gideon.

"You're sure you can lift us both, Gryphon?" Ronan looked over his shoulder but saw nothing, so he lifted one arm in the air, his hand extended. Bacchus copied him just in time.

There were several booming thumps and the resounding snap of wings before Gideon snatched them from the roof, their arms almost wrenched from their sockets at the sudden liftoff. The brothers reached up with their free hands, securing Gideon's tenuous hold on them before catching a look at the crowds below. No one looked up. The Glamour was working.

The Gryphon's flight was silent as they swept along, gliding high above the pier. With a sharp thrust of his wings and an upward tilt, Gideon deposited the Syreni on the luxurious flybridge of the Black Widow. The open platform was spacious for sunning and entertaining, with plush couches around a modular coffee table.

Gideon changed forms mid-flap, landing neatly on his feet beside them. He was naked, a soft glow highlighting the muscular perfection of his birth form. Gideon was not shy, and his sculpted body was on proud display.

Ronan yanked Gideon's longsword free from the glamoured holster on his back and pulled out the dry shorts tucked within. Eyes up, he handed them both to Gideon.

"Put these on before you blind me," he growled. Ronan's eyes glittered with a vengeful eagerness, gold leaching into them as he shot the Knight a sharp smile.

"Ronan, stay calm. We need complete control for this," Bacchus warned.

A long slide of metal on leather pulled their attention to Gideon and the golden longsword gleaming in his hand. The crossguard was lengthy and ornate, its intricate details shimmering in the sun.

Bacchus hefted the prickly homemade mace onto his shoulder, and they slipped silently down the stairs.

***

Cal and I walked down the dock holding hands. Mine was slippery with nervous sweat; Cal's was like holding a piece of ice-cold steel. I gave him an anxious look. I had expected him to be afraid like me, but Cal was seething with an angry, let's-spill-blood vibe. My friend never ceased to amaze me.

Cal looked down at me, his sun hat at odds with his aggressive expression.

"You're not going to scare anyone in that hat, Cal." The joke sounded hollow, even to my ears.

He squeezed my hand.

"I've got you, Eddi. We all do. It's time to end these monsters, once and for all. What was it that your father said? Never run from a fight for the greater good."

I nodded and swallowed. My Bowie knife was invisible at my hip, the Glamour working perfectly. I had a small piece of my father and my friends with me. Strong friends. I wasn't alone this time.

Taking a deep breath, I hardened my resolve. My father did not deserve what they did to him, nor did Ronan's mother. I let the slow burn of anger rise, my steps growing bolder.

When we got to the Black Widow, we stopped at the water-level swim platform and, without hesitation, stepped on board. We were halfway up the wooden steps before a curvy blonde woman appeared at the top, blocking our path. Her lovely form was too perfect to be authentic. This one was a shifter, no doubt about it.

"This is a private yacht," she said, narrowing her eyes.

"We're here to see Cain," Cal said. "Cream suit, long fangs, sleeps all day?"

The woman looked over her shoulder at someone, then turned to face us.

"Well, then. Welcome aboard." The malicious glitter in her eyes brought the whole "spider welcoming a fly" saying to mind.

As I crested the stairs, with Cal right behind me, I turned to see who she had consulted before admitting us. Only one other woman was on the deck, standing against the far wall, her short black bob capping off a body built for the runway—another gorgeous shifter.

Cal must have felt my fear because he looked at me and rubbed my hand with his thumb.

"Hang in there, Eddi," he said in my mind. *"They'll get here, don't worry."*

The Black Widow's main deck was bigger than my apartment and fully covered. Barely visible through the smoked glass patio doors, a modern open-concept kitchen and lounge area blended in luxurious harmony. The tinted glass made it hard to see inside the living space, but the captain's chairs were visible in silhouette on an integrated bridge beyond the kitchen. Though terrified, I could appreciate the dreamy yacht.

Someone approached the dark patio doors from across the lounge, a petite figure in a sundress. The blonde slid the door open, and I felt a blast of air conditioning.

"It's ok, Sophia. They can stay."

I recognized that voice.

A woman appeared. She had a magnum of wine and a handful of glasses, holding them upside down by the base as she sauntered past the blonde.

"PATSY!?" I almost shouted it, shock blasting across my nerve endings.

"Hello, Edaline. Why am I not surprised to see you here?"

With her hand full of glasses, Patsy motioned to us. "Why don't you and your friend Cal have a seat over here by me? We were just going to toast something."

She indicated a padded gray loveseat sitting opposite a massive wingback chair done in leopard skin. The furnishings were luxurious and arranged under the long, spacious overhang of the deck roof to keep the sun off. Open on three sides, it allowed a panoramic view of the bight.

Her voice was friendly, but the blood froze in my veins. Something really, really bad percolated in my brain.

How is Patsy involved in this shitshow?

She paused at the glass side table beside her chair, looking out across the bight, before setting the wine bottle and glasses down and taking a seat. She tucked her feet under her and started pouring like she'd been to finishing school, her mouth pursed as she concentrated on her task.

I resisted the urge to give in to my shock and let my mouth flop open. Instead, I pressed my lips together and stood tall.

Panic gets you dead, right, Father?

Quickly cataloging the scene, it was just as Miri said. The covered deck area was extensive and set up like a living room. The only other people here were the two pretty women standing off to the side, just inside the roofline. They were behind a padded chair occupied by a guy in a suit who was fidgeting in his seat and looked ticked off.

"Well, if it isn't my tasty little darling."

Inside, I cringed, and it felt like someone pressed pause on a horrible movie. I turned my head. Cain lurked in the shadow of the molded roof, standing in the darkest corner and leaning against the smoked glass patio doors. He smiled, his arms crossed and his cream suit spotless as usual.

Something seems different about him.

My shock turned to anger, which morphed into cold fury. My eyes burned with the rage in my belly. I opened my mouth to say something, but Cal spoke.

"What's wrong, Cain? Don't you want to come out here with us and enjoy the afternoon sun?" Cal snarled, his eyes boring into the blood-sucking bastard. I felt him shift his weight like he would make a move, so I squeezed his arm.

Patsy chuckled as she poured the wine. The two women by the overhang sauntered over, helping themselves to a glass and bringing one back to suit guy. The blonde trailed her hand up his arm as she strolled back to where she had been hovering.

"Now, Cal, don't be mean." Patsy glanced at my face, a momentary frown quickly hidden by her fake smile.

"Edaline, your eyes are lovely when you're angry. So frosty!"

Cal's mental shout almost made me cringe. *"What the everloving fuck is going on here, Eddi?"*

His confused eyes darted around the room, trying to make sense of things. Then he looked at me, and his eyes shot wide.

I reached my hand to my face, but nothing felt out of place.

Something about the man in the suit caught my eye, and I glanced over. His fingers twisted nervously, running through his hair and rubbing the back of his neck before returning to tap on his leg. His leg twitched again and again. He shifted his weight. Left side. Right side.

The suit wasn't nervous. He was tweaking, and I'd bet my Huckleberry Holster hooked on *Gush*.

Tall, dark, and addicted wasn't what you'd expect. Sitting on a plush black wingback chair, he looked every bit the wealthy businessman, his long legs crossed, his expensive gray suit perfectly tailored to his form.

Cain pushed up from the patio door and strolled across the room, looking at me and licking his lips as he passed. He picked up a wine glass and poured. His hand briefly passed through a sunny reflection, and a tiny trail of smoke wafted from it. He flinched before standing and returning to his post. As he passed Cal, he pointed a finger at him and mouthed, "You're mine," with a wink. A burn marked the back of his hand.

Ok, that was gross, and I was over the gawking.

"Patsy, what are you doing on a Spectre Yacht in Key West? What am I missing? Because your choice of friends is *surprising*," I snapped, looking at Cain.

Patsy sat back and took a sip of her wine. "You're not missing anything, dear. Come and have a seat. I promise I won't bite."

Under her dark, curly hair, Patsy's eyes shone with the promise of death, a faint reddish tint making me shiver.

I wondered if Bacchus and Ronan were on board yet because this was about to get ugly.

"Cain, good call using James to get these two on board. And Galahad, help Eddi and Cal sit over there on the loveseat, will you, dear?"

I looked at the guy in the suit, but he didn't respond to her command.

I felt a sudden presence behind me that made my skin crawl, and a frigid hand grabbed me by the arm, lifting me off my feet. I stifled a scream as Cal, and I were dragged across the room, kicking at nothing because the only thing touching me was a black mist wrapped around my bicep. It was transparent and without substance, with no visible body attached.

As it dropped us on the loveseat across from Patsy's chair, I tried to see what had grabbed us, but it was gone, black motes evaporating into the air. My skin crawled with prickles, and I sensed something evil had touched my skin.

Crossing her legs, Patsy settled back in the chair across from us. She wore a casual but well-fitted sundress with slip-on sandals, a simple and fun attire for any sun lover. She was in charge here; that was obvious.

She was the Patsy I'd known and loved for years—yet wasn't. Because her eyes were Van Gogh crazy, and she was—*giving orders?* There could only be one reason for that.

I wanted to vent with a scream loud enough to wake the dead. Because the woman who had helped me to my feet, cared for me, and given me a livelihood for the last ten years ... *was Hex.*

I resisted the urge to vomit and pulled myself up straighter.

"Now, where were we, Warren? You were saying?" she asked the man in the suit.

Warren looked at Cal and I, then back at Patsy, raising his brow.

"Don't worry, hun," she said with a wry smile. "Let's resume our little meeting, and please, speak freely. They aren't going anywhere." Patsy turned and gave me a vicious smile. "Ever."

The leer she gave me made my skin crawl.

Where are Gideon and the Syreni? What's taking so long?

Warren cleared his throat. "As I was saying, at my urging, the Security Council has voted to give your experimental operatives a try. We are assessing your location in South Carolina and setting up a training program with your staff. The council would like a demonstration within the next six months, and if they like what they see, they are asking for a start date of early winter 2024."

He cleared his throat and adjusted his tie, shooting a sidelong glance at Patsy.

"You will be heavily monitored. You will be expected to follow our experimental protocols and submit to periodic review from an independent third party. I'm sorry, but that's how it's done now."

Patsy looked unconcerned by the news.

Scratching at the back of his neck, Warren asked, "Do you have any issues with the proposed timeline?"

Patsy clapped her hands together, a smile lighting up her face. "We'll be ready to show you the incredible capabilities of our Security Units within three months, not six. Thank you for the wonderful news. You won't be sorry."

She held her wine up. "A toast?"

She raised her wine, and everyone lifted a glass, their delighted expressions making me shiver.

"To intelligent, biddable weapons—she looked at Warren—and to *Gush.*"

Warren looked like he'd rather be burning in hell than sitting on this yacht with these creeps. His leg was jumping, and his eyes darted to a small decorative box on the table beside Patsy's chair.

My mind was scrambling, processing what I saw and coming up with a big, fat zero. *Security Units? Biddable Weapons?*

"Patsy, what the ever-loving fuck is going on?" I snarled.

Patsy grimaced and put her glass down.

"Well, for starters, you took the bait a little too easily, my dear. Not very clever."

She took a sip, her eyes reflecting the red of the wine as she peered at me over the rim. She set down her glass and clapped her hands.

"I know! Instead of telling you, why don't I show you? It's time Warren sees a sample of our work anyway." She looked at Cain.

"Galahad? Bring the child."

Black whorls of mist appeared next to Cain and disappeared through the patio doors. A few minutes later, a slender child of about eight or nine years appeared from beyond the lounge, unconcerned about the barely visible haze drifting beside her.

She was a sweet-faced, huggable child with shoulder-length blonde waves and petite features. Wearing an immaculate OshKosh floral print jumper, the soles of her tiny denim shoes gleamed an immaculate white against the gray carpet.

Her eyes snatched my attention—a jungle of greens that shimmered as she took a measured look around the patio. Face by face, she examined each adult staring back at her.

"Matilda, there you are, sweetheart. How are you this morning?"

At Patsy's cloying words, I wondered whether to cry or go postal on these monsters. Now they've gotten their slimy hands on a child. A freaking cute as a button, innocent child that someone was missing right now.

Sweat beaded on my forehead as I flushed with rage. When I blinked, my eyes burned, the warm ocean air barely finding my lungs. Waves of wrath rolled under my skin; I was about to explode.

Cal, sensing my distress, squeezed my hand. My eyes found him, and he stilled, sucking in a sharp breath. He stared into my eyes, and I resisted the impulse to raise my hand to my face. I turned to look at the glass patio doors and froze. My irises were white, and they glowed, just like my father's. I stifled a gasp.

"Come and show Aunt Patsy what you learned this week, dear?"

I dashed the sweat from my forehead and focused as I watched the little girl cross the shaded patio to stand beside Patsy, who pointed at Cain.

"See that pale creature? You know him. He's the vampire that looks after your mommy."

The child nodded, her expression clouding over.

I looked at Cal, who was as dumbfounded as I was.

Do they have her mother?

Patsy mulled over the things on her side table, then, smiling, she picked up the corkscrew and handed it to the child.

"He needs a little poke once in a while. You can save me the trouble. Use your dissipation so everyone can see, dear."

Matilda lifted the corkscrew, examined the wooden handle and curly point, then stared at Cain, unmoving.

"It's OK, Matilda. I'm not asking you to hurt him." Her gaze shot to Cain. "*Yet.*"

With an offhanded wave, Patsy added, "Oh, don't you worry about him. It's just a little poke. He heals quickly. I want to see what you learned this week, that's all. I've heard you've been doing well, my dear."

With a troubled look at Patsy, Matilda closed her eyes, pinching her lips together in concentration. At first, nothing happened, then slowly, satiny gray wisps curled away from her skin, strip by wavy strip. Within seconds, she was hazy, and then she was gone. A faint gray shadow swirled and billowed across the room.

A Djinn. The kid is a Djinn?

Cal shot me a surprised look.

Warren watched the twirling mist with a bland expression, unconcerned that a child had disappeared into thin air. He seemed more worried about the lint on his pant leg, which still bounced up and down.

Why isn't he freaking out? Does he know about the Others?

Cain didn't move when the vapor arrived to hover before him. Something darted out of the whirling mass, and the vampire yelped, jerking his hand to look at it.

He laughed. Laying in his palm was the corkscrew, but when he turned his hand over, there was a small red hole and a trickle of blood.

"How about that?" Cain said. "Already quite tractable, isn't she, Hex?" He smiled at the black-haired bitch I used to consider a friend.

The haze drifted back across the room, and when it became solid again, Matilda stood beside Patsy.

"Thank you, Matilda." She reached out to pat her on the head, but the child stepped back, a defiant look on her face.

Cain had spoken too soon because quietly, her eyes blazing, Matilda addressed Patsy. "I don't like it when you ask me to do things like that. It's mean. I don't like being mean." She looked over at Cain, the apology plain to see. "It's not right."

The expression on her face broke my heart. I wanted to run over there, put my arms around her, and get her away from these maniacs.

Her eyes frosty, Patsy snarled, "Unfortunately, what you like is completely irrelevant, Matilda. We do unpleasant things. You'll just have to get used to it."

Her expression went cold. "And someday soon, you won't have a choice."

Matilda took a step back from Patsy, her eyes wide. She glanced around the room, looking for something, her eyes worried.

Patsy raised her arm and snapped her fingers over her head, her eyes still on the child.

With a sound like whispers and a stiff breeze, a man appeared out of nowhere, blinking into existence beside the leopard print wingback. Black wisps drifted away when he solidified.

He was strikingly handsome in a cold, malicious way, his features chiseled and his bronze-colored eyes glowing with hatred. Muscular yet lean, his fighting leathers molded to his perfect body like a second skin. His appearance screamed *assassin*.

Now that I finally had eyes on him, death by orgasm was the first ridiculous thought that came to mind.

His attire may have been immaculate, but his hair was disheveled. Black as pitch, it flopped around his ears and ageless face. He was neither old nor young, but the expression in his odd-colored eyes was flat, hateful, and cruel, and he wore a perpetual scowl. I'd bet my boat there was a glamoured weapon hanging behind his back.

I knew someone else who could turn to mist and move around undetected. He could fly, too—my father.

This twisted, evil thing was a Djinn. But his species was their only thing in common; a vile coldness clung to this creature. I shivered.

Patsy reached out and touched his arm, giving him an icy smile.

"Galahad, take Matilda to her room," she said, running her hand over his muscular forearm. The flirty smile she gave him made me want to retch.

The Djinn looked down at Patsy's hand on his arm, and his jaw hardened. He raised his lifeless eyes to Patsy's, and for a moment, I thought he would refuse.

Then he was gone, wafting away on the breeze. Matilda turned and followed him through the glass doors.

I felt the floor tilt beneath my feet at what I'd just witnessed. They're both Djinn. But while Matilda appeared to be a typical, pleasant eight-year-old, there wasn't a trace of humanity in Galahad.

The dark-haired Djinn was a killer.

CHAPTER 27

Cain burst out laughing, clapping his hands in delight.

"Amazing, isn't it Hex?" She's certainly come a long way, hasn't she?"

My ex-boss looked at him with a frown, her jaw clenched.

I couldn't help myself. I'm not sure if it was the cocktail of fear and anger bubbling under my skin, or relief that the child was gone from this pit of vipers. I burst out laughing.

"Wow, Cain. Trouble in paradise, I see. You're definitely on her shitlist. What did you do? Try to drain one of her prisoners dry?" With an acidic smile, I raised one brow.

Cain snarled at me, and that's when I saw it. Four empty craters, top and bottom.

Cain had no fangs.

I looked at Patsy and lost control of myself. I started to laugh.

"Cain, you're all bark, no bite these days." I held my side, the laughter making my eyes water.

Cal stepped on my foot, and Patsy put down her drink, her eyes promising a slow death if I didn't shut up.

"Well then. It seems, Edaline, that you still haven't learned to control that mouth of yours. You do realize who is in charge here, don't you?"

"Well, Patsy," I spat. "Last time I checked, it was a free world. And I wouldn't be so quick to label yourself 'in charge' of anything. Why are you doing this—and why me?"

Patsy turned her head and ignored me, addressing the suit guy instead.

"I have something for you, Warren. You can go now, and I'll be in touch. Keep up the good work, and you'll never run out of *Gush*."

She motioned to the black-haired runway model. "Emma?"

The long-legged shifter slunk over, taking something the size of a matchbox from the box beside the wine bottle. She brought it to Warren, who took it with a greedy smile.

"You girls should accompany him. I'm sure he would appreciate some entertainment this afternoon while he enjoys his—*gift.*"

The two girls smiled at Patsy and followed Warren down the steps to the dock, their heels clicking on the lacquered wood surface.

Once they'd left the boat, Patsy turned to look at me, all pretense of civility gone from her face. Her eyes were blazing, a glowing blood-red filling her narrowed gaze.

"Why am I causing chaos? Well, dear, because I can—and *it's a riot.*"

Patsy's expression was brittle, tainted with something dark and vile. She grinned at me, and I watched as the sharp tips of vicious spikes slowly replaced her human teeth.

A small part of me died right there. All this time, I had been working for a monster. The same malignant beast that had killed my father. My gorge rose, but Cal rubbed his thumb over my hand, and I held it down.

"And why you? Oh, you already know the answer to that question, Eddi. I've watched you since *long* before you came to our lovely tropical paradise. And you have something I want."

She lifted her glass and took a sip, the tips of her fangs clinking on the glass.

"It was like tending a garden, really. I watched you grow, comfortable in the knowledge that when I was ready, I had only to pluck you from the vine. And your employment at the restaurant was perfect. I knew exactly where you were every single day. The security cameras—" she gave a hollow-sounding chuckle—"those were sheer entertainment."

Her eyes went hard, the glow intensifying. "The original Patsy wasn't too happy when I let Cain have her, but it was, shall we say, unavoidable." She grinned. "Her screams were almost as bad as listening to your pathetic whining all these years."

My skin prickled with heat, and my eyes felt on fire again. I shook out my fingers to stop the tingles, itching to grab the Bowie and go to town. But Gideon told us to get as much information as possible and sit tight.

We're waiting, Gideon. Where the fuck are you?

Patsy's eyes went to Cal.

"And you. The perfect babysitter all these years. I should thank you, but I'm not the thanking kind. I don't think I'm quite done with you. That Octopus of yours will come in quite handy, I think."

She brought her glass to her lips, and her eyes shone over the rim, waiting. Watching.

The room was like a powder keg, and I wasn't the only one about to explode. Cal dropped my hand and stood up, his face like thunder. I'd seen those devil-be-damned protective instincts before. He was about to throw himself into danger. I reached for him.

Before I could grab Cal, a black cloud materialized, and Galahad stood before him. The dark Djinn snarled, a Damascus longsword shimmering in his hand, the tip at Cal's throat.

Patsy giggled and took another sip of her wine.

"I'd sit down if I were you. He bites."

Patsy's hooded eyes traveled over the Djinn with a possessive stare as she licked her lips.

My god. She's fucking him.

Cal sat down, but the anger was rolling beneath the surface of his skin. As in, actually moving. His Octopus wanted out.

Where the hell is Gideon? They should have been here by now.

"I can't have you damaged, kiddos. I've got some plans for you two. I have a special room reserved for you, Edaline. Oriana will love having company for a change. It may even increase our production."

I ran the name through my mental database and came up empty. Who was Oriana? I'd heard that name before...

My attention shifted because Patsy looked at Cal and said, "You? I think you'll be heading to South Carolina. We can get a much better look at what makes you tick there. The main lab is very well equipped."

An inferno blasted across my skin, and I growled, the deep sound surprising me. I shot a look at my friend. Cal's face glowed faintly. His eyes darted to mine, fury and desperation shining from them. His control was shot—a change was imminent.

"Where are Gideon and the Syreni? What's taking so long?" The mental shout made me squint one eye. My friend was not calm. Cal was losing control.

"You're both plotting, trying to decide how to attack me." Smirking, Patsy looked around. "Is the bird-kitty here too? Come on out, Gideon," she trilled.

"Oh, wait. Is it the Syreni you're waiting for? I saw you together this morning. Such a cute couple. Having them come to our little party would be most advantageous. I need a bit more of their wonderful secretions, and I know Layla wants another go at your sexy Syreni, Edaline," she purred. "His cock is delicious."

Oh my God, this freak was going to die. I was sweating, and my fingers were twitching, wanting to grab my knife.

"You two don't think I will be an easy kill, do you? Better men than you have tried."

She tapped her finger on her chin, the red of her eyes deepening. "Now, who was that last one? Oh, yes—*your father*. And that did not work out for him whatsoever," she taunted.

Patsy turned to Cain. "Get over to the lab and take Matilda with you. I'm not leaving her unattended with the Gryphon hanging about. And prepare a spot for our new guests. I'll be there shortly."

Cain had scarcely left the deck when Galahad straightened, his spine stiffening. He cocked his head, listening. Patsy's head whipped around, searching, then she looked back at us, her lips an overly dramatic "O."

"They're here? How exciting! Maybe I'll stick around this time to watch Layla suck off your lover, Eddi."

She turned to Cal. "Or maybe I'll get her to fuck you while she's at it and start the countdown to your death, Octopus."

She tucked her chin and laughed, the sound deepening. Her body jerked and seized, her face contorting as fleshy clunks and sharp snaps echoed through the room.

Then all hell broke loose.

The Djinn disappeared so fast that I felt a breeze.

Patsy's face darkened with pain, her fingers cracking as they grew. Talons slid from her fingertips, her shoulders blooming with fur until a thick mane framed her vaguely humanoid face. With the sound of a growling stomach, her bulk surged forth, the grotesque form that used to be Patsy elongating and sprouting upwards. She stood to her full height in mere seconds, her bulk so massive that the roof crooked the furry triangles of her ear tips with a slight bend. The area rug moved as six-inch talons flexed into the luxurious threads.

Shining and black, a monstrous tapered scorpion tail swung over her back, the hardened carapace clicking as it curled. The limb rocked back and forth, the sharp tip oozing as if anxious for a target.

Patsy wasn't my mild-mannered boss anymore. She was Hex. And her voice was a jarring mess that ended with a hiss.

"I've waited a long time for *thisssss—*"

I'd listened to her maniacal bullshit until I almost blew apart from the strain. I'd had enough, and it was time for her to pay. I yanked my Bowie from my hip and launched myself at her.

***

GIDEON

Were they too late?

Ronan's eyes had gone yellow, and his fangs were showing. Bacchus was on the balls of his feet, his hands tight on his log mace.

As they sprinted quietly across the Spectre's main dining area, the covered rear deck came into view through the smoked glass doors. Gideon heard the two Syreni take a sharp breath.

The enormous Manticore was mid-shift, with Cal and Eddi standing before it. Cal was fighting a change to Octopus form, but Eddi was off the rails.

Her eyes glowed like icy spotlights, a thin translucent aura coating her entire body like a second skin. She reached for the Bowie knife at her hip and attacked, the glowing halo trailing powdery blue wisps as she moved.

Gideon felt a surge of hope at the sight. Edaline was expressing her powers.

Crouching, he turned to the brothers, using his thoughts and hoping the Djinn didn't hear him.

"The Djinn is unbeatable. Leave him to me. Can you two handle the Manticore?"

Ronan's eyes glowed yellow when he looked at Gideon, his expression bordering on a senseless rage. It was too late to worry about that now. He glanced at Bacchus, who was staring at the giant beast, his eyes wide, his mace hand white with a strained grip. He started forward, but Gideon stopped him.

"Watch the tail. Death is instantaneous."

"Now you tell me," Bacchus snapped, then raced through the open glass doors after his brother.

Gideon's eyes darted across the scene before him, using his sixth sense to track the Djinn, who, until a split second ago, had been standing near the beast.

There was no need to join the fight because the battle had come to him. The Djinn overheard them and already tracked across the room. The element of surprise disappeared in a puff of smoke—just like the mist that had quietly slipped in and was creeping up behind him.

Gideon drew the longsword from over his shoulder and turned to face Galahad, who materialized a few paces away.

"You don't have to do this." Gideon circled him, his sword tip extended.

"Oh, but I do, Gryphon."

Disappearing in a puff of mist, he tore past Gideon, who narrowly dodged the sword that shot out of the roiling cloud as it swept past him.

"Help me kill her, Djinn, and you will be free."

Gideon lifted his weight to the balls of his feet, feeling the sweat trickle down his bare chest.

The dark-haired Djinn was solid again, standing on the kitchen island across the large dining area. Galahad's black leather boots paced up and down the marble countertop, and he frowned as if considering Gideon's offer.

Then, with a snarl, he shook his head. "Not possible."

Again, Gideon dodged the murky black whirlwind full of sword, his eyes darting to follow his opponent's nearly invisible trajectory. The sweeping haze was a mere shadow in the shaded lounge.

Galahad materialized beyond the glass coffee table. His head was down, his bronzed eyes glowing from under furrowed brows. His lips curled in a snarl.

Gideon frowned, his surprise evident. "You've changed, assassin."

Galahad's scowl deepened, and his hand clenched on the ornate handle of his sword. The patterned blade winked in the filtered light coming through the tinted windows of the lounge.

"You would gift the offspring of your Prince to an enemy of the Court?" Gideon spat.

His bronze eyes turned orange as Galahad raised his head, straightening.

"He is not my Prince. Not anymore. I renounced my loyalty the moment I agreed to her bargain."

Galahad leaped over the table, dematerializing as he attacked.

Again and again, they parried back and forth across the lounge and through the open kitchen, knicks, and slices appearing on Gideon's bare chest with each pass.

The Djinn solidified, blood dripping from the tip of his steel. He was close, mere steps away.

"I can do this all day, Gryphon. Why don't you give up now? Let me end you quickly to avoid the pain and suffering she will surely inflict when I beat you."

Gideon lowered his sword to the side and opened his arms, palms forward in a placating gesture. It was a risky move.

"I don't want to kill you, Galahad. You can trust me. I will not harm you. Work with me. Together, we can regain what you lost."

The Djinn shook his head, his eyes glittering with a sinister light. "You will have to kill me because I have no interest in your offer." He spat in the Gryphon's direction and moved his feet.

This time, Galahad came straight at him, and Gideon hurled himself into the air, hoping there was enough room for the Djinn's rampaging black mass to pass beneath him.

There wasn't.

***

Cal slipped into his Octopus form as I charged the monster in an absolute rage. No one would touch my friends as long as I was alive.

My heart swelled as the memories of my father's lessons sprang from where they lay hidden for ten years.

Always go for the weakest spot—I charged straight for her head.

I left the ground, lighter than air, turning my knife in a reverse grip as I shot across the short distance.

Like a lightning strike, she wasn't expecting it. I rammed my knife straight down, slashing across her temple as she jerked her head back just in time.

I flashed over her crouching form, my feet tapping down just out of range. I pivoted on the balls of my feet, ready to move. I glanced down, surprised to see my hand glowing with a faint light.

"You dare!" she screeched, blood running down her face and dripping on the white carpet. Hex lowered her head, lips quivering as she pulled them back in a snarl, exposing the white cage of ice picks in her mouth. She changed, her enormous bulk and slashing tail making the covered sitting area much smaller.

I bounced straight up and to the side, hovering for an instant, and she sailed past me, missing me by inches. My head bumped into the low ceiling, and I dropped haphazardly onto her back, righted myself, and, with two quick stabs, I pierced the front of her carapace. It would have been a direct shot to the kidneys of any other animal. I slid to the ground and darted away, the speed at my fingertips making me dizzy with excitement.

The shrieks from the Manticore would have awoken the dead if there weren't incredible wards shielding the yacht.

Her tail snapped toward me, and I dove between her legs, sliding through the blood dripping from her fur. As I scrambled up on the other side, I lost my balance and nearly fell. The beast bellowed with rage, spinning to find a target. She was unable to see me through the blood sheeting across her face.

I found my feet and darted around her, heading to where I'd left Cal. He was gone.

My head whipped back and forth, looking for his white Octopus form, and my blood ran cold. His strong tentacles wrapped tight, Cal clung inside the elbow of one front leg, out of the range of Hex's stinger. Judging by the blood trickling to the ground, he was busy with his beak.

Hex roared and shook her head, reaching down to bite him, but he was too fast for her. Two thick, muscular arms snapped out and twisted around her muzzle, and he let go of her leg and let her head pull him into the air.

It would have made me laugh if the situation wasn't so dire.

Like a giant wad of bubble gum had fallen from the heavens and landed on her head, Cal changed his hold. His body covered her eyes and part of her face, and several of his strong tentacles winched her mouth shut. The arms that weren't actively blinding or muzzling her pulled like mad on any bare skin they could find. Red seeped over his slippery white skin and dripped off the end of her snout. He was going for her eyes.

Hex tossed her head, trying to slam him on the ceiling, but Cal quickly slipped to the side of her head for every strike, constantly biting her as he moved. His tentacles, made of solid muscle, formed several layers around her face. She couldn't open her mouth, and her waving tail couldn't strike for fear of hitting herself.

Out of nowhere, Bacchus and Ronan appeared and charged into the fray.

As the Manticore whirled around and around, struggling to shake the Octopus from her head, Bacchus attacked. His feet pounded the decking as he swung, his mace thumping her shoulders and sides, blow after punishing blow. He dodged her wildly swinging tail between each strike, each stabbing thrust barely missing him. He would have been in grave danger if she had not been blinded and distracted. Blood sprayed as the nails did their job, the sound having a sickening similarity to tenderizing meat.

Legs braced, Ronan raised his short sword, then hesitated, letting the Manticore turn. He stabbed downward with perfect aim and every ounce of his strength, catching her foot dead center. The force of the blow buried the sword into the decking. With Hex pinned, the noise coming from her mouth would have been ear-splitting had it not been clamped shut by the solid wrap of Cal's tentacles.

Ronan lifted his head, and what I saw made me freeze.

This creature was not Ronan.

His face was like granite, and his irises were thin yellow rings around blown pupils. Strands of viscous fluid swung from his bone-white, pinky-sized fangs. Thick black talons curved from his fingertips, and when he let loose a furious bellow, my ears rang. I startled and let out a yelp, briefly catching his attention.

He didn't recognize me. He stared through me, his bare chest heaving, before returning to his sole focus—killing the Manticore.

Circling the pinned beast, Ronan snarled, his bulging thighs pounding with a burst of speed before they bunched, propelling him upwards. He landed on her neck with predatory precision and snatched at her head with his clawed hands, the talons hooking in and shredding her skin.

His broad shoulders bulged and strained as he wrestled her head to the side, with Hex fighting him the entire way. Grunting and snarling, he jerked and twisted until he had room, then buried his fangs in the side of her neck. His face disappeared into her fur.

My mouth hung open in shock as I watched him, the horrific sounds of his attack turning my stomach. I felt hollow; had I lost him to this... *MORS?*

But there was no time to think about that because Ronan had forgotten Hex's tail.

As the toxic barb swept forward, Bacchus saw it when I did, and we both screamed. With two running steps, I jumped, my lighter-than-air form sailing forward with incredible speed. I beat Bacchus there.

I landed on Ronan as it struck, the barb slamming into my back. The pain was unbearable, and my numb fingers slipped from where they clutched onto Ronan's torso. My lungs weren't working.

He looked over his shoulder and blasted an enraged snarl into my shocked face. Blood dripped from his chin, mixing with the strands of his toxin. His eyes were distant, his face furious.

With a frightened yip, I slid over the Manticore's side, headed for the ground. My arms were numb, my hands unfeeling. Ronan's hollow eyes darted to the scorpion tail, already swinging for another strike.

Unable to hang on, I fell.

Letting go of the great beast's head, Ronan turned and reached for me, snatching my wrist. With unbelievable power, he hauled me up to his bloody chest. The scorpion stinger stabbed into empty space, and Ronan dragged me over Hex's opposite side and back to the ground, then pulled me clear.

The poison from Ronan's savage bite was working. Hex gave an agonized yowl, muffled by the Octopus smothering her, then sagged, almost going down.

Bacchus rained down blow after blow, hitting the same place repeatedly before leaping to avoid the tail. The sickening crack of ribs and bones filled the air, and he'd hit her so many times that his face and shoulders shone red with her blood.

As Ronan trotted away with me under his arm, I helplessly watched it unfold.

The Manticore, now desperate, rallied against our efforts to down her. Leaning to the side, she used her free foreleg, and reaching up, she scraped Cal off with her claws and tossed him through the air like an insect.

Her mouth now free, Hex grabbed the hilt of Ronan's blade from where it pinned her foot and yanked it from the ground. Blood puddling, she swung around and groggily focused her demonic eyes on Bacchus.

"You insolent whoremonger," she bellowed, a mighty swipe of her good leg taking him to the floor. She scrambled forward and slammed a taloned foot on his chest, pinning him. Her claws burrowed into his muscular torso, sending blood pouring down his sides. His face turned crimson, and his eyes bulged—he couldn't breathe!

Ronan threw me onto a chair, his glowing yellow eyes raking over my face as I tried to suck air into my lungs. His focus swinging between Bacchus and me, he snarled.

"Bacchus!" I choked out, pointing. He pushed hard enough to bounce me on the cushion, growled an almost incoherent—"Stay!"—and raced to help his brother.

The scorpion tail hovered over the fallen Syreni, the segments clacking angrily.

"Say goodbye, fish."

I screamed. Ronan was too late.

I caught movement from the corner of my eye as something flashed over the railing behind the beast, water splashing across the deck. It pounded across the floor with a streak of glittering gold and blue, sliding to a stop beside Hex.

The Manticore paused and looked over her shoulder, a costly error she realized too late.

Sleek shoulders bunching, the golden-haired Syreni raised a shining Cutlass high over her head, and with a ferocious swing that hacked directly between tail segments, she severed the poisonous tip. It landed on the carpet with a dull thud.

Pointing her saber at Hex, she opened her mouth and roared, her neck straining and her face a mask of fury.

Bleeding, bruised, poisoned, outnumbered, and minus her most potent weapon, the Manticore staggered backward, releasing Bacchus.

Ronan scooped up his weapon, and together, he and the newcomer went at the retreating creature, their blades swinging.

The Manticore was outmatched. Hex's ugly cat-like face looked toward the railing, and she scrambled for it, hobbling on one front leg and dragging half a tail. A blood trail marked her passage until she tumbled over the ship's side and splashed into the bight.

Sagging into the soft chair, the throbbing pain from my back turning my insides to mush, I said a little prayer. I rolled my head to look for Cal.

He lay against the short wall closest to the marina dock in his human form, gasping for air but seeming uninjured. His tired arms were flopped out on the floor, but he smiled and raised one rubbery appendage to cover his junk, giving me a weak thumbs-up with the other. Then he laid himself out, his head plunking on the glossy wooden walkway, his chest rising and falling with gasping breaths.

Then Ronan was back, his eyes and fangs slowly returning to normal. He tilted me forward to see where the barb had struck me.

"I saw her sting you," he said, his voice distorted by his receding fangs. "The Manticore's toxin is instantaneous. How is this possible?"

He ran his hands up and down my spine, lifting my shirt and pressing on what felt like the mother of all bruises. He laid me back in the chair and gently eased me onto the soft cushions. Then his eyes found mine.

"You are unharmed. There is no mark!"

I laid my head back, laughed, then choked because it hurt like hell. "I'm not sure why I'm alive, but I'm not complaining."

I turned my head to look at the female Syreni. She and Bacchus were standing by the patio doors. She yelled at him and waved her cutlass around in the air, blood dripping from it and splashing the walls.

"Who is that?" The tiniest flash of jealousy sparked when Ronan smiled fondly at the female with shimmering blonde hair that hung to her hips.

The flash of color I'd seen was her skins, the gold base with striations of blue and a subtle hint of green blended in beautiful swirls. The delicate skin of her waistline extended over her flat belly before splitting into a V over her chest. The effect was a discreet covering of fine, smooth scales blending with the skin of her ribcage and ending just below her collarbone. Her features were delicate yet strong, and her eyes glowed a luxurious green beneath dark eyebrows.

She was absolutely gorgeous.

"Bacchus, are you ok?" Ronan called across the room.

His brother was bloody and pouring with sweat, but he smiled at us between huffs, nodding his head and coughing.

Hunched over, his hands trying to staunch the bleeding on his chest, Bacchus struggled to catch his breath. The blonde looked like she'd just stepped out of a Diver's Direct catalog.

She flicked her wavy blonde hair over her shoulder and marched across the deck to see Ronan, who held me close and rubbed my shoulders. The throbbing in my back would hurt for a while because I'd pushed his hands away when he tried to heal me.

"You must be Edaline."

Giving her a hesitant smile, I looked at Ronan.

"My sister, Tabitha." He smiled up at her. "Thank you, sister."

Tabitha's lips twisted into a smile.

"Don't you mean, thank you *AGAIN*?"

Ronan frowned. "What are you doing here? How did you find us?"

She turned to me. "Do you see what I put up with?" Her eyes glittered with mirth. "My brothers always leave me home. Yet, here I am again, rescuing them from another near disaster."

With a smirk, she glanced at a scratch on her hand and said, "I left home this morning and wasn't here ten minutes before I felt your *MORS* sizzling down our bond. How do you get into these situations?"

She frowned. "I was truly concerned when the sensation reached me on the other side of the island. You had me worried."

I tried not to think about the crazy way Ronan looked when he showed up. It was too disturbing. I had a lot to learn about the Syreni race.

My head cleared, and scanning the deck, I realized we were missing someone.

"Gideon! Where is Gideon?"

Ronan and Bacchus looked at each other, then ran for the lounge, disappearing through the patio doors.

Tabitha looked at me, her eyes searching the room. She saw something and smiled, darting away and returning with the wine bottle.

"Score!" she said, taking a swig and holding it to me.

***

Bacchus and Cal disappeared for a time, searching the boat for Gideon and the Djinn with no success. When they returned, Cal was swimming in someone's shorts and T-shirt.

There was no sign of Gideon, the Djinn, or the little girl, Matilda, although they did find her room. Cal told me there were no toys, books, or artwork decorating the walls.

I leaned into Ronan's neck, wanting to cry. But there were no tears. A trembling started in my legs and worked its way up my body. Soon, I was shaking from head to toe.

Ronan scowled and pulled me closer.

"It's adrenaline. It will pass," Cal said, his legs vibrating hard enough that he slid to the floor with a grunt.

CHAPTER 28

Cal stood by the gunnel, his eyes darting around the calm waters of the bight. He stopped pacing and started chewing his nails. His hair stood straight up from his hands constantly dashing through it.

"Where the hell is Gideon?"

The three Syreni had hit the ocean for a top-up after we left the Black Widow but were back on the *Wanderlust* with us. The stern deck looked small right now, with every bench and bucket occupied.

Ronan's soft snores drifted up from the cuddy cabin. Apparently, a MORS rampage lent tremendous strength, but the cost was significant.

When I positioned myself where I could see him through the shutter doors, Tabitha gave me a knowing smile, her eyes sparkling. Every time I looked at her, she winked, and I looked away.

The bottoms of Ronan's feet were visible through the doorway, and I marveled at how soft they looked. My eyes traced the contours of his muscular calves, but the view ended at his buttocks, their firm curves tight even as he slept.

Tabitha caught me looking again and cocked one finely arched eyebrow at me. My face turned red, and I covered the smile that sprang to my lips.

"It's the damnedest thing," Bacchus said. "We searched the entire yacht, but there was no sign of Gideon. No mess, no broken furnishings, and only a few drops of blood. It's like they vanished."

Gideon and I had a love-hate relationship, but my scalp prickled when I thought of what might have happened to him. Cal looked positively ill, his leg constantly juddering. He kept getting up and looking across the rippling water as if Gideon might somehow rise from the depths and make everything right again.

James' possible involvement weighed heavily on us, but we weren't going there now. Cal called to give our nightly update, but James' phone went straight to voicemail. We'd unpack that mess when we found the Gryphon.

My eyes went to Miri's dream RV. Still empty. I'd told her to lay low at the boat, but the sun was setting, and she hadn't returned. I felt queasy and had to resist grinding my teeth together. Is this how it felt to be a parent?

We'd won the fight. Well, if you didn't count that Cain and Hex still breathed. The only blessing was that Hex was licking her wounds and trying to grow a new tail.

Cain had disappeared into whatever black hole they used for cover in this town. They were here, somewhere. The knowledge of their oily presence was an undercurrent that tainted the evening.

"What do we do about Gideon? Who can we contact?"

Cal shook his head, moving on to the next nail.

"Is there any way to reach out to this Sovereign person or something?" I felt dumb as dirt, having no clue about the hierarchy of the *Others*.

Cal tore his eyes from the water and sat down with a thump.

"Gideon IS the contact. It's all hush-hush—a security thing. There is a Sovereign for this corner of the country, but where? Who? I have no idea. We're floundering here."

What in the name of God will we do now?

Bacchus frowned, his eyebrows pinched together as he looked down at his chest. His fingers traced over the four perfectly round punctures marring his perfect skin, the technicolor bruising slowly spreading across his chest. I was no nurse, but permanent scars were a definite possibility.

"Are those going to heal, or will we need to amputate?" Tabitha teased.

Bacchus shrugged. "I think it's the tail you need to worry about as far as poison goes. My chest will heal, eventually. Fucking Manticores," he muttered.

"Oh my god, Bacchus. Get over yourself." Tabitha said, poking him with her foot.

With a solemn smile, I added, "Girls think scars are sexy, Bacchus. But you'll have to make up a story about alligator wrestling."

The jokes weren't working, and the mood was bleak. It didn't feel much like a victory with our leader missing.

Cal wasn't listening and was back at the rail, his eyes scanning the purpling horizon. "How can you all be so calm? What are we going to do about Gideon? It just doesn't happen. Gideon is the law around here, and we need him. We have to find him!"

I got up, dug a cold soda from the cooler, and brought it to him. He took it but didn't snap the tab.

Cal clenched his teeth and said, "We're completely fucked. Our boss—no, our friend—is probably involved in this shitshow, the Knight is missing, and we have no idea how to contact the Sovereign. On top of that, the Manticore is still slinking around somewhere, pissed as hell because Tabitha took her tail."

Tabitha beamed. "You're welcome."

I rubbed my eyes and sighed. "You forgot something there, Cal. My boss is a freak, and I'm currently unemployed."

I sat down on an overturned pail and watched Cal fuss.

My eyes shot open. "Holy crap. What do we do about Ada and Miguel? And do you think Bert—*Gideon*—knew Patsy was Hex? Is that why he worked at the diner?"

Cal looked at me, his frown deepening, then at the blood-colored Yacht across the bay.

"The Black Widow is a huge problem. Gideon always mopped up the messes that could expose the *Others*. Who would clean up the blood and damage on the Spectre?"

Sitting back down on the rear bench, Cal put his head in his hands. "I don't know what to think. This is a fucking disaster."

I went to sit beside him and rubbed his back. My friend was usually the calm one.

"I'll tell you what we do, Cal. We take it one step at a time. Starting with getting a bit of rest." I looked up at the sky, which was fading to black.

"We're safe at night as long as we're on the *Wanderlust*. We can ask James some careful questions to see if he had a legitimate reason to be on board."

Cal stiffened under my hand and shot me a black look.

"I know it's far-fetched, but Gideon did say not to be hasty. And if push comes to shove, we leave the Spectre for the authorities and take the *Wanderlust* home. We keep our mouths shut, and it'll be business as usual until we figure it out. We'll make it work."

Cal lifted his head and gave me a wet look. I moved my massage from his back to his neck.

"It will all work out, Cal. You can bunk with me tonight, okay?"

***

GIDEON

The Djinn was a skilled swordsman and blazing fast. When I sprang into the air to avoid him, I cracked my head on the low ceiling, crashing down on top of him. Messy, but effective. I ignored the throbbing slice in my arm from the mishap.

We scrambled to our feet, and I pressed him, striking and lunging so fast he couldn't change forms on me.

Retreating from the onslaught, Galahad pulled back to the stairs and upward to the flybridge. Neither the battle raging on the patio nor the clanging of our swords raised any alarms or sirens. The wards on the yacht were strong.

At the top, we paused, circling each other.

"Galahad, this is madness. Help me kill the Manticore, and it will release you from your oath."

The Djinn backed away and leaned on his thighs, a river of sweat dripping from his chin and tracking down his long, patterned blade.

Eyes glowing a vibrant orange, he snarled, "She is my master. I am sworn to protect her." He pointed his sword at me, and with a sinister smile, he said, "You will die, Gideon, and things will continue as they must."

I leapt forward and stabbed, narrowly missing his shoulder, but the Djinn phased to smoke and swept around me, forcing me to spin and throw up my guard.

"There are ways to break the bond of the Oath, Galahad. Let me help you."

Our swords rang as we exchanged blows, and I could see that his legs, like mine, had turned to Jello.

"You presume too much, Gryphon. I took the Oath willingly." I lunged, but Galahad rocked his head to the side. A line of blood trailed down his cheek.

With a mighty surge, I swung my sword and brought it down on his, then with three strikes, I had him back at the railing, his shoulders hanging over the edge.

"Don't make me do this, Galahad."

As he strained under our crossed swords, the Djinn frowned, his eyes fading to bronze.

"She is alone. Hex will make her suffer." He looked into my eyes, and his expression turned fierce, his eyes blazing orange again.

The outcome of this fight would not change. I pulled back and swung my sword in an arc, aiming for his neck.

But at the last moment, he phased out and whipped behind me, solidifying and giving me a push. I toppled over the railing, grabbed his arm, and pulled him over with me.

As we tumbled through the air, I dropped my sword and shifted, my Gryphon wings snapping to the sides and my feline legs unfurling. I reached for him and snagging his leg in one taloned grip, I tilted my wings, and we shot across the water, my Glamour hiding us from view.

His sword still in hand, Galahad swung, but at every slash, I tipped a wing and dipped so that he missed. Again and again, he struck, his arm tiring but his determination strong.

I crossed the channel and headed for Wisteria, a small vacant island. Keeping one eye on my flight path and one on my captive, it was inevitable that I would make an error.

So when I crashed head-first into the lighthouse mid-swerve, the only surprise was that it didn't hurt much when my skull collapsed and my right wing snapped in two.

As we tumbled to the rocks below, the Djinn smiled, and then I buried him like someone dropped a tank on his head.

***

MIRI

When someone tells me to stay put, I usually ignore them. Today was no exception.

As promised, I stayed out of the fight, which must count for something. I saw it all unfold from the safety of the railing, my invisibility a safe option as long as I didn't use my wings.

When Eddi started shooting her mouth off, I almost screamed at her to shut up. Instead, I bailed. I didn't want to watch her die; I just met her. Running a jerky hand through my hair and pasting my smile back on, I pattered down the railing and slipped through a smoky glass window into the lounge. The dummy could get her damned self killed, but I wouldn't watch it.

I couldn't help them in the fight, but I could use my stealth as a weapon.

So when the little girl left for her chambers, I followed. I kept quiet, stayed out of the way, and avoided getting killed, just as Eddi asked. I peeked around the corner and watched from the end of the corridor.

When the Djinn materialized, the child turned to him and hugged his legs. Her eyes were bugging out of her head, the poor kid.

"Keep your door locked, Matilda. Don't let anyone in but me."

He touched her shoulder and turned away, his expression going cold before he faded and blinked out of sight.

Running on my tiptoes, I whisked through the door as it closed, quickly climbing the teak dresser. My invisibility made me a master at stealth, but apparently, Matilda had a few tricks of her own.

She sat down on the bed and looked right at me.

"Are you here to hurt me, Bluebird?"

I blinked into view, my hands on my hips—the nerve of this kid.

"The name is Miri, and I'm not a bird. I'm a Sea Sprite."

Her eyes widened, and she pulled the pillow onto her lap, clutching it tightly.

I stalked back and forth on her dresser, looking over my shoulder every time I turned.

This kid was cute. A little too perfect but pretty enchanting, if I was being honest.

"I'm not going to hurt you. I just have a couple of questions, ok?"

That got me a tentative smile.

"Ok." She lifted one hand and chewed on her nail, her denim sneakers swinging where they hung over the edge of the bed.

I took a deep breath, but honestly, I'd never been in this situation, so I had no idea what to ask her. I thought back to the day I met Eddi.

"Who are you?" There. Perfect opener.

"I'm Matilda."

I stared at her, scrambling to think of another question.

"Ya, I already knew that." I tapped my chin with one finger. "That's some talent you have there, Matilda. You can do the ether thing, like the Djinn hottie. Are you a Djinn?"

She hesitated. "I'm not allowed to talk about that."

"Says who?" I snarked.

Her eyes widened, and she glanced at the door, pulling the pillow tighter.

Scowling, I crossed my arms and tapped my foot, then gave her my most mischievous smile.

"No one tells me what to do. I'm *independent*. No one except Eddi—but only because I let her."

Matilda went still, her sparkling green eyes looking inward.

"Listen, chiklet. I have a pink Barbie RV over on our boat. Well, it's a dream camper. I can take you to the *Wanderlust*, and we can hang out for a bit so you can check it out. What do you say?"

Matilda's eyes widened, and she asked, "What's a Barbie?"

My mouth fell open.

"It's a toy. For little girls to play with. It's a doll that you can dress up. It comes with all kinds of cute dresses. I'm pissed they don't fit me, by the way. And the camper is like a big car, but it's to go and stay in the woods, with nature all around you."

She looked confused, and frowning, I tried again. "Not really nature, of course. You're on the boat when you play with it. But you can imagine you are in nature."

God, it sounded pretty damn stupid when you explained it out loud.

"Let me put it this way. It's way nicer than sitting in here," I looked around her barren room, "and I'll play with you. But I get the Ken doll. You can have Barbie, OK?"

Matilda mulled it over, biting her lip, her eyes darting between me and the door.

"I'm not allowed to leave the Black Widow. Hex will get mad."

I laughed. "Well, if Hex doesn't watch it, she will get dead. My friends are no joke."

I realized what I'd just said and cringed, but when I looked at her face, it wasn't horror that I saw there.

I took a chance and fluttered down to stand on the bed beside her.

"Listen, Matilda. Hex and that bast—um, vampire, are bad news, and I'm sure you don't need me to tell you that. We need to make tracks right now and get the hell outta Dodge before someone comes. Do you know what I mean?"

She shook her head. Okay, wrong choice of words.

"We need to blow this pop stand." She shook her head again.

"Get the lead out. Hit the trail. Vamoose. Split. Take a Powder."

Matilda shook her head, giving me a confused grin, her eyes shining brightly.

"Oh, for the love of Pete! Don't they teach you anything here? You need to get out more." I laughed, and she laughed back.

"Ok, here's the scoop. This lady is mean and horrible. She's not good for you. Come with me, and I'll take you home. It's early, so we'll have all day to play with the Barbies." I held up my hand. "But the RV is where I live, so you can't be messy."

More tears. Great.

"Listen, there's a gigantic world full of people having fun every single day. I can take you to the beach! We can get ice cream or go shopping. Have you ever heard of Disney World? It's amazing! You can shake hands with Mickey Mouse!"

She sobbed, "What about Galahad? I don't want to leave him here."

I gave her my most confident smile. "He's a big boy. He can handle himself. Once we get you settled, where you're safe, we'll return and get him, okay?"

Tears overflowed, and as they tracked down her face, her stricken look killed me.

"I know you're afraid, Matilda. Eddi will know what to do. She'll help you. She's amazing that way." I cocked my head. "I'm guessing you're not very happy here, right? You have no one to play with. No friends, no pets. And Hex is pretty nasty and makes you do bad things, right?"

Matilda bit her lip and nodded, looking down at her shoes.

"You don't know me, but I'm the wingman for a great crew of people—uh, beings—who stop creatures like your crazy boss upstairs from hurting folks. We can help you. I promise."

Matilda thought about it for a minute, wiping her eyes on her sleeve. With a sniff, she stood up and held out her hand.

I shook my head, and crossing my arms, I snapped, "What the hell am I going to do with that? I can't hold your hand. You'll squish me!"

She sniffled, and swiped away her tears.

"No, silly. You sit on my hand, and I'll take you there in my cloud."

I shook my head. "No way. I'm not getting into any damn cloud. I may end up in another universe or something. I have a hot date with Ryker tonight. I can't miss it, and if my molecules scatter into nothing, I'll never get laid again."

Frowning, Matilda said, "You know a lot of bad words, Bluebell."

I wanted to fight her on the whole name thing, but I figured I'd get her out of here first and give her crap later. Plus, the shit was about to hit the fan because I heard footsteps coming down the hall.

"You're imagining things. Those are perfectly acceptable words in Sprite language." My eyes darted for the door, listening to our visitor, who was closing fast.

"Listen, if we are going to do this, we must do it. NOW." I tipped my head towards the door, and Matilda's eyes shot wide.

"Do you know where to take us?"

She nodded her head, her eyes sparkling over her flushed cheeks. "I do! It's the white and blue boat across the water, the one Hex always watches with binoculars."

Ok. That made my skin crawl.

"Someone is just outside that door. It's now or never, kiddo."

Matilda bit her lip, and her hand shot out, her palm flat.

I stepped on and crossed my arms, my foot tapping. She giggled at the tickling sensation and wiggled her chubby fingers. A subtle scent of verbena and the salty sea enveloped me, making me sigh. It reminded me of home.

If Eddi survived the fight upstairs, she better thank me for this dangerous dive into insanity. The colors around me dulled, and the room blurred. A split second before things went black, the door opened. Cain's shocked and terrified face made my day.

My glittering eyes triumphant, I mouthed. "Gotcha, motherfucker."

CHAPTER 29

Twelve twenty-one. That was the time on my watch when something woke me from a sound sleep.

Cal lay beside me on his back, his hand across his chest, and some sort of goblin oratory happening in his throat.

What did I just hear?

I looked around the cabin, the glow from the distant street light coming through the portholes bright enough to get my bearings.

Someone whispered outside the shuttered door.

I climbed out of bed, trying to be quiet. Only a few people could pass through the wards, and they were all here, except for... I opened the shutters to peek out.

"Miri?"

The Sea Sprite looked up, her hand on the open door of her pink RV.

"Sshhhh," she hissed. "You'll wake everyone up."

"Where have you been?" I whispered.

"Listen, I'll tell you everything tomorrow, promise. I'm beat." She closed the plastic door, and I heard her rustling around. Then everything went quiet.

I looked across the stern. Tabitha and her two brothers were sprawled in a heap on the floor, the warm night perfect for sleeping.

I caught my breath. There was a fourth figure curled up on the back bench, her head pillowed on one of my fleecy sweaters. A thick bath towel was draped over her body and tucked under her chin.

Feeling my stare, she opened her eyes and peered at me, dark rings of exhaustion bruising her face. I released the breath I held and stared at the two emerald eyes glowing brightly in the darkness. She blinked, smiled at me, then closed them and snuggled into the soft towel.

At that moment, I knew the world around us was about to explode into chaos. The little flower in my chest shivered, then leaned toward the child.

EPILOGUE

Cain staggered into the Cigar Factory, his eyes haunted. He was a dead man. Hex would tear him to pieces when she discovered the child was missing.

Ten minutes ago, when he opened the door to retrieve her, Matilda faded away right before his eyes. The little blue bitch had stolen her from under their noses. Cain could still taste the bile that flooded his mouth when he stared into the empty stateroom.

Hearing the ruckus at the stern, he had escaped using the blackout van, his exposed skin peppered with stinging burns from his mad dash over the railing. He clattered down the factory stairs, his pulse racing, searching his breast pocket for the key. The leather soles of his Gucci Oxfords tapped out a staccato beat on the ancient bricks as he hurried to the chamber holding their greatest prize. As he unlocked the door, his hands trembled.

It was time to make his move. After tonight, the Syreni gold mine would be his to plunder. He anticipated a celebratory sip of her delicious claret, saliva welling at the prospect. But he mustn't dawdle.

As he hastened across the cool brick room, a wall sconce cast shadows into Oriana's enormous tank. The meager glow revealed her motionless form, huddled in the furthest corner.

Long foxy hair drifted over pale, slumped shoulders; her striking face tipped forward in sculpted perfection. Dull and peeling, a lifeless tail sagged on the tank bottom.

Cain hesitated. Was she dead? He cursed the shiftless junkie for running off and not properly tending to her.

Oriana lifted her head, offering a sluggish side-eye. Still alive—thank goodness. Cain expelled a relieved breath and pictured Eric minus his limbs, the craters in his gums throbbing painfully at the thought. Hissing under his breath, he hurried to the corner cabinet.

"Oriana, today is your lucky day, darling. It's time to move on to a nicer hotel." Cain clapped his hands. "Pitter Patter!"

Snatching a pry bar from the toolbox, he jogged up the stairs beside her aquarium, the salty scent of seawater teasing his nostrils. He loved the smell of the ocean, but being aquaphobic, he never learned to swim. How ironic.

Inserting the pry bar into the heavy cowl latch securing the mesh lid, he leaned into it. It didn't budge.

"Dammit." God, he hated opening this thing. Eric was always here to help with the stubborn spring and the unpleasant task of restraining their captive.

"Why do you have to be such a bitch, Oriana?" He grumbled, prying on the clasp. "If you were better behaved, you'd have more freedom. You understand that, don't you?"

There was no response.

When he switched to two hands, the rebellious clamp flipped open with a thunk. The bar clanged as it hit the bricks below, and Cain yanked at the thick strap securing the lid.

His plan was half-baked, and that irked him. Cain was always meticulous with his schemes. But losing the child had stripped him of choices. Hex wouldn't hesitate to destroy him. He'd lose more than his teeth if she caught up with him.

Cain climbed the remaining stairs of the wooden deck bordering the watery prison and shoved the lid back.

"Come, Oriana. It's time to expand our horizons."

The Syreni female turned, eyes downcast, rising slowly to the platform's edge. Chestnut hair plastered her face as she surfaced, exposing pale shoulders mottled with dead skin.

"Good heavens! You look worse than I anticipated."

Oriana ignored him and averted her eyes.

"Now, now. A change of scenery is just what the doctor ordered. Be a love. Don't make me get the noose. I'm on a tight schedule today and want a quick top-up before we skedaddle."

As her jade eyes fluttered closed, her arm lifted. Reluctantly, she offered it to the vampire.

Careful to avoid staining his costly cream suit, he turned her hand and bent it back, exposing the delicate veins threading her wrist. His crimson eyes sparked, and razor-sharp barbs slid from his fingertips. Leaning over the tank, he paused to inhale the tangy aroma of her salty skin, then brought the sharp tip of one claw to her wrist.

In his final moments, Cain recalled how the sudden predatory sparkle in her eyes spilled his bladder and spoiled his suit.

With a hair-raising cackle, Oriana's free hand snaked forward and snared Cain by the hair, hauling him into the tank. Bubbles poured from his mouth as he struggled to right himself. Water in his nose. His mouth. Over his head. His arms flailed as blind terror overrode survival instincts.

Oriana hadn't languished in her tank. She hadn't helplessly counted the bricks on the walls, waiting to die. No, she was a proud Syreni Doyenne. Biding her time, she hunted him. Ten endless years of waiting led to this glorious moment. Patiently stalking a singular tick of the clock—the nanosecond when Cain suffered an inevitable lapse of judgment.

Needle sharp spikes filled her yawning jaw, and snapping his head back with her talons, she struck, her fangs clicking home inside his neck. With an inhuman snarl, she twisted her head and yanked, removing his throat.

Blood clouded the tank as she choked down chunky mouthfuls of her prize, the ambush seasoned with expensive aftershave. Cain lived just long enough to see her skin healing, a healthy glow suffusing her features. Her smile was sugared with malice. In his mind, she spoke.

"This is for the Shoal."

Her glittering green tail morphed into legs. Swinging her feet to Cain's chest, she fisted his hair, threw her shoulders back, and yanked his head free. Dropping her messy handiwork,

Oriana smiled as it tumbled to the bottom of the tank before coming to rest on one perfectly groomed cheek.

Not wasting any time, she turned and pushed off, lunging over the side of her prison in a red tidal wave of seawater. Her lungs expanded as she gulped greedy mouthfuls of air for the first time in weeks. With a cough, she rolled to her feet and fell down the stairs, her water-softened soles tender on the bricks. It felt wonderful.

Hot-footing it across the floor, she wrenched the door open, marveling at the speed of her recovery. She had never eaten human flesh, and the thought sickened her. She growled softly to herself, her wet feet leaving a crooked trail as she fled down the darkened hallway. Hope bloomed in her chest as she reached the main room and darted across it.

Almost there. Soon, the salty breeze would tickle my face, and I would hug my children. Tears sprang to her eyes at the thought. She staggered up the stairs, the outer door before her. She grabbed the handle and hesitated. Then, with a ferocious yank, she pulled it from the hinges and headed for the ocean.

THE MOON TIDES

BOOK THREE
THE TIDES SERIES

PENELOPE AUSTIN

This book is a work of fiction.
Any references to historical events, real
people, or real locations are used fictitiously.
Other names, characters, places, and
Incidents are the product of the author's
imagination, and any resemblance to actual
events locations, or persons living or
dead, is entirely coincidental.

THE MOON TIDES
Book Three
Of the Tides Series
Copyright © 2023
by Penelope Austin
All rights reserved.

No portion of this book may be reproduced
in any form without written permission
from the publisher or author.

DEDICATION & THANKS

My husband is a saint, as are my dogs!
All of them put up with me reading bits
and pieces of my work to them, constantly
asking for advice. (And never vacuuming,
at least as long as there's a book on the go.)
Thanks for being so patient.

Thank you, Flirty Quill, for helping me
polish my story, ensuring it's the
the very best it can be for my readers.

And for the readers who reached out
*to me, and told me how much they loved
Ronan, Eddi, and the Florida Keys gang*

~ THANK YOU ~

*When you write a long story like this, you
never know how it will be received. Hearing
your wonderful words of praise made my day.*

PROLOGUE

~ HEX ~

Pain. Such agonizing pain. And blood, trickling down her legs. Three blocks, and it had already soaked through the fancy clothing stolen from her kill. New lows had been met and exceeded today; she stunk of the lowest life form on the planet. Damn humans.

Cloaked inside the shell of Patsy's body, Hex staggered over the cobbled bricks of the old cigar factory. Leaning against the walls of the dark corridor, she stumbled to check on her greatest asset, safe in her—

A hiss bubbled from her throat.

Wet footprints. And they came from the bitch's cell. When Hex shoved open the door, the last thing she expected to see was a traitorous vampire on the bottom of Oriana's tank. Her beast struggled to rise as she hobbled closer.

Cain's severed head rested at an angle, his lifeless eyes staring at nothing. Even in death, his smile was cocky. With a bitter laugh, she picked up the crowbar that the vampire used to free the bitch—then imagined turning his head to liquid with a thousand swings of it.

Oriana was gone. *Gone.* Ten years of successful Syreni egg production brought to a screeching halt.

A hellish sensation rolled through her veins, the steel bar clattering to the bricks. Her control vaporized—and she shifted. The human body snapped and tore until slowly, her beast stretched tall in the center of the room. The claws on her hind feet curled chunks from the bricks as she rose, her tufted ears brushing the ceiling.

She roared. With a slash of her claws, Hex raked the thick glass of Oriana's tank. Threads of water sprouted, the fine streams misting the air. Panting, fast and hot, as if she'd run a marathon through Hell itself, Hex closed her eyes and tried to think.

When her breathing finally slowed, she glared over her shoulder at the bloody stump of her tail. She was a *mess*. Her flesh was in tatters, her ribs broken, poking through her fur like oversized matchsticks. A walking disaster, and all because of that bastard Gryphon and his flunkies.

With a high-pitched whine, Hex lowered herself to the cobbles. Her slitted eyes swept over the vampire's remains as silently, they mocked her. Then, she remembered. Before the fight, she sent Cain after the child! *Where was the child!?*

Bitterness drenched her throat. Matilda had escaped, too. Why else would Cain have tried to flee with Oriana? Fearing her wrath, the vampire had run, and lost his head regardless. She would have laughed at the irony, if not for the pain of her injuries.

Injured, yes—but *far* from dead. Hex's stiff whiskers perked up at her reflection in the glass, a crimson flash lighting her eyes. She did NOT live for four millennia by giving up easily. Being Immortalis, the infernal boredom that plagued her *required* ongoing challenges; she *thrived* on them. Her blood boiling with anger, or plunging with dismay made her feel alive. NO—at this stage, it probably *kept* her alive.

Her mood lifted. The lab in South Carolina had stockpiled an astounding supply of nectar, and it would keep coming. There was enough for—well, for *everyone*. Chuffing a throaty laugh, she thought of Warren. National security advisor, indeed. That idiot was so addicted to *Gush* that he wouldn't dream of turning on her now.

She would hunt for another Syreni egg factory. Oriana wasn't the first, and she definitely wouldn't be the last. In fact, now was the perfect time to play her trump card. It was time the half-breed Djinn was brought to heel.

Binding Galahad had proven it; Djinn were powerless to resist the Talisman. Hex's heart soared as she imagined Edaline under her thumb. No more fighting back. No more running. Edaline, and every child she bore, would put up, shut up, and do what they were told.

Rising, she gimped to the storage room next door to find the glass cabinet full to the brim with *Gush*. Half the population of Key West was under its thrall—but to rock the world, she needed to think bigger. *Much* bigger. Maybe something fun, like spiking the water supply.

The thrill of getting high would soon become an all-time low for the human race. Man would tumble from the top of the food chain and find themselves nothing more than a portable feast. The demons she released from hell would pay handsomely for human snacks—or as she liked to call them, pre-marinated party favors.

She laughed so hard that blood splattered the glass before her. Sweet images swept away her pain. The streets filled with monsters, high as a kite on human flesh. Fighting like fiends, fucking whatever moved ... it would be her finest work.

And she would sit on the throne and rule it all. A new era of demonic supremacy would enslave mankind forever. And they'd be so strung out on *Gush* they wouldn't even see it coming.

Turning, she closed her eyes and concentrated. Bones popped, fur shrank, and soon, Hex transformed back into Patsy. Blood still trickled down her buttocks and dripped onto the bricks, but the infirmary down the hall would do nicely to patch herself up. She sucked in a breath and smiled.

Time to head to Charleston.

CHAPTER 1

His mouth open, his eyes popping from his face, Bacchus pounded down the dock toward the *Wanderlust*. His arm waved in a circle above his head—the universal symbol for "fire it up, let's GO!" Looking behind him, I saw why.

Girls. At least a half dozen, and they were closing in on Ronan's brother, whose shoulder length sand-colored hair flew behind him as he ran. I would have laughed if he didn't look so frightened. Ronan growled, hopping onto the jetty.

"Eddi. We should go, don't you think?"

I nodded, and the twin Yamahas rumbled to life, Cal quickly unhooking us from the dock cleats, and holding on as we waited for Bacchus.

"Matilda, Miri, would you girls mind going down and making sure that the cabin is secure?" Miri saw my expression and grabbed Matilda's arm, buzzing and pointing below deck. Thankfully, Matilda complied, because there was a shitload of sexual aggression heading our way.

I turned back to the scene just in time to see one of the women snag a fistful of sandy hair and almost bring Bacchus down. Her breasts bounced, her thighs jiggled, and her open mouth moaned as she tried to climb the bulky Syreni male.

The gaggle of human females were entirely naked, and their white, glazed-over eyes made my blood run cold. Bacchus let out a tiny scream as he grabbed her hand, still wrapped in his hair, and kept running, dragging her along as he tried to extricate himself.

Ronan, his mouth set in a thin line, jogged down the dock to intercept the women, who were obviously high on *Gush*. As the Syreni brothers converged, Bacchus whirled, disentangled the woman from his hair, and tossed her into the Bight. He and Ronan braced for impact.

As the remaining five women swarmed over their muscular bodies, their velocity brought everyone down in a tangle of naked skin and glittering skins. I bit my lip, Cal's concerned look making me nervous as hell. I needn't have worried, though.

Ronan got his feet under one of the writhing maniacs, lifting her from his body and shoving her off the dock and into the water, her arms flailing as she performed a spectacular back flop. Bacchus snagged another two by their wrists and, squatting to gather power, he lifted them off their feet long enough to heave them to the edge and send them into the ocean with their friends.

That left the red head, and wow, was she fast. In a flash, she had Ronan in a front headlock, and I growled when she gave him a boob facial. Then Bacchus was there, grabbing her from behind by the forearms. She locked her legs around Ronan's hips, dragging him with her as Bacchus dragged everyone to the edge of the jetty.

After Ronan finally managed to detach her legs from around his waist, the two males teamed up and gave her the heave-ho into the water with her friends. Then, panting like a pair of greyhounds, they sprinted to the boat.

Not a moment too soon, I throttled forward, spraying the jetty in my haste, because the school of *Gushers* also happened to be good swimmers. They were closing fast, and I didn't want to catch them in the props. Once we were out in the middle of the Bight, I slowed down, turning a concerned stare on the two brothers.

Bacchus, his hands on his knees, panted up at me.

"I'm sorry—Eddi—but I dropped—breakfast."

I bit my fingernails, my eyes checking him over to make sure he was alright. "It's ok, I'm sure we'll live for the hour and a half it takes to get home. Maybe we can grab a coffee at the Hurricane Hole when we fuel up." It was the last planned stop on our way out of Key West, and about twenty minutes on the other side of the island. But damn, a coffee would have been lovely.

Cal had read the reports of a wild party in town last night when he checked my phone this morning. I didn't realize things had gone this far. My stomach soured at the thought of how fast *Gush* was gaining ground in town. Just a few days, and things were out of control.

Our very early morning hadn't been any better than the night prior. Gideon was still missing, and when Ronan found the Enforcer's golden longsword on the bottom of the bay not far from the Black Widow, Cal nearly lost it. We split up, and after two hours of searching, had found not a sign of the Gryphon.

We did get Miri's story, though. She'd gotten nervous when she saw Hex splash into the bay, and snuck off with the child to hide in a local landmark. They'd fallen asleep until the wee hours, and then returned.

It was early yet, but not daring to call attention by hanging around the *Black Widow*, we decided to leave Key West. As it turned out, without a morning snack. My stomach rumbled, and I cursed the horrifying lack of caffeine in my bloodstream.

As I idled us through the enormous marina filled with all manner of boats and boat houses, I kept the speed down because of the mist rising from the water. As we passed Ronan's bench on the pier across the bay, I heard more moaning. I was afraid to look.

As we got closer and the fog lifted, a couple came into view. First were the two pairs of feet, then a rather well endowed male, on his back and driving into a voluptuous blonde female, his hands dug firmly into her buttocks. They were naked, they were wild, and their eyes were glazed over like the women who had attacked Bacchus. My stomach flopped at the sight, and I looked away.

When Miri and Matilda poked their heads out of the cabin, I told them to hold on a bit until I said it was ok to come out. Matilda was getting a crash course on my crazy life, the poor kid. Half a day in our company and—well, welcome to "The Edaline Show." Age inappropriate, naturally.

We saw two more groups of *Gush* addicted humans as we circled the island. A huge gathering at Mallory square, and a smaller one at Fort Zachary Taylor. In both cases, the Sheriff's office was handling things. Or, trying to. I wasn't sure Key West had enough manpower to round up that many crazed humans, but they were giving it their best.

Ronan appeared beside me, his face grim.

"Hex has not wasted any time. I cannot believe how quickly our stolen nectar has consumed the city. It is appalling."

Bacchus stepped up beside him, the two of them watching the ruckus on shore as we idled past. "I'll admit, I thought it was funny the first time Ronan and I ran into an affected female at a bar downtown. Now, it's—incredibly *distressing*." Bacchus turned his green eyes on me. "We must stop the demon. This will not end well for the human race. And if the authorities figure out where the drug originated, the Syreni will be exposed."

Ronan snarled. "It may already be too late, at least for some of those humans. Who knows what the drug will do to them in the long term."

When we passed the Fort and the Southernmost Point, I opened the *Wanderlust* up, and headed for the Hurricane Hole and the Cow Key Marina. Unfortunately, before we got close, it was clear we wouldn't be enjoying any breakfast this morning. The marina was on fire.

As we paused in the channel to sort out what happened, one of their tanks exploded, a fireball rolling skyward. The acrid stench of unburned fuel overwhelmed my nostrils, and the horrifying visual splashed my throat with bile.

Ronan stood close, his hand massaging my shoulders as everyone on board took in the carnage on shore. There was nothing we could do to help, and going closer would be a mistake. After a quick check of the fuel gauge, I threaded through the boats accumulating in the bay, and headed out to deeper water. We had enough gas to get home. Hopefully.

When we called down to them, Miri and Matilda rejoined us on the deck. After that, things settled down. It was almost impossible not to feel ill about what we'd seen. After a half hour out on the water, my stomach settled down, and Ronan's firm grip on my shoulder settled my nerves. His encouraging smiles did wonders.

The *Wanderlust* powered through the heavy chop, the wind treating me to a salty shower with every shuddering slap of the hull. Surprisingly, it was a wonderful sensation. The sun, the wind, the cooling effect of the spray on my skin—it reminded me. We were still alive. My back was killing me today, but thankfully, the ten foot scorpion tail from yesterday—hadn't.

In no time at all, Miri drove everyone crazy as Matilda smiled at the tennis match of words flying back and forth. Our new normal decorated the deck before me, and I was glad for it. The bow glittered with a blue and gold tangle of legs as Bacchus and Tabitha's skins reflected the sunlight. They had perked up, and were enjoying the ride, but Cal—well, he wasn't so good. Chewing like mad, his nails worn to nubs, my friend's eyes never left the horizon. He'd need skin grafts if we didn't find the Gryphon soon.

Like the smooth ridge of blue water carving alongside the hull, the rest of our trip home to Marathon was a moment of quiet in the maelstrom of crazy. Ronan lounged on the seat beside me, the smooth scales on his legs glittering when he stretched. I resisted the urge to run my hand along the hard curves of his thighs, opting to curl them around the steering wheel instead. We were in mixed company, after all.

Sensing my thoughts, Ronan darted sly, ultra-steamy looks at me between his quick scans of the horizon. I was weak when it came to him. And so were my legs, every time those beautiful peepers of his looked my way. The little flower in my chest preened for him, the saucy minx.

Finally, I asked the question that had tortured me since leaving Key West.

"How will we get time together when we get back to Marathon? Will you be returning to your people on the *Shoal* now that the fight is over?"

My eyes remained glued on the water ahead as Ronan's baritone voice hit me with a little thrill in all the right places. "We will find a way. How hard could it be when we both desire it?"

"I'll take you however I can get you," I said, shooting him a quick look. His smile ... oh my god. His short black hair, tousled from the wind, and the shallow cleft in his chiseled chin, pushed his striking features into breathtaking territory. I clamped my thighs together at the image of him licking my—*ugh*.

Seeing me squirm, Ronan darted glances at the shuttered door of the bow cabin. I bit back a grin. I didn't need any reminders of what we'd been up to down there. Our time in Key West had its moments, most of them terrifying and life-threatening. Finding our way back together again—*it was heaven*. I swallowed around the lump in my throat.

"I ... uh ... can you stay over at the apartment tonight?" Cringing at my desperate words, my fingers tapped the captain's wheel to cover my embarrassment. When he didn't answer, I looked over at him, tension coiling in my shoulders. He wasn't on the bench. No, he was right beside me.

At Ronan's beaming smile, I let out a long breath, and he slid his arm around me. It was warm, and reassuring. He leaned in and placed a sweet kiss at my temple.

"Of course," he said. "Bacchus and Tabitha can warn the *Shoal* of Hex's escape. I will tend to your needs tonight, and return to the *Shoal* tomorrow."

At his sultry words, a curling heat pooled between my legs. Every time he opened his mouth, I—*dammit*.

Ronan stood and moved behind me, his muscular arms cradling my shoulders. He nibbled beneath my ear, raising goosebumps.

"How is your back?" he mumbled into my neck. "It was quite colorful last night when I ... inspected it." Ronan's hand slid lower, his fingertips creeping over my shorts to massage the apex of my thighs. Slanting a look at his face, the sly grin there released a basket of butterflies in my chest. I covered his hand to stop its downward trajectory, my eyes darting to the gang at the bow.

No one noticed what Ronan was up to, thank the gods. Feeling my stare, Miri shot a suspicious look through the windshield before turning her attention back to Matilda as she laughed at Bacchus. For safety's sake, Miri rode in the back of Cal's hoodie, a splash of blue against his white hair. We couldn't take a chance on the wind blowing the sea sprite overboard.

Ronan pushed my hand away and added his thumb, rubbing it along the seam of my jean shorts. The pleasant ache teased a soft sound from my throat. When his fingers threatened to slide under the fuzzy strands of my cut-offs, I stopped him. Pulling the plug sucked; I wanted him—*badly*.

With a sigh and a cautioning hiss, I eased his hand away. Based on the boyish grin on his face, he'd heard my frustrated thoughts. Thank goodness no one noticed because *playful* Ronan wasn't the least bit shy.

The boat sputtered as I bumped the throttle, my laughter drawing a few sets of eyes from the front. Reluctantly, my tormentor moved to stand beside me as his gaze drifted back to the horizon. The corner of his mouth held a sexy curl ... the tease.

I almost forgot that he asked me a question before all the groping.

"Right. My back. I'm fine, really. I took some pain meds. I'm a lovely shade of prune, though. I got off pretty easy, so I'm not complaining."

I had yet to unpack yesterday's events. The Manticore was a walking nightmare; it took the five of us to bring her down, and still, we didn't kill her. During the fight, an overwhelming rage had pulled a strange power from deep inside of me, saving my life. The blue glow coating my skin deflected a deadly strike of Hex's venomous tail. I shivered, remembering the gross sound of Tabitha hacking it off with her cutlass.

Ronan frowned, his eyes reading the tension on my face.

"You're thinking about Hex."

I nodded.

Ronan watched me for a moment, his eyes flicking over my face. "Do not trouble yourself, Eddi. It *was* a victory. We will finish the job, as soon as we find the Gryphon."

Turning his eyes forward, Ronan smiled at Matilda's happy face. You wouldn't know a monster raised her for all eight of her formative years. Until we stole her. Well, Miri stole her. I was the getaway driver.

"Matilda is safe now," he drawled. "And Hex's stinger is her greatest weapon. Losing it will set her back until it can regrow. It will lend us valuable time."

I raised my eyebrows at him, and shivered. "You're kidding, right? Like the rest of her isn't terrifying and deadly?"

Ronan treated me to one of his heartbreakingly beautiful smiles.

"Oh. You were trying to make me feel better. *Gotcha.*"

He chuckled, reaching to cover my hand on the Captain's wheel.

"All will be well, Eddi. We will find Gideon and get to the bottom of James' involvement. We will uncover all the details of Hex's seemingly endless supply of nectar, and we will destroy it. All of it." The last words came out on a snarl, and I caught a flicker of yellow in his eyes.

I tried, but I didn't share his optimism. Easy for him to say. He was Syreni. They had power to spare and the confidence to back it up. And a tail. Let's not forget the tail.

With a frown, I said, "Did you forget the people we watched banging like bunnies on the point this morning? This *Gush* thing isn't going to die down. Sooner or later, the authorities will start looking for answers. If they figure out the source of the drug ..."

Ronan frowned, his eyes meeting mine. The furrowed brow and tight lips told me I'd hit a nerve.

"And what if Hex comes looking for more Syreni nectar? Your males will never be safe until she's caught."

"My people will stay close to home. Hex will not be successful, and when the supply in Key West runs out, things will return to normal." He turned to face me, his eyes lit with a fierce light. "I will protect my people to the last breath. And I will not allow her to take you from me again."

He took my hand and brought it to his lips, pulling a long sigh from me. Ronan's confidence was astounding, but together with the rhythm of the waves pounding the hull, I began to relax. My thoughts drifted as my eyes scanned ahead of the boat.

I had some power but no idea how to use it. So I had some sort of shield thing and could fly short distances. What good was that without a user manual? My father would have helped me, had he survived Hex's attack in Tennessee. I pushed the excruciating memories away. My grief would wait. There was plenty of time for that at night, under the covers, when things were quiet.

Gideon had answers—that he never shared, the bastard. The Gryphon was the key to everything. But where the hell was he? One minute, he fought Galahad, the next, he disappeared along with his "unbeatable" opponent.

My eyes found Cal, who had his back to the windshield. His hoodie pulled up, the loose strands of his white hair whipped around Miri, still tucked inside. He wasn't watching the others, his worried eyes scanning the horizon. I had no idea he was so fond of the Gryphon Enforcer.

The ocean swells gained some height, so I headed closer to shore. Matilda had never been on the ocean in a small vessel, and although her face radiated excitement, I was cautious. Being a charter boat captain, I knew the kid might be okay now, but that could change in a heartbeat. I didn't want to make her seasick on the way home.

A tug on my shorts startled me, and I looked down to find Matilda biting her lip and wiggling like a worm on a hook.

"What's wrong, honey?"

She motioned for me to bend over, then whispered in my ear, "I have to use the bathroom."

My heart clenched at the tearful admission. She must have heard me talking to Cal about the head being full this morning.

"No problems, cookie! You hang on for five minutes and we'll get you sorted." I angled the *Wanderlust* toward shore, heading for an island not far from Ramrod Key. It was an excellent place to stop, with easy boat access. The locals called it Picnic Island, and I'd been to a few memorable parties with Cal over the years.

There wasn't a boat in sight as I eased into the shallow water surrounding the island. Bacchus hopped over the rail and held the bow line as his brother joined him. Reaching for Matilda, Ronan carried her to shore, putting her down on the little beach tucked in the mangroves. When he turned his head to give her privacy, she found a good spot in the bushes to do her business.

What the hell had we gotten ourselves into? I knew nothing about raising a child, although I'd had a crash course on patience with Miri the last few weeks.

I glanced through the window and swallowed a snort. Cal, his arms crossed on his chest, pretended to sleep while the sea sprite stood on his arm, her chin wagging and her arms gesturing wildly. I caught something about her male "friend" Ryker *carrying tackle* with another female sprite in Key West. I guess we wouldn't be seeing Miri's little stud muffin again. Dang. I really enjoyed her Victorian curse words.

Ronan was back, but as he handed the smiling bundle of Oshkosh and sneakers up to me, he froze. His eyes flashed wide.

"What's wrong?" I hissed, my eyes racing along the shoreline.

He didn't answer, his gaze searching the mangroves that ringed the island. Bacchus hesitated, stilled, then sucked in a breath, and his eyes followed Ronan's. When Tabitha scrambled to the bow, I considered going for my knife. All three siblings were as still as statues, their eyes glued to the shore.

And that's when I caught wisps of a soft melody, so quiet that I strained to hear it. Like nothing I'd ever heard before, it came closer; it whispered in the breeze; wordless, it sounded ... *bittersweet.*

Bacchus and Ronan took a few hesitant steps toward the island as Tabitha leapt from the *Wanderlust*, splashing to their side. As if in a trance, Bacchus dropped the bow line, his hands balling into fists.

I sprang into action, scrambling to find my spare anchor, throwing it over the side, and snubbing it to the railing. The boat secured, I turned to watch the Syreni. My heart pounded as fear tap-danced through my veins.

"Ronan, what is it?" He didn't answer. The song came closer, tugging the tiny hairs on my neck to attention; then I remembered. We were safe as long as we stayed on board. Meeting Phoebe in Key West was a stroke of luck because the talented witch warded the *Wanderlust* weeks ago. But my friends were in the water. They were sitting ducks. I couldn't breathe.

Ignoring me, Ronan marched forward, his eyes locked on something around the point. I was about to grab the speargun when I saw what seized everyone's attention.

It was a woman. My eyes flicked over her form, and it hit me—*no*, not a woman. A beautiful Syreni female with emerald eyes and glittering green skins that, like Tabitha, covered her legs and belly. Miniature scales smoothed upward over her ribcage and breasts before fading away. The effect was discreet, and positively stunning. The dark jade pattern of her scales was a striking complement to the lustrous red hair cascading over her shoulders.

Thigh deep in the ocean, she hummed to herself as she splashed around the point, then stopped and looked up. She turned to stone, her face stiff with shock.

"*Holy shit,*" I mumbled under my breath, my hands reaching protectively for Matilda's shoulders before remembering the wards.

Ronan's expression made my heart stutter. His chin trembled as fat tears clumped on his lashes, then rolled down his face and dropped into the ocean. He took another step, raising a shaking hand as if reaching for the lovely redhead.

"*Mother!?*" The throaty word was tangled with a sob, the broken look on his pale face bringing tears to my eyes.

Holy double-shit burgers. Mother!?

Pushing through the water, Ronan bolted forward, Bacchus and Tabitha bumping his heels. Together, they plunged through the sandy shallows, met halfway by the stranger. Her vibrant eyes were a perfect match for the siblings I had grown to love.

Ronan got there first, stopping to grab her forearms and stare into her face before crushing her in a hug, his shoulders shaking with emotion. In seconds, the four Syreni were tangled in a sea of arms and legs, their tears causing sympathetic waterworks to run down my face.

Ronan's mother was alive. She was singing to herself on Picnic Island. The fates must have decided we needed a break because there was no other explanation for it.

When Ronan finally looked my way, his eyes were red, his face lined with grief. I thought of my father, joy and sadness battling in my chest. I let the tears flow so that I could breathe again.

On fire with excitement, the reunited family chattered in a strange language. Ronan's mother pulled back to examine Tabitha and stroke her hair before turning to smother Bacchus. She laughed as she tugged his long sandy tresses with a tearful smile.

I felt Cal move beside me. He slid his arm around my waist and said, "Well, how about that?"

CHAPTER 2

Cal and I watched the reunion, sharing the emotional explosion from a distance. A pang of jealousy had me flushing red with embarrassment. His mother's return was a cause for celebration. I should be happy for my friends. I would have Ronan back as soon as he was ready. *Right?*

After a lengthy huddle, Ronan's family returned to the *Wanderlust*, still hanging onto each other as they waded through the deep water. When they reached the boat, Oriana hung back, her face uncertain, but Ronan put his arm behind her and drew her forward with a soft smile.

"Eddi, this is Oriana, my mother." His face still flushed with emotion, Ronan beamed down at her. Feeling awkward, I leaned over the railing and extended my arm.

"Pleased to meet you."

Oriana stared at my outstretched hand, giving Ronan a concerned look.

"It's ok, mother. She is—" his eyes met mine *"—very special to me."*

At his urging, Oriana reached up and took my hand with a tentative smile. The skin on her fingers was cracked and peeling, mottled patches dotting her arms and shoulders. It was all I could do not to gasp.

"Greetings." The word rasped like rust from her dry throat.

My welcoming smile faded quickly as Oriana's eyes trailed over the boat, taking in the sleek lines and the twin Yamahas at the back. The silence stretched into awkward territory. She looked into my face and paused at my light gray eyes. Her stare pinned me in place.

"You ride on this thing, Ronan?"

I bristled, my eyes flicking to Ronan as I struggled to understand her tone.

What does she mean, this thing?

Ronan's brows pulled together, dipping along with the corners of his mouth. "We return from battle, Mother. It was the fastest way."

Oriana turned to stare at him, her lips a tight slash. He looked flustered.

"Eddi required my protection. It was the right thing to do." His shoulders tight, Ronan refused to meet my eyes, his gaze remaining locked on his mother. Bacchus and Tabitha shifted uneasily behind him.

"It is a landwalker's boat, my son. Have I been gone so long that Syreni now accept rides on human vessels?" Her throat scratched out the words, but her head was held high with pride. Even weakened, there was power in her. What was it Ronan called her? A Syreni Doyenne. *A respected female.*

I looked over my shoulder, but thankfully, Miri and Matilda had disappeared into the cabin. This conversation wasn't a sail through the sunset of my expectations, and Matilda didn't need any more drama right now.

My friends' expressions shut down, except for Tabitha. She bit her lip as she took in her mother's skin condition, her eyes flicking over every patch and bump. Oriana wasn't thin, but her complexion was sallow, her eyes dark with exhaustion.

Maybe Oriana wasn't well, and her words were an unintentional insult. I tried to ignore the lump of cement in my stomach as Ronan attempted to smooth things over.

"Mother, we can take the *Wanderlust* home with Eddi. You don't have to swim. It will be easier for you." Ronan's eyes flicked to mine for an instant, and then they were gone. Pain lashed my chest, and I struggled to breathe. It was as if we were reunited, only to have him pulled away again. And dammit, it hurt.

Oriana squared her shoulders, her eyes glittering like facets. "I will swim. It has been a decade since I felt the ocean rushing over my skin. I am halfway there and will finish on my own. *This* Syreni does not ride in *boats*."

Ronan frowned, his brows drawing together as a look passed between the three siblings. Bacchus, who up until now had been very quiet, said, "It's fine, mother. We will accompany you and take breaks if needed. You've been through enough. We know this must be difficult for you. If you wish, you can tell us your story along the way."

I was happy for them, really. But my heart fell when Ronan took his mother's hand and gently pulled her away from the *Wanderlust*. He wouldn't look at me, and he didn't say goodbye.

The Syreni staying together was natural. I couldn't imagine how they felt right now. I swallowed around the knot in my throat, knowing I should be happy for them. If that had been my father back from the dead— Still, in a selfish corner of my mind, it hurt.

Mentally slapping myself, I backed the *Wanderlust* away from shore and swung her toward home, feeling the loss of the masculine presence I'd longed for. He was here, then he was gone. The story of my life.

Cal stowed the anchor and joined me at the helm, and once we were underway, Miri and Matilda reappeared, looking subdued. Whether it was exhaustion, or the disappearance of our friends, I didn't know. Cal answered their questions while I pulled myself together. Keeping my eyes on the water, I was able to hide the defeat on my face as the reality of my situation slowly sank in.

I wasn't a Syreni. I didn't live at the *Shoal* and never would. I had no claims on Ronan. I had to remember that. My stomach soured as I recalled the vast differences between our worlds.

Why did I always set myself up for heartbreak? There was a reason we had parted company weeks ago. *How had I forgotten that?*

Cal slung an arm over my shoulders, his eyes inspecting my stiff expression.

"It's alright, Eddi. Relax, ok? He'll be back. He needs this time with his mother. You're sore, you're tired, you need a shower—*and something to eat*. It'll be fine. I promise."

My eyes burned as I struggled to keep the waterworks at bay. Matilda and Miri were in the shelter of the cabin with some sticker books. I was bound and determined not to cry. Matilda didn't need to see that. I stuck out my trembling chin and forced my breathing to steady. Hard to do with a bowling ball in your chest.

"Hey! What am I? *Chopped liver?*" Cal's arm tightened over my shoulders as he rocked me to cheer me up. I dashed the back of my hand under my nose and sniffed. Then I slid my arm around him and squeezed.

"Thank you for being here for me Cal. I'm ok. You're right. Let's get home."

Ronan would come to me as soon as he could. Four Syreni were more than capable of protecting themselves. Hex was lying low. I needed to force the child living inside of me—the one who feared abandonment above all else—to see reason and enjoy the peace and quiet.

***

Forty minutes later, tired and windswept, I eased the *Wanderlust* into her slip at Davy Jones Locker. It was lunchtime and there wasn't a soul in sight. Something wasn't right.

"Where is everyone?" I hissed to Cal. He shrugged, his wary expression making me nervous. This was *not* what we expected. The marina always hopped, especially on Friday afternoons.

We docked the boat and headed up to the shop, my feet telling me to run, but my brain telling me to toughen up and stop panicking. Matilda trailed us, and Miri snuggled up in Cal's hoodie, cloaked from human eyes.

As the door to the shop tinkled, Evan came out of the stock room. Happy to see us, his hazel eyes locked onto Cal.

"Hi, guys," he said with a cheerful nod. "How's everything down in Key West?"

I looked at Cal, whose eyebrows drew together in a scowl. "Where is everybody, Evan?" He glanced through the bait shop door. "It's pretty dead out on the docks. Where are James and Brian?"

Evan dropped the stack of t-shirts he carried onto a chair behind the counter and shrugged. "I have no idea. I came to work this morning, and I've been flying solo ever since. James disappeared in a hurry yesterday, and Captain Brian came in before me and took off with his boat. Something about a group he had to pick up at Palm Island. They planned on going offshore to fish for Mahi at the humps."

Evan began folding the shirts by size as he glanced back and forth to the muted TV hanging from the ceiling. Cal looked at the clipboard with the booking sheet and stiffened.

"There's no snorkel or family charters today. Didn't James schedule something?"

With a genuine smile, Evan looked down at Matilda, pulled a purple sucker from the jar by the till, and handed it to her.

"Hello, pretty thing! Where did you come from?"

I threw together a hasty story about me babysitting for a friend. When Cal raised his eyebrows and tapped the clipboard, Evan finally answered his question.

"Right. James. Charters. No, he took off yesterday morning and turned the closed sign when he left. He mustn't have returned to man the phones, and I was gone on a charter with Brian. I never saw him."

Cal looked at me, his expression tight.

Evan, his eyes glued to the TV, said, "I tried calling James' cell, but there's no answer. So I started working. I figured eventually, someone would show up." Evan glanced at Cal, taking in the gulf stream hair and dark circles under his eyes. "You ok, man?"

"Yeah, we're fine. No worries at all, just tired. We'll check on James. See if you can get something booked for tomorrow, OK?"

Prickles skittered along my spine, and judging by the fingers twisting at his sides, Cal was freaking out too. His Octopus wanted out.

As we turned to leave, I followed Evan's eyes to the TV. It was a newscaster, and they were talking about *Gush*. I asked him to turn it up.

In the corner of the screen, police loaded a thrashing crowd of naked men and women into cruisers. One of the cops had a slice under his eye, and every one of the officers looked exhausted. The Newscaster's next words turned my blood to ice.

"Authorities have reverse-engineered samples of the drug plaguing Key West and have determined it is not man-made. It is organic, and from natural origins. It's like nothing they've ever seen. Preliminary reports suggest the biochemical composition originated from an ocean-dwelling mammal with a genetic link to the species Delphinidae. Yes, folks, dolphins."

The newscast cut to a commercial, and I turned to Cal. He looked as pale as I felt. I grabbed Matilda by the hand, giving it a squeeze. The clever kid stared at the TV screen with her bottom lip between her teeth. Her eyes were enormous.

Telling Evan to call if he needed help, Cal and I headed to the bike rack. Sizing up Matilda, I looked at my ride and drew a blank. How the hell was I getting this kid to my apartment?

Feeling a tug on my sleeve, I looked down as Matilda treated me to a ghost of a smile. Holding up one of the beach towels from the boat, she pointed at my basket and said, "Maybe we can use this for padding."

"Why do you have a towel, Matilda?"

"I didn't know if you were keeping me."

She bit her lip and stared down at her feet. "I'm sorry. It smelled nice, and I was cold last night. I thought I might need it again if you didn't want me to stay with you. I ... *I took it.*" Her face crumpled, her chin twitching as she tried not to cry.

I frowned at Cal, whose eyes misted over. Dropping into a squat, I took her gently by the shoulders. "Do you think we can use it as a cushion for the basket on the front?"

Matilda nodded, her eyes glistening. My chest tightened at the sight of her tears.

"Let's get this straight right now, OK? You're ours, kid. You're not going anywhere. You'll stay with us as long as you want. You. Me. Cal. And Miri, naturally. We're a team."

A fit of sobs burst from her as she threw her thin arms around my neck, burying a wet face against me. Cal turned away, his Adam's apple bobbing as he unlocked his bike.

With one hand, I swiped at the wetness under my eyes while rubbing her back with the other.

"Alright, Matilda. Good thing one of us knows what we're doing. Hand me that towel, then hold up your arms, and Cal will lift your cute little butt up there."

***

A satisfied warmth spread through me as I closed the door to my bedroom. Matilda snuggled under a comforter on my bed, having a nap that would hopefully remove the dark circles from her eyes. I didn't blame her. I was exhausted, too, and the aches crisscrossing my upper body felt like I'd gone three rounds with a meat tenderizer. Getting stabbed with a stinger the size of a volleyball would do that to a girl.

Cal stood at the window watching the seabirds as they coasted high above. The glittering ocean visible at the end of my street lifted my spirits a bit. When he turned, the bags under Cal's gray eyes cast a shadow over his face. He opened his mouth, but I cut him off.

"So what's first? James' potential traitor status or Gideon's disappearance? Or hey, how about the return of Ronan's mother and what it means? I mean, really. Just pick one. I can pop some corn."

Cal shook his head. "I don't know what to think about it all. What a shitshow. You heard the news cast. They're already halfway to finding the source of the drug." When he lifted his hand to bite his nails, I gave him *the look*.

Going to the fridge, I grabbed a can of soda for each of us and looked inside at the bare, filthy shelves. My heart sank. I had some adulting to do today.

Cal snapped the lid on his Fanta and plunked down in his favorite chair with a moan. "It's too much, I swear. Do we look for James and fish for some answers? How do we do that without tipping our hand? Because that's the only way forward that I can see. We can't sit on our thumbs and wait for Gideon. Who knows what happened to him?" He looked down at his twisting fingers. "What if he's *dead?*"

I stared at the top of Cal's head, his white hair much longer than when we left for Key West a few weeks ago. When he looked up, his eyebrows scrunched together. He lifted his fingers to his mouth and started chewing, and I sighed.

"You're pretty close to Gideon, aren't you?"

Cal looked away. "I've known him for a long time. He came to the Keys a few days before you showed up. I always wondered about that, but now we know the whole story, don't we?"

The bastard had taken my memories ten years ago to hide me from Hex. Not giving me a say in things and leaving me wandering the highway without a single memory was unforgivable. I still hadn't come to terms with his actions, but I cared about what happened to him.

I gave Cal a sympathetic look. "Gideon is a Knight of the Sovereign. An Enforcer. Doesn't that mean something? He must be tough enough to go a few rounds with a talented swordsman, don't you think? Galahad may be a Djinn, but Gideon once told me that Gryphons are hard to kill."

Cal lifted his feet onto the table, then leaned back and closed his eyes, laying his arm across them. "Yeah, well, he told Bacchus that Galahad was unbeatable. Enforcers are tough, but even Immortalis can die. They aren't Gods, Edaline. There are ways."

"Maybe it's not what we think, and he got held up." I cringed at the unlikely words. Gideon was in deep shit somewhere, and we might never find out what happened to him.

Cal sat up, scrubbing his hands over his face. "Or the Djinn kicked his ass, and Hex is doing God knows what to torture him." He turned to look out the window. "If Gideon doesn't come back, we're screwed. We have no idea who is next in the chain of command. We'll be completely on our own down here."

I took a sip of my drink, mulling over how to move forward from here. Waiting for something to happen was the easy option. Gideon would expect more from us. Hell, *even I* expected more from us.

"Why don't we find James and fish for information about why he was on Hex's yacht? Maybe we'll find out he was completely innocent."

Cal rolled his eyes, taking a giant swig of his soda.

"Ok, I admit, it's not likely. But we don't know for certain that he's involved, Cal. Gideon said not to rush judgment."

Looking over at the bedroom door, Cal lifted an eyebrow at me. "And our precious cargo in there? What do we do with *her?*"

"Shit, I don't know. She's eight. We can't just leave her here alone." My warded apartment was the safest way to protect her from Hex, at least for now. But who would babysit her while we were gone?

Something moved on the counter, and I watched Miri slide from my messenger bag. She stood up, stretched, and yawned, her hands fisted high over her head.

"You guys are really stupid, you know that?" With an evil grin, she swung her hands around with a flourish and bowed. "Built-in babysitter, at your service." She fluffed her dragonfly wings and buzzed over to stand on the coffee table.

I rolled my eyes. "Miri, you took an eight-year-old child on a bootie call. I'm not sure that qualifies you as babysitter material." I slid my pop away before she sipped from the rim.

Miri growled. "Not fair. I had no choice! I saw Hex plop over the railing into the bight, and then you guys never came back. I got nervous! Hiding in that rotten old jalopy advertising fish tacos—it was the perfect solution, and you know it. Ryker showed up, sure, but there was no fadoodling! *I swear.*"

She gave me a saucy smile and crossed her heart. "Are you forgetting they never found us? And here she is, safe and sound." Miri spread her arms, wiggling all ten fingers. "Ta DAH!"

At the sour expression on my face, she snarled. "I let her scatter my molecules for you guys! I should get a full pass for that!"

She had a point. Wards, if pressed hard enough, could be broken. If Hex swam over to the *Wanderlust*, she may have been furious enough to do something drastic to get Matilda back.

I thought about Tennessee and my father's cabin burning. It had top-notch wards, and with one match and a can of diesel, my whole life went to shit.

"Ok, fair enough. I'm sorry, Miri. I still can't believe you got her off the *Black Widow* right under everyone's nose. Well done. And for the record, I'm glad your molecules survived."

"You're welcome. Now, you guys go ahead and do what you gotta do. When she wakes up, I'll keep her busy and make sure she stays here. She's pooped. She may not even wake up."

Fluttering over to the fridge, Miri tugged for all she was worth, eventually opening the door. Frowning, she looked over her shoulder and hissed, "Who are you, Old Mother Hubbard? Go shopping, already."

CHAPTER 3

CHARLESTON
~ FELIX ~

I ducked my head, hiding my smile at throaty rumbles filling the air this morning. The cafeteria, jammed full of male Servus and Argenti, hummed with excitement. Everyone loved Mondays, and it showed with the rising volume around me.

Well, we *Servus* loved Mondays. The Argenti males were all snarls and dirty looks, as usual.

Glancing down the lineup of bare-chested males sitting at my table, I marveled at the long row of emerald eyes glittering with excitement. An occasional splash of white stood out, and I frowned. Those males displayed an unfortunate variation in eye color, much like me.

My eyes were bi-colored, one white, the other a vivid green, making my face appear lopsided. Sometimes, I looked in the mirror and cursed the genetic twist that made me stand out. Jovi said something about genetic variability—whatever that meant. Life was easier now that I was grown and had hard fists, but the teasing had been merciless as a youngling.

The rising noise in the room caught my attention. Many Servus already rubbed at large erections swelling eagerly beneath their finely scaled skin. I fidgeted on the plastic bench as I tried to get comfortable, willing my cock into submission.

God, I loved collection day.

Growls exploded at the next table when Anton, a large Servus male, attacked an Argenti named Ivan, snatching up a handful of his short white hair. Showing his fangs, Anton shook the ghostly male until his teeth clacked. Ivan's white eyes bulged as he panicked, spreading long pale fingers to expose his webbing and claws. With a screech, he raked welts along Anton's hands.

Tossing him away with a snap of his jaws, Anton kept one eye on a group of Argenti gathering behind their friend, their lips pulled back in threat.

The dining hall went silent as chairs scraped and several tables of Servus got to their feet. A burst of telepathic warnings spiked between my ears, shooting through the Servus fighters—then ebbed away. The Argenti were outnumbered and they knew it, slowly backing down. Everyone returned to their tables, and I heaved a sigh of relief, as did the males around me. No one wanted a fight on collection day.

An Argenti caught me staring and glared, his piercing white eyes making my skin itch. Frowning, I tucked my chin and looked away. It wasn't worth it. If their boots came off, we'd get more than a few scratches when they let loose their long claws.

The Argenti hated Mondays. They had no nectar to donate to the program. It wasn't their fault, and I pitied them for missing out due to a genetic roll of the dice. I'd be angry, too, if I didn't have Monday.

The cafeteria pulsed with low growls as the Argenti stood and stacked their trays, then zipped up their black fighting leathers. Their days consisted of beating each other with wooden practice swords and learning how to kill rubberized dummies.

Watching them shove their way out the door made my shoulders throb. We trained together in the practice yard five days a week, and my muscles still ached from being thrown against the stone wall yesterday.

I sighed, thankful that it wasn't Friday. I *hated* Fridays.

Sucked back into reality when the bell sounded, every bench in the room rocked on its legs. Eager Servus lunged to their feet, threw their trays in a sloppy stack, and lined up at the swinging doors. I stifled a grin when I wound up behind Gallis, who was fully extended and enjoying a stroke before the collections.

His confidence never ceased to amaze me. The large-framed male was the envy of our barracks, his impressive cock legendary. Gallis was popular with our controller because his output of nectar was unrivaled. He was so heavily favored that even his spendings were preserved for the Benefactor's breeding program.

As the doors opened, a tide of jostling males pushed me along, everyone eager to get down the long white hallway. My groin throbbed, the tight skin there threatening to release my thickening arousal.

With gritted teeth, I pictured the beating I took at yesterday's practice, heaving a sigh of relief when my twitching phallus eased. Extending before collection annoyed me. Jovi said I was a control freak and needed to see the counselors.

I glanced at my eager companions, who had no qualms about swinging free as they bulldozed down the hall. Dozens of erect penises poked skyward by the time we reached the lab. I shook my head and smiled, my eyes scanning the white room as we entered.

In the long line of comfortable black recliners, one space missed a chair; that was my target. I pushed forward through the crowd of excited males, a few following as we vied for the spots closest to where they collected Axel.

Rumour said the bearded male was rescued from a rebel clan of Syreni hiding in the oceans to the south. Nearly identical to Servus in appearance, the Benefactor said that Syreni were distant cousins still living wild on the reef. No one knew the full story, but Jovi heard they were driven mad by toxins in the fish, their food source. Insanity seemed plausible, given their senseless efforts to resist our Benefactor's help. Axel's brethren had turned on him, their vile tortures ruining his mind in the process.

A full-blooded Syreni, Axel was a ferocious beast, his struggles on collection day always a spectacle. His strength and courage would benefit our cause if he ever overcame the brainwashing.

But entertainment wasn't why everyone fought to sit near him—it was the ancient and powerful Succubus that controlled the snarling beast. As she helped him release his nectar, her magic had a side effect. Any lucky Servus sitting adjacent enjoyed an overflowing blast of her very potent magic.

The euphoric sensations were mind-blowing to the point of pain, with lingering after-effects. Anyone who claimed what we dubbed *"The Splash Zone"* was forced to sleep outside for a night. Otherwise, no one got any rest with all the jerking and moaning.

"Watch it, Felix," Max snarled, giving me a shove. The diminutive male loved to get in my face and stir up trouble

I smiled and ignored him. Last week, I won a chair. My phallus throbbed and threatened to slip through my skins at the remembered intensity of my climax.

Today, my luck ran out. Max elbowed me in the ribs at the last moment and slipped into the padded seat before me. His friend Hector grabbed the one opposite, but I snagged the next in line with a burst of speed. Leaning forward, I shot Max a dirty look. Then, with a sigh, I settled back and put my hands behind my head.

As the long rows of donors settled in, everyone grabbed their receivers. The plastic mouthpieces clicked neatly over our teeth, leaving room for our fangs to slide into place. The network of tubing gathered every drop of liquid secreted from our canines during arousal. When our nectar drained fully, we were allowed to ejaculate.

I turned my head as two dark-haired beauties strolled through the outer door. Our regular Succubi had arrived, my throat bobbing at the sight of them. With a seductive smile, the pair started at opposite ends of the lab, their skin-tight t-shirts and jeans showing off their physical perfection. Soon, their lusty whispers and gentle strokes would help us express our nectar while their magic strengthened our arousal to increase its flow.

I grinned at Jovi, now sitting beside me with a lusty smile on his face. We were fast friends and stayed close at all times. He looked at me, his green eyes glittering with excitement.

"How in the hell do you control your dick, Felix?" My friend's swollen shaft bounced on his belly, his sapphire scales a vibrant backdrop for the turgid length that had already slipped through his skins.

I glanced at his erection and chuckled. "I like to test myself. I imagine the pain of your kicks at practice, and I shrink like a raisin."

Jovi reached across to give me a shove, a grin on his handsome face. "Well, if you ever managed to score a kick on me, I could certainly give self-control a shot. I'm not sure why you care, though."

His swollen penis jumped, and he reached down to stroke it, a bead of fluid seeping from the tip. His breath hitched, and his thighs flopped open. "I'll take as much as I can get of those Succubi. I sure wish they would suck it." He poked his tongue in and out of his cheek as he rolled his eyes theatrically.

I laughed at his antics. "I'll try extra hard to score a hit tomorrow, Jovi. I've been taking it easy on you in practice." I looked around the room, noting the eager faces of my brothers. "I want to show respect for the Benefactor, not hang myself out and spew everywhere. Serving our country is a noble cause. I would give every drop of nectar in my body if it saved one human child from that horrible disease."

I glanced over my shoulder at him. "Besides, it keeps Stephen's prod in his holster. I'd rather not have it rammed up my ass by spending too soon."

Jovi chuckled and dropped his engorged shaft onto his belly, looking around nervously for Stephen. Jovi wasn't thinking about honor at the moment. Stephen had nailed him good last week.

Every week since we were younglings, our training sessions included a study period about the plight of the human race and how a rare infection methodically killed their children. When the Benefactor discovered that nectar was the only cure, she set up facilities to produce, raise and train us not just for nectar production but also to protect the country.

Donating nectar solved the human health crisis; developing an underwater military defense kept everyone safe. The monsters who released the virus were a constant threat, and we were to be the country's first line of defense. I smiled to myself. We would single-handedly save the human race from extinction.

I settled back in my chair, clicking the collector over my teeth so that I didn't get in trouble when Stephen came by to check the lines. I caught a glimpse of him as he headed down the first aisle.

As usual, the bastard was all business, his black glasses sliding down his nose every time he bent over to adjust something. Stephen was a slender, dark-haired human male who constantly fluttered around the lab. He passed Gallis, thrusting eagerly into his tightly clenched fist, ready to ejaculate.

"Stop that," Stephen barked. "If you spew before I get you hooked up, I'll give you the shocker, you cocky bastard."

The well-endowed male looked up and grunted, his nectar streaming from his canines and dripping down his bare chest. Rolling his glazed eyes, Gallis stopped fondling his phallus long enough to slip on the plastic mouthpiece.

With a frustrated sigh, Stephen finished adding lubricant and slid the mechanical stroker over Gallis' truly impressive erection. He grunted, pressing his shoulders into the chair and clenching the arms with white knuckles. As his nectar slipped down the lines, the stroker began vibrating and with a jerk of his hips, Gallis' balls popped from his sheath. He groaned, and I grabbed myself to keep from sliding free at the sight of his pleasure.

Lucky asshole. Gallis' semen was in high demand, and he never let us forget it. I grumbled to myself, frustrated that my bi-colored eyes made me unacceptable for the Benefactor's breeding program. I slanted a look at Gallis, wondering what life would be like if younger versions of *His Highness* joined our ranks.

We never met the younger Servus and Argenti. Separated in locations throughout South Carolina, the age groups weren't mixed. I had fond memories of the salt marshes Jovi and I had played in at the other facilities, which were much nicer than this one.

Crammed with fifty mature males of fighting age, our latest facility was small. Having little space to roam was a sacrifice, but a small one when it came to doing our sacred duty.

I stretched my arms and ran my tongue along my mouthpiece, reassuring myself that at least I was providing something of value. Whenever our Benefactor visited, she preached that nectar was a God-given gift. Her eyes glittered with encouragement when she reminded us— production was vital to our survival.

A commotion in the hallway snapped my attention to the doors. *Axel was coming.*

An attractive female prowled into the lab, her potent magic preceding the tap of her stiletto heels. Layla.

Lust tickled my nostrils, and I lost the battle as my cock slipped through my skins. I hissed, my hips rolling as my member swelled. I reached down and pinched my smooth pink head to avoid a climax.

The powerful Succubus was a striking female with large, round breasts and buttocks to match. I imagined running my fingers through her shining hair, the golden strands tumbling from my fingertips.

A moan slipped over my lips as an image of my hands fisting her hair nearly sent me over the edge. Turning my head away, I bit down on my tongue, the pain giving me a shred of control. No coming until *after* my nectar drained. A potent culmination was worth the effort of control, and following the rules meant avoiding that damn shocker. It hurt like a bitch, and if you pissed off Stephen, he got creative with it.

I focused instead on Axel, groggy from Layla's magic but still fighting as they rolled him into the room. Strong leather straps at his thighs, chest and wrists secured him, his ankles cuffed at the base of the cot.

His rumbling snarl tore through the room, and I jumped at the sound. The gigantic male struggled in his bindings, his eyes blazing with fury as Stephen helped roll him into position.

"You little weasel," Axel spat. "When I get loose, I'm going to rip your head from your shoulders and shit down your neck!" The Syreni's wild eyes rolled, yellow flicking through them. Spit flew from his mouth as he bared his fangs at Stephen, who laughed in his face.

"You're not going anywhere, you Syreni fuckwit. Now shut up and enjoy the ride, or we'll send you for fertilizer."

Poor Axel. How badly had he suffered out there on the reef? I lay back and watched, keenly focused for a glimpse of Layla's buttocks.

As the Succubus strutted around Axel's chair, it occurred to me that she enjoyed the procedure as much as the rest of us. Axel's aggression was a drug to her. Layla rubbed her legs together, a pink tongue darting out to lick at her lips. Spreading her fingers over Axel's bulging pectorals, she gave his nipples a tweak. He snapped at her, and she rewarded him with a giggle and a playful slap on the nose.

"You bitch! Keep your fucking hands off of me. My people will come for you, and when they do, I'll kill you with my bare hands!" Axel's chair rocked, his head slamming back against the cushion as he fought.

Layla was my muse. She always wore a skin-tight dress of either black or red. My cock throbbed, and I moaned, my fingers reaching to throttle the head again. Before it was too late, I pictured Jovi kicking me in the groin.

Deftly avoiding his snapping teeth, Layla clawed her fingers through Axel's bushy brown beard, grabbing a handful and holding tight. Leaning over, she whispered in his ear, then nibbled his straining neck, a fine mist rising from her skin to shroud his face.

Stephen reached for Axel's device, a fucked up smile pulling at the corners of his lips as his eyes devoured Layla. The tent in his pants sparked a surge of jealousy in my chest, and when he reached down to fondle himself, I growled under my breath.

Thin, visible wisps of magic now hovered around the angry Syreni. Drifting on the air currents, it slipped into his nostrils and ears, then slithered into his mouth when it fell open on a sigh. Axel's growls soon turned to groans, his long thick shaft pressing against his skins.

At Layla's stroking caress, Axel's eyes hazed over and his gigantic cock popped free. Slack-jawed, his mouth fell open, and Layla clicked his mouthpiece into place. I watched as clear liquid pulsed down the long tubing before disappearing into the collector behind his chair.

I lay my head back and tried to feel the outer edge of Layla's mist now spreading toward me. From the corner of my eye, I watched Max in the chair next to Axel, his head rolling back and forth and his mouth hanging open. Across the way, Hector panted through grit teeth with his eyes crimped shut in pain. Both were fully engorged, their hands hovering over their cocks without daring to touch them. Lucky bastards.

As Axel gave in to the Succubus magic, Stephen hastened down the aisle, returning with another stroker to collect Axel's rare wild semen. Sometimes I wondered if the addlebrained Syreni appreciated his good fortune. I'd give anything to feel that thing massaging my cock until I climaxed.

The outer edges of the Succubus' cloud reached my chair. My eyes drooped, and I turned my head, sucking it in eagerly. I couldn't help a subdued laugh at Max, his face frozen in a contorted grimace. Overwhelmed by the mist, he lost control and ejaculated all over his chest—and Stephen.

Our controller looked over his shoulder, handed the stroker to Layla, then turned around and jammed the shocker into Max's thigh with a string of curses. At his friend's shrieks, Hector strangled his cock in a desperate attempt to stop his orgasm.

I rolled my head back to stare at the ceiling, my hazy eyes taking in the slogan there. Rumbling quietly to myself, tension oozed from my limbs as I wallowed in the edges of Layla's magic. My cock was rock hard, my nectar was flowing, and soon, I could ejaculate.

From the sounds of his strangled cries, Stephen hadn't let up on poor Max, and I wondered if this chair wasn't the best option after all.

The Benefactor's words painted above had it right—*Whatever it Takes*.

As my balls swelled inside my sheath, an erotic tingle spread upward from the base of my spine. My fine thread of control held fast until the moment the collector clicked off behind my chair. I roared my release, my hips surging into the chokehold of my fist. Like the other males in this room, I was proud to serve.

CHAPTER 4

After a quick trip to Publix to stock my fridge, Cal and I called a cab. James lived about ten minutes from my apartment, which was too far to bike. As Cal paid the cabbie, I stepped onto the curb and checked out James' bungalow.

Like most older Keys homes, it started as a trailer, but James had renovated. Freshly painted and sporting new windows, the house sat neatly in the burnt grass of his yard. Much larger than others in the neighborhood, it extended into an attached garage taking up most of the back yard. Cute and Keysie, the pink walls were decorated with colorful tin lizards.

Several young palms bordered the short driveway where James had parked his truck, crooked and with one front tire flattening a shrub. The bumper had some damage from the broken porch railing, currently held on by one brave bolt. His keys were still in the ignition.

Rapping on the door got no answer, and after several attempts, Cal shaded his eyes and peered through the front window. He looked at me with wide eyes.

"He's on the couch."

"What the hell?" I mouthed the words as Cal knocked harder. When no one answered, he tried the handle, which turned easily.

James sat on the couch, his hands in his lap, his eyes unfocused and staring into space. The TV was going, playing a commercial for ladies' hand cream. I opened the door and we slipped inside, approaching our boss where he slumped in a trance.

"James?" I reached out to wave a hand past his eyes. He blinked and slowly turned his head, his eyes cloudy. I bent down, and he met my gaze.

"Eddi?" he said, his voice cracking. "What are you doing here?" James blinked, and his hands flexed in his lap. "What time is it?"

I looked at Cal and said, "It's three o'clock. What are you doing here? Shouldn't you be at the marina?"

James looked at the wall clock and mumbled, "I don't know. What day is it?"

I was so baffled by James' mindless expression that when Cal spoke behind me, I jumped.

"It's Wednesday. Evan told us you didn't come to work today."

"Wednesday," he said, looking at his hands. "I thought it was Tuesday." He yawned and closed his eyes.

Cal's snarl inside my head made me flinch. *"What the fuck, Ed? He's so messed up. What the hell happened? He wasn't like this when we saw him in Key West yesterday!"*

Reaching out, I took James by the chin and pulled him to face me, his eyes slowly opening. "James, you need to wake up." He smiled at me but showed no sign of rousing. I sent my thoughts to Cal.

"This is nuts. We need to get some caffeine into him. Do you know where he keeps his coffee?" Cal headed through a door at the back of the living room.

I grabbed the remote and clicked off the TV, but not before seeing a blurred shot of human asses plastered across the news feed. I reached down and lightly patted James on the cheek.

"Wakey wakey, sunshine."

James turned his head as if to pull away, so I grabbed his chin. He mumbled something unintelligible, and my anger bubbled to the surface, my next pat a trifle harder than I intended. His eyes shot open.

"What the hell, Eddi!"

"You have to pull it together, James. I'm not sure what happened here, but you're pretty messed up. Did you drink or do drugs or something?"

James shook his head and yawned, his jaw cracking. "No. Not that I know of, anyway. I'm exhausted."

I sat in the overstuffed armchair opposite James and watched him while waiting for Cal. He kept closing his eyes and lowering his chin, but when I snapped my fingers and yelled, "OY!" he woke up a little. The cloudiness in his eyes began to clear.

"Here you go." Cal put a steaming cup of black instant coffee in James' hands, but when he stared at it, Cal helped him drink.

After we got half a cup down the hatch, James looked more himself. The grogginess cleared, along with the freaky cloudiness in his eyes. Cal sat on the coffee table, holding James' cup as he started with the questions.

"What is the last thing you remember, James?"

"Well, when you texted me from Key West, I grabbed the truck—"

"What? You got a text from us yesterday?" I asked, my eyes meeting Cal's. I scrolled through my phone to check, but there were no messages to my boss.

"Yes, in the morning, I think," he mumbled, his head tipping down. Cal handed James the cup, and he swigged what was left.

Wiping the back of his mouth, James said, "You texted that the boat was having issues and needed me immediately." He leaned forward and fished his phone from his back pocket, unlocking it and handing it to Cal.

A few seconds later, Cal looked at me, his eyes wide. He turned the phone to show me one text. The time stamp was right around when Ronan and I crawled out of our love nest.

James squinted as if trying to remember. "Brian and Evan took out my charter and I closed up. I had a bit of trouble parking but found a spot at the end of the bight by the Cuban restaurant. I had to walk all the way down the jetty."

He looked up at nothing, thinking for quite a while, then said, "The last thing I remember, I was looking across the bight and admiring the new four strokes I got for the *Wanderlust*." He smiled at me. "They work great, don't they?"

"Yes, they sure do. What do you remember after that?" I asked.

"Nothing. That's it. Now I'm here, and my employee is slapping me on the face," he said with a scowl.

Cal finished looking at the cell phone and handed it back. James stretched and winced. "God, my ass is sore. How long have I been sitting here, for crying out loud?"

Cal reached out and grabbed his hand, helping him to his feet. James could barely walk, pins and needles making him hobble.

"Thanks, Cal. If you'll excuse me for a sec ..." He minced down the hallway, and the bathroom door clicked shut.

"What do you think?" I whispered. "Did we get this wrong? Who could have messed with him?"

Cal growled. "That fucking vampire, I bet. I mean, he's the one that met James and brought him on board." Cal snapped his fingers. "Wait a minute. Didn't James turn around *after* passing the Black Widow?"

I thought back and realized he was right. And having been on the receiving end of Cain's talent, I knew his compulsions were powerful. He probably had some range.

"It sounds right, but who texted him? That message didn't come from my phone. Can a hacker do something like that?"

Cal nodded. "It's not a stretch that they would have someone capable on the payroll. I mean, it worked great, didn't it? We weren't long boarding their boat. Gideon suspected it was a trap. I guess this proves it, doesn't it? They used James to lure us on board—*before* we were ready—planning to take us out, then capture you. If Tabitha hadn't happened along, they might have succeeded."

Cal looked at me, relief written in the relaxed lines of his face. "There's no doubt James is messed up right now. That counts for something."

The toilet flushed, and we stopped talking. When James came back into the room, he looked much better. He walked over to the windows and looked outside.

"I'm hungry, and you guys didn't bring your bikes. Do you want some McD's? My treat," he said, his quirky smile returning.

It was the best thing I'd seen in days.

CHAPTER 5

James recovered quickly from whatever the vampire had done to him. After we ate, he dropped us off at Davy Jones to get our gear from the *Wanderlust*, offering to drive us home after he caught up on some work. There wasn't much we could do to verify James' story, but my gut feeling was that he spoke the truth. Cal agreed.

The marina was still quiet, but everything appeared normal as we walked down toward the docks. Cal sat on one of the benches near the Tiki hut, his shoulders drooping as he clasped his hands together between his knees. He looked down the channel, his eyes scanning the turquoise ocean visible through the palms.

"Well, what next? I'm glad James is alright, but we're still missing one grumpy-ass Gryphon," I said.

"I have no idea. I think Gideon's been captured. We still don't know where Hex hid her lab in Key West, and now we may never know." Scrubbing his face with his hands, Cal sighed. "If we can't find Gideon, we have no choice but to wait. We're at the end of our rope here."

I nodded, my eyes going to Bert's boat. Well, Gideon's boat. The Bert persona was a glamor. To others, Gideon looked like an overweight, balding human. The derelict and dirty glamor masking his vessel fit Bert's character to a tee, but I saw through it thanks to my budding powers.

Gideon's true form was spectacular, and to my eyes, the boat bobbing at the slip was the same. Hidden beneath the glamor was a brand new Ranger Tugboat, special edition. And now it sat, the windows dark.

HOLY SHIT.

"Cal, what's going to happen to Mr. Darcy? There's no one to feed him and give him water!"

Cal stiffened, grabbed his sun hat, and we headed down the docks to the end slip. As we got closer, it struck me how quiet the boat seemed without Gideon running the grill as his damn parrot shot me dirty looks.

Gideon's wards recognized Cal and me, so we hopped aboard without getting zapped. He cautiously opened the sliding glass doors and peered inside. Nothing moved.

Then, with a burst of feather confetti, a blue and gold macaw shot past Cal and walloped me in the chest, his sharp beak pulling up a hunk of my skin and hanging on for dear life. I screamed. Without thinking, I turned and jumped over the side of the boat, landing in the ocean with a tremendous splash. The parrot wisely let go.

The little monster slapped his wings across the surface, working his way to shore, then dragging himself onto the sand. He looked over his shoulder and shot me a corrosive glare.

"HOLY mother of OUCH!" I screeched, pulling my t-shirt away to look at the nasty v-shaped wound on my chest. It dribbled blood and was already sporting a bruise. My temper igniting, I snarled and scrambled to shore. That fucking parrot was going down.

Mr. Darcy must have realized my intentions because, dragging his sodden wings and tail, he started running and hopping down the sandy shoreline. It amazed me how fast the little prick could move without his wings.

I clambered onto shore and took off after him, my pants and shoes squishing with salt water. Cal hollered something at me, but I didn't care. If I got my hands on that damned bird, it wouldn't end well for him. Mr. Dickhead must have read my mind because he flapped his saturated wings like mad, zig-zagging to stay just out of reach.

"Eddi, stop!" Cal yelled, scrambling onto the dock to try and head me off. "You can't hurt him! Stand down—*stand down!*"

Too late. With a lunge, I scooped the little prick up in my hands and held him away from my body, turning back toward the Ranger.

Someone should have pressed pause on the Terminator movie playing in my head because picking him up turned out to be an asinine move. When he clamped his sharp beak down on my finger, I nearly lost a digit. *Again.*

The curse words that rang out across the bay would have gotten me into a ton of trouble had the marina been busy. As my shouts echoed around the cove, no one heard except Cal, who was busy prying Mr. Darcy from my mangled hand.

With considerable effort, he succeeded, and Cal put the wet parrot back into the living area of the tugboat, refilling his food and water. Then, he followed me up to the office to tend my wounds.

As the tinkling door announced our entrance, I tried to hide the blood dripping through my free hand. We bumped head-first into James.

"Crap, Eddi. Have you been messing with Bert's parrot again?" He shook his head. "When will you learn to leave that poor bird alone?"

I glared at my boss and trailed Cal to the back office, where we kept the first aid kit. Sitting down, Cal cleaned me up, stopped the bleeding, and bandaged my hand.

"Eddi, I don't mean to laugh because you know I love you dearly ..." Cal's lips barely held back his laughter. "But you and that parrot—I don't know why he hates you so much."

Hissing, I pulled my bandaged hand from his and tucked it against my smarting chest. "Are you going to clean and dress the wound on my freaking boob, too?"

Cal shook his head with a snort. "I think you're on your own, there." He stepped out of the office, and I went to town with the Bacitracin and bandages.

As I worked, something on James' desk caught my eye. With my bandaged hand, I pushed the top paper aside, my skin prickling when I read the page. It was an invoice made out to James from a wholesale meat supplier on the mainland—for twelve hundred pounds of beef.

I pushed the top invoice back, and right underneath was another one, this time for fifteen hundred. It was from the month prior. I pushed back six pages, and every one was a similar order, one for each month. My face flaming, I swept the pages back together and gathered up the first aid kit.

Feeling guilty for snooping, I tried to appear calm as I returned to the dive shop. James was there.

"Have you seen Cal?"

He looked up from what he was doing and said, "Yeah, Cal's down on the docks." He looked at my bandaged hand. "Are you ok?"

I nodded. "Nothing that time and a parrot club with fries wouldn't fix." I hesitated, trying to decide if I should ask about the meat. We'd had a close relationship for ten years. What would it hurt?

"James, I couldn't help but notice you had a receipt on your desk for a bunch of beef. Are you planning a party for us?" I winked.

James looked up and went still, his hazel eyes probing my face. He said nothing for a minute, then stood up and straightened the papers before him.

"My friend in Key West is getting married. It's for the party."

My eyes met his, and I saw the lie as plain as day. But what could I say?

"Ok, I just wondered. Sorry, I didn't mean to snoop. I'll go see if Cal is ready to go." I turned to leave, and as the door jingled, I looked back. James watched me, a strange expression on his face.

***

"Are you sure you didn't read it wrong?" Cal pulled our gear off the deck of the *Wanderlust,* setting it on the dock. It was getting late, and we had to get back. I was worried about Miri and Matilda.

"I'm not stupid, Cal. James bought huge quantities of meat for at least six or seven months." I did the math in my head. "Rough guesstimate, at least seven thousand pounds, mostly beef, but some chicken. My God, how much would that *cost?*"

Grabbing my phone from my pocket, Cal clicked away. "Okay, I googled tigers, and they eat about four to seven hundred pounds of meat a month." He looked at me. "I don't think James has two tigers." We stared at each other.

"There's no wedding, is there?" I asked.

Cal shook his head. "What possible reason could he have to need that much meat?" He glanced over at Bert's boat. "The only one who might know is missing."

Cal's head snapped around. "Wait. Do you think it was for Gideon?"

I shook my head. "That would mean James knows about the *Others*, and I don't think that's the case. And Gideon ate fish most of the time. I smelled it on his breath pretty much every time he harassed me."

I climbed off the boat, Cal right behind me. We dropped the subject and took the stairs to the parking lot, where James waited by his truck to give us a lift home. Ten minutes later, we opened the door to my apartment. I expected to see Miri at the wheel of the mayhem-mobile, but it was quiet.

A movie played on the TV as two sets of eyes turned to watch us come through the door. Matilda and Miri were cuddled together on the couch.

"So, what did you guys do all day?" My eyes darted around the apartment, looking for damage. It was hard to believe that nothing went wrong while I was gone.

"Oh, this and that," Miri said, her eyes sparkling.

Matilda giggled, then turned back to the TV. They watched *Frozen*, the music making the apartment feel lived in. It felt ... *good.*

I looked at Cal, who was at the fridge poking around for something to nibble on. He returned with cheese and crackers and set them on the coffee table. As Cal visited with the girls, I kept snooping. How did they spend the afternoon here and not get into some sort of mischief?

It wasn't until I went to use the bathroom that I found the answer. The tub was half full of water, with an inch of grit on the bottom and a two-pound bag of salt lying empty on the counter. The floor was soaking wet, and Cal's rubber ducky floated in the tub, mocking me. With a fluttering sound, Miri landed on the counter behind me.

"*Shh,*" she hissed, putting a finger to her lips. "I can explain."

I crossed my arms but humored her. "That was my last bag of salt, Miri. I needed it for Cal's visits."

"It's the kid. We had a problem while you were gone." The concern in Miri's eyes told me she wasn't yanking my chain this time.

"Matilda needed to soak in salt water. I don't know why, she wouldn't say. After lunch she looked restless and pale, so I asked what was wrong. Matilda said she needed salt. Once she had a good long soak, she was good as new."

Miri looked at the water and frowned. "You know what this means, right?"

CHAPTER 6

Matilda was in bed as Cal and I climbed the ladder to the Widow's walk. Miri hung out in the apartment to watch our new guest. I'd mentioned the bath to Matilda, but she clammed up, so I didn't press. She would tell me when she was ready.

"Interesting," Cal said, pulling his chair closer. He looked up at the night sky, sighing at the light show going on above. "That poor kid has been through hell."

"Cal, something is bothering me. When Hex was shooting off her mouth just before the fight, she mentioned the name Oriana. *'She'd love some company.'* That's exactly what Hex said. Oriana was her prisoner, wasn't she?"

Cal nodded. "I remember that. Hex also said that Cain looked after Matilda's mother." His eyes hardened. "You think Oriana is Matilda's mom."

"That's exactly what I think. You saw Matilda's eyes." I looked at him, goosebumps lifting my skin. "Today has been really chaotic, so I didn't put two and two together at first. All three siblings have the same eye color. It fits, doesn't it?"

"That would be pretty freaky, wouldn't it?"

"Yes, totally crazy. I wish Ronan was here so that I could ask him." Something moved behind us, and I jumped, nearly falling from my chair.

"Ask me what, Eddi?"

Ronan climbed through the hatch and grabbed his pink plastic chair, dragging it over to the table. With a groan, he sat, then stared into my eyes. His bronze torso gleamed in the moonlight, the salty scent of the ocean drifting to me from his wet skin. At the intensity of his gaze, my breath hitched, and I faltered.

"Uhhh ... Where is everyone? Did they go back to the *Shoal?*"

Ronan smiled a raw, pained smile, and nodded. "Yes, they are together there. It was a joyous occasion for everyone. My mother has many things to tell our people. I am very tired." He lifted a hand to his neck and rubbed, then stretched his legs with a long, drawn out sigh.

I reached out and squeezed his hand, leaning over to hug him. "I'm so happy for you, Ronan. It must have been amazing to be reunited. I can't even imagine how that felt."

Ronan caught my wrist and pulled me closer. His soft lips pressed above my collarbone with a kiss that made me shiver. "It was better than you can imagine. I am still in shock."

"But how did she end up on Picnic Island? Where was she all these years?"

He tensed, a throaty snarl vibrating along my nerve endings. I flinched and pulled back. Ronan's eyes flickered between green and yellow, raising the hair on my arms.

"Cain had her. For ten years, he and Hex held her in Key West." Ronan's face was murderous.

"What!?" *This whole time?"*

Bile rose to coat the back of my tongue as memories of my nightmarish time with Cain came flooding back. "Ten years," I whispered, my eyes finding his in the darkness. *"I can't—"*

Ronan nodded. "My mother is a strong Syreni female, but it has ruined her. She is not the same as when she left. Her glow has faded." His eyes glistened, and he looked down. "She says she is fine, but she is lying. She is not fine."

The plastic of his chair creaked, and I watched the armrest bow under Ronan's grip. Cain and his disgusting games. I shivered.

"How did she escape after all this time?"

"It happened during our fight with Hex," he growled. "For some unknown reason, Cain rushed in to move her. He was impatient and distracted. My mother is a clever female. She waited all these years for him to make an error. Finally, on that very day, he was not so cautious." His eyes sparked with rage and pride. "She tore off his head."

I jumped to my feet, my chair falling back. Cal grabbed it, then stood and put his arm around my shoulders.

"He's DEAD!?" A numbing cold flashed through me from head to toe. I didn't know whether to laugh, cry, or vomit.

Ronan nodded. "My mother finished him." For a brief moment, Ronan's eyes flickered yellow. "My mother is a good fighter. It is done. She did what she had to do."

My mouth hung open, a surge of happiness flooding through me, followed closely by a thread of regret. Deep down, I wished it was me that ended his putrid life.

"He's dead for sure? Not breathing, never going to rise again, dead?"

Ronan nodded, and a sad smile pulled on the corners of his mouth. "Her patience was rewarded." His voice thick with sorrow, he went on.

"She did what any good Syreni would. She held on until she saw an opportunity to strike, then killed him and escaped to the sea. That is why we found her on the island. She was returning home to the *Shoal*."

At my expression, Ronan reached out and pulled me onto his lap, wrapping his arms around me. "My mother would like to meet you." His soft words in my ear made me shiver.

Ronan looked at Cal, who righted my chair. "You too. I told her about my new friends on land. She was—*surprised*." He grinned, his tension dissolving.

"Has Oriana told you anything about her time in Key West?" Cal asked.

"Not everything. Why?" Ronan looked at me, curious. I frowned, letting Cal take the lead on this one.

"It's about Matilda. Did you notice her green eyes?"

Ronan nodded, his expression sharpening as he stared at Cal.

"Before you and Bacchus joined the fight, Hex shot off her mouth to Eddi and me. She let something slip, and it might be important. But you should brace yourself."

"Tell me, Cal."

"Hex mentioned they had Matilda's mother. Ronan—I think she's your sister."

Ronan froze, his tightening grip on my knee bordering on painful.

"My sister? Hex said that?" His eyes wide, Ronan scowled at Cal. "How could that be?"

Cal shook his head. "I don't know, but your mother is holding back things she may not be ready to tell. Not yet, anyway. You need to ask her about it."

As Ronan stared out at the ocean, deep in thought, Cal said, "I wonder how long it will take us to unravel the chaos that Hex is causing in the Keys."

We sat for a while, quietly enjoying the cool night breeze from the ocean. Ronan shared everything his mother had relayed about her time in captivity. It had been a living nightmare for her.

The details of Cain's death made me smile, even though I knew it was wrong. No one was more deserving of a vicious end than the unhinged vampire.

I crossed my arms as Cal and Ronan laughed about the parrot's recent attack. Ronan was pleased about our hunch that James wasn't a traitor. When I told him about the vast quantities of meat James had been buying, Ronan raised his eyebrows.

"You think James is *Other*?"

I sighed. "No idea, but he doesn't even have a house cat. What is he doing with all that beef and chicken?"

We tossed around a few ideas, none of them very plausible. When it got late, we descended the ladder and Ronan stopped beside me at my apartment door. He took my hand in his.

"I'm sorry, Eddi, but I must return to the Shoal," he rumbled, his eyes glowing with a subtle light. "I do not wish to leave you, but Mother ..." His eyes pleaded with me to understand. "She is not well. It's been ten years ... "

Cal slipped through the apartment door, his cheeks rosy as he clicked it shut with a wink in my direction.

Ronan watched my face, the corridor so quiet that I heard something scrambling behind the wall. Slowly, he leaned closer, the galaxy of green in his eyes coming into focus. He lifted one arm and pressed his palm to the wall beside my head. His breath fanned my cheeks when he sighed.

Mesmerized by the intensity of his scrutiny, I raised my hand and smoothed it over his chest. Spreading my fingers, I explored the bare skin of his pectorals, the sun-kissed curves flexing beneath my fingertips. As I touched him, a soft purr came from his throat.

"I need to see you, Eddi. I do not wish to be away from you. I am sorry that your first meeting with my mother was ... *difficult*." With downturned lips, he whispered, "I did not handle the situation well. I was ... *torn*. Being overwhelmed does not excuse my behavior. I am sorry for hurting you."

Quiet, rough, and heavy with emotion, the timbre of his voice sent a shiver down my spine. Goosebumps peppered my skin as he lowered his lips to mine, then hesitated. His soft breath tickled my face, the scent of peppermint drifting across the tiny space between us.

"You smell wonderful," I whispered. "Minty."

His throaty chuckle teased a smile to my lips. "Bacchus. My brother is wise in the ways of women, is he not?"

Ronan closed the distance, and our lips met with the gentlest of touches. It was a slow, sensual kiss, the kind that made your heart take up too much room to breathe. When his free hand found the nape of my neck, and his thumb stroked beneath my ear, I pressed into his touch.

Encouraged, his tongue swept my lips apart before dipping to taste me. I devoured him in return. Eager for his touches, breathing in his scent like I would die without it, I was lost in a sea of feeling. As his muscles twitched beneath my fingertips, I moaned. The warmth of his mouth, the gentle caresses of his tongue—they consumed me, my senses flaring with an eager response.

After the stress and anxiety of being apart, the intensity of our connection stole the air from my lungs. He was here. He was mine. I kissed him back, pulling him closer, molding my body tightly to his solid frame. He felt like—*home.*

Drawing a ragged breath, Ronan moved. His hand abandoned the wall to pull me in, one arm firmly across my shoulders, the other sliding down to squeeze my buttocks.

My lips melded to his as our tongues twined, and I slipped my fingers into his soft hair, still damp from the ocean. He tasted of mint and the salty tang of the sea. The teasing caresses of his lips on mine made them tingle. I wanted more of him. When I nibbled along his jawline, Ronan groaned.

Pressing his hardened length against my hip, he tucked his face into the crook of my neck and panted his frustration. Strong shoulders bunched under my hands, and I rubbed his back, dotting tiny kisses on his shoulder.

"I am afraid to lose you again," he breathed, his voice muffled against my throat. His arms slid in like two boa constrictors, leaving me little room to move. "Hex is still roaming the Keys. I don't like it. She is wounded, but not for long."

Ronan held me for a while as he caught his breath. Then, with a resigned sigh, he eased back, his glittering eyes finding mine. Raw emotion reflected back at me. After a long moment, he looked down and lifted my necklace. Smiling, his eyes flicked over the golden filigree cage, taking in the pinks and creams of the magnificent pearl within. He growled.

"I cannot go through losing you again. Finding you with the pearl was a slice of good fortune. We may not be so lucky next time." Leaning in to press a lingering kiss on the corner of my lips, he whispered, "I need you, Eddi."

I wiggled loose from his hold and ran my hands over the soft emerald skin at his waistline, remembering the first time we kissed on the Widow's Walk. We'd come a long way since then. My fingers slid over his hips, memorizing the feel of the slightly irregular scales there—tiny, soft, and slippery to the touch, yet completely dry.

"I miss you when you're away." Looking up, I drank in the sheer perfection of his face, his tousled hair caressing his forehead. I wanted to sweep my fingers through it. "Getting time together will be hard now that we're back in Marathon. I hate this. I want to be with you."

Pulling me in for a suffocating hug, he mumbled, "We will find a way." Ronan pressed his lips on mine as if in promise, then reluctantly let me go. "I must go. I will ask my mother about Matilda."

His eyes flicked to my apartment door, then focused inward. "Another sister. That would be special." He looked at me, his eyes bright. "Female births are exceedingly rare for Syreni. If it is true, there will be a celebration."

As he turned to jog down the stairs to the ground level, he glanced over his shoulder, his eyes meeting mine. I smiled and raised my hand. I didn't have the heart to remind him that Hex's involvement with Matilda could throw a curveball into his festivities.

CHAPTER 7

The next day, I watched as Miri cleaned her Barbie Dream Camper—*for the first time ever.* As the Sprite fluttered by, a crooked smile on her face, I stuck out my hand to block her path.

"What?" Miri paused, buzzing angrily as she glared at me.

"Since when do you clean up after yourself? Have you even been outside the door since we got back to Marathon? What gives, Miri?"

"I go out all the time!" she snipped. "I was outside today. That idiot next door has a Chihuahua. I may or may not have teased it for a while."

I laughed. "Was that the barking I heard? I wondered. It sounded like someone skinned it."

Miri giggled. "No, but the dancing bone may have caused a doggie nervous breakdown." Zipping down to stand on the coffee table, Miri gave me an expectant look, so I sat down and stared back at her. She crossed her arms and cocked her head at me.

"So? When is the Syreni hottie going to make an *honest woman* of you?"

I laughed so hard I choked. "What?!"

"You know what they say, "Why buy the cow when you can get the milk for free?"

My mouth opened and closed.

"Doesn't it tick you off that mommy is more important than you?"

I closed my mouth with a snap and frowned.

"Oh, come on, Eddi. You need to give him a kick in the ass. He's stalling."

Snapping out of my funk, I blasted her. "Now, you listen here. He thought his mother was dead—for ten years! He's not getting the milk for free, ok? We don't have anywhere — *private*—to spend time together. That's all!"

"Are you sure about that?" Miri raised an eyebrow.

"Listen here, you little blue pot-stirrer. It's none of your business. He cares about me. We're stuck in the middle of this nightmare, and until it's over, it's going to be tough, alright? I know how he feels. YOU ... don't. So stay out of it."

Miri laughed. "Sure, toots. I'm sure that's all it is."

Something inside of me snapped. My relationship with Ronan had issues, sure. But our feelings were solid—*weren't they?* My sudden misgivings caused a surge of anger and loosened my tongue.

"Who are you to be giving ME relationship advice? I don't see your little blue stallion prancing around this apartment now, do I?"

Miri's face fell, and her lip quivered. Her hands dropped to her side, and giant tears beaded on her lids. My heart plummeted.

"I'm sorry Miri. I didn't mean it."

With a whimper, she zipped into the air and tore across the apartment, slipping through the door to my bedroom. I sighed, feeling lousy about my foolish words. Matilda was in my bedroom with a book, working on her reading skills. Maybe Miri would settle down enough that I could apologize later.

Whether I liked it or not, Miri's words scored a direct hit. To lessen the sting, I got busy, launching into cleaning the fridge and putting the new groceries on the shelves. Key West had us all on edge and tempers were flying high. Thank goodness the apartment was warded up the butt and Hex couldn't touch us here. I had asked Phoebe to make sure she protected the apartment against fire. After what happened in Tennessee, I wasn't taking any chances.

I closed the fridge and glanced at the corner of the living room Cal set up for Matilda. A Little Mermaid lamp that he surprised her with lit the space with a cheerful glow. A bright pink curtain made from one of my sheets lent some privacy. Miri and I helped her cut out sea stars to fasten to the outside, and my lips curled up at the cutout traced from the sprite's body. Inside, Matilda's few belongings were arranged with precision in the small space. It was unnerving, and made me wonder, yet again, what she'd gone through while under Hex's thumb.

Curious, I headed to my bedroom, opening the door to find Matilda sprawled on her stomach. Miri lounged on a pillow while she listened to the child reading quietly aloud. At my soft steps, Matilda jumped up, the book slithering across the bed to fall off the edge. She stood to face me, her hands clasped behind her back and her eyes downcast. My heart squeezed.

"It's OK, Matilda. You keep going." Smiling brightly, I motioned for her to crawl back onto the bed, which she did, hesitantly. I pretended to rummage in my drawers to cover the stiff look on my face.

"Ronan wants to take you swimming, Matilda. Would you like that?" At the stifling silence, I turned to find Matilda biting her lip, her beautiful green eyes shining too brightly. Sitting down on the edge of the bed, I reached out and rubbed her arm.

"What's wrong, sweetie?"

After a long pause, Matilda whispered, "I don't know how to swim." Matilda's face was a heartbreaking shade of pink as her chin quivered. I pulled her to my side, partly to hide the threatening tears in my own eyes.

"It's ok. We'll teach you. We have a great spot to swim, and it's very safe. The water is shallow, and there's even a swing!"

Matilda pulled back to stare at me as if looking for a trap in my offer. Whatever she saw must have satisfied her because she smiled, rubbing her eyes with a sleeve.

"It's ok, you'll see." I looked up, pinning a misty-eyed sprite with my smile. "Miri will come too. We ALL need to get out and have some fun. Starting today. What do you say we kick this off with some shopping?"

A smile spread across both faces, proving that no matter who you are, buying stuff was the bomb.

***

When Ronan and Cal arrived later in the afternoon, Matilda sat politely on the couch. Her shining golden hair was brushed and her clothing was immaculate. I vowed to get some dirt on the kid, mess up her hair, and make her laugh at the earliest opportunity.

I knew that having a child in the apartment was a short-term thing. I was already looking for a bigger place, but it was impossible, with rent in the Keys being astronomical. Secretly, I wondered if I had what it took to raise a child.

There were so many questions. Schooling, babysitters, and how to explain her presence were all high on the list. I sighed. Tomorrow's list. Today, we would have fun. The rest could wait.

As we walked to the Big K, I resisted laughing at Ronan's brand-new bright pink t-shirt. In bold letters, embossed around a cartoon pirate, it read, "I have a little Seaman on my shirt." I slapped Cal.

"What!? I found it on Amazon!"

Walking down the street in a happy group, Cal, Ronan, and I chatted in our heads about what we called *the meat mystery*. The more we talked, the more it seemed that James was *not* human.

Even Ronan was in on the game. *"The only animal in Florida that would eat that much is a panther. It has tan hair. James is a panther."* Ronan smiled down at Matilda as she walked along beside him, holding his hand.

I shook my head. *"Nah. Florida panthers are small, and they don't eat enough."* I put my finger to my lips, tapping. *"James is a gentle guy. He never yells. That leaves out all of the nastiest predators."* I hummed, and then it hit me.

"Maybe he's a giant? Giants are huge." I shuddered when I thought of the stone giant that killed my Guardian, Imara, back in Tennessee. *"I mean, he'd have to cook the meat, so that would be tricky, and I can't recall ever seeing James barbecue anything."*

Cal swallowed, his face paler than usual. *"I hate to tell you this, but Giants don't cook their meat. They eat it raw. And they prefer human flesh."*

Ok, that was a mood killer. I looked at Matilda, happy she couldn't hear us.

Cal shrugged. *"A bear. James has to be a bear. With his sandy hair, he could be a brown bear. Shifter bears eat a TON of meat. I looked it up, and a brown bear will eat seventy pounds of meat a day in the summer."* He held up his finger. *"James told me he has a cousin in Alaska—and his last name is Winters."* He gave a triumphant nod. *"Yep, brown bear."*

Everyone's mood lifted as we walked into the cool comfort of the Big K. This little trip cheered everyone up. Matilda needed clothes, and there was safety in numbers. What could it hurt?

Cal was a professional shopper, his hands already rubbing together with excitement. You would think helping Matilda pick out cute, colorful clothes was the next best thing to a Disney vacation.

As it happened, he was also a natural-born *fun uncle*. Ronan and I found ourselves alone within minutes of entering the store. We tracked them down in the Kids' department, as, clapping his hands, Cal had Matilda do another twirl.

"OH my GAWD look at that. It's the perfect color for you, too." He jumped up, and taking Matilda's hand, led her around the corner to the shoe department. "We can find some cute sandals to match over here—"

"Are you getting this, Miri? I want to pull out my phone and record it, but that would be awkward."

Miri wiggled around in my bag and it flipped open. Tinkling laughter reached my ears. "Yeah, I heard. Who does he think he is, RuPaul?" Her disembodied voice caused more than one customer to look our way. I smiled at them as we walked past, my hand tucked into Ronan's.

We wandered down the center aisle, browsing for sales. Well, I did. Ronan gawked at the colorful displays. As we stopped at the TV department to look for earbuds for my phone, I looked up at the vast display of units and a shiver raced through me. Every single TV had the same scene playing on its colorful screen.

Police in riot gear swarmed past the Garden of Eden in Key West. The sound was off, so I followed the captions from a live reporter who stood beside layers of barricades.

"Police have cordoned off Old Town from Caroline to Elizabeth Street to contain the issue. No one is allowed entry, and homes and businesses have been evacuated. We are receiving reports that a large number of residents are behaving erratically, taking over local businesses en masse. It is becoming clearer as the reports come in, but it looks like more than half of the residents are badly addicted to the new drug, Gush. They are out of control and the sheriff's office still struggles to contain the rioting."

The reporter tucked her head, touching her earpiece before speaking again.

"There have been reports of shots fired. Police are moving in, with units from the Upper Keys and Miami assisting."

She looked back at the camera, her expression grave.

"Hold for our drone footage. What you are about to see may be disturbing to some viewers."

The scene cut to an aerial view over Old Town, and ice flooded my veins. The streets were crammed full of people, most of them naked. There had to be five hundred humans milling near the pier, some thrashing in piles on the street doing god only knows what. Others fought each other with fists and crude weapons.

The drone filmed from a high altitude, likely to mask the gruesome details, but it was clear. These people were high on *Gush*. They were addicted, looking for more, and apparently, willing to do anything to get it. The scene was utter chaos, and my stomach curdled at the sight.

As the scene panned over Garrison Bight, Ronan's hand clutched mine, and he gasped. Cal came up behind us, catching the end of the newscast over my shoulder.

"The *Black Widow*," Cal hissed, his face going pale.

I looked back at the screen, my eyes darting around the aerial view of Garrison Bight. The *Black Widow*, all 100 gleaming red feet of her, was no longer docked at the pier. Instead, a giant gap marked the Spectre yacht's previous location.

I looked at Cal, then glanced down at Matilda, who gawked up at the screen. I grabbed her hand and quickly steered her away from the electronics section. We headed to the checkout, Ronan's jaw clenched tightly and Cal chewing his nails.

I heard Miri in the bag, her voice muffled. "We're in some deep shit, aren't we?"

Surprisingly, it was Matilda who answered, her voice quiet. "You don't know her. She won't stop. They're going to catch me and take me back." She looked up at me. "Hex will hurt you."

Matilda's lip trembled, and although she tried to hold it back, her face crumpled as tears filled her eyes. I motioned to Cal and Ronan, who took care of the cashier while I ushered Matilda outside.

We were under the shady overhang when I stopped, turned to her, and squatted down. "Now, you listen here, little Miss Worrywart. How did you come to be with us in the first place, hmm?"

Matilda's lips squirmed as she wrestled to keep her distress hidden. One rebellious tear pushed its way out and tracked down her face.

"You and your friends stole me away from Hex."

"Exactly. We aren't letting her take you back. You're with us, and that's final." I clenched my teeth. "Next time, she won't get away."

"But what about your friend? The one who's missing?" Matilda's chin trembled.

"We'll find him, don't you worry. Your safety *and* your happiness is our focus right now. Stop worrying, because we've got you, and we won't let you go."

I picked her up and hugged her close, the guys joining us with our loot. Cal grinned and waved the packages in the air, which teased a smile from the poor kid.

I looked out across the scorching parking lot and watched the cars whizzing past on Highway 1. The sky was a cloudless blue today, and the heat was off the charts. But somehow, it couldn't chase the chill that crept through me. We'd see whether my bravado was misplaced soon enough.

It was bad enough with people hooked on *Gush* and tearing apart Key West. But with the *Black Widow* out at sea, it was anybody's guess how this would play out.

CHAPTER 8

"A cigar factory?" I thought about Ronan's description, trying to remember if I had seen anything like it while wandering around Key West.

"Yes. Cain held Mother there the entire time she was missing. It is on the edge of Old Town. She tells me a very talented witch from Savannah came down to ward it. Mother saw this witch, Sybil, when she came into the tank room to set wards on the tiny window there."

We were relaxing at the island, Matilda and Miri playing in the shallow water nearby. Cal brought a kayak and paddled double with Matilda while I carried the gear. After scaring the crap out of her in Big K, we put swimming at the top of the to-do list for the day. A distraction was on order.

Cal jerked upright from where he lounged in the water. "Did you say Sybil? From Savannah?"

Ronan nodded.

"Eddi, that's got to be the witch we planned to meet before the Tortuga's trip. Do you remember?"

I zoned out, trying to recall the conversation, then snapped my fingers. "Her shop was Witches Brew, right? I thought it sounded dumb at the time! *THAT'S* the witch that made these assholes practically invisible?"

Cal clenched his teeth. "When we walked back to the *Wanderlust* that first night in Key West, I remember passing a huge empty parking lot. I wondered why no one had developed it yet. It's not like there's an inch of empty land on the entire island."

He growled, and using his fist, he bumped his forehead. "I should have noticed it. Dumb, dumb, dumb."

I grabbed his hand. "Gideon didn't notice either. Hell, he had shifters scouring the entire island for weeks. It must have been one of those *look the other way* wards. Remember, Phoebe said a good witch could hide things, even from an Immortalis. This Sybil must be one helluva witch."

Leaning back, I splashed water on my shoulders to cool off. With a wry smile, I nudged Cal. "Going to Savannah might have changed things in so many ways."

Ronan quietly watched Matilda as she splashed and played with Miri. When I poked him, he jumped.

"What else did your mother say?"

"They have a lab in South Carolina." Briefly, Ronan's eyes flashed a solid yellow, his fangs peeking from his mouth. I wanted to touch him but hesitated as he struggled for control.

"It's OK, Ronan. It's over. She's safe." I lifted my hand and rubbed his back. He turned as if finally seeing me, his eyes fading to their usual brilliant jade.

"They stole her eggs, Eddi. Every week for ten years, they froze them, and sent them to their lab in South Carolina." A low rumble sounded, growing louder as his lips curled back.

"They are breeding Syreni. Mother heard them speak of 'crosses,' but we cannot be certain what it all means." He looked at me, his eyes strobing yellow and green as he fought for control. His voice cracked.

"It is likely that Matilda is one of these—*crosses.*" He looked at me, his pupils blowing out and his irises blasting a bright yellow. "She is my sister."

His last words came out on a garbled growl as he looked at Matilda. Although she couldn't have heard his words, her tiny body went stiff at the brilliant color of Ronan's eyes.

He was up in a flash, and in three giant steps, he dove into the drop-off, his glittering green legs morphing into a muscular tail that sliced through the water. He disappeared with a splash.

I whipped my head back to Matilda, who watched where he had disappeared without a trace of fear on her face. Calmly, she turned back to play with Miri.

Cal's mental voice eased into my mind. *"I often wonder what Ronan would be like if he didn't have so many crappy things happening to him right now. Being abducted by Hex's gang was bad enough. But having his nectar extracted against his will, then at the same time, your rocky start together ... "*

He shook his head. *"His mother went through hell for ten years, and now he finds out he's got a sister produced in a lab. It's mind-boggling."*

I hissed my agreement under my breath. Watching and waiting for Ronan to return, I tried to relax and take in the beautiful afternoon. Everything gleamed at this time of the day. Nearby, a Flats boat hooked a tarpon, the angler's whoops and hollers carrying across the turquoise water.

I turned to scan the horizon and saw Ronan's head bob up a few hundred yards from shore. Something splashed beside him, but he was in silhouette, so it took me a moment to realize a pod of dolphins surrounded him. I smiled, remembering our first meeting here at the island.

"Uh, Eddi—what is that?" Cal shaded his eyes with his hand, looking further toward the horizon.

I followed his gaze and stiffened, my eyes taking in the contours of the approaching vessel. Silhouetted against the sunny backdrop, it was hard to make out details. But as it came closer, it looked familiar. Blood red—with a graphic of a black spider on the hull. Hex's boat was here, and heading straight at us.

When he noticed our expressions, Ronan looked over his shoulder. With a splash, he disappeared. In a few moments, a wall of water pushed ahead of him as he blasted out of the drop-off, seamlessly changing to leg form and running through the shallows.

"We must get back. We are defenseless out here," Ronan growled, his eyes darting to Matilda. I looked at the shore where she and Miri stared at the approaching ship, their faces ashen.

We had everyone packed up in no time and Cal and I paddled with deep strokes toward the marina. Luckily, it wasn't far, and Ronan sped things up by taking turns giving us a push from below. It would have been fun if my heart wasn't in my throat, choking off my air.

When we pulled up to Davy Jones, we dragged the kayaks on shore, left our hastily tied gear, and made a beeline for the marina. As our wet, sandy feet slapped against the cement floor of the shop, I realized I'd forgotten our flip-flops at the island.

James looked up from where he manned the till.

"What's wrong, guys?"

SHIT.

"Uh, nothing," I panted, grabbing Matilda's hand. "Just a little bathroom emergency." Matilda didn't need any encouragement, trotting beside me down the hall. I tugged her past the bathroom door, opened the supply closet, and pulled her in behind me. I squatted to speak at eye level.

"I'm so sorry, Matilda, but this is the best I can do." A blur of blue popped into view. "Miri, will you stay with her?"

She nodded, and I gave Matilda a brisk hug. Her heart pounded against my chest, and I whispered, *"Shh,"* and smoothed my hand over her soft blonde hair. "Remember, you're ours. Stay here, and hang in there. We'll handle this."

I pulled back to look into her wide green eyes, and with a reassuring smile, I tried to rise. Her hand locked onto mine, but with some gentle words, she released me.

Popping back into the hallway, I trotted past James and tried to look casual. I found Cal standing on the end of our longest dock. Out of breath, I watched the channel with him.

"I don't know what's about to happen—*let alone* what we're supposed to do to keep it quiet." He looked at me with panicked eyes. "We don't even have a *fucking gun.*"

After what felt like a lifetime, sure enough, the stylish bow of the hundred-foot Spectre yacht drifted into view around the corner at the end of the channel, gradually making the turn and easing into the deep water canal. Cal and I ducked into the Tiki hut as the massive vessel finished the turn.

It was a tight fit through the entrance, and I prayed the damn thing would run aground. What the hell was Hex doing, bringing the fight here? And what would we do without weapons or backup?

Glancing across the channel, I noticed Ronan tucked into a mangrove, the tips of two fangs poking from beneath his lip. His eyes locked on mine, a ferocious snarl rippling over his face. He had his short sword clenched in one fist. I let out a relieved breath at the sight of him.

Still as statues, Cal and I watched as the driver used bow thrusters to nudge into the deepest spot in the bay. The engines stopped. With the rattle of heavy chains, the windlass kicked in, plopping the anchors into the water. Soon, the *Black Widow* was eerily quiet, not a soul moving on board.

Gnawing on my lip, I looked at Cal, who blanched a ghostly white. His fingers wiggled with tension, his octopus threatening to erupt from beneath his skin.

"We have no weapons," he bit out through white lips. "We're fucked."

Something moved behind the tinted glass of the helm. A human shape shuffled the length of the dining room, then limped across the covered rear deck, weaving through the luxurious leather furniture before coming to the rail. My heart thumped so hard I choked.

Gideon was back.

Tall and tanned, his torso gleaming in the afternoon sun, he was in his birth form. And he looked like hell.

Adrenaline forced tears to my eyes, and I dashed them away.

From the side of my mouth, I choked, "Are you seeing Gideon, or Bert?"

"Bert," Cal said, yanking the Tiki door open, his long, athletic legs launching him down the knoll and across the sandy beach, where he grabbed a kayak.

Right. The Black Widow can't dock. We're going to Gideon.

I spun on my heel and tore up the path to the shop before Miri and Matilda had a heart attack. As the door slammed open under my hand, the crash of the jingler made me realize I needed to tone it down a bit. James looked up from his paperwork with a frown.

"Sorry, James," I said, hustling down the hall to grab my two most prized possessions. I stopped at the door to the broom closet and straightened my shirt, taking a deep breath and letting it out. I opened the door.

It was empty.

Frantic, my eyes darted around the small dark space as I flicked on the light switch. The closet appeared empty, but I heard a small gasp behind a recycling box. Matilda slowly misted back into view.

"My goodness, girls. You gave me a heart attack!" I waved them up, and Miri blinked into view momentarily, her eyes wide and relieved when I announced the coast was clear. I had to pry Matilda's hands from around my leg before coaxing her into the hallway.

I gave James a friendly smile as we passed, but he wasn't buying it. His eyes followed me to the door. He knew something was up, but I kept quiet. How did I explain a multi-million dollar yacht in the bay? *Screw it.* That was on Gideon. Bert. Whatever.

Matilda was reluctant to go anywhere near the yacht, but I got her onto a kayak with some sweet talking. Miri helped by disappearing herself to the Black Widow, then returning to reassure the terrified child that there were no baddies on board.

"The only nasty thing out there is a big, grumpy Gryphon in his miserable human form," she quipped. Matilda cracked a hesitant smile, her body hunching in on itself as I paddled over.

In short order, everyone was on board, including Ronan, who left wet footprints everywhere and wouldn't leave my side. I don't think I'd ever seen Cal so happy. I wasn't there when he greeted Gideon, but I'm sure some awkward octo-hugs were involved.

Gideon watched as I boarded, his face set in stone. Irritated, miserable, and looking like he'd gone two rounds with Rocky Balboa, I was surprisingly happy to see him—like I'd hoovered a glass of champagne.

Waving us into the dining lounge with his good hand, Gideon followed us in. We all dropped onto the comfortable, top-of-the-line furniture and stared at each other. Being on the yacht again felt—well, it made my skin crawl.

My eyes traveled around the lounge area, still streaked with blood from the fight. Dents dotted the walls where we'd slammed into them, and one of the chairs sported a crimson splatter. The carpet—well, it was best to forget about saving that. The scorpion tail was gone from the floor, but—my God, *what a mess.*

I was about to open my mouth and make a Molly Maid joke when Gideon did what he did best. He read my thoughts.

"Returning from Key West was challenge enough, Edaline." The snappish words were rough, even for Gideon. Someone was hangry and needed a snack.

"So where have you been, Gideon? We've been looking everywhere for you." I searched his face, getting a good look at the mess that was our Enforcer.

Half-healed slices crisscrossed Gideon's chest, his right arm tucked against his body in a tight sling. Blood seeped through a bandage around his temple, his heavily wrapped head making him resemble a muscular Q-tip. As he settled into a chair, I gasped at the major case of road rash blazing a trail down his right side. Surrounded by patches of raw skin, the raised scabs still oozed.

But what blew my mind was the bruising. The Gryphon's tanned body was a rotten plum of purple and brown from head to toe, the white of his right eye now a three-dimensional red. I had a troubled relationship with the Gryphon, but seeing him like this made my heart ache.

"Where do you think I've been, Edaline? Convincing a boat full of humans to take my naked ass across the channel while reassuring them that I didn't need an ambulance. Then, driving a one hundred foot yacht—by myself." Gideon reached over to tuck a piece of sling back into place, his eyes avoiding mine.

"The Djinn was a remarkable opponent and a skilled swordsman. Galahad gave me a difficult time." Gideon raised his eyes, the burst blood vessel a nasty crimson blob in his tanned face. "I lost my cell phone. I am sorry."

I thought I heard Cal choke back a laugh before he asked, "IS. Not WAS. Galahad is still alive, then?"

"Yes, the assassin lives. The fight went overboard, and we crashed into a lighthouse while I tried to subdue him in flight. Before I crushed him, he blinked out of existence and escaped. I awoke in my Gryphon form, my wing shattered and my skull crushed."

"It is unclear whether the Djinn assumed I was finished"—Gideon closed his eyes—"or whether he showed mercy. I assume the former, with his being under Hex's thrall."

The room went quiet, the only sound the turning of pages. I looked over my shoulder. Matilda flipped through a magazine on the chair behind us.

I broke the uneasy silence. "How on earth did you manage to steal the *Black Widow*? It's not like you can just take it from Hex. *Can you?*"

Gideon looked up with an icy stare. "We have laws, Edaline. Of course I can take it. I would have also taken her head had Galahad not kept me so busy. The *Black Widow* is now the property of the Sovereign of the south-eastern seaboard."

Moving to readjust his position, Gideon groaned. "The *Black Widow* may come in handy for the next phase of our quest to rid the world of that demon bitch." The Enforcer leaned back to put his feet up on the footstool, sucking in a harsh breath.

I covered my surprise at his uncharacteristic outburst. Getting to my feet, I headed into the attached kitchen to find him a drink. As I popped open the fridge, I wondered if there were any aspirin in the staterooms below.

I screamed—a short, high-pitched shriek—and slammed it shut. The glass bottles on the door rattled with the impact. Resisting the urge to lose my lunch, I whirled to find every eye in the lounge locked on me. It must have been the smell.

"We're going to need another trip to Publix," I said, then ran to the sink. Leaning into the stainless steel perfection, I promptly tossed my cookies. Wiping my mouth, I looked back at my wide-eyed friends.

"Unless you want a nice ripe head for lunch."

SHIT. The kid.

I shot a horrified look at Matilda. She completely ignored me, calmly flipping through her magazine—but it was there. The stiffness in the shoulders, the trembling fingers. I had to wonder what she had witnessed under Hex's thumb.

Ultimately, I never had a chance to think about her calm acceptance of a rotting head in the fridge. We had an unscheduled visitor.

In a flapping whirlwind of blue and gold, Mr. Darcy made a grand entrance through the open glass doors. Making a beeline across the living area, he landed in a sploosh of feathers on Gideon's chest.

Clawing his way up that golden, heavily marred expanse of muscle, Mr. Darcy settled himself into the crook of Gideon's neck and began preening his shoulder-length blonde locks. His weird tongue traced up and down each clump of hair, but he kept one narrowed eye on me.

Gideon's eyes misted over, and he raised his good hand to scratch the bird's head and neck. "I'm sorry, my friend. I never intended to be gone so long."

He looked up at Cal. "Thank you for taking care of him." Gideon stared fondly at the parrot, then stiffened as if listening. His hazel eyes bored into mine.

"It's a very good thing you did not injure him during your fit, Edaline. There would have been consequences."

"WHAT!? That flying menace attacked ME! I had nothing to do with it—*how did you ...?*" I rolled my eyes. Of course he could speak to the winged gangster. I sputtered and grumbled, almost slapping Cal when he hid a grin behind his hand. Fucking parrot.

"I don't know if you can hear me, you feathered menace, but you've messed with the wrong girl." I shoved the thought out to the macaw with a loud snarl.

Gideon winced. "Edaline, *please*. My throbbing head can't take your caterwauling today."

I contemplated getting up and stomping off, leaving everyone to their sappy reunion, but my tantrum sputtered out when James appeared at the patio doors.

To my surprise, he didn't mention the giant yacht sitting in his docking area. Or the streaks of blood across the walls and the floor. Nor did he question Gideon—who would have looked like Bert—about how he came by such a lovely vessel.

With a pleasant smile, James said, "I'm sorry, Gideon. Mr. Darcy got out when I opened the door. I'm glad to see you're still in one piece. I've been worried about you."

CHAPTER 9

As shock set in, the skin on my face felt three sizes too small. Judging by his expression, Cal felt the same. Ronan, who until now had been quietly leaning against the wall, went rigid, every muscle tensed for action.

Hello, Gideon—not Bert. James KNEW.

As my boss sauntered into the room, his brown eyes flicked over the beautiful trappings of the multi-million dollar yacht before settling himself in a chair near Gideon.

"What's that smell?" James asked, wrinkling his nose.

Everyone stared. Except Gideon, who answered without flicking an eyelid. "Hex's lunch, apparently."

"Ohhh. Yeah, that's not good. That's going to take some bleach."

In typical Eddi fashion, I didn't wait for this cozy scene to play out.

"What the hell, Gideon? James knows about—*everything?*" I waved my hands for emphasis. "This whole time, *James knew*, and you never thought to mention it?"

My face flushed with anger, and I clenched my fists until my knuckles turned white. The information hoarding bastard! Days of worrying. Stressing. My fear that Cal would have a meltdown. And all for what? James *knew* Gideon and could have helped us find him.

Waves of heat wafted from my face as I stood up and pointed at Gideon. "Do you have *any* idea how worried we've all been while you were missing? We had no idea who to contact or where to start looking for you! And all this time, James was in on *your little SECRET!?*"

Ronan stepped toward me, but I shook my head. I was just getting rolling. "And let's not forget James"—I shot him a glance—"cozying up with Cain and Hex the other day."

James looked uncomfortable at the mention of his boarding the yacht. I turned on him. "All this time, you never said a word. You let us put ourselves in harm's way. We kept getting into trouble, but you never lifted a finger to help. Do you know how many times I ended up *in the hospital*? And Cal! He almost died! *Holy shit,* you two *really* take the cake!"

My eyes burned as an odd warmth wafted across my skin. I looked down to see my hands glowing. I needed to settle down, and without thinking, I started for the fridge to grab a drink. Remembering the smelly package, I threw my hands up and turned back to sit in my chair with a thump, struggling to slow my breathing.

James' lips formed a thin line. "Edaline, I know this is difficult for you to understand, but our world doesn't revolve around you and Cal."

"What!? Oh no, you don't. You aren't turning this back on us. This isn't about Cal and me. It's about you two. I'm going out on a limb here, but the pair of you are suddenly thick as thieves. That can only mean one thing. Either you are equals, or one of you is in charge." I bit my lip. "Ok, that's two things."

I looked at James and remembered the meat. "And thousands of pounds of meat!? A wedding, my *ass*. You flat-out *lied,* James!"

My face flamed as I lost it. All this time stressing about our messed up situation had taken an unseen toll. The aches. The pains. The exhaustion and worrying about Matilda. And now that I had built a head of steam, I couldn't stop.

"Either you tell me what's happening, or I'm outta here. I'll take my kid, my sprite, and hop a bus to—*somewhere else*!" I leaned back in the chair and covered my face with both hands.

Ronan came to my rescue, pushing off the wall and standing beside my chair. I groaned through my hands, then ran my fingers through my hair, my breath slowing as I tried to suck air through my nose. A firm squeeze of his warm hand on my shoulder helped.

"Are you finished?" Gideon barked. "Because if you pipe down, I have something to tell you." He looked at Ronan, Cal, and Matilda. "It's time you knew the truth. We were clearly wrong, and keeping things from you was a bad idea. That will change, as of now."

Gideon turned his head, fixing me with a cold stare. "If you'll shut up for two seconds, *Edaline?*"

I stared into his face, the blood red of his injured eye making my stomach churn. Breathing deeply as Gideon stared me down, I calmed myself. After a long silence, he spoke.

"James is the Sovereign for the southeastern seaboard. It is my job to protect him and all of you. We could not disclose his identity for security reasons. We are well beyond that now."

I closed my mouth, which had fallen open, and glanced around the room. Everyone stared at James except Matilda, who gazed out the expanse of tinted windows. Her toes tapped the air, so she wasn't missing a thing as Miri sat on her shoulder, a small blue hand over her mouth.

James spoke. "We have reason to believe that there is an informant among our people. Information that should be classified has reached Hex and Cain—now deceased, by the way." He smiled and nodded at Ronan.

"The meat is private and nothing you need to concern yourself with, Eddi. It has no bearing on this situation. Knowing my station shouldn't change your behavior toward me. It is vital to conceal my identity for as long as possible."

Cal frowned. "But what about the *Black Widow?* You went on board. And you were so messed up when we found you the other day." His eyes ping-ponged between our two leaders.

James sighed. "When I got your text that day in Key West, I was unaware of its authenticity until I passed the Black Widow. When I felt the force of Cain's compulsion, I had no choice but to play the part, or expose my ability to them.

They had no idea I was unaffected. Cain thought I was human. There were no choices at that point. I let him bring me on board, hoping to gather information. Under the same circumstances, I would do it again. We learned many things that day."

I let out a sharp breath. "You *pretended?* Then why were you so messed up when we found you yesterday? There's no way you were faking *that.*"

"Because after they brought me to Hex, they gave me something that snowed me under." He shrugged. "I guess it was their insurance policy. I was your bait. They wanted to create chaos. I don't know how I made it home because I barely remember anything." He grimaced. "It was all I could do not to blow my cover while I swallowed it. The stuff tasted like flamingo piss."

Gideon snarled, the arms of his chair cracking under the force of his grip.

"The Sovereign was in a desperate situation, and I could do nothing to stop it." He rounded on James. "You were very fortunate. *WE* were very fortunate. Humans are disposable to them. They could have killed you."

James frowned. "It was a calculated risk. They also used it on me the day they abducted Eddi on the *Wanderlust*. I was useful to them in the past. I took the chance that they would keep me around. As it turns out, I was right."

Looking around the room, James' eyes flashing a strange silvery hue. "Our people are still trying to determine what they used to drug me, and where it was purchased. Right now, everything points to a witch's shop in Savannah. The practitioner—Sybil—is known to us."

Cal and I looked at each other. He mouthed, *"Witches Brew,"* and I nodded. What were the chances?

Gideon mumbled something about James being lucky it wasn't truth serum, but the Sovereign ignored him. He looked at Cal and me, his expression filled with sorrow.

"I am truly sorry about your injuries. Seeing you two in the line of fire tore my heart out. I wanted to bring you home, but you insisted, Edaline. Your service to the *Others* has been exemplary and won't be forgotten."

Looking around the room, James added, "Ronan, please thank your mother on behalf of the Sovereign Council. But for now, we need to keep my identity secret. From everyone, including your mother—and *the Shoal.*"

Ronan nodded, his eyes glittering. "You have my word."

Of course, I never could keep quiet when stressed, so I blurted out, "So, what are you, James? You're not human, *that's clear."*

Cal gasped. "Edaline! You're talking to the Sovereign! You can't ask him that!"

James gave me a wry smile. "While I am certain it will eat you alive, Eddi, that answer is intensely private and not common knowledge. I'm afraid you'll just have to stay curious."

Gideon snapped, "Edaline, asking someone their species is considered rude. Apologize this instant."

I stared at James, then looked down. "I'm sorry. Getting used to the new—*dynamic*—might take me a while. I'm having trouble picturing you being in charge of all of ... *this.*" I waved my hands around for emphasis.

James smiled. "Leaders can be kind, Edaline. Our chain of power is simple. I am a figurehead. I oversee our corner of the country, and Gideon is my muscle. He reports to me, and I inform the council."

I represent all of you. Think of it like a Governor. A King does not rule us—we're a council of twelve nationwide. And, like Gideon, I have a measure of my own power."

His eyes flashed that creepy silver again, leaving me wondering what sort of creature ate thousands of pounds of meat every month.

James turned to Matilda, who, until now, had watched quietly with Miri sprawled on her shoulder. It dawned on me that a child probably shouldn't be privy to the tennis match of tension streaking around the lounge.

"Matilda, are you happy staying with Edaline?" James asked.

She nodded, her face solemn. "I like it there. Miri keeps me company." She reached up and patted Miri's legs.

The sprite buzzed her wings, pleased as punch. Spreading her arms wide around Matilda's neck, she said, "Where she goes, I go."

"Sounds alright to me, then." James frowned at Gideon. "What's next, Enforcer?"

"I need time to recover. My injuries are extensive, and I was unable to hunt while securing the vessel and traveling back to Marathon. I haven't eaten for over two days." He wiggled around in the chair until he was comfortable again. "I need to question Ronan's mother, and from there, we can form a plan of attack. We must defeat Hex now before she gets any stronger."

Gideon turned to me, his expression firm. "Edaline, keep your thoughts to yourself about the Sovereign. I cannot stress how vital it is that James' identity remains a secret. Can you manage that?"

CHAPTER 10

Our little surprise party broke up, with Ronan heading out to catch some fish for Gideon while Cal and I grabbed Matilda and Miri and headed back to the apartment. We decided it was wise to stick together with Hex injured and on the loose.

James quickly called a shifter in Marathon, who agreed to come and take care of the mess on the yacht. I wondered what they would think about cleaning the fridge.

Cal and I headed home, with Matilda riding in my basket again. Her tension disappeared as soon as we left the yacht, and she was Chatty Cathy all the way home.

Ronan popped back to the apartment later that evening, the pounding on the door rattling its hinges. After I yanked it open, ready to give an earful to whoever was being so disrespectful, I let out a screech when he lunged through the door. Ronan scooped me up into his arms, and ran to the couch. He tossed me over the back and followed me, his heavy body crushing me into the soft cushions.

His blazing eyes glittered inches from my face. *"Gods,"* he groaned, then kissed me. My legs crept over his hips, and my arms threaded around his neck. I sank into the taste of him, my body pressed tightly to his writhing frame. Thankfully, there was an adult in the room.

Ice water slid over Ronan's shoulders and cascaded into my face. Spluttering, I came up for air, Ronan looking over his shoulder with a growl.

"Don't give me your *big badass* glare, you heathen. There's a child in the room." Miri hovered over us, an empty glass in her arms. Matilda's eyes twinkled, both hands over her mouth.

"Uh, er, sorry kiddo. Sometimes I forget we have an audience." I chuckled as Ronan pulled himself upright, letting me slither from beneath him. I pulled my t-shirt down over my hips and licked my lips. The barest suggestion of a growl simmered in Ronan's throat as he lounged beside me, a pillow in his lap. I covered my mouth to stop the laugh threatening to erupt at his red face and obvious discomfort.

"Uh ... so ... what brings you here, Ronan?" He rolled his eyes at me, then sighed.

"My mother would like to meet with you."

Shocked, I jerked my head up. "Your mother. Wants to meet ... *me?*"

Oh shit.

"Yes. As soon as possible. How soon can you get a breathing machine organized?" Ronan and I had discussed visiting his home, but with the entrance underwater, I had to dive to access the tunnels. Once inside, natural ventilation filled the caves through openings in the ceiling above the waterline. There was plenty of breathable oxygen inside the Syreni caves.

"How about tomorrow? I'm sure James will let me take the *Wanderlust*."

Davy Jones Locker was a certified dive shop, and although I didn't use the equipment very often, the staff got free rentals. It was tough for me to get out diving because the only other diver was Evan, and we were always busy. I felt a little thrill at getting out again for a dive—with Ronan. In *his* world. *Together.*

Ronan nodded. "The entrances are not far from shore. I will take you there." He turned and gently gripped the back of my neck to give me a small massage. "Do not concern yourself about the trip. My mother is very kind. You will have no problems, and I will enjoy showing you my home."

Inside, a nauseating sea of emotions rolled through my belly. I had never gone home to *meet the parents.* And let's face it. Our first meeting wasn't the most encouraging.

Naturally, by the time we dropped anchor the next day, my nerves were a jangling mess. I set up my tank, checked the regulator, strapped everything together, and heaved it onto my back. Carefully, I did a back roll entry from the gunnel, cleared my mask, and we were off.

I loved diving. While equalizing, I had time to *experience* the ocean around me as I sank to the bottom. Snorkeling was fun, but diving was *special.*

Setting up my buoyancy control vest, I leveled off, and looked around for Ronan. Slowly rotating in the water, I got quite a start to find out he was suspended behind me, his long green tail gently waving beneath him. The enormous smile on his face was contagious.

It was moments like this when I appreciated being able to communicate with him telepathically. *"I look ridiculous to you, don't I?"*

Ronan chuckled, tiny bubbles rising from his lips. He shook his head. *"I will take you however I can get you, little Barracuda."* His eyes roved up and down my gear, his head rocking sideways to watch my bubbles rise to the surface. *"Is that comfortable for you—breathing like that?"*

I nodded. *"It's not as bad as you think, especially with us diving shallow. Deeper than thirty feet and the game changes."* I reached out and took his hand. *"This is perfect. I love being able to do this with you."*

As we hung suspended above the sea floor, I marveled that here I was, going for a swim with a handsome Syreni male to meet his mother. *Mind blown.*

"This way." Ronan nodded toward the shore, and we set off along the bottom. The reef was scattered here, with small patches of coral poking up from the sand. Although sparse, small clusters of colorful fish hovered over the coral patches, playing a massive game of musical chairs.

Off in the distance, a school of jackfish eased by, drifting with spatial precision, never touching each other as they swam in tight formation. I looked down, noticing a small patch of coral covered in purple fans. They were pristine, not one branch twisted or broken by the fins of careless snorkelers. The giant swaths of coral on the main reef took a pounding from the daily onslaught of tourists, well-meaning as they might be. Seeing a perfect patch of untouched fans was a balm to my soul.

Ronan kept glancing at me as we swam along, his eyes bright. The sun filtered through the surface ripples, stamping dancing patches of shadow over his darkly tanned torso. Watching those sexy hips of his as they slowly undulated to move him through the water was mesmerizing. Like a dolphin, he could drift for great distances with little effort. His muscular tail left little doubt that he could disappear into the murky depths with a few quick strokes.

"Why are you watching me so intently, Ronan? Is there something you're not telling me?"

"You will see—I think."

What was he hiding? I wasn't concerned because I felt safer with Ronan than anyone else in the world.

As we moved along the ocean floor, and the scene turned to turtle grass as far as the eye could see, I watched for green turtles. They were nature's remarkable canvas, their beautifully marked shells too intricate to be duplicated by artists. In the end, I saw three, one utterly unaware that he was about to be tested by a young bull shark. I froze when I saw the barrel-chested predator ease into view through the murk. Ronan squeezed my hand, and I relaxed.

Ever since Cain threw me into the ocean at night, I'd developed a hesitation around sharks. I had never feared them before because I usually met them head-on at the reef. Those yellow eyes would flick over you, and when you met their stare, they would move off to go about their business. The only time I'd ever felt uncomfortable was when young bulls found their way to the reef. They weren't as timid as Caribbean reef sharks and often came too close for comfort.

This bull was a five-foot youngster, slowly tracking the sea turtle as he moved past us. He was about to give the poor thing a run for its money. The shark completely ignored us, barely flicking an eye our way.

We'd been down for about ten minutes when I gasped at the sight that unfolded before me, appearing through the underwater haze and gradually filling my mask with color.

A reef. Not just any reef but an expanse of coral formations that stretched on as far as I could see. Brain coral, their swirling grooves so reminiscent of a human brain, with colorful Christmas tree worms popping out like jack in the boxes. This coral was so healthy it made my chest tighten with sentimental delight.

As we drifted along, Elkhorn coral came into view, its clusters of tan, white-tipped branches giving shelter to schools of young damselfish. Some coral was two and a half feet in diameter, something I'd never seen on the main reef. Not far from it, a massive Staghorn coral spread its flat palms over the open water, at least six feet in diameter. Not one sign of bleaching. It was a miraculous sight.

Purple fans, purple branching coral, and ocean whips swept and fluttered in the current, the expanse of colorful movement blowing my mind. It was the healthiest coral I'd seen since arriving here ten years ago. Tears of joy sprang to my eyes inside my mask.

I looked at Ronan, who studied my face.

"You see it, then?" He nodded toward the tapestry of natural beauty before me.

I nodded, my eyes wide. "How is this possible? There's no sign of any damage— it's pristine!" I looked around, wondering how the tour boats hadn't found this place.

As if he heard my thoughts, Ronan said, "The Shoal has been protected since the beginning by a powerful glamor. Humans cannot see it and are magically redirected if they wander near. For thousands of years, it has existed undetected."

He frowned. "Lately, our elders are struggling because the water is too warm. Keeping it healthy has been a challenge."

His smile returned as he waved me on. My heart swelled with emotion. To see an uninjured reef was something I never thought I'd experience in my lifetime.

Ahead, a large shelf of coral gradually rose until it nearly touched the surface, and it was to this structure that Ronan led me by the hand. Poking from the sandy ocean floor, it extended as far as I could see into the underwater gloom, gradually rising out of the water in the distance. We were a little closer to shore, the water about thirty feet deep.

"Follow me." Ronan headed to the middle of the shelf, pausing before the almost vertical face. His green eyes blinked as he watched me come, then he pointed.

My eyes focused on where he indicated. Nothing was there, just a solid wall of ancient coral. But as I watched, it shimmered, turning lighter until it faded to a glowing shade of blue, revealing an opening big enough for me to stand in. The limestone tunnel was lit by a dim light shining from somewhere inside.

Ronan nodded, and we swam into the entranceway. I hesitated to touch the sides, not understanding what I saw. If magic was involved, it might behave in strange ways. Ronan sensed my concern and stopped to touch the wall with a finger, smiling at me.

"It is limestone. My ancestors carved it out."

We continued for a few hundred feet, and when I looked up, I saw silvery patches of surface water here and there along the length of the tunnel.

I pointed, and Ronan nodded. "Yes, we are near the surface here. The tunnel is always underwater, but the water level drops if there is a moon tide. I have seen the tide low enough to wade through. On those days, you could walk into the chambers." He grimaced. "We have someone watching the tunnel during the moon tides in case a human somehow sees past the magic and wanders in."

"Has that ever happened?"

"Never, at least since I've been born. It is said that a mariner wandered in five hundred years ago." He gave me a feral grin. "He disappeared and was never seen again."

I nodded, a shiver racing down my spine. I was glad that the Syreni had reeled things in under Sovereign rule. They had a violent history but now lived quietly and peacefully. *Thank goodness.*

Ahead, the soft blue light of the tunnel transformed into a gold hue. We were getting close to our destination. Those were lights ahead.

Ronan turned to rise toward the watery ceiling. I followed him, bobbing into a low-slung chamber. What I saw made me gasp.

The pool we floated in was dead center of a small cavern cut into the limestone. The islands of the Florida Keys were compacted ancient minerals, the sedimentary rock interspersed with fossils. This chamber was a breathtaking view of ancient history.

Whoever had done the initial work to carve it out had paid particular attention to the fossil patterns in the stone and followed them wherever possible. The result was a three-dimensional wall that showed, in relief, the creatures that had died when the stone was formed. The effect was absolutely stunning.

A few low-hanging wall sconces glowed with tiny lights that chased the shadows from the furthest corners of the chamber. It must have been magic because there was no fuel. The primary source of light was a narrow crack in the ceiling. About six inches wide, the sunlight filtering through it lit the cavern with a beautiful glow.

Ronan held my hand to help me from the water. It dawned on me that I didn't need my regulator, and spat it out, unclipping the snaps on my vest and removing my tank. I shut it off, and Ronan took it from me, piling it by the edge of the pool.

"What's overhead?" I asked, stunned.

"A small glamored island that is invisible to everyone who passes by. It looks like a mangrove tussock to them, so they steer their boats away. We are far enough from shore that we do not get much traffic. More adventurous kayakers occasionally paddle by, but they are usually fishing. They are not interested in visiting a clump of mangroves."

With a proud smile, he looked around the alcove. "What do you think?"

CHAPTER 11

CHARLESTON
~ FELIX ~

"Friday. *Fuck.*"

Resigned, I watched from my bunk as Jovi slipped his shin pads over his glimmering blue skins, the brightness of which made the clunky black footwear look ridiculous. I hated our boots. They cramped my feet and squished my toes.

I hated everything about training in the yard five days a week, but I loathed the stomach churning nightmare that was Friday.

"Don't you wish we could skip training, hit the ocean, and enjoy a good long swim?" I asked my friend.

Jovi smiled at himself in the mirror, fussed with his bangs, and looked again. Unsatisfied, he wet his short hair with hot water, then scrunched it in his hand to give it a more touseled look.

"Oh, for heaven's sake. You are such a pretty boy, Jovi."

He grinned at me and gave it one more fluff. Stephen kept us sheared like sheep—said it was safer in combat.

"You're just jealous, Felix." He grabbed the bulge under his skins. "Maybe if you're lucky, I'll let you suck on this."

I jumped up and pummeled him once or twice, then we shoved each other and headed to the yard. Jovi didn't like Fridays either, but he handled the stress in his own way. Overgrooming.

As we headed out into the humid darkness of the approaching dawn, I looked up at the balcony on the far end of the ring. The Benefactor watched from there on days she chose to attend the facility. Today, the space was empty, save for a few scattered chairs. Disappointment flared through me. The Benefactors' applause and encouraging smiles helped dull the ache of our painful duties.

"She's not here," I hissed in Jovi's ear. "Do you think that means we won't have to—

"If we're lucky." He frowned down at his boots, bending over to knot a stray lace before we headed over to the weapons rack. I grabbed some leather bracers and handed a pair to my friend, then we laced each other up. After a final inspection, we headed to the milling group that congregated in the moonlit courtyard.

On cue, that bastard Stephen slunk into the yard, his electric prod in one hand. Three vampires shadowed him, and behind them strutted Boris, a real swine and the bane of our existence. Sauntering over to the weapons rack, our trainer picked up a spear before turning to address us.

"It's Friday," he said with a malicious smirk. "Give me twenty laps, and we'll get started."

As instructed, the entire yard of Argenti and Servus headed in a clockwise direction, jogging around the perimeter of the expansive yard. Twenty laps was more than enough to get our blood pumping. One hundred boots pounded the dry earth, the few remaining blades of grass disappearing beneath the thundering mixmaster of our passage.

Even in the dewy pre-dawn hours, dust rose to clog my lungs, but my flickering glimpses of Stephen through the churning mass kept my arms pumping on every circuit. He leaned against the entrance arch, his arms crossed and his hard eyes gleaming through the spectacles perched on his nose. He saw me looking and sneered, tapping his prod on his shoulder with feigned nonchalance.

There were times that I thanked the heavens for our telepathy. Like now, when breathing was a challenge.

"That bastard. Are you seeing this, Jovi? Do you think he will use that thing on anyone today?"

Jovi thumped along beside me, turning his head slightly with a grimace. *"As long as it's not me, I don't much care."*

After a torturous warmup, we lined up in the center again to face Boris. "In a circle, please—*grunts.*" The way he said it made my skin itch. I knew what was coming.

As everyone pushed outward to form a haphazard barrier, Stephen disappeared into the darkness of the archway.

"Shit. Stephen just left." The skin on my face tightened, a sick feeling blooming in my guts.

Jovi groaned, his eyes shooting wide before remembering where we were. He lowered his head. It wouldn't be wise to call unnecessary attention to either one of us.

Stephen returned, the vampires dragging a monstrous male human between them. Thick hair covered the man's beefy arms and neck, his long beard knotted like a Viking warrior. Jeans and heavy boots skidded against any forward progress, the man hurling obscenities at his captors as he realized he would never free himself. A narrow chain attached to his vest, and the knotted rag covering his bald head tumbled to the ground. A colorful patchwork of tattoos crisscrossed every inch of exposed skin. This man lived to fight.

Stephen's nasty smile widened as he nodded to Boris. Watching the man struggle in vain, our trainer grinned, his fangs briefly denting his lips before he closed his mouth.

"Now, recruits. Who's first?" Boris turned his head, surveying the milling circle of green and silver eyes, the latter gleaming with anticipation.

"You Argenti favor your Djinn side—far too easy to compel. Where's the fun in that?" he chuckled, his eyes roaming the lineup. "Let's have a Servus for a change, shall we?" Boris strutted down the line, staring into the eyes of the waiting males. My stomach lurched as he stopped before me.

Boris's eyes ran up and down my bare chest, narrowing slightly as he watched the beads of sweat tracking down my neck. He rocked back and forth on his feet, then, as if it was all a misunderstanding, he turned his head. His eyes locked on my friend.

"Jovi. Get over there and choose your weapon."

The only sign of hesitation was the bob of his Adam's apple before Jovi turned and trotted to the weapons rack. He stared at the gruesome assortment, his eyes flat. Finally, he pulled out a short sword. Boris grinned and shook his head.

"The mace. A sword is too easy. Please demonstrate your weapon's three main strike zones with our volunteer." Boris tucked his chin, his fangs lengthening as his eyes glittered a devilish crimson in the darkness.

Through our connection, a soft whimper shot prickles across my shoulders. Jovi plucked a mace from the rack, then walked reluctantly to the center of the yard. My stomach churned as I watched, powerless to help.

His hesitation wasn't lost on Boris. "I'll time you, *grunt*. Please keep your prey alive for more than ten seconds this time, will you?"

With a disgusted look, the vampire turned on his heel and strode back to the perimeter to stand watch. He crossed his arms, his head tipping back as he stared down his nose, a wicked smile teasing his lips.

Jovi's green eyes flicked to me for the briefest of moments, the flayed strips of his soul shining dully before he looked away. Staring down at the wooden handle of the mace, he squeezed until his knuckles whitened. The chain rattled as he lifted the heavy weapon, the air whumping as he began to swing.

"Human—" Jovi's deep voice nearly broke as he addressed the now terrified biker struggling to free himself. "You need to run, and hope you're faster than me."

My guts pitched, the sensation of the ground tilting making my breakfast shove into my throat. It all happened so fast.

The Argenti released the human, and he turned to run. Jovi leapt forward, and with one mighty swing of his mace, the sickening crunch of metal on bone announced the man's departure from this world.

Mere seconds, and Jovi stood over a bloody crumpled form, his lungs working like bellows. With only one swing, my friend looked like he'd run a marathon, his jaw clenched and his nostrils flaring, his eyes as hard as granite.

I knew that look.

Standing tall, Jovi turned to Boris, the hollow whumps of the mace filling the air as it sped up.

"Why don't you come over here, Boris? You're bigger and stronger than that poor fellow. Maybe I'll be able to keep *you* alive for more than ten seconds."

Boris snarled, long fangs fully extended from beneath his lips, his irises sparking to a crimson sheen. "I thought you'd never ask."

The vampire was on Jovi in a blurred heartbeat, the mace missing him entirely as he ducked in faster than the eye could track. The two bodies shot across the courtyard as one, the sound of Jovi's snapping ribs like a shot going off. The ground furrowed as they landed. When the dust cleared, only the top of Jovi's brown hair and his shimmering green ankles peeked from the trench. He wasn't moving.

Boris lurched from the hole, his heavily booted foot stomping down right where my friend's belly would be. The vampire hadn't even cracked a sweat.

I choked on my thumping heart as I swallowed. I didn't dare look at my best friend.

"Anyone else have any bright ideas about mouthing off this morning?"

The yard was still. A dawn breeze stirred the leaves of a sycamore clinging to life inside the stone wall of the courtyard. Restless feet broke the tense silence.

"That's what I thought." The bulky trainer looked across at Stephen, who nodded and disappeared into the creeping gloom of the archway. A moment or two later, he and Boris's guards appeared with another male victim, this one slightly younger than the first.

"Who's next?"

I watched as the vampires trotted across the yard to drag Jovi out of the hole containing his motionless form. My friend's head swung on a loose neck as they dragged him across the grass, the only sign of life the pained moans that floated faintly through my mind as they hauled him away. My eyes misted.

Dimly, I became aware of someone watching me. Turning my head, I met Boris's glowing red eyes right beside my face.

"I think you can go next, Felix. Let's see if you can show us where to use a spear to incapacitate our enemy—"

***

"It's beautiful, Ronan!" I spun around, taking in the three-dimensional limestone walls, and lifting one hand, I traced my fingers along the tiny shelled patterns. Textured fossils, with elegant hand-carved additions in the spaces between them, made the entire wall a textured masterpiece.

"Who did this?"

Ronan shook his head. "It was long ago, made by those living here at the very beginning." The viridescent shimmer of his eyes took my breath away. He seemed more alive than ever in the faded light of the cavern. "Come, let me take you to the inner chamber."

As we left the alcove, the reflection of the water cast shimmering movement upon the wall. *So beautiful.*

The pathway, worn smooth from centuries of use, followed gentle curves as it wound through the solid limestone. I realized there were more sconces here, as there was no natural light. I looked closely at one of the features as we passed, and just as I suspected, there was no smoke. Fascinating.

We passed a large male and petite female Syreni heading in the opposite direction. Ronan gave them a respectful nod as we passed. The female, a tiny slip of a thing, had luminous hazel eyes and long black hair woven into an intricate braid. Her eyes darted away nervously as if afraid to make eye contact.

"Do your people know that I'm coming?" My thoughts startled him, and I realized he had tensed as we passed the pair disappearing behind us.

"Yes, they do." Ronan looked at me. *"Some are unsure of the wisdom of my mother's choice to see you here. We have never had a non-Syreni visitor at the Shoal. It has caused some—anxiety."*

GREAT.

Ronan squeezed my hand, which was suddenly slick with sweat. "Do not worry," Ronan whispered. "I am here. Bacchus and Tabitha are here." He frowned. "My mother is here." The smile he gave me didn't quite reach his eyes, and I shivered. Ronan was nervous.

Soon, we popped into a large, low-ceilinged chamber. Seating and flat surfaces resembling tables were carved into the limestone. It had no real order, but it was beautiful in a surreal way. The sconces were fewer here, a long, narrow crack in the ceiling letting in plenty of light. I felt a breeze and was glad because although it was cool here, I felt claustrophobic. Whether that was the low ceilings or the crowd of eyes staring back at me was unclear.

My back stiffened, and I pulled myself up to my full height, what little there was. At least I wouldn't bang my head anytime soon.

A long-legged blonde with shimmering blue and gold legs leapt up from a low-slung bench. Smiling, Tabitha trotted over, throwing her arms around my neck and squeezing me until my shoulder blades popped.

"Eddi! I am so glad you are here!" Tabitha leaned back and gave me a big, sloppy kiss on the lips, her jade eyes dancing with laughter. She winked and whispered, "Just go with it. I'll tell you later."

My eyes bulged, but I couldn't stop the grin that popped to my lips. "Tabitha, has anyone ever told you you're crazy?"

"A time or two," she chirped.

I looked over her shoulder to see Bacchus approaching, his sandy brown hair brushing his shoulders, an infectious grin on his face. He grasped my arm and squeezed my elbow before leaning forward to kiss my cheek lightly.

"So good to see you, Eddi. I am glad to hear you found your Enforcer." He looked behind me. "You didn't bring your octopus friend along?"

I shook my head. "No, he had to work. He wanted to come, though. Maybe next time." I peeked around his bulky torso and saw the Syreni lining the room. Some had returned to chatting quietly, but most were still staring.

Bacchus leaned down and spoke quietly in my ear. "Don't concern yourself with the stares. They're nervous about meeting you. Syreni are sensible folk. You have nothing to fear down here." He stood up, then smiled. "Besides, you're with me. You'll be accepted—whether they like it or not." With a wink, he headed back across the room, his fingers squeezing mine as he released my hand.

"What now?" I whispered to Ronan, whose eyes scanned the space. I followed his gaze and saw the beautiful redhead coming our way. Oriana.

It wasn't fair to call her beautiful because, in the muted light, Oriana pushed the envelope way past stunning and into breathtaking. She had an ethereal quality, her creamy skin glowing in the natural surroundings. Her eyes, I knew very well. They glittered with the same faceted shades of green as the male holding my hand. At a firm squeeze from Ronan I tilted my chin up. Ronan's mother was stunning, but she was still a person. Creature. *Whatever.*

Oriana smiled, although it lacked warmth. As she came to a smooth stop before me, it felt as if the room faded away, and the three of us stood alone, staring at each other.

"Hello again, Edaline," she said, her voice as smooth as buttercream icing. Her voice had improved. "Welcome to our home."

I had the insane urge to curtsy, but luckily, I went with a nod and a smile. "I'm happy to meet you. Officially, I mean. *Uhh* ..." I shot Ronan a desperate look, cursing myself for not thinking this through earlier.

"You may call me Oriana. May I call you Eddi?" A moment passed as we stared into each other's eyes. As if making a decision, a sudden warmth crossed the space between us. I must have passed muster.

"Yes, Eddi would be perfect." I glanced over the redhead's shoulder and saw Tabitha grinning and giving me a thumbs up. It was then I realized that Oriana was not a tall Syreni female. In fact, she was barely an inch taller than my five foot and a smidge.

"Ronan has told me so much about you, Eddi. I understand you have been helping rein in the monster that attacked the *Shoal*." She looked at Ronan. "And it appears I owe you thanks for saving my son from that demon and her tribe." She frowned, her eyes taking on an icy cast before her expression cleared. "I'm sorry I was not more gracious when we first met. I was ..." Her voice trailed off.

"We must show you around. Please, come with me." Oriana turned and drifted away, her bare feet silent on the damp stone floors. Tabitha surged ahead of her mother, and Ronan placed his hand firmly into the small of my back. Shooting him a thankful look, I turned to see Bacchus standing with a group of pretty Syreni girls. No surprise there, although he did smile and wave as we left.

I discovered the *Shoal* was the Syreni name for the beautiful coral reef outside the caverns, and this inner sanctum was included in that moniker. The entire thing was stunning, and I had to force my mouth closed as we walked through the tunnels.

The Syreni weren't big on creature comforts, each family or group having their own small nook in the underground system. Carved into the wall, bunks and a few low benches dotted the rooms. Being creatures of the sea, it appeared their residences didn't require furnishings, or a kitchen. Apparently, the Syreni wrote the book on "eating out."

There was one central gathering place, the cavern where Oriana greeted us. Syreni congregated there for various reasons, but never to greet a land-walking visitor, it seemed. I didn't know whether to be terrified or in awe of the strange looks I received as we trucked around the place.

Eventually, we ended up back in the main chamber, and my entire body vibrated with shock as we stepped into the cavernous room.

Tara.

Oh yes, my archnemesis, seated on the edge of a carved nook, chatted with a group of stunning female Syreni. Judging by the toxic look she shot me, I would be a fool to think she didn't know of my visit and planned ahead. The other females froze, their eyes flicking over me with disdain and dismissal. I felt so loved.

Never one to lay down in the face of tyranny, I gave her a sarcastic smile as we passed by.

"Well, hello, *Tara*. I never thought I'd see you here today."

Flicking her long blonde tresses over one shoulder, the Lionfish shifter smoothed her hand over her brown and white brindled skins and sneered. "I'm here all the time, *Edaline*." She emphasized my name just to make sure I got the point.

Tara's ice-blue eyes roved over Ronan's muscular torso, and she licked her lips. "It's a wonderful place, *the Shoal*. Full of so many handsome males. How could I resist?"

Ronan squeezed my hand, so I bit back the retort that sprang to my lips. I glanced over my shoulder and realized that Oriana stood behind Ronan, watching our exchange with great curiosity. I turned back to Tara with a sugary smile.

"I was honored by Oriana's invitation. I agree. The *Shoal* is fascinating. I'll be sure and visit more often." I smiled at Ronan's mother, whose eyes glittered with approval.

Oriana held out her hand. "Come, Eddi. We should move to our *private* chambers so you and I can get to know each other better." A look passed between she and Tara, and I grinned inside. Tara was *pissed*.

I followed Oriana, but when I glanced back, Tara spoke to the Syreni females, her face an ugly mask of hatred. She hadn't changed a bit. Being threatened with death by the Enforcer for almost exposing the *Others* should have rattled her cage. Apparently, she had thicker skin than I thought. Or she was too stubborn to fear death. Typical Lionfish. Toxic until their last breath.

CHAPTER 12

Oriana's chambers were adjacent to one shared by the three siblings. Spartan but pleasant, the numerous wall sconces cast a beautiful glow over the walls. Cushions made of finely woven bulrushes were stuffed with dried grasses, surprising me with how comfortable they were.

When I glanced into the adjacent room, I noticed the recessed bunks had sleeping mats woven of the same materials. It dawned on me that their families stayed together after maturity, and males and females shared a room. It made sense, with space being at a premium down here. I had to wonder where Bacchus took his harem of conquests. Probably under a palm tree somewhere.

Ronan chuckled, and said, "Palm trees, rocks, at the reef...."

I elbowed him.

"You think too loud," he whispered between my ears, then leaned down to nuzzle me. It tickled.

Oriana cleared her throat, and my attention snapped to my first good look at Ronan's mother. Her skin wasn't as flawless as I first thought. Raised patches on her arms and shoulders still healed from her time in captivity. Ronan said her light was dimmed, but physically, she looked better than when I first met her. I shuddered at the thought of her lengthy imprisonment under Cain. Mental damage was an invisible wound that took longer to repair than a few patches of skin—*if it ever* healed.

"I am not as beautiful as I once was," she said with a quiet sigh. "I suffered greatly at Cain's hands. Ten years was an eternity." Her gaze turned inward, and I almost gasped at the pain in her expression.

She lifted her eyes and said, "I understand you knew Cain's—*disposition*— quite well. Ronan tells me you barely escaped the vampire with your life." Tucking her chin, she gave me a once-over. "I guess you might say we are soul sisters."

Nodding, I frowned. I spent most of my days trying to forget what happened to me at the hands of that sadist. Hashing it over with Ronan's mother wasn't part of the plan.

"I see. I am making you uncomfortable, Eddi. I apologize. Bringing things into the open is a Syreni trait. It avoids ... escalation. When our people become troubled, talking helps."

Oriana wiggled closer on the shared bench, reaching up to lift the beautiful pearl nestled against my chest. "Did Ronan give you this?"

I nodded.

Oriana looked at her son, and I'm not sure what I saw there, but it didn't give me the warm fuzzies. It wasn't anger in her eyes. *It was fear.*

Ronan's chin tightened, and he squeezed my hand. "I swore an oath of protection, mother. Nothing more." He looked at me, his eyes soft. *"Yet."*

Whatever was going on between them dissolved as Oriana shuttered her thoughts. The topic turned to Key West.

"I heard many things during captivity," she sighed. "Eric was helpful to me. I daresay he was blissfully unaware of the danger until it was too late." She cast a long look at me, and I nodded.

"Yes, I met Eric. He inadvertently saved my life."

"That sounds like Eric. He was a lost soul, that poor boy. Once Cain got his claws into him, he was in over his head. Eric kept me sane in his time there. He told me tales from the outside."

I stiffened. "What kind of tales?"

Glancing down at the fanciful patterns on her legs, Oriana smoothed her hands over them, elegantly crossing her ankles. "Eric was lonely and fond of chatting. I think, in his own way, he wanted to help me." She looked up. "He gave away many things, but most importantly, he let slip the location of their main laboratory."

She swallowed and looked to Ronan, who lifted his hand to caress the rough skin of her arm. "Mother, you don't need to talk about this if it troubles you." His beautiful eyes clouded over, a frown tugging at his lips.

Oriana waved her hand with a sharp motion. "No. This is important. I need to help." Her throat bobbing, she added, "It helps *me* as well."

She swiveled to look at me. "Charleston. The lab is in Charleston. They have done terrible things there. Hex is holding captives in the cells below the ground, and I understand they have captured two male Djinn and a Syreni male."

The skin on my forehead tightened, my scalp flushing with a tingling heat.

"Male Djinn? Did Eric have names?"

She shook her head and sighed. "He did not. Eric had only snippets of information. How you would find this facility in a large city is beyond my comprehension. It's a dilemma for younger souls to rectify. I have spent too much time on the end of Hex's spear. I am sorry."

At the sorrow in her voice, my eyes burned with anger and unshed tears. Ten years. Imagining it was painful. Living it must have been hell.

I changed the subject, trying to hide the cartwheels happening in my mind. Filled with hope, I struggled to remain calm.

Two male Djinn. In Charleston. But to what end?

As the conversation steered to more comfortable subjects, my visit netted me a ton of information on the male who had my heart. Funny stories of the three siblings as children, the sad tale of what happened to Ronan's father, and a fun fact that Tabitha was happy to expose.

"Yes, *little seal*. That is the meaning of the name Ronan. Although I wasn't around to enjoy it, Ronan was a chubby runt of a male when he was born." Making a ridiculous face, she flapped her hands tightly at her sides and made barking noises as she waddled in a circle. It earned her a teasing growl from her brother.

Tabitha poked at me hard enough to bruise my arm. "Not so little *now*, is he?"

My face flamed, and Ronan laughed, pulling me to my feet to leave. But Oriana reached out and touched my arm. "If you wish to talk, Eddi—about *things*—I'm here for you. I know what you went through." She looked up at the gentle expression on Ronan's face. "If my son has taken a liking to you, then that is enough for me. We will get to know each other better."

At Oriana's encouraging words, the last dregs of my tension melted away. I held in a sigh, and instead, I gave her a warm smile.

Tabitha walked us back to the entrance pool, chattering away about the goings on of her life. Finally, she explained her lip-smacking greeting.

"One of the males is getting pushy with his advances. I told him I liked girls. I hope that's ok?"

We rounded a corner in the tunnel, passing a massive blonde Syreni male. She grabbed my hand and jerked me around, locking lips with me again. Grabbing the back of my neck, she slid her fingers into my hair, her head tilting as her tongue dove deep. I resisted the urge to shove her off, remembering her words. After a thorough tongue lashing, I couldn't help it—I laughed into her mouth and accidentally bit her tongue. She pulled back and smacked me, which made me laugh harder. Not a very romantic goodbye kiss.

When she pulled back, making a huge fuss, I glanced over her shoulder and saw the large blonde male grinding his teeth. My laughter bubbled just below the surface, but I kept up the ruse until we were back in the entrance cavern.

Picking up my tank, I did my safety checks, hoisted the heavy kit and shrugged it over my shoulders. As I strapped my gear on, I asked, "Tabitha, he's a hottie. Why the heck are you avoiding that male?"

She groaned. "I'm not ready to settle down, sister! I have places to go. Things to see. I'm not ready for embryos just yet." She winked at me. "Enzo is very insistent. It rubs me the wrong way sometimes." She snorted. "He's going to run out of pheromone lure at the rate he's going."

Ronan hopped into the pool and bobbed to the surface, his tail unfurling in a flash of iridescence. Treading water with slow undulations of its massive length, he held his hand up and helped me down into the pool. I cleared my mask and we headed down the tunnel toward the open ocean.

We were halfway to the entrance when I pulled in a breath and nothing came through my regulator. *I was out of air.*

I froze. Time and again, we were taught not to panic in *out of air* situations. I looked around wildly, grabbing for my second regulator.

Nothing.

Mere seconds had passed. I ran out of air on an exhale, my chest now burning with the hysterical need to breathe. Ronan looked over his shoulder, somehow registering the scene in an instant.

He grabbed my hand and yanked me to him, crushing me in an embrace as he turned to race toward the mouth of the tunnel. His giant tail churned a cloud of sand behind us as we barreled along. I fought, resisting his hold, my lungs on fire as I desperately tried not to suck in a breath that would be pure seawater. I couldn't stop myself. I gave up and tried to breathe.

Ronan crushed his lips against mine, forming a seal. Frantic to take in air, I tried to pull away. He clamped down tight, forcefully blowing into my mouth until he parted my lips with the pressure of it. At first, I choked, my struggles nearly breaking the seal. Then I relaxed into his arms and drew in long sips of the air he offered.

My mask popped up onto my forehead, and water flooded my face. I screwed my eyes shut against the blasting current as Ronan flew down the tunnel, my body following the powerful thrusts of his hips as he accelerated to what must have been his top speed.

My tank and vest dragged against the force of the seawater, the straps choking me as we raced down the tunnel. My mask tore away, the tank sliding down my back with the force of our passage. Ronan held everything together as he powered forward. Then, through my clenched eyelids, things brightened.

Sunlight. Air. Almost there.

Ronan turned and shot vertically to the surface, breaching with a tremendous splash. Too soon, I sucked in a gulping breath, then choked as salt water washed back into my mouth.

Ronan pulled me close, gently patting my back, whispering soothing words of encouragement as I hacked and coughed. When I stopped choking he leaned back, his wild eyes darting over my face.

"What happened? You scared the life out of me!"

I coughed, my throat burning from the seawater I'd swallowed, then rasped, "I'm not sure. I did my safety check. I had air when we left."

As we bobbed on the surface, Ronan holding me close, I reached down and checked my regulators. There was no air when I tested them.

"I can check once we are on the *Wanderlust*." I looked around.

"*Shit*. My mask! I dropped it." My voice sounded like sandpaper, and I stifled the urge to hack up a lung.

Ronan disappeared, the water swirling from the swipe of his tail. I kicked my fins, barely able to stay on the surface, and terrified that I couldn't see below. The terrifying sensation of not knowing what was beneath me transported me back to the night Cain had thrown me overboard. I clenched my arms around myself and quietly tread water, breathing in through my nose and out through my mouth.

A wall of water pushed up from below and I shrieked, then Ronan's arms were around me. When he saw my face, he tucked my cheek against his shoulder and made soothing noises.

"You'll make an excellent father one day," I coughed into his neck.

Trying to hide the heart lodged in my throat, I rinsed my dive mask and slipped it back over my face before mouthing my snorkel. My hands shaking, I adjusted it, keeping eyes on Ronan, who watched intently.

My intention was a surface swim to the *Wanderlust*, bobbing quietly on its anchor a few hundred yards distant. I eased away from him and started swimming, but with my buoyancy vest empty, and the few weights I carried pulling me down, it was tough.

"*Uhh* ... I'm going to need your help," I gasped, my throat still raw. Ronan gave me a grim smile and rolled onto his back, pulling me, and my mess of gear, over his broad chest. As we started toward the boat, the gentle undulations of his tail brought me back to a certain day, not so long ago, when I threw caution to the winds and—

"Do you remember?" he murmured in my ear. "Because I do." His rumbling drawl tickled, and I smiled. Relaxing, I curled my arms under my chest and lay my head down.

"Oh yes, I remember. Very well." With the tank and weights, I was quite heavy, but Ronan handled it with ease. He took his time swimming us back to the boat. Adrenaline from the incident coursed through my bloodstream, weakening my arms and legs even as the hormone drained away. A quiet numbness settled over me now that I was safe.

I snuggled close as his shoulders raised to form a wake, keeping most of the water from my face. Small waves tickled past my bare thighs, the sensation bringing me right back to the day we made love for the first time. The heat pooling between my legs reminded me—we hadn't had five uninterrupted minutes together since coming back from Key West. His strong arms had aroused the sleeping sex fiend in my shorts.

I squirmed, biting my lip as desire raced through me. I couldn't resist and rocked a bit harder than necessary to meet the upstroke of his slowly swaying hips. Ronan was not oblivious to my teasing, and soon, a hard ridge poked along my belly. He tightened his hold, the slow undulations of his tail pushing into me a little harder than necessary. He grinned down at me, two tiny fangs peeking from beneath his upper lip.

"Be careful what you start, little barracuda." The softly purred threat made things worse, an electric throb shooting straight to my pussy. Frustrated, I clenched my thighs together.

Now was not the time. I knew my stimulation was a reaction to the ebbing adrenaline and the post-panic desire to cling to him. With a sigh, I concentrated on the boat, now looming before us.

Ronan wasn't through with me, though. As he approached the ladder, at the last minute he swung away from it in a swirl of seawater and dropped his tail. I laughed as the ocean splashed up my neck, the feeling of soft scales sliding between my legs setting off shivers.

Two large hands grasped my buttocks and yanked me closer, his lips meeting mine. Warm, wet sweeps of his tongue undid me, setting off fireworks as I curled my legs behind him and pulled him close. His tail curled up so far that the tips of his dolphin-like fin poked through the surface behind my head. The sound of its lazy flops against the water, and the intense look in Ronan's hooded eyes had my pulse fluttering. Grinding against the ridge beneath his skins, I enjoyed a few firm rubs along his arousal before ending his playful side trip.

Work was calling; I had a charter and time was running short. Ronan wasn't just my lover, he was far more. I knew that, now. I took comfort in the fact that things would be fine, as long as I was with my handsome, capable, and incredibly sexy Syreni. The porno playing in my head would have to wait.

CHAPTER 13

Tara. It was the only explanation. I climbed the ladder and hauled myself aboard, shucking off my gear. In seconds, I found the culprit. A small, perfectly round hole in my buoyancy vest. The kind of hole a claw could make. And it was cleverly placed beneath a wide strap, where I wouldn't notice it.

A buoyancy control vest was the perfect piece of equipment to help divers stabilize underwater—*unless it had a hole.* Then, it continuously drew air from your tank, and under the right circumstances, you drown.

I had been talking to Tabitha when I did my dive check. I should have been paying more attention when I opened my valve, and checked my gauges closer. There was no excuse for running out of air. It was my fault. But it left me wondering if Tara intended to kill me. *Again.*

When he heard my theory, the snarl coming from Ronan raised the hairs on the back of my neck. So did the dent in the boat railing when he clenched his fist tight enough to warp it.

"I will end her," he spat. "That Lionfish is a stain on the *Shoal.*"

Reaching up, I slid my hand behind his neck and pulled his face to mine. Eyes blazing and nostrils flared, he sucked in short angry breaths as his eyes flickered gold.

"It's OK, Ronan. We can't be sure it was Tara. Suspicion isn't proof. I lived to tell the tale. Just keep her the hell away from me, and we'll be fine." In truth, I was being overly generous because inside my head, I pictured her slow death. I'd kill the bitch if I saw her again.

My hands still trembled when, after stowing my gear and hoisting the anchor, I brought the *Wanderlust* around. Gazing out at the nearly flat calm ocean I marveled at how the day was perfect for a dive.

Or a drowning. Whatever. Moving on.

I shook my head and started back to Davy Jones Locker. As we skipped over the gently rolling ocean, from the corner of my eye, I noticed Ronan staring at me. His tongue kept darting out to lick his lips as he focused on my neck. Tilting his head, he rubbed his chin with one hand, a long-suffering sigh coming from his puffed cheeks as he shifted back and forth on his bare feet. The effect was adorable.

I grinned at him. "What?"

"You are so beautiful." Ronan's voice was soft, his look sincere. The combination did very naughty things to my vagina.

I glanced ahead of the boat. We were getting close, the marina coming into view on the distant shoreline. My responsibilities were all piled on that shore, waiting for me. I made a decision.

I throttled back, turned the boat, glanced at my sonar screen, and hit the button for the windlass. With a hum and a rattling plop, the anchor raced for the bottom. I shut off the motors.

Turning to Ronan, I got a surprise closeup of his tanned chest. Thick arms snaked around me as I looked up at his hungry expression. His lips met mine with a frantic urgency, his tongue teasing my lips apart. The sounds of seabirds and our quiet, urgent breaths pushed the moment along, the two of us lost in the idyllic atmosphere surrounding us.

I wasn't sure if it was the beautifully calm ocean or the after-effects of my near-death experience, but I was desperate for him. My hands were in his hair, tugging the silky strands as I pushed him back against the helm console. Our tongues twisted together, our eager lips devouring each other with delight. I ground against his bulging sex, throbs radiating in all the right places between my legs. I pulled away for a moment, panting for air.

Ronan licked his bottom lip. "I enjoy this side of you," he purred.

We launched at each other in a flash of urgency, his hands quickly shucking my damp rashguard. Smoothing his large palms down my back, Ronan paused to knead my ass and pull me close, pressing me against the long rigid length beneath his skins. A finger slid under my dive shorts from behind, and with a husky groan, he stroked my wet folds, hauling me off my feet and onto his chest for better access.

His finger traced over my slick contours before sliding deep inside, massaging firmly over the knot of nerves there. The intense sensations turned my limbs to jello, and I stilled, spreading my legs further and tucking my forehead against his chest with a groan. As he probed and caressed with just the right pressure, my breath hitched, starving me for oxygen. Looking inward, I sank into the sensations stroking to life in my core.

My feet shook against his calves, my hands clutching his shoulders as I trembled and moaned through his rhythmic invasion. The desperate pants from my lips laced the air as his finger snaked into just the right place, another one joining in. The dynamic duo turned me into a writhing mass of nerve endings as Ronan's heavy breathing puffed past my ear.

His soft, hot tongue was everywhere—my neck, my cheeks, my lips. I couldn't get enough of him, and those long fingers undid me. Under the shade of the canopy, the pleasant breeze floating over us cooled my skin, but nothing could quell the fire rolling through my body.

With a muffled grunt, Ronan lifted me, swung me around, and laid me belly down over the railing of the *Wanderlust*. With a deft crook of his wrist, my wet shorts flopped onto the deck next to my shirt, and the breeze teased my bare ass. Molding my cheeks with firm squeezes of his hands, Ronan's soft sigh of pleasure trailed off as he surveyed my honeyed labia spread bare for him.

I reached back. I wanted to feel him. Ronan moaned as my hand found his cock, already slipped through his skins and pulled tight against his belly. The erotic sound that burst from his throat sent a pulse straight to my clit.

Nudging the head of his hard shaft against my entrance, Ronan groaned, then slowly slipped into me. I curled my chin to my chest and closed my eyes with a sigh. I felt every inch of him as he spread me wide, my hands tightly clenching and unclenching on the railing.

As he began to stroke in and out with slick precision, our wet sounds heightened my arousal. The railing rattled under my grip as I turned to look over my shoulder, his slack-jawed expression sending a surge of wetness through me. His fingers dug into my hips as he threw his head back and moaned, thrusting hard.

All hell broke loose. The gate, apparently unlatched, swung open beneath my hands. *"SHIT!"*

With a splash, we tumbled head-first into the Atlantic, coming up for air with laughing sputters—only to stop and stare into each other's smiling faces.

Ronan closed the distance between us, his tail brushing my legs as he dragged me into his arms. His intense stare swept over my face as he reassured himself that I was unhurt. The world around us faded as we bobbed at the surface, slow strokes of his tail keeping us afloat.

"I love you." The declaration raced from my lips, my brain waking up and hitching a ride on the last word out. I hesitated, suddenly afraid of what he would say, or do.

Ronan froze. He cocked his head, his mouth open as he digested the three words; he cocked his had the other way. I saw the moment he understood. With a rumbling purr, he crushed me to his chest.

Shoving his tail between my legs, he slid his hands up the back of my thighs, parted them, and entered me with a determined slide. With gentle but firm swings, he stroked his length into me and out, his eyes closing as he pressed his smooth cheek to mine.

The hard squeeze of his fingers dug into me, his hands palming my ass as he thrust; my chest squirmed with emotions as we floated, nothing between us. His soft, gasping growls sparked an earthquake in my pussy, his pumping hips lifting me slightly on every glide of his shaft. I gripped his shoulders and lowered my head, burying my face in his neck as he curled his tail to pull me closer. He filled me, and filled me, and filled me, my inner walls welcoming his plunging cock.

The inside of my thighs and calves slid over the soft scales of his tail, their smooth texture adding another layer of sensation that spiked my arousal into the clouds.

Ronan's lips traced the length of my neck, my head tilting back to lay on the surface of the water as, delighted, he fastened his lips on the bead of my breast and sucked. A warm tongue flicked and teased, his teeth lightly catching my nipple before he hunted the other. His whispered endearments made my spine tingle, given in a language I'd never heard before— soft, lilting, and exotic.

Pulling me close, Ronan's fingers gripped my hair as he devoured my lips with his and thrust into me. Water sloshed around us as a hot, electric tingle snapped along my spine.

Wildfire flashed across my lower back, my pussy clenching his cock as I threw my head back and rode a blissful cresting wave, crushing myself to Ronan with the force of it.

In a spasm of thrusts, Ronan screwed his eyes shut and roared his release, my back creaking under the force of his hold as he thrashed against me. His cheek crushed mine and his lips parted, desperate for air. Nectar dripped from his fangs and trickled down my neck as he groaned, the low guttural sound sending tingles over my skin.

My heart swelled with affection for him as Ronan held me in a post-orgasmic cuddle. The fingers of both his hands splayed over my buttocks, holding me close; he jerked through the final echoes of his orgasm, his huffing laughs soft against my ear.

"*Mmm*," I sighed, my eyes closing as he nuzzled me. "You didn't bite me."

"Boat—drive—home."

I laughed. Right. We were in the middle of the Atlantic, having sex with the sea turtles. I opened drowsy eyes and gazed at the flat ocean surrounding us. This was heaven. And I was with *him*. In this moment, I felt a part of something—a part of *someone*. I wasn't alone anymore.

Ronan lifted his head, his hooded eyes probing mine. "You are *mine*," he whispered. "And my heart is yours."

As he kissed and cuddled me, the two of us floating on the sea, my overstuffed ticker melted into a gooey puddle inside my chest. Tipping my forehead to his, I closed my eyes and slid my fingers into his hair, enjoying the last of this beautiful moment before we had to get back on the boat and face reality.

My eyes popped open, and I sucked in a sharp breath.

"*SHIT!*"

Ronan froze. His head whipped back and forth, looking for what alarmed me. His tail pushed harder, and he spun us in a circle, his neck arching to scan the ocean around us.

I grabbed his chin and turned his head to face me, my eyes wide.

"Protection! *We forgot protection!*"

Ronan frowned, puzzling over my words. I saw the moment it dawned on him what I was going on about, and he relaxed, one eyebrow arching.

"It is of no consequence," he mumbled, his face darkening. "Syreni do not worry about these things when they tangle—"

I pushed against his shoulders, my anger flaring. "No consequence? How can you even think like that, with all the shit that's been going on?" I looked down at his tanned chest, the water sloshing over it as he waved his tail, keeping us afloat. "What if I get pregnant?"

I turned and pulled away from him, clambering awkwardly up the ladder, my legs not entirely with the program. My foot slipped on a wet rung, and I almost fell back into the ocean.

His big hands grabbed my ass, but catching myself, I patted his hands away and heaved upwards, wedging one foot on the deck, my legs still parted as I struggled to pull myself aboard. His chuckle, likely at the bird's-eye view of my poonanni, sent me over the line.

I heaved myself aboard and stomped across the deck to the opposite railing, crossing my arms over my stomach in distress. Looking up, I watched the seabirds riding the air currents and tried to control my breathing. Ronan came up behind me, reaching for my bare hips. Comforting hands thumbed the small of my back in a pleasing caress. Then, sliding one arm around me and across my breasts, he pulled me back against his warm chest.

Tears poured down my face at the loving gesture. I grabbed his hand, pressing it to my cheek. He wiped away some tears with a masculine sigh.

"Ronan," I groaned. "What if I get pregnant?"

"Then we will have a child." He leaned forward to meet my gaze, his eyes serious, his expression soulful. He ducked down to make me look at him.

"Perhaps our offspring will be like Matilda. Or a clever male with your silver eyes and my tail. Either way, I am happy. Our offspring will be perfect." With a smug look, he turned me to face him and pulled me forward, his lips finding mine with a sweet, gentle kiss.

I couldn't relax, a terrifying fear of the unknown dragging me down into a simmering stew of anxiety. I was out of control. There were no plans. The "what ifs" choked me as I sobbed.

"What if it's deformed? What if it has—*issues?*" My lip stung beneath the bite of my teeth, and tears threatened again.

Ronan tipped my head up, a finger curled beneath my chin. "Our child would not be an 'it' Edaline. Do you think the two of us could produce a babe that wasn't perfect?" He shook his head, tutting about us having an "*it.*"

I laughed—a cold, defensive reaction that tainted the air between us. "I think you're being a bit optimistic. With my luck, our kid will have six legs."

Ronan grinned and pulled me into a tight squeeze, his chin sliding over my head as he tucked me close. "Stop worrying, Eddi. Everything will be OK. Matilda is a healthy, intelligent eight-year-old who is Syreni *and* Djinn. That means something."

As we eased apart, I swiped the back of my hand under my nose to catch a sniffle and turned to fire up the windlass. The anchor chain clanking into place grated on my nerves, but I tried to talk some sense into myself and ease the fear munching on my confidence.

You didn't get pregnant last time. He's not going anywhere. Relax.

As we headed to shore, my thoughts went to better places as Ronan cuddled me from behind. Racing over the flat calm of the Atlantic, his gentle massages chased away some of the fear, and the little kisses he pressed on my neck were a reminder—our connection grew stronger every day.

He cared for me. His mother had accepted me. Why was I so terrified? What if I lost him? I had no idea how I had ever managed without him in my life, and the thought of being alone again hollowed out my chest. I couldn't raise a child on my own!

As if hearing my thoughts, Ronan placed his hands over mine where they clutched the Captain's wheel. He squeezed his fingers and leaned forward to breathe into my ear.

"Stop torturing yourself. It's giving me a headache," he teased. When he saw the moisture beading on my lashes, he whispered, "No matter what happens, we will find a way to be together. I will not leave you alone, Edaline."

Too soon, the engines rumbled to silence as I nosed the *Wanderlust* into its slip. The marina was quiet, the looming menace of Hex's yacht sending chills across my neck. Nothing moved on board, the calm waters of the bay reflecting the spider graphic.

"I'll never get used to seeing that thing here," I whispered as Ronan hauled me onto the dock. His use of excessive strength told me someone hadn't settled after my recent brush with danger. Either that, or he needed exercise weights. Lord knew, he slung me around like a wrecking ball.

Ronan's eyes traveled over the crimson hull of the yacht, pausing at the empty decks. He looked at me with cold eyes. "After I deal with Tara, I will kill the abomination that owned that vessel. Hex will *not* escape again."

I squeezed his hand in solidarity, then tramped to the office to get my gear stowed. Writing out an incident report for James, I blamed the out-of-air incident on a dive-related puncture rather than outing Tara. I figured Ronan would take care of that little bitch on his own.

CHAPTER 14

The next day, we took Matilda to the island again. He was right. She was a natural. After patiently showing her how to hold her breath, Matilda stayed under for longer and longer periods. Every time they bobbed up, Ronan gave me a thumbs up. It was adorable, really. A rugged Syreni male teaching a delicate child how to hold her breath made me feel all sorts of warm and tingly.

Even Cal got into the act, flashing into his octopus form and crawling over to where Ronan held swim class. When a wall of water shot into the sky, and Matilda shrieked with laughter, I knew Cal had pranked Ronan. It was his favorite pastime.

Miri buzzed over and landed on my kayak. "Well, now I've seen everything. The suckered slug remembered how to let his hair down. Cal's been a real stick in the mud since we left Key West."

I nodded. "He's not himself. We needed this, and Ronan was right. Matilda loves swimming. Do you think she'll end up with some of her mother's Syreni traits? Gideon says they can take a while to show up, especially without training."

Miri laughed. "Let's hope not. The apartment smells like a fish cannery as it is." She dodged my playful swat, then settled back on the gunnel.

She chewed her lip. Something was up. "Eddi ... " At my raised brow, she continued. "Your neighbor stopped by yesterday. He knocked, and knocked, and I tried to stop her, but Matilda answered the door."

My eyes shot open. "What?!"

Miri turned red. "I was afraid to tell you. Matilda listens alright, but she's smart and has a mind of her own. I couldn't stop her. She left the chain on, though! Of course, she couldn't reach it ... "

I frowned. "What did my neighbor say?"

"He wanted to know where you were. Matilda is smart. She said you'd gone for groceries and would be back in a minute. He didn't look happy." At my deepening frown, she added, "I'm so sorry. I didn't know what to do."

I reached out to grab her little hand. "It's ok, don't worry. We'll figure something out. Thanks for the heads up."

Miri looked relieved, and we sat to watch the show.

Ronan took Matilda closer to the drop-off to get her accustomed to swimming in deeper water. The kids' goggles I bought her landed on the kayak beside my snorkel gear after she decided she didn't need them. Unconcerned and swimming with her eyes open, her vision was perfect beneath the surface. How it didn't sting like mad was beyond me. Eager to watch, I snorkeled over to where they played.

Ronan dove down, Matilda clinging to his neck. After each shallow dive, he surfaced for her to breathe. Then, something strange happened.

As Ronan coasted beneath the surface, Matilda stopped lifting her head to take a breath. Did Ronan know she wasn't breathing?

Panicked, I swam to them, my fins pushing hard. Getting closer, I caught a glimpse of childish smiles wreathed in bubbles. Matilda wasn't concerned. Then, I saw why.

Three small slits on her neck, each no longer than my pinky, flashed open before closing just as quickly. Seconds later, it happened again, confirming that I wasn't losing my mind. Matilda breathed seawater.

Ronan glanced over his shoulder, and Matilda nodded, and together, they dove a little deeper. Childish squeals of excitement crossed the ocean gloom between us, the muffled underwater shrieks a boon to my frayed nerves.

She can breathe underwater. With gills. Holy Hogfish.

Seconds later, when I thought the youngster couldn't surprise me anymore, she shocked me. Her little feet, kicking wildly—*changed*. They lengthened, then widened. Stretching to three times their original length, her toes spread open, and a thin membrane appeared between them, tiny hooked claws tipping each toe. Matilda waved at me. Her hands were webbed, pale skin stretching between each finger.

I jerked in surprise, choking on the seawater that poured over the top of my snorkel. I followed it up with a scream as a suckered tentacle grabbed my arm from behind and yanked me about-face.

Cal, his goat-like eyes rolling in his bulbous head, frantically pointed two of his eight arms in Ronan's direction. The rapidly curling tips of his tentacles made me laugh with shared excitement.

"I see it, you knucklehead. Don't scare me like that!"

Cal flinched, his eyes squinting at my shrill tone. *"Sorry. I got excited. Can you believe it? Gills!"*

I looked back to where Ronan had surfaced, his beautiful tail waving enough to pop them out in a small breach. Matilda screamed, then laughed hysterically as the water splashed over them, and they sank into the drop-off.

"Cal, these days, nothing surprises me."

His octopus clung to my arm, and together we hung over the deep water to watch the fun. Soon, Matilda swam alongside Ronan, her hands and feet learning to coordinate for more speed. It wasn't Syreni fast, but much faster than a human swimmer.

When they took a break, Matilda chattered away as she told us how it felt to use her gills. She turned her hands for me to see the webbing, and I fussed over the tiny claws sprouting from where her fingernails used to be.

The pink, hard nails curved to tiny points, then retracted when she pulled her fingers straight and relaxed. We spent five minutes watching Matilda sheathing, then unsheathing her claws as she stared at them in wonder. Ronan lounged behind her, a brotherly smile lifting his lips as he showed her his claws.

I looked at Cal, now back in his human form, sprawled on the kayak behind me. The brim of his sun hat fluttered in the strong ocean breeze as he smeared zinc cream over his sunburned nose.

"She's half Djinn, half Syreni," I mused. "It makes sense that she has some of the traits from each species. It's wild, isn't it?"

Cal nodded and turned to look at me. "Yeah. and I read somewhere that the mother contributes sixty percent of the genetic material to her offspring. It makes sense that Matilda is a natural in water." He was quiet for a moment, then added, "Galahad is a Djinn. Do you think he's her father?"

I mulled it over, then shook my head. "It's possible, but I don't think so. She looks nothing like him, and doesn't have his black hair." I frowned. "Oriana said Hex is keeping two Djinn up in South Carolina. Why? They had to ship Oriana's eggs there in dry ice."

With a shiver, I remembered the room that Cain held me in after kidnapping me. Eric had rolled in a trolly with a tall canister and a box of dried ice. They were planning on gathering my eggs that day. But why?

Cal tapped his long fingers on one knee, eyes scanning the horizon. He was quiet for a while. As the sun began to ease into the mandarin hues of late afternoon, he shared his thoughts.

"Oriana wasn't well when she escaped. I've often wondered how the half-Syreni they're breeding can live so far from the magic of the reef. Ronan mentioned Syreni needed to stay close to coral, remember?"

Yes, I remember that."

"Well, I looked it up. Scientists recently discovered a new deep-water reef offshore from Charleston. It's a long way out, but maybe it's enough to keep the hybrids healthy. Cain must have suspected the distance from coral would affect the fertility of Oriana's eggs."

He looked at me, his expression grim. "The reef in Key West is only seven miles from shore, and Oriana still had health issues living in a tank. Charleston would never have worked. She would have gotten sick, maybe even died."

"That makes sense," I said. But why not move the Djinn males to Key West, then?

"I've been thinking about that too. Djinn turn to mist. They must be pretty hard to contain. Maybe they have something special up there to hold them? Then, they can collect sperm and ship it here. I can only imagine how they collect—"

Cal grimaced. "God, it sounds horrible, sitting here talking about *breeding* them. It's sick. It makes my skin crawl just thinking about it."

I mulled it over as we sat quietly, watching Ronan and Matilda getting ready to leave. Djinn were powerful. Keeping them against their will would be tough.

Cal stood, picking up my kayak anchor and coiling the rope. "I guess the real question is ... *what's in Charleston?*"

I looked out over the ocean, watching the sky change to a pale violet as excitement thrummed beneath my skin. Was my father one of the two Djinn in Charleston? Thinking about him made it tough to breathe. Soon, we'd get some answers.

***

After a beautiful day on the water, we returned to the marina, Cal taking the girls back to the apartment. Watching the swirling footprints of Ronan's tail as he headed back out to sea, I smiled through the pain in my chest. This was the part I hated. The leaving part. It reminded me of Miri's comments, and my eyes misted over.

I tied off my kayak and trotted up the curved steps of the *Black Widow* to find Gideon sprawled in one of the comfortable leather lounge chairs, his feet up.

"I see you're making good use of your downtime," I quipped, plopping down in a chair across from him. My eyes found the fridge. I didn't need to say anything because he read my mind.

"It was taken care of. If you'd like to help yourself, the fridge contains drinks now. No heads." The smile he gave me barely concealed a cold stare that surprised me.

What had I done? Gideon was a lot of things, but he wasn't cruel. At times, I wished I could read *his* mind.

As I rose and walked past him, I noticed his chest lacerations looked better, pink scars now criss crossing his bare torso. His broken arm remained clamped to his side, bound tight enough that his hand was puffy and tinted pinkish-blue. The notion of a flightless Gryphon, unable to police his area, was disturbing. It made me wonder who was minding the fort.

I padded into the luxurious kitchen, hearing him snort as I cautiously opened the stainless steel monstrosity in search of a beverage. Flushed from the sun, I paused to enjoy the blast of cold air on my face. I sighed and grabbed two Corona beers, popping the tops off and bringing one to Gideon before sitting down. He looked at it, his face blank.

"What? It's beer. I assumed alcohol was your beverage of choice."

Gideon grumbled. "I prefer the juice of fruits and vegetables. And chicken broth." He set the beer down on the side table, and I jumped up, adding it to my stash before spinning to head back to the kitchen. I paused, put my hands on my hips, and pointed my finger at Gideon.

"Wait a minute—*Bert*. I saw your flask when you cooked at the diner. You used to swill booze all the time at work." I crossed my arms and frowned. "And you smoked! What's up with that?"

"It was chicken broth. The Gryphon requires a constant supply of nutrients to maintain its strength." Gideon ran the fingers of his good hand through his hair and looked down at his cast. "Cigarettes were a habit I picked up in Mesopotamia five centuries ago. I gave it up recently." He sighed.

"I have been unable to care for myself since *this* ..." He tried to raise his arm and flinched. "The humerus bone shattered on impact." At my confused expression, he rolled his eyes. "One of the major bones in my wing. It will take weeks to heal, slower still without proper sustenance."

"I'm not confused about your bones, Gideon. You smoked for *five thousand years*? Talk about a hard habit to kick!" He didn't laugh. With a sigh, I grabbed my beers and trucked back to the kitchen. I couldn't look at him because his weakness stirred up feelings of ...

I don't know. *Feelings.* I felt terrible for the grumpy prick. His discomfort and obvious frustration were hard to watch, especially knowing his powerful creature so well. The Gryphon *lived* for prowling the skies every night. And for bossing everyone around. It must have been hard to sit here doing nothing.

I rifled around the fridge and pulled out a plastic bowl with a snap lid. Cautiously, I looked inside. Raw chicken. I popped it into a pot with some water and snapped on the gas burner to let it simmer. I peeled the carrots, onions and celery I found in the fridge, rummaging through the cupboards for salt and pepper.

While I worked, Gideon refused to look my way. His stiffly squared shoulders and rigid jaw spoke volumes. Our Gryphon was a protector, not a patient.

When my concoction warmed, I ladled some into a giant beer stein from the cupboard, leaving the rest to simmer longer. As I turned toward him I saw Gideon's tawny eyes staring back at me, his neck craned, and his nose flared at the delicious smells wafting his way. I brought it to him with a satisfied smile.

"I get that you're hurt, but last time I checked, there wasn't anything wrong with your legs." I set the mug down on the side table and thumped back into my chair, crossing my feet on the table. Gideon looked at my feet and frowned.

Ignoring him, I asked, "How did you get it so clean in here? I mean, there were holes and blood everywhere. I didn't know Molly Maid did crime scene cleanup." I laughed at the framed print of Foghorn Leghorn covering the biggest hole on the wall. Cal's work, *no doubt.*

"I have my ways," he said, taking a big sip of his broth. I must have gotten something right because he kept going, downing half the mug and licking his lips.

"I'm guessing this isn't a social call, Edaline."

His mood seemed better, so I took a deep breath and relayed everything Oriana told me back at the *Shoal.*

"This is excellent news indeed. Did she have a name for this lab facility?"

"Eric never mentioned the name, if he ever knew it. But he did mention a location. It was across from Fort Sumter. You know, the Civil War fort on the island in the middle of Charleston Harbor?"

"I am well aware of Fort Sumter, Eddi. I was there and saw that first unfortunate shot."

His words stalled me out, and my chin dropped. "You were *there* in April 1861? The first day of the Civil War? *Wow.*"

"I passed through the skies above Charleston that day. When I saw the commotion, I went to investigate. We cannot intervene in human problems, so I could do nothing but watch." He sighed. "It was a terrible time in history, and I strive to forget it. There was far too much misery."

I chewed my nails for a moment, letting the subject drop. "So, I gotta ask. What's up with you these days?"

Gideon's eyes shot to mine, and his lips formed a thin line in his hard face. He stared at me for a minute. I shrugged.

"I'm sorry. It's just hard to see you ... I'm not used to ... *to this*." I waved with a flourish at his scowling face. "You've been different ever since Key West." There was more staring, and then a huge sigh left him and his tension melted away.

"Edaline, I am an Enforcer. Everyone is my responsibility. YOU are my responsibility. Being injured has been—" He looked down at his lap, his lips drooping. "It's been hell. I failed you. I failed all of you." He looked up at me, his expression overflowing with guilt. "I should have done better."

HOLY SHIT.

I sat there in shock. Then, I imagined how he felt. My eyes glistened with tears by the time I responded.

"Gideon. Last time I checked, Immortalis weren't GODS. They screw up. They get hurt. Sometimes, *they die*. When you become a God, let me know. I'll come and visit you at your palace in the sky. But until then, you might have to accept that even you aren't perfect." I smiled, and circled my finger at him. "Galahad must have been quite a fighter to get one over on you, big guy—you scare the shit out of me."

I laughed. Slowly, the corners of his lips turned up, and his whole posture straightened.

"Ok, nice talk. So, what's next, Boss?"

Gideon lifted his good arm, pointed at his heavily bandaged head, and then curled his lip in distaste.

"First, I heal this mess. Then, we head to South Carolina."

CHAPTER 15

Gideon said he was fine, and didn't need help. So I ignored him and got into his business, poking around the yacht every day. I brought Matilda and Miri, and sometimes, Cal tagged along. Being on board the *Black Widow* helped Matilda get over her fear of the boat.

If I happened to make a bit of broth, or do some cleaning while I was onboard, it was worth the effort to see how much it irritated Gideon. Annoyed meant he wasn't stewing in a vat of self-induced misery.

The Gryphon had an astounding appetite. I wondered how he got any policing done, with how much time it took to feed himself properly. I guess wild-caught fish was his go-to when he was mobile. It was a good thing he ate his meat raw.

In a few days, Gideon looked healthier and was able to get around better. Unfortunately, he couldn't shift to Gryphon form. That fact frustrated him to no end, so I made sure to vacuum each and every time I visited.

One day, I lounged on the flybridge, taking a break while I enjoyed a soft gray couch. The splendid Spectre yacht featured top-of-the-line Italian furnishings. It was heaven. I closed my eyes and tried not to picture Hex sitting here.

Miri lounged on a throw pillow at the end of my couch, while Matilda played with a Barbie that Miri gave her.

"Matilda, do you need to practice your *cloud thing?* I mean, since we brought you home with us, you haven't tried transforming, have you? Well, not since the broom closet episode."

Matilda frowned. "No. I haven't tried." She bit her lip. "I didn't think I should, in case someone saw me." She squirmed in her chair, then added, "I hated when Hex made me do it. It was always to show off to someone. But I do—I like how it feels when I go cloudy."

Sitting up, I slipped on sunglasses and a ballcap to ward off the brilliant afternoon sun. "Do you want me to help you practice now?"

"It's not like that. You can't help. I try hard to concentrate, and it just ... *happens.*" Matilda looked around the flybridge. "Sometimes it helps to have a target. Before you found me, I practiced carrying things in my cloud." She pointed to the stairs leading down to the living area, then grinned at me. "Do you need anything from the fridge?"

I laughed. "Always. Do you know what a Corona looks like?"

"Yes, it's yellow." With a shy smile, she closed her eyes. I watched her face, stiff with concentration. It didn't work, and after a moment or two, she opened her eyes and gave me a frustrated look.

"I'm sorry." Her hands trembled in her lap, and my heart melted.

"Oh, honey. Don't be sorry. It will come when you're ready."

I leaned back on the couch keeping one eye cracked open. As I expected, she didn't give up. Closing her eyes, her face scrunched until it turned red, her hands clenching and unclenching on the Barbie she held. After contorting her expression for a moment or two, it happened.

Slender gray wisps drifted away from her body until gradually, the last of her misty form lifted into the air, joining the rolling mass of gray nearly invisible in the bright sun.

The virtually transparent cloud hesitated, then tumbled away, churning down the stairs. If I hadn't been watching, I might not have seen it. I was amazed how such a small child could master such an incredible power.

In the past weeks, I had struggled over and over to revisit my unexpected flying, the weird blue barrier over my skin, and the added strength that appeared during our throwdown with Hex in Key West. Sadly, I was a dud. I had no idea how to manage the skills from my Djinn side, and no one to ask for help.

It was incredibly frustrating. I couldn't count how many times I stood in front of my mirror, looking like I was constipated as I tried to levitate. No amount of straining would recreate the incredible thrill of the glowing magic that had transformed me that day. I decided to ask Matilda about her technique when she got back with my beer.

She was only gone a moment when an ear-piercing shriek startled me off the couch. I leapt to my feet and thumped down the stairs. Miri, buzzing behind me, kept bumping into the back of my head as she struggled to pass.

"Stay in your own lane!" I hissed. Hitting the bottom of the curved stairs, I slid to a stop on the polished tile floor of the kitchen.

Gideon, buck naked, towered in the middle of the open space with a tea towel clutched over his junk. Cookie Monster eyeballs rolled wildly in his face as he tipped his head toward the fridge.

Matilda stood frozen, a smashed Corona bottle lying in the puddle at her feet, her hand over her mouth and her eyes scrunched shut. As my eyes flicked back to Gideon, I noticed a feather on the island, and a few on the floor.

His Gryphon form had returned. Wonderful news. Too bad he couldn't shift back fully clothed—or in the privacy of his stateroom.

Choking back a laugh, I motioned for Gideon to beat it, then squatted down to block Matilda's view of the muscular butt cheeks pounding down the hall. Gently taking her by the shoulders, I couldn't resist peeking at Gideon's glorious backside as it fled the scene.

Sue me. It was impossible not to look, especially with Miri hovering in the doorway, making ooo-ing and aww-ing noises as she enjoyed our Enforcer's hasty retreat.

I grinned at Matilda and eased her hand away from her mouth. "Shh, it's ok, he's gone. Gideon gave you quite a fright, didn't he?"

Matilda, her eyes wide, nodded. "I've never seen—*boy parts*—before."

I cringed. Worst Mother Award, coming right up.

She looked down at her little gray runners with the white soles. "I never saw anybody before I moved in with you." Matilda peered down the empty hallway. "There were no boys. Just Galahad."

Looking into her eyes, I wasn't surprised to see the tears shining there.

"I know you miss him. Someday soon, you'll see him again. When things are ... *better*." Pulling her to me with a huge hug, I kissed the top of her soft blonde hair. "I miss my father very much, so I know how you feel, kiddo. But you'll always have us. We're here to stay."

As Matilda sniffled into my shoulder, my own heart bled a little. Lately, a fresh hope had blossomed that Father might still be alive. I knew that was unlikely, but when Oriana told me of the two Djinn being held in South Carolina—well, Djinn were rare creatures. What was the chance that one of the two captives was my father?

There was only one way to find the answer to that riddle. With a sigh, I picked Matilda up and said, "Do you want to help me cook up something for the big jack—*jerk* that just scared the daylights out of you?"

***

As Gideon healed, Matilda, Miri, and I pumped him full of healthy snacks between my shifts at the marina. I had more time now, having lost my second job. The closed sign on the door of The Crazy Conch had temporarily solved the problem of how to protect my friends from the demon.

Hex, having stolen my boss's old body, wasn't exactly employer of the year. My friends knew nothing about the paranormal world around them and would have been in constant danger at work. When I called to check on her, Ada filled me in.

"No one even called to say we were closing," Ada sniffled. "Patsy acted so strange this past year. But now this! I don't know what to do." On the other end of the line, her voice broke. "I'm sorry. You don't need this right now. It's just—well, I'm lonely as hell, and miss you guys, and the fun we used to have working together at the diner. And Bert! Have you seen that miserable slacker around town? I even miss his terrible gas ... "

I almost laughed out loud at that. "Ada, I think I have just the job for you."

***

The next day, I finished work and once again boarded the *Black Widow* to check in on our fearless leader, who currently watched me with a thoughtful expression.

"Have you been practicing?" Gideon asked.

"Practicing what?"

"Your powers. During the battle on the yacht, you manifested a shield. I think it would be wise if you worked on controlling it."

"My shield ... ?"

The blue glow hovering over my skin was a shield?

"I *knew* it! What the hell kind of power *is* that? I've never heard of a Djinn having a shield!"

Gideon stared at me until my skin prickled. When he answered, the *I'm hiding something* vibe tagged along with his words.

"Djinn wield many powers, some unknown even to me. Each one manifests depending on the family bloodline. Yours have, on the odd occasion, exhibited what is known as an *air shield*. The mechanics of it are unknown, but it is formidable—light as air, switched on and off with a thought, and completely impenetrable."

Before the words were out of his mouth, I bombarded him with questions.

"Why can't I call the thing back up? I've tried! I concentrate and nearly have a coronary holding my breath, but nothing happens."

Gideon looked down at the broth in his hands and finished it. Using his weaker arm, his hand shook with the effort. He placed the mug on the glass side table before speaking.

"You were under duress during the fight in Key West. Powers manifest in strange ways, especially without proper training. I know *Others* who lived well past maturity with no idea they had powers, only to have them appear during a high-stress situation."

"As a rule, family members develop a youth's budding skills. It is understandable that you cannot call the shield forth on command. Your father—*your training* never happened when it was prudent."

My face had gone pale, and Gideon frowned. With a sigh, he said, "Do you have any memories of expressing the air shield before the fight on the *Black Widow?*"

I thought about it, recalling that my eyes glowed white when Cain and Hex made me angry. Gideon, reading my mind, nodded.

"Yes, white eyes when angry is a common Djinn reaction. Some, like your father's, stay white. Now that you are fully mature, if you master the powers of your heritage, your own eyes may very well go silver and remain that way."

I bit my bottom lip and frowned. I wasn't sure I wanted to prance through life with headlights beaming from my face.

"How do I make the shield appear when I'm not pissed as hell about something?"

At my rough language, Gideon's eye twitched. "You must learn to control the magical energy flowing through your center. It is there, untapped."

"When Hex attacked your father's cabin in Tennessee, you were untrained. Then, when I took your memories, it is likely that you lost the ability to connect with your innermost powers. Without knowledge and training, it lay dormant until now. *You must train.*"

I glared at him, working my lips between my teeth. I wasn't prepared to enter another argument about what he did to me ten years ago in Knoxville. He had no right to take my memories. I wanted to accept that he had good intentions, but being homeless and adrift ripped giant holes in my soul. I wasn't sure I could forgive him. Not completely. If it hadn't been for Cal, I would still be dumpster diving.

"I know what you are thinking, Edaline. You must let it go. There is no way forward when you are constantly looking back."

I mumbled, "How convenient," but the words lacked starch. "So, who will train me then?" Our eyes locked in a challenge.

The fridge hummed and clicked, the tap in the kitchen dripped, and my heart thumped along with the quiet sounds in the room. Gideon held up his broken arm, his expression hedgy. "I am incapacitated. James will train you."

The big chicken.

CHAPTER 16

"Close your eyes, and forget about the peanut gallery." James cast a resigned look at Cal, Miri and Matilda, who sat on the sidelines waiting for the fireworks to start. We were in James' garage, which was surprisingly well-outfitted. You would be hard-pressed to find a piece of workout equipment he hadn't stashed in the large structure.

James stood facing me, and I mirrored his pose from a few paces away. I wore shorts and a muscle shirt, which felt like the right choice for this morning's inaugural *let's kick Eddi's ass* training session. Unfortunately, James had the temperature cranked, so I roasted even in my state of undress. Sweat inched its ticklish way down my butt crack, distracting the hell out of me. James, on the other hand, looked cool as a cucumber.

I closed my eyes and listened to his instructions. "Now, picture something that makes you feel connected to yourself."

My eyes shot open, and I laughed. "Ok. What the hell does that even mean, James? Connected *how?*"

James sighed and rolled his shoulders. "Think of people who meditate. They slow their breathing and think of a meadow, a rolling blue ocean, or something that makes them feel calm and centered. To tap into your powers, which are dormant inside of you—" He looked at my face. "Are you listening?"

I wasn't, actually. I stared at Matilda, who watched the entire proceedings with such focus that she began to mist over. My God, having your ass kicked by an eight-year-old sucked. A hand appeared in front of my face, and the fingers snapped. "Pay attention, Edaline."

I looked back and, for the first time, experienced the shocking sight of James looking annoyed—at me. That was a first. I wondered whether he was the kind to stay calm until he detonated, went on a killing spree, and ended the world.

"OK, sorry. It's just that Matilda over there is showing off." The soft giggle behind me teased a smile to James' lips.

James darted a look her way as he pointed. "Exactly. Do what she just did. Think inward, Eddi. You have to connect with yourself. Picture something that makes you angry, if it helps. When you find something that works, you will use that every single time until calling on your power becomes second nature."

I closed my eyes again. My brain ticked through a bunch of things that were *me*. Sarcasm. A short fuse. Impatience. And then it dawned on me. Anger was my number one emotion these days, so I concentrated on that. I closed my eyes and frowned, grunted, tensed my neck, and clenched my fists while I growled. Nothing.

I opened my eyes, and James laughed. I lunged forward and gave him a playful slap.

"What the hell! Learning is hard enough without you making fun of me!" I looked ridiculous, and I knew it.

"You aren't trying to have a baby, Edaline," Cal giggled. Without looking, I shot him the finger over my shoulder.

Miri shrieked with laughter. "I think she needs a laxative!"

"Shut it, or I'll come over there, and you'll both need a stretcher." I cast a suspicious look at Miri, who was very quiet this morning. I frowned. My mind drifted past the notion that we may have a traitor, but just as quickly, I dismissed it. There was no way Miri would turn against us.

A hand appeared, and the snapping fingers brought me back to James' sweltering garage. "I can do this all day, Edaline. Get it together." The frustration on his face was plain to see. "You can't get anywhere if you don't try. Don't worry about making a mistake. There are no mistakes. There's practice, and there's slacking. Dedicate yourself, and everything will come together."

Closing my eyes, I let out a long sigh, then plunged deeper into my head. I needed something that made me angry. The first thing that came to mind was Cain. The vampire had hurt me in too many ways to count. I recalled the night he'd beaten me half to death, dumped chum into my pants, and threw me overboard. *At night.* Anger lanced through me as I pictured his leering face—

Matilda gasped, and my eyes snapped open. I lifted my arm, stared at the glowing film that coated it and smiled. Holding up my hand, I turned it, closely examining the air shield for the first time. I had taken on a powder blue glow, soft and opaque, the details of my skin obvious beneath it. I raised my hand and sniffed, the faint smell of ozone tingling in my nostrils. I touched my nose, and the shield felt like a firm water balloon.

My eyes changed focus, and through my fingers, James beamed.

"Well done, Eddi. Now let's see if you can hold it."

Out of nowhere, a wooden sword slapped hard across my thigh, making me jump into the air with a yelp. I snarled and looked at James, who held out the handle of a practice sword. He shook it.

"Take it. No time like the present to see what you can do."

Rubbing my leg, I took the handle, stepped back and took a basic fighting stance. It had been a long time since I'd fought with anything other than my Bowie knife.

"OK, Edaline, let's start with something simple. The Oberhau."

As I raised my wooden practice sword before me, I saw my pink hands. No shield.

"What the f—" I glanced sideways at Cal, who had his hands over Matilda's ears.

"Hilarious, Cal."

James took a relaxed stance and lowered his wooden tip. "OK, back to square one. Rinse and repeat. You need to learn how to hold the air shield."

Impatient to get going, I pinched my eyes closed and dove into angry thoughts of Gideon, picturing his golden eyes beaming into my face as he stole my memories. I opened my eyes, and I glowed again.

Quickly, without taking my stance again, I dove at James, giving him a solid whack on the top of one shoulder. He winced.

"OW! That's fighting dirty." His lips twisted, and I cringed when his eyes rolled to silver momentarily.

"I like it," he said, then flicked the tip of his practice sword at me.

The session dragged on. At first, the air shield held until my thoughts drifted away from Cain or Hex. Gradually, I held it longer, but only with my anger front and center.

Every time James slapped me with that stupid sword, I got ticked again, and my shield glowed brighter. When it shone its brightest, I felt nothing except the hardest hits. If I lost focus, it dimmed, and I felt everything. James didn't hold back, and soon I felt like an old banana.

Panting, I stopped to wipe the sweat pouring from my chin. "What is this, James? Christmas? Why do you keep it so freaking hot in here?"

A strange look flickered across his face, then he shrugged. "I like it hot. Stop stalling." He lunged forward, giving me a mighty slap with his weapon. Rage flared, and prickles danced over my skin. I quickly learned that I sensed the rising of my shield without looking. That was good because James never allowed me to look down—*for an entire hour.*

My muscle shirt stuck to me by the time we finished, and sweat pooled in the crack of my butt. Cal had covered Matilda's ears at least seven or eight times. Miri zipped over, bringing a towel and dropping it into my hands.

"That's a healthy glow if I ever saw one," she tittered. As Matilda popped up and grabbed Cal's hand, we followed James to the stairs. Watching him jog up the steep incline, I grimaced at his irritating perkiness after over an hour of slapping me around.

That made me think about the meat. Even after our lengthy session, I hadn't a clue as to what sort of creature I followed into trouble.

***

The next day, I had a surprise knock on my door, bright and early. A little too early to be my new babysitter.

That situation was solved, thankfully, and I no longer had to worry about the neighbor nosing into my business.

Recognizing the knock, I opened the door, expecting to see Ronan. What I got was my Syreni male—and his mother.

"*Uhh*. Well! This is a surprise. Please, come in."

I settled Oriana on the couch, and my eyes shot to Ronan, whose expression was apologetic.

"I'm sorry, Eddi. We should have notified you. We came ashore to meet with Gideon."

As I hastily picked up Barbies, Oriana reached for my arm.

"Do not concern yourself, Eddi. We were unannounced. I am sorry for that." She looked around the room. "Is it possible to see—the child?"

"I guess. I mean, *of course.*"

I went to my bedroom door and tapped, then slipped inside. Matilda sat on the bed in her pajamas. She had a nightmare and crawled in with me last night. "Hey, sleepy head. I know it's early, but someone is here to see you. Are you ok with that?"

Matilda's eyes were wide, and she had a pillow tucked into her belly.

"You heard us talking?"

She nodded.

"Are you alright to see Oriana? Because if you aren't, we can ask her to return when you're more ready."

Matilda nodded her head, her teeth worrying her lip. She slid out from under the covers, stifled a yawn, and then tried to smooth her tousled hair.

"You're such a cutie in the morning. Have I told you that?"

Matilda stopped biting her lip and threw her arms around my thighs. I knelt down, bringing myself to her eye level, and gently grasped her shoulders.

Her eyes brimmed with tears. "I don't want her to take me away. I like it here."

"No one is taking you anywhere. Not unless you want to go. So don't you worry about that, OK?"

She nodded, dashed her tears away, and I followed her.

If I lived to be a thousand years old, I would never forget the look on Oriana's face when we walked into the living room.

She sucked in a sharp breath, one hand flying to cover her mouth while the other clenched against her shimmering emerald belly. Tears trucked right over those beautiful lashes and poured down her face. Delight and dismay warred there, and my heart ached.

Matilda stopped walking, and I bumped into her. Seeing the child's reaction, Oriana quickly got hold of herself and dashed the tears away.

"I'm sorry, little one. I didn't mean to frighten you. Meeting you is a joyful moment for me."

I gave Matilda a gentle nudge, and she moved to stand closer, her hands clasping her top. She stared at Ronan's mother, her lips tight.

"Do you know my name, child?"

Matilda nodded, then, in a small voice, said, "Oriana."

"Your name is Matilda, correct?"

She nodded again.

I felt for Ronan's mother, the awkwardness of the situation tripping her up. I took Matilda's hand and guided her to the chair across the sitting area. Plunking down, I pulled her onto my lap.

A pea soup of tension filled the room, my nerves jangling in the quiet. Oriana's eyes flicked greedily over Matilda; jealousy and a sudden desire to protect her flooded me.

Don't be ridiculous, Eddi. Her mother deserves to see her.

"Ronan has told me so many things about you, Matilda. I wanted to meet you in person. I remember when you visited me at the—*in Key West.* You were so little then. You've certainly grown."

Luckily, Matilda decided to open up and help out the awkward adults in the room.

"Yes. I remember." Her voice was quiet, her eyes glued on Ronan's mother. "You look much happier now." Matilda's fingers curled into her pyjamas.

"Hex told me you're my mother." Matilda's eyes looked over Oriana's beautiful red hair, luminescent eyes, and glittering legs, then the bare feet. Her visual examination ended with a long, steady look into Oriana's face, where she noticed the trembling chin.

"You have the same eyes as me. You're very pretty. Especially your hair. Just like a Barbie doll."

Oriana drew in a breath, then let it out slowly as she struggled for control. A tragic battle raged in her eyes as Ronan's soft voice whispered into my mind.

"I'm sorry I sprang this on you. Mother has been distraught since returning home. She is fixated on meeting Matilda. It was the only way to calm her—and since we were here already—"

"It's ok. It needed to happen. It might as well be today."

Oriana looked at me, her expression pained. "I am sorry about what happened to your breathing apparatus while you were visiting us at the *Shoal*. It has been dealt with."

"What did you do to Tara?" I wasn't sure I wanted the answer.

"She was banished from the *Shoal*. Permanently, this time. She will not get a chance to wheedle her way back in. Tara is now living at the main reef where she belongs."

I could handle that. As much as I disliked the Lionfish shifter, I wouldn't want to see anything bad happen to her.

Matilda listened intently to the conversation, her eyes darting back and forth between the three of us. Sliding from my lap, she walked over to stand before Ronan's mother. She reached up, taking a strand of Oriana's long, beautiful red hair in her fingers.

"Why is my hair a different color than yours if you're my mother?"

"You share the same color hair as your sister, Tabitha." Oriana smiled. "You are fortunate you did not get this fiery red. It comes with an equally hot temper."

Matilda let go of her hair and said, "Can I touch your legs?"

Oriana chuckled. "Yes, you may. They are very soft."

Matilda ran her hand over Oriana's knee and lower thigh, then made a soft sound.

"It's so soft. And slippery. But it's dry. Why is it slippery *and* dry? Why don't I have legs like that?"

Oriana said, "When we are out of the water, our skin dries and seals to stay safely on land for long periods. Our tail returns when we touch sea water and will it." She looked at me, her expression tight. "I suspect you do not have scaled legs like mine because you also resemble your sire. I understand he is a Djinn."

Matilda watched her talk, her head slightly cocked.

"Ronan showed me his tail. It changes so fast!" There was a pause, then Matilda said, "I have webbed feet. It's strange, but I like it. I can swim better when they stretch out." She curled her lip in a shy smile as she plucked at her pyjamas.

"I can move in a cloud. I got that from my father, I think. Maybe I could show you sometime."

Oriana's eyes met mine, and we both melted. I swear to God, this kid could defrost the polar ice caps.

CHAPTER 17

Oriana left with a radiant smile in place of the worried frown I'd come to expect since meeting her. Ronan stopped at the door and turned to me, leaning forward to place a chaste kiss on my lips. I heard him in my mind.

"Thank you, Eddi. As I hoped, meeting Matilda—the only good thing from all of this—helped my mother in ways you cannot imagine."

With a quick hug, he vowed to return, but as they headed to the street, sadness swept through me. His mother—*my God*—how hard would it be to know you had hundreds of children out there you would never meet? It boggled my mind. How did anyone heal from that?

Emotional issues were the theme of the day, because I had some of my own. Seeing Ronan standing in my apartment, but unable to touch him, ripped at my insides. It reminded me that I had no idea how we would blend our lives. Getting time together had been nearly impossible since our return from Key West. Before Ronan slipped through the door to the street, he looked back at me, his expression torn. Maybe I wasn't the only one struggling.

I felt a tug on my hand and looked down to see Matilda staring up at me. "You're going to be late for work," she said, her expression grave.

Smiling, I looked at my watch. "Thanks, kiddo. Ada will be here soon. Do you want some breakfast?"

A tiny voice from the corner startled me. "Breakfast? Yes, please! And quick, because I'm starving. You guys took forever to get that shit out of the way." Miri's Dream Camper rattled as she slammed the door. She stretched, and I covered my mouth to hide my laughter. She wore nothing but a Kleenex tucked around her Barbie-sized body like an oversized bath towel.

"Miri, you owe me a quarter," Matilda giggled. She looked up at me. "I'm getting rich on her bad words."

Miri shrieked, "WHAT!? No way. Excrement words get a pass, kid." She whizzed over to the countertop and plunked herself down on the edge. "Whatcha' makin, Edaline?"

"Shouldn't you be putting on clothes, Miri?"

She rolled her eyes. "I'm having a bath today. As soon as you leave."

The sprite sat on the counter, rubbing her stomach and flashing her eyelashes at me as she ran a tongue over her lips.

I growled at her and looked at my watch again. Where was Ada?

On cue, the street-level door slammed and Ada's brisk steps skipped up the stairwell to my apartment. Miri popped out of sight with a yawn, and I heard her ruffle through the air to the bathroom.

"Make it a bird bath. You're out of time!" I whisper-yelled after her.

Flinging the door open, I pulled my sixty-something, pink-haired co-worker into a bear hug. "I'm so glad to see you!" I chirped, pulling back to give her a look. Other than having a faint shadow beneath her eyes, Ada looked right as rain, her newly manicured nails sporting the cutest flamingos.

"Darlin', I'm happy to see you too. You have no idea how much I'm looking forward to hanging around with your boyfriend's little sister today. I can't wait to meet her. Where is she?"

I nearly choked when I heard my horrible excuse for an explanation roll from her lips. I mean, Matilda was Ronan's sister, so it wasn't like I lied. Ada peeked around me to where Matilda stood motionless, a *deer in the headlights* look on her face.

"Well, how about that!" Ada crowed. "You're bigger than I expected! And look at those bee-you-tee-ful golden locks!" In standard Ada form, she rushed forward, squatted down, and grabbed Matilda into a tight hug.

I watched that tiny face as Ada's fierce pats on the back made her jiggle. Matilda's expression went from petrified to begrudging to smiling in moments. Ada had that effect on most people.

"I'm hungry," Matilda said, shooting me a guilty look over Ada's shoulder.

"Well, sweet dumpling, I can do something about that right now. How about pancakes!" Ada jumped up and grabbed Matilda's hand, hustling her to the kitchen while shooing me off to work.

At the sound of the bathroom sink draining, I bit back a laugh. The fastest bath in history. I wasn't sure how the sprite would manage to get her breakfast without being seen, but I knew she'd find a way.

"I'll be back after work, Ada. Thank you so much for doing this for me." I looked down at Matilda and asked, "Are you going to be alright, kiddo?"

She nodded, her face solemn but with a touch of mischief lighting her eyes. She'd taken to Ada like a duck to water. Happy days.

***

When I walked into the shop at Davy Jones, Cal and Evan stood by the cash register, heads together and conversing deeply. Cal looked over his shoulder and cleared his throat, stepping back from the counter. Evan shot me a quick hello and headed out the door.

I looked at Cal and raised my eyebrows. He shrugged and said, "So, how's it going with Matilda? Did Ada babysit?"

"Yes, and it went great. Ada is a natural. They're having pancakes." I rubbed my stomach, and Cal rolled his eyes.

"You and food," he grinned. "Come on, I have an extra bagel for you. You're so predictable."

It was busy, and the day flew by, a steady stream of customers in and out of the shop. At the end of the day, I hummed as I headed to the docks and grabbed a kayak. I passed Cal and Evan, their heads together as they organized the life vests. I was so happy to see him spending time with someone he seemed attracted to. Now, we just had to find a way for him to find love without dying for it.

I tied off to the swim deck on the Black Widow, my happy buzz making everything around me look brighter, the tropical colors popping as I glanced up and down the channel. I never tired of sand, palm trees, and that vibrant aquamarine.

As I marched up the stairs to check on Mr. Grumpy Pants, I thought about Matilda. Who was her father? The question had plagued me ever since we put things together.

When I crested the stairs, I found Gideon standing on the coffee table. It groaned and creaked under his heavy muscular frame and the enormous golden longsword in his hand.

"What the hell are you doing!?"

"What does it look like I'm doing?" Gideon swung the sword using his good arm, slowly rotating it while using the height of the table to give him extra range on each stroke. He stretched his arm up, then down, like some sort of swordsman's yoga. The sword gleamed in the indirect light that filtered from beyond the overhang. Sweat rolled down his torso, his arm shaking slightly at the effort.

"Well, the good arm looks better. How's it going with the *other* one?"

The Gryphon had recently removed his bandages, a scab on his right temple the only sign of his head injury.

I constantly teased him about *having a dent*, which made him snarl. Thankfully, as he told me long ago outside of Knoxville, he was hard to kill.

Watching the Gryphon stretch while he completely ignored me, I couldn't help but worry about the weak arm clamped across his stomach.

"It's going great, Gideon. Just fine. Thank you for asking. And how was your day, darling?"

Gideon kept his eyes up, the sword making a whooping noise as he went faster, the shimmering blade slicing through the air.

"Stand back unless you want a haircut, Edaline." His breathing heavy, the sweat poured down Gideon's torso, large veins bulging in his now pumped-up forearm.

I laughed, tapping my finger on my lips. "So ... what about the other side?"

Gideon's growl rained down on me, but he didn't stop.

"No, seriously—let's see it. Maybe I can help."

The sword stopped rotating, and the tip tapped down on the carpet, Gideon gleaming with sweat. He was out of breath but trying not to show it.

When I raised an eyebrow in challenge, he passed the sword over to his injured right side. His grip was knuckle white as he slowly raised his arm. Carefully, he did one complete circuit, his face paling at the height of his arc.

I watched him do five rotations before I took pity on him. His sallow complexion and trembling muscles made me feel like a first-rate bitch.

"OK, great. Looks much better. I have something I need to talk to you about. Are you ready for a break?"

My reward for being nice was an imperious look down the end of his regal nose. Then he hopped onto the carpet without wincing and laid his sword on the loveseat. The same loveseat that Cal and I sat on the day we battled Hex. I shivered and wondered if I'd ever feel comfortable on this yacht.

When Gideon toweled off and grabbed himself something from the fridge, my reward for not getting lippy was a cold bottle of Corona. As Gideon handed it to me, he smiled—an *actual smile.*

"Where's the lime? Lemon? Whatever, I'm not fussy."

No answer, the corners of his mouth twitching ever so slightly. Gideon definitely felt better.

As he settled himself into the leather chair like a King on his throne, he did that thing where he stopped moving and became eerily still. His eyes bored into me, a tingle starting between my ears.

I growled under my breath, conjuring up an image of Mr. Potato Head, wearing his cowboy hat and a pink thong, his butt hanging out as he wiggled it in circles.

"Get out of my head or he's doing a porno just for you, Big Bird."

Gideon laughed, his power disappearing from between my ears as he waved for me to get on with the reason for my visit.

"Uh, well, OK. So here's the thing. Matilda is half Djinn. I've been wondering who her father is. I only know one person to ask. *YOU.*"

"And just how do you think I would know that, Edaline? My crystal ball?"

"Cut the crap, Gideon. You know exactly what's going on most of the time. If you don't know for certain, then you have a hunch."

"That information is none of your concern."

"Enough with the posturing, Gideon. I've been thinking, and I decided that if you want my help, you're going to answer my questions and tell me what you know."

At his stoic frown, my eyes misted over, and my voice caught. "My father, Gideon. Don't you get it? He could be alive. Not knowing if he's up in Charleston is killing me. I've been alone for so long. What if my father—*is Matilda my sister!?*" My voice broke, my chin quivering as I struggled to contain tears.

I didn't know if his workout wore him out, or if he felt bad about the tears, but Gideon sighed. I nearly fell off my chair when he answered.

"I cannot confirm the identities of the two Djinn at this time. But we now know the lab's location. My sources have confirmed it is across from Fort Sumter, on the water. James and I have shifters staking out the facility. The Manticore may have enslaved the Djinn she holds there using the Talisman of Tenebris."

I stared, gawking at his stoney expression. I forgot to breathe for a minute. The room was eerily silent; the only sign of life was the sound of some distant pelicans fighting over a fish.

He answered me. He actually answered me.

"And? What is this Talisman of ... whatever you said." When he answered again, I bit back a triumphant smile.

"It is a powerful piece of black basalt, chipped from an Egyptian artifact in the sixteenth century BC—the pillar of Tenebris." At my blank look, he added, "A ten-foot-tall volcanic rock pillar—inscribed with magical laws crafted by the Immortal Gods. It carries the code that all their Immortalis children must live by. Well, all of their children except for Hex, apparently."

Well, now, that was a mouthful.

Gideon looked out the window. "I was young, then. Hex broke into the palace in Karnak and hacked off a chunk from the top of the pillar." He snarled. "Even then, she was up to no good. She covered her tracks well after the theft. We have been trying to find and destroy the Talismans ever since."

I whipped out my phone and Googled it. Sure enough, the top of the pillar was a very rough triangle.

"It used to be square," he snapped.

Even now, the flying feline couldn't resist invading my thoughts. Gideon growled when Mr. Potato Head stuck one finger into the strap of his thong, his eyebrows wiggling in threat. At the expression on the Enforcer's face, I laughed.

"So let me get this straight. Hex was in Egypt. She broke into a palace. She cut off a chunk and disappeared. Is that about right?"

"Yes. Hex had the hunk of basalt split into pieces and used them to create ten Talismans. The power of our magical laws still resides in these specimens, but she has corrupted them through blood magic. They now hold the power to enslave a Djinn."

"You've got to be kidding me." At his words, the blood drained from my face.

Gideon shook his head. "All but three have been found and destroyed. Hex has them." He saw my wheels turning and saved me the trouble. "One Talisman can imprison the will of a single Djinn. She has three."

I stared at him, mulling over his words. Like a bug in flypaper, I froze on the whole *Hex and Gideon were youngsters during antiquity—thing.* I mean, I knew they weren't Immortal, but I guess *Immortalis* lived a freaking long time. It didn't hit home until this moment what that meant. Eventually, the cogs grinding in my head came to a screeching halt, and I looked up at him.

"How do they work?"

"I cannot share that information; you do not need to know it."

Why was I not surprised? I took another tack.

"So, Hex enslaved Galahad with this Talisman of Tenebris. That's how she gets him to do terrible things."

Gideon nodded.

"So, is it permanent? Are they stuck with that monstrous bitch for all of eternity?"

Gideon nodded. "Unless we break the blood magic oath connected to the Talisman, or she dies. That is the only way."

"Holy shit." I ran my fingers through my bangs, pulling on them. "This is horrible."

As Gideon watched me, a thunderbolt of understanding tore through my mind. Nausea rolled as my face flushed with heat, almost pulling my lunch and one slightly warm corona from my guts.

"She's trying to enslave me."

Gideon's eyes glimmered with a ferocious light. He nodded. "She is, indeed."

"I don't understand. Why? What use could I possibly be to her? It's not like I have great powers or anything." I stared into Gideon's face, my eyes searching for the secret hidden behind his eyes.

"For the love of God, Gideon. This is my life. You owe me the truth!"

To my surprise, that elicited a nod, but he wouldn't look at me. He stared out the shaded window at the bay.

"When you were sixteen, and I had to drop you off on the highway—"

"Listen. Let's get this straight, Enforcer. You didn't *have* to do anything. You *could* have done everything differently. You have no idea the hell I went through!"

Gideon shook his head. I may have imagined it, but I swore I saw his eyes mist over. And then it was gone, and he glared at me again.

"You don't understand. Hex was everywhere. She planned this thing for decades. You were but a cog in a huge machine of moving parts. I had no choice. You don't believe me, but your random disappearance was hard to trace. Hiding you safely in the human world was the best I could do at the time."

He stared into my eyes, probing my mind while he had his say. I was so mad I didn't even try to stop him.

"I didn't *want* to do it, Edaline. Circumstances forced my hand. But don't for one minute think that I *enjoyed* it."

"Fuck, Gideon! Did you ever come and check on me? See where they took me? Follow my progress? I bet you didn't, did you?"

Gideon looked down into his lap.

"Yeah, didn't think so."

A strange light shone in his eyes when he finally looked at me. "Would it help if I apologized, Edaline? Because fine, you have my humblest apologies. I lived with the horrible burden of my actions for the last ten years. Better?"

I scowled, my arms slipping together tightly as I crossed them and tried to decide if he was sincere, or yanking my chain.

"You have no idea what goes on around you. This world you live in is treacherous. You have but scratched the surface of what transpires in the shadows under your very nose. Some things I cannot—no, I WILL NOT share with you. It is not your concern. I am here now and *will* do my best to keep you safe. And if you can't accept that, you know where the door is. I will gladly release you from your assistance in this matter."

Well, that was an interesting tack. I should have let it rest, but like a hound with a bone, I went right back to digging. "So why does Hex want me so badly? What am I to her?"

An entire feature film played behind Gideon's eyes as he contemplated how to answer. At that moment, there was no doubt in my mind that he held all the pieces of the puzzle. After a long, tense silence, he answered.

"You are the key to producing an army of willing slaves. If Hex manages to snare you, she will own you—and your children. Every single one. *Forever.*"

CHAPTER 18

We were almost ready. The *Black Widow* swallowed supplies all day, and Gideon called a meeting that night. We had two days left to prepare. Gideon filled us in on final details.

"The Charleston facility houses at least fifty properly conditioned, well-trained fighters. We don't have exact numbers. We have confirmed that, for over two decades, the demon has bred Syreni-Djinn hybrids using eggs harvested from Syreni females."

Gideon glanced at where Ronan and I stood, and added, "There was another Syreni Doyenne before Oriana—the mother of the Charleston hybrids. Embryos were routinely flushed and frozen in a cryo chamber; estimates are 10 eggs per cycle. We are unsure of the identity of the first Djinn sire, but have confirmed that it was, indeed, a Djinn."

Watching Ronan, Gideon's eyes flicked briefly to Bacchus as he said, "Frozen embryos only last ten years, which is why Cain needed Oriana ..." His gaze jerked back to Ronan, whose eyes glowed a solid yellow. At the squeeze of my hand, they faded to green again and our Enforcer continued.

"We are still searching for the facilities where the youngsters are being raised. We WILL find them. Doing the math, there may be as many as twenty four hundred hybrid children waiting in the wings to join Hex's army when the time comes."

There was an audible gasp from Tabitha, but Bacchus and Ronan snarled, low and menacing. The vibrations tingled along my fingertips and all the way to my elbow. I squeezed his hand, and Ronan quieted, his eyes an unnerving chartreuse.

Gideon took a deep breath, and looked at me. "Djinn females are incredibly rare. One in a thousand. If Hex ever succeeded in wielding an army of hybrids raised from a Djinn mother line—"

Gideon's voice trailed off as he glanced sideways at James, whose eyes flashed that strange silver again as he looked straight at me and spoke.

"A Djinn mother line would give Hex complete control over her army. The Talisman would guarantee total compliance." James' lips were a tight line. "Counting Galahad, Hex has three Djinn. But we have no idea whether all three are bound. If there is an unused Talisman—"

At James' words, Gideon's lips turned down at the corners. He glanced at Bacchus and Tabitha, who only knew that James was *Other*, both of them unaware of his Sovereign status.

"James has put himself in grave danger, several times, against my wishes. Twice he was drugged while trying to gather information. It was a miracle he wasn't captured right alongside Edaline."

When James turned to the Enforcer, his expression harsh, I resisted the urge to gawk. Bacchus and Tabitha's eyes bounced around the room, aware that something was up—but not what.

"We don't have the luxury of me sitting idle, Gideon. It was a calculated risk." James stared Gideon down, his face like granite. "I wasn't captured. And here I am. *With information.*" He crossed his arms and raised a brow at Gideon as if daring him to argue. "Mission accomplished."

Breaking eye contact, Gideon grumbled. "As I was saying, there was some important intelligence gleaned from James' short time on the *Black Widow.*"

Tension coiled like a serpent in my gut. I knew it. Anger surged at the knowledge that even now, important information was denied us even as we struggled to help. Reading my mind, Gideon turned to me, his expression troubled.

"They are holding Edaline's father Ezen in Charleston. Your father, as far as we know, is still alive."

Between one heartbeat and the next, the blood in my veins turned to sludge, my mind straining to absorb his words.

My father. Alive? After all these years. In Charleston!?

"He's alive. My father isn't dead?" The only reason my quiet voice registered was that the room had gone silent, every eye on me.

Gideon nodded, his eyes glittering. "One of my spies has, at great risk, infiltrated the compound in cloaked form. She has visited Hex's cells. I must caution you, Ezen is not well, Edaline. There are no guarantees we will get there in time to save him."

I tried to swallow, but my throat turned to dust. With a head suddenly stuffed with cotton, all sounds came as if from a distance. My lips were a perfect match for my numb fingers as Ronan reached down to grab my arms. Effortlessly, he pulled me onto his lap and whispered into my ear, "This is wonderful news. Now breathe."

Gideon continued, all eyes turning to the Enforcer. My father was alive. ALIVE! I didn't know whether to laugh, cry, rage, or empty the contents of my stomach.

Resting against Ronan's chest, I followed the steady beat of his heart and let his incredible warmth soothe me as he rubbed my back. Then, I allowed the conversation back in, Gideon's words muffled by the shock ebbing from my system.

"We will pay Hex a little visit in Charleston. We are taking everyone. And we're going to end this, once and for all." Gideon looked at James, and with a wicked smile, he said, "This time, we have backup."

The meeting lasted an hour, with Gideon filling the gaps for everyone. I had already heard most of it. I say *most* because I knew the Gryphon loved his secrets.

As it turned out, the Talisman of Tenebris was a stylized black statue of an Arabian stallion that fit in one hand. If we wanted to free the enslaved Djinn, we had to take out her fighters, then either kill Hex or break the blood magic oath—*thing*. No one mentioned how to do that, of course. Minor details.

After the meeting broke up, Cal and I sat on the dock with Ronan and his siblings as we quietly discussed the plans Gideon had outlined. I thought of nothing but my father.

The idea that a malignant being like Hex had kept him prisoner—I couldn't think about it. Every time I did I started to glow so brightly that Cal nearly had a heart attack, worried that someone would see me. Ronan cradled me in his arms, pressing encouraging kisses to my hair. Bacchus and Tabitha bobbed in the water, watching us.

My father was alive. And so close I could be there in one day. To take him away. To see him again. It was almost too much to fathom. I could barely contain myself, because deep down, I feared we were already too late.

Gideon and James were optimistic, but we wouldn't storm an undefended laboratory. Hex had fifty musclebound lab rats at her beck and call, waiting to take us down—on their home turf.

There had been no sign of the Manticore since our battle in Key West, but that didn't mean she wasn't out there, healed and ready to give us another dose of pain.

"Cal, do you think the other Djinn could be Oliver? I mean, Phoebe did say he disappeared eight years ago. Maybe Hex found him and forced him into her service. Djinn are so rare..."

"I thought of that," he frowned. "I asked Gideon if we could bring Phoebe on board for this. She's a witch. We could surely find a use for her, even if only to crack and replace the wards on the *Black Widow*. He said no."

My fingernails poked into my palms. "Well, that's not ok with me. Is it ok with you?"

Cal shrugged.

A nasty grin on my face, I said, "We'll have to make sure she gets an invite, and not tell the flying furball."

The Syreni chuckled, but Cal's eyes went wide as he shook his head. "No way, Ed. We can't. He'll kill us. And I mean, actually kill us."

"No, he won't. He's full of shit. When was the last time you heard of him offing anyone? He didn't do anything to Tara, and she almost killed me in plain view of a bar full of humans."

Cal stared into the night sky, his fingers twisting in his lap. Finally, he looked at me, his face shocked.

"You know what? I've never heard of anyone, to be honest. Shifters disappear, and they blame Gideon, but I've never actually seen a beheading. You think all this time he's been *bluffing?*"

"That's exactly what I think. But you know, it pays to be smart about it. We don't have to go off all willy-nilly and get ourselves into trouble."

Ronan cocked his head. "You don't know for sure he won't retaliate. You must be careful, Eddi."

"I know. I will. I can leave all of you out of it, okay?"

Cal's brows knitted, but I was no fool. My friends wouldn't let me leave them out of anything—*I knew that.* Especially Cal. His protective instincts were strong where I was concerned.

Cal looked up at the moon, which was almost full. "I don't know whether to be excited or terrified."

"Yeah, well, we have to get Gideon up on his feet again. The sooner the better."

A restless anger swept over me. I pictured Hex, and what she had done to my father—and what she must have done to poor Patsy to be able to take over her body. My eyes burned, and I sensed my air shield as it whispered over my skin. I looked at my hand to see the silvery blue coating throbbing softly in time to my heartbeat. It reflected against Ronan's tanned skin.

"It's not just Gideon who needs to be stronger before we go. I've got work to do. When did James say he was off work tomorrow?"

***

I took a walk with Ronan before the Syreni left to go back to the *Shoal.* It was wonderful to see him again, and to feel my hand in his. The kisses weren't bad, either. My heart ached at the thought of him leaving, the petals of my little flower curling inward as he walked into the ocean and turned to wave goodbye.

After the ripples disappeared across the bay, Cal and I headed home, the moonlight easing my anxiety about being out at such a late hour.

When their ripples disappeared across the bay, Cal and I headed home, the moonlight easing my anxiety about being out at such a late hour. As we came upon the only stoplight before my road, we stopped to check out a traffic accident.

Two cruisers were parked against the curb, a three-car pileup blocking the center lanes. Other than the occasional car that moved over to pass the mess, it was late and there wasn't a soul to be seen. I turned to Cal, the blue and red flashes across his face making my stomach flip.

Where were the cops?

We moved closer to the nearest cruiser, listening to the radio. The dispatch was going non-stop, calling all available units to the junction of Roosevelt and Overseas Highway in Key West.

"All available units?" I whispered.

Cal shrugged, his eyes fixed on the accident.

"Cal, what the hell? That's the only bridge into Key West. Are they barricading the Island?"

My friend wasn't looking at me, he was staring at the pileup in the center of the road. Cal dropped his bike on the grass and motioned me to follow.

As we approached the tangled wreckage, the moans and groans made my skin crawl. Those weren't pained sounds.

In a small clearing in the center of the wreckage were five bodies writhing together in a sexual frenzy. Two were cops, their uniforms twisted, their pants down as they—

Open-mouthed, I looked at Cal, who was equally shocked at the scene before us. As I took in the signs of a massive struggle, I put two and two together.

The faces of both officers were covered in scratches, a taser lying smashed on the pavement nearby. The coils were deployed and lying in a tangle. Next to it lay one of the officer's firearms, still in the holster, the buckle broken in two.

A woman's purse lay open on the pavement, small colorful strips of paper tumbling out to scatter across the scene. Dozens of microdots ran in organized lines down each slip—hundreds of those innocent little slips fluttering everywhere. The ground. The air. All the way to the curb. Microdots, thousands of them, had come loose, fluttering free in the breeze like so much confetti. We hurried to back away.

Was this woman a dealer? Because that was definitely *Gush*. And there was a *shit-ton* of it.

Cal looked at me and pointed to his cheek. It wasn't until a slack-jawed officer looked my way that I saw the tiny microdots stuck to his face. Cal and I looked at each other, our eyes wide.

"What are the fucking chances *of that...!?*" Cal hissed.

The three females, who belonged to the cars, thrashed together in a sexual craze, the two male cops pounding into whichever woman they could get their hands on. As we watched, an officer reached out his tongue and sucked in another microdot, his eyes glazing over as he swallowed the papery orb, then toppled over on his side and grabbed for himself.

I looked at Cal. "Holy mother of God. How many did they swallow? We need to call an ambulance!"

The radio dispatch came back on, and over the roar of a truck racing past, we heard a distraught voice say, "They've breached the barriers. Calling all available units ... I repeat ... the barriers are breached ..."

I reached for my phone, but when I called nine one one, the line was busy. After ten minutes, we still hadn't gotten through. I called the hospital, and luckily, I reached someone, who agreed to send an ambulance.

"You'll have to be careful," I told the woman on the phone. "There's *Gush* all over the place, and the officers...." I swallowed. "They got an accidental dose, possibly an overdose. Please hurry."

Cal and I sat on the curb until the ambulance arrived, watching to ensure no one got into any worse trouble than they already were. I was cold, my stomach curdling as we sat on the curb listening to the frantic orgy going on between the wrecks.

"It's already moving north," Cal said, his eyes downcast. *"There's so much of it!* What are we going to do?"

Anger spread through me, the now familiar whisper of my air shield sending me a warning. The flashing lights coming up the highway were a relief, so I stood up and grabbed my bike, and we moved along. We needed to get to Charleston, and fast.

CHAPTER 19

~ FELIX ~

Jovi was in the infirmary for days, and when he finally returned to our dorm, he wouldn't speak to me. He lay on his bunk, refusing to talk. Curled in a ball, he faced the wall, only getting up for meals and modified practice. That meant glorified calisthenics for the Servus that Boris constantly injured.

I tried to cheer him up, but it didn't work. Something was different about my friend after his beating. He seemed—*broken*.

"Come on, buddy. It's Sunday. You know what that means." I waggled my eyebrows, but there was no one to see. Jovi faced the wall.

"You won't even get up for smoked salmon bites? They're your favorite!"

"Go away, Felix. I want to sleep."

"That's all you've done the last few days. Come on. Let's go and see if we can get you some of your favorite food, my friend."

Jovi groaned and pulled the pillow over his head.

"Come on, what's wrong? You can tell me."

Jovi threw the pillow off the bed and flipped over, his face like thunder. "You want to know what's wrong? I'll tell you. Every day we swallow their bullshit. Give them nectar. Sperm. Fighters. And what do we get?"

My eyes wide, I stuttered, "We get to fight for our country! Protect humans from their attackers. It's a noble cause—you know that!"

He looked at me, his face falling. "Do you believe that? Do you think killing an innocent human being every Friday is *helping*? Where do our collections go, Felix? How is it that Stephen can strut around, blasting whomever he wants with that stun gun of his? Does that sound fair to you? And what about Axel? I'm starting to think he's the only one who really knows what's going on."

I laughed. "Axel is traumatized—the wild Syreni tortured him for years! You know that!"

Jovi scoffed. "You're dumber than I thought, Felix. Give your head a shake. Why would Axel fight so hard? And if he's been *rescued*, and he's still unhappy, why don't they just let him go free? I've been in the library, reading. To me, it sounds like they're breeding us like a bunch of livestock."

I hesitated. My friend was smart, and I usually listened to what he had to say. I reached down and picked up his pillow, then stood and took it to him. I had an idea.

***

"Just for the record, if we get caught, this was your idea, Jovi."

My friend responded with a quiet laugh as we casually strolled past the Argenti leaning outside the door of the barracks. I ignored him completely, just as I would on any other day. When we reached the courtyard, Jovi poked me, and I stood up straighter, the two of us pretending to chat as we headed over to the library together.

Once through the library doors, we hot-footed it as quietly as we could through the foyer. A long wooden table and chairs were placed on each side of the spacious entrance, but we headed down the long aisles of the stacks which started at the back of the lobby. A modest but well-stocked library, muted light from the windows and the well-conditioned air made this a sanctuary for any Servus like my friend, who enjoyed reading.

Jovi always complained that the books were bland and one-sided; I'd never know if that were true. I didn't like to read, preferring to leach information from the sharp mind of my friend.

Reaching the end of the main aisle, we turned right. Jovi's eyes darted back the way we came to ensure no one watched our route. Instead of heading back up the next row of books, we crossed straight into a hallway exiting behind the stacks and followed it all the way to the end.

There was a door there. One frequently used by lab personnel, judging by the worn handle. Jovi, who spent plenty of time in the library, had watched countless Argenti using this corridor. They often carried tall, narrow containers marked with what Jovi said was the dry ice symbol: a square on its end, and long black stripes on the top half.

"I think they keep Axel down here." Jovi's eyes bulged with excitement, my own pulse racing with the knowledge that if we got caught, there would be pain. Or worse.

The door was locked. Looking back at me, my friend smiled, then with a clench of his teeth, he gave the handle a sharp twist. Metal snapped, and the knob turned easily in his hand. In a flash, we were through, the door closing with a snick behind us. The landing was dark, but we saw well enough to find the stairs, heading down them quickly and quietly.

At the bottom, we heard voices coming from one of the two corridors stretching out before us. We ducked behind a skid of supplies in time to avoid the two guards strolling past.

We headed down the darker passage of the two, the hall the guards had just left. It seemed the logical choice. My skin prickled with a combination of fear and excitement as we trotted down the corridor.

It opened into a room filled with stainless shelves and cabinets full of supplies. There was an elevator in one corner, and the stark white walls made me nervous for some reason. Jovi poked me, and I looked where he pointed.

Axel's chair. It was pushed against the wall, an assortment of vicious looking tools organized neatly on a rolling cart beside it. A tall canister sat on the counter, with the sticker Jovi had described.

"Dry Ice?" I hissed. Jovi nodded, raising his finger to his lips and pointing at the floor. Splatters of blood covered the space around the chair, each droplet a tiny dot in a galaxy of crimson. Shackles hung from a bolt in the ceiling, and a whip hung on the wall. On a tray lined shelf, there were metal clips, pieces of chain, and a few large paddles. That wasn't all, though.

The counter behind the chair held an assortment of ropes and leather face masks laid out neatly in a row. Strange objects that were long and smooth and a variety of pretty colors soaked in a tray of soapy water. Some were fat, and some were thin, and some were cone shaped.

I opened my mouth, but Jovi slapped a hand over it, his eyes rolling at a large metal mask in the shape of a human head tucked away in a glass cupboard. It was two pieces held together by clamps. There were small eye holes, and a large, padded opening at the mouth. Bile choked me.

Jovi grabbed my arm and nodded in the direction we were going.

It took no time to reach the end of the corridor, which had three doors facing into it. The thick plexiglass window panels, large and webbed with inner wire, were solid except for a small shelf and center slot large enough to fit a food tray. We had found Axel's quarters.

The first small room held the irate Syreni, his full beard and thick arms making him resemble an ornery grizzly bear. Axel looked up to see us peering through the window at him. A rumbling snarl filled the air, startling me. Rising to his feet, the Syreni ran at the door, slamming both fists against it like a battering ram. The metal frame rattled under the pressure.

"*Shh!*" Jovi hissed. "For the love of God, shut up, or you'll alert the guards."

Axel's chest rose and fell like a bellows, his teeth grating together hard enough to hear the enamel scrape. Two fine points poked from beneath his upper lip, and his eyes flickered between yellow and brown as he glared at us through the window.

"What do you want, you Servus scum?"

That got my back up. Keeping my voice low, I growled, "Hey now. That's not necessary. We're here because we have some ... *questions*."

Axel rolled his eyes and turned, his hulking frame thumping back to a pallet in the corner. He picked up his food tray from the bunk and grabbed the raw fish from it, jamming it into his mouth. "Go away, mindless little minnows. You're of no use to me."

The Syreni's dark blue skins were dull, his once tanned torso now pale and peeling. For all his bluster, the male was not well. I looked at Jovi and shrugged.

My friend was made of sterner stuff than me. "Axel, I know the truth. Well, I suspect I do. I want you to confirm it."

The hulking male stopped chewing, spitting a wad of fish bones onto his tray.

"Do you, now?"

His long reddish-brown hair swayed as his head cocked toward us. Flinging the tray down with a clatter, he stomped back to the door, his eyes snapping with hatred.

"You're not very clever, are you? You've been under her boot for what, *twenty years?*" His mocking tone made me bristle.

Axel leaned forward, his face inches from mine, the glass the only barrier between us. His hazel eyes flicked over me with searing intensity, his voice lowering to a quiet but deadly tone.

"I listen. I watch. I've been here three months—and I know the sickening truth about this place. *What's your excuse, you Servus twat?*"

He snapped his teeth at me, then stormed back to the tray lying upside down on the floor. Picking it up, he hurled it against the wall, shattering it into pieces.

"How's this for a story? Your boss is a cock-sucking demon, and *you* butt-kissing little guppies are a bunch of half-breed spawn stolen from the womb of a Syreni Doyenne."

He curled his lip, his eyes flickering to solid gold. "You aren't fit to carry one drop of that blood, and never will be."

He spat out a curse and bent down to pick up a jagged piece of the tray, holding it up to his face, his massive hand flexing until a drop of blood tracked along his wrist. The narrowed six-inch edge slowly turned toward where we stood. Axel pointed it at us and laughed, the sound harsh and grating.

"One of those two Djinn across the way might be your daddy. Why don't you go ask *them* for advice?"

Muttering an unintelligible curse, he bent over and slipped the makeshift weapon beneath the mattress before flopping down and rolling to face the wall.

My scalp prickled, my head swimming with the Syreni's words. A Demon? A Djinn father? A breeding farm—*Doyenne?* For a moment, the darkness swam around me in a confusing muddle. Rubbery legs made me consider sliding down the wall to sit on the floor.

I looked at Jovi. His wide eyes were already focused on the door across the corridor, tucked into a small shadowy vestibule. As one, we turned and padded over, our faces filling the window.

On a cot in the farthest corner of the tiny room lay an emaciated creature, which, according to Axel, was a Djinn. He appeared to be old and in terrible condition. With both sunken eyes closed and one arm hanging from the bunk, his chest rose and fell with labored breaths. A rack of protruding ribs pressed upward against the loose skin of his abdomen. Dirty bare feet twitched as if dreaming. He made no sound other than his thin gasps for air.

I smelled something and looked down to see a food tray still resting on the opposite side of the slide-through shelf. A hard biscuit, a pile of unidentifiable slop, and a glass of water were untouched. I watched a fly buzzing across the surface of the water glass, and my stomach lurched—

"He won't hear you. He's been unconscious for two days now."

I yelped, bumping Jovi as we whirled to face the third door, which sat at the end of the hall with a clear view of the corridor. Pressed against the plexiglass, another white-haired male watched us from the shadows.

His pale face pressed against the window; his upper lip curled back to flatten on the pane. It called to mind a long pink snail, a trail of saliva streaking the filthy glass. The male's eyes glittered with a strange light, his silver irises flashing in the darkness.

"Hey, kids. Coming to check out the breeding shed?" The Djinn leaned back, his lips twisting into a smile. Athletic, if a bit thin, he was a handsome male with eyes brighter than the Argenti on the compound. I let out the breath I held, knowing I was safe on this side of the door.

Raising both forearms, the Djinn leaned them against the sides of the window, his white skin spreading across the reinforced glass. He leered at us, his eyes keenly flickering over our chests and scaled legs as he snickered softly to himself. Wild eyes peered out from beneath dark, sculpted eyebrows. I shuddered at the sudden realization that bad things would happen if he ever got loose.

"You can call me Oliver." He cocked his head. "Stud, if you prefer." Then, he laughed, a cold sound that matched the icy, predatory eyes now glued to us.

He leaned forward again, pressing his forehead against the pane, the roll of his head adding another smear to the glass. "He's in sorry shape, our little Ezen. Spent all of his life force resisting the demon. *SUCKER!*"

His shout made me flinch, and Jovi grabbed my arm. He was as unsettled as I was at this ... whatever *this* was.

The Djinn's eyes widened as he hissed, spit spotting the door as, in a singsong voice, he whispered, *"Hells bells, ten years fighting spells, and now he's a rotting shell..."* The Djinn's hums trailed off before he burst out laughing.

"She's a mighty hard one to resist, our *Benefactor*. It hurts like a *BITCH!*" He bellowed the word, then pulled back, slammed his head on the glass with a rattle, then pressed his bloodied forehead against the window. Pink added another layer to the streaks already there.

His soft giggle made my skin crawl. "Oh, I'd kill the demonic bitch, alright. If it wasn't for the fucking horse. Gets me every time." He cackled, his eyes rolling in his head.

Jovi grabbed my hand and pulled me back down the hall. The tromp of approaching boots spurred us to action, the two of us skittering away as quickly as we could manage without making a sound.

As we neared the end of the darkened corridor, I looked back. Two white orbs penetrated the shadowed passage, eerily following our progress until we hit the stairs and bolted to safety.

We made it into the library hallway where I took a gasping breath.

"That was intense. What the hell is going on here, Jovi?"

He wasn't listening. His sharp eyes peered toward the library, and he cocked his head. "Did you hear that?"

Jovi hissed and grabbed my arm, pulling me behind a planter. As we watched, the door of a room down the hall opened, and one of the vampire guards stepped out.

Or, *stumbled* out. Laughing quietly to himself, he wiped a sloppy hand across his gasping mouth. Breathing heavily through his nose, his pants undone, his erect shaft jutting out, the vampire wove drunkenly down the hall. Falling against the wall a few times, he finally overcompensated and landed on his ass, his cock pointing straight up. The vampire looked down with a hearty laugh, then folded himself back inside his pants with a pained hiss and zipped up. He struggled to his feet and disappeared around the corner.

Jovi and I exchanged a look, then I followed my friend down the hallway toward the stacks. Halfway there, he stopped at the room beside Stephen's office.

"Shh." Jovi grabbed the latch and silently slid the bolt across and opened the door.

Humans. At least ten were sprawled across the vinyl-padded floor of the room. They were naked, moaning, and their eyes were glazed over with a white film. Every one of them was covered in puncture marks—like a room full of hairless pincushions. The vampires had been feeding on them. *And worse.*

How long they had been here was anyone's guess. A hose on a spring hung from the ceiling. It looked like it was designed for washing down work areas. The thought made me queasy.

High on the wall, a gray metal box with a glass cover held small vials with clear liquid inside, and packages of syringes. I wanted to look closer, but Jovi held me back. He opened the door a bit wider, and the light filtering through illuminated exactly what went on in this room.

The humans writhed in a ball of twisting arms and legs. Slick sounds filled the air as they slammed into each other, their slapping and choking sounds punctuated by grunts and groans. They had not a lick of sense in their actions—three males on one female, or males on males—it didn't matter.

I yanked the door shut, gulping for air.

"Jovi. My God—"

My friend slid the bolt back, and we hustled down the hallway to safety.

CHAPTER 20

"Harder. Harder! Oh, baby!"

Glaring at Mr. Darcy, I yelled, "Shut up, you stupid bird. I'm concentrating!"

Gideon was babysitting for a change. Well, *training* me. Same thing.

After we told James about our trip home and the accident with the drug dealer, the Sovereign headed to Key West to get eyes on what was happening down there. So, for our last two days, Gideon would work on my flying.

Judging by the frown that greeted me upon arrival, the Gryphon was an unwilling participant. And let's just say he didn't have James' patience. Add his blood-thirsty parrot into the mix, and I was getting angry.

"Edaline, if you aren't going to concentrate, we should quit for the day."

Taking a page out of the Gideon handbook, I ignored him and his damn parrot, bending my knees and closing my eyes. There were no issues with finding my anger today. The idea was to call up my power and fly—or die trying.

I wobbled, nearly toppling from the railing into the black water of the bay. Naturally, flying wasn't something I could practice in broad daylight. I shuddered to think what might be swimming around under the surface, waiting for a midnight snack.

"Now, what were you saying, Gideon?"

He grumbled, the low growl percolating from somewhere hollow.

"Close your eyes. Pull on your power, imagine something lighter than air, and then step off the railing."

"What? That doesn't sound right. I'm not jumping overboard because you have a sick sense of humor. Why can't we do this on the grass?"

"Because if you don't have air beneath you, you won't have any reason to lift off. This will work, trust me." His eyes sparkled with mischief.

I sighed. Thinking about Cain's compulsions, I immediately felt my blood pressure rise. Heat whispered over my skin. Concentrating, I thought of light things as Gideon instructed.

"Will feathers and bubbles work? Maybe I should picture your brain. That's light enough."

Gideon rumbled an answer, but it sounded suspiciously like laughter. I lifted my foot to step off the railing when a large boot planted itself in my ass and pushed.

Tumbling from my perch with a shriek, I rotated end over end until crashing into the water twenty feet below. I came up sputtering, and when I looked up, four eyes stared back. Gideon smirked with a satisfied smile while the damn parrot bobbed his head and laughed, dancing around on the railing in the darkness.

"Very funny, you featherheads!" Remembering where I was, I skedaddled to the swim platform and pulled myself up, water sluicing from my legs and draining overboard. Hearing footsteps, I looked up to see Gideon jog down the curved staircase from the main deck, his face wreathed in smiles.

"I hope you enjoyed that, Gideon. Because we don't have much time, and if I don't figure this out, you're basically down by one helper." I rubbed the salt water from my eyes.

"Fine. I apologize. But you had it coming for all that vacuuming while I tried to relax. Let's go over to the lawn. We'll train there."

"I KNEW IT! You ... you ... *argh!*" I stormed to the edge of the deck and slid onto my kayak, paddling over to the marina and stomping up the grassy knoll behind the shop.

Wings snapped overhead, making me duck, and the Gryphon blinked into existence a scant second before landing. Losing his balance and almost falling, his four furry tree trunks staggered forward until he regained his balance.

I would have laughed, but seeing the powerful beast in such sorry shape was a sobering experience. He was our protector, and we were out of time. Gideon needed to get back on his feet and fast.

After midnight, and with the place deserted, Gideon stayed in his Gryphon form. He couldn't talk when shifted, so mind-speak it was.

"Edaline, pay attention. The only way to fly is to decide you can. It's not about magic. It's about believing in yourself. Now, take it from the top. Call your power, and when you have it spooled, run down this hill and categorically believe you can leave the ground. You may have to jump into the air to get things started."

"Wait a minute. How do you know this? It's not like you downloaded the Djinn training manual, right?"

Gideon's eyes glowed gold in the darkness. *"You doubt me, Edaline?"* He stood motionless, a small curl in the corners of his beak.

"You remember you just pushed me off the boat, right?" I sighed. "Ok. Let's do this, then." I turned, thought about how much Gideon was annoying me right now, gathered my power, and then with a deep breath, hauled ass down the hill.

As I closed in on the dark water caressing the beach, I thought of flying. I was halfway there when my footsteps felt lighter, so I concentrated on the image of a feather and felt a sudden lift. Unsure what to do about my feet, I kept moving them, then changed my mind and stopped. I guess that was a bad idea, but luckily, I was out over the shallows. My efforts ended with another salt water bath when everything just ... *fizzled out.*

I leaned back on my hands, spitting the sand from my mouth, then scrambled up. As I stomped up the hill, my sneakers squished and squeaked, and I pictured taking them off and beating Gideon over the head.

"It's not my fault, Edaline. You need practice. This is the only way."

At my frustrated grunt, he added, *"You will get better. Soon, you will not need to trigger the magic with action. It will become as natural as breathing. Try again."*

So I practiced, Gideon offering helpful suggestions and laughing in my head when I got dunked. It took over an hour and about seven or eight head-firsts into the bay, but finally, I saw progress.

I ran down the hill and jumped, comfortable with the knowledge that the water would catch me if I messed up. This time, something felt different.

As I rose through the air, my trajectory was forward as usual. But when I thought, "STOP," I came to a halt and hovered. I looked down at the water and saw my reflection on the dark surface. I glowed, the ripples in the water making me appear to sparkle.

Holy crap! I'm an angel!

In my head, Gideon roared, his laughter spiking through my brain. *"I wouldn't go that far. You're more in need of receiving a blessing than qualified to give one, Edaline."*

"Will you STOP eavesdropping on my every thought!?" My voice echoed over the bay, and I slapped a hand over my lips. Whoops.

My magic sputtered, and I gasped, then dropped like a stone. This time, I sank all the way to the bottom, my toes squishing in the sandy muck down there. Something hard and slippery snaked across my legs, and I screamed.

Power blasted through me, and I shot straight up, launching through the surface without stopping. No, I kept right on going, higher and higher, until I realized my situation and stopped myself.

Looking down, terror iced my veins. I was way, way too high. The grip on my power slipped, but fear gave me strength. I grabbed hold of the slippery tendrils of magic and held onto them like lifelines.

"That's it. Hold it steady, Edaline. Now, come down slowly so I don't have to save you from yourself."

The Gryphon was a speck on the hillside, his eagle head tilted as he eyeballed my progress. The laughter in his words usually distracted me, but I ignored him. Instead, breathing deeply, I concentrated. Slowly drifting down, I landed with a soft thump at the bottom of the hill. It took forever. I let out my breath with a gasp.

"Did you see that? That was incredible!" I turned to look up the hill, and Gideon stood there, his tail flicking softly and his golden eyes smiling at me.

"Well done, Edaline. Well done."

***

I was so excited that I didn't hear the footsteps coming up behind me. When a pair of strong arms snaked around my waist, I shrieked, and Gideon disappeared. A quiet chuckle in my ear turned my legs to jello.

"Ronan!"

He whirled me around, his lips meeting mine for an enthusiastic kiss. Feeling his touches, smelling his salty skin—it was heaven. I sank into him with a sigh, diving into his exploring lips with abandon. When we finally pulled apart, our heavy breaths filled the air.

"That was amazing, Eddi. You can fly!" Ronan beamed at me, the luminescent pools of his eyes sparkling in the darkness. "You looked like a celestial being."

I laughed, but somewhere in a quiet corner of my mind, I heard a sarcastic snort. Mentally, I shoved Gideon out and slammed the door.

Ronan's arms clamped tight as I melted into them. "Where have you been, Ronan? I thought you'd never come." I stretched to kiss his soft lips, and he returned my caresses, then eased away with a breathy moan. Softening his hold, Ronan pulled back and gazed into my eyes, then examined my face, one feature at a time.

"I've been gathering our people. Gideon has called on everyone to join forces."

I pulled back and stared at him. "Who's coming to Charleston?"

He listed off some names, most of whom I didn't know. But Tabitha and Bacchus were coming, and it sounded like Tab's wanna-be lover would be there as well. That could be entertaining.

"What about your mother?"

Ronan shook his head. "She is too weak to join the fight. In fact, she wanted me to ask you if Matilda could stay with her at the *Shoal*. The child would be safe there."

My heart sped up at the thought of leaving her behind. In reality, it was a fantastic suggestion, because I'd been struggling with how to keep her safe while I was gone.

"That would be perfect. I will check with Matilda, but I'm sure she'll be excited to visit the *Shoal* and get to know Oriana better."

Ronan smiled. "It is done, then." He gazed into my eyes, his brows pulling together in a frown. "I don't like the idea of you joining us, Eddi. Your powers are still developing. You are putting yourself at unnecessary risk."

With a shake of my head, I said, "Oh no, you don't. You're not going anywhere without me. You *or* Cal. I'm in this whether you like it or not. I'm sorry. Besides, you know I'm no safer here, right?"

Ronan pursed his lips but nodded. He reached up and pushed his fingers through my bangs, then slid his hand to the back of my head and pulled me in for a long slow kiss.

Melting into his arms, the darkness that shrouded us lent a privacy I had longed for. It was incredible. The sound of gentle waves rippling along the shore. The warm night heating my skin, then cooling it with a whisper of the ocean breeze. Coming together in the peaceful oasis of the cove, everything tickled my senses, my heart swelling with want, my body aching with need. I drown in a breathtaking slew of emotions, and all for the male who held me close.

My hands slid over his powerful back, exploring the contours of his smooth torso before stealing down to his hips. Ronan murmured against my lips.

"You feel so good, Eddi. I missed you terribly."

The soft scales of his curved buttocks flexed beneath my palms, each one so tiny that they slipped like silk under my hands. I answered him with another kiss, standing on my tiptoes and rubbing my body against his with a sexy purr.

"Stop that," he teased, a hand rising to palm my breast. "Gods, Eddi. You feel so good." His light pinch on my beaded nipple sent a shockwave to join the heat spiraling low in my belly. "Being apart has been hell," he whispered against my ear.

Pulling away, I rested my forehead on his heaving chest. "Oh my god. I hate this. I can barely stand it when you're away." I looked up into his eyes, mine bright with unshed tears. "I try to stay busy and not think about it, but it's ... it's *awful.*"

Ronan's eyes glittered down at me, flicking over my face before he answered. "It won't be forever. I promise." Pulling me closer, his voice rumbled under my ear.

"I don't know what to do, Eddi. I have obligations at the *Shoal* now that my mother has returned. A Moon Tide is coming, and we must prepare."

I was so busy smelling his skin and snuggling into him that I barely registered his words. When I did, I pulled back and looked at his face.

"A moon tide? You mentioned that once before."

Without answering, Ronan's eyes roamed the hillside, his feet restless on the grass. Smiling, I couldn't help but notice his hard length pressed against his skins.

"Come. We must find a quiet place to talk." With a twinkle in his eye, Ronan took my hand and led me up the hill. I jimmied the door of the Tiki hut, then propped it open to let in some moonlight. He pulled the staff bench from beneath the rustic service counter and we spooned together on the end nearest the door. Ronan pulled my back to his chest, his hands massaging up and down my arms as his lips found my neck.

"There, that's much better," he rumbled. When he slid one hand down to cover my mound, I giggled.

"Ok, I love it, but what's a moon tide?" I grabbed his hand, pulled it to my lips, and kissed his palm.

He sighed. "You know that the moon causes the tides, yes?"

I nodded.

"Well, the Syreni are secure in the tunnels as long as the tide doesn't drop too low. Every month or two, we get an extreme low tide, and the entrance is shallow enough that anyone can walk into the tunnels. I have seen the water level as low as the knee. We plan for it by adding extra security."

"Coral sticks up from the water all around the entrance. The beautiful purple fans attract human eyes as they flop on the surface. We have two Syreni on patrol all day, strengthening the glamor to avoid detection during the moon tide."

I grabbed his other hand, which had moved to massage my breast, and pulled it up to my lips. "Quit distracting me, Mr. Busyhands. Who is going to do the extra security if everyone's gone to help Gideon and James?"

"My mother and the youngest Syreni males. They are all in their second decade and are too young to risk at battle." I turned my head, and he smiled down at me, his eyes glowing with pride. "Both male and female youngsters are powerful. Together with my mother and the other adult females, they will keep the *Shoal* safe. Matilda will be secure there while we are gone."

I gazed out at the moon-soaked grass surrounding the Tiki and sighed, leaning back and playing with his strong, thick fingers.

"It can't be helped, I guess. We have to do this. I'm sick at the thought that they might have my father. If that's true, what has Hex been doing to him all of these years? Do you think Matilda could be my ...?"

My voice trailed off, the idea that she could be my half-sister stirring a blend of excitement and dread.

"Your sister? Quite possibly. Would that bother you?"

"No! Absolutely not. I love her. She's so clever and smart. I looked over my shoulder at him, unsure how he would take my words. "She's your sister, too. How weird would that be?"

Ronan chuckled. "It will be fine, Edaline. Syreni have many extended families. In fact, in the old times, there were no rules about mating. Things got ... *interesting*."

"What?!" I sat up and turned my head. "Are you serious?"

"Yes. But those times are long gone. They disappeared when we stopped eating humans." With an exaggerated growl, he leaned forward and bit me on the shoulder. Rather than making me shriek, it had the opposite effect.

At the sudden pulse of heat, I ground my thighs together and pushed back on the bench, pressing against the growing bulge beneath his skins. He rumbled in my ear and moved his hands to my chest, massaging me as I squirmed.

"Stop that. We can't do that here!"

"Why is that?" His lips traced down my neck, my flesh rippling with bumps that raised shivers and pebbled my nipples. Ronan growled. "It's quiet now. Everyone has gone. The darkness can hide *many* things. *Pleasant* things."

Sliding his hands up my front, he grasped my jaw with one hand and pulled my neck to the side. Tipping his head, he mouthed my neck, and two tiny fangs grazed over the sensitive skin without breaking through.

It tickled. I reached to brush my neck with one hand and it came away wet.

"Ronan. *What ... ?*"

"*Shh.* Wait," he rumbled. Probing up and down my neck, his fangs scraped over my skin as his tongue licked at whatever he was doing. The rasping sensation shocked the tiny hairs of my arms and neck to full attention, and pressure bulldozed through my vagina, flooding me with desire.

A tingling sensation followed his nibbles, then slowly sparkled down my spine before dancing into my arms and legs. I was spineless jello, but my pussy was a swollen, aching inferno.

"Oh my god ...*fuck ... Ronan.*" Squirming beneath his hand, I curled my legs around his bare ankles. His long fingers slipped beneath my cotton shorts and snuck down to the V of my thighs, the steady pressure up and down my wet folds coaxing a groan from my throat. Up. Down. Slow and sure. My limbs quaked, my mouth pulling so tight that I had to pant through my nose.

He circled my entrance until I whimpered, my feet leaving marks in the sand below the bench as I writhed on his fingers, desperate for more. Between the gentle nips of his dripping fangs, Ronan was relentless. Pressing and sliding back and forth, he stroked me, then teased my entrance and stroked again.

When I struggled, his arm clamped down and held me tight. Adding a finger, then curling them both, he found the knot of nerve endings deep inside of me, and rubbed.

I gasped. My head rolled, my eyes shutting against the torturous sensations heightened by the hard arousal pressing into my backside. As I writhed in his arms, Ronan's fangs skated along my neck, his tongue lapping, his huffing breaths at my ear adding to the tingles that suddenly shot to my clit, then ricocheted all the way to my curled toes.

Nudging my head to the side, he kissed me, his tongue coated in a sweet sticky liquid that tasted divine. My mind drifted away. I floated on a cloud of bliss as more nectar trickled into my mouth from his slightly distended fangs. His tongue swirled with mine, his soft moans mingling with my own.

I stuck out my tongue, teasing a drop from the tip of one tiny nub. It prickled. I licked at him, my teasing igniting something in Ronan. His powerful arms constricted around me, crushing me to his chest and driving his fingers deeper.

"*Eddi...*" A satisfied growl rolled from his throat, joining the breathless sounds that hung in the darkness of the hut. Caught like a fly in the euphoric haze of his nectar, I pushed into his hand. Faster, and more firmly, his fingers stroked, hitting my clit with every slippery circle.

My head jerked back against his chest, the two of us like a tangle of snakes wrapped in a passionate knot. My hips jerked under his ministrations, my shoulders pushing against his pecs, and I reached down to cover his hand with mine, helping him find the perfect angle.

In moments, I was there, crashing into the abyss on a wave of pleasure that had me stretching tight under his hold. The noises we made could easily get us busted, but I didn't care. Not now.

As the last of my orgasm ebbed away, I moaned into his mouth, my tongue greedily dabbing like a bee searching for honey as his fingers played with me. The sensations stretched out, until finally, I grabbed his hand.

His soft huff of laughter against my lips brought me back to earth, and I lay back against his arm and stretched.

"Jello," I said, my voice dry.

"Hmmm?"

"I can't move my legs." My voice, slow and drawling, sounded far away. I smiled and enjoyed the buzz of his nectar as he cuddled me close.

Ronan was rock hard against my hip, and with my eyes closed, I lazily curled into a ball on his lap, reaching one hand down to feel him. He mumbled something incoherent, then pulled my hand away and tucked me against his chest. With a sigh, Ronan rubbed his cheek against my hair.

Drifting on a blissful cloud, I left my heavy eyes closed and enjoyed the feeling of his arms around me. His hot breaths puffing in my ear were intoxicating, a happy haze threading through me at being so unbelievably close to him.

Rubbing my arms, nuzzling my neck, Ronan's contented rumbles tickled my heart with pleasure. It was heaven. When I reached down to explore the outline of his shaft through his skins, he groaned.

"You're very good at ... *that.*" My throat, dry from panting, cracked at the words, and he chuckled into my ear.

"Pleasing you makes me very hard." Ronan rolled his thickened ridge against my hip.

I leaned back and tilted my head, finding his lips and sharing a pleasant, gentle kiss, our tongues tangling. When we eased away, I smiled, the Tiki so quiet that I swear I heard the pounding of his heart.

"Oh, really? How hard?" I smiled, his eyes sparking in the darkness at my playful expression.

Sliding down his lap, my knees came to rest on the sandy floor as he tried to pull me back into his arms. I shook him off. At eye level with his bulge, I rubbed my hand over the soft, smooth scales there.

"I can never get over how soft you are, Ronan. It's amazing." I lay my cheek on one muscular thigh and brought my hand up to gently massage his hardened length. Ronan's lips parted as he looked down, his hand covering mine, forcing it to press harder as I massaged up and down the bulky ridge of his arousal.

Leaning closer and opening my mouth, I closed my teeth gently over the ridge of his erection, and gently bit him. His scales were smooth against my lips, and when I touched them with my tongue, they were salty, like the sea.

He hissed, and his legs shot wide, his cock popping free. It was beautiful, so hard and thick, the pale skin of his shaft bright in the moonlight filtering through the doorway. I grabbed him with both hands and slid my mouth over the purpling tip. Slowly, my tongue rolled around and around until he was slippery with my saliva.

The noises coming from Ronan made my pussy clench, the hissing and grunting erotic in a way I had never imagined. I smiled to myself as I worked up and down, each time taking him further and further into my mouth.

Ronan was beside himself, his hands touching my hair, my shoulders, and my neck as if unsure where to hold on.

"Oh my god. Eddi. It's ... *nggggh.*" I had him almost all the way down my throat now, the slick bubbly sounds an erotic backdrop to his strained panting. Ronan's hips rolled under my mouth, and when I peeked up, his head was back. The only thing visible was his tense chin, the corded muscles in his neck strung tight.

Not yet ready to give up control, I pulled back, but he gently grabbed my hair in his fist, his wild eyes blazing into mine. I smiled an evil smile and began exploring.

Running my fingers along the now slippery length of him, I found the base of his cock where it slid free from his skins. I explored the hidden mounds of his testicles, and rubbed. He gasped and grabbed my hand.

"Don't," he hissed, his eyes rolling back in his head.

"Shh."

Slipping my mouth over his cock, I sucked and swirled, massaging the two hard lumps beneath his skin, his legs shaking with excitement. My other hand stroked him up and down, and with a final swirl of my tongue, he moaned, and his smooth testicles swelled into my hand. I squeezed, very gently, and bobbed my drooling mouth up and down on his cock.

Unintelligible words poured from his lips, his head slamming back against the wall as he jerked in my grip. Gently, I rolled his balls in my hand as incoherent noises came from his open mouth. A smattering of words and sounds cobbled together on his tongue, his ecstatic response was punctuated with powerful surges of his hips.

The visual caused an ache in my core that was almost painful in its intensity. My slippery mouth, my stroking hand, and my gentle massage of his testes sent him over the edge. Ronan came undone. He grabbed my hair in both fists and pulled me down onto his throbbing cock, his hips thrusting until he bellowed, a sound that carried down the hill and across the quiet bay like a foghorn.

Tipping forward, his chin dropped to his chest, nectar streaming from it as he came, the thick jets of cum coming so fast that I almost lost some of it. I swallowed it down, and it was salty, and a little sweet. My Syreni male was full of surprises.

I smiled as I licked my lips, then swallowed him again. Ronan spasmed, his head denting the wall of the Tiki hut as it slammed backward.

He jerked and twitched, his head rolling on his neck, his eyes closed, and his mouth open. Nectar trickled from his lips, tracking down his chin and leaking onto his chest. His long fingers released my hair and began caressing me in a gentle, loving way.

Leaning forward, he grasped me by the forearms, hauling me up in one powerful yank that sprawled me across his damp chest. His wet cock jerked against my thigh, his long low groan of happiness filling the hut.

"You," he whispered, his mouth dry. Still breathing heavily, he struggled to catch his wind. "That was ... *I don't ...*"

I sighed, nestling my head under his chin. "You don't have to explain. I know. I loved it, too. Watching you was very hot," I said with a grin.

With a weak laugh, his hands feathered over me as if to make sure I was okay. He grunted as he stuck his legs out in front of himself, wincing at a cramp in one thigh.

"We need to find a place to do that again. Somewhere softer," he said, smiling down into my flushed face. "I have not done that before. I would like to do it again *very soon*."

With a laugh, I spread my hand over his rock-hard pecs. "I can arrange that, handsome."

As we lay there, cuddling in the woozy aftermath of our lovemaking, I thought about how far we'd come. The way I felt about him was so right. I cared so much for him that it hurt. I spent half my time worrying about him and the other half wanting his touch.

Ronan must have caught the gist of my thoughts because he answered in my mind. *"In the Syreni world, when two become as one and cannot part without pain, that is a sign from the Gods that it is a true mating."*

He looked down at me, his hooded eyes soft with desire. *"That is how I feel about you, Eddi. It hurts when you are not with me."*

I wiggled against him and smoothed my hands over the broad expanse of his chest. Absent-mindedly, I caressed him, thinking about how to answer that.

"Ronan, I don't know about you, but if I never had to say goodbye to you again, every day would be perfect."

I felt him smile against my hair, and his hands pulled me closer. All hell might be breaking loose, but in the safety of Ronan's arms, in a quiet thatched hut with the moonlight streaming through the door, my life was perfect.

CHAPTER 21

Before we left for Charleston, I had one more stop to make. I packed my away bag and tossed it into my basket, taking a side trip to Ada's house on my way to the marina. She was like a mother to me, and I had to say goodbye. Just in case.

Similar to James' house, but much smaller, Ada's home was at the end of a quiet street. There was a clear view of the turquoise ocean through the palms. When I knocked, Ada opened the door, surprised to see me.

"Hang on, hun." She disappeared inside and popped out a few minutes later with some sweet tea. Ada motioned to a shady spot and some comfortable chairs on her veranda. As I settled in, I took a sip of the tea around a lump in my throat. Sitting in the shade with her, taking in the beautiful view, and hearing her voice—possibly for the last time—brought tears to my eyes.

"What's up, Eddi? Are you alright?"

"I'm ok. I have to go away for a bit, and I wanted to let you know. I feel badly that you were counting on the babysitting money and now I'm letting you down."

"Don't worry about me, child. I'm fine. I have a little nest egg. And I can wait until you get back. I'll be fine." She reached out her manicured hand, taking mine in hers. "What's really bothering you?" Her kind face, wrinkled with concern, and her pink hair—well, it undid me. I burst into tears.

"There, there, Eddi. Don't cry." Ada popped into the house and came out with a box of Kleenex. "What's going on? You can tell me. I've known you for what, ten years? I'm family! Spill it."

I couldn't tell her I might never return, so I told her about Ronan—not everything, of course—I focused on my worries that we'd never be able to combine our lives because of his responsibilities. Like any good friend, she tutted and frowned, and offered encouraging words in all the right places. It wasn't a true conversation, seeing as she didn't know the real story. But it helped. When I was done blubbering, she smiled.

"See? All you needed to do was get that off your chest. Now you listen to me, and listen good. You are a wonderful human being, Edaline. You are kind to everyone around you, and protect your friends like we're solid gold. If your boy has half a clue, he'll scoop you up and never let you go. You're a keeper, kiddo."

"Ada, you're so special to me. No matter what happens, I wanted you to know how much I cared about you, and how much I appreciated all the times you've helped me over the last ten years. You and Patsy saved my life."

Ada rolled her eyes. "Don't you talk like you're never coming back, now. And don't get me started about Patsy. I don't know what's going on with her, but I'll get to the bottom of it, trust me. Closing up the restaurant with no warning? It's bizarre, don't you think?"

I nodded, but didn't add anything. I finished my tea and got up to leave. Ada gave me a hug, then walked with me to my bike.

"Eddi?" I threw my leg over the seat and turned to face her.

"If you see that damn Bert, you tell him I've got a bone to pick with him. He needs to get his damn act together, and get his shit sorted." Her face was thunderous, her hair glowing a bright pink in the sunlight. Finally getting a grip on herself, she sighed. "I think Patsy closed because she couldn't get reliable help. This is all his damned fault."

I laughed. "It's ok, Ada. Everyone has their issues. We'll all get by. With any luck, I'll be back in a few days."

As I pedaled away, I turned back, and almost sobbed at the tears glistening in her eyes. I think Ada knew that our time together was ending, and we all had to move on. Life was such a bitch sometimes.

***

The engines of the *Black Widow* thrummed to life, then slowly backed us out of the bay. The smooth power of the Spectre yacht's nineteen hundred horsepower engine sent happy chills along my skin; knowing what awaited us at our destination made it crawl with fear. I was conflicted, to say the least.

Tired of the spider graphic peering at us across the bay every day, Cal peeled it from the hull one extra-hot afternoon. Now, our luxury yacht was minus a monster and christened with a much simpler moniker—the *Spectre*—a great name. Somehow, the change made the last taint of Hex's presence fade away.

We were finally on our way, and the thought that my father might be alive haunted my every waking moment. A stomach-clenching eagerness to see him overshadowed my fear of how the coming days would unfold. Hex wouldn't go down easily.

I thought back to the night in the meadow in Tennessee—the night the Manticore took everything from me. Hex was a blight on the world and deserved to die. Whether or not I'd have the courage to kill her weighed heavily on my mind.

I had so many happy memories with Patsy; that monster killed her. When I first arrived in the Keys, the diminutive and pleasant woman helped me get back on my feet. I'd never forgotten her kindness the day she hired me, her short black hair gleaming in the sunlight as she waved goodbye from the kitchen entrance.

Finding out she was gone, the shell of her body now housing a deadly creature, knocked me on my proverbial ass. I tried not to think about whatever horrific process she'd endured before dying. I'd kill Hex for what she did to Patsy, and I'd die before becoming her vassal.

I knew in my heart that the third Talisman was for me. Killing Hex was now job number one. Patsy on the surface but unbridled evil on the inside; her death was the only solution.

Something jabbed me between the shoulder blades, and I turned away from the railing. It was Tabitha, a bottle of Corona in her hand. An olive floated inside.

I laughed and took the beer from her. "Uh, Tabitha, it's supposed to be a lime, not an olive."

She shrugged. "You say potato, I say tomato. It works." She took a big sip, her eyes sparkling a shamrock green as she winked at me.

I turned back to watch the ocean roll by, the funk of my thoughts lifting. I wasn't alone. Powerful backup had come along for the ride. We could do this.

Tabitha bounced her shoulder off mine as she leaned onto the railing, long strands of blonde hair finding her mouth in the wind. The velvety soft scales that covered her chest always drew my eye.

Syreni females—their chests, at least—featured smooth scales so fine that they looked like form-fitting fabric. Suntanned and athletic, their backs were completely bare, the flesh on their sides blending into the belly scales in a seductive, curved fashion.

I admired the brilliant blue and gold pattern on Tabitha's legs. Stunning, like her mother Oriana—pop a t-shirt or tank over the upper half, and she blended into a human crowd.

With a mischievous side-eye, she said, "I know you can't help looking at all this glorious perfection. No one can." Then she shoved me, spilling my beer, and laughing as I almost dropped the bottle.

"Sorry, Tab. I can't help myself. It's not every day you meet a beautiful creature spawned in your nightmares."

We clinked bottles as her lips curled up so tightly that her tongue stuck out.

Glancing over her shoulder, Ronan's sister peered through the smoked glass of the helm above and behind us. Gideon and James manned the console, deep in conversation. Ronan, Cal and Bacchus sprawled on the couches of the flybridge, their eyes glued to the small TV screen there.

I caught a glimpse of a bare male butt as riot police hauled him to a cruiser, a sea of naked bodies in the background. Key West was in dire straits. I couldn't watch and turned to stare at the ocean instead. Behind the Spectre, the reef spread out in a patchwork of turquoise and greens. The vibrant color brought tears to my eyes as it faded into the horizon. Would I ever see it again?

Tabitha whispered, "I can't believe James is here with us. What do you think his creature is? Doesn't this break some sort of rule, having an unknown *Other* with us?"

I followed her gaze to where James, barely visible through the window, spoke with Gideon. He appeared downright relaxed compared to the tight-lipped Enforcer beside him. Tabitha had no idea he was the Sovereign, but how did I explain his presence?

"Rules? Hell, I don't know the bloody rules. James must be a high-octane critter of some sort, otherwise Gideon wouldn't have brought him along." I faced the ocean, hoping my explanation would do the trick. Tabitha was clever.

"I wonder about James' form, though. Do you have any idea what he is?"

Tabitha shook her head. "Judging by the meat I saw them hauling below deck, it's something big." Her eyebrows waggled. "Big is good!" Then, she punched me, adding another bruise to my arm. At the rate we were going, I'd be banana brown by the time we reached Charleston.

We stood by the railing, watching the sun begin its daily climb to its scorching best. I marveled at the confidence Tabitha exuded. She leaned over and grinned directly into my face.

"What is going on in that pretty little head of yours, Eddi?"

"I'm nervous. And excited. Terrified really. How do you Syreni appear so calm all the time?"

She shrugged. "I don't know. I guess it's part of who we are. I mean, we come from the sea, and when we die, we go back to the sea. I don't fear death. It's natural."

"I don't want to die. I want to live a long life. Have babies. Lots of hot sex ... " I turned red as Tabitha pulled her lips tight to hide her smile.

"Well, if I know my brother, he makes you beg for it." I cringed and changed the subject.

"What do you think will happen in Charleston? It's not like we can show up, say hi, and storm the fort. We have a handful of fighters compared to Hex."

"We won't win if we aren't positive, Eddi. Courage makes an enormous difference."

"What are we, though? A ragtag group of paranormals, a Gryphon, and whatever James turns out to be. Sure, you Syreni are strong. But, my powers are nothing to brag about. Cal's octopus is handy with all those legs. I'd seen him fight—he's positively ferocious when antagonized. But how does it compare to what we're facing in Charleston?"

"First of all," Tabitha said, "Gideon is worth all of us put together. I'm betting—and this is going by his show of confidence—that James is something powerful. We'll do fine. Have a little faith."

"You're forgetting. Gideon's Gryphon hasn't fully recovered from his injuries yet."

Tabitha sighed. "I don't know what he has planned, but I do know that we are a strong group of fighters. And Gideon is clever. Splitting the extra thirty Syreni males onto different boats was wise, especially if a traitor is helping Hex."

With a shrug, her luminous green eyes focused on me. "Gideon has a long and powerful reach. Who knows how many more he has coming to aid us? He will throw what he has at the demon, and we *will* win."

Taking a sip of my beer, I sighed. "I hope Gideon knows what he's doing. He's being tight-lipped, as usual. It drives me crazy when he won't give us information." I caught sight of something and watched as a green sea turtle, floating thirty feet from the bow, dove back under the turquoise water.

"If the Gryphon was female, we would know everything," Tabitha whispered. "The flow of information is sometimes the key to success in a large conflict."

I smirked at the thought of a female Gryphon. I'd love to see THAT.

***

"We shouldn't be doing this, Cal." I looked over my shoulder, anxious that the Gryphon would somehow read our minds and roar down here to throttle us both. "What if we get caught?"

Cal laughed, gripping my hand tighter as he pulled me down the stairs to the lowest deck of the Spectre. He wanted to explore and find the storage room where he watched them pack away the big meat coolers.

"Aren't you a little curious, Ed? I mean, come on. We're talking a thousand-plus pounds of meat here. I counted thirty Igloo coolers. Curiosity is killing me!"

We hit the bottom of the stairs, the darkness closing in as the light from above faded the further we went.

"Uh, how about a light, Cal?"

"Shh. We have to be quiet. And no light. Geez, Eddi. You'd think you'd never done this before," he giggled. This wasn't the first time he'd led me into trouble. Octopuses were curious creatures, and my friend was no exception.

We tiptoed down the hall, and when we turned the corner, a strange sound trickled through the silence. I pulled him to a stop, my eyes wide in the darkness. He squeezed my hand and pulled me behind him, speaking into my thoughts.

"I'll protect you from the hamburger, Eddi." His laughter chased the words through my mind, and I poked him.

At the end of the corridor, a sliver of light sliced across the narrow passageway. A solid gray door, open a crack, blocked our view of what made those soft noises; something was inside that room. I turned to hightail it back up the stairs, but Cal held me firmly in his grip. He put a finger over his lips and soundlessly mimed, *"Shh."*

Offices lined the hallway stretched before us, the large rectangular windows made from mesh-reinforced glass—protection against rough seas, no doubt. Every one of the rooms was dark, and when I peeked inside, they were empty except for cots, having one or two in each room.

Not offices. *Medical bays.* A splash of crimson splattered across the walls of the first room made my stomach clench. The restraints on a cot in the second room gave me chills.

What the hell was Hex up to down here?

Our bare feet were silent, so we reached the room at the end of the hall without any surprises. Cal peered inside while I waited behind him, feeling stupid for being so frightened. It was a dark hallway on a yacht. What could happen?

Relax, Eddi. Breathe. Don't be silly.

"*Holy shit!*" Cal's voice ricocheted through my mind.

I slid into the space he made for me and peeked inside the room, my hands clenched at my sides. I had to bite my lip to keep the curses inside.

The long reptilian tail caught my attention first because its narrow tip lay mere inches from the doorway. The tan coloring was the exact opposite of what you'd expect to see on an alligator. This was no alligator.

My eyes followed the long, studded tail past musclebound hips, which were folded to hold the weight of a creature that must have weighed a few thousand pounds. Brushing the ceiling when it lifted, the reptilian head and swept-back tufted ears were an oddly handsome addition. Thin, spiky scales swept backward over its body, each coated in short, downy fur—like a fuzzy cat tongue with legs.

The elegant, narrow face turned in our direction, one slitted eye snapping wide as it cocked its head. It listened.

I jerked back, mentally hissing at Cal as I turned to stone, hardly daring to breathe. Cal went rigid and pulled me tightly to his chest. We waited, starving for oxygen as the seconds ticked by. The noises resumed, and pursing my lips, the air slowly eased from my lungs. I looked back into the brightly lit room.

Wings. It had wings, and they hung loosely at its side, the smooth, bat-like skin flopping as they darted back and forth. Hooked claws at the tip of each wing arch busily stabbed at the dripping meat in the Igloo cooler at its feet. The wet sounds made my stomach roll.

Packed tightly into a blocky jaw, the rows of slender white fangs reminded me of a baby gator, needle-sharp and as long as my fingers. And currently, this thing needed a toothpick.

Holy crap. At the rate it was shoveling the bloody entrée into its mouth, it might not fit back through the door.

Intent on its snack, the creature didn't look up, blood trickling down a long, curved neck that rolled in fat waves as it stretched to swallow. A membrane flicked over the eyes with each gulp, the eerie sight making me happy its sole focus was the meat and not us.

At least it *was*. Mid-chew, the head snaked toward the door, and two golden, slitted eyes locked onto mine. A shred of raw meat slid down one fang and plopped onto the linoleum.

I couldn't stop myself. *I screamed.*

It roared.

Cal yelped, and the tail lashed out, the door slamming shut. We both ran for it.

CHAPTER 22

CHARLESTON
~ FELIX ~

I stood tall beside Jovi and our entire complex of fighters. We were all that stood between the country and certain doom, my chest swelling with pride at the thought. Axel wasn't here, and after meeting him face to face, I'd given up hope that he would come to understand the importance of our mission. The humans were depending on us.

Longing to know the real story about the unfortunate souls in the library, I resigned myself to the fact that the vampires had needs and were ferocious on the best of days. Jovi didn't understand how I could be so obtuse. My friend, and his big words.

Our pending demonstration washed away my misgivings, excitement racing through me when I thought about swimming free in the ocean and testing my skills against someone new.

I watched our diminutive Benefactor as she strolled through the training field, thoroughly inspecting the lineup of Servus and Argenti. Hex's glittering stare roamed over our contingent, a tight smile and the occasional nod marking her approval.

Her short black hair shone in the Charleston sunshine, perfectly styled and lending an aura of authority to an already powerful figure. Hex paused before me, her eyes flicking over my chest as they narrowed, then tracked the heavily beaded sweat rolling down my belly. She licked her lips, and my sex responded with a badly-timed throb. Her golden eyes lowered, stopping on the outline of my member, now visible through my skins. Her lips curled upward with a hungry smile.

"I like this one. Bring him to my room tonight."

Stephen shoved his glasses up his nose and scribbled something in a white notebook. The envious look he shot me on the way by made me groan. I'd be targeted after the demonstration, no doubt about it.

Behind Hex came a tall, stately man who seemed important. His messy brown hair was in stark contrast to his perfectly tailored suit. The poor man already showed signs of heat stress thanks to Charleston's typical summer inferno. His face held a grayish cast, his sleeve constantly dabbing at the sweat threatening to drip from his chin. As he lowered his arm, his hand shook. I glanced at his eyes, red-rimmed and hazy and scarcely able to focus. This man was ill. As he passed me, I smelled it on him, a sweet and sickly aroma that teased my nostrils in his wake.

"Aren't they fantastic? And ready for a demonstration two weeks early." Hex glanced back at the man trailing her. "We will be observing from my helicopter." Her expression soured as she took in his pallor. "Relax, Warren. It's air-conditioned."

Today, we performed an exercise out in the ocean that would seal our position within the Department of Homeland Security. After many years of training, we would win the mock battle and enjoy a meteoric rise in station. How I'd longed to put to good use the things I'd learned here. My skin prickled with goosebumps at the glorious images flickering through my mind.

I didn't relish the thought of killing, though. It wasn't something I enjoyed. I'd been forced to kill during our training, and my stomach still rolled at the memory. The look in those humans' eyes when I dealt the final blow—

This would be different. Training wasn't the same as killing in the defense of your homeland. I repositioned the metal helmet under my arm and took a deep breath.

As our inspection ended, Stephen stepped forward and gave the signal. As one, all fifty fighters slid the heavy medieval Barbute helmets over our heads. The hammered iron scrollwork decorating the sides of the cumbersome headgear resembled a galloping horse. The metal protected our face and nose, and the T-shaped opening in front provided much-needed ventilation.

At least, that's what Jovi told me after he grumbled non-stop about Hex having a fascination with the history of the Crusades. My friend claimed our ancient headgear was outdated and useless and refused to use it when they were distributed. I smiled at the memory of Jovi holding his bleeding nose the last time we sparred. He'd get used to the cumbersome things. I thought they looked regal.

Stephen yelled out, "To the boats!" and the entire yard emptied, every fighter jogging into formation. A smooth river of gray metal, black fatigues, and sparkling blue and green legs flowed through the open gate before marching down the hill toward the docks.

Despite my misgivings, my heart raced. This was it. We would show off our skills to the Benefactor and her superior. Passing through the wrought iron gate, I slanted a look at Hex and the tall man as they watched us file past.

"What you are about to see will change history, Warren." Her eyes glittered with a strange reddish light that made my skin itch.

"Everyone will be QUITE surprised by how this all pans out."

***

The warm ocean splattered across my bare chest as a wave side-swiped our vessel. It was a rough day to be on the water. I turned to check on Jovi, who stood beside me on the narrow walkway of the tugboat. We'd opted to stay together throughout the exercise. Neither of us trusted Stephen or his Argenti pets.

Slowly, we chugged for open water, our destination a shallow patch reef not far from shore. Being daylight, Boris and his pals were ... *unavailable*. I smiled at the thought, happy that the vampires would miss all the action. The Argenti became holy terrors when under Boris' influence.

Turning my head, I watched as the Argenti closest to me kicked off his boots and, with a satisfied grin, snapped open his fingers and toes to expose the webbing there. Sensing my stare, he curled a lip at me and flexed his arms in a thinly veiled threat. White eyes bored into me as he ran his claws through his short hair, then slipped his helmet over his head. The glowing orbs staring back at me through the t-shaped slits made me shiver.

"Don't drown today, fingerling." With a dismissive grunt, he turned and spoke to the Argenti next to him.

I ignored him and leaned forward to see what was happening down the walkway. Our fighters stood ready for a quick water entry, helmeted, barefoot, and shirtless. The Argenti were in their usual black dive leggings, the rows of colorful Servus skins lighting up the sunlit deck of the vessel. Goosebumps rose across my skin at the sight.

On the horizon, a low-slung vessel waited. A helicopter slowly tracked back and forth across the ocean, the chupping blades and fat body of the flying machine backlit by a cloudless blue sky.

The idea was to get to the target ship and take out its defenders, some of whom were already in the water. The final goal was to overwhelm the defending force onboard, then capture our country's flag and seal our victory.

It wouldn't be a simple exercise. The independent contractors in the water were mercenaries hired to defend the ship, a decommissioned Avenger minesweeper. Sleek and layered, the three tiers of decking got progressively shorter as you went up the levels, providing great opportunities to practice our boarding skills. With plenty of uprights to climb thanks to its extensive radar systems, the Stars and Stripes waited at the very tip of the highest tower, flapping hard in the offshore wind.

Stephen strutted up and down the length of our tugboat, shouting last-minute directions. "Remember, maim, but don't kill." His eyes glittered. "Unless you have to."

He shoved at some of our soldiers, making them stand up straighter or being an ass in general. I snarled softly to myself when he poked my helmet to straighten it.

"What's that, Felix!?" Stephen shouted, putting his weight behind a shove that almost sent me overboard. "You think you're so much better than everyone, don't you, boy? Straighten your helmet!"

He leaned forward to hiss softly in my ear, "You'll be sorry if you displease the mistress tonight. You better at least have your *cock* straight by then."

A smattering of malicious chuckles down the lineup made me bristle, then my eyes shot open in surprise. I looked at Jovi and hissed into his mind, *"I thought going to the Benefactor's room was a joke!"*

He shrugged, ignoring my concern as he squinted at the ship in the distance. Worry curled in my guts. I wasn't sure if I was honored or horrified. I mean, she was not a young woman; her experience far surpassed mine. What did she expect of me? What if I was found wanting and disappointed her?

"Keep your mind on the job, *BOY.*" I turned my head at the ugly sound in my ear, almost bumping noses with Stephen. "I'll be watching you."

Shaking out my hands and feet, I was glad to be in the Servus group. Our job was to take care of the deep-water fighting. The Argenti would go hand to hand after breaching the enemies' on-board defenses.

The thumping of feet vibrated through the deck beneath me as everyone shook off their nerves and prepared to disembark the tug. It was now or never.

A shrill horn blasted, and as one, dozens of sleek male bodies catapulted over the side. The Servus immediately morphed to tail form while the Argenti swarmed across the surface, their hands and feet snapping wide to make use of their webbing. They were quicker than humans but nowhere near the speed of the Servus, their eerie crawling motions so ... *unnatural.*

I sped through the water, staying close to my friend, whose anxious expression told me that he wasn't wholly comfortable with our task. He shot me a glance, the water pulling at his face with the speed we traveled.

A sea of thrashing blue and green tails surrounded us, the noise from our sheer numbers sounding like a mixmaster. We'd clocked our fastest swimmer at 35 miles per hour. Any faster and the pain of collapsing cavitation bubbles in our tail became debilitating. Swimming deeper helped, and that was exactly what we did as a group.

The mine sweeper was only one mile out, so in no time, we streaked into range and split into groups. The Argenti should arrive by the time we finished taking out the underwater defenders. At least, that was the plan.

Jovi and I paired up, focusing on a small group of mercenaries clustered behind a tiny patch reef well below us. The rebreathers they wore created no bubbles, but their black wet suits stood out in stark contrast to the sandy bottom. A bottlenose dolphin hovered nearby, and I grinned.

Stephen had forewarned us of the possibility that our opponents might use dolphins. The US military employed an extensive training program for marine mammals to great success. But we had trained on how to manage them, and it wasn't nearly as hard as one would think.

I turned my head, and Jovi smiled, bubbles coming from his lips. He nodded, and I followed him as he shot downward.

We marked four men, each carrying long knives and two with underwater guns. The MK-1. Not very effective, but it was the best option the military had at the moment. Underwater, the dart it fired had a range of only 30 feet. I wasn't worried, and neither was Jovi.

Sweeping in, he shot past the dolphin, which startled. An excited squeak reached my ears, and after a quick defense arc to identify the intruder, the dolphin swung its head and raced after Jovi.

I laughed, bubbles tickling my face. Dolphins were curious creatures, and our tails always fascinated them. They also couldn't resist a wake, and Jovi just gave him an enormous one to ride—so predictable. If that didn't work, my friend would wrap his arms around the barrel of the creature and pull him away from the battle. He'd be safer at a distance, either way.

With a curl of my tail, I launched, pumping hard to gain momentum before I confronted the men. Sweeping behind them, I circled at top speed, their heads rotating wildly as they tried to follow my arcing path. A diver aimed and took a shot with his MK, the dart sailing through my bubble trail.

Thrill-seeking behavior wasn't clever, but I couldn't resist. I'd waited a lifetime for this, and giddy excitement emboldened me. Back and forth I swam, streaking over, then beside, then on my last pass, between the divers. Darts rained onto the patch reef, the slashing blades of their knives no match for my speed.

I felt bad for them, their wild eyes bulging behind their masks. Taking pity, I made a final loop. Grabbing them by the back of their dive suit, with one in each hand, I hauled the first two straight up, careful not to disrupt the rebreathing apparatus on their chests.

At top speed, I dragged them to the surface, bumping their heads together and tossing them into the waves. I glanced over my shoulder, and when they started their swim to the Zodiacs dotting the area, I smiled.

Slicing back through the waves, I dove for the last two, who were now back to back. Looking upward, their heads twisted back and forth, trying to spot me through the underwater murk.

I moved in more slowly this time, easing down from above so as not to disturb the water. One looked up, and having lost the element of surprise, I smiled ... then attacked.

The MK1 fired, the dart grazing my helmet with a clank as it swept past. I snarled, grabbing both men by the collar and repeating what I had just done to the last two. This time, I may have smacked their heads together a little too hard before dropping them next to one of the Zodiacs.

Laughter bubbled in my chest. This training exercise was far too easy. My speed must have frightened the humans for them to try a kill shot. Still, there was no excuse for using excessive force today. I reeled in the adrenaline pumping through me and sliced back into the ocean.

Sweeping downward, I searched for Jovi. He hovered over the patch reef, feeding fish to the dolphin as it whistled its approval. I clasped him on the back of the neck and put my forehead to his, our helmets banging together.

"Well, that was fun. Aren't you glad you didn't stay back at the barracks, Jovi?"

He never had a chance to answer. The first Argenti powered into view on the surface, a group ten strong. Their speed was more impressive than I imagined. Born with a fitness level far exceeding a human's, they powered past us as they made good use of their webbed feet and hands. Their expressions were ferocious, every glowing eye focused on the hull of the nearby ship. I shuddered, glad I wouldn't be on the receiving end of their attack.

Jovi and I, and our new dolphin friend, followed along the bottom, ready to defend from below. We were uncontested all the way to the boat. A Servus tidying up the stray frogmen darted past, dragging his latest victim. It was a good thing for the humans that the exercise took place in thirty feet of water. Any deeper, and their human bodies would not have withstood the sudden depth changes.

Under the mine sweeper, the sea floor was littered with discarded weapons and the odd piece of scuba gear. A black rubber fin drifted past at eye level; Jovi and I looked at each other, then burst out laughing. Our revelry excited the dolphin, who went to investigate the fluttering object before drifting off, presumably to find his trainer.

Adrenaline made me giddy, and I punched my friend before slapping him with my tail. Jovi grinned and tapped the dent in my helmet with a questioning look. I shrugged, and he shook his head.

"You shouldn't borrow trouble, my friend. It will get you killed one day."

I ignored him, tilting my head back to watch as the first of the Argenti boarded the minesweeper. The urge to see the second phase of our battle was overwhelming.

"Jovi, do you want to go watch the action? We can hide onboard somewhere. I want to see!"

With a conspiratorial smile, my friend nodded. We eased up under the minesweeper, following the hull until our heads popped above the surface. The waves were higher now, a wind whipping up from the Atlantic.

The sides of the craft rose fifteen feet from the waterline, within easy reach of our muscular tails. A quick thrust and we hauled ourselves over the railing. Changing forms, we trotted out of sight, squatting down behind some communications equipment.

Just in time. The thumping of feet made me duck, but I peered between two antennae to watch the show. Jovi popped his head up beside mine, and we took it all in.

My smile faded as a human pounded into view, his black tactical clothing ripped in several places. The terrified expression on his face sent ice through my veins. An Argenti raced after him, his clenched fists pumping, his nostrils flared with excitement. With a burst of speed, he pounced.

Grabbing the mercenary by the back of his shirt, the Argenti whipped him around. The sharp snick of a knife leaving its sheath startled me. With a satisfied smile, our soldier punched the ten-inch blade into the human's chest, all the way to the hilt. The mercenary went limp, and after a few vicious twists, the Argenti let him drop to the deck. As the body slid from his blade, he chuckled, the raw violence of the sound skittering over my nerves. Spitting on the dead soldier, he stepped over the body and raced away.

Acid burned my throat. He killed him. Just like that, and for absolutely no reason, a man was dead. One of the very lives we were tasked to protect. I wrenched my eyes from the grisly scene to look at Jovi.

He wasn't breathing, his white face slowly turning blue. I pulled him down, spinning in the confined space to shake him.

"Jovi, snap out of it!" I hissed into his mind, fearful of discovery.

With a gasping cough, he sucked in a breath, his color returning to a healthy pink.

"Are you ok?" I ran my hands over him, my chest squeezing at the memory of what I had witnessed.

His eyes shining with unshed tears, Jovi looked at me and shook his head. I looked back through the opening, only to see another Argenti snag a second soldier. Hands gripping the throat of the wild-eyed human, the bastard grit his teeth and wrung the life from him.

With a snarl, the Argenti yanked out his knife and with an arcing swing, sliced right through the human's neck. The soldier's eyes widened, then faded as his head fell forward onto his chest, a thin thread of skin holding it on. Breathing heavily, the Argenti's icy stare darted up and down the outer passageway before he dropped the lifeless body and took off toward the bow.

Jovi leaned against my legs, his head hanging between his knees. He whispered to me, his voice rough with emotion. "What ... *I don't* ... what's happening here, Felix?"

"I don't know. I don't fucking know." I squeezed his shoulder. "But we'll find out."

***

The exercise completed, we lined up in formation on the deck of the minesweeper. The sun had dipped below the horizon, so Boris appeared, joining Stephen, Hex, and our guest Warren.

The man in the suit didn't look very happy, his fingers twitching as sweat poured down his face despite the cool evening breeze. Looking down at the five dead soldiers piled on the deck, Warren raged.

"Are you out of your ever-loving *mind!?* How do you 'accidentally' kill five men in a training exercise? What is the meaning of this, Hex? Because from what I can see, your little experiment is *out of control!*"

Our Benefactor smiled at him, unrepentant. "Oh, Warren, give it a rest. Our boys were just showing off. We can't blame them for wanting to impress you, now, can we?"

Warren turned a peculiar shade of purple, holding his breath until he finally answered, the spit flying. "I didn't sign up for this, you *fucking monster*. You're going to cost me my career!" His face was wild, the sweat pouring freely from his chin as his lips curled with disgust.

Hex turned away, her claws lengthening as she moved. Warren couldn't see it, but her eyes glowed a ruby shade of ... *not human*. I sucked in a shallow breath. I had suspected, of course.

"Warren. You must understand something about me, right here, right now," she whispered. Turning to face him, her eyes flared crimson, and he recoiled. "If you want to live, you'll keep your mouth shut, sign the paperwork, and fade off into the sunset with your whores."

Warren froze, his eyes bulging at the hellish sight before him. He raised a shaking hand to cover his mouth, trailing a shocked gaze up and down the lineup of men on the deck as if he only now realized his colossal error.

Hex reached out, something tucked into her balled fist. She flipped her hand over and opened it, and Warren froze. "Would this be enough of an incentive to get you to shut your trap and let us continue with our—*training?*"

Warren gawked at her offering, his throat working as if he might vomit. Then he grabbed the box, staring at it with a greedy smile before stuffing it into his jacket.

"I thought so. Now, I'm sure you can come up with a suitable explanation as to how these men *tragically* lost their lives this afternoon ... *hmm?*"

Hex strutted around the pile of bodies, grimacing at the one whose head hung by a thread of skin. She nudged it with a toe, the lifeless eyes staring up at the darkness as it rolled.

"Well, this one might be a tough sell." She looked up at Warren. "A great white showed up today, *my god!* How positively horrifying," she cackled.

The small hairs on the back of my neck stood straight up at the sound.

Warren wasn't listening. His shadowed stare focused inward as the reek of desperation poured from him.

Without turning my head, I whispered into my friend's mind, *"What is in that fucking box?"*

Jovi twitched his cheek to show he'd heard me.

I would find out. Tonight.

CHAPTER 23

When Gideon hauled us to the lounge, I had no backup, because Ronan and his siblings had taken to the ocean to recharge. I hung my head, feeling the weight of James' disappointed stare.

Gideon perched on the white padded bar stool at the island, completely still. His granite expression was devoid of life, the fury rolling from him in waves. We had embarrassed him, and he was *pissed*. I'd never seen Gideon angry before, and it was *terrifying*.

Cal looked like he wanted to disappear. His long fingers twisting in his lap, he kept glancing at the stairs to the stern deck of the Spectre like he considered bolting. I was with him. We were in deep shit with the two most powerful paranormals in the southeastern states.

"You wanted to see what was in the coolers. That's your excuse?" James' words were clipped, the disappointed look that accompanied them making me feel even worse.

Cal nodded, looking up into James' face. "I'm sorry. We overstepped."

I looked at my friend with a frown. Was I the only one having trouble seeing James as anything other than the happy-go-lucky boss I'd known for the last ten years? My thoughts churned as I tried to digest this latest bombshell.

James was a *fucking dragon?*

"Wyvern!" Gideon snapped, thumping his fist on the island.

I looked at Cal, mouthing the word. He gave me a tiny shrug before turning his attention back to James.

I didn't bother to blast Gideon about staying out of my mind. At the moment, I was on thin ice with the Enforcer. The dark glare coming my way made my neck itch.

"I'm sorry, James." And I was. I felt terrible, not only for interrupting his meal but also for nosing in where we didn't belong. I'm sure it would have come out eventually, though. And to be fair, I wasn't a completely willing participant.

Gideon's attention snapped to Cal. He narrowed his eyes and a thready growl came from his chest.

SHIT! *Nothing like throwing Cal under the bus.*

James sighed. "I guess it would have come out eventually. But you two need to show some respect. It was fine when you didn't know my true identity. But now that you do, others will follow your lead. You simply cannot continue going around, thinking this is fun and games and putting me on the spot like that."

I swallowed, my heart sinking. He was right. I had been acting like a complete ass. I heard Gideon mumble something nasty as he read my thoughts.

"That's right, Gryphon. I'm apologizing. Enjoy it while you can."

He glowered at me, and I'm fairly certain I saw fur sprout along his arms for a brief moment before it disappeared. He was *ticked*.

"So, what exactly can a dragon do?" I asked.

"WYVERN!" Gideon bellowed, startling James. My boss narrowed his eyes at his Enforcer, who settled down and rubbed his face.

James pulled up a stool, his lips still tight. "A Wyvern isn't as large as a dragon, but our skills are similar. Flying, speed, strength—the ability to incinerate boisterous maidens who irritate them."

With a gasp, I looked at my boss. James' lips were a firm line, but a ghost of a smile lit his hazel eyes. Gideon grunted and rolled his neck to stare at the ceiling, stretching his muscles. The crack of his jaw sounded loud in the quiet lounge.

The three Syreni came through the sliding glass doors, and Ronan padded up behind me, his bare feet silent on the tiles. He must have sensed my distress.

"Is everything alright?" He rubbed my shoulders, and my tension eased. His warm touch was the pillar of support I needed right now. I wasn't alone in this. He would protect me, even if I didn't deserve it right now.

"Edaline? What is going on here?"

I covered Ronan's hand with mine. "Everything is fine. We met James' creature. He's a Wyvern."

Both of Gideon's fists crashed down on the island, cracking the marble. "Edaline, keep your mouth SHUT! *Or I will shut it for you.*"

James covered his eyes with one hand, his shoulders bunching. Tabitha and Bacchus made tracks, scuttling down the hallway and trotting up the stairs to the flybridge. Tabitha glanced over her shoulder, her eyes wide as her lips mouthed the words, *"Wyvern—wow!"*

Quietly, James said, "Will you all just stop it? We have a huge mission that we are about to face—he glared at Gideon—*together*. Each and every one of us is about to put our lives on the line. We don't need to go into this *arguing*. A united front is an absolute *must*."

He turned to me. "Edaline, just keep quiet about it for now, alright? I know you mean well, but no one else needs to know. The longer you are in this game, the more you will realize that information is the key to success." He stood up with a stretch.

"I'm feeling a little peckish. I'm going down to finish my dinner." James walked past us, nodding to Cal, who lowered his eyes.

Stopping before me, James leaned down to look straight into my face, his expression serious. "Edaline. Make sure you keep training. Your powers will be critical in this thing."

I looked into his eyes, seeing concern there. My chest tightened at the notion that James might get himself hurt during the fight. I lifted my hand, wiping a little red blob from his cheek.

"You have a little something there, big fella."

James chuckled as he stood, nodding to Ronan as he swept out of the room, his footsteps disappearing down the hall. The lounge went silent.

Gideon refused to meet my gaze.

"Oh, for crying out loud, Gideon. It's not like we divulged some sort of top-secret weapon."

The Gryphon ignored me and took another swig from his flask, his foot tapping on the base of his stool. The sound of the waves rushing against the hull filled the room. Even the engines, their quiet grumble barely noticeable through the lush carpet, thrummed their way into the uncomfortable silence.

Nope, he's definitely not letting this go.

Finally, Gideon spoke, his voice harsh.

"Cal, I am *incredibly* disappointed in you. You have, for the first time ever, embarrassed me in the eyes of the Sovereign. When I tasked you with keeping Edaline safe, I never expected you to behave like this."

Gideon turned to me, his expression nasty. "If we're laying things on the line, *Eddi*, we may as well get it all out there, right?"

I nodded. "Absolutely." Something told me I wouldn't like what was coming.

"Cal, you're such great pals, perhaps you should tell Edaline exactly what it is you do for me. Tell her your place in all of—*this.*" He waved his flask in the air, his eyes glittering.

Cal sucked in a breath and shook his head, his eyes round. He looked at me, and I saw ... *fear.*

"What is it? Tell me—Cal?"

"I ... um ... well, it's like this ... *Ahh* ... "

"TELL HER!" Gideon roared, the glasses rattling in the racks above the island.

Cal blurted, "I'm Gideon's Ensign. I report directly to him." At my horrified look, he said, "I'm a part of the Enforcer's security detail."

The evil chuckle that filled the air came from Gideon, whose eyes blazed a bright yellow. "Keep going, *Cal*. Tell her what you were *supposed* to be—*to her.*" The last two words came out a throaty baritone, as if Gideon fought a shift.

I shook my head, tears brimming on my lids. "Don't. I don't want to know." I wanted to run. I didn't want to hear the words. The only thing keeping me together was Ronan's grip on my shoulder, his thumb rubbing my icy skin.

Cal sat up straighter and took a deep breath, resolve tightening his expression. "I was tasked with rescuing you from the street and making sure you stayed safe. All these years, I've been working for Gideon."

Staring at the Enforcer, Cal's eyes were ice chips. "There. Are you happy?"

Gideon snarled at him, his fists clenched on the table. "It's time she knew the truth, *Ensign*. Or have you forgotten—*you work for me?*" The last words came out a garbled mess as tiny feathers sprouted across Gideon's bare shoulders, and faint stripes appeared across his skin.

Turning his head, Cal looked into my eyes. "I'm sorry, Eddi. I never meant to hurt you."

I couldn't breathe. As I stared at my friend—my only true friend in this whole damn world—I realized he'd never been ... *what I thought*. Not in the ten years since I'd met him behind that dumpster. It wasn't real. It was all a big, fat lie. All these years, he was paid. Every movie night. Every trip to the island. *Paid* ... to *babysit.*

"How *could* you!? All these years, *you LIED to me*." My voice trailed off, and the tears flowed, a waterfall sheeting down my face. I couldn't see. Behind me, Ronan's warning growl made it worse. Choking on my tears, I struggled to come to grips with Cal's revelation.

His shoulders slumped, and Cal looked down at his hands. "I'm sorry, Eddi. It's not like you think. I did enjoy spending time with you. I promise."

I shook my head, the tears flying. The pain that roared across my temples was excruciating. I couldn't feel my hands. My chest heaved, and I stood, clenching and unclenching my fists as I reeled in the tears as best I could. When I finally got it together, my voice was deathly quiet.

"All this time, I thought you were with me by choice. I thought I wasn't alone. But I was alone this whole time and never knew it. I wasn't *your friend.* I was your—*assignment."*

Ronan stepped forward and reached for me, trying to pull me into his arms. I shrugged him off, hearing a grunt as my fist connected somewhere unintentionally.

Shaking even though my skin was on fire, a hellish anger rode my tongue like a rodeo star. "You're nothing but a fucking liar, Cal. You're no better than him." I punched my hand toward Gideon, then turned to leave. At the patio doors, I looked back at Cal.

"You stay the hell away from me ... *Ensign*."

There was a sudden flash of blue over Cal's head, and I heard a yelp as Miri appeared, kicked Cal in the nose, and then hauled ass across the room to perch on my shoulder. She landed hard enough to bruise.

"Loser!" she snapped, an L-shaped hand waving in his direction.

Gideon watched the exchange, his form blurry through my tears. "This was low, even for you. *You fucking bastard*."

With that, I turned and charged out of the room, leaving the three most important figures in my life behind.

***

For once, I was glad it was nighttime. I could brood like a two-year-old on the upper deck, and no one would bother me. The Spectre traveled closer to the shoreline now, the moon rising above the dark trees on the horizon. The moon was so bright that it illuminated the entire deck.

I lay back on the comfortable gray sofa, staring up at the night sky. Miri sprawled beside me, her legs crossed and one hand behind her head, the little dent in the pillow next to mine making me realize I still had one friend. Or one-fiftieth of one. *Whatever.*

If my life hadn't flipped on its ear moments ago, this was the perfect place to relax. The breeze from the water caressed my tight, flaming face; the humidity was gone with the sun. Soft, fleecy cushions large enough to sprawl upon hugged my backside like a comfortable glove. I sulked in absolute comfort. Yay me.

Misery spread through me like a creeping plague. All this time. All those movie marathons, the trips to the reef, the nights spent enjoying the stars on the widow's walk—he was simply doing as he was told. Protecting me. Because he worked for Gideon. Cal was a cog in the Sovereign's wheel, and I had not one clue this entire time that he was paid to be my friend.

I thought back to the day he found me behind the dumpster. *"God, you're so prickly. I didn't expect that,"* he had said. Hot embarrassment flooded me every time I realized—even in those first few moments, Cal had hidden the truth from me.

I gasped, the pain in my chest almost unbearable. Miri reached out and rubbed my cheek, her tiny hand scrubbing at the fresh tears.

"It's ok, toots. Just another bump in the road—right?"

I turned my head her way, but she was a blurry blue blob.

"This isn't a bump, Miri. It's a fucking iceberg. What am I going to do now?" I covered my eyes with one arm, sobbing as Miri patted my hair. Without expecting to, I eventually fell asleep. I awoke to someone poking my leg.

"Hey, grumpy. My brother wants to know if you're ok."

I opened my eyes to see Tabitha leaning back on the cushions at my feet.

"Are you ok? Ronan is worried about you."

I glanced at the top of the stairs. "Where is he?"

"They're all at the dining table, going over plans for tomorrow night. He came up to check on you but you were asleep. He asked me to get him when you woke up."

She raised one eyebrow. "I'm sure you've noticed we aren't moving. While you were trying to get rid of this"—she circled her finger at my puffy face—"we pulled in and anchored in a sweet little spot outside Savannah. They'll organize everything this evening while we still have time to hash out the details."

I sat up and rubbed my eyes, which still burned from all the crying. The shitty details of the last few hours came crashing back, and I hung my head to pull myself together. I sucked in a breath, then let it out as a long, slow sigh.

"Savannah, huh? What a shame we can't go to shore and see it. It's supposed to be amazing. Cal and I booked a ghost tour—"

Tears sprouted, and with a sob, I covered my face. Tabitha pushed closer, her hand hovering over my back before she shrugged and patted me like a dog.

"It's ok, Eddi. This will all be water under the bridge soon. He's your friend. No one spends that much time together without developing a bond. Trust me. Enzo certainly has a bond, and it's impossible to shake him."

At the look of sheer misery on my face, she bit her lip. Then, her eyes lit up.

"I know! She thumped her chest, then waved her arms with a flourish. "Your newest, greatest, *bestest* friend ever—*me*—will take you on a ghost tour! Let's go, snookums!"

Miri screeched. "Me too! I want to see a ghost!" Launching off the couch, she buzzed in circles around our heads.

Tabitha raised her hands and shrugged. "See? We'll all go. Now get up."

"How the hell are we going to get ashore? The guys will never let us leave, and you know it."

Tabitha stood, looking down at my dry shorts. "Well, if I'm not mistaken, those clothes you are wearing are meant to dry quickly. Which means you can get wet. Which means we can go!*"* She spread her hands as if it made perfect sense.

Looking up at the night sky, her eyes focused on the moon, which was halfway to its zenith. "Ghost tours run at night if I'm not mistaken?"

I nodded my head. With a sudden wrench of my shoulder, Tabitha grabbed my hand and hauled me from the couch. She frogmarched me over to the railing, my feet barely touching down as I sputtered in surprise. Then with an over-exaggerated groan of effort, she yanked me off my feet and held me over her head like she was Hulk *freaking* Hogan.

I screamed.

"Bombs away!" Tabitha yelled before dropping me overboard and jumping in after me.

I came up sputtering, and when she split the surface beside me, I gave her a rough shove.

"*Jesus*, Tabitha! Don't scare me like that!" I shoved my bangs out of my eyes, spitting out a mouthful of brackish grossness. Treading water, I looked around me, my eyes widening at the waving marsh grass and dark tussocks that surrounded the little bay. The Spectre rose behind us, the gentle waves lapping at her hull.

A symphony of frogs bloated out their throaty songs, the high-pitched whine of cicadas making my ears ring. A fresh, wild scent filled the air—the earthy smell of decaying vegetation. I breathed in deeply, somehow enjoying the smell of the salt marsh that surrounded us.

Then, at the not-too-distant shore, a pair of silver eyes blinked open, glowing back at me. Then another pair. And another. All told ten or more pairs of glowing orbs soon stared back at us, some appearing to grow larger as we hovered next to the yacht.

"*Uhh,* Tabitha. You do realize this is alligator country, right?"

She laughed and rolled her eyes. "Of course, silly! You don't have to worry about them while you're with me."

She grabbed my arm and started swimming, the water jetting over my face in a solid sheet as she picked up speed. Choking, I slapped at her with my free hand.

Above us, a blue light sped along, hopping from tussock to tussock and waiting for us. Apparently, Miri wasn't about to be left behind.

Tab glanced over her shoulder, saw me submarining behind her, and stopped to sling me onto her back. As I wrapped my arms around her neck and spat out some unidentified vegetation, I didn't know whether to strangle her or hug her.

CHAPTER 24

The skin sticking to my dry shorts itched. Semi-dried brackish water was no fun at all when you couldn't change your clothes, and they were damp in all the wrong places. Tabitha was blissfully unaware of my discomfort as she chatted away with Miri, who was currently invisible on her shoulder.

As we relaxed at a cafe on River Street, the moon put on a breathtaking show over the Savannah River. At its highest point now, it cast an eerie glow over the cobblestones, the ethereal view like staring back in time.

The well-preserved history of the town was certainly a sight to see. Buildings still carried signage from the eighteen-hundred textile boom. The cotton warehouses lining River Street were now a row of interesting shops, restaurants, bakeries, and other touristy places. The famous Stone Stairs of Death tested my fitness when we climbed them earlier.

There were still plenty of people around, looking in shop windows or watching the river flow by as they leaned on the decorative railing. The Georgia Queen, a massive historic riverboat, was back from a dinner cruise, the guests long gone. It was quiet, and I enjoyed the mellow vibe spreading through the warm Savannah night. I tried not to think about Cal.

My glass of sweet tea sloshed as Miri took a drink. I could only imagine how she was doing that, with her little cup still back home in Marathon. On second thought—

"You're not swimming in there, are you?"

Miri giggled. "Of course not. I fell in, silly!" Sticky, wet footprints splatted across the table and ended on a napkin, which immediately soaked through. I rolled my eyes and took a sip of my coffee, which went better with my flaky pastry anyway. Tabitha was lucky I had cash in my pocket when she threw me overboard.

"Well, what's next, kids!?" Tabitha exclaimed. "The night is young!"

"We really should get back, Tab. They're going to be worried about us, and we left in such a hurry that I forgot my phone on the coffee table ..." I glared at her, but it was half-hearted at best. In reality, this side trip was just what I needed.

The ghost tour was amazing. We went with Patrick Burns, a kilt-wearing, enthusiastic guide who had been at it for years. He only used newsprint-verified sightings, which lent an air of authenticity to the tour. It wasn't hard to imagine how Savannah got the Most Haunted City in America designation. Patrick was an amazing storyteller, raising goosebumps at each stop on the tour.

In truth, a ghost tour was the best way to see Savannah if you didn't have a ton of time. Walking through the historic park squares, checking out creepy older homes ... entertainment at its finest. If you were a history buff, even better. I especially loved seeing the old-style lanterns still working on some of the streets. The cobbled roads flickering eerily beneath the flames took you right back in time.

Walking back toward River Street, we passed a row of stores and lingered to look in the windows. My favorites were the metaphysical shops with their spell kits, crystals, and colorful tarot cards all on display. One shop was packed to the rafters with witchy stuff and had a cool artsy sign hand-painted on a wooden piece of ship's hull. Hanging by ropes from the rafters, it was displayed on an angle that caught the light from a ship's lantern in the window.

"Witches Brew," I read. "Welcome to the witchy world of Sybil Metoyer."

Tabitha leaned over to look at the antique-framed picture propped in the window display. "Yeah. I wouldn't want to tangle with that one anytime soon."

I followed her gaze. A beautiful, dark-skinned woman stared back from the photo, her thin, lustrous braids artfully twisted to hang over one shoulder. Striking features and a haughty frown lent her an air of authority, her intelligent eyes pools of sabled midnight that sparkled from the frame. Lovely and luminous, an aura of power radiated from her image. I had the oddest sensation that I was being inspected in turn. Prickles skittered across my shoulders. She was absolutely stunning, in a freaky, *I could fry you with a snap of my fingers* way.

"Wait a minute! I know her! Cal and I were supposed to come and see her before our trip to the Dry Tortugas. Before we found Miri."

I looked at Tabitha who was still checking out the photo. "What a small world. And to think I almost came up here to get help with my past." A ghostly shiver whispered down my back. "She's involved with Hex somehow. It's hard to imagine her as a dark witch when you look at that picture. I mean, she looks powerful—but she doesn't seem *evil*."

Tabitha shrugged. "What makes you think she's a dark witch?"

"Your mother said she helped Hex and Cain cloak the cigar factory with powerful wards. They were so strong even an Immortalis couldn't pierce them. And Gideon hinted that she supplied the potion they hit James with. She's gotta be a dark practitioner, don't you think?"

Tabitha shrugged, her eyes trailing over the goods in the front window. "I'm not sure you can tell from a photo. I don't know about you, but there's something powerful inside this shop. I wouldn't want to mess with her if I didn't have to."

"I wish Cal could see this," I whispered. Tabitha raised an eyebrow.

"No, I mean it. As upset as I am with him, I don't think he was faking ... *that part*, anyway. He used to get so excited when he talked about going to Savannah. He set up an appointment with Sybil, but we had to cancel it."

God, I was talking about him like he was dead. I shuttered my thoughts because they were pointless. I might as well enjoy one night before going back to face the music. Still, it was impossible to ignore my clawing sensation of loss.

Eventually, we wandered back to River Street and enjoyed some freshly baked pastries from the last shop to flip its sign. Together with a nice rich coffee, it was a pleasant experience at the end of a really shitty day, even if Miri did just take a swim in my sweet tea. That made me think of Cal again, my hand coming up to rub my chest—

Miri screamed. Like, full-on, eye-squinting SCREAMED. It went on and on, the napkin flying up into the air as the table wobbled. She took a breath, then her wings snapped like tiny firecrackers as she launched herself from the table. The shrieking resumed, only this time, in short, ear-splitting bursts.

"GOD, be quiet!" Tabitha hissed, looking around. "Where did she go?"

I gawked at the tourists around us, whose eyes searched for the source of the racket. All except for one man. He stood in the middle of River Street, on the cobblestones, with his head cocked to one side.

Long, lithe limbs were the first thing I noticed, followed closely by the devilishly handsome face with a smooth olive complexion. Physically stunning, his matching hazel-green eyes screamed "shifter" to me.

Tabitha hissed, "Do you see him? Holy smokes, check out that body!"

I looked again. Yep, he was athletic, his muscular shoulders and chest obvious in spite of the floppy, ill-fitting cotton dress shirt he wore. It looked like he'd pulled it out of a dumpster, yet did nothing to detract from his beauty. The man wasn't a bodybuilder type, but if he had a muscle on his body, it was tight and true. My gawd.

Tabitha slapped me *hard*. "That was from Ronan."

"You *told* me to look!" She shot me a sideways grin before turning back to ogle the man on the street.

Who was, at this very moment, holding his hands over his throat and choking.

What the hell—?

He muttered something, and the coughing trailed off, followed closely by a smile that would have made a nun drop her pantaloons. Carefully, he pulled his hands away from his neck and held them cupped in front of his face. Gazing into them, his eyes glimmered like he had discovered a priceless artifact. A breeze teased his messy brown locks, and I sighed. It was like watching a love song playing out right in front of us.

There was no doubt in my mind that was Miri in his hands. I'd bet my life on it. And that would make him ... *who?* I had an idea, but I would find out for sure. I tapped Tabitha's arm and rolled my eyes in the hottie's direction. She nodded and jumped to her feet.

As we approached, my mind ticked over possible scenarios. I could think of only one that made any sense. When Tabitha and I stopped before him, his twinkling hazel eyes lifted—and an eerie, ageless quality drew me in as if I stared straight into the Cretaceous Period.

"Don't you think we need to move this little reunion somewhere more private ... *Cleatus?*"

He didn't answer, but he nodded, his eyes continuing their inspection of my face with an unnerving intensity. Still invisible, Miri fluttered to his shoulder, the sound of her sobs stirring a twinge in my chest.

Happy for her, I assumed this was the one and only Cleatus, the crocodile shifter of Dry Tortugas fame. He kept Miri company for years while she was stuck at Fort Jefferson. The Civil War Fort was a lone sentinel standing guard seventy-plus miles off the coast of Key West. We found her on a trip there and brought her home. I still laughed whenever she insisted that humans ate him.

Something wet trickled down his neck, accompanied by a host of sniffles and soggy hiccups. And dammit, if I didn't mist up at the sound of it.

Tabitha marched over to a bench tucked away from the streetlight under a magnolia tree. Cleatus followed and sat down, crossing his legs in a rather elegant way.

Interesting. I didn't know what I expected. Maybe I pictured someone—I don't know—shorter and more musclebound. With a long nose. I chuckled at the thought and settled down beside everyone.

Miri popped into view on the shadowy side of Cleatus' neck. He turned and gave her a warm smile, his odd-colored eyes rolling to silver in the reflection of a nearby lamppost.

Wow. Freaky.

"You are well, Miri." His voice was a throaty purr, and the deep, rumbling baritone echoed through his chest. "I have missed you more than I care to demonstrate in mixed company."

Tabitha and I looked at each other, our eyes popping wide.

Miri wiped her eyes and hugged his neck, rubbing on him like a little blue kitten. "It was horrible, I thought they *ATE* you!"

I hissed, "Miri, keep it down!" and looked around to make sure she hadn't called attention to us. The crowd was thinning, thank the gods.

"I'm sorry. I'm so excited to see him!" At my sharp look, she brought it down a notch or two, her lips pinching together as she clutched his short brown hair and squirmed.

"So, how did you come to be in Savannah, Cleatus?" Tabitha asked.

His eyes never leaving Miri, he said. "Well, as you know, my sense of direction isn't the best." Miri giggled. "When the humans took me away, as soon as I was freed, I tried to find my way back to you, flutter butt."

Oh my god, he has a nickname for her. How cute.

"I got turned around. They released me far from here. A place that was familiar, in a sea of grass. It was beautiful." He frowned, his eyes narrowing on the sprite.

"All I could think about was you, Miri. I had to know if you were safe. I didn't trust the other creatures on that godforsaken island. I left almost immediately to find my way back to you. I swam and swam, hugging the shoreline. For a long time, I didn't shift. I don't like asking for directions."

Tabitha leaned over and whispered from the side of her mouth, "Not that I told you, but Ronan doesn't either. Just sayin'."

At the soft expression in the shifter's eyes, my heart fluttered. I had to bite my lip to keep from sighing at his sweet declarations.

Cleatus let out a long breath. "As you can see, I chose badly. I was soon spotted, recaptured, and put into a wildlife rescue here in Savannah." He looked at me, his odd-colored irises flashing. "I'm assuming this is precisely the opposite direction that I desired?"

"Well, you might say that. You went about five hundred miles the wrong way." I resisted the urge to laugh.

Frowning, Cleatus lifted his hand and laid his palm out flat, and Miri hopped over to sit on it. He brought his hand to his face and stared into her eyes.

"I cannot tell you how relieved I am to have finally found you, sweetling. He pulled his hand closer and rubbed his cheek against her. Miri's high-pitched giggle was met with a low rumble from her handsome beau. I must say, they were an odd couple. How would they even—

Behind them, Tabitha opened her eyes as wide as they would go, then crossed them. I couldn't help it. I laughed. Miri had a boyfriend. A very tall, stunning, and completely unsuitable crocodile ... shifter ... *boyfriend.*

Miri, I never should have doubted you. I guess love isn't always physical.

I cleared my throat, and when they both looked at me, I had the sense that I was intruding on their *moment.* They might not have been able to do *the deed,* but I guess their bond was strong. *Weird*, but strong.

"Well, Cleatus. What do we do now? We obviously can't leave you here, but we have a bit of an issue—something that I'm fairly certain you'll want to avoid."

At his raised eyebrow, I added, "We're headed straight for a huge battle with a demon who is trying to enslave me, kill all the humans, and destroy the country."

The crocodile shifter leaned into my space and stared straight into my eyes. I resisted the urge to crane my neck away, swallowing nervously at the odd gesture.

With a throaty hiss, his chin jutted forward, revealing two-inch fangs as they slid up from his bottom jaw. One hand lifted, and he pointed at me, his long finger rippling with scales as a shining black talon stretched out from the very tip.

Then, he wiggled it, and Miri laughed.

"May I be of some assistance with this ... *issue?*"

CHAPTER 25

~ FELIX ~

My mouth slobbered around the smooth round ball crammed into it, the leather holster digging into the tender skin behind my ears. Two iron shackles gouged into my wrists as my weight pulled down, the very tips of my toes whispering over the carpet as I rotated. The position made it difficult to breathe around the mouthpiece, my torso and arms stretched to the point of pain.

The Benefactor sipped on a drink of some sort, her eyes traveling up and down the curves of my body while her free hand massaged her privates. As attractive as she was, the painful ache of my arms stifled any chance of arousal.

Being tied had the tiny hairs of my neck standing at attention. I wanted to growl, everything inside of me saying, *FIGHT!* I didn't dare. My twenty years at the end of Stephen's electric prod had taught me that. And this was Hex. She had been responsible for my care since I was a babe. She would never hurt me. So I waited, closing my eyes to hide my traitorous thoughts.

"You don't like that very much, do you." I opened my eyes at her voice, an oily whisper that vibrated with something foul. As I struggled to breathe, she smiled, her eyes dark with desire. Raising her hand and licking her fingers, she watched my reaction. I held my breath ... and my thoughts. There were no guarantees she wouldn't hear them.

When I didn't respond, she snapped her teeth together, walked over to the wall and cranked once more on the ratchet secured there, raising me another inch.

My toes brushed back and forth across the plush carpet, and I squeezed my eyes closed as my mouth moved around the ball. Saliva bubbled down my chin and neck. All I could focus on was how badly I wanted to wipe it away with my hand.

"No, you don't like that one little bit." She prowled over, setting her drink down and running both hands up and down my hips. Hex's eyes followed her hands, and when she curled her fingers, black polished claws slid forth, leaving shallow furrows in my scales. My body tensed at the burning pain of the scratches as a satisfied smile slid across her face.

"You creatures are my finest work. Positively spectacular."

She rolled her hand over my sex, still flaccid beneath my skins. I mouthed around the slobber-covered ball and a large wad of drool dribbled down my chin. Some splashed on her hand.

Lifting it to her mouth, she licked it off with a moan. "Salty with a hint of nectar," she purred. A frown aimed at my groin marred her perfectly made-up face.

All these years, we were taught she was the savior of humanity. That the great Hex would rally a world-renowned army to secure everyone's lives under a blanket of protection. I was part of that noble plan and loyal to my Benefactor.

I wanted to believe, even after what I saw. Everything inside me howled, "Give her a chance. Let her explain." Jovi told me I was naive, whatever that meant.

This uncomfortable experience was a test. It had to be. To ensure I was tough enough to serve her. At her hiss, I opened my eyes.

"There you are. No drifting away, Servus. I need you awake for this." A giggle bubbled from her crimson lips as she rubbed my groin again. When there was no response, she screeched in frustration, the high-pitched sound hurting my ears. It reminded me of the noise the feral cats in the yard made when the Argenti caught them.

With a dissatisfied grunt, she lifted her phone and spoke to someone. "Send Layla and Charles. *Now.*"

She sat on the bed and took a few more sips from her glass, watching me as I slowly rotated. There was a thump on the door, and a male and female walked in. One was a dark-haired man, quite handsome, his head bobbing with curls. The other was a blonde beauty—my favorite Succubus.

My cock stirred at the sight of her lovely golden tresses before I accidentally moved. At the jarring pain in my shoulders, my phallus shrank.

Hex nodded toward where I hung.

Layla smiled, coming to me and unbuckling the gag from my mouth, then sponging the drool from my chest with a cloth. With a final dab at my lips, she tossed the rag away and rubbed her hands over my pecs and shoulders.

"*Ohhh*, I remember you. You're Felix." She rubbed her cheek against my chest, then pulled back and slipped off her robe, draping it on the bed. Never before having seen a naked woman, let alone Layla, my response was instantaneous.

Her perky breasts were as full as melons, the cherry red berries of her nipples making my mouth water. My eyes trailed down her perfect body to the small sculpted patch of hair around her sex. When she turned away, her round, curvy ass made me groan. The Succubus looked over her shoulder and noticed my bulge, giving me a sultry smile.

The dark-haired male reclined naked on the bed, his elbows beneath him as he lay back and smiled up at Hex, his erection hopping. The benefactor put her drink down, then, in one smooth motion, straddled him and began to grind herself down onto his considerable length.

Without looking up, Hex barked, "Layla? Nectar!" She snapped her fingers over her head, and Layla's bright laughter tinkled through the room.

"Of course!" The grin on her stunning face made me flush. She came to stand before me, and when her magic hit, it was what I had always wanted—what I had always desired. Her sole attention was *mine*. My heart sped up to match the pulse in my shaft as it swelled beneath my skins, then burst free.

The wave of lust that rocked through me made my hips jerk, the answering pain in my wrists somehow intensifying the sensation. A moan wrung from my lips and my head fell forward, my breath suddenly heavy under the euphoric blanket that swaddled me. With a heady throb, a stream of nectar cascaded down my chin and dripped onto my chest.

With absolutely no control over myself, my cock strained against my belly, hard and long and throbbing painfully. Layla smiled up into my face, and when she reached out to smooth a hand over the weeping tip of my cock, I hissed.

My testicles, still buried inside my sheath, swelled and hardened, their agonized pulse joining the one in my phallus. My breaths came in short, sharp bursts as finally, Layla's hand gripped me. My legs shook, the chains above me rattled, and a ragged moan wrenched through my gritted teeth. Layla's magic washed over me, and my nectar poured.

"Now, that's better. *Lovely.*" Layla stood back with a satisfied smile, licking her lips as if she'd just had a meal at the finest restaurant in Charleston.

Her eyes glowing a faint crimson, Hex rose and dropped her robe before sauntering over to where I hung, my chest slick with nectar. She wore a slinky black piece of clothing, her breasts pointing up and out, fully visible through the gap in the frilly ruffles. I closed my eyes but jerked them open at her warning hiss.

Through hazy eyes, I watched as she leaned in and began licking my chest, the long, lazy swipes of her tongue gathering the nectar there. She looked me in the eyes, and her pupils shrank to pinpoints, then blew out so far that the color was gone—a solid black, with no white. Ever so slowly, her eyes drooped, becoming unfocused; her mouth parted, and her pink tongue slowly dabbed at her lips.

"*Yumm,*" Hex moaned, grabbing my cock in her hand. I grunted, thrusting into her strokes, my hips seeking friction as a thick haze seeped around me from behind.

Layla. She snuggled against my hip, her fingers gently probing my finely scaled buttocks, searching. Rubbing. Pushing, and finally finding the small hole there. As she slipped into me, my cock swelled to a painful state in Hex's hand, my legs shaking with powerful sensations as I dangled. The chain rattled over my head, the agony of my shoulders replaced with a cloud of bliss that pulled incoherent sounds from my throat.

Running the fingers of her opposite hand around the outline of my ear, Layla breathed gently beside my face and whispered, "Relax. You're going to love this."

A damp mist, sweet and cloying, feathered across my face, sneaking into my mouth as it opened with a gasp. Layla's finger prodded—*by the gods, yesss ...*

The soft erotic magic coated my body, whispering into me through every opening and filling me up with sensations too vast to comprehend. I was lost in a sea of arousal, tossed on waves of ecstasy that flirted over my skin, teasing me up and down, side to side, tugging on every sensual nerve ending in my body. My cock swelled until it ached, my balls spilling from my sheath and pulling tight beneath my shaft. A hand smoothed in and gripped them, squeezing tight, followed by a warm, wet mouth. Male whiskers bristled against my tightened sac, but I didn't care.

My eyes rolled back, and the world faded away. I jerked. I spasmed. Another wet mouth sucked me in, as something long and large enter me from behind, the pumping fullness prodding against nerve endings and pushing me over the edge. I screamed out an orgasm that rocked me to the very core of my existence.

And still, so painfully hard.

My body was lowered to the ground, my aching shoulders sinking into the luxurious carpet. An enormous shaft slid down my throat, two fists in my hair holding me while I slobbered and coughed around it. Something tight and wet gloved my throbbing cock, sliding up and down as my frenzied hips pumped into the slick opening. I came undone, my full throat choking through my release.

The suffering weight of an overwhelming bliss sank me beneath wave after wave of pleasure, my head tossing, my teeth biting through my tongue as I came, and came, and came.

Glistening folds settled onto my lips, my tongue dancing and thrusting of its own volition, hungrily taking the sweet dew that was offered. My overworked cock pounded until pleasure turned to pain. Claws raked my chest, my thighs, my buttocks, my belly. Nectar poured from my fangs, filling my mouth before being greedily sucked up by three lapping tongues. I didn't care.

I bled. I sobbed. I sank my dripping fangs into willing necks, and I came. And came.

And then, everything went quiet. My muffled, overtaxed mind sensed only darkness, although somehow, I was semi-conscious. The door clicked as two pairs of feet padded from the room.

I was on the floor, Hex's warm body lying on top of me, my hard cock tightly gripped inside of her. She rubbed up and down, bouncing and moaning, before screaming out her release. Finally, she slipped from me, my hard shaft jumping against my belly, unable to subside.

"You will go far under me, *Felix*."

Booted feet thumped into the room, and someone grabbed my arms and lifted me. Still fully aroused, I grunted as my member dragged across the floor, then brushed against fabric as I was carried somewhere. Unable to stop myself, I thrust into the sensations, earning a vicious slap across my buttocks.

I didn't care. I was lost somewhere in my own head, riding on waves of ecstasy through the darkest caverns of depravity.

***

I opened crusty eyes to see Jovi's anxious face peering down at me.

"Thank God you're awake! I was so worried." He had a cloth in his hand and resumed wiping my skin. The rag was white until he pulled it away, a bright red stain in his hand.

"My god, Felix. What did they do to you?"

I licked at my cracked lips. My throat was so dry and raw I couldn't speak around the bruising. Memories of the acts of savage passion that I experienced aroused me in spite of the pain of it. I winced and mashed my head into the pillow, my eyes screwing shut. I couldn't get comfortable, the sheets prickling against my irritated skin.

Jovi looked down at my hips, his eyes worried. Then the cloth was down there, too. It stung at first, but when Jovi was done, I felt clean. *Less dirty.*

I slept, waking again when Jovi fed me a tablet of some sort. "This will help with the pain," he said, his voice catching on a sob. I must have been a sight.

"You're feverish," he said, a tear tracking down his cheek. "Don't leave me, Felix. I can't do it without you." I wanted to comfort him, but I couldn't open my eyes long enough to say anything.

The next time I awoke, my vision was better, although the pain was worse. I wondered how it would have felt if Jovi hadn't given me that pill. When I tried to sit up, scabs had formed over the lacerations on my body, and they pulled painfully at the motion.

I flopped back down with a groan. At least my penis was finally tucked away inside my skins, although it stung so badly I wondered if it would ever heal.

Jovi went to practice, but thankfully, no one called my name, and I was allowed to stay in my bed. After everyone left, I had a long time to reflect.

The truth was, I couldn't think. I was in shock, something we learned about in our training. My head felt like it was full of cotton, and I had trouble seeing things clearly. But as the day wore on, I knew. It came gradually, the knowing. But when I weighed what I had seen, and measured what I had experienced, it all came down to one explanation.

Our benefactor was sick. Something dark and rotten ate away at her. She was no longer sane. We needed to—*she just needed some help*, that was all. I allowed myself a slight measure of relief at the thought.

A few more hours of soul-searching passed, and I thought about the men that were killed on the minesweeper. Hex reacting the way she did wasn't an illness. She enjoyed it. It made her happy. This was not a sickness.

After Boris nearly killed Jovi, and he wound up in the infirmary, my friend used a word that I couldn't quite remember. It was on the tip of my tongue. Something that described our trainer's vicious behavior.

What was it?

Psychopath. Or was it Sociopath? Maybe both. I couldn't remember.

I lay there a while longer, the cuts and slices that marred my body slowly healing. I slept, but when I wasn't sleeping, I was thinking. About the training we had undergone. The weekly horror of Friday. The Argenti's vicious cruelty. Axel, and Layla. Stephen's electric prod. The humans in the library. The way I felt when I saw these things unfold.

In the afternoon, I rolled over and stared at the wall. Axel said Hex was a demon, and the Servus were spawned from a Syreni Doyenne and a Djinn. Could he be telling the truth? Were we all just a bunch of pawns in a twisted plan? Did I have a father down in that cell?

After our visit to the depths of the facility, Jovi looked up the word Doyenne in the library. It meant a highly respected female. If Axel was right, the Argenti and Servus were not just brothers in arms—we were full-blooded brothers from a powerful Syreni female. Jovi had explained why Argenti and Servus were so different. Genetic variability, he said.

Where were the females from this cross? *Our sisters?* I had a terrible feeling that Hex wouldn't hesitate to dispose of anything that didn't serve her purpose.

Thinking about it made my head hurt, so I fell back to sleep.

The door slammed, and Jovi was there, his face anxious. "How are you now, Felix?" I opened my eyes, wondering why he whispered.

"I'm fine. Better. Thank you for caring for me." I looked at him. "Jovi, I had all day to think. Something occurred to me. In the library—have you ever looked up anything about our race? About the Servus?"

Jovi's eyebrows disappeared into his hairline. "Yes, I looked it up. I couldn't find any information about our heritage. It's just a name."

I shook my head. "I don't think it is. I need you to look it up again. Look harder." I raised my head, and it throbbed at the motion. "Please."

Jovi nodded. "I have some library credits. I will use them this afternoon." He reached out to grasp my arm and squeezed it before leaving. As the door slammed shut behind him, I fell into a restless sleep.

CHAPTER 26

Gideon cocked his head, looking up and down the full length of our new friend. Cleatus lay sprawled across the swim platform in his crocodile form. I must say, he was an impressive beast at over thirteen feet long. His eyes were the same as his human form, an olive green. But now, they had a catty slit that made him look wickedly dangerous. And at the moment, they were narrowed—at the Enforcer.

His lips thinning, Gideon snapped, "What do you propose I do with *THAT?*"

Miri gasped and flew down to sit between Cleatus' eyes, her chin shoved forward. "He's not a *THAT*... he's a crocodile. And he's *fierce!*" Miri's blue aura throbbed in the dim light of dawn as she stroked the end of the croc's nose. The rumble coming from Cleatus sounded suspiciously like laughter.

"Yes, I see that. But what can a crocodile shifter *do?*" Gideon looked at Miri, his expression flat. "We will not unnecessarily risk the lives of *Others* in this venture, *Sprite.*"

A reptilian tail came out of nowhere, thumping down where the Enforcer had stood a second before. Slightly off balance from his evasion, Gideon staggered backward. Cleatus launched himself across the swim deck, his low-slung form scrambling forward and upward, knocking Gideon flat on his back.

In a flash, the croc was on top of him, his substantial weight holding down the struggling Enforcer. With a toothy hiss, Cleatus opened his mouth, his head twisting to snatch Gideon's head between his jaws. It was over before I could blink.

Framed by a pair of crocodile jaws, Gideon screwed up his nostrils as if smelling something foul. His face went red, his voice strained under the grip of one hundred thick, pointed teeth.

"Alright. I see your point. Now let me go."

With a long, slow hiss, Cleatus backed away, settling near the edge of the platform as if nothing had happened.

Gideon rose, straightened his shorts, and scooped some water from the bay to scrub off his face. A row of fat dents marred his tanned skin. The disgusted grimace as he cleaned himself up made me laugh on the inside.

A head popped over the railing on the main deck, then James thumped down the stairs. "I heard we had company. What did I miss?" James gave the massive croc a once-over, lifting one eyebrow. He looked at Gideon, who shrugged.

"Welcome, friend," James said. "Any chance we can get you into your human form and have a conversation about how to utilize your skills?"

I expected a flash-bang like I'd seen with other shifters, but that's not how our croc shifted. It was gross, actually. Bones popped and snapped, cringe-worthy sucking noises coming from his gaping jaws as slowly, one by one, Cleatus's limbs reshaped themselves back into human form. It reminded me of those weird black firework snakes in reverse. No wonder he didn't stop to ask for directions.

After quite a few rather gross and painful contortions, Cleatus lay face down on the deck, his bare ass pointing at the sky. It was completely undignified, to be honest. I had to stifle a giggle because Miri kept shooting me dirty looks as if reading my thoughts.

Cleatus let out a slow groan before pulling himself to his knees and standing up. He was naked. *Aaannd* now I knew why Miri loved this guy so much.

Holy jumbo hotdogs, Batman.

James smiled into the newcomer's eyes, refusing to look down. "Gideon, I think his clothing is about your size. Do you mind?"

Our Enforcer grumbled but trucked up the stairs and disappeared. I looked around, wondering why Cal hadn't appeared by now. It was probably for the best. I wasn't sure I could handle that conversation just yet.

James said, "Gideon took Cal ahead to Charleston. He'll scout the bay for us."

"The bay? As in, he's going to be in the ocean?" My stomach plummeted, and then I realized ... *James heard my thoughts.* Perfect. Another mental peeping Tom.

"Don't worry yourself. Cal is smart, Eddi. He'll keep himself safe." James looked into my eyes. "FYI, I don't read your mind. Not often, anyway. But for the record, you do think pretty damn loudly. It's hard not to hear you," he chuckled.

I ignored him, and for a moment, I couldn't breathe. Cal's very white, very obvious octopus was a crawling sushi appetizer every time he went into the ocean. Conflict raged in my brain, the push and pull of anger and fear making me seasick.

James reached out and placed a hand on my arm. "He'll be fine. Don't worry. He's well trained."

Like a yo-yo, my mind snapped back to anger. *Trained. As in my trained guard dog for almost ten years. And I didn't know it.* I frowned, and my stomach settled along with my resolve.

Tabitha appeared at the railing and trotted down the stairs, coming to a full stop. Her eyes narrowed, and her lips curled in as she took in a *very* exposed Cleatus.

"Wow," she breathed.

Miri snarled like a rabid blue chipmunk. Reaching out, she gripped Cleatus's ear, howling, "He's mine! No looking! No touching!"

When the Sprite shook a fist at her, Tabitha rolled her eyes, but that didn't stop her from checking out the impressive view. Thankfully, Gideon appeared with a set of swim trunks. Cleatus slipped them on, and there was a collective sigh of relief.

James motioned for us all to move to the covered lounge deck, and soon, we were all situated for an impromptu meeting. There was a splash near the stern, and Ronan and Bacchus trotted up the steps, Bacchus carrying a large grouper over one shoulder. He took the fish to the kitchen and flopped it into the sink before returning.

Gideon yelled, "HANDS!" Bacchus sulked back to the sink to wash up, grumbling the entire time.

James opened a laptop and put it on the coffee table, turning it so we could all see. It was a detailed map of Charleston Harbor, showing the location of the lab.

"Cal is currently watching the comings and goings of their facility. As you can see, it's not a huge place. We estimate there are fifty or so of their—*creations*—on site. I'm not sure what to call them, actually. As you know, they are Djinn-Syreni hybrids. Our initial reports say that most resemble Syreni males, with almost no physical differences. The other third or so resemble their Djinn sire. Other than general appearances, we know nothing about her force."

At my wide-eyed look, James added, "We're working on it. It takes time, Ed. I'm told that besides being very aggressive, the Djinn look-alikes have webbed hands and feet. Very unusual."

My God. I didn't know whether to be excited about the prospect of seeing another Djinn or horrified that they were mutants.

"Not mutants, Eddi. *Hybrids*. There's a difference," Gideon mumbled.

He'd been much quieter today, and I had caught him giving me strange looks all afternoon. If I didn't know better, I'd say that Gideon felt bad about hurting me.

Right. Now he grows a conscience.

James continued. "They outnumber us, but the remaining thirty Syreni warriors from *the Shoal* will arrive this evening and are outstanding fighters. We'll head to Fort Sumter at midnight and avoid detection using the far side of the island for cover."

So far, his plan sounded pretty good.

"Gideon aims to organize everyone and storm the building just after midnight."

My stomach fell. Right. There it was. It was time to head straight into hell.

***

As the Spectre powered across the Atlantic on a crash course with Charleston, Ronan and I cuddled on a couch on the flybridge. Tabitha and Bacchus sat opposite us, while Cleatus and Miri were on the rear deck catching up.

The sun was high in the sky, its blazing heat whisked away by the wind. Lying back against Ronan's warm chest, I felt at peace. I knew bad things were coming down the pipes, but for now, I was content to laze in his arms.

His hands stroked up and down my arms, his warm breath tickling my ear as Ronan talked with his siblings. His rumbled words vibrated through my back, relaxing me until I stifled a yawn.

"So let me get this straight," I grumped. "We're just scrambling over the wall, plopping down on the other side, and scattering? Does anyone else think this is a bit ... I don't know ... *suicidal?*"

Tabitha shrugged. "Maybe Cal and whoever is helping him inspect the site know something we don't. It sounds very awkward to me as well." Her smile was sharp. "I have no doubt our warriors will meet any challenge with a tremendous show of strength. They are fearless males, every one of them, and incredibly strong. I look forward to seeing Enzo in action." The words were out of her mouth before she realized it and turned a flaming shade of red.

Ronan sounded quiet but confident. "All of our lives, we have trained to protect the *Shoal*. We are ready for whatever comes our way."

Stretching, I snuggled into my Syreni pillow as something hard poked into my back. I stifled a smile and said, "James says we're not to kill our opponents unless we have no other option. How is that even possible?"

I leaned back to look into Ronan's eyes. Ok, his chin. "Do you think he's planning something and not telling us? You know Gideon, the information miser. He's got a trick up his sleeve, or he's not giving us an important detail."

Ronan chuckled into my ear, and I crossed my arms to cover the headlights poking through my t-shirt.

"It seems like something he would do, yes." Ronan gazed down at me, his eyes finding mine. "I am worried about you, Eddi. Are you sure there is no way I can talk you out of joining the fight in Charleston?"

I shook my head, and he sighed. Pulling me up, Ronan dropped a kiss to my lips, then went back to gazing at the ocean racing by. James and Gideon had picked up the pace, the Spectre plowing along at it's max speed of 52 knots, which was about sixty miles per hour. The wind whipping over our heads was an amazing feeling, the luxury yacht soaking up the bumps for a smooth ride.

Getting up, I reached for my phone. I had been texting Phoebe all day, filling in the details. Augusta, Georgia, where Phoebe ran a small occult shop, was a few hours from Charleston. As soon as she heard my news, she insisted on joining us, hoping that Oliver was one of the captive Djinn.

Gideon had no idea, of course. I didn't trust him, not completely. Ronan agreed with my decision not to tell him. While he wasn't keen to see my new friend in danger, I think he hoped Phoebe would be another layer of protection for me.

Phoebe made some calls to friends in Charleston and asked about the lab building. One of her friends owned a food supply company that delivered to the facility several times a week. In no time at all, she had cooked up a plan, and it was brilliant. As I scrolled to see her latest message, my shoulders tightened.

There was a message from Cal, brief and to the point—sent from Gideon's new phone.

"I know you're mad at me. I'm sorry. I never meant to hurt you."

Eyes misting, I grit my teeth and kept scrolling, finding Phoebe's message.

"I'll be there before you. My friends don't know the details but are on board. They scheduled a delivery for tomorrow at the end of the work day. I'll be waiting inside if I can manage it. Can't wait to see the fireworks!"

In spite of my happiness to see her again, the words dug into my stomach like a dull knife. I was exposing Phoebe to a deadly situation. A sudden desire to cancel her efforts made my fingers hover over the keys, my teeth worrying my lips.

Ronan reached out, setting my phone aside and taking my shaking hands into his warm, steady grip. "I am glad your friend can make it, although I'm not sure how a ward witch can help during a battle."

"You're right. I should never have mentioned the Djinn captives to her. She's hoping it's Oliver, of course. I warned her not to get too excited." I rolled my head back to meet Ronan's soft gaze. "Maybe she has a few tricks up her sleeve. I just hope Gideon doesn't kill me when she shows up without an invite."

"Oh, he's definitely going to kill you," Tabitha grinned. "I can't wait to see his face."

CHAPTER 27

Ronan and I stood on the bow, the sun slowly beginning its drop to the sea. We made excellent time, and watching Charleston Harbor creep closer intensified the sick feeling in my stomach. On any other day, at any other time, I would have thoroughly enjoyed this experience.

The boat traffic was impressive, and yet there was plenty of room to maneuver, the beautiful harbor a flurry of vessels of all sizes. Squatting at the mouth of the harbor was Fort Sumter, its red brick walls just visible above the water. I would have loved to see it under different circumstances.

We anchored in the mouth of the Ashley River. Gideon tucked the Spectre as far inside the cluster of boats as he could manage, although I doubted it would help much. A crimson boat stood out, even *without* a spider on the hull.

As the giant windlass clanked out its spool of chain, the metallic sounds raked across my nerves. I couldn't stop picturing my father, less than a mile away, suffering beneath Hex's thumb. Under what circumstances had he lived these last ten years? Was he in pain? Was he hanging on, or was I too late? Deep down, I feared the worst, wavering back and forth between hope and grim resignation.

The constant tension turned my stomach into a churning mess, and I hadn't been able to eat this morning without tossing my cookies. I resolved not to let my fear show.

Ronan wrapped his arms around me and whispered into my ear. "It will be alright. I will protect you."

After anchoring, a steady stream of traffic to the helm marked the final stages of planning. The dinner table was quiet, not a word spoken, the only sound the clinking of silverware and glasses. At about ten pm, several boats slipped up beside the Spectre to quietly drop off the Syreni males that would join us for the coming shit storm.

Every jaw set like granite, the massive Syreni males climbed on board the Spectre. As a stream of burly bodies thumped up the curved stairs, my eyes grew rounder.

Tabitha stood beside me, and it was obvious that she scanned for Enzo. I watched her expression from the corner of my eye, the straight line of my lips curling up when her face brightened. When the striking blonde male powered up the staircase, Enzo's eyes locked onto Tabitha as he beamed a knowing smile. She sucked in a breath when I elbowed her in the ribs.

"What!?" she yelped, pink flooding her cheeks. Tabitha looked down her nose at me and turned away with a haughty sniff. I would have been offended had I not caught the sparkle in her eye.

Soon, our forces crowded under the overhang of the outer lounge deck, a sea of sparkling skins and tanned torsos gleaming beneath the full moon. Light wouldn't be an issue tonight. Whether that worked for or against us was unclear. It was too late to worry about that now.

The windlass hauled up the anchor, the motors grumbled to life, and James and Gideon eased us forward into the channel. We headed to the far side of Fort Sumter, and from there, we would launch our attack. The trip was short, and soon, we were in position.

Cleatus and Miri hugged the shadowed corner near the patio door. It was the same place Cain had stood in the moments before we confronted Hex the last time. Thoughts of the vampire made me shudder, and I pushed them away.

The crocodile shifter might be a looker, but he wasn't much of a talker. With Miri standing on his shoulder, holding onto his hair, his hazel eyes rolled over the lounge as he examined the restless fighters. Preternaturally still, his gaze flicked from body to body as if memorizing every detail. It looked oddly predatory. I was glad he was on our side, especially with the eerie glow every time his eyes hit the right angle in the moonlight.

Everyone on deck had weapons. Most carried short swords like Ronan or daggers like mine. A few, Tabitha included, held the short, very practical cutlass. The cup guard covering the handle always made me think of pirates, who favored them during that era. Short, light, and easy to use in tight spaces, they were perfect for close-quarters fighting..

Bacchus and one or two others had homemade maces, the protruding nails transforming the crude wooden logs into something deadly. Two gleaming golden tridents were visible over everyone's heads, their wielders taller and more heavily muscled than the other Syreni. I asked Ronan about them.

"They are the finest weapon for the sea, better even than the short sword I carry. Because they are slender, the water does not push back on them. The long, narrow shape makes it perfect for underwater combat, should it come to pass."

Neither James nor Gideon carried a weapon—they were weapons already. They didn't need any help.

As James' voice droned on, with occasional remarks by Gideon, I tuned out. I knew what was coming. I wondered, deep down, if my magic would come when I asked for it. I could only hope.

Checking my texts, I scrolled to see that there was no word from Phoebe. A lump lodged in my throat and stayed there. Closing my eyes, I prayed she was alright.

Hearing a familiar voice, I turned my head to see Cal trot up the curved stairs from the swim platform. He immediately noticed Miri and Cleatus, raising his eyebrows. Blank gray eyes swept over me as his expression flattened, a casual mask sliding into place. It hurt like hell.

Crossing the room to stand behind Gideon, Cal leaned forward to speak quietly into his ear. The shifter shadowing him was a female Syreni.

Leaning over, Tabitha whispered, "She's from the Key Largo *Shoal.* Her name is Chloe."

A sparkling blue, her eyes were bright and constantly moving. Chloe took in her surroundings, her confidence and poise making me a bit jealous. Tabitha saw me staring.

"Syreni females are rare. *Special.* Of course, we're confident," she whispered, then shushed me.

Cal didn't look my way again. A burning ache raked my insides, the desire to speak with him making me antsy. For a second, I thought about going to him. Now that the shock had subsided, I wanted to know—*why?* Why didn't he tell me?

I needed to know, dammit! *What next* would have been a great subject, too. But there wasn't time.

I swallowed the lump in my throat, choking on the thought that I may never get a chance to have that conversation with him. I let out my breath with a long, shuddering sigh. At least I could relax, knowing he wasn't shark bait.

Ronan, sensing my distress, put his arm around my shoulders and pulled me close. As he held me, he nodded to Syreni males as they moved around us, the group restless to get moving.

Soon, everyone had gathered. It was time, Fort Sumter looming just off the port side. My hands clenched into fists, my damp palms slick under the press of my fingernails. How would I have the guts to follow through with this? What if something happened to my friends? And what if my father was already dead? If he was, the heartache would kill me quicker than Hex ever could.

There was a brilliant flash of light, and the fighters around me jostled as Gideon transformed. His wings stretched out over everyone's head, showing not a trace of stiffness. His neck arching upward, the Gryphon's tufted ears brushed the ceiling as his eyes blinked open, yellow lighting up the surrounding faces.

The Enforcer snapped his beak a few times as if stretching his jaws. The furred tip of his striped tail twitched, thumping between the wall of the lounge and the brightly scaled legs gathered around his massive form. Raising his shoulders in a cat-like stretch, the six-inch black talons on all four of his thick feet hooked into the rug, lifting it a few inches before letting go.

Gideon turned his head to nod at me as he padded toward the open end of the lounge. He looked so regal, his wings ruffling as the ocean breeze teased the long tiger-striped feathers. The fighters parted to let him through, and I heard him in my mind.

"*Follow your orders, Edaline. Do not stray from the plan. Be safe.*"

A familiar tickle buzzed between my ears. Not wanting to give away my Phoebe secret, I thought about Mr. Potato Head baking some pot brownies. Gideon's stare jerked toward me, his golden eyes narrowing.

With a subtle hiss, he turned toward the ocean and crouched, the Spectre holding firm as he launched himself into the night. The silvery backdrop of the moon briefly displayed his silhouette, his broad wings beating the air once or twice before he blinked out of sight.

In his absence, the mood on board shifted. Filled with a nervous energy, my eyes went to the beautiful full moon. A face peered back at me, and I wondered if I imagined the smirk there tonight. Laying down a silvery trail across the black waves of the harbor, the glowing orb lit us up like we were players on a stage. Whether the light of the damn thing would be a help or a hindrance, we'd find out soon enough.

CHAPTER 28

~ ORIANA ~

Once again, I checked the jagged wound on the young Syreni male. I was concerned about his color. He had not regained consciousness since the vampires stormed our home, stealing every single Syreni. Matilda clung to my leg, her lip trembling, her eyes like a lighthouse beacon. I bent down to soothe her.

"Don't worry, little one. I am here. They will not hurt you as long as I still breathe."

Matilda looked up, my heart twisting as my own eyes shone back at me. They glittered with unshed tears. The child was positively terrified.

"I miss Miri and Eddi. Do you think they're ok? Will they come and save us again?"

I nodded. "If I know anything, it's that nothing will stop them."

As predicted, the moon had brought an extreme low tide to the *Shoal*. We left all of our young males patrolling for stray humans or guarding the entrance. When night fell, the tunnels of the *Shoal* were still fully accessible, the water at knee height.

By dusk, the ocean had begun to rise again, but a sixth sense made my scalp tingle for hours on end. Our young force pulled back inside the caverns, a small group of the oldest males tasked with guarding the entrance until the water level returned to normal.

When night fell, it wasn't curious humans who breached our home—it was vampires. Horrible and cold, their eyes glowing a deathly red, they'd charged in and taken everyone. Our young males fought back, killing a few of the invaders with their swords; some were badly injured, and a few now hovered near death. It was clear that the undead filth were instructed not to kill, but it didn't stop them from cracking heads and feeding off some of their victims.

Compelled to obey, we were herded onto a ship, where they shoved us inside a long metal container. Dawn came, and as we rocked along on rough seas, the blasting heat of the rising sun began to take its toll.

We'd seen no one since they shoved us in here. The doors were secure. We were stuck. I stood tall for my people and fought back the tears.

Our prison was barely large enough if everyone stood, so there was little room in the container to lay down our wounded. The injured boys were together at my feet, and I tended them as best I could.

Our captors provided water, which was something, at least. Matilda had torn off a piece of her t-shirt, and I washed away the blood of our fallen as we bounced along. I was not a healer like my son Ronan. The rare trait was a blessing, but sadly, I didn't possess it.

My heart raged at the familiar helplessness and lack of control. Yet again, I was shackled, the natural beauty of my home lost to me, possibly forever this time. But it was the younglings that made it so much worse. My lip trembled whenever I thought of what was in store for them.

So I sucked in my frantic thoughts and calmly organized the terrified group, preparing them for what was bound to come. My words of encouragement sounded hollow in my throat. In the last hours, I had begun to lose hope, fearing that we were doomed.

It had been a hellish ride. After what felt like a lifetime of rolling on the open sea, the sounds of loud voices and beeping filled the container. As one, we stumbled against the walls as the floor rocked beneath our feet. There was another smoother phase of our journey where I heard loud traffic, but after a time and a few bumps and scrapes, we were still.

My eyes drifted up to the small round holes along the top of the container, the only ventilation in this miserable place. We lifted a young male up to peek through a hole, learning we were in the shade of some trees. There was a brick wall and dead grass, but that was all he saw from the tiny vent. Even in the shade, it was far, far too hot.

The cries of youngsters mixed with the tearful whispers of the adult females as the temperature rose inside our prison. I tried to comfort them, telling them that we were valuable to our captors. They wouldn't go to all the trouble of taking us only to let us die. In truth, I wasn't entirely sure about that. What were their plans for a bunch of females, young boys, and babes?

One thing was for certain—our captors would return. And when they did, we would be ready for them. I would not make the same mistake that put me under Cain's thumb. I would fight until the last drop of my blood seeped into the parched earth outside our prison.

Beside me, Matilda tugged on my arm. When I looked down, her emerald eyes shone at me through the tears. "Galahad is here," she whispered.

CHAPTER 29

~ CHARLESTON ~
GALAHAD

I watched the tiny ball of mist, no bigger than a plum, as it twisted and swirled, nearly invisible in the moon-kissed darkness of the courtyard. Had I not possessed the sharp eyes of a Djinn, I would have missed the tiny sliver of someone special. A clever little someone inspecting the hazards around them.

Tendrils of magic reached out like a curious child, testing and teasing and drifting along the ground. The mist trailed over the weeds, then swerved into the corner of the yard where a pile of brush covered Boris, Hex's vampire trainer, who was currently enjoying a dirt nap.

The mist recoiled, then turned to investigate the stone walls and the massive rack filled with weapons directly behind the container. I watched it drift above the vast selection of swords, lances, and archery equipment, touching each sharpened tip and feathered arrow. My heart swelled with pride. Matilda had been practicing what I taught her.

I opened my mind, and the mist paused, then came toward me with steady purpose. Speeding up the stone wall, it darted between the leaves of the ancient tree that hid me from prying eyes. Gently, it came to rest on my outstretched hand.

It smelled of verbena and sunshine and tickled me as it twisted against my palm. I lifted it to my face, breathing in the sweet, flowery scent of the child I had grown to love. For the briefest of moments, my cold heart thawed, but the warmth gave way to an icy reality.

All afternoon I had watched from my perch, my chest throbbing, as I concealed myself in the canopy of an overgrown sycamore trailing over the wall. The container arrived at sunset, a crew of Hex's vampires watching from the shadows as it was lowered into place beneath me.

The box was full of Syreni. Their heat signatures lit up my mind—at least twenty of various ages, a few prone bodies close to death.

I snarled softly to myself at the knowledge that Matilda was captured. When Edaline and her friends stole her from Hex, I had hoped she would finally be safe. Now, the child was back under the Manticore's cancerous influence.

Pain spiked through me, a grim reminder of my years of service—resisting the demon's directives meant paying an agonizing price. The oath may be unbreakable, but for Matilda, I would try. No one deserved a life of forced servitude, especially her.

Time was not on our side. Hex had plans for the little Djinn in that container and for Edaline. I blew gently into the misty sphere in my hand and smiled as it swirled in response.

"I am here." Narrowing my eyes, I filled the tumbling haze with positive, reassuring thoughts and sent it back to its maker. As it slipped through the ventilation hole, I thought back to the surprising events that had put me in this tree.

***

When Gideon crashed into the lighthouse with me in tow, I narrowly escaped with my life. Blinking to mist a millisecond before he crushed me was a well-timed stroke of luck. The Gryphon had not fared as well.

My legs wobbled, and I fell to the sand, dropping my forehead onto my knees. My sides heaving, I caught my breath under the hot afternoon sun.

Wisteria Island, two miles from Key West, lay vacant due to the greed of men and an indecisive human power chain. How fortunate for the Gryphon, who was clearly visible on the rocks behind me. His powers had fled with his life force, leaving him exposed to prying human eyes. The Sovereign, whoever he was, would have a hard time covering this one up.

Rubbing my neck, I raised my head. Gideon's broken body lay draped over the jagged rocks below the lighthouse. Like broken tent poles, the bones of his wings jutted in every direction. Relaxed in death, four thickly furred legs and his orange-striped tail dangled over the edges of the jagged boulders that had sealed his fate.

My eyes traced the long smear of feathers, skin, and blood that streaked the side of the tower. A twinge of regret flickered through my mind but was quickly snuffed out by the insistence of Hex's command. I must ensure he was dead.

Dusting the sand from my black leathers, I crawled over the rocks to inspect the carcass dangling above me. The Gryphon's crushed skull, hanging over the ledge in a matted mess of blood and feathers, turned my stomach. His long, forked tongue dangled and swayed, already drying in the ocean breeze.

Definitely dead.

Lifting my eyes to the horizon, I watched the boats of Garrison Bight darting like bees from a hive—close enough to see, yet here I was, stranded. The sun had begun its descent, signaling the end of another miserable day in my life. I needed to hurry.

Hex's talisman dangled under my shirt, a black weight that dragged me under even as it pulled me back to her side. Killing her was a solid guarantee of my own miserable end, so here I was, doing devilish deeds in her name.

Looking up at Gideon's gaping mouth, my heart eased at the knowledge that I would not have to end the beast after all. Now, the only question was how to get back to my puppet master.

A faint sound froze me in place.

Cocking my head, I listened. Then, I heard it again. A single, struggling thump.

Gideon.

Unable to resist my directive, I looked up at the horrific mess leaking from the rocky shelf above my head. Crouching beneath his neck, I hefted my sword. I would honor him by delivering a tidy, efficient kill.

Flipping my sword tip up, my hands clenched the golden hilt. I bent my knees, my mouth open in anticipation of the effort it would require to punch through his thickly feathered neck.

Sickness swirled through my guts, and in my mind's eye, the sweet face of a child came into focus.

"Is it hard for you to kill things, Galahad?"

I hesitated. A throbbing pain began in my temple, quickly radiating down the side of my neck and into both arms. I clenched my jaw, the imperative to end the creature shoving away the memory of the child.

"I don't like it when you kill things. It's not fair." Tears—fat shining tears that melted my heart. The memory of her words hurt worse than the oath that scored my insides as I delayed.

As my mouth hung open in anguish, I looked up just in time to catch a fat drop of blood as it rolled down the dangling tongue. With perfect aim, it landed at the very back of my throat. I choked and dropped my sword.

"Fucking Gryphon! On death's door, and you're still a pain in my ass."

Bending over, I spat until the coppery tang disappeared, then looked for my sword. It had clattered into the rocks, the tip lodging in a crack. The Gryphon stirred, and I scrambled for it.

"Will I be like you someday? Will she make me kill things, too?" More tears, the thought of her sparkling green eyes whisking prickles across my skin.

My blade was firmly lodged. I couldn't pry it loose. Back and forth, side to side, I worked at the wedged tip. Another heartbeat and Galahad's mouth began to bleed in earnest, crimson droplets splattering my face like rain when I looked up. It pooled in my eyes, making me blink as I dashed it away with my fingers.

"Will you just die already!?"

At last, the tip scraped, and the sword came free in my bloody hands. I raised it again, another much louder thump of Gideon's heart startling me. The tip of his tail twitched, and I hesitated for no good reason other than curiosity. How was he still alive?

I growled, then repositioned my blade, but sorrowful emerald eyes stayed my hand. Eight lonely years, the child had suffered under Hex's thumb. Year after endless year, scattered with only rare, stolen moments of joy to mark their passage.

Tears poured down my face at the thought of Matilda. She would never forgive me for this terrible deed.

A faint whisper in my mind sparked a lightning bolt of jaw-clenching spasms that burned beneath my skin, ricocheting through me like a high-speed train. My eyes shut against the fiery sensation, an inferno licking the very shell of my being. My body locked, and I fell onto the rocks in a spasm. I had felt pain before, but not like this. *Never like this.*

Something inside of me snapped, and I screamed. My sword slipped around in my trembling hands as mindlessly, I rose to my knees, raised my arms, and stabbed downward, ramming the steel home between two large boulders. Gasping against the excruciating burn beneath my skin, I threw my entire weight behind the wobbling blade and snapped it in two.

Clambering down the boulders, my eyes squinted against the pain. I ran into the sea, striking out for the sailboat drifting along a few hundred yards distant. My shouts echoed across the water as I began to swim, leaving the Gryphon and my broken sword behind.

CHAPTER 30

~ EDALINE ~

The oppressive heat made breathing difficult as I waited on the river bank below the lab facility—made worse because of my jean jacket. Did I wear it for luck, or because I was sentimental? Either way, I regretted it thanks to the sweat dripping from my chin.

Slick muscular bodies appeared around me as the Syreni arrived and our forces left the water. The intimidating males swam over from the Spectre, while the rest of us landed a short way downriver in a Zodiac. Miri met us there, looking tired and filthy as her lumbering crocodile led us through the wetlands. The Sprite rode on his head, her eyes wide. Things were about to get real.

The pair had been here all day, the croc digging several holes under the stone wall to create an escape route. Branches hid their handiwork. No one noticed one extra reptile hanging around Charleston, even with the long, narrow snout.

So we crouched here, my racing heart making me feel oxygen-deprived. Cleatus and Miri slid back under the wall to wait on the other side in the shrubbery. Their job was simple: help if they could.

It was happening, and I wanted to puke. I still hadn't heard from Phoebe. The possibilities were terrifying, so I tried not to think about them.

Gideon's wings snapped open above us, startling me. A loud thud vibrated the ground as four heavy feet landed, his creamy tiger stripes shining in the moonlight when he blinked into existence.

"There's been a slight change." Gideon's voice throbbed in my skull. The gleaming eyes around me stared straight at the Gryphon. *"You know your targets. When I say the word, do not delay—get over that wall and engage. Do not kill unless necessary. I will be there, but first, I must free some unexpected captives."*

Ronan's curious eyes found mine. Gideon's fondness for smoke and mirrors was pretty old news, and I shrugged it off. Ronan's frown told me he wasn't so sure.

"The Enforcer suspected a traitor in our midst," he whispered. "Something has happened, but what?"

Gideon must have heard him speaking quietly to me and turned his eagle eyes our way, his golden stare boring into Ronan. But his expression wasn't anger. It was— *worry?*

"We're walking into a trap, aren't we?"

He didn't answer, but Ronan's worried eyes flickered over my face as I swallowed around the lump in my throat. We were here now, and there were no other choices. The only option was forward, carried along on a tidal wave of insanity.

What happened to my nice, peaceful life?

Ronan squeezed my hand and gave me a reassuring smile. I looked over his head across the bay but saw no sign of James in his Wyvern form. He had disappeared as we left the yacht.

My eyes rose to the top of the square brick wall above us. It was tall, but no sticky metal things. I could do this. I welcomed the action. Doing something other than sitting here freaking out seemed like a fabulous idea. We all knew the general layout of the facility and the plan. It was time to get moving.

"Be careful, everyone. Follow your directives." Gideon blinked out of sight, and I heard him take off over our heads. A few minutes later, muffled screams on the other side of the wall were followed by the sight of two limp bodies flying off into the night, carried by the invisible Gryphon.

"BEGIN." The command shot through my mind, and I lurched into action.

Heavy breathing and thumping feet filled my ears, and I called up my power. A mental image of Hex torturing my father inside these walls was all it took, and I was on fire. With three running steps, I jumped, my form lighter than air as I sailed over the wall. I briefly hovered to allow the Syreni beneath me to move away before landing next to Ronan. He asked that I stay close, and I didn't want him wigging out and going *MORS* on me. His dangerous side needed to stay buried tonight.

Clearing the wall, we split into groups. Most headed for the barracks, my much smaller outfit taking the library. According to Gideon's spies, the basement held the prisoners.

Ronan shoved the glass doors wide, and we hustled into the dark, empty building. Bacchus and Ronan went left; Tabitha and I went right. I gripped my Bowie knife with practiced ease, but my unhappy guts twisted like fighting cats as I raced after my courageous friend.

A dark hallway led from behind the stacks, and it was here that we encountered our first resistance. Guards. Four of them, heavily armed and—*human?*

Ronan and Bacchus knocked them out in seconds, the guards putting up absolutely no resistance. Adrenaline choked me, my fingers trembling as I helped Tabitha zip-tie the guards, who were clothed in ill-fitting fatigues. Every inch of their skin was covered in bite marks, their eyes a glazed white.

"What the hell is this?" I hissed to her. "Why would they use a bunch of fucked up humans?"

Tabitha shook her head. "Did you see their eyes? A bit of vampire compulsion, and they save their good soldiers."

"Hex knew we were coming tonight. I'll kill that fucking traitor myself when I find out who it is."

The sound of tearing metal echoed down the hallway, and I looked up in time to see Ronan twist off a handle and fling open a metal door. The muffled sound of pounding fists got louder as he opened it. Ronan and Bacchus charged into the darkness.

I shuddered as, outside, sharp screams and the clash of weapons filled the air. Tabitha's eyes widened, then she stepped over the humans and raced down the hall, pulling me by the hand.

"DOWN HERE!" a deep voice boomed.

We followed, hitting the bottom of the metal stairs to find ourselves in an expansive, block-walled basement with two hallways. There were no guards in sight. We followed the banging, passing through a creepy little lab that made my skin crawl when I saw the implements there. I couldn't look.

Near the end of the passage, a monstrous Syreni pressed against the reinforced glass window of a small room. His snarls curled the hair on the back of my neck.

Ronan didn't recognize him but quickly looked over the industrial locking mechanism. Designed to open from the outside, it was simple but heavy. It took both he and Bacchus to break it. As it fell to the floor, their bodies slammed against the opposite wall as the Syreni male burst out of his cell.

"Whoa, brother!" Bacchus yelled, pulling Ronan to his feet. "We are friends, not foes!"

Chest heaving, the burly male looked down his nose, his eyes wild and tinged with yellow, two tiny fang tips protruding beneath his upper lip.

"Apologies," he panted, turning to Ronan and clasping his arm. "I am Axel." His eyes flicked the way we came. "Are there more of you? Please say there are more of you." The bearded male frowned, a low growl coming from his throat. "Something is wrong. There are usually two Argenti guarding these cells."

I looked at Tabitha, and she shrugged. I didn't want to know what an Argenti was.

Bacchus rounded on Ronan, his shoulder-length hair swinging as he lifted his mace. "We must be quick and get back into the open. Tab said the human guards were a distraction. They know we're here."

Before we could move, a voice came out of the darkness.

"Aren't you forgetting someone?"

I squinted my eyes, and in the window at the end of the hall, a pair of glowing white eyes stared back at me. Tangled white hair and a handsome face appeared from the darkness, tight lips framing a vicious smile. The Djinn slanted a strange look at us.

"I won't hurt you. I *promise*." The way he said it sent a shudder through me.

Our burly new friend shook his head. "No way. You can't let him out. That door is of special design and warded to keep his damn mist contained. Release him, and everybody dies. We must hurry!"

I looked into the predatory eyes of the Djinn, and my stomach sank. I don't know how, but in my heart, I knew this was—

"*OLIVER!*" The heartrending cry came from behind me, and I whirled to see Phoebe race down the hall toward us. Her face said it all as she rushed past me, slamming herself against the door.

"You're here! Oh my God. *You're here ...*" Her voice trailed into hysterical sobs as she pressed her body against the glass. Phoebe slapped the flat of her hands on the window, looking over her shoulder at Ronan. "Help me get him out! *Please!*"

Tears poured as Phoebe's chest heaved in and out, but Oliver's expression never faltered. Staring through the glass, his chilling white eyes narrowed. He cocked his head at my friend, and a lip curled back to expose his teeth. He punched the glass near Phoebe's face and snapped his teeth together. With a shocked cry, she jumped back.

"Oliver, what are you doing? It's me! Phoebe!" She spread her fingers over the glass and leaned close, fat tears clinging to her lashes.

Oliver laughed, low and vicious. "Sure it is, *Phoebe*. Just like it was last week and the week before that. He snarled so close to her face that his teeth bumped the glass. "It won't work this time, you *FUCKING WHORE!*" The guttural words shocked me, but the devastated look on Phoebe's face was tragic.

Pulling back, Oliver slammed against the window, his forehead splitting open on impact. His eyes were wild as he did it again and again until soon, blood ran down the glass, his forehead, and into his mouth. He smiled, his teeth a bright red.

"Stop! *What are you doing!?* Oliver, calm down, and we'll get you out of there!"

Ronan looked at the hulking Syreni male, who shook his head. "He's too far gone. You'd have a better chance of saving the other one."

My eyes shot open, and I noticed a third door tucked in a short vestibule beside Oliver's cell. I jostled past Phoebe, leaned against the glass, and peered through the inky darkness.

There were whispers at my back, and the air moved behind me as Axel appeared. "Let me help you. Stand back."

I did as he said, and with the screech of shearing metal, the entire door ripped from the hinges, the handle clenched in his meaty fist. Moving quickly, Axel rested it against the wall and nodded to me. "Hurry."

I raced inside, nearly falling in my haste. Through the gloom, I saw the prisoner, a white head of dirty hair and an even whiter face coming into focus as I approached. His eyes were closed, his arm hanging over the cot's edge.

"*FATHER!*"

Scrambling to his side, I grabbed his cold hand and rubbed it. "Wake up! I'm here. Oh my God, it's you. *It's really you.*" I choked back a sob as happiness and horror battled for supremacy in my chest.

Ronan appeared behind me to lean over my father's form. He reached out to touch the dry skin of his forehead, and after a moment or two, he looked down at me, his expression grim.

"He is in a bad way, Eddi. He needs help, or he won't leave here."

Without another word, Ronan sank to his knees, and a green light pulsed in his fingertips. I reached out a hand to stop him.

"You can't," I sobbed. "You need your strength, or Hex will have you in a heartbeat."

"I can give him a small dose of my power, and his chances will improve." Ronan bent his head and closed his eyes.

Powerless to help, I watched my father's features, so pale and drawn that fear swam circles in my guts. I let out a long, slow breath. We had him. Now, we just had to get out of here.

Feet shuffled behind us, Axel's low rumbles scratching along my nerves. Seconds later, Ronan raised his head, then stood, lifting my father's lifeless body into his arms.

"Let's go."

Phoebe's white face met us as we emerged, her eyes pleading. "We can't leave him!" she sobbed.

I looked at Ronan and then at the window, squirming at the blood trickling down the inside. Oliver had retreated into the darkness of his cell. In the end, it didn't matter. From the entrance to our corridor came a low, demonic laugh.

"Well, look what we have here. A family reunion."

Down the hall, the lights of the lab flicked on. I stared into the glowing crimson eyes of the creature that had tortured my father.

Behind Hex stood a large group of white-haired soldiers armed to the teeth, their eyes gleaming as they hovered, poised for action. Fifteen strong, their weapons flashed under the lighting.

"You're outnumbered, Edaline. It's time to give up and stop letting your friends die. You'll never escape me, and the sooner you realize that, the better."

***

GIDEON

Folding his wings, the Gryphon slammed onto the lid of the shipping container, a hiss leaving his throat at the terrified sounds coming from within. Sobs and moans, the sharp wails of terrified youngsters—a stew of miserable sounds slipped through the ventilation holes. His golden eyes flashed, lighting up the roof of the container. With a flex of his muscular shoulders, his sharp nails punctured the metal roof of the prison, still hot beneath the pads of his toes. Hex would pay for this.

His heavy feet thumping down the lid of the long metal box, the Enforcer was halfway to the end when a dark shape materialized before him, blocking his path.

Galahad.

Gideon's eyes narrowed to slits as they lit up the Djinn's cold features. He didn't need to speak to convey a clear message—Galahad's death was imminent.

"I see you've recovered, Gryphon."

Despite the assassin's frigid smile, Gideon noticed something off about him. Something was *different*. The Enforcer shook his majestic head, his tail lashing. Talons scraped as he crouched, his wings flattening, poised to strike.

"Now, let's be reasonable," Galahad drawled. "Something in there interests me, and I want it. Let's come to an agreement, shall we?" He opened his arms and spread his hands in appeasement.

Gideon rushed the Djinn. He was on him in a flash, too fast for the assassin to draw a blade. Grabbing the leather-clad warrior in his enormous beak, he shot skyward.

In seconds, hundreds of feet in the air, he flung the Djinn away, then folded and streaked back to his charges. Tucking his wings, Gideon pounded toward his target, tearing around the side of the container, raising furrows as he slid to a stop at the door.

Grasping the handle in his beak, he pried and yanked at the lever, but when that didn't work, he crouched and added fumbling paws. At last, the door swung open, the onslaught of desperate thoughts and emotions—

A seething mass of bodies erupted from the doorway, a Syreni with fiery red hair leading the charge. Her hand drew back, a piece of metal trim gleaming in the moonlight before arcing toward him. Just in time, Oriana stopped her swing.

"Gideon!" she cried. "Thank the Gods."

His eyes glowing, the Gryphon searched the sea of faces, quickly finding Matilda peering from behind her mother.

"Come, child," he projected. *"We must get everyone out of here. Can you hear me?"*

When Matilda nodded, Gideon turned with a sweep of his tail and headed for the wall, tripping over a crocodile as it scrambled around the corner of the container. The Gryphon tumbled in a flash of feathers and scales. Righting himself, he hissed, slashing his beak at Cleatus.

Miri snapped into view, so close to Gideon's face that her shining blue body blinded him for a moment. Buzzing like a furious bee and waving a tiny plastic sword, she slapped him on the soft coating of his nostrils.

"Back off, Toucan Sam. He's with me." Spotting Matilda and the crowd of Syreni behind him, Miri gasped. When the Sprite looked into his golden eyes, her expression was horrified. "We'll get them to the water and safely onto the yacht. And make sure you *kill* the bitch this time!"

As the captive Syreni followed Cleatus and Miri, Gideon turned to find five male younglings standing behind him, their eyes glittering in the darkness. He examined each face and saw the anger there. The rage. The pain of seeing their families injured by monsters. The Enforcer's protective instincts flared, and he motioned for them to follow their families.

One young Syreni jutted his chin and lifted the short sword hidden behind his back. The blade gleamed in the moonlight as, one by one, the rest of the boys revealed a bristling array of weapons. Where they had gotten them, he had no idea.

Gideon raised his head and chuffed his approval, then looked into the air and wondered where the Djinn had gone. The clang of metal and the screams of pain from the barracks jerked his attention from the skies. Shaking his feathered head, he gathered the young warriors.

CHAPTER 31

~ EDALINE ~

A feverish heat ignited my eyes at the sneer on Hex's face. I knew without looking that my air shield was back. There was no need to call it—the rage curling up my spine had sparked the pulsing light. My father hovered near death because of the monster standing before me.

I raised my arm and pointed the tip of my Bowie knife at Hex. "I'm going to end you, you *fucking bitch!*"

Hex chuckled, straightening the sleeves of her fancy leather jacket. When she raised her eyes, they flared with a color straight from the fires of hell.

"Well, you can try." She cocked her head, her lips curling in the corners. "Brave words for a foolish girl. You're as bad as your father."

Hex nodded toward where my father dangled in Ronan's arms and tutted. "Poor Ezen. It didn't turn out so well for him, the stubborn fool."

My harsh breaths spiked the charged silence as something imploded inside my mind. My glowing fingers slid around the handle of my Bowie knife, the urgent need to remove her head stealing the oxygen from my lungs.

Behind me, Axel growled something about Argenti scum as Bacchus rumbled low in his throat. Ronan, frantic to protect me, hissed into my mind, *"Eddi, NO! Wait!"*

My friends were ready to fight despite being outnumbered three to one. We were well and truly fucked. They had us right where they wanted, trapped at the end of a hallway with nowhere to go. Ronan moved closer, my father's arm brushing against my shoulder.

And that was when I heard it—insane whispers, chuffing grunts, and a deep rumble that didn't belong to Bacchus. Slanting a look, I knew Axel heard it too because he smiled. Bacchus nudged me from behind, and with an almost imperceptible nod in return, I sucked in a breath.

All hell broke loose.

Bacchus shoved everyone down the side hall. With a quick burst of strength, Axel turned and yanked Oliver's door from its hinges. Metal squealed and snapped; Axel held the thick steel door like a shield; two thousand pounds of enraged Polar Bear erupted from the darkness. Knocking Axel flat, the bear scrambled over the door and launched straight down the hall at his tormentors.

Hex's eyes snapped wide as she turned to run, her face beginning to shift. Too late, a monstrous white freight train bowled her and the Argenti over, thumps and frantic screams filling the small space of the lab.

Blood flew. So did limbs and a few heads as Oliver tore into Hex's fighters. A torso slid down the hall, coming to a stop by my feet, and I choked at the sight of trailing blood and sinew.

"Go, *GO!*" Tabitha hissed, trying to push around me. I wasn't budging. Oliver was out of his mind, his furious roars mingling with the sound of tearing flesh.

Tabitha screeched, "She's getting away!" and jumped over the body at my feet.

Chasing Tabitha down the hall, I saw Hex bolt up the far stairs, a half-formed scorpion tail waving behind her. Axel ducked into his room and popped out with a homemade weapon before joining the others. Ronan, still behind me, reached out a hand to grab my shoulder.

"Stay here. They will handle it." I shrugged him off and ran, fury and adrenaline making me bold.

An Argenti met me in the corridor, teeth clenched and a bloody sword swinging. I ducked and tilted my neck, the blade glancing off my shield to strike the wall. He looked at his weapon in surprise.

Ignoring the ringing in my head, I slashed his wrist and his sword clattered to the cement. He screamed and clutched the stump of his arm, his chin trembling in shock as he stared back at me.

A backhand to his carotid with the butt of my knife, and he was down, his white eyes rolling back in his head. Laughter bubbled in my throat as I tore down the hallway, Ronan following. High on adrenaline, my fears fell away.

The carnage in the lab was shocking, the Argenti scattered in pieces on the floor. The tables in the lab lay on their sides, cupboards shattered, glass frosting the floors. A wave of relief rushed through me—until the bear turned to face us.

Oliver's white fur was slick with blood, his gaping muzzle dripping red as he stared at us, his eyes bright and narrowed. His lips curled back and a low rumble vibrated along my nerve endings. When the bear lowered its head, a puncture in his shoulder gaped. He bunched his muscles to charge at us.

Bacchus raised his mace like a baseball bat as he crouched, Axel stepping to his side. With a cry, Phoebe shoved forward, pushing between them and the bear.

Oliver bellowed at Phoebe but halted his charge to growl at her outstretched hand. Hunching his shoulders, his giant paws thumped the floor over and over, his head swinging back and forth. He curled a leg and swiped the air between them.

"Oliver. It's me," Phoebe whispered. "Let's get out of here, ok? We'll go somewhere quiet, and I'll make you your favorite pancakes."

Oliver's eyes rolled back as his mouth gaped in a glass-rattling roar, his head lowering and bloody saliva trickling from his lower lip. I reached out and grabbed Phoebe's arm.

She shoved me away and once again stretched her hand toward the bear. "I know you don't want to do this, Oliver. I don't know what they did to you, but whatever it was, we'll fix it. Please. Let's go home."

Her face a mask of anguish, Phoebe kept up with the soft crooning. "Please don't hurt my friends, Oliver." She took a step, a sob lodging in her throat. "I need you to come home."

The bear's eyes narrowed, but he stilled.

Her fingers fluttering at Oliver, Phoebe whispered, "Do you remember when I came home and found your bear sitting on the couch? You big bugger. You chased me all the way out to the backyard before letting on. You scared me half to death!"

Oliver chuffed, a low moan easing from his chest. I swore I saw his lips turn up as the mountain of white fur settled. His pumping ribs slowed, and he sat down, his lower lip hanging as he lifted his head and sniffed in our direction.

Above us, a door slammed against a wall and shattered the spell. Everyone froze except Oliver. With a vicious snarl, he whirled and tore up the stairs, his fur rolling as he pumped all four massive legs toward the sound.

The metal stairs clanged as we raced after the gigantic white rump, following him into the library. At the entrance, the manticore crouched in the doorway, her tufted ears brushing the header. Slitted red eyes flicked over us as Hex snapped her fangs together with a wet, hollow sound.

"You didn't *really* think that was it, did you?" A laugh slithered up her throat as she lowered her head, a vaguely human smirk wrinkling her lips.

I glanced over Hex's shoulder into the yard. What I saw sent a wave of heat across my skin, shock freezing my lips. The underground chamber had muffled the noise of the absolute carnage that had been taking place above ground. Things had gone badly. Very badly.

Oliver didn't care about any of that. He had eyes for only one thing, and that was the gigantic creature crouched before us. With a wide-mouthed roar, he charged, tearing after Hex as she turned and scrambled into the training yard.

CHAPTER 32

At the thud of boots behind us, I whirled. More of Hex's soldiers stepped out from behind the stacks. They wore matching medieval helmets, the scrollwork of a galloping horse etched in gold along the sides.

Argenti—but this time, there were others. These athletic males were very different. With sparkling green or blue eyes and colorful scaled legs, they looked almost identical to Syreni.

Every male before us was bare-chested, their skin glistening in the moonlight that filtered through the doors. Cold stares pinned us as they closed in. We were outnumbered two to one, and Ronan still cradled my father in his arms.

Bacchus lifted his mace, swinging it at his side as he prepared to face them head-on. Tabitha raised her cutlass, her expression fierce, but Ronan stopped them, giving Axel a firm look where he crouched.

"Bacchus, NO. We cannot win this. Be patient, brother. We will find a way," Ronan's voice was calm, but the veins in his arms bulged and his eyes flickered yellow. He looked five seconds from losing it.

Bacchus lowered his mace, his knuckles flaring white as he snarled through his clenched teeth. Hex's soldiers stepped forward, pressing us backward toward the open door. From the corner of his mouth, Axel huffed, "The Servus are soft. Go for the Argenti first if you get a chance."

Out of nowhere, an arrow whizzed over my head, the feathered tail a sudden splash of color between two white eyes. An Argenti toppled forward.

Bacchus and Axel charged, Tabitha right behind them.

Swords waved in the air as Hex's men attacked, Tabitha taking down a Servus with a swipe of her cutlass across the back of a knee. She leapt into the air, bringing her blade down on an unsuspecting head. It glanced off his helmet and sank into a neck beside him. The Servus dropped to the floor, blood pouring down his chest.

Beside her, Bacchus kicked into the air, catching an Argenti in the gut, then landing and swinging his mace. The nails stuck through his helmet with a final clunk.

Tabitha fell backward into me, two Servus rushing her. I hauled her to her feet with a grunt.

"Thanks, Sister," she huffed, then launched back into the fray. I followed on her heels, Ronan roaring at me to stop.

For every soldier we knocked back, another took his place. Axel threw bodies into the air as he kicked, punched, and slashed, doing minimal damage with his makeshift blade. The stabs were far too shallow when he missed something vital.

Swinging and hammering with my heavy knife, I hovered and leapt, trying to avoid the blades whistling through the air. Twice, I was knocked into a spin as a sword bounced off my shield. Every time I swung, I came down on a helmet or a blade. It was useless. There were too many of them.

Ronan, my father over his shoulder, swung his short sword, knocking back any attackers who got past the rest of us. Terrified for them both, I swept over the crowd of fighters and landed by Ronan, turning to help him defend my father's lifeless body.

Outnumbered, they beat us back to the entrance, and when a slash to the hamstrings took Axel down, Bacchus dragged him to safety. Soon, we were right back where we started. Only six of their fighters were down.

As we retreated to the yard, I looked for the source of that arrow. The stone walls rose around us, with no sign of our would-be savior.

The breeze was a refreshing change as it whispered over my hot skin. I turned, and my heart wept at the sight before me. Dead Syreni males dotted the bloodied field, the spears through their chests pinning them to the ground. Mouths gaped with deathly grimaces as blood sheeted from their fatal wound.

Enzo, Tabitha's beau, lay among the fallen. His chest smeared with blood, he twisted backward with his mouth open in one last, agonized scream. Tabitha cried out, but Bacchus grabbed her with his free hand to stop her from running to him. She struggled, scratching at him with frantic claws. He pulled his sister to his chest with soft words, a brawny arm lifting her feet off the ground. Axel swayed beside him, unable to walk. It was over.

Half our fighters remained, held on their knees in a far corner of the yard. A helmeted group of Servus surrounded them, their sharp weapons hemming them in.

A tiny spark of hope flared in my chest when I noticed the horrified looks on the faces of the Servus soldiers flanking Hex. Their helmets hid their expression, but I saw their eyes, and with one fleeting glance, I knew—it wasn't over yet.

A Servus with strange coloring snagged my attention. Beneath his helmet, his eyes—one white, one green— made his face appear lopsided. His gaze flicked over Hex with an expression of—*disgust?* Pure, unfiltered horror, perhaps. This male was unhappy; both he and the warrior beside him shifted their weight with a restless energy.

At the lull in the action, I lost the battle with my stomach. It erupted, and I turned and emptied the entire contents on the grass. Before I straightened, I cried out at the sight of Oliver lying off to the side, a feathered dart lodged in his back. He'd been lured right into a trap.

Phoebe crouched over his body, which slowly returned to human form. Her flushed face was focused on Oliver, her mouth trembling—but not with shock. Her hand twitched along with the subtle movements of her lips. I couldn't be sure, but she was up to something.

A sharp hiss behind me made me jump. I turned to face the monstrosity that had killed so many of my friends. Hex shot me a curdled sneer.

"What a weak stomach you have, my dear. Don't worry. My controller will toughen you up."

A dark-haired man with specs stood behind her, his mocking laughter raking over my last nerve. A small black figurine swung on a leather cord from his hand.

Hex laughed, the deep gashes on her face gaping. The thick carapace of her scorpion tail waved over her back, clacking like slow-moving castanets as she paced over to the man holding the necklace—

The Talisman of Tenebris.

"Your attempts at defiance are amusing, Edaline. But that shield of yours will come down the moment I give the word." She looked over her shoulder at me.

"Stephen will be doing the honors for us tonight."

Behind me, a strangled sound came from Ronan. Handing my father to Tabitha, he turned to face Hex, his body appearing twenty pounds heavier. Ronan's eyes flashed gold as he stalked forward, his lips peeled back in a snarl—a picket fence of fangs shot into his mouth.

"Ronan ... *NO!*"

Hex howled with laughter. "Oh yes. Yes, yes! Your plaything has such a short fuse, doesn't he? Just wait until he sees what I have in store for him. I have big plans for tonight."

Stephen stepped forward, raised a gun, and fired darts into Axel and Bacchus. Their eyes rolled back, and they fell face down in the dirt.

Ronan snapped. Talons tore free from the tips of his fingers, thick strands of clear goo trailing from his fangs as an unholy sound came from his chest.

"Oh, pipe down," Hex sneered. "Layla and I will have plenty of fun with you later. Your fuse may be short, but your cock—*mmm*."

Ronan's eyes narrowed on his target as he picked up speed.

"Uh-uh-uh," she tutted. "If you don't stand down, your mighty Enforcer here won't live to see the next moon tide."

The crowd of men behind her parted, and my stomach plummeted. On his side, Gideon's great wings flopped listlessly as a low moan soughed from his chest. A spear stuck through his heart like a skewer, impaling him to the ground. It was all I could do not to break down.

Ronan didn't care. He was lost somewhere in a bubbling cauldron of fury. His pounding feet lifted trails of dust as he attacked. He made it halfway there, then slowed. Grabbing his head, he staggered, then stopped, weaving where he stood. My blood froze at the groan that came from his lips.

A familiar taste tickled the back of my throat. Cloying sweetness tainted the air, and Layla sauntered forward from between the soldiers. When Tara appeared behind her, my shield flared so bright that Hex's men had to cover their eyes with one hand. The traitorous Lionfish at least had the good sense to look frightened.

"Hello, Ronan," Layla purred, walking toward him. "I'm so excited you're here. I missed riding your glorious cock." When Ronan pulled it together and snarled, Layla sucked in a lungful of air, then opened her mouth and heaved a breath at him. A hazy stream of magic flew from her lips, hitting him and billowing around his body.

Ronan's eyes rolled back and he fell to his knees, his hand reaching for the bulge beneath his skins. Moaning, his eyes slowly drifted back and forth, his throat bobbing as his thick pink tongue reached out to lick at the air. An erotic growl rumbled from his chest. A growl that should have been reserved for *me*. My shield crackled as I struggled to stay calm.

The edges of Layla's magic scraped across my skin, and my hand creaked on the handle of my knife. But I didn't dare move, thanks to the soldier beside Gideon. His short sword balanced on its point above the Gryphon's throat, an evil white glare daring me to try something. Torn between saving the Gryphon and ripping Layla's arms from their sockets, I froze.

"Leave him alone!" Tara darted toward Ronan, her tiny fangs bared at Layla as she brushed past. The shifter's skin flashed the brown and white of her Lionfish as she threw her arms around his broad shoulders. With a sob, she tucked her face into his neck.

Ronan didn't notice her, his lazy gaze struggling to follow Layla. His eyes, still yellow, were now cloudy and pale.

"You said I could have him! *You owe me!*" Tara shrieked, glaring at Hex's hideous face.

"I lied. I owe you nothing. No one trusts a traitor, you foolish little Lionfish."

Her red dress creeping up her thighs, Layla reached her victim. Tara whimpered, pulling Ronan closer as the Succubus stopped to slide her hands through his black hair. Parting her lips, Layla sipped the air with a sigh, drinking in his power.

I'd had enough. My air shield flared, my eyes flicking to Gideon. I couldn't let him die—I just couldn't. Despite our issues, I loved him like the father dangling in Tabitha's arms.

I had to be quick. Save Gideon, then attack. The distance to the Gryphon was short, twenty feet max. I pictured my trajectory, preparing to lunge as I resisted the urge to glance skyward. Where the hell was James?

Confusion flickered through me. I hesitated, my legs suddenly weak. My eyes drifted around a sea of blurry faces. I put my hand to my head, cursing at the pink skin of my fingers. The psychedelic smile of the Manticore ripped a snarl from my throat.

At least, it started as a snarl. It ended in a grunt, and I fell to my knees as wetness slicked the apex of my thighs. Tipping my head down I closed my eyes, desperately trying to hold back a moan.

"You fucking monster," I choked. Black dress pants appeared before me. I looked up to see curls. A perfect face. Someone leaning over to peer into my eyes.

Charles.

"You know, I would have made this something epic. Something orgasmic that you would *never* forget. But after that painful little stunt you pulled at the bar"—he rubbed his balls with a sneer—"I don't think I will."

And then he smiled as daggers of lust sliced through my skin, my knees giving out. I sprawled on my face, one hand going to my crotch. I screamed as my feet raked clumps of grass from the parched ground. Mindless, I floated on agonizing blades of need.

A tire-sized paw landed beside my face, six-inch black claws flexing into the dead grass. Punctures marred Hex's hairless wrists, but I couldn't focus on them as I gagged on the desire spearing my throat.

"Stephen? The Talisman, if you would," Hex's voice sounded muffled as I rolled in misery between her feet.

Through the haze, I thought of Cain, and power whispered through me—then snuffed out as Charles blasted me again.

"Stop it, Edaline! You're making me hard with all that rage you've got going on in that pretty little head of yours," he taunted.

I stared up at the blurry moon above. Trying to focus, my eyes tracked a black shadow that slashed across the face of the moon. I smiled, my soft laughter filled with tears and snot. James was still here.

James! Oh my god, hurry!

Something moved over my face, and I twisted my neck to avoid looking at it. It dropped down in front of my eyes, shiny and black. Swinging in circles. A sculpted horse figurine, tiny and smooth. The legs curled quaintly into its belly, a stylish Arabian head arched high in triumph.

Something tugged at my mind, and I turned my head to admire the casual elegance of the stallion as it drifted back and forth above me. It was stunning, dropping a violet trail of mist at every swing.

My mouth opened in awe of the beautiful black horse galloping through the desert sands of my mind, dust billowing into the air as it ran. It snorted, and chills raced down my spine. My strength disappeared with the breath that left me on a long, tortured sigh.

Treacherous fingers grasped at my soul and twisted; words filled the air, their power rushing through me.

"*OBEY! You are BOUND. A willing SERVANT until the END.*"

The words weren't English, but I somehow understood every single one.

Thick, coppery liquid slid down my throat. Blood, tangy and rich, burned all the way to my stomach. My body was made of butter, and I was standing in hell.

And then it stopped.

My aching chest heaved with the effort of breathing. Sucking in the night air, I welcome the muffled quiet of the courtyard.

"Open your eyes." The words of a snake, rasping and sharp. I wanted to lay here and keep my eyes closed forever. They opened against my will, and I peered skyward into two crimson eyes gleaming back at me.

Hex's enormous paw disappeared, a trickle of blood dripping from a slit on the inside of her leg. I was ruined. Something dark raced through my blood, its head held high as it galloped through my veins.

Hex sat back, raised a paw, and licked the inside of her leg with a thick tongue that was forked at the very tip. Countless eyes watched, unmoving except for Tabitha. She cradled my father as tears poured down her face, her brother and Axel motionless on the ground beside her.

"Well, that was far easier than I expected." Hex dropped her leg with a nasty snarl and barked, "Edaline, *get up*."

I didn't want to, but I lurched to my feet. Hex heaved herself onto all fours, her segmented tail swinging through the darkness. The curved tip reached for me, a smooth black needle slipping under my chin to lift it. I didn't dare move. I stretched my neck and complied, my heart sinking at how fast Hex's poisonous tail had regrown since our last encounter.

"You know what? Slavery is a good look for you, Edaline." Hex's tail retreated into the darkness.

The group of Argenti around her laughed. Charles joined in, his eyes boring into me. My lazy gaze found the Servus male with the bi-colored eyes. He looked furious.

With Hex distracted and Charles no longer pinning me down with lust, I could see again. Ronan was still cradled in Tara's arms. She crooned softly into his ear, pausing to nuzzle his straining neck. His once beautiful eyes were opaque, the yellow faded to a washed out cream. Layla's mist coated his face, his fangs no longer strung with poisonous strands of *MORS*.

Now they streamed with nectar, the thin liquid dribbling from his chin. Layla smiled at me and mouthed, "*he's all mine, BITCH.*"

My stomach rolled. Even enthralled, Ronan was lost. *MORS* had seized his mind. In my heart, I knew he might never come back to me. He'd struggled so long to contain his fury. Now, there were no signs of the proud Syreni male that I loved.

Was this it? Everyone dies? Then I remembered the dark shape hurtling past the moon.

Where are you? What are you waiting for? JAMES!

Hex spoke, breaking the silence. "Well, enslaving you was a blast, but it's time to test your blood oath, Edaline. I can't wait!"

She raised her arms in the air and howled at the moon, her face wreathed in smiles as she shifted. The sound of crackling skin and popping bones filled the courtyard, a pained whine at the very end the only sign of discomfort.

With a final snap, Hex stood front and center—in Patsy's form. She raised her fists in triumph like a female Messiah. The Argenti roared their approval, thumping their weapons on the ground. The Servus didn't move.

Hex turned to her warriors, a crazed grin on her face.

"We've done it, my lovelies. We have broken the only force that can resist us. It's time to celebrate!" She clapped her hands together and turned to face me, her eyes glittering.

Her ageless, naked body strutted forward, her perky breasts swinging as she came, stopping close enough that I smelled her rancid breath. Hex looked me up and down, then addressed the man in the lab coat.

"Stephen?" He stepped forward, handing her a short sword. I recognized the sweeping scrolls along the handle. It once belonged to a pirate—*Ronan's* sword.

"Edaline, a gift for you." She pressed the weapon into my hand, then pointed at Ronan with a vicious smile.

"Kill him."

CHAPTER 33

~ FELIX ~

From our hiding spot in the shrubs, Jovi and I watched as the wild Syreni poured over the stone wall. A glowing blue female with a Bowie knife hovered above them before landing. The wall of muscular bodies glistened in the moonlight, their ferocious expressions curdling my blood.

Their resemblance to Servus was uncanny, but these creatures looked wild and untamed. A lump popped into my throat as they broke into groups. The glowing female and a small group headed to the library—straight to the prisons in the basement, no doubt. They would release the prisoners.

"What do we do?" Jovi hissed. Moonlight flashed along the blade of his sword. His hands were shaking.

"The truth will set us free," I whispered.

***

Yesterday, Jovi had returned from the library with answers about our origins. Searching high and low, he found no mention of Servus or Argenti. Luckily, my friend went one step further this time. He looked up the Latin definition of the words.

I would never forget the prickles that swept my neck when I learned the truth. The word Servus meant *slave*. It wasn't solid proof, but the word Argenti—*silver*—lent strength to my suspicions. Our Benefactor wasn't very imaginative, it seemed.

All this time, we believed in our directive. For years, Fridays had nibbled on my soul, but I had held fast to my loyalty.

Until the killings on the minesweeper. Boris attacking and nearly killing Jovi. The humans he and his guards fed upon. The debauchery in Hex's quarters; I still ached from the acts I endured. These were not the trappings of a *just cause*. They were the workings of a madwoman.

Another puzzle piece came from a newspaper stolen from Stephen's office. Apparently, Jovi was both brave *and* foolish. The grim reality stared back at us in black and white. Literally.

"Strange Drug Wreaks Havoc in Key West." Jovi read the article to me, his eyes wide. It wasn't hard to connect the erotic drug to our nectar. I'd seen the effects on others firsthand. Hex, Layla, Charles—they'd gotten obliterated when they stole it from my mouth the other night. Savage lust. Aggression. Arousal that wouldn't quit.

But the final straw lay hidden in Stephen's office closet. Thousands of vials of our nectar, each labeled with dates back to the beginning—to the very first day we donated to the human cause.

It was all a lie.

Jovi and I agreed—Hex had deceived us for years. Our loyalty was gone, our minds wide open. Who could we trust? We knew nothing about our enemies, other than what Axel told us. We had no choice but to wait and see how things unfolded. As it turned out, we didn't have to wait long.

***

We received word at supper hour of an imminent battle, and prepared accordingly. Jovi and I had swords, our weapon of choice. We did our best to pass what we learned about Hex to other trustworthy Servus. Whether they believed us or not was out of our hands.

As the wild Syreni warriors cleared the fence and hustled across the yard in our direction, I clutched my weapon, held my breath, and hoped that at least some of our brothers were on board.

The first intruders charged past, their shoulders low as they headed for the barracks. Most of our forces were out here, hiding around the courtyard, the remainder lying in ambush in the barracks. Most of the Argenti went with Hex to the lab beneath the library, two remaining on watch. Those two were missing.

When the Syreni attackers crossed the yard uncontested, I shot Jovi a relieved smile. Our comrades were sitting tight, like us, waiting for a clear path forward. One that didn't require fulfilling Hex's heinous designs.

The bunkhouse door slammed open, and the Syreni streamed inside, the sounds of a fight erupting. Swords clashed, males shouted, and I saw Max go down in the doorway under a Syreni blade. I hissed at his stupidity, but Jovi and I could not delay. We were needed elsewhere.

Running along the edges of the training yard, we headed to the shipping container at the far end of the field—the one whispering with terrified, breathless voices.

When it arrived in the yard earlier today, Jovi's curiosity was piqued. He snuck over to find it full of female Syreni and their offspring. Fury masked his face when he gave me the news. It made planning easier; our side in this fight was clearer.

Pushing ahead of me, Jovi reached the end of the makeshift prison, but when we rounded the corner, it was open—and empty. A Gryphon the size of an elephant stepped into view, his wings flaring. A cluster of child warriors chafed at his back.

Jovi lay his sword on the ground, spread his arms, opened his hands, and spoke to the snarling brute.

"We are not your enemies. We've been fed lies by the demon that runs this place. We want to help. Some of our brothers want to help."

The great beast cocked his head, his eyes glowing as bright as the sun. I felt a strange tickle between my ears, and as I watched, Jovi scratched at his nape. In my head, the creature spoke.

"Where are your forces?"

Jovi answered. "The worst Argenti are with Hex in the library. The Servus and a few Argenti soldiers are split between the dorm and the yard."

The Gryphon narrowed his eyes on the shrubs surrounding the courtyard.

Jovi's eyes glittered with emotion as he said, "The Argenti are loyal to Hex, but most of the Servus are not. Please—*don't hurt them.*"

"Take me to the back of the dorms." The Gryphon turned and motioned for us to lead the way. Jovi waved him to the right, picking up a jog as we passed the library, ducked between two buildings, then raced to the rear of our quarters.

With a swipe of his massive talons, the door blew to pieces, the Gryphon charging through the opening. My heart bled when I saw the carnage inside.

Scattered across the room, a few Servus and two Argenti lay dying, their missing arms and legs littering the floor. Blood pooled everywhere, and as we slid to a halt among the struggling warriors, I saw Gallis, a Syreni mace arcing for his head.

"STOP!" Jovi screamed.

The tall blonde Syreni pulled his swing, knocking the Servus flying with a fist instead. Gallis fell back against a bunk with a pained cry, clutching at his face with both hands.

The Syreni warriors in the room pulled to attention, their chins lifting. The Gryphon stared into their eyes, then they broke to charge into the courtyard.

My eyes wide, I looked at Jovi. "The machines! *Stop them!*"

The Gryphon turned his face to me. My head buzzed, then the massive beast charged for the door. Behind me, the younglings lifted wounded Servus onto the bunks, their stern faces focused on the injured. We raced after the beast, but we were too late.

Hex was fascinated with historic weaponry, and somewhere, she'd found an old harpoon gun and fitted it to fire spears—*four at a time.* Eager to test it tonight, she'd had it rolled into the furthest corner of the yard and hidden with brush.

Jovi and I cleared the doorway in time to see an Argenti hit the lever and fire into the swarming Syreni. All four spears whistled across the space and found their targets, screams of pained surprise filling the air. The warriors fell, their hands clenched into fists, their mouths wide. They shuddered a final breath as their lungs collapsed.

The remaining fighters saw the contraption and thundered straight for it. With a grin, the gunner flipped a switch, and another load of spears rotated forward and launched.

More screams and another four males went down. It was a bloody massacre.

Thankfully, only a handful of Servus burst from the bushes to take on the survivors, weapons ringing as metal met metal. A towering Syreni fighter thrust a trident through Hector's collarbones, removing his head. Yanking it free, the warrior swung it in an arc, slicing another throat, then turned to thrust it into an Argenti rushing him from behind.

The harpoon clanked as it reloaded, two Argenti rushing to complete the task.

With a roar, the Gryphon thrust himself into the air, sweeping over the wall and rounding on the frantic gunners. With talons outstretched, he landed on both Argenti, crushing them beneath thousands of pounds of furious fur and feathers. An arm, then a leg rotated through the air, landing with a thump in the courtyard. Satisfied, the creature tore the machine to pieces with his claws, the sound of cracking wood and metal piercing the air.

As the last pieces showered the ground, the creature lifted his bloody face and stared across the courtyard—straight into the eyes of a monster. It scrambled from the library with a cat-like face that looked remarkably like Hex.

Seconds later, a polar bear charged through the library doors, focused on the creature as it scuttled away. The bear's bellowing roars rolled across the distance between us. A loud pop and the bear went down, a dart hanging from its back. Stephen stepped out of the shadows, gun in hand. The same weapon I'd seen him use on Axel on more than one occasion.

The battle had taken on a life of its own, our pleas for leniency lost on a tidal wave of adrenaline. Horrified, Jovi and I backed into the dorms, motioning for the Syreni youths to hurry out the back. Saving their young was the least we could do.

They ignored us, scrambling to the windows to watch.

The bear no longer a threat, the monster from the library slowed to a swagger, crossing the dried grass as it huffed with laughter. Its jaw gaped to reveal four-inch fangs, its terrifying face swinging to catch the scent of its foe.

Jovi, his eyes round, turned to me. "Is that—*Hex!?*" I didn't answer, but we both knew the truth. The thing had a scorpion tail that rattled as the demon picked up speed, scuttling across the yard straight at the Gryphon.

They met in the center with a thundering crash, rolling in a frenzy of claws and fangs, chunks of feather and fur flying skyward as deafening shrieks pierced the night air. My skin flushed with bumps at the sheer power of it.

A handful of Argenti raced in for backup, their weapons waving. It was Hex alright, and it was clear that our Benefactor came straight from Hell.

Two Argenti ran past us from the right, spears hefting to their shoulders as they closed the distance. Before I could react, a pair of knives whizzed past my ears, taking both Argenti down mid-stride. I glanced over my shoulder to see two young lads puff their chests. The little one spoke.

"You are lucky we are here. You are far too slow to be a Syreni." His glittering blue eyes trailed up my body, stopping on my helmet. He pointed at it. "You must be very soft up there to need so much protection." The other boys snickered at his comments, but I ignored them and turned back to the fight.

Hex's loyal soldiers clashed with the remaining Syreni as the winged beast rose into the air, its claws gripping Hex's furred ankles hard enough to draw blood. Hauling her skyward, his beak hacked at her face as he fended off snapping teeth. Shiny black segments clacked together as Hex's tail writhed to strike, each hit deflected by the Gryphon's kicking hindquarters.

Enormous wings rent the air, debris flying across the yard as the brawling pair gained altitude. The Gryphon had almost cleared the height of the stone wall when I saw a horrifying scene unfold across the yard. A Servus—*Anton*—was locked in combat with an Argenti, who slashed his throat, then turned toward the Gryphon and loosed his spear.

It whistled through the air, punching into the Gryphon's chest with a thud. His wings folded, and the grappling pair crashed to the earth, the spear sticking into the ground on landing. The magnificent creature was down, its wings fluttering weakly in the dust.

The Gryphon raised its head, one yellow eye blinking weakly at Hex.

She rose and moved in, smiling at the struggling form at her feet. "I hope you're enjoying my little surprise, Gideon." She swung her tail around in front of her face and smiled. A small drop of venom oozed from the very tip.

"My Argenti spent all afternoon coating their weapons to ensure all it would take was a scratch. And now look." She tutted, shaking her cat-like mane. "Leave it to my favorite creations to go for a bulls-eye. I can't say I'm going to miss you, Gryphon."

She turned, her hind feet tossing scoops of sand onto the Gryphon's still form. Snarls sounded across the yard, and Hex's eyes snapped to the library.

The pretty blue female and a handful of Syreni fighters backed through the doors, a team of Argenti and Servus pushing them into the courtyard. The old Djinn from the cells dangled from the arms of a male.

Not far from the barracks, our surviving soldiers had gathered what remained of the Syreni force, pushing them against the corner with their weapons. As Servus stragglers swarmed around Hex, Jovi motioned to the youths to escape. We slipped into the courtyard, blending with the group closest to the demon.

The next ten minutes were a living hell as, powerless, we watched Hex reveal dark magic beneath the moonlight—Layla weaponized to great effect—and Charles tormenting the glowing female who seemed powerless to stop him.

And Stephen. By the fuck, I would kill that bastard myself.

CHAPTER 34

~ EDALINE ~

"Kill him?" I looked at the sword in my hand and then at Ronan, who was still lost to lust and fury. Hex's compulsion swept through me, my brief moment of horror dissolving as I fell headfirst into her spell.

My feet moved without permission, my resistance snuffed out like a lamp in a hurricane. And then, I realized—Hex was right. The Syreni were a scourge on this planet, and we needed loyal soldiers to champion her cause. I could do this. Ronan was lost to *MORS*, so he might as well be dead.

I lifted the tip of the sword and ran my eyes over it. Very pretty. I'd keep this for myself as a souvenir. I stalked forward, my steps sure, a wry smile pulling at my lips.

Tara rose to block my view of Ronan. "No, Edaline! You can't! He's mine! He's *always* been mine!" She snarled as I stopped before her, my arm raising to the side as I angled my blade to strike.

Barbed fins flashed across Tara's face and arms, her fingers morphing to ten long barbs tipped with a dangerous poison. "You can't have him! Just try it, you *bi—*"

I swung, her blue eyes popping as her head hit the ground with a thud.

My laughter filled the air. One sure swing and it was over. I should have done this long ago.

Laughter erupted from the Argenti behind me. Tara deserved it, the bitch. I looked at Ronan, who hadn't noticed Tara's absence whatsoever.

Stephen stepped behind me, the electric prod in his hand crackling. "You heard Hex. *Kill him.*"

I turned. "You use that thing on me, and I'm going to ram this sword so far up your ass you'll have a pointy steel hat."

Stephen held his hands up, his eyes wide.

I smiled, leaned over, and stared into Ronan's hazy eyes. Glancing down at the hard ridge pushing against his skins, I snorted.

"You won't be needing that where you're going." I raised my sword.

I hesitated when, deep inside, a cry of resistance whispered frantic pleas into my ears.

"Don't kill him. You love him."

The voice was soft, tragic. The snorting scream of a black horse raked through my mind. There was no time for this. My shortsword flashed as I raised my arm.

In a final moment of clarity, Ronan looked up, his vision cloudy. Even through the creamy glow of his eyes, I thought I saw forgiveness there. My heart cracked into ten million shards of microscopic powder—then the oath galloped through the dust of my resistance on a shining black horse. I swung.

Without warning, I staggered backward, an arrow through the palm of my sword hand, my blade flying through the air. I looked into the trees by the stone wall and saw movement. The archer was in the damn trees.

"You'll die for that!" I screamed.

But someone else was screaming, and I whirled around.

"Pull it out! Pull it out! Oh my god, *it hurts!*"

I doubled over with laughter. My sword had landed—hitting Stephen's foot dead center, the razor-sharp blade slicing through his dress shoe to pin him in place.

"Fuck, Stephen! All the way to the hilt!" I laughed. "What are the chances?"

I snapped the arrow from my hand, feeling nothing. Reaching down, I gripped my sword to pull it out, but a second arrow set a blaze of ferocious activity into motion.

Yanked off balance by a shrieking Stephen as he jerked and hopped in place, I saw the second arrow had skewered the hem of my jean jacket—and pinned me to the controller's thigh. I wobbled as Stephen tried to pull away, the pain making him scream harder.

"Stop moving, you fool!" I elbowed him in the groin, unable to free my sword with all the antics. "Shut the fuck up and hold still!"

With a hollow grunt, Stephen curled. Behind him, Hex stared open-mouthed at the night sky, her eyes blazing crimson as she screamed at nothing. Her naked body looked odd, her breasts swinging as she shook her fist in the air. I looked up, seeing nothing.

The sharp sound of flapping wings filled the courtyard. Something enormous swerved over the ten-foot stone wall, a long armored neck snaking down as glittering bronze eyes swept over the training yard. The dragon's mouth gaped, and from between long rows of serrated teeth billowed a fire straight from Hades. A thick wall of flames traced the length of the compound as the dragon swept past, narrowly missing Gideon's still form.

"Wyvern, Edaline." The words whispered through my mind, and my chest pinched tight. I brushed a tear from my cheek, then narrowed my eyes on the Gryphon. It didn't move.

Heat billowed around me, a blast furnace straight from hell scattering the fighters. Stephen tried but couldn't move, his foot still pinned by the sword and the arrow holding us together. I jerked, and the feathers slipped through my jacket, the shaft still lodged in Stephen. With a twist, I yanked it free, the controller's screams reaching a fevered pitch.

Wasting no time, I gave up on the sword and went for Ronan, turning the arrow in my hand. His back was to me as I stomped closer. This was too easy. He didn't hear me, but as I got closer, I saw why.

Wild with *MORS*, Ronan's hands crushed Layla's throat. Her face purpled as she struggled for air, her eyes turning crimson as darkness spread across her beautiful features. I halted, fascinated by the transformation of the previously beautiful woman.

Pruning looseness dragged her skin downward, a raisin texture replacing the smooth lines of her body. A horrifying mess of puckered warts rose from her flesh, and beady eyes glared from within the folds of her ruined face. Ronan shook her, his savage snarls powered by rage.

His mouth stretched wide, then he struck, ripping her throat free with a wet, tearing noise. Ronan spat out the mouthful, then shook her so hard that the widening gap of her neck left her head flopping like a pulpy hoodie.

He dropped the Succubus and turned my way. Panting, his face coated in red slime, I watched something white drop from his chin.

Was that a tooth? Gross.

Before I could react, a searing heat razed my backside, a wall of flames rising in the grass and flaying my skin. I scrambled forward as it swallowed Stephen's shrieking form. Massive leathery wings acted as bellows, the flaming wall bowing toward me and driving me away from Ronan. All around me, burning bodies ran. There was no sign of Hex.

I turned and came face to face with two blazing yellow eyes and thick strands of death dripping from a fat pair of canines. Ronan's fists locked around my forearms, and he bellowed into my face.

***

~ FELIX ~

When the fire-breather came over the wall, like everyone, we ran. But when I saw the enraged Syreni clamp his hands around Layla's throat, I turned to help her. Jovi's hand shot out and stopped me.

"She's not worth it, Felix. *Come!* The youngsters and the wounded! They're still in the barracks!" Fireballs rained down around us, and instinctively, I ducked. But not before I saw Layla's beauty fall away, and bile rose in my throat. I retched at the horror of her true form.

"FELIX—*RUN!*"

A wall of flame billowed across the ground, and we scrambled toward the dorm. Young male faces peered back at us from the windows.

To my left, an Argenti pulled his arm back, a spear ready to fly at the creature in the sky. I swerved toward him and drew my sword.

Jovi screamed, but I ignored him. My blade rang on the steel shaft of the Argenti's spear as I slashed downward. Gritting my teeth, I twisted my wrist, my sword skittering along the spear toward his face. Like grapes from a tree, all five of his fingers tumbled to the ground, followed by his weapon.

Whirling to gather momentum, I swung with everything I had. My sword met no resistance as it slid through his neck, his head landing next to the fingers. His body fell away with a thump.

I looked up to see the tan-colored beast hovering above the yard. His eyes locked with mine, his lips curling in the corners. As I watched him in awe, a flash of blue crossed my line of vision.

"JOVI!" I hollered. With a clash of steel on steel, my friend slammed into the white-haired bastard that, unknown to me, had come up on the other side of my opponent, a spear balanced over his shoulder—and leveled at the Wyvern.

With a snarl, the Argenti dropped his projectile and threw his weight into my friend, who was pushed backward by the sheer force of the hit. Jovi dropped to the ground, throwing the fighter off balance, then bounced back up beside the surprised male and ran him through with his sword.

The Argenti cried out in agony and hit the ground, his helmet rolling away. With a ferocious scream, Jovi brought his blade down across the exposed neck, then looked up at me, his chest heaving.

The Wyvern streaked over my head, and I jumped, a blast of hot air buffeting my helmet. When several lithe bodies raced past me, I yelped. The Syreni youths, heading straight into the fray. I looked over my shoulder as the largest youngsters followed, the wounded Servus dangling from their shoulders. My jaw dropped at the ease with which they carried their burdens.

At a yelp from Jovi, I turned in time to see him crouch, a helmet bouncing off his head with a clang before tumbling into the darkness. A blast of heat from the dorm startled me out of my stupor, the melting windows lending wings to our feet as Jovi and I raced after the youths. Chaotic screams and clashing metal hung in the air as we pounded between walls of flame.

Left! *Right!* If a clear path in the fiery wall opened, the boys took it, their end game clear, at least to them. A youngling in the rear stopped to knock an arrow, grinning as it sliced through an Argenti running straight at him. As I ran through the choking smoke, I curled my knees and let my momentum carry me over the falling body.

"Felix, DUCK!" Jovi's voice hit me like a cannonball and I dropped to my knees just in time to hear a sword whoop over my head. I looked up into a pair of narrowed white eyes.

"Servus *traitor!* I should have killed you a long ti—" Jovi's sword sliced through his neck at the exact moment feathers replaced his eye. His mouth a surprised O, the Argenti toppled backward, his head rolling away and disappearing into the wall of flames. A youthful laugh brought me to my senses, a slender form disappearing ahead of us into the smoke.

Jovi hauled me to my feet, his head twisting to watch for threats as he dragged me across the grass. My lungs burned as sweat poured down my face. We didn't get far before an Argenti appeared before us, stepping from the orange glow of the smoke—Ivan, the asshole who constantly ruined breakfast with his damned fighting.

"What have we here?" he coughed. "A few traitors, trying to fly the coop?" He grinned, his hair fluttering in the breeze from the roaring flames creeping in around us.

Ivan lifted his arm, a throwing knife in his hand. "This will be my absolute pleasure." His arm pulled back behind his head, but before he could let his knife fly, a shadow appeared above us. The flames billowed outward, and Ivan looked up in the air—straight into a gaping mouth.

With a hiss, the Wyvern snapped his jaws and inhaled Ivan all the way to his thighs, then lifted him into the air, his wings flapping wildly. Tossing his head back, with just a few swallows, Ivan's feet disappeared.

Jovi and I looked at each other, then back at the Wyvern, who let out a low belch, winked at us, then shot into the air and disappeared.

We darted forward, only to come up against a wall of flames. Jovi and I were hemmed in. We'd waited too long, and lost sight of the youths. Frozen in place, the two of us turned in horror, but in every direction an inferno blocked our way. I turned to my friend, and we looked into each other's eyes. The firestorm rose around us, blasting heat flaying our skin, and I knew— we were done. We tipped our helmets together, Jovi giving me a sad smile as he panted into my face.

A blast of wind rushed to the ground as the leathery creature in the sky swooped through our airspace, breathing life into the fire around us even as his wings shoved it outward, a slight reprieve from the crackling maze.

A path appeared, the fire-breather floating above us, driving the flames back with repeated gusts from his wings. We followed a curve in the hellish inferno, tracking beneath the beast above, then rounding a curve to see the youths waiting. Through choking tears, they pointed at the towering stone wall.

My friend stopped and I crashed into him, my eyes following Jovi's. A dark-haired male dressed in black leather dropped from the Sycamore tree hugging the wall. He stood to face us, a bow in his hands, an empty quiver on his back. His cold eyes traveled over our group, flicking to the young males. He smiled.

"You two Servus are smarter than I thought. Come." He pointed to the hole at the base of the wall just as the tip of a scaled tail disappeared from view. "Follow the croc. He'll show you the way."

I'd seen this Djinn before. For years, he'd been stuck to Hex's side like glue. This was the first time I'd ever seen him smile, the cold-hearted fucker.

"Ladies first," he said, bowing to sweep his arm in a grand gesture.

The Syreni youths chuckled, then gave us a shove.

***

~ EDALINE ~

I was fucked.

Hanging over me, Ronan paused, thick strands of death sheeting from his teeth. Golden eyes boring into me, his clenched hands nearly snapped my forearms.

Grinning, I thought of Cain, and power flooded my air shield, pulling an enraged scream as it sizzled Ronan's grip. He released me, and I bolted straight to the charred short sword still embedded in Stephen's smoking foot. Ronan charged after me.

My air shield protected my hands as I wrestled the sword free, then swung the blackened blade. It missed a hastily tucked belly, and Ronan caught my wrist, yanking me off my feet. The scorched blade waved in the air over our heads as we wrestled. My boot caught him in the groin. He grunted but held fast, his fingers tightening.

Out of nowhere, a thick tentacle grabbed Ronan around the throat and wrapped tight, squeezing. Two more slapped around his wrists, a white octopus dangling behind him like a cape. Choking, Ronan released my arms, the tentacles around his throat cutting off his air. When his eyes rolled back in his head, I had my opening.

With a vicious smile, I swung my sword, but a rubbery vice grabbed both my wrists and pulled down, twisting viciously until my fingers released the blade.

"Eddi! STOP! You can't—HOLY FUCK!"

The frantic words of my friend tore through my mind, making me gasp. I didn't care. I struggled, my eyes rolling downward to follow Ronan as he slumped to the ground, unconscious. Then, those tentacles were on me, wrapping tightly around my body and pushing the air from my lungs. I couldn't speak, so I grunted my fury instead.

Wide with terror, goat-like eyes peered into mine as slowly but surely Cal cut off my oxygen. I collapsed, barely registering as he began pulling me across the courtyard. Inch by inch, he hauled me to the wall.

The screams and shouts of fighters mingled with the wet rasps of the octopus. Cal's breathing tube pumped like a bellows until finally, he yanked me into the flickering darkness of the shrubs. A crocodile thudded past, Ronan unconscious and dragging from his jaws.

The battlefield was visible through the shrubs, Gideon's body still lying near the center as, around him, long thin walls of flames streaked toward the sky. Thunderous screeches rent the night, the ring of steel on steel peppering the air. The buildings were ablaze, all but consumed by the Wyvern's breath.

There was no sign of Tabitha, but Phoebe jogged beside a young Syreni male with Oliver's unconscious human form draped over one shoulder. Seeing him handed under the wall, Phoebe turned, whispered something, flicked her fingers, and a shimmering barrier rose across our end of the yard.

Just in time—a handful of Argenti slammed into it, their flat hands pounding as they screamed in terror. A fiery hurricane consumed them, their hands falling away into the orange inferno. The barrier held.

As the last of our forces disappeared into the shrubbery beside me, my compulsion flared, and pain raked over my skin. I screamed. Cal hissed at someone who dragged me under the wall.

As my head bumped across the ground, I watched the Wyvern drop into the training yard and snag Gideon by the wings. Flapping hard, he lifted the Gryphon into the air, deftly avoiding the waving metal spear. Then they were gone, the heavy whumps disappearing into the darkness.

Defeated, I let my head fall back. I cried out as pain raked my skin, every inch of me lit with punishment for an incomplete mission. Cal stopped, and Galahad reached out to feel my forehead.

"You need to get her as close as possible to her target. The pain will kill her if she isn't actively seeking to carry out Hex's command. Proximity will help."

As I lost consciousness, I saw Matilda's bright eyes and wondered why she was here. She should have been back at the *Shoal*. Matilda held the hand of the leather-clad Djinn, and I felt a different kind of agony—one that was far, far worse.

You didn't keep her safe. You failed her.

The excruciating pain of both unfulfilled directives pulled me under.

CHAPTER 35

Groggy, I slowly came to. Reaching out, I ran a hand over the soft material beneath my fingers, confused by the smell of diesel tickling the back of my throat. Then, through the haze of something that felt suspiciously like a sedative, I caught a hint of the warm, salty scent I knew and loved. *Ronan.*

I sat up, but flopped back when my forehead throbbed hard enough to bring tears to my eyes. I had no idea where I was, but Ronan was close, which calmed me.

The deep vibration of the Spectre's engines lifted my spirits. Hopefully, the nightmare was over, and the GPS was aimed at our marina in Marathon. The memory of mangled Syreni bodies caused a heavy roll in my stomach; nothing came up, thank goodness.

I swung my legs over the bed and opened my eyes, but what I saw wasn't what I had expected. I was in the hold of the ship, and the shackles attached to my cot told me it was one of the rooms we'd passed when we discovered James was a Wyvern.

Mumbling to myself, I stood up, dizziness hitting me hard. For the first time, I noticed reinforced windows between the infirmary rooms. A plain beige curtain covered each one.

I wobbled over and pulled back the first one. Oliver was naked and huddled in the far corner, covered in blood and holding both arms over his head. Squatting, he rocked back and forth. He must have felt my stare because he twisted to face the corner. I covered my mouth in horror at the scars criss crossing his back and buttocks. A pink glow around the windows and door told me, Phoebe was here, and had warded him into the room.

What did they do to you, Oliver?

I walked to my door, as weak as a kitten, the pain in my head pounding like a jackhammer. I would kill for an aspirin. I looked down at my hands, and they were pink. My magic was asleep.

I grabbed the door handle and twisted, anxious to get out and discover what happened after the battle. It was locked. I yanked and jiggled, but nothing budged. With a growl, I checked the other window.

It was Ronan, sitting on a cot in the next room, his muscular back to me. Pounding on the window to get his attention, a strange feeling of anger curled in my gut at the sight of him. Aggression speared through me, I was confused to realize it was directed at the male I used to love. I felt nothing but anger toward him, now.

At the thumps on the window, Ronan's shoulders tensed. Jumping up from the cot, he whirled to face me, his lips curled back in a snarl. His yellow irises flared when he saw my face, and he charged. I jumped back as he slammed against the window, pounding hard enough that the glass flexed under his fists. Wild eyes drilled into me with a deadly promise if he found a way through the barrier.

"Hey! Watch it!" I yelled. A sudden desire to hurt him cut through the haze of whatever drug made me groggy. Those bastards. They'd drugged me!

Ronan hit the glass again, his teeth snapping as toxic secretions flipped up to stripe the glass. He pounded so hard that his fists turned red. The sight of the blood made me growl, but I needed to plan my attack. I tossed the curtain back across the glass and stepped back.

A strange mixture of sorrow and anger came over me, and I fell back onto the mattress. My head swam as I cried against the pain in my head, my body exploding in agony. Heat scorched through my chest, whisking outward to the tips of my fingers and toes.

Laughter, sad yet fierce, bubbled from my chest, the solution suddenly clear. The pain would go away if I killed him. I shouldn't feel bad. He was a danger to everyone around him. He had to die. My mind made up, I looked around the room for a weapon, but my cot was the only thing in here.

At my retreat, the pounding and snarling had slowed and finally stopped, and when I teased the curtain for a look, Ronan was back on the bed. His head hung between his shoulders, both hands crushing the edge of the mattress in a white-knuckled grip. I looked around his room. He had destroyed everything. Even his side table lay in pieces.

Long, splintered pieces. With very sharp ends. The perfect weapon. I needed to get in there. I went to the door, my brain working overtime on ways to get out of this godforsaken room. It opened as I reached for the handle, and I had to jump back to avoid getting hit. It was Cal.

Seeing my opportunity, I tried to blast past him, but he reached out a hand to stop me. James and Galahad were in the hall, their strong arms catching me and shoving me back inside. The door slammed shut with a click. Someone was outside the door.

Three sets of hands forced me back onto the bed, and my chest heaved as I sat pinned on the edge. My angry screams must have roused Ronan because he renewed his assault on the window, the curtains fluttering with the force of his fists.

James and Cal exchanged wide-eyed looks as I struggled against their hold.

"Calm down, Eddi," Cal said, his voice soothing. "It's ok. I'm here."

"Fuck you," I bellowed. "You're a dirty traitor, and I'll kill you if you get in my way." Cal's face went gray.

"Edaline, calm yourself," James said, his voice soft. "Hex enslaved you. You're not yourself right now. You don't want to kill Ronan."

I glared at him. What did he know about what I wanted?

Galahad snapped his fingers, and I focused on him. "If you kill Ronan, the compulsion will release you, and the pain in your head will disappear. You will feel well again. Unfortunately, you will also wish for your own death."

"Then, you will see everything clearly. You are a slave; she has used you and will continue to use you. You *must* find it inside yourself to resist. If you don't, your guilt will be like a thousand blades on your soul—far worse than anything you can imagine."

He looked at James, his expression tight. As they became distracted by an inner conversation, I took that opportunity to lunge upward with everything I had, breaking their hold.

I piled into Galahad's stomach, his lungs collapsing with the force of my attack. We both went down in a heap and then I was up, Cal and James grabbing at me as I pounded on the door, ripping at the handle and screaming like a mad thing.

Strong arms wrestled me to the ground as Cal scrambled for the door, opening it to speak to someone outside. Moments later, Bacchus entered, holding a large white piece of material.

In moments, I was trussed up like an Asian wrap, my arms pulled across my stomach, and the straight jacket winched down tight. Someone shoved a padded helmet on my head and shackled my ankles to the bed. I hissed in fury and fought against my restraints.

Bacchus produced a syringe, and Cal held me down while James squirted a nasty-tasting liquid into my mouth.

"This will calm you down, Eddi, so we can talk," Cal said. "We'll explain everything so you can resist the pull of Hex's talisman. Thank god she never got a chance to hang it around your neck."

I had no choice, with all the muscle in the room and my head beating like a drum. As the drug took effect, my breathing slowed, and my muscles relaxed. It was a blessed relief, although my head still pounded with angry dwarves carrying sledgehammers.

James ran a hand over my forehead, pushing my bangs back with a gentle touch. "That's better. Now, let's see what we can do to help you fight this thing."

"What happened? There was so much blood out there on the grass ..." My voice trailed off as I lifted my eyes to James' grim face.

"We lost many Syreni yesterday." At my surprised look, he added, "You've been out for quite a while."

James frowned down at me. "I'm sorry, Eddi. I was too late to stop her. Hex transformed into her Manticore too early. The carapace is virtually fireproof. I needed her in human form before I could intervene. Gideon hadn't counted on her being so quick at changing shapes."

His eyes dropped to examine the hem of his shorts. "Gideon isn't in a good way right now. I don't think he's going to make it this time."

Tears misted my eyes even through the haze of the drugs and the pain of the compulsion. Gideon couldn't die. *Could he?*

Reading my thoughts, James answered. "Even a being as powerful as a Gryphon can die, Edaline. It just takes a lot more to finish the job. Hex tipped the spear with Manticore toxin."

James' face went white as he looked at the window. "Ronan is—well, he's stuck in *MORS*. He lost control. We can't bring him out of it, so there's no one to heal Gideon. Or any of our injured, for that matter." His eyes softened. "Even your father."

My father. Gideon. All those Syreni. *So much death.*

"Go ashore! Take them to a hospital!" In my mind, a voice whispered that Ronan *should* die, but I closed my eyes and tried to ignore it, letting the drugs do their work.

James shook his head. "Your father can't be moved. And doctors will know Ronan isn't human when they look under his skins. Gideon is stuck in his Gryphon form. It's his only chance to heal. He hasn't regained consciousness, and we can't even take the chance of pulling the spear out of him because it will restart the bleeding. It's a miracle he's not dead already."

The hopelessness of it all hit me. It was all for nothing. All those people dead, Oliver a total mess, and Ronan—I gasped as the urge to kill rocked me to the core. Remembering Galahad's words, I fought it.

"Did the bitch get away?" I knew the answer before asking. Her death would have destroyed this horrible thing inside of me.

James nodded. "She did, but I have no idea how. She was in her human form and got part of the blast that almost took you, too." He grimaced. "Her superior staff and most of the hybrids are dead. We saved any Servus who came willingly, about a dozen all told. Ronan killed the Succubus, but the Incubus escaped with Hex."

His voice droned on, but my eyes drifted closed, tears seeping between my lids. I thought of losing my father and Gideon and—*Ronan*. Even Cal was lost to me. Once again, I was all alone.

CHAPTER 36

~ MATILDA ~

Holding my form at the ceiling, I watched the scene in Eddi's room. I had been practicing; my cloud was so clear now that I could explore the ship all I wanted, and no one saw me.

When Eddi woke up, I wanted to smile, but the rocks in my stomach wouldn't let me. She was sick, and it was all my fault. It wasn't fair. Why did bad things always happen around me? I shouldn't have let them help me. I shouldn't have let them take me from Hex.

Hovering against the ceiling, I waited until Bacchus reached for the door handle. A quick breath, and I slipped out the door as soon as he opened it.

Gideon was here. I needed to find him. As I worked my way through the yacht, I remembered the horrible things I had seen here—the things Hex did. As if sensing my shudder, Bacchus looked over his head. I dropped back and held my breath as he took the hallway to the engine room.

Sensing a cold space at the back of the Spectre, I soon hovered over the swim platform. Gideon's broken body sprawled motionless on the deck below. The water swirled past the swim deck as we headed home, the body of the Gryphon glamored from prying eyes. It didn't stop me. I saw through everything.

Seeing the great beast in so much pain made me cry. Irresistibly drawn to him, I wisped down the stairs and whirled around each curve of his enormous body, the feathers of his wings ruffling as I passed.

There was so much blood puddled around him on the deck that I lost my concentration and tumbled into a heap, landing on one giant paw. Gideon's sharp nails poked into me as I scrambled to safety, leaving a deep scratch below my knee.

My eyes burned with tears as I crept around him, anxiously watching for his chest to rise. I began to lose hope, my stomach tight with fear that I might be too late. I could have sat with him. I could have eased his passing like the others—the ones Hex killed.

Gideon was too beautiful for this to happen. It hurt to see him this way. At least I made it before he died. Before his body looked like an empty suitcase. That part was always horrible.

There. A small sip of air, drawn in so quietly that I held my breath until it came back out again. Gideon's chest cavity, bigger than my whole body, slowly went flat. I was just in time.

When a quiet moan made the floor tremble under me, I jumped. The Gryphon's massive feet twitched, the claws curling as if he still fought a battle somewhere. Like his feet, his eyes moved, the gray membrane twitching as if he dreamed.

Wide-eyed, I glanced up at the long steel pole still impaled behind his elbow. I couldn't contain the sob that rose to my lips this time. I wanted to pull the horrible thing out. It didn't seem right to leave it in there while he died.

Feeling more comfortable that he wouldn't wake up and eat me, I reached out. I ran my fingers around the edge of a gigantic feather that hung from his neck, marveling at how stiff it felt. I cocked my head at the crispy paper sound.

When I kneeled and sunk my fingers into the thick fur covering his front leg, it was stiff, like a soft hairbrush. The intricate patterns that covered him mesmerized me, my fingers tracing the stripes on his chest. So beautiful. Such a waste. I wouldn't let him die alone.

My arms slid around a foreleg so thick my hands couldn't touch. I lay my head onto the sleek fur, catching a subtle beat of his heart beneath my ear. It sounded far away and getting further with each slow bump. Soon, it would stop. I always imagined that dying things looked for a doorway to somewhere nicer when they sounded like that.

As I cuddled against him, I thought about never seeing his beautiful wings lifting him into the air. I had heard stories about him, Hex spitting and sputtering whenever his name came up. Like so many things, she took him away from me.

He would never fly down, lift me onto his back, and carry me somewhere safe. I always wanted to fly away with him, and now, I never would. My lips shook; I couldn't hold back the tears any longer.

When his heart gave a final, shuddering thump, I wept, my tears trickling into his fur. I cried for him and all the other creatures that had found the door to somewhere nicer. I cried until my heart was empty, and the coat beneath my cheek was wet with transparent pearls straight from my soul.

CHAPTER 37

"Ok, Eddi. We're going to let you go to the bathroom. Behave yourself, and maybe we can take off the straight jacket." Cal unbuckled me as I faked being calm. I was far from calm.

For an hour, I'd lain on that cot, fuming about the restraints. I hated them for standing in my way. Ronan needed to die, and the sooner the better. Everyone looked exhausted, so it was the perfect opportunity for me to strike.

James and Tabitha watched from inside the door, their arms crossed and their lips in a tight line. Tabitha's eyes narrowed on me, suspicious of my relaxed smile.

Clever girl. No wonder I used to like you.

As soon as Cal dropped the jacket onto the bed, I lashed out with a kick that sent him flying across the cot. I backed over to Oliver's window, my hands out like claws. I had to get next door. It was now or never. I lunged, swinging at James, who sucked in his belly and jumped back, then darted forward to grab my wrist.

I brought up a shin, took him between the legs with everything I had, and then kicked out to the side to catch Tabitha in the chest. With a surprised *"Bitch!"* she fell backward, thumping onto her ass. Cal lunged toward me from the floor, briefly grabbing my arm, but I called on my shields and turned up the heat until he let go with a gasp, holding his burned hand.

"Get out of my WAY!" My bellow echoed through the small room, and I lunged for the door, jumping over James, who lay curled in the fetal position.

I made it to the hallway, but a dark shape hurtled down the corridor toward me. Enormous talons clicked around my neck, choking me as I was lifted and pushed back into the room. An impossible weight pinned me to the floor, and as my head slapped the ground, I closed my eyes. *Ow.*

Ronan snarled, hitting the glass as the noise worked him into a lather.

Thick, leathery digits shook me back to reality, my head bumping up and down on the floor.

"Gideon!?" Tabitha's shocked voice filled the room.

Shit. Now, I'd have to kill the Gryphon first.

I twisted my neck, struggling to breathe, and from the corner of my eye, I noticed a sliver of steel lying on the floor by my hand. When I rolled my eyes toward the door, I saw it twisted in the frame and hanging by one hinge.

The golden eyes above me narrowed, two tufted ears perking forward.

Grimacing at the handsome face above me, my fingers wrapped around the makeshift weapon. Choking on a laugh, I drove the shard into Gideon's thick wrist.

The Gryphon didn't snarl or snap. Instead, the fleshy corners of his lips turned up with a wry smile. As the blood poured from his wound, Gideon chuckled.

"Perfect timing as always, Edaline." Then, he released my neck and jammed his dripping leg into my face.

I tossed my head, gurgling under a coppery waterfall of blood as it splashed on my face. Thick crimson liquid filled my mouth, spraying into the air when I coughed. That made him laugh even harder, the echo in my head making my ears ring.

I froze. Flames licked over my skin as my legs jerked straight, and my head smacked the floor as my neck pulled guitar-string tight with a full-body seizure. As fiery waves of shock hit me, I screamed.

I'd endured a defibrillator in the not-too-distant past, but I was unconscious then. This time, I felt every jolt of the maelstrom of power that flooded through me, my teeth clicking home inside the tip of my tongue.

As I went limp, a quiet voice in my head said, *"I release you from your bond."*

My eyes were open, so I saw the moment Gideon leaned too far one way and flopped onto his hip, his head lowering, his forked tongue dragging on the ground. Blood trickled down his leg, pooling beneath his enormous foot.

Abject horror flooded me at the sight of the majestic Gryphon, reduced to a weak, trembling disaster.

What have I done?

I heard pounding and rolled my eyes to see Ronan's face pressed against the glass, his fangs dripping and his eyes wild.

I was going to kill him. Kill the best thing that ever happened to me.

My eyes blurred with tears. In my feverish mind, I fell, plummeting into the hollowed-out shell that was the last ten years of my life. The loneliness. Finding my way alone. The nights of sleeping by the sea. The tears and pain of having no one.

My thoughts were deep, and dark. I was a terrible person. I would have killed for Hex. I let her win. I was just as big a monster as she was.

James lurched upright with a groan, staggering across the room. I watched as he pressed his forehead to Gideon's, smiling so hard that his lips pulled back. I thought I saw tears, but my eyes and ears weren't working very well. Snippets of conversation reached me.

Then, a loud, rumbling purr filled my mind as Gideon spoke.

"As I said, my mother favored tigers to lions." He looked up at everyone, his golden eyes pale with exhaustion. *"Unfortunately, she also enjoyed the sexual prowess of a demonic scorpion."*

The room went church quiet as his words sunk in. James caught on first, his mouth opening and closing. Then, he smiled. But it wasn't a happy smile. It was a *funeral* smile—the kind you gave to people who'd lost a mother or—*a sister.*

I licked my lips, my throat dry. *"Hex is your sister?"* At the croaky question, Gideon nodded his head.

"There were no guarantees it would work. But as siblings from the same mother line, I believed my blood would trick Hex's magic. I was right." He looked down at me. "How do you feel, Edaline?"

I closed my eyes and threw my arm across my face. "Like shit. Thanks for asking."

Tabitha came over and nudged me with a bare foot. I opened my eyes to see her glowering at me. She snapped, "You owe me a box of pralines and a double brownie whoopie pie." With a half-hearted kick, she reached out her hand and yanked me to my feet.

The room spun, and Tabitha pulled me close, wrapping her arms around me. She smelled like the sea—*like Ronan*. Sobs burst from my lips, her hands patting my back in comfort.

Through the curtain of my tears, I noticed Matilda. She stood in the doorway with eyes like saucers. She looked exhausted, her knees trembling as much as her bottom lip.

I rasped, "I thought you were dead, Gideon. How are you here, kicking my ass yet again?" I hurt all over from the ten thousand-watt spa treatment, but I was happy—*ok, overjoyed*—to see him alive. Our love-hate relationship could resume unhindered.

Gideon sat up straighter, his striped tail reaching to hook around Matilda's waist. Slowly, he pulled her into the room and tucked her under his wing.

"It seems I have a guardian angel that cries the healing tears of the Gods"—he looked at Ronan's window—"somewhat like another healer we know."

At the incredible news, I would have been amazed along with everyone else, if Ronan hadn't suddenly decided he was done playing games. With one final meteoric thump, his window came at me in an explosion of glass and wire.

CHAPTER 38

Lucky as always, I attracted his gaze and became the object of his aggression. He charged, and my shriek came a millisecond before my shield slapped into place. He grabbed my head and yanked, his slick fangs biting down in the crook of my neck. The very place where he'd teasingly licked and nibbled not so long ago.

The thought made me gag, although that may have been the crushing weight of his jaws trying to push through my shield. I didn't want to hurt him, but I had no choice. With a push of power to my air shield, he staggered backward, his feet crunching on the glass that littered the floor.

It was enough time for everyone else to react. Gideon couldn't rise, so Tabitha and Bacchus snatched Ronan under his arms and hauled him through the broken door and across the hallway.

Snapping and yowling, Ronan kicked and struggled, but he was no match for his siblings. They wrangled him onto another cot with restraints, and as he hit the end of the shackles, the cot rocked beneath him. When they were sure everything held fast, Tabitha and Bacchus backed out and locked the door.

What happened to my peaceful life? Why did I have to lose everything I held dear?

I pulled myself together and padded across the hall to his window. With tired eyes, I watched Ronan struggle. It was all too much. I had to get away. I turned to James and, without raising my head, asked, "Where is my father?"

"Up one deck, at the end of the hall. The room beside yours." He reached out and put a gentle palm on my shoulder. "He is not good, Edaline. Prepare yourself."

I walked down the darkened hallway, passing rooms filled with Syreni and Servus, the injured males sprawled across cots and floors in the infirmary rooms. I nodded to Axel, propped on the floor with his leg bandaged. His sad smile almost undid me.

I trudged up the stairs, passing the bi-eyed Servus male and his friend—the gentle one with the blue skins—as they jogged by. They nodded, but I barely responded. I didn't even have enough energy left to feel bad about it.

My fingers tingled as the magic that Gideon pumped into me slowly left my body. I was empty, hollowed out, ready to throw in the towel and call it a lifetime. But first, my father. Even the thought of finally seeing him brought me no joy.

As I crept into his room, I left the door open a crack to see where I was going. My eyes darted around for any sudden movement as I approached where he lay on the bed.

His eyes were closed, his face peaceful. An IV hung from the headboard. I didn't want to know why Hex needed IV bags in her infirmary.

My father was so thin that his cheekbones pressed against the skin of his face, his chin sharper than I remembered. Gently, I lifted his hand and ran my fingers over each frail digit. Skin and bones. That pretty much summed it up. The sheet came up to his belly, where the white skin hung so loosely that I counted every rib.

Grief overwhelmed me, twisting into something horrible that battled with the joy of seeing him again. When I lifted his arm to cross it over his chest, I saw scars peeking up from his back: long, thin stripes, each ending on his ribcage. I didn't look further. I couldn't handle it right now.

Weaving my fingers into his, I remembered him at the cabin, so brave and strong. He fought so hard for me. I clenched my hand in his as a sob escaped, and he stirred. I released the pressure, but it was too late.

His eyes opened, and two white irises sparked in the darkness of the room. Dull. Confused. They rolled back and forth until they came to rest on me, and he smiled.

"Daughter." The soft dry sound caught my heart in a stranglehold, and I began to glow. His eyes widened.

"You look like an angel."

My hands shook, but I held back the tears by reaching for the glass of water and straw on the side table. I brought it to his lips, and he swallowed, his throat clicking at the effort.

"Don't speak, Father. You should rest. You're safe now." I brought his hand to my lips and kissed the protruding veins, the skin there tissue paper soft.

"Seeing you is like a dream. Is this a dream?" He coughed, and I gave him another sip. When he settled back on the sheets and closed his eyes, I ran my fingers through his hair. It was long and knotted, and the smell of sickness wafted from him.

"No, it's not a dream. We got there in time. You'll get better soon. Just rest, ok?"

He shook his head, his eyes still closed. "It is over for me, Eddi. But seeing you fills my heart with joy. It was worth the wait." His trembling hand reached for me, his fingers spreading over my belly. "You will have a family after I'm gone. You can name him after me."

He opened his eyes, and seeing me shake my head, he smiled, his lip cracking at the motion. "I will watch over you both."

My tears had a mind of their own, pouring down my face. Not wanting to upset him, I caught them on my sleeve.

"You have to fight, Father. You can't go—I only just found you again!"

He sighed and closed his eyes. "Fighting to deny Hex's spell took everything I had. There is nothing left to hold me on this plane." He drifted off, then spoke again. "She hated me for it. She punished me, but I got the last laugh, didn't I?" He coughed, his breath rattling in his chest.

A band tightened around my heart, squeezing until I couldn't breathe. After all these years and all that fighting, I would still lose him. I would never know who my mother was or what led to that night at the cabin. He would leave me alone again.

Father frowned. "You are never alone, Edaline. You are part of something grand." He opened his eyes, his lids heavy. "You want to know about your mother."

I nodded, leaning down to hug him, my cheek resting against his bony sternum. His hand came up, trembling as it smoothed over my hair.

"Ariya. Her name was Ariya. Your mother was a beautiful creature. I loved her with all my heart." When he gasped in pain, I pulled away to look at him. He was paler than when I came into the room, if that was possible.

"Don't speak, father. It's too hard for you right now. I can wait."

He shook his head. And then I heard him in my mind.

"My time here is over, Eddi. I must tell you the truth of your birth before it's too late." He squeezed his eyelids tight as if the memories pained him.

"I worked for Hex for a time. She stole the body of an acquaintance and hid her true form from me. Hex lived to hurt things and captured a hostage—your mother. We fell in love. When she got pregnant, I stole her away. Having you was the best thing that ever happened to us. We managed five wonderful years before they took her from me."

"Who took her, father?"

He coughed a wet and horrible sound. I tucked a pillow under his shoulders and rubbed his arm. His breathing settled, but he didn't answer. I thought he had drifted off to sleep.

When he opened his eyes, I was startled. They glowed a little brighter in the darkness, and for a moment, he seemed better.

"My family plotted to kill her after we sought their help." His eyes stared off into the darkness. *"She wasn't considered good enough for my station. They refused to accept her. With the help of Fitzwilliam, my valet, we ran. We were so happy when you were born. You were a joy to us both."* His chin trembled, and a tear rolled from the corner of his eye.

"They found us. They waited for me to leave and killed her. It was a miracle that I took you with me that day."

I gasped, barely able to comprehend what he was saying. "Why? Why wasn't she good enough for your—*station*? I don't understand." I tried to keep my voice quiet, but it was hard.

Pain filled his eyes, and he closed them. *"I killed her. When I trusted my family, and took her to the palace. I should have kept her hidden—kept you hidden. I am sorry."*

He opened his fingers, and I slid my hand into his with a gentle squeeze.

"It's not your fault, father. None of this is your fault. The world is full of monsters."

"I am so proud of you, daughter. You are like her in so many ways. You make our sacrifices bearable. You are every bit the royalty that runs in your veins." His lips turned

down, and even in my mind, his words were choked with grief. *"They will never know the treasure they lost when they promised you to Hex."*

I gasped, a spreading sickness filling my guts. I felt numb. Royalty? Promised to Hex? They killed my mother, but who are—*they?*

It was only when he answered that I remembered he could hear my thoughts.

"You are a half-Djinn princess of the Court of Seas. They are corrupt and greedy. I did not fall in line, and they took steps to destroy what I wanted most. Your mother. You. My chance at happiness. When they promised you to Hex upon your birth, we ran. You were born five days later."

His lip curled as he took a deep, rattling breath. *"To them, you are a bastard. If they find out you are alive, they will kill you. Stay simple. Live your life. But you MUST kill Hex first. She has not revealed your presence because she will lose standing with the Djinn council. They hire her for their dirty dealings. Her failure to bind you would be a black mark."*

My head reeled with the news that sparked every nerve in my brain, the implications coming hard and fast. I was a princess. They would kill me if they knew I was alive and unbound.

Fuck my life. Fuck my fucking life.

My father grimaced, squeezing my hand. *"Edaline, princesses do not swear like sailors."*

I smiled through my tears and leaned down to hug him again. He was so frail. I climbed onto the bed, snuggling beside him, pulling his hand close and rubbing my fingers over it. I closed my eyes, and we lay together for a long time, his breaths easing. Before he drifted to sleep, with a faint voice, he told me about their escape from the palace.

"If it wasn't for Fitzwilliam, Ariya and I would never have escaped. He was Fae and despised the Court of Seas. They enslaved him, then compelled him to serve as my valet. Fitzwilliam became my greatest friend, and when we fled, he risked everything for us. He covered our tracks. He lied to the court. We ran, and I never saw him again."

A tear trailed over his cheek, and I wiped it away. After a long pause, out loud, he whispered, "I think he would have liked you, Edaline."

Finally, I asked the one question that burned brightest in my mind.

"Father. What was my mother? I need to know. I know it's not polite, but please tell me?"

When he didn't answer, I knew he had drifted off to sleep. There would be more time to discuss this tomorrow when he felt better.

I smiled as I pictured him, strong and fit, teaching me to fight—the picnics in the forest, hiking through the meadows on the mountain. Him snipping about his fighting leathers, freshly washed and hanging on the line. The look on his face when he whispered into my mind to run. Away from Hex. Away from him. I should never have left him that day. I drifted off holding his hand, and dreamed of palaces.

When I awoke, he was gone.

In a daze, I crawled from the bed and looked down at him one last time before pulling the covers up to his neck. I couldn't cover his face. I couldn't bear it.

I wasn't thinking clearly, but somehow, I made it out of his room. I turned and trudged down the hallway, climbed the stairs, and crossed the lounge. It was bright in there, and I realized we were no longer moving. When I lifted my head, I saw the familiar sight of the marina going about its daily business.

That was a different life, and I wasn't interested. I continued on my path, and when I got to the swim platform, I stepped off the deck and slipped into the water, swimming to the kayak beach.

I remembered my bike was still here, so I went to it, unlocked it, and rode home, narrowly missing several collisions at the few intersections on the way.

I couldn't think. Everything was a haze of pain and sorrow.

When I unlocked the apartment, for a moment, I felt a sense of peace. My home was as I left it, and it smelled like my life. I stripped my wet clothes, dropping them along the way before slipping under the covers of my bed.

Then, I pulled the blankets over my head and wept.

***

Nausea greeted me when I opened my eyes to a hammer renovating the inside of my skull. It took me a minute or two to realize it wasn't my head. Someone was set on removing my door from the hinges with their fist.

I knew that knock. I covered my face with a pillow and ignored it.

The sound of splitting wood made me cringe, and then Cal was there, standing beside the bed.

"Eddi, are you alright?"

"Go away, Cal." The pillow against my mouth muffled the words.

"I've been worried sick about you!"

The edge of the bed dipped, and I slapped at him. "Go away!"

No response. I lifted my pillow and looked up. I must have looked pretty horrible because his eyes rounded, and he sucked in a breath as he reached for me. I shoved him off.

"Doesn't Gideon need you to ruin someone else's life now that you've finished your work here?"

He winced, but his hands wrapped around my wrists and pulled me over to where he sat. "You're being ridiculous."

My head reached atomic levels of pain as my eyes pushed out of their sockets.

"You ... what? Fuck you!"

I tried to slap him, but he had my wrists, and with a burst of strength he pulled me into his lap and forced my head under his chin. I struggled, but Cal's strong arms clamped down like an octopus, trapping me with an unholy grip.

I promptly burst into tears, my struggles weakening as I sobbed into his t-shirt—which did nothing to ease the volcano of pain raging against my skull. When I pulled back and saw it was the shirt he bought in Key West on our trip, I lost it. The howls that came from my mouth would have woken the dead.

"*Shh*, it's ok, I'm here. Cry all you want," he said, gently rocking me as he pressed his cheek to my hair. "It's alright. I've got you. You're not alone, Eddi."

A tsunami of tears later, my bladder was the catalyst that pulled me out of the crying jag and back into reality. My eyes burned as I pulled away. I'm sure my hair was a fright because Cal chuckled.

"I've always been your friend, Edaline. You know that. When we met, I might have been performing a duty for Gideon, but not since then. I've loved you like a sister since the very beginning."

He hugged me tight. "You're everything to me, and you know it." He leaned back and used a finger to pull a strand of bangs out of my mouth. "What do you say I get you something for that headache that's putting those ugly purple rings under your eyes?"

I squirmed my protest, but there was no force in it, and he let me up. After I relieved myself and settled on the couch in a miserable heap, he brought some aspirin and a cold glass of water, then sat down close beside me.

"I'm so sorry about your father. If it makes you feel any better, I'm here for you."

Staring at his familiar face, framed by the afternoon sunlight filtering through the curtains, I let out a long wet sigh. Having him here was a comfort beyond words.

Then, the world crashed in again. I shoved my head under his chin and sobbed.

"Ronan," I choked. "He's not coming back, is he?"

Cal rubbed my arm. "We don't know yet. Oriana thinks it's possible, and they'll give it all the time they can. Then, if he hasn't come around in a month, we'll worry about it. But not today."

I let out a shuddering breath as Cal leaned over and grabbed a wad of Kleenex. Handing it to me, he said, "We're *all* here for you, Eddi. Even Gideon. He feels terrible about what happened and wants to help."

I rolled my eyes, which actually hurt. "Sure he does. He's always been so worried about my welfare, hasn't he?"

"He worries more than you think." Cal stiffened. "I don't know what we would have done if he hadn't figured out the whole blood thing. He freed Galahad, too. The day they crash landed, Galahad accidentally got a dose of his blood. It broke the bond. The Djinn has been a loose cannon ever since. Lucky for us. He took out at least five of those Argenti bastards and all of Hex's vampires with a bow and arrow."

I didn't bring up the whole *Galahad shot me through the hand* subject. Cal explained to me the differences between Argenti and Servus and how there was so much variability even from the same cross. It was confusing, but I was glad to hear some of the Servus were alright. The one with the bi-colored eyes— *Felix*—his friend, Jovi, and a few others were at a safe house in the Keys. Gideon had plans for them.

"That damn Gryphon never quits scheming, does he? It made me sick to see him lying there in the training yard. I can't believe Matilda saved his life." I sucked in a breath, hope rising in my chest. "Maybe she can help Ronan!?"

Cal frowned and lowered his eyes, picking at the seam of the couch. He shook his head. "We already tried. After she rested a bit, we restrained Ronan. Matilda did her best, but there was no response. Glancing up, he added, "We'll try again in a few days. It took a lot out of her, healing Gideon like that." He shook his head in awe. "It's incredible what she did. We know nothing at all about her powers. Gideon has never seen anything like it."

Cal tucked his chin. "Oliver is her father."

Deep down, I knew. My father died resisting Hex, so it had to be Oliver. I didn't know whether that made me happy or sad.

I gave him a soggy smile and leaned back onto the couch. Cal scooped up the throw blanket and arranged it across us. "Hang in there, Ed. Things will work out. You'll see." He gave me a squeeze. "Just remember, you'll never be alone. We're here. All of us. *Especially me.*"

CHAPTER 39

When I said goodbye to Cal, I walked him down to street level and hugged him goodbye. Then I remembered I left my phone on the *Spectre*. Matilda was with Oriana, so I didn't need to worry about her, but Miri was still on the yacht with Cleatus. She may want to come home.

"Crap. Can you give me a ride back to the marina on your way home? I have to pick up the missing pieces of my life," I said with a soggy smile. "Can you manage me on the handlebars?"

Cal grinned, sweeping his hand in an arc. "Your chariot awaits."

After some awkward positioning, I managed to get safely stowed and we tottered off down my street. It was just like old times.

As we came out onto Highway 1 and headed toward the shop, we rode up to the Crazy Conch, which looked dark and dismal. The sign hanging over the door creaked as it swung, unlit and dreary against the night sky. After so many years spent building a life here, seeing it empty was depressing.

I swallowed my thoughts as we approached, resigned that my life had changed, and I had to change with it. It wasn't like Ada and Miguel could return to working there, especially since they had no idea our boss was a bloodthirsty maniac—and was still on the loose.

That was when I noticed the light. Cal did, too, and stopped before we passed the enormous picture windows and glass door. With a suspicious glance at each other, Cal pushed his bike over to lean on the outer wall, and we peered around the corner. Someone was in there.

The skin on my scalp tightened as my eyes adjusted to the darkness. A light over the long counter illuminated someone sitting in a crumpled heap in a booth, their back to us and their head in their hands. It was ten o'clock at night. There shouldn't have been anyone in there.

It was Hex, a stump of her black segmented tail hanging over the end of the bench.

What the fuck—!?

I pulled back and looked at Cal, who stood beside me chewing his lip, his eyes round. My phone was at the Spectre. We couldn't call for help. Cal wasn't about to back down. I saw it in his eyes.

He stood up straight, and I nodded. We tiptoed around to the back door, which was unlocked. Opening it, I hoped the desiccated wood didn't creak, then crept through it. The floor was mopped, and everything was tidy, although a layer of dust and a few dead bugs dotted the counter.

Making our way to the swinging doors, squinting through the darkness of the kitchen, I used the light from the tiny window to find a weapon. Handing a butcher's knife to Cal, I grabbed one for myself, then with a nod, we burst into the dining room.

Bolting through the swinging door, we found Hex hunched in the same booth facing us. When she didn't look up, we slid to a stop, Cal hissing in surprise.

Raw and patchy, the top of her head was burned beyond repair. Her hand rested on the Formica table, half of her fingers missing. She still had her pinky and ring finger, the jagged claws broken to the quick. They started tapping, the *tic-tic-tic* making my skin crawl. Cautiously, we approached, and when she looked up, I gasped.

Hex's body was a charred mess, a spiderweb of cracks crisscrossing the solid charcoal scab covering her torso. The leather jacket had saved her, but raw skin showed through scattered holes. Half of her lower lip was missing, her fangs showing in a perpetual snarl. A wad of spittle slid out of the ruined corner and dripped onto the table.

"You think I didn't know you were out there? *Fools.* You always were too self-absorbed for your own good, Edaline." Her voice was a raspy slur, her lips unable to form the words correctly.

Hex pushed up from the table with difficulty, standing to face us. She must have tried to shift during James' attack because what remained of her charred scorpion tail hung lifeless behind her. It made a strange scratching sound as it dragged over the worn linoleum.

She raised her hand, a 9 mm Springfield gleaming in the dim light. She flicked it toward the counter.

"Drop the knives and move away from the door. Haven't you ever heard not to bring a knife to a gunfight?" Her half-hearted chuckle made me gag, the wet noise sounding like it came straight from hell.

Our options being non-existent, we did as she asked and moved across the room. When Cal tensed to leap at her, she drooled, "I wouldn't do that if I were you." She snicked off the safety. "Shooting you would be my absolute pleasure, octopus." I stifled a laugh when the last word sounded like *octopush.*

When our backs were to the front windows, I glanced over my shoulder. The center glass door was locked, so that escape route was out. Never in a million years did I consider a gun. We were so screwed.

"Hang on, Eddi. I'm trying to connect with Gideon. We may be close enough, if he's still on the Spectre." Cal's inner voice was terse, his eyes unfocused. I kept Hex talking, hoping she didn't notice. It was our only chance.

"You're looking a little worse for wear ... *Patsy.*" I spat the name at her, and she grinned, wincing with pain at moving her deformed lips.

"That Wyvern sure did a number on you, eh?" I chuckled, watching for her reaction. That damn gun was steady in her hand. She wouldn't miss.

"You're a mouthpiece, you know that, Edaline? All these years, I waited for the right time to scoop you up and use you to strengthen the control over my army. I can't tell you how many times I almost killed you just to *shut you up.*"

She waved the gun. "But I couldn't very well kill my biggest success now, could I? Your father"—she choked on her laugh—"he was such a fool, falling for your mother and stealing her away from me. Did he not think I would find out about you?"

A wet-sounding growl rumbled through the room. "You've all played into my hands this entire time, and I'm not giving up now." Her eyes blazed. "Kill the octopus."

I stared at her. *She didn't know.* I laughed, and it came out a tad hysterical. "You're the fool, Hex. You don't think we found a way around your oath?" I stopped laughing and glared at her. *"Go fuck yourself."*

A flash of light blinded me as she fired the gun, a pop and a puff of dust telling me she'd hit the booth beside me. I nearly jumped out of my skin, and Cal may have screamed a little.

"Well, that might be true," she hissed. "But I still have a gun, now, don't I?"

Startled from his mental search for the Enforcer, Cal refocused on the situation. His downturned lips said it all, and my heart sank. We were on our own.

I turned back to Hex, and that's when I saw the kitchen door soundlessly ease shut. Someone had crept in behind the mangled bitch. It was dark, and I couldn't see who it was, so I kept talking.

"So that night your hoodlums abducted and almost killed me—what were they doing on the *Wanderlust*, anyway?"

She snorted. "What better way to receive shipments from Charleston than stealing someone else's boat?" She looked down her crispy nose at me. "You'll never win, *Edaline*. I have far too many irons in the fire. I'm taking you out of here, and he will die." She pointed the gun at Cal. "No hard feelings, *shifter*."

She pulled back the hammer, but before Hex could fire, an enormous cast iron frying pan came out of nowhere, slamming down on the top of her head with a resounding crack.

Hex's hand fell open, her gun clattering to the floor. The red blaze in her eyes snuffed out as they rolled back in her head and she slumped to the ground.

Behind her, our savior sent a gleaming smile our way, her pink hair bouncing as Ada laughed with delight, her hands on her knees.

"That *fucking CUNT!* Who does she think she is!?" As Cal and I stared in shock, Ada curled her ringed fingers around the handle of the heavy pan. Then, with a snarl, she hammered for all she was worth on the crumpled form at her feet. Her face drawn tight, she smashed the heavy pan into Hex over and over again, unidentifiable goo splashing up as she connected. Ada paused, her chest heaving, then spat on the bloody mess she'd made.

"You killed *Patsy,* you *demonic piece of shit!* She was my *FRIEND!*" Ada leaned over, snatching one of the butcher's knives from the counter. Her manicured hand curled into Hex's hair as she lifted, wrenched the head back, and began sawing at her neck with the knife. The grisly disaster came off with a wet pop, and Ada shook it, her face contorted with rage as she glared into the demon's lifeless eyes.

"Now die and go back to hell where you belong!" she screamed.

With a disgusted sound, Ada threw the head on the heap at her feet and turned to face us. "I've been watching the place and was coming to borrow some frozen shrimp. I saw everything. Are you kids ok?"

I looked at Cal, currently staring at my friend with his mouth open.

"Uhh—ya. *Are YOU ok?"* I asked, my voice croaky.

Ada shot us a maniacal grin, the bloody splashes across her face making her look positively *nuts*. Something didn't look right. Ada was always a trim, fit woman, but now she looked narrower—more angular.

What the ... are those feathers?

Yup, those were tiny feathers, and in a rush, they popped free across her face, her arms lengthening and her legs shrinking.

"Ah, *SHIT!* Ada cussed. "Now look what she's made me do!" She glanced up at us with wide eyes, feathers continuing to replace her wrinkles. "Sorry, guys. I *just* wanted a *freaking* bag of shrimp. And now look! What is it with the Keys these days? Everyone stirring up shit, demons coming out of the woodwork ... "

She threw her hands in the air with an exasperated sound, and when they came back to rest on her hips, each finger was covered with plumage. The knife in her hand clattered to the ground, and she groaned, the sound high pitched and garbled.

"*DAMMIT.* Sorry, kids. Gideon will have to take care of this mess."

With a rapid series of tiny popping sounds, bright pink feathers swept over Ada's skin, her legs shrinking to stick size and her arms sweeping out and coming to rest against her round body with a satisfied ruffle. The entire thing happened in seconds. A curved bill, tipped in black, shook back and forth, and her neck stretched to a long, graceful curve.

With a confident ruffle of her feathers, the flamingo turned and strutted behind the counter, her beak hooking around the handle of the upright freezer and pulling it open. Reaching inside, Ada plucked out a frozen bag of shrimp, then kicked the door closed with one splayed foot.

With a sideways look, she winked a shiny orange eye at us, then slammed her smooth body against the swinging door. Raising one wing over her head and flapping it in our direction, she slipped through the gap, the door swinging shut behind her with a soft sweep of rubber.

I looked at Cal, whose mouth still hung open. There were no words. We turned and looked at Hex—or what remained of her—then looked away. I wasn't sorry, but I sure was grossed out.

"Well, that was ... *interesting*," Cal huffed. He turned to me, his face shining with a strange look of grim exhilaration. "I guess we better go find Gideon."

As we crept around the mess on the floor, I hopped over the discarded frying pan, trying to avoid the splashes of unidentifiable muck on the floor.

With a bewildered shake of my head, my stunned brain searched back for that snapshot in time—the last, wonderful moment when my life had been simple.

Cal wrapped my hand in his, squeezed it, then pushed open the swinging door.

CHAPTER 40

Hex was dead, my father was laid to rest, and Ronan was a disaster. The news still carried reports of the occasional *Gush* party, but the subject slowly fell out of the spotlight.

James burned the Charleston facility to the ground taking the stockpile of nectar with it. Sadly, no documents were recovered to help us find the other facilities—the ones with youngsters. Knowing Gideon, he wouldn't rest until he found them all.

Soon, life would return to normal for us, *and* for humans—even those struggling with the physical after effects.

According to the news, withdrawal was a bitch, but a task force had been set up to ease the way. It turned out that *Gush* wasn't very different from other drugs when it came to recovery. With its disappearance from the party scene, things slowly returned to normal.

I could have focused on the worst of the fallout, but tried not to. Matilda was safe— and for now, living with Oriana—the *Shoal* was recovering, and Gideon was—well, *he was alive*. And I couldn't have been happier about it.

If fighting Hex had taught me one thing, it was that families were messy. Life was chaotic. And backup sometimes came in large feathered doses with an annoying side order of striped orange fur. At least, it did in my world.

The only thing keeping me going these days was positive thinking. I hung onto that as much as I could, working my way through each agonizing day, one after another, one moment at a time. Because for me, there was no happy ending. Ronan was leaving me, slipping away more and more with each passing moment.

I was not alone, thank the Gods, and Miri brought me out of my funk for a time. The day after Ada dispatched Hex, I got an unexpected surprise when I returned from Publix with an astronomical number of groceries. Cleatus had chosen to stay with us at the apartment until the dust settled, and he was a big eater. Like, *really* big.

As I came through the door, I almost dropped my bag when I saw the enormous crocodile sprawled across my living room rug. *Dammit!* Cleatus had agreed to remain in his human form during his stay. I didn't need a call from the Florida Wildlife Commission.

"Cleatus? What are you doing?"

I dropped the bag on the counter and came around the couch as he hissed a welcome, his lips cracking into a reptilian grin. That was when a dozen or more tiny blue marbles rolled out of his mouth.

Wait. Not marbles. *Sprites.* Tiny, skittering sprites, spreading everywhere like little blue cockroaches. My eyes popped open, and I stifled the urge to scream.

"CLEATUS! You *fopdoodle!* I asked you to hang onto them for a second! *One ever-loving second!*" The door of her Barbie RV slammed, and Miri appeared, her tiny hands gripping her hair in frustration.

Miri marched over to the croc and began gathering up tiny hands, herding her babies—*oh my god, so many babies*—into clusters that she hauled into the air. They squirmed, four in each of her hands. I leaned over to get a better look. Every wriggling infant was a tiny blue mini-Miri, the itty smiles on their bitty faces making my heart clench.

So freaking cute.

Miri sighed, then marched back to the RV and tossed them through the door with a slam. She came back for the second load.

"*SIXTEEN!?*" My mouth fell open in shock.

With a shrug, Miri grabbed the last eight wrigglers and lifted them over her head, their excited chitters making her smile. She lowered her arms and kissed each one—which took a while—before tossing them into the RV with the others.

She leaned hard on the pink door as it bounced against her hip, and wiped her hands on her thighs. "Yeah, sorry about that. I wanted to tell you, but I wasn't sure you wouldn't kick me to the curb. I should have skipped the Key West canoodling, because apparently Ryker shoots super sperm and Walgreens doesn't carry sprite-sized condoms."

Cleatus bobbed his head with breathy laughter, a fishy smell wafting through the room. But I was too busy dashing away tears to complain about it.

"Miri, I would *never* kick you out. We'll make this work. But sixteen! *Impressive.*"

When she gave me a tearful smile, I cringed, hoping I was right. My life was a mess, but at least I wasn't alone. And by the looks of Miri's brood, I never would be.

As the weeks rolled by, nothing changed for Ronan. His siblings moved him back to the *Shoal.* Shackled in a bare room cleared of anything that could hurt him, Ronan was well cared for despite the threat of his aggressive condition. I visited him as often as possible, taking the *Wanderlust* and scuba gear to reach him.

Whenever I passed through the beautiful coral surrounding the caves, melancholy swept over me, and I was more and more certain it was too late for him. *For us.*

Every time I donned my scuba equipment, I thought of Tara. I wasn't sorry she was dead. Not really. I went through a period of remorse for killing her, but Cal talked some sense into me. It wasn't me that swung the blade. It was the monster that Hex tried to make of me. So, I forced the guilt away and went on with my life.

Four months after Charleston, Ronan was the same. His golden eyes haunted my dreams, and I felt sick most of the time. Life was a rollercoaster ride of stress and emotions, the occasional surges of hope dashed by the reality that day after day, he remained locked in a struggle with madness.

One morning, as I settled onto the cushion at the entrance to his room, I heard the approaching footsteps and knew his time was up. I stood to face Oriana, Bacchus, and Tabitha. Their expressions said it all, and when I looked her way, Tabitha burst into tears.

"When? How?" I whispered. For a moment, my friends went out of focus. I couldn't think straight, tears streaming from my eyes like raindrops.

Bacchus cleared his throat, his eyes on the floor. "Syreni are difficult to"—he glanced at Oriana—"well, there's only one way. Are you sure you want to know this, Eddi?" Bacchus' voice was dust, the life gone from his usually happy face.

Tears poured as I nodded. "Yes. I'm going to be there. You can't stop me, so don't even try."

Oriana took my hand and gave me a wet smile. That was when I knew it was done. His own mother had given up on him. I would lose the most important being in my life, and there wasn't a damn thing I could do about it.

My gaze turned to the darkened room where Ronan sat chained, his back to us, his muscular frame rigid with barely contained fury. He rocked and moaned, grunting and snarling to himself. It was the right thing to do. I knew it, and so did those closest to him.

That didn't make it any easier.

* * *

The *Wanderlust* cut through the waves as we headed out past the humps. The unique underwater mountain made for outstanding sportfishing, the drop-off plummeting to over a thousand feet. The pressure at those depths was catastrophic for a Syreni body. Their Gods took their soul at eight hundred feet, and raised it into everlasting light at a thousand. At least, that's what Bacchus told me.

A stifling numbness haunted me all morning. I was about to drop the love of my life into an ocean canyon with enough weight to drag him to certain death. But I wasn't backing down. I could have stayed home, but I knew that if I ran away from this, I would never come to grips with him being gone. I needed to be there. I needed to say goodbye.

Back at the *Shoal,* Oriana led the Syreni rituals attached to the act of humane euthanasia. I didn't go to the ceremony—I just couldn't.

I was fortunate they let me be present during this final act, which was an intensely private Syreni ritual. Usually, the strongest swimmer in the family carried both the weight and the victim out to sea. Today we used the *Wanderlust,* even though memories of Ronan's last moments might make my future charters a living hell. It seemed appropriate, with Ronan and I having so many happy memories here.

Oriana didn't make it. Bacchus said she wasn't eating and had taken to her rooms, not allowing anyone to enter. My heart went out to her. She'd returned from hell only to be dragged into a new one by losing her eldest.

Tabitha was in the cabin, completely unable to function. She helped get her brother on board; even with Bacchus carrying most of the weight, Ronan was a struggle. As I watched him thrash and snarl, there weren't enough tears in my body to release the pain in my chest.

When Bacchus brought the weight aboard, it was smaller than I expected. The hunk of coral had a metal ring hammered into it to hold the rope that would be tied to Ronan's feet. Seeing the ten pound weight made this traumatic, mind-numbing process real.

Nausea rode me all the way to the humps, even though I had barely eaten the day before. When I glanced in the small mirror hanging in the cabin, I looked like hell, my face a puffy gray mess. My weight loss was significant, and Cal had urged me to see a doctor. There was time for that later. He didn't push.

The whole thing being too much for him, Cal stayed home. I envied him. I had spent so much time trying to reach Ronan—every moment I could spare was at the *Shoal*—that admitting defeat was like a weight around my own neck.

Ronan seemed subdued today, as if he knew what came next. The grunts and snarls were intermittent, the bindings no longer creaking with his struggles. I stopped looking at the ruined skin of his wrists and ankles. I knew there were no solutions, we had all done what we could, and soon, he would be at peace.

We arrived at the coordinates and Tabitha appeared from below, her eyes mere slits in her swollen face. She hugged me and then helped Bacchus lower Ronan into the dark blue water. The weight rested on the deck, ready to drop.

Bacchus and Tabitha jumped in and surrounded their brother, who was unable to shift to his tail form because of the rope bindings. An extensive basket weave of knots covered the length of his body. The ceremonial design was ancient, safely containing any Syreni locked in *MORS* until the act was completed.

As soft noises drifted on the light breeze, my head twisted back and forth until I realized the beautiful sounds came from the Syreni. Their lilting hums and whistles formed a song that seemed to relax Ronan, his snarls ebbing as his head nodded sleepily.

I grabbed my mask, slipped over the railing, and swam as close as I dared to Ronan. His yellow eyes gleamed as if being in the water made him happy. His eyes were unfocused as he lay his head back and stared into the sky as his brother and sister sang to him.

When the music stopped, and the only sound was the waves slapping at the boat, the Syreni climbed back on board. Tabitha ran, her wet feet slapping as she threw herself into the bow cabin. Before we left shore, Bacchus had agreed to pilot the *Wanderlust* so that I could say goodbye to the love of my life.

His face a shocking white, Bacchus bent over and grabbed the hunk of coral, which was the size of a bowling ball, and handed it to me.

The rope was twenty feet long, and I let it out halfway, then clutched it tightly, watching Ronan's face as he bobbed just off the stern.

His bound legs slowly swept back and forth, barely keeping him afloat, his golden eyes alert now that the song was over. Lugging the weight, I pushed off and kicked like mad, my human legs struggling to keep me afloat as I moved behind him.

Quickly, to avoid a bite, I squeezed myself against his spine while he whipped his head back and forth trying to snap at me. The weight tugged against my hand.

"I love you. I will always love you, and I will never forget you. You were the best thing that ever happened to me." I slipped my mask over my face and let go of the rope.

Pressed against his shoulder blades, with my arms wrapped around his chest, my stomach continued to argue. It pitched—hard. But I hung on for all I was worth, clinging to the beast still struggling to kill me as I sucked in one last breath. The rope pulled tight, and we were both hauled below the surface.

As the ocean closed over my head, I cried, holding tight as the weight pulled us down. The buoyancy of two bodies slowed our descent, giving me more time. Time to feel his body. Time to hear his heart. Time to let go.

And then, I felt it again. A thump, this time. Not the bubbling sensations I had felt the last few weeks, but a hard, solid knock of discomfort.

At first, I didn't know what it was. It was forceful and very determined to make me lose my lunch. And then, as Ronan and I drifted down into the murk, I remembered.

The day I visited the *Shoal* for the first time, Ronan and I got carried away. We hadn't used protection. My eyes widened as realization hit me.

I'm pregnant. Holy shit. I'm going to have a baby.

Another firm kick pushed against my diaphragm, and Ronan stopped struggling. Whether he felt it or simply heard my thoughts wasn't clear. He cocked his head to the side, then tried to turn and bite me, yanking from my grip.

We were out of time. I shoved myself away, Ronan's fangs snapping past the end of my nose. Without my added buoyancy, he sank faster, and with a heart full of lead, I sent a final thought to him.

"Goodbye, Ronan."

I twisted my body downward, struggling to swim further to watch until he drifted out of sight. My lungs cried for air; I needed to surface.

For as long as I could, I watched, my heart shattered. Peering up through the navy gloom, his hair, now quite long, fluttered around his face as he sank. Yellow, staring eyes watched me, a curious look in his eyes.

"I love you." In my mind, my quiet words were barely audible.

Ronan began to struggle. He roared, bubbles pouring from his mouth, his eyes wide as he stared up at me. As the vast ocean slowly claimed the details of his face, his eyes blinked. First, a golden yellow—then a dull chartreuse—and then a brilliant emerald green. The beautiful eyes that had captured my heart focused on me, and he frowned, his features disappearing into the blue shroud of the ocean.

"I'm sorry, Edaline. I never meant for this to happen." The words whispered into my mind as if from a distance, and panic hit me like a train.

"RONAN!" I swam deeper, but it was no use. My lungs were on fire. I kicked and pulled with my arms, but I was too slow. The need for air began to suffocate me. I didn't care. *His eyes were clear*—I had to save him! Down I went, shrieking in my mind, calling for him as loudly as I could.

"I'm coming! Hang on RONAN!"

For a moment, I saw his shadow as it faded into the murk. Ronan watched me, his green eyes flashing; then he was gone. I was too late. My time had run out.

I broke—a profound numbness sweeping any lingering fear of death from my mind. I didn't care if I lived or died. I couldn't live without him. I slipped off my mask and let it go, my sick soul uncaring as it drifted away. Then, with a final look at the empty darkness below me, I sucked in a giant breath of water and let the ocean take me.

Hovering in the endless navy depths, I felt a light, fizzy sensation in my lungs, and I choked, then breathed again. Water rushed in, but nothing came out. My lungs were full. But it wasn't death that filled the space. *It was oxygen.*

My neck tingled, and I raised my fingers to where three ridges lifted and fell along both sides of my neck. I pulled in a giant slug of seawater, and my head cleared.

What the—I could BREATHE!?

I didn't hesitate. I jack-knifed and headed after Ronan, my strokes feeling odd. I looked at my hands, spreading my fingers; the webbing between them made me jerk in surprise. Without pausing to think, I spread my toes and fingers, then angled down and kicked for all I was worth.

"RONAN! I'm coming—!" He wasn't far away because I heard his whispers between my ears.

"Stop. You must go back, little barracuda."

I knew we were deep, at least fifty feet, the ocean around me growing darker as I descended. Finally, after a lifetime of pulling and kicking like a maniac, I saw him. At least fifty feet below and falling faster, he gazed upward, his breathtaking eyes glittering through the gloom.

I couldn't reach him. I wasn't fast enough. In my head, I cried out, the bumping thing in my belly clearly unhappy about what we were doing.

"Eddi, NO. Leave me. You must live—for him."

As Ronan's voice faded, I stopped swimming, bubbles rising toward the surface as I sobbed. Balling my hands into fists, I closed my eyes and screamed into the depths. I wailed into the darkness below, and when my cries ebbed away, I hung there, looking down at an empty wall of blue.

I was alone. I'd always be alone. Confusion took over my body, and I closed my eyes. Inside, I died.

And that was when a wall of water, that burgeoning swell of force that usually signaled a shark attack, shoved me. Hard. Straight down.

As it passed, that forceful blast knocked me sideways, and I tumbled end over end, righting myself in time to see the glittering flash of an enormous blue tail as it blinked out of sight. The rushing cavitation of sound pummeled my eardrums, then he was gone.

Bacchus heard my screams!

I grew old in the moments that followed, sucking in seawater and trying not to panic. Here I was, hanging fifty feet below the surface, breathing water. It barely mattered, my eyes glued on the cobalt expanse below.

I have always marveled at how the ocean hides things, even when visibility is good. Things moving toward you start as shadowy shapes, then gradually gain substance until they are crystal clear.

As Bacchus came into view, his eyes looking up and his hair swirling, I tried to see past his tail. The rope in his hand appeared, and the steel band squeezing my chest snapped. When Bacchus smiled, not just with his teeth but with his sparkling jade eyes, my heart exploded with a shockwave of joy. I bet they heard it all the way in Georgia.

Ronan, still bound, tugged along behind, his feet pointing to the sky. As he passed, Bacchus grabbed my arm, looking at my hands in surprise. Then, with a shrug, he hauled me along behind him.

As his tail bumped against me, his smooth scales reminded me this was home to the Syreni. It was where they were most at ease; their speed and strength were not just part of their DNA but the reason for their survival.

Looking down, I watched Ronan curl to look up at me. He smiled, the galaxy of greens in his eyes taking my breath away. I didn't know if it was possible to die of happiness, but I did—all the way to the surface.

Halfway there, I pulled away from Bacchus and latched onto Ronan as, upside down, he drifted past me. Latching onto his bindings, I lowered myself until we were face to face. His eyes sparked with curiosity at the gill slits in my neck.

"You can breathe?" A sly smile crept over his face.

"Hex kept saying that I was her greatest success—her first. I thought she meant my special spot on her 'must-catch' list. It wasn't that at all! My father didn't get a chance to tell me, but my mother—she could only have been one thing."

Ronan drank in my features, his hair wafting as he cracked a smile that showed his teeth. His lovely, beautiful, *normal* teeth.

"Your mother was Syreni."

"My birth started it all. Ronan, I'm the very first Argenti. And I'm female. No wonder Hex wanted me so badly!"

There was so much to discuss, but that conversation would have to wait because we reached the surface. Tabitha waited on the *Wanderlust,* her puffy face hanging over the water as she watched for us. When Ronan smiled at her, Tabitha screamed, launching herself into the water and attacking her brother's ropes.

Soon, he was free. We were *all* free. And my God, it was the best feeling in the whole damn world.

***

As we hauled ourselves back onto the boat, my spare parts disappeared into my body, and other than a lingering itch, I was myself again. Tiny ridges ran along the inside of my fingers and toes, but that was the only sign that I'd just done a stellar impression of a goldfish.

My gills disappeared entirely, which was a relief. Ronan seemed disappointed that he couldn't explore the wondrous new changes in me, but I had the feeling he would get another chance very soon.

I couldn't keep my hands off of him. Unfortunately, I also couldn't stop crying. As Ronan held me close, Bacchus and Tabitha wrapped their arms around us both, and for a while, I wasn't the only soggy mess on board. Overwhelming relief and excitement filled the air during our joyous reunion.

Tabitha wanted the whole story, then smacked me a little too hard when she heard I was Argenti. I didn't blame her. After meeting them, I wondered if I should be happy or horrified.

"Don't be ridiculous," Tabitha spat. "Hex ruined those creatures from the moment they were born. *She* made them into monsters. You, Edaline, are no monster." She tilted her head. "You're more of a swashbuckling damsel in distress. And just think, you can lose the clunky metal tanks when you visit us at the *Shoal!*"

I hadn't thought of that, but she was right. Life held exciting new options for me now. I didn't mention the pregnancy to her, though. I still had to unpack that surprise and face my fear about what might be swimming around in my belly.

I was part Syreni. If I thought about it right now, I would explode—so I concentrated on Ronan and the feel of him against my side.

When Ronan's hands began to wander into inappropriate places, Bacchus and Tabitha hopped overboard to swim back to the *Shoal;* there was joyous news to spread.

I watched them leave, my heart aching at the mixture of joy and sadness in Tabitha's eyes. My friend still grieved Enzo's death. Guilt nibbled on me as I waved goodbye while trying to hide my happiness.

"Don't." Ronan slid his arms around me from behind, his chest a comforting warmth against my back. "She will recover in time. You should not feel guilty about being happy. Today, the Gods chose us. Sometime soon, it will be her turn."

I reached up to cover Ronan's broad hand with mine, memorizing the smooth texture of his skin. I loved how soft he was, and the sensation of touching him again made me cry.

Ronan rubbed his cheek over my hair, the rumbles in his chest telling me how much he had missed me. I was still numb, the lingering fear and tension clinging to me like a second skin. I closed my eyes and held back the sob lodged in my throat.

"*Shh*. Don't do this to yourself. It's over. I'm here." He pulled my back tighter to his chest, his lips pressing into the base of my neck, his warm breath fanning my skin. "I feel like I've been gone a lifetime."

Ronan slid a hand over my breasts and down, stopping over my belly. He palmed the small bump between my hip bones, his thumb feeling where my joints pressed sharply against my skin.

"Gods, you are skin and bones!" Feeling the other hip, Ronan hissed with displeasure. Turning me around, he tucked his chin and stared into my eyes.

"I will fatten you up. Our babe must be strong so I can show him how to fish for stone crab and lobster."

My eyes popped open. "*Uhh*—is there something I need to know about Syreni babies? They slide out and *what*—get a slap on the ass, and handed a lobster snare?"

Ronan chuckled and pulled me into a hug. "No, no, not like that."

I sighed with relief until, with a chuckle, he added, "Not for a month or two, anyway." At the look on my face, he palmed the back of my neck and gave me a gentle shake. "Eddi. I tease! You are too easy—"

I burst into tears.

With a sigh, Ronan pulled me close and tucked me under his chin. His hand stroked my hair as he whispered in my ear, trying to calm me. Riding hard into a full-on meltdown, I couldn't stop the choking sobs. He grasped my shaking hands, and pulled them to his lips, crooning soft whispers of comfort.

The pressure from four months of hell, fisted under a fine thread of control, burst like a dam. All the nights without him, and the loneliness that ate at my soul. Seeing him, day after day, locked away from me behind a wall of fury. Being totally helpless to do anything but watch him slip away. Hoping he was better one day, only to have him nearly take my hand off the next. Oriana's face when she told me it was over. As Ronan held me, I sank into the sea of misery I'd been swimming through and poured it all out on his chest.

At some point, he lifted me into his arms and settled us on the bench at the stern, cradling me in his lap. I gave in to selfish tears and bawled, thanking Heaven that the only thing watching me were a few frigate birds. I hadn't cried hiccups since I was a toddler, and yet here I was, trying to breathe through them. Ronan held me until, finally, I sputtered to a stop.

"Do you feel better now?"

"I think it might partly be hormones," I rasped.

Ronan laughed. "I do not know this 'hormone' thing, but it must be very scary to make you cry like that."

I huffed a laugh through my stuffy nose. "Scary for *you*, maybe. But you'll get used to it."

As we drifted along on the Gulf Stream, I couldn't care less that we might end up in Cuba. I'd always wanted a holiday. So Ronan held me, and as the heat of his skin and the thump of his heart calmed me, the band around my chest slowly slipped away until I could breathe again. My little flower and I clung to him as if our lives depended on it.

I lifted my puffy face to see him staring down at me, his expression soft and his eyes lit from within. I marveled at all the different colors coming together to form the intense shade of green that I loved so much. I drank in his glorious smile, my hands roaming his curves with trembling delight. Drifting on the ocean wrapped in his arms was a surreal experience that slowly brought me back from the brink of despair.

Tilting his face down, he kissed me, his mouth firm and insistent. My sighs mingled with his as he parted my lips with his tongue and pulled me right out of myself.

There are treasured moments in your life that you remember with profound clarity. I would never forget the feeling of drifting out to sea with him, the salty breeze cooling our skin as passion flared between us like a brushfire.

Our bodies wound together with feverish kisses and thick moans, our hands everywhere. His hot, teasing lips drew me along on wave after wave of delight as he worked every curve of my body. My chin tucked to watch as he entered me, our soft groans mingling as he slid himself home.

Ronan's hooded eyes, flushed with pleasure, shot arousal straight to my core. When his neck strained, and his eyes closed, I trailed my lips along the whipcord of his throat, and he roared his release. I held him close, his powerful thrusts stirring a spiraling pressure around the base of my spine before billowing heat lashed across every nerve ending. Bliss swallowed me whole, then ebbed away, leaving me panting weakly into his neck. Slowly, my senses returned.

We drifted together, the *Wanderlust* bobbing in the waves as we held each other in one exquisite moment of absolute peace.

The ocean brought us together, only to have a monster tear us apart. I walked through the flames of hell to have him, and I would do it all over again. I was his, and he was mine; nothing would come between us.

CHAPTER 41

"You're not going to tell her, are you."

Gideon turned from the moonlit scene on the reef below, tilting his eagle head at the blue and gold macaw. Mr. Darcy clung to the red iron grating, waiting for an answer.

"Tell her what?"

"That you've been tailing her like a pathetic little kitten ever since you left her on the side of the highway in Tennessee."

Gideon clenched his taloned feet where they clung to the side of the lighthouse. He tossed his feathered head and said nothing, ignoring the parrot.

"Or that you left a trail of crumbs to lead her all the way to the Keys."

Gideon tuned him out and watched Edaline and Ronan as they played with their wee Syreni babe, his tiny orange tail flashing under the strawberry moon. A sleek and clever youngster, his bold green eyes flashed a brilliant white whenever Edaline scolded him. Gideon chuckled with delight at the thought.

Flashing the parrot some side-eye, he rumbled, *"I think little Ezen got that glorious orange tail color from me."*

Mr. Darcy squawked out a laugh, which drew Eddi's attention. Her gaze snapped toward the lighthouse where the pair had perched to watch the show for over an hour.

Gideon's paws flexed, the talons clicking on the rusty metal as he adjusted his grip. *"What! I gave her my blood while she was pregnant, remember? It could happen!"* Focused on Edaline's narrowed eyes, he shushed the parrot, who ruffled his feathers in indignation.

"Gideon, your arrogance is unparalleled. You can't even hide from her anymore," he chortled, his head bobbing. *"It's good for you that my Fae glamor works on her. Otherwise, you couldn't spy on her every five minutes."*

Gideon huffed and turned back to watch the youngling.

Shuffling sideways, his friend inched down the iron rail until he brushed against the Gryphon. *"I'm stuck in this pathetic form because of her, and you'll never say a word, even though it's all her damn fault,"* he spat, shaking his head and flapping his wings with annoyance.

Gideon turned and gently nudged him with his enormous beak, nearly pushing the parrot from his perch.

"That was all you, Fitzwilliam. It's not her fault you were fond of her father and helped him escape." He gave the parrot a reproachful look. *"Nor is it her fault that the Court of Seas decided to punish you in this manner."*

At the bird's angry glare, Gideon sighed. *"Let it rest, Fitzwilliam. Let her be. She deserves a chance at happiness—and no more BITING."*

With a fond look at the peaceful scene, Gideon watched as Ronan picked up the youngster, his orange tail flapping with delight, and tossed him up and out. The giggling pup sliced into the water with a happy slap of his tail, Eddi's smile rivaling the glow of the moon. The Enforcer's chest swelled with pride at the unusual splash of color on the youngster.

"Definitely. That tail definitely came from me. When have you ever seen an orange tail on a Syreni?"

The parrot's sarcastic snort made him bristle, but the cell phone that went off in the holster around his ankle caused a scramble. Quickly, he reached down with the point of his beak, tapped a key, then looked up to see if they'd blown their cover.

Cal's voice rang out a tad too loud. "Gideon, you need to get to the Big K right away. Two panther shifters are heading for a throwdown over a female. By the bank. *Hurry!*"

Gideon sighed, lashing his tail in annoyance. When he dipped his shoulder, Mr. Darcy leapt across the short distance and snuggled down into the thick fur of his neck.

Below, Edaline froze, her gaze locking on the Sombrero lighthouse tower. Her eyes narrowed as she tread water. When Gideon dropped away from the metal framework and spread his wings with a snap, Eddi's mouth shot open in disbelief.

With a surprised screech, the parrot grabbed on with his beak, and Gideon stretched his wings to catch the updraft, the pair shooting into the air currents above the moonlit reef.

But Mr. Darcy was on a roll.

"So I suppose we're flying over to 'behead' another tactless shifter? I swear, Gideon, if you don't get these morons under control, you will run out of places to drop them off. I mean, really. The last time you went as far as Georgia! And for what? Another bumbling fool wandering on the side of the road with no memories. You're getting soft in your old age, my friend."

Gideon chuckled, partly at the parrot's ranting but mainly at the image of the potato creature that flashed into his mind, the middle finger of each gloved hand raised in defiance.

The Gryphon let out a roar of laughter, which was unusual considering he couldn't speak. His throaty whistles sounded loud in the moonlight; *they were so busted.*

As he turned toward Marathon, Gideon folded his wings and dropped, snapping them wide just in time to swoop low over Eddi's head. The wake of his passage lifted her bangs on a blast of air, her joyful laughter reaching his ears as he streaked past.

And for the first time in five thousand years, Gideon's heart was full.

Did you enjoy The Tides Trilogy?
BE SURE TO READ OLIVER

Our Next in Series

~~~~~~

With your support, I will gladly write more epic tales for you!
WHAT CAN YOU DO TO HELP?
LEAVE A REVIEW FOR EACH BOOK!
You'll be helping this Indie Author more than you know!

~~~~~~

News from Penelope's desk...
One of my favorite characters
from the Tides Trilogy
CAL'S STORY
~ COMING FEBRUARY 2024! ~

~~~~~~

OTHER BOOKS BY PENELOPE AUSTIN

~~~~

THE MARTYR TIDES
BOOK ONE OF THE TIDES TRILOGY
THE BLOOD TIDES
BOOK TWO OF THE TIDES TRILOGY
THE MOON TIDES
BOOK THREE OF THE TIDES TRILOGY
(FINAL IN TRILOGY)
OLIVER
A STAND ALONE SEQUEL ROMANCE

Printed in Great Britain
by Amazon